HENRY, KING OF FRANCE

Henry,

KING OF

France

by HEINRICH MANN

TRANSLATED FROM THE GERMAN BY
ERIC SUTTON

ALFRED A. KNOPF : NEW YORK

19  39

Originally published as
DIE VOLLENDUNG DES KÖNIGS HENRI QUATRE
Copyright 1936 by Querido Verlag N. V. Amsterdam

Being published in England in two volumes under the title of
HENRI QUATRE, KING OF FRANCE

Manufactured in the United States of America

CONTENTS

BOOK ONE: *LUCK OF WAR*

BOOK TWO: *VICISSITUDES OF LOVE*

BOOK SIX: GREATNESS AND POSSESSION

BOOK SEVEN: WITH FACE AVERTED

BOOK EIGHT: *THE GREAT PLAN*

Contents

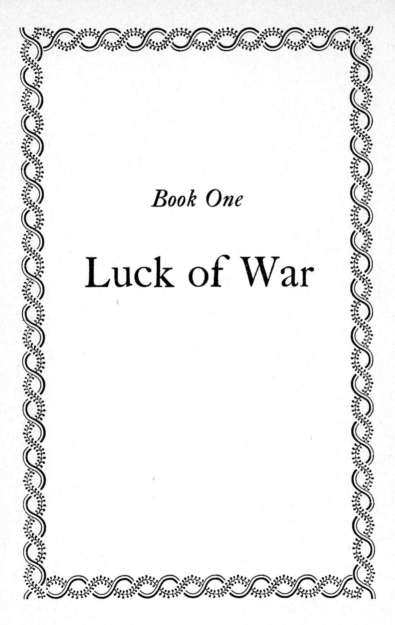

Book One

Luck of War

THE RUMOUR

THE KING had won his victory. He had flung the enemy back
and laid him low. But he had not destroyed the mightier power
nor brought him to a stand. His kingdom was still in deadly
peril; indeed, it was not yet his. It still belonged to the League;
for the lawlessness of those days, the common defiance of decency and of reason, had risen to very madness. Worse even than
madness, a dull subjection to disorder and unreason had laid
hold upon the people, and they had sunk into a melancholy acceptance of their shame.

The King's one victory could not alter their condition. One
fruitless, solitary success — how much of it was accident and
how much was destiny? It brought no change of heart to what
was still the stronger side. And yet this Protestant from the
South was no bandit captain, he was the veritable King. What,
then, were all the great leaders of the League — they who each
ruled a province or a county, in their very persons and in full
authority? The King's writ barely ran save where his army lay.
The idea of the kingdom stood for the King; so much was recognized by many, to their disquiet and regret. An idea is both less
and more than actual force. The kingdom was more than a territory and a domain, it was the very essence of freedom and of
justice.

If eternal justice then looked down upon the earth, she must have seen a sorry sight of humiliation, and, what was viler still, of hypocrisy and self-betrayal. Frenchmen who, to serve the needs of every day, had subjected themselves to the traitors and were like, through them, to pass under the sovereignty of Spain. From mere fear of their fellow-men they endured serfdom in their own land, spurned the spirit, and flung away the highest treasure of all, freedom of conscience. Poor noblemen serving in the armies of the League or holding the offices of State, worthy citizens who trafficked with it, and humble folk who joined it; not always fools, and often not dishonourable. But what could they do? A whisper among trusty friends, a secret prayer to God, and after the King's unlooked-for victory at Arques, hearts leapt with hope that the day might not be far off!

Strange it is that people at a distance mostly conceive a larger notion of events than those near at hand. The King's victory was won beside the North Sea; and within a compass of two or three days' journey men might well have marvelled. In Paris, most of all, they should have searched their hearts and rid them of their abiding errors. Far from it. Up in the North, as the scattered bands of the League's great beaten army overran the countryside, many saw with their eyes what did not penetrate their heads. For them, the League was still unconquered; the King, thanks to the sea mist and a turn or two of luck, had possessed himself of an insignificant strip of territory, and that was all. But for the inner provinces the hour seemed indeed about to strike. By the Loire and in the city of Tours they believed, from ancient experience, that in the end the King would always come among them in person. Time and again as a poor fugitive, but at last as their master, thus had they received him for centuries past. As for the outlying domains of the West and South, they viewed the battle of Arques as though it had been refought and won before their very eyes, and decreed by Heaven itself. The stormy Protestants of the fortress of La Rochelle sang: " Let God, the God of Battle, rise! " — the very psalm with which their King had conquered. From Bordeaux slantwise across the land, the whole South, afire with enthusiasm, conceived as accomplished what was far from done: the subjection of the capital, the punishment of certain powerful traitors, and the glorious union of the kingdom under their own Henri, who had been born among them, had marched out thence, and was now so great.

Did his countrymen in fact go farther than the rest? Great! — it was easiest to call a man so who was not even known by sight. His Southern countrymen knew from their own encounters that he was of no more than middle height, wore a felt hat and a threadbare doublet, and was always in need of money. They remembered his kind eyes; did these really bespeak a cheerful humour or much grief endured? Well, he was a man of ready hand and understood how to deal with common men — and, better still, he understood the ways of women. Many of them, none could tell how many, held his secrets. And, usually so garrulous, they did not tell them. Enough; here he was known by sight, though they had not indeed been with him in the North, among the sea mists, when, to the strains of the great psalm, the attack was made and a mighty army routed. That was a great deed done, and heaven and earth had held their breath the while.

And now far-off lands had learned of what was going forward. Hitherto no news of him had reached them. At great distances so new a fame is a vision of pure glory. Thus he loomed all the greater when he suddenly appeared. The world was waiting for him, sick of the incubus of Philip of Spain, the tedious, dreary Philip. The burdened world had long yearned for a deliverer; behold, he is here! His victory a trifling battle, no shattering blow that changed the face of Europe, and yet more significant than had been the defeat of the Armada. Here had a man by his own strength dealt a blow at the throne of the Ruler of the World that set it rocking. And that shock, faint as it was, was felt across the frontiers, across the mountains, and beyond the seas. In a famous city over the great sea they were said to have carried his portrait in procession through the streets. A doubtful portrait. Faded, discovered in a dealer's shop, and cleaned: "The King of France!" cried the populace, and marched off behind it; even the priests marched in their ranks. Rumour knows everything and is winged.

THE REALITY

He himself held no celebration of victory. A task brought to fullness leads on to another, and he who has not conquered by guile, but in open fight, knows nothing of victory and feels none of the dazzlement of joy. The King thought only of taking his capital of Paris by surprise, before the Duke of Mayenne with the beaten army of the League could reach it. The King was the quicker of the two; moreover in Paris they let themselves be persuaded that he had been beaten by their beloved Mayenne and was in full flight, which gave him yet more start. But before he arrived in Paris, the citizens had recovered their nerve and had set about providing for defence — though in very clumsy fashion. Instead of manning the massive walls and bastions round the inner city, they decided to hold the outlying wards as well. This was much to the mind of the King, who thought to overwhelm them outside and then to dash through the gates with the fugitives.

He stormed the outer works with ease, but in the meanwhile there had been time to shut the gates. And so it was that his troops — Switzers, German landsknechts, four companies of adventurers, four thousand Englishmen, sixteen French regiments — plunged into a welter of butchery and pillage. Otherwise nothing came of the assault. The King was indeed received with plaudits, but the pillage and the butchery went on. He cannonaded over the walls into the city, but knew he would not win his capital that time. So he retired to rest in a palace called after his family: Petit Bourbon. Henri had to force his way in like a stranger, and indeed found nothing to lie on but fresh straw. There were three hours left for sleep, and part of them he passed in meditation.

In the city stood the palace of the Louvre; there he had endured as prisoner through many profitable years, he bore the mark of them yet. Was he never to see the city again as a free man and a King? On a certain night of Saint Bartholomew nearly all his friends at court had fallen; and in the city, most of his fellow-believers. After eighteen years they were avenged! At one single cross-road his soldiers had that day cut down eight hundred of the enemy, crying out as they did so: " Saint Bartholomew! " How terrible it was that all things are fated to return and nothing can be banished from the world! He would be for forgetting and forgiving, he would be for humanity. Where lay the truth in those old conflicts? Who could tell? What remained certain was that killing still went on, without as within. If only he had reached the gate in time! He would have shown them a merciful conqueror and a true King. The kingdom would have had its capital, and the citizens could have looked in peace upon an end achieved. But no; only a little sated vengeance, the usual slaughter, and the luck of war.

Henri, a man of thirty-six, who had behind him much horror and much patient toil, though his natural gaiety had indeed brought him many joys, lay on fresh straw under a huge refectory table. For the last time he sat up — to command that the churches should be spared — "and the men too! " he shouted to his captain. Then he really fell asleep, for he had learned self-mastery, in failure and disheartenment not less than in times when fortune smiled. Sleep was his good friend, appeared punctually, and mostly brought what Henri needed — not fears, but visions of good omen. In his dream that night Henri saw ships passing by. They hovered first in the haze of the horizon, grew larger and set forth on the sunlit sea, great galleasses full of power and glory; they came nearer, they bore down upon him. His heart began to throb, and the sleeping man grew aware of what that visitation meant. There had been talk of such matters after the battle he had won. He had not listened, because of the many urgent tasks that lay to his hand. One does not listen to fairy-tales at such a moment. But when he awoke after his three hours the vision of the ships had quite vanished from his memory.

All Saints' Day dawned; the royal army, all of it that was Catholic, went to the churches in the outer city. Behind the walls they had not the heart to celebrate the feast; they lamented their dead and feared for their own lives. But towards evening they were saved, for the League troops appeared, and the King could not now prevent them occupying the city from the farther side; the moment had passed. He allowed one more abbey to be taken by his men, and three hundred citizens of Paris were cut down. That was his farewell, and a sorry one, as he himself was well aware. He paid for it too; to get a view of the city he mounted a church tower, taking a monk as his guide. Alone with the monk on the narrow roof he shuddered suddenly as he thought of the late King, who had been murdered by a monk. He himself had often seen a knife peeping out of the sleeves of a habit. Quickly he stepped behind his companion and grasped both his arms. The man, though tall and powerful, made no movement. Henri did not look upon his capital for long; on the way down he made the suspect walk before him, he himself remained several steps behind. At the bottom he met Marshal Biron. " Sire," said Biron, " your monk took to his heels and fled."

At that moment came a roar of joy from the people of Paris. Their commander, Mayenne, had appeared in person; his troops were feasted in the streets. Next day the King drew up his army in battle order and gave the enemy three hours to come out. In vain, Mayenne was too wary; so the King withdrew. On his way he took some fortified places; but some of his regiments, their pay being in arrears, broke up. With his remaining troops the King rode to his city of Tours, there to receive the ambassadors of Venice. The ancient republic had sent her ships from far away, the rumour had proved true. The mission had landed, and while the King was taking certain towns, they rode slowly through the kingdom on their way to bring him homage.

A Fairy-Tale

He learned daily of their approach and grew disquieted, so he pretended to be gay. " It is raining! The wise men from the East will get their incense wet! " He was really afraid that the League might capture them and snatch them from his grasp before they could arrive, with all the honours and all the visible glories that they meant to lay before him. While they were still several days' journey from the Loire, he sent a body of troops to meet them, ostensibly as an escort of honour, but in fact with more serious intent. Then he awaited them in his castle at Tours, and he had to wait some while. One of the elderly Venetian gentlemen had fallen ill on the way. " It is a very old republic," said Henri to his diplomat, Philippe du Plessis-Mornay.

" Sire, the oldest in Europe. Once one of the most powerful, but now the most experienced. He who speaks of experience does not usually know that he means decay. But to those who now approach, that too is known. Now pray consider the event! The most astute of governments, concerned now only to carry the frailty of age with dignity and postpone the hour of dissolution, she has the most sagacious observers at all the courts and is most assiduous in reading their reports; suddenly she rises up and acts. Venice challenges the World Power, and offers you her homage on your victory over it. So it was indeed a mighty victory! "

" I have begun to ponder on my victory. Victory, Monsieur de Mornay — " began Henri; then he stopped and fell to pacing up and down the stone-flagged hall of the castle at Tours. The companion of his youth watched; and he felt, as he had so often done, that he had chosen his Prince aright. He gave God alone the honour for that victory. The stern Protestant doffed his hat as the thought was borne into his mind. There he stood, a man of forty years, in dark array, with a plain white collar after the fashion of his fellows in the faith, a Socratic mouth and chin, and a high forehead, very smooth and polished with reflected light.

" Mornay! " cried Henri, facing him. " Victory is not what it used to be. We have both known it otherwise."

" Sire! " answered Henri's envoy, in clear unruffled tones. " In your former dignity as King of Navarre you brought to reason certain obstinate and misguided cities. Ten years of toil and striving, and a notable battle, which fame has celebrated, made you heir to the Crown. The King of France, as you now are, will fight with less toil, will win greater victories; and fame shall, on his behalf, flap her wings with even more ado."

"If that were the only difference! Mornay, since my victory, which has brought the Venetians hither, I have besieged Paris and had to raise that siege. Don't the Venetians know that?"

"It is far to Venice, and they were already on their way."

"They could turn back. They are sensible men and must know what it means when a King has to besiege his own capital and even so cannot take it. Butchery, pillage — and retreat, after I had looked down upon the city from a tower, in fear of assassination by a monk."

"Sire, the luck of war."

"So we call it. But what is it? While I am watching one gate, Mayenne enters by another. He approached by the bridge; by my orders it was to have been cut, but had not been. Such is the luck of war. I have a suspicion that matters scarce wear a different aspect when I win."

"Sire, the handiwork of man."

"None the less, there should be commanders." Henri broke off: he thought of one commander, called Parma, who, by the reputation of his art, relied upon no luck of war, nor excused himself by talking of man's handiwork.

"Mornay!" cried Henri, as he grasped his counsellor's shoulder and shook him. "One word! Can I win? My duty is to save this kingdom; but my mind was more at ease when none were making their ways hither to pay me homage before the time."

"Venice regards you as having conquered, Sire. She would not recall her ambassadors even if your army were utterly broken up."

And Henri answered: "So I am to believe that fame is a misunderstanding. I deserve it, and yet I get it without my own desert." Whereupon his face changed, he swung round on his heels, and with an air of high good humour he greeted some persons who at that moment entered — several of his most trusted followers, elegantly arrayed in new clothes. "Bravo, de la Noue!" cried Henri. "An iron arm, and you swam across the river. And bravo, Rosny! Your jewels come from good houses, though not from your own; I wonder how much money you found and pocketed in the outer wards of Paris. Suppose I appoint you my Minister of Finance instead of that fat rascal d'O?"

He looked about him, for they barely smiled. "Gloomy faces, gentlemen — above all things do I fear them and mistrust them."

They were silent. He looked from one to another until he guessed. His old friend d'Aubigné nodded — d'Aubigné, once his fellow-prisoner and afterwards the companion of his campaigns, a bold man and a pious, in verse and in deed. The kindly face nodded and said: "Sire! It is so. A messenger, all wet, arrived when we had already arrayed ourselves for the reception."

A quiver shook Henri. He let it pass. And when he had completely mastered his voice again, he said to his old friend genially: "What would you have, Agrippa? It is the luck of war. The ambassadors have turned back. But they may yet change their minds, for I shall soon fight another battle."

A hubbub could be heard outside the door, which was then thrust open; between two guards appeared a dripping messenger, out of breath and speechless. He was put in a chair and given a cup of wine. "It is a different one," observed d'Aubigné.

At last the man spoke. "In half an hour the ambassadors will be here."

As Henri heard this, he clutched at his heart. "Now I'll let them wait till morning." And he hurried away.

Now overnight a miracle happened; November changed to May. A soft breeze blew up from the south and banished all the clouds, the blue canopy of heaven shone down upon the park and the river, winding its way through the meadow-land in the heart of France. The birches stood up tall and almost leafless; from the castle the ambassadors could be seen disembarking from the ships in which they had crossed. They were lodged in garden-houses on the farther side. Under tall windows level with the ground the court awaited them — gentlemen and ladies as richly clad as they were able, or thought decent. Roquelaure was the most elegant. Agrippa wore the largest feathers, Frontenac stood in rivalry with Rosny, who carried on his hat and collar more jewels than were sewn into the women's dresses; though his still young, smooth face bore its usual air of understanding gravity. When the King's sister entered, she appeared at once as the loveliest woman of that company. The delicate fair head was poised against the high lace collar sewn with diamonds; and her air of courteous decision only masked a childlike humour that she would never lose. She was still in the doorway when her gold-embroidered veil caught on some projection; or it may have been her lame foot that played her false. The entire court stood arrayed to welcome her, when at that same moment she saw her brother approach through the opposite door. A little cry of joy — and, heedless of herself, she ran a few tripping steps towards him. " Henri! "

They met in the middle of the room. Catherine of Bourbon bowed the knee before her brother — they had been playmates in their childhood, and they had travelled through the land in heavy antique coaches with their mother Jeanne. Their dear mother had indeed been sick and restless, but how strong in virtue of the faith she taught! Her cause had triumphed in the end, though she had been fated to die first, poisoned by the wicked old Queen, and much terror and much toil had been their lot. However, now there they were, standing in a hall in the very heart of the kingdom, the King himself with his sister, about to receive the ambassadors of Venice. " Catherine! " cried the brother with a gush of tears; he lifted his sister from her curtsy and kissed her. The court joyfully applauded.

The King, in white silk with a blue scarf, led the Princess by her trembling hand; the court fell back, but closed their ranks again behind the royalties. They halted under the tallest window, and the company thronged round them — those who thrust to the front were not always the most considered. The sister said in her brother's ear: " I don't like your Chancellor Villeroy. And still less your Treasurer d'O. And you have worse than those about you. Dear brother Henri, if only all who served you might be of our faith! "

" I would it were so," he said in his sister's ear, and therewith he beckoned to the two courtiers she had named. She turned away in disgust; and the farther she went, the kindlier grew the faces that she met. By the wall Catherine came upon a bevy of old friends: her brother's companion in arms, cavaliers of the former Court of Navarre, though in those days coarse leather doublets had been their usual garb. "You have indeed made yourselves very splendid, gentlemen! Baron Rosny, when I taught you to dance, you had no diamonds. Monsieur de la Noue, your hand!" She took the Huguenot's iron hand — not the living hand, the iron one — and said, for him and Agrippa d'Aubigné and tall du Bartas alone to hear:

" God had but to let a single grain of sand fall otherwise than on its natural course, and we should not be here. Do you know that? "

They nodded. On the darkened face of tall du Bartas could be read the verses that were forming in his brain; then came a blast of trumpets from without. They were at hand! The company hurriedly stiffened into the presentment of a powerful court. Most of the faces assumed an air of grave magnificence, tempered by curiosity; rigid and straight they stood, even the Princess of Bourbon. She eyed the women, of whom there were few to be found in that wandering court and camp. With a quick decision she took one hand and came forward with Charlotte Arbaleste, the wife of the Protestant Mornay. There followed a sudden pause.

There had no doubt been some misarrangement of precedence in the procession of the envoys. The trumpets had sounded too soon. The path up the river-bank was steep; perhaps the gentlemen from Venice were too old to climb it? It seemed as though the King made merry, those around him were all laughing. The Princess, his sister, led her companion to another window; she had been startled, for beside her royal brother stood Soissons, whom she loved. It was fortunate she had this stern Protestant on her arm, thought Catherine, as though she had not been one herself. Indeed, she forgot herself, as she did all her brief life long, at the unexpected vision of her cousin. Her heart throbbed, her breath came in gasps, and in self-defence she assumed her haughtiest expression, but she scarce knew what she was saying to her neighbour. " Palpitation of the heart," said she; " Madame de Mornay, have you not suffered from that affection? In old days in Navarre, when you had dealings with the Consistorium on account of your lovely hair? "

Charlotte Arbaleste wore a coif that reached almost to her eyes — limpid, shining eyes that knew no awe of men. And the virtuous wife of Protestant Mornay answered: " I was accused of immodesty because I wore false curls, and the pastor forbade me the Lord's Supper. And he refused it to Monsieur de Mornay. And even today, after so many years, all those troubles have left me a flutter at my heart."

" How unjust our Church can be! " said the Princess quickly. " You endured banishment and poverty for our Religion, after your escape on the night of Saint Bartholomew. All of us here, now awaiting the ambassadors, were once prisoners or exiles for the faith. You yourself, Monsieur de Mornay, the King my brother, and I also."

" And you also," repeated Charlotte, her bright limpid eyes looking straight into those of Catherine, who trembled in disquiet. No use for her to talk; that she realized. The woman saw through her.

" But despite the pastors, you kept your red curls for a long while," poor Catherine persisted. " And rightly, say I. What? Persecuted and exiled, and when you came back, your sacrifice rejected, just because of your hair."

" It was wrong," confessed the Protestant's wife. " I was immodest." Wherewith, by admitting her own transgression, she really reminded the Princess of herself and her more heinous fault. She made this quite clear. " My immodesty was not merely venial; it was deliberate, and despite all warning. But I received the light through prayer, and at last laid aside the evil thing, since when I have worn a modest coif."

" And suffer from palpitations of the heart," said Catherine. She glanced angrily at the other's face, now pale and drawn and pious. In earlier days, when Charlotte was pretty, they both went to balls together, thought she. This banished her wrath. Pity possessed her — pity that soon turned to penitence. She still looked as she had looked then — and so did her sin. She knew herself, and had learned many things, but was incorrigible; there would be no pardon for her, she thought ruefully. " Lord help me, that I too may put on the coif this evening and wear it for ever! " She prayed in a low and urgent voice, though with little hope of being heard.

The Count of Soissons stood before them, and said: " Ladies, His Majesty desires your company." Both bowed their heads obediently, both in silence. He took their finger-tips and led the ladies by their lifted hands. Gently he tried to press his cousin's hand. She did not respond and kept her face averted. Courteously he handed her to her royal brother.

Among the birches could be seen a metallic glitter; the thoughts of all turned to weapons and to war. But the ladies knew the flash of jewels; or, at the least, of embroidery. Such, indeed, was what they saw, and yet more sumptuous and surprising visions: a ship of silver that floated, or seemed to float, towards them, ahead of the rest of the procession which was just coming into view. The silver ship was so large that people could have gone aboard — and, indeed, hands were setting a sail, but they were children's hands. The ship was manned by children, in sailors' garb, and singing sailors' songs to a tinkling accompaniment; but whence it came, and how that magic ship was moved, none could tell.

Twenty paces from the castle it stopped, or rather it was set down, and from beneath the rich fabrics hanging from its bow sprang forth dwarfs, who had been carrying it. Humpbacked dwarfs, dressed from head to foot in red, who promptly took to their heels, amid the laughter of the court. Meantime a sort of chair was seen approaching — no, it was a throne. Moving just above the level of the ground, it then rose upwards; only the most elaborate machines could so noiselessly uplift it; and behold — it was a throne. The sparkling air rippled over the fair hair of the lady there enthroned, her blond head piled high with tresses and huge pearls. The throne was tapestried in purple, and the woman — a proud creature in golden draperies, like a painting by Paolo Veronese — who could she be? Her eyes hidden by a black velvet mask — who could she be? The whole court fell silent. The King bared his head, and so did all the rest.

By the side of that lofty throne walked, or rather marched, certain stark figures in black cuirasses, arrayed in dark and motley colours, their uncovered heads a tangle of red or black hair. But they were recognized by their formidable teeth: Slavonians, conquered subjects of Venice. They were followed by fishermen, true sons of the sea city, unkempt, with patched clothes and splintered oars, as they had been taken from a canal bridge. They sang — in high, clear voices, and there was little mystery about what they sang, though few understood their speech. Into that gay singing came a graver note that carried to the listeners the vision of a church, the distant shimmer of a church across the waters.

The singers broke off, in the middle of a rhythmic cadence, for the lady on the throne stretched out her hand. It was a wonderful hand, a shapely hand with pointed fingers slightly upturned. Hued like a rose-leaf, it wore no rings, and beckoned in imperious but alluring fashion, as though to a suitor whom so great a lady was graciously admitting to her arms. The court realized that the Ambassador was at hand; and the King of France went out alone on to the terrace to receive him.

At the same moment the fishermen fell back from the throne and knelt. The warrior Slavonians also moved aside and knelt. The children knelt in the silver ship, and the red dwarfs beneath the bushes in the distance. The space about the throne was empty, and across it came a slender figure in a robe and biretta; a scholar, as the court conceived. Why a scholar? Did the republic send a scholar as her highest representative? The two others, grey-bearded captains, gave him precedence.

Agrippa d'Aubigné and du Bartas, two humanists, who bore many scars on their bodies from battles new and old, took hurried counsel while the Ambassador came very slowly towards the King. Monsieur Mocenigo, a kinsman of the Doge and himself quite old; he had fought at Lepanto, the famous sea victory over the Turks. Now he taught Latin at Padua, and hence had first become known in Christendom. " What an honour! " said the poet Agrippa exultantly. " Monsieur Mocenigo to pay homage to our King! I'm so overjoyed that I could write a poem about the battle of Lepanto as though I had been there myself."

" Write a poem about our next battle," said the tall du Bartas grimly. " I'll be mum," he muttered to his own foreboding heart.

The King was again wearing his feathered hat with upturned brim, but his unshadowed eyes beneath it were wide open that they might lose nothing. But he was moved, and perhaps the tears had come into his eyes; it was indeed for that reason that he kept them so wide open, and his eyelids were as rigid as his hand or foot. The Ambassador bowed his head on his chest in salutation to the King. Then he raised it once more, and for the first time it could be seen that one eye was closed, and barred by a red scar.

He began to speak in marvellously cadenced Latin — smooth, but hard. The court thought of marble. Then too the man's face could be seen for what it was — its bony contours, sharp and sunken mouth, like the busts of Dante, the face of an old sage. The court did not understand every sentence, for the familiar speech came from foreign lips. But they observed from the orator's expression that their King was being highly lauded; measured by the pattern of the Roman commanders and found worthy of their company.

Henri, and he alone, grasped every word, not merely what was actually said, but what lay behind it, which was this: Your cause is at issue. Who are you? That you may learn from this harangue, or think you may guess while it is uttered. The one-eyed sage appears to be comparing you with the first conqueror of the kingdom, the Roman Cæsar, your predecessor. But he is in truth warning you to remain what you have always been, a horseman bold and debonair, great in little things, unequal to high deeds. You know whom he thinks a better man than yourself: his countryman, Farnese, Duke of Parma, the most celebrated strategist of the age. And you are no strategist, merely a rough and daring horseman. . . .

He began to grow uneasy and opened his eyes yet wider. The

stranger, who had so curtly acquainted him with the truth, now for the first time looked in earnest at that face. It was thinner than at first glance; its very gauntness stamped it with ardour and devotion; the Ambassador had not thought to look on such a face. He broke off his harangue and clasped his hands.

When he resumed, his voice had softened and mellowed; and he uttered but a few words more, the chief of which was " love." Though a man were rich in art and victory, and had not love. . . . The Gospel in place of Cæsar, which was quite unlooked for, and surprised everyone, most of all the speaker, who thereupon closed his address. Then Henri, too, did something unexpected. He did not, as had been arranged, give his hand to the Ambassador, to invite him up on to the terrace; he himself leapt down, gave him the accolade, kissed him on both cheeks; and the court applauded. The children in the silver ship saw it, and so did the throned woman in the golden draperies — and as she was the daughter of one of the fishermen in patched clothes, she forgot her majesty and clapped her hands. The warrior Slavonians clapped their hands likewise; so did the fishermen and the two grizzled captains.

Henri looked about him and laughed joyfully — although a strange shudder quivered through his shoulder. Not as when the murderer had stood behind him — no, this time it was the faint flutter of a wing. Fame had brushed against him for the first time when he was nearly forty, — fame that was true fame. In aspect like an Eastern fairy-tale, it had passed in a flash, leaving a shudder of fear behind it.

" Master Ambassador, when the ceremony is over, I want a word with you alone."

" On what matter, Sire? "

" The Duke of Parma."

The Heraldic Beast

" I must have my battle," thought Henri, almost before the ambassadors of Venice had departed; indeed he had so determined when they appeared with such display. That odd pre-

monition of fame had likewise shown him how he stood. A
commander of his sort has no money, and if his army is not to
melt away, he must take a city as often as he can — to raise pay
for his soldiers. They were the cities of his kingdom; it was a
hard matter to remain the father of his country, and beloved as
such, while he ranged the land subduing his enemies and collecting contributions. Not a week passed since the festal fairy-
tale at Tours before he was plunged in the struggle once more.

He cleared Touraine, as well as the neighbouring provinces,
of the enemy, and then marched into Normandy — but his victory at Arques was won on Norman soil. What had been the
issue of that victory? The conquered places he had left behind
him had in the meantime fallen away. His enemy was not a man,
like himself, but a many-headed hydra. Cut off seven, and eight
grow in their place. So was it with the League. His subjects all
thronged the streets to welcome him when he rode among them
as their master. Never had they dreamed of bearing weapons
against him — though he had merely to dig up their gardens to
find the buried muskets. All of which would have been good entertainment had he been made to spend his life in such fashion.
And if in truth he were not made for such a purpose, but for
something greater, he had better keep his mouth shut.

" My health is as good as it has ever been," he said to everyone that winter, when snow fell often and many nights were
spent on frozen ground. " And there's no disease in my army,
which will soon be greater still, for this wretched little town
alone is paying me sixty thousand crowns. Will you wager that
the next one will surrender by Thursday? "

He did indeed make such a pact with the town of Honfleur.
If Mayenne or his son, Nemours, had not arrived by Thursday,
the gate was to be opened, and so it came about. Mayenne, the
leader, was content that his League should be a league and took
his ease in Paris, " as I shall do in days to come," observed Henri
confidently. But in his own mind he thought: " I must have my
battle." And he pondered it in alternating mood — now as a
swift and joyous stroke, now as the decision of his life.

In his baggage he carried a singular object, an alarm clock,

which he kept in order most carefully. He spent less time in
sleep than did the fat Mayenne at table. Which was a new thing
for a man of his hearty temperament; and sometimes he missed
even those few hours. " I must have my battle — and not as in
other days, when I could win or lose. This one I may not lose,
or all will be at an end. There are too many eyes upon me, the
world is watching me — my allies, who paid me homage before
the time had come, but especially the King of Spain, who wants
this kingdom. And he would have it the moment I were no
longer there. There's none to prevent him. The nation is at
odds over religion. If all of them had the true one, then Don
Philip could do nothing. Meantime, what care I? Every man
has his own, I am a Huguenot and I lie on frozen earth. If Don
Philip comes, and if he comes in power — 'tis all one whether
my religion is the right one; creed makes no matter here, it is
the kingdom that's at stake, and that, whatever may befall, is
from God. The game is played between the Almighty and myself." So much was very clear to the King, on a pitch-black night,
while in his tent a night-light sputtered and at last went out.

The alarm clock struck; the King rose and called for his officers. On that day there was much to do and far to ride. A moat
had to be drained, so that the besiegers could press up to the
walls of the fortress. This done, there was much desultory can-
nonading, until the early evening. Henri had long been ahorse,
over other matters that took him far afield. He was very hungry
when about dinner-time he reached the town of Alençon and
drew up with a small escort at the house of a certain Captain,
who was very much his servant; but the man was away. The
King was not known to the wife; she took him for one of the
royal commanders and received him as was his due, but also
with marked embarrassment.

" I fear I am unwelcome, my good lady? Speak freely, I would
not embarrass you."

" Then I'll tell you, my lord. Today is Thursday; I have sent
all over the town; there's nothing to be had, and I'm in despair.
Only a worthy mechanic near by tells me he has a fat turkey on
a hook; but he'll not give it up unless he sits down to table too."

" Is he fit for company? "

" Yes, my lord, he's the merriest fellow in our quarter. A decent man too, fire and flame for the King, and with a prosperous little business."

" Then let him come, dear lady. I have a rousing appetite; and were he tedious, I would sooner eat with him than not at all."

Whereupon the mechanic was fetched, and appeared in his Sunday attire, bearing the turkey. While it was roasting he entertained the King, though he did not indeed appear to recognize him, or he would scarce have talked so freely — such gossip, jests, and sallies, and all so good that Henri forgot his hunger for a while. He very soon dropped into his companion's tone — without intention, and did not notice it himself. It was no hard matter to remain father of his country, and beloved as such, while he compelled his subjects to obedience and levied contributions from them. The whole secret was his good conscience, born of the honourable task he had in hand. To bring his countrymen to reason and save the kingdom without flurry or guile. This thought was always in the forefront of his mind, in sleep and even in cheerful talk. The worthy mechanic opposite was telling him tales, but he, too, did not forget his workshop.

The King thought: " I must have my battle. It is not now far away. I have taken enough strong places to make my fat friend Mayenne uneasy. My cousin Marshal Biron is harrying the League, and I have all our successes reported to the Queen of England. We will now besiege the town of Dreux; Mayenne can't look on at that, he must advance and offer battle. Indeed, the Spaniards will insist on it. That is the sole purpose of the Spanish auxiliaries, the first that Philip has ever granted to the League. They are from the Netherlands, sent by the Governor, Farnese. Am I never to get a sight of him, the great strategist, the most famous artist of war? I wonder what Farnese says about me."

As the name came into his mind, Henri instinctively leapt to his feet. The mechanic kept his mouth open. But Henri was able to repeat the story the man had been telling. " When the glove-maker found the tall farrier with his wife, he stretched out his hand in forgiveness and said: 'Of you, friend, I cannot believe such a thing.'" Henri laughed. "A merry tale, brother."

"Merry indeed, brother," repeated the worthy fellow, relieved of his disquiet at his companion's wild demeanour. At that moment the hostess called her guests to table. All three sat down to the great bird, but hostess and mechanic ate with reserve, the guest was given the larger portion; and so hugely he ate, and so heartily he laughed at his neighbour's stories, that the worthy mechanic grew droller than ever. So it was all the more singular, after the last glass, when they were about to leave the table, to see his plump face lengthen and his eyes close in fear. The King had indeed taken it for a jest, but there lay the man at his feet, pleading for pardon: "Forgive me, my lord, forgive me! This has been the greatest day of my life. I knew Your Majesty and have served you, and fought at Arques for my King; and now I have had my desire, which was to sit at table with Your Majesty. Forgive once more, Sire, I had to feign to be a fool that you might laugh a little at my jests. And now the dreadful thing has happened, a menial like myself has sat at dinner with the King."

"What are we to do about it?" asked the King.

"I see but one way."

"Well?"

"You must ennoble me."

"You?"

"Why not, Sire? I work with my hands, but I carry my sense in my head; and in my heart — my King."

"Excellent, my good friend, and what would be your blazon?"

"My turkey. I owe it all the honour."

"Your neatest jest. Rise, Knight of the Turkey!"

A Romance of Chivalry

The new knight took care that his exploit should be talked about and do much good to the King among his people. At last a good fellow like ourselves! Not proud, nor aloof, although as a heretic his damnation was sure. Why, the King's heresy would even be accepted, so far as it was God's intention. Would God let him conquer?

The King also asked himself that question. He had made no such careful preparations for any of his battles. He raised the siege of Dreux, withdrew his troops from every side, and allowed himself to be forced to the frontier of the province of Normandy; but not within it. He halted at Ivry, in the Île de France, the vital point that covers Paris.

The Duke of Mayenne had believed that this time his superior numbers would suffice and that a battle would not be needed. The Spanish General, Farnese, Duke of Parma, by Don Philip's orders had had to hand over to him the flower of his army, six thousand musketeers, twelve hundred Walloon spearmen; in all, there were twenty-five thousand men under Mayenne's command. Against all these what could avail a King without a country, with an army scarce a third as large, and faced by the regiments of Spain? These were the as yet unconquered arms of the World Power. But the King halted at Ivry.

It was the 12th of March of the year 1590. That day, and the night that followed, Henri spent quite otherwise than was his wont before a battle. He did not ride from company to company, to hearten them, nor did he bear a hand at entrenchments. There were none, and none were dug. A broad stretch of country, a little river, on the farther side of it an army thrice his own; and on the hither side a man with a plan ripening in his mind.

He lay on the ground, drawing plans. His marshals, Biron and Aumont, did not recognize him, so possessed was he by the thought of Parma. The famous commander had not come in person, the issue did not seem important — not yet; Don Philip would send him later as his last resource. Pray God it might be so. Lord, we call upon Thy name!

Henri also prayed. As often as he rose from his plans, he exchanged his strategic ambitions for the devotion of one who stands under the highest arbitrament of all. He prayed with his troops, he even gave orders that those of the other religion should be allowed to receive the Sacrament in their churches, and many did so; the churches round about were full. Most of the men, regardless of their creed, wanted to hear the King utter a prayer — and this he did, in the midst of a throng of troops, with face upturned above them towards the flying clouds, as though he were committing to Him who sits enthroned on high all that moves man's heart below. But the heart was his own, and its throbbing shook his chest. Hence his voice carried farther than ever before. Then it failed in the stress of his emotion, or was carried away by the wind. His Huguenots in the front ranks knelt, bowed their weather-beaten heads, and if the tears came, they let them fall.

After this intercourse with Heaven, Henri was especially cheerful, and inspired everyone with his confidence. And this indeed received its due in the domains above the clouds; for Huguenots came continually riding in from far away, to help win the battle. In the night it rained, which was to the disadvantage of the enemy: the Royalists lay in the villages. In the morning the King drew up his forces in accordance with his plans; Mayenne, who was watching from beyond the stream, marvelled at the ease of these manœuvres. It was but the 13th, and Mayenne did not want to give battle so soon. The gamecock yonder should be discomposed by waiting; raiding horsemen wasted his precious time; a Swiss Colonel caught under an apple-tree, and a handful of landsknechts captured. So in the evening the gamecock had to unman his elaborate battle array, which had served no purpose.

The 14th. Patiently Henri drew up his line once more: the cavalry of Marshal Aumont, those of the Duke of Montpensier, his own in the centre, then Baron Biron, the old Marshal's son — and every mounted unit carefully secured by infantry, French regiments, Swiss regiments, and even landsknechts from across the Rhine. All together they made no more than six or seven thousand men on foot, and two thousand five hundred mounted; in close formation as they stood, the enemy from a distance took them for even fewer. The enemy, on the other hand, lengthened out his line, to make play of his superiority in numbers. Great as this was, it had in the meantime lessened. First, because new arrivals were continually joining the King — the new Knight of the Turkey and many of his sort, who came because they trusted Henri, and likewise at the bidding of their consciences. But on the other side many had of late deserted the League — not alone because of the rain and other hardships, but also from naked fear. They had discovered, none could tell how, that the King was going to win the fight.

He himself held fast to reason and did but hope that God would do so likewise. Between nine and ten his battle order was arrayed as on the day before, though slightly slanted with an eye to the wind and sun and the smoke from the arquebuses. Henri moved about in the mood of ethereal exultation which always came upon him before his battles, when prayer was over and only the fight remained. Indeed, it was marked by all as an omen of victory. A poet among his officers, du Bartas, eight years older than Henri of Navarre, the companion of his youth through many ups and downs — the night of Saint Bartholomew, the long captivity in the Louvre, the battles, the victories, the ascent of the throne, the shifting luck of war — du Bartas, a tall, dark-faced man, who thought more of death than of life, and, as time passed, still less of life and even more of death, saw Henri in that hour. And again he looked at him with utter love, and with as strong a faith as, long ago, in their youth, when they had ridden in a long cavalcade, stirrup by stirrup, through the land. Huguenots — to their winged spirits this land was holy, they held themselves ready to encounter the Lord Jesus in bodily guise at the next turning of the ways, and indeed they would have hailed him: Sire! They would have followed him and won his victories. And all this came back into du Bartas's mind as he watched the King at Ivry.

Henri stopped, for the man's eyes held him fast. "Well, we are to fight for the Religion once more," said he. "You were always troubled, du Bartas, over the blindness and the wickedness of men. Will our victory and kingdom teach them a lesson, do you think?"

"Perhaps," said that foreboding heart. "I hope so. Those, at least, that are called to see the victory in the eye of God. Sire, you must give me my discharge."

" No," said Henri sharply, lowering his voice. " This should be a piece of life — old friends, the time of joyous darkness. I would not miss it nor lose it. Stay with me, whatever else becomes of me. Du Bartas, awhile ago I sent you secretly to the courts of Europe. What did I pay you for your journeys? "

" A hundred and fifty crowns the first time, and eighty-five the next."

" Next time you shall be governor of a great city."

" 'Tis no matter now," said du Bartas. " Lord, today I still serve you, tomorrow someone greater. I have even composed the song you shall sing, in thanksgiving for victory." And he gave the King a parchment. " And it is not mine, but yours, invented and composed by you yourself. And you are to proclaim it, that in your fame something of me may yet survive upon the earth."

Here they were interrupted, not altogether to Henri's displeasure. It was in fact the Swiss Colonel Tisch, who came about his men's pay. Just before the battle was the right moment. No sooner did the King see him than he burst into a tirade — making more of it, indeed, than he really felt, that his wrath might put the money out of Tisch's head. The Switzer's face grew purple and he kept his lips firmly closed or he must have answered the King's onslaught. Henri watched him as he marched off in his great boots, and reflected that it was too late for the Switzers to desert him then. They would have to fight, and would fight all the better, as plunder was their sole hope of getting paid.

But without the resolve to fight, nothing can be done. The other Switzers, yonder with the enemy, who also had not been paid, knew moreover that the King of France was the ally of their Confederation; and they did not mean to strike a blow in that battle. They had so sworn; and since both, Henri and Colonel Tisch, knew this, neither master nor man was seriously perturbed. They were to win that battle. Henri had thrust a gigantic plume of white feathers in his hat, and another such nodded from his horse's head. He rode down the front of the line and cried: " Comrades! God is with us, yonder stands the foe, and here your King. At them! And if your standards go down, mark my white plume, you will find it where victory and honour lead the way! "

He rose in his stirrups, and behind that lean face and those flashing eyes came the thought that his hat was indeed worth looking at! It had cost a hundred crowns, with the white ame- thysts and the pearls. Not including the plume. And the Swiss would fight. Then he noticed that the enemy army was in mo- tion, led by a monk, who had promised the Leaguers that the heretics would flee at the sight of his great cross. Henri, with the order to attack upon his lips, during that last minute gal- loped along his line till he reached his Switzers. " Colonel Tisch! " He embraced him from horse to horse. " I did you wrong, but I will make all good."

" Ah, Sire! Your graciousness will cost me my life," retorted the old Colonel. Then they parted, and each galloped ahead of his own men against the enemy line. The first to strike it was Marshal d'Aumont, who drove in the enemy light cavalry. But the German horsemen promptly threw back the King's squad- rons in disorder against the infantry, which made much confu- sion among the Royalists. To add to the disaster, Count Egmont with his Walloons fell upon the Royalists, who were thus faced with Spain and the House of Habsburg; for they had never seen so close into the eyes of the invincible World Power. Terrible it was, and that first unlucky clash might well have led to rout and ruin. One Royalist cried to another before the mêlée swept him away:

" Well, old heretic, who wins the battle? "

" It's lost for the King. Pray God he be not killed! "

Rosny, usually a dashing horseman, took no more favourable a view — he had five wounds already, from pistol bullets as well as swords and lances; he conceived he had done enough, slipped out of the turmoil, and found refuge under the hanging branches of a pear-tree. A man so full of wounds was deaf to the noise of battle, and Rosny, later known as Sully, promptly fainted. Nor was he awakened by any thunder of cannon.

As in his other battles, the King had the cannon in his fa- vour, and he knew how to make good use of them. The enemy guns fired over his head; his found their mark. The first to turn and run was the too sanguine monk. Now, the army of the League was compact with superstition and false foolhardiness; when the lies that puffed it up were blown away, the heart was gone from out of it. This was the achievement of the King's cannon. In a flush of fury Count Egmont rode in a mortal charge against those guns; he thrust the hind-quarters of his horse into one of the fire-belching tubes, by way of insult to what, in his opinion, was the weapon of heretics and cowards. And indeed it belched no more. Instead, the King's horsemen fell upon the unsuspecting enemy and cut them to pieces, including Egmont himself. The Duke of Brunswick fell in the attack of his German horsemen, who promptly fled. Henri! In press and tumult do not fail to notice that the flying Germans have crashed into their own front, which has begun to waver towards the right.

A moment — beyond mark or measure; miss it, and it is gone. The King halted, he stood up in his stirrups. But as though the moment must indeed be measured, he felt for his watch, but he had lost it: eighty crowns, and a moment that could not be measured. His plan was otherwise; truly had the ambitious strategist never designed nor purposed what he was now about to venture. A glance behind him, where silence had fallen, a sudden, utter silence: "Turn your faces to me! And if you will not fight, then see me die!" He dashed forward about two horse-lengths, plunged wildly into the forest of enemy spears, seized them with his hands, and held the enemy until his horsemen could come up. He held them not only with his hands, he showed them his face, which spoke of majesty and power; of other things, perhaps, at other times, but here only of power and majesty. First their humiliation by the monk, then their terror of the guns, and now the face of the King. They had missed the moment — all those Spaniards and Frenchmen, and the German riders. The Royalists were on them, cutting them down and bursting through the shattered line of the once dreaded enemy. A rider brought the King back his watch, which was indeed surprising, and said in so doing: " Sire! Less than a quarter of an hour ago we were defeated."

" Spare all Frenchmen! " shouted the King after the pursuers. The Switzers of the League surrendered, they had not struck a blow. The King himself, at the head of but fifteen or twenty horsemen, pursued a throng of more than eighty fugitives. When he pulled up, he had killed seven with his own hand and taken a standard. Where he halted ended the battle and the victory of Ivry. The King dismounted and knelt. He flung his hat upon the ground. No one else should now follow that great white plume, he longed to be alone and far from all his fellows; but from every side came the noise of the now scattering struggle. The King, on his knees, drew from his doublet a sheet of parchment, the song of thanksgiving written by his old comrade, du Bartas.

Far away, Mayenne, of the House of Lorraine, leader of the almighty League, strove, corpulent as he was, with the two surviving members of his suite, to collect some sort of force. Far away too, in another direction, awoke a sorely battered horseman — who was one day to become the famous Duke of Sully — from his fainting-fit beneath a pear-tree.

Rosny felt his limbs and his members; not one of them was whole — swords, pistols, and spears had done their work upon him, and he had also fallen with his horse — his first horse, when its belly had been slit; of his second he had lost all recollection. Wherever he touched himself he came upon dried blood. " I must look horrible," thought the Baron, who was much attached to his smooth face. Dusk was falling. His sword in fragments, his helmet battered, he made an effort to get out of his cuirass, but the dented iron hurt his bruised body almost beyond endurance. " Hey, arquebusier, whither so fast? Come — fifty talers for that nag you're leading by the rein. But you will have to help me mount."

Scarce had the fellow taken the money when he ran. The rider, swaying in his saddle from loss of blood, hunger, thirst, and weakness, missed his direction and strayed over the battlefield; he fell in with some enemy horsemen, their standards starred with the black crosses of Lorraine. He supposed that the battle had been lost and they meant to take him prisoner.

" Who goes there? " cried one of the noblemen of the League.

" Monsieur de Rosny, in the Royal service."

" What! Why, we know you. Permit us, Monsieur de Rosny, to introduce ourselves. Will you have the courtesy to take us prisoner against a ransom? "

" What! " he too began. But the word " ransom " promptly cleared his head. Five wealthy noblemen, and each one ready to pay according to his value. Rosny grasped the position. Beneath his pear-tree he had been unwittingly transformed into a conqueror.

Song of Thanksgiving

In the meantime his King knelt upon the battlefield, his only company over a wide compass being the dead, lying in heaps or scattered singly, and darkness was about him. His horsemen of the last encounter had left him, for they observed that he was reading from a paper and his lips were moving. Night fell; he put the paper away; it indeed contained a song of thanksgiving — but it sounded to him too vainglorious, and also too sad. His own thanksgiving to the Lord was to conceive Him as the God of Reason — God is always on the side of reason, said Henri, on his knees there after the battle; and later on, erect upon his throne, he said no less.

His enemies had poor swollen heads, full of lying and deceit; and so they failed. They made boast of a power and a glory far beyond their claims; hence the anger of the Lord. Their creed was surely false, if only because it was theirs; and the reason of God was against them, being arrayed on the side of the kingdom.

Such was his confession of faith, and it rang clearer to his inward ear than ever before, in the shadowed stillness of a deserted battlefield. Wherefore, for the first time, he was touched by no sympathy for the fallen. A thousand must have been cut down, certainly five hundred taken prisoner, and how many had been drowned in the river, who could tell? Meantime the Lord's pa-

tience had its limits. They would drop all their baggage, but
Henri and his men would be at their heels, and however light
they travelled, the Royalists would be in Paris before them this
time. " Grant this, O Lord, for Thy patience has its limits."

Such was his supplication after the victory; nor did he, as was
his habit, shed tears over each of his slain countrymen. But evil
was truly beyond all pardon, as Henri felt most deeply at that
moment, and he would have had fat Mayenne hanged. Now in
the distance a few lights were moving from place to place. The
King approached his noblemen, who were looking for their own
dead among the corpses. " That is Monsieur de Fouquières," he
suddenly observed. " He should not have fallen, I still had need
of him."

They told him that the dead man had left a wife, who was
expecting a child.

" I'll give his pension to the child she carries," said the King.

They carried the lanterns from corpse to corpse until they
reached that of Colonel Tisch. The King recoiled and covered
his eyes. If only he had not embraced him! They had ridden to
the attack just afterwards; it must have happened then. He
meant to make too high a payment for his master's favour. " My
Cross of the Holy Ghost for my brave Switzer," said the King,
and was about to take it from his breast. But there was no cross
there; it had been lost in the battle, and no rider brought it back.
The King bowed his head, stricken by his own helplessness.
They depart, and he had nothing to send after them. What did
they care now for his brief victory, when they were sitting at the
seat of eternal victory? Suddenly he recalled the whole song of
thanksgiving, as he had read it by the failing light, and found it
too vainglorious and too sad. But he felt his heart contract with
pain.

Quickly he snatched a lantern from one of those about him
and hurried on until he found the dead man whom he knew that
he must find. He could not weep, for the pain that gripped his
heart. But he moved the lantern back and forward over his old
comrade as he lay there, and held his hands to see whether there
were any last message in those broken eyes. None. Of course

there was none. Indeed, he was but one of several who had ridden in that train of horsemen many years ago. There were enough Huguenots left. But this one meant to go — why? Had the hour struck for du Bartas? How stood it then with Henri?

By way of answer to the questionings of his agonized heart, he announced to his noblemen that they would sing a thanksgiving to the Lord, and he would sing it to them first. Then he recited it to a psalm tune, very simply and in an undertone. The others knew the tune, and all hummed it together.

> *Now, Lord and God, cometh at last the day;*
> *In human guise, compact of earthly clay,*
> *Thy loved Son, in a chariot of fire,*
> *Descends awhile to us and these dominions,*
> *In love and justice; while the angel choir*
> *Circle the starry vault with whirring pinions.*
>
> *O glory of the battle we have won;*
> *For God hath sent to us His only Son,*
> *That we might see the victory in His eyes.*
> *My Christ and King, now Thou art Lord below,*
> *Let me go whither I have longed to go,*
> *And stand before the Throne of Victories.*

When the King had finished, he was weeping bitterly, though no one had really understood what he was saying. Indeed, the last few lines were scarce heard. The pious humming of the noblemen had drowned the words.

In the village tavern there was high rejoicing, but a few left the revelry and waited outside for the King as he came back from the battlefield. " Sire, your orders! "

" We start for my capital before dawn."

" Sire, your fame indeed demands it. . . ." " This time nothing and no one shall withstand you. . . ." " The gates shall

fly open before you." These utterances, from various lips, were
rapped out in sharp succession, as had been arranged. Such was
the King's impression, especially when this sentence reached his
ears: "A great and victorious King will never abjure his religion."

Henri glanced from one to another; and in their eyes there
was mistrust of him and his constancy. He had long known it,
and he had understood that many a man was secretly wavering
because he thought his master was so. He could best conceive
of this from his own anxieties and doubts. Again the contrac-
tion of the heart that had come upon him as he stood by the
body of his old comrade. "God permits the Huguenots to conquer, my lords." He spoke with majesty and force. "The Lord
my God hath taught me to respect both creeds, and to be true
to mine." It was just that of which he was no longer certain —
and he was convinced as he looked about him that several of
the Protestants who heard him disbelieved his words. Except
Mornay. His virtuous Mornay, his Ambassador, that astute man
of affairs, who had damaged his enemies by his dispatches no
less than by a cannonade; Mornay believed in his good faith.
But how could he know what the King did not know himself?
Strange it was that the virtuous Mornay's confidence annoyed
Henri, and he turned away. At that moment someone said:

"Sire! Paris is worth a Mass."

The King swung round; the speaker was a man by the name
of d'O, just O, and looked as much, a corpulent youth, whom
the favour of the late King had turned into a drone and a thief
— one of the adventurers who had divided the land and its
revenues between them. For that very reason Henri had allowed
him to remain what he was, Treasurer of the kingdom. It was
a business that could best be managed by such as meant to make
a profit on it; and he was saved the trouble of persuading honest
men into the needful devices. As the King's questioning gaze
fell on Mornay, the latter said:

"All honourable Catholics serve Your Majesty."

Henri had made the very same answer to d'O and his satellites
when they first urged him to abjure his religion. This had happened at the deathbed of the murdered King and had been a

perilous warning. However, Henri himself had then used the words, and now his Mornay had uttered them again that day. But he slipped his arm through Mornay's, drew him aside, and said in an undertone:

" Were we fighting for the Religion? Was this the best of our battles? "

" It should be," replied Mornay. " Sire, you no longer have the right to risk your life as you did today, when you dashed on to the enemy spears. It was the bravest folly of your life."

" And how should we stand now? What words are these, Mornay? "

As the King came among the revellers, the laughter and the shouting were stilled. The feasting and the wine-cup were put aside, all stood up, and with their eyes upon the King they struck up the song of thanksgiving. It was the same that Henri had first sung on the battlefield, with but a few companions round him. These had marked it carefully; especially Agrippa d'Aubigné, the King's old friend. A stocky figure, he drew himself up to his full height, and sang in resounding tones. Quite distinctly too he brought forth the last lines, which Henri had but muttered, or even swallowed.

> My Christ and King, now Thou art Lord below,
> Let me go whither I have longed to go,
> And stand before the Throne of Victories.

Agrippa's naturally bold and humorous face here became so expressive that the King was left in no doubt. Their old friend du Bartas had shown the song of thanksgiving to both of them before he fell. Someone said:

" That is the song composed by the King."

" Yes," said Henri, as his departing friend had bidden him do. He spoke under the bold and humorous gaze of Agrippa, who nodded. But Henri felt it was not true — nor anything else that was happening in that place. Only in outward aspect was this like the Huguenot victories of old days.

A FEAST WITHOUT GUESTS

The march upon the King's capital did not proceed as quickly as had been ordered. Even a conquering army falls into some disarray, all the more when there is much booty to be taken and a fleeing enemy to be pursued in all directions. The King could only wait until his commanders had got their men in hand again. Meantime he recovered from the strain of battle by the aid of hunting and of love. Of the latter he had for some while been deprived. It was indeed the essential force within him, as the Venetian Ambassador had recognized at once. In all that he had done the deep-set impulse had been sex and the heightened energy born of its enchantment. After the battle the enchantment persisted, and Henri thought of his women, of those once loved and lost and of those whom he had looked on and desired.

He wrote letters to Corisande — the Muse of his journey towards the throne. Her face had grown blotched; he was ashamed of her and glad that she was in the South, a hundred miles away. None the less she lay before his senses as happiness possessed, and once again he wrote to her whom he no longer loved, the Countess of Gramont, letters in which he showed himself a master of romantic adoration. For the heightened vigour of the ecstasy born of sex had made him also a master of his pen.

She who had once been Corisande saw through his self-deceit. She had long known herself deceived. She wrote bitter comments in the margins of his lively letters, which she hated for their very liveliness; her life had no place in them, only his battles, his murderers, enemies, and victories, his tremendous hopes, and his kingdom. In days gone by, whether he remembered it or not, it was agreed between them that she should stand upon a balcony and be the first to greet him when he rode into his capital. Faithless creature, he had flung it from his mind. She picked up a pair of scissors and drove it through the letter at the place where he had signed his name.

He was impervious. In those days he even wished the Queen of Navarre were with him, but had to take his pleasure quickly

with any passing adventuress whom he happened to encounter.
In his youth he had most often possessed his Queen, and, what
was more, in disaster, in mortal need. In those days she stood
by him despite the many men she had preferred from time to
time; she stood by him, saved his life, and followed the fugitive
to his land of Navarre. " Never again, Margot? And when my
fortunes rose, you became my bitter enemy, raised troops against
me, and would do so again, had you any money left. But you
sit alone in your bleak castle, hating me. I would love you again
and love you always, Margot of the night of Saint Bartholomew."
So thought he after Ivry; and Marguerite of Valois, in her bleak
castle, smashed most of her majolica when she heard of his
victory.

The castle of the widowed Countess de La Roche-Guyon
stood in Normandy; not far for Henri to ride, and he rode
thither often after he came to know the Countess. Until the
battle of Ivry he had almost always gone by night, for work and
fighting kept him busy in the daytime. In the grey dawn he
would appear beneath her windows, she would step out on to her
balcony; he in the saddle and she at a safe height would converse
for a while. He told her she was beautiful, as beautiful as the
fairy Morgana, if indeed that fairy was more than the figment of
a dream. But here above his head the dream appeared in bodily
form, a fair-haired lady, tall and lissom, and her flesh, were a
man allowed to touch it, would not dissolve into air in fairy
fashion.

To which Antoinette replied with gallant banter to the same
effect. She would let her floating draperies slip apart, then wrap
them round her, while she could make her blue eyes look grave
or roguish, mocking or very still. On each occasion that astute
and highly honourable lady gave her fiery lover hopes. But when
his brief interlude was over he had to ride away without ever
having been admitted. Her excuse was that it was still night.
Now his toil was over, that should avail no more. Soon after
Ivry he announced that he purposed coming at high noon. " We
have sniffed at the lily long enough, 'tis time for Antoinette to
confess a little love for Henri. Dear lady, my body is quite whole

again, but my soul will never be disburdened until you have leaped the fence. Dear heart, do not delay; love me as one who will worship you until the grave. In true token of which I press a thousand kisses on your white hands."

Thus he wrote; but later, when all was long past and he had never possessed Antoinette, he felt no regret, either for her resistance or his devotion. Indeed, from respect for her virtuousness, he promoted her Lady of Honour to the Queen.

He paid that promised visit, like all the others, alone and unattended. She feigned astonishment, received him half-way down the outer stairway, and led him within to a table which had been set for at least twenty people. Mystified at first, he looked inquiringly for the other guests. She laughed, so that he could not but understand how he stood with her. Whereupon he recovered his wits and requested that the lackeys who were arrayed against the wall should hand the dishes to the invisible guests. She dismissed the lackeys, and he promptly repeated what he had written about sniffing at the lily and leaping the fence, but in rather more gallant and expressive fashion than he could do in the best of letters. Truly she need fear no faithlessness, she had his word — and his heart went with it.

"Sire! Worship until death? I am young and would not see you die because you no longer worshipped me."

They were seated alone at the long table with the twenty covers. The calm and watchful look masked the lovely delicate face once more, and the lady spoke:

"I jest, Sire, because I am afraid; as one might sing in the dark. It was much harder to win the battle of Ivry than a victory over a poor solitary woman."

Then he fell at her feet, kissed her knees, and besought her humbly. But she was firm: "My House is not great enough for me to be the King's wife, and too great for me to be his mistress." As he persisted, she pretended to retire to her room, but left the house by a doorway at the back and got into her waiting carriage. Before Henri noticed her absence, she was saved.

He had, while searching for her, gone through several rooms. In the last a door opened and someone came towards him. Just before they met he recognized his mirrored image. It would not commonly have misled him for so long, but he was confused by the lady's demeanour. " Well met, old friend! " — and he waved at the mirror; what he saw there stirred the suspicion that the lady might in truth have run away from him because he was no longer young enough for her. It was his first suspicion of the kind. A shock, a searching gaze, and then a burst of laughter, because, as often and often, a man is bemused by his own heart, and by the enchantment of sex that heightens energy. But what could avail against sunken cheeks, a greying beard, and that deep furrow from the root of the nose up into the wrinkled forehead? Indeed, he laughed deliberately, that he might see the tension in the lifted brows, and the sadness in the wide eyes.

" Why so sad? " he wondered in all seriousness. " Deep within me I am gay; and they all enchant me." He meant women, the whole sex. She had found his nose too large, he decided; too curved and drooping. It was ridiculous on so thin a face as his. In the end he came to the conclusion that he must take more trouble " with them " than he used to do. The easy luck of youth was past. What else was changed he did not observe. " Henri! " said the Countess Antoinette at that same moment, and the creaking of her coach on the rutted road covered up her cry and what she suffered. " Henri! Had you not been the victor of Ivry. Sire, I should have encountered you when you were an unknown Prince, when in the forest you found a charcoal-burner's wife and made her happy. You had the tapers put out at a ball, and in the darkness took the one you wanted. I would have been she. All would have been over and forgotten, and you would have been gone long since. Now it is your notion to endure; a faithful lover, it was to be seen upon your forehead, my Henri, and I read it beneath your brows. I would gladly follow you everywhere, except into your greatness and your fame. Forgive me. Your too bright light would fall upon me. Sire, for ten years long you would promise to marry me and never do it. . . . Drive back, coachman, at a walk." He had surely gone by now. She wept.

An Easy Question

Hunting had to console Henri for this failure; and as he was galloping with horses and dogs across a plain, at the end of which stood a castle-crowned hill, what did he see? A most curious procession climbing the hill — very slowly, so that the huntsmen easily caught up with it. " Hello, fellows, what may this be? " Ahead walked two great horses with slit hides.

" Sire, they are Monsieur de Rosny's chargers. The largest was his first at Ivry. It fell under him, and we caught it later on."

" Why is the page carrying a suit of armour and a white banner? "

" It is Monsieur de Rosny's page carrying the chief standard of the Catholic army, captured in the battle. The other page is carrying Monsieur de Rosny's shattered helmet and a splintered lance."

" Who are those behind them? "

" The one with the bandaged head is Monsieur de Rosny's equerry; the other, on the English palfrey, is his chamberlain, dressed in his master's orange and silver cloak, and in his hand the trophies of victory, swords and pistols, which Monsieur de Rosny broke and captured in the fight."

" But in the centre, on the litter? "

" Sire, Monsieur de Rosny."

" I hope all is well with him; indeed, he could scarce otherwise have given himself so splendid an ovation," said Henri, turning to his suite. Then he asked another question: " Who are those riding on donkeys behind the litter? "

" Sire, those are the noblemen whom Monsieur de Rosny took prisoner."

" No doubt they are discussing the luck of war. And what are you doing at the rear of the procession? "

" We are Monsieur de Rosny's servants and are following him to his ancestral castle. Yonder rides his banner-bearer with his company of guards and two companies of mounted arquebusiers. More than fifty are missing, and those that survive have bandaged heads and arms."

Henri felt like laughing at this pompous display; but ought vainglory to be derided when it lies upon a litter? He rode up; the litter was constructed of branches and barrel staves, but upon it were the gorgeous mantles of the prisoners, black silk and richly embroidered with the silver crosses of Lorraine, and their battered helmets with black and white plumes. And among them all lay, triumphant but sadly damaged, the cavalier himself.

"My good friend," said Henri cordially, "I congratulate you. You look much better than might have been expected. Is there no broken limb? We cannot have you left a cripple. There are hair-raising stories told of your adventures."

At these simple words the excellent Rosny's self-complacency faded and was gone. He rose from his prostrate position and would even have got out of the litter, but the King would not suffer him. So the Baron said in cool, calm tones, omitting the quaver with which he had lately been speaking: "Sire," said he, "Your Majesty brings me comfort, and honours me too much by your concern. I cannot express my feelings, and will but say that I have recognized the visible aid of God. Thanks to His goodness, my wounds are in good case, even the large one on my hip, and in at most two months I hope to gain some more in your service, and for the same wage — love of Your Majesty."

At this, Henri was much nearer weeping than laughing, so deeply was he moved. He embraced Monsieur de Rosny, who had spoken with such modesty and composure, and without a hint of arrogance. "Look, my lords," he cried, "here is a true and noble knight!"

He accompanied the train for a short distance, bent over the litter, and said in an undertone:

"Make haste and recover, Rosny, you obstinate old heretic; we have to take Paris."

To which the Baron, in a whisper too: "Your Majesty scarce speaks like one of the Religion."

Henri, in an ever lower voice: "Would that trouble you?"

Rosny, into the King's ear:

"Sire, you may not ask an obstinate Huguenot like me to advise you to go to Mass. But one thing I will say to you, that this is the quickest and easiest way to counter the machinations of your enemies."

The King sat erect in the saddle. As though he had not heard, he pointed to the castle, now not far distant. " Farewell, my friend. If I succeed and am increased in power and greatness, you may be very certain of your share, Monsieur de Rosny."

So saying, he set spurs to his horse, and with hunt and pack behind him the King of France dashed off at a gallop through the woodland domains of his astute and faithful servant. Suddenly the trees thinned and he came out upon fields edged by tall birches, quivering faintly against the blue of heaven. Bent over the ground, peasants stood toiling — looked up when they heard the clatter of hoofs, and made ready to leap aside. But the hunt halted suddenly, and the King, whom these folk did not yet know, pointed to the purple walls towering above the distant peaks. And he said to the oldest of the men: " Tell me, friend, to whom does that castle belong? "

" Monsieur de Rosny," answered the old man.

" Give me a handful of earth," said the King to the man's sturdy son, who reached it up to him on his horse. The King poured the earth from one hand to the other. " Good rich earth. To whom do the fields belong? "

" Monsieur de Rosny."

" Look! " The King crushed a clod in his fingers; in it shone a silver crown. " That is for Madelon. Whisk up your apron." The girl did so, he tossed the coin into it, and she laughed up at him with half-closed eyes — in them a glint of roguery and secret understanding, familiar to him from his youthful days.

As he rode on he shouted back:

" You have a good master, and he will always find me a good master too."

The peasants looked at each other open-mouthed; then, speechless with amazement, they ran a little way after the cavalcade. The galloping horsemen departed in a cloud of dust, the hounds bayed exultantly, and a huntsman wound his horn.

A Pit of Hell

" Praised be God, the King is dead," said the people of Paris,
and they did indeed believe this time not merely that he had
been defeated, but that the game was played out. And the King
let them so believe. Rain fell interminably, the highroads were
deserted, and nothing was heard of him, though he was but a
day distant at Nantes. He had had to take the town by assault,
like all the others. Once within its walls, he gave the bakers a
feast. The Craft had heard tell that the King owned a mill down
in his native country and was known as the miller of Bubaste.
To do honour to his name, he played ball with them; they won
all his money and then wanted to stop. He demanded his revenge, and when they refused he ordered bread to be baked
throughout the night. Next day he sold it at half price; whereupon the bakers were truly eager to play once more.

He took care that this affair should be reported in Paris. Thus
they learned not merely that he was alive, which was disastrous
enough, but that he was buying up corn everywhere. His army
must be enormous! Suddenly everyone knew and admitted that
the King had won at Ivry. He had utterly defeated the Duke.
Fat Mayenne and his shattered army would never get to Paris
on those sodden roads. They were lost. Nothing would stop the
heretic; they could but sit and wait for him. Last time he had
pillaged the outer wards and killed nine thousand citizens.

Eight hundred in fact, but the terror of the great city exaggerated on every count — Henri's ruthlessness and their own
impotence. He was waging war on the mills and the grain-
merchants of France. They would starve, said they, paralysed by
foreboding, while they watched the Spaniards getting in supplies. The Spaniards were the Ambassador Mendoza and the
Archbishop of Toledo, the latter on a special mission, that he
might report to Don Philip what was the most pressing need of
those next to be subjected to the World Power — faith or money.
It was, in truth, bread, as was very plain to the Archbishop. He
and the Spanish party made provision, especially the sixteen
prefects of the city wards, and, above all, the religious houses.

The Dukes of Aumale and Nemours commanded the garrison, and were, come what might, allied with Spain, but at heart they were for France, as was not too common in Paris at that time; only older folk, lying in prison, remembered the meaning of freedom, religion, and sound sense. A certain Bernard Palissy wrote from the Bastille offering the Duke of Nemours, a Guise, the philosophers' stone. This was the name he gave to a certain petrified skull — and he really meant that the sight of such an ancient relic of humanity should warn Lorraine to abandon the futile and disastrous ambition of his House and recognize the true King of France. " We shall soon appear before God," observed the sage, and he never learned that Nemours had actually been stricken with remorse when he touched that " philosophers' stone."

Then there was Lorraine's sister, the famous Duchess of Montpensier, whose husband was serving in the army of the King; she herself was his enemy, and proud of having suborned the late King's murderer. Not satisfied with that exploit, she wanted to see the Huguenot upon the scaffold. Nay, on the wheel and gallows! The Fury of the League once more from her balcony harangued the student youth of Paris, until they carried her cry of murder through the streets. Meantime the beautiful but now ageing Duchess lay within, clutching her heaving bosom. The hatred and the thirst for vengeance that so wrought upon her had grown to torture, and in the end she began to doubt her senses. Navarre's victory at Ivry she had heard of through her defeated brother, Mayenne, before even the Spaniards themselves, but she had long kept the knowledge to herself and would not admit the reason until it mastered her. " Navarre," she said, that she might not say " France "; but in her passionate breast his name was merely Henri, and her hatred was as much a torment to her as his good fortune. She heard that he had captured the Prior of the monastery whence came the monk whom she had suborned to murder the King. Henri handed the Prior over to his tribunal at Tours; the Prior had been torn asunder by four horses; the Duchess lay three hours unconscious. Ambroise Paré visited her, an old surgeon whom all respected, though he was

a Huguenot. He bled the lady, and when she awoke she said:
" Has he come? " — in a tone and with an expression that made
the old man recoil, though he had seen the night of Saint Bartholomew and several times looked upon the face of hell.

The great city believed every rumour. They believed him
come while he was still reflecting whether he should again
launch his soldiers against the outer wards of Paris. They cried
that they were starving, when their markets might well have
been full; but they were betrayed by the prefects of the sixteen
city wards, whose minds were Spanish though their speech was
French. On the 8th of May in the year 1590 the King had his
capital completely beleaguered at last. This time he left no outlet, neither to the right nor to the left of the river, took the outer
wards, put down violence, and kept up a desultory cannonade
over the walls — but did no more than beset them closely, so
that none could pass.

On the 14th the processions began. The monks marched at
the head of the city guard. They had all eaten, the monks more
heavily than was needful; they panted painfully under the cuirasses in which their portly persons were confined. Habits were
belted up, cowls thrown back, the men of God were helmeted and weaponed. When the Papal Legate appeared, these
ghostly warriors, in offering him due salutations, shot his al-
moner. Whereupon the Duke of Nemours said, as man to man,
to the Duke of Aumale: " How long are we to take part in this
scandal? I am a Lorrainer, and a Frenchman too; but this is
Spain. We are on the wrong side. We should be outside the
walls, with our seventeen hundred Germans, eight hundred
French infantry, and six hundred cavalry. Guise or Navarre —
that could be decided outside in honourable fashion."

And d'Aumale replied: " Do not forget the city guard and
the slaughtered victims; nor the terror of reprisals, always so savage in a civil war. Suppose we withdraw now; Paris will sink into
an orgy of terror and massacre, and swear that all was done in the
interests of the true religion."

The other stretched out a hand towards the swaying, shouting procession in token that he had understood. " Paris would

be Spanish," said Nemours. "We Guises are betrayed. Don Philip no longer even sends the soldiers' pay. Mendoza coins beggars' pennies and throwns them out of his windows. To what purpose? The people are eating cats' meat, and that only on Sunday."

The two noblemen were always heavily guarded when they rode through the city they were charged to defend. The passers-by commonly fled, from evil conscience or because none trusted their fellows. No one cared to be seen alone. The bands that ranged the streets would venture nothing unless they were in outnumbering force. They searched the religious houses, headed by the city guard; but they found no more than what they could devour on the spot, all else was securely hidden away. Whereat they jeered at the monks and told them that on a derelict ship the fattest are eaten first. When they were filled, and not until then, came Mass and a sermon, that courage and zeal might be fortified.

Others crowded round the towers and wanted to climb up to see the fields and the ripening crops from far away. Then they stormed the square outside the Parliament and cried hoarsely for bread. Among the women madness had broken out; they offered themselves to be slaughtered and their flesh sold, if only their children might be fed.

Brisson, President of the High Court, had done what he could for these poor folk. He himself had no resources, being an honourable man. Many had indeed been fed in his house on that suspicious flour, brought in by smugglers, not from any mill, but from the cemetery by night. Brisson, a humanist, and devoted to the law, and hence at heart a King's man, treated with Monsieur de Nemours to save this besotted city. They conducted the most perilous talk upon which a great burgher and a great lord could venture under the iron sky of fanaticism. They both agreed that the revolt of godless unreason had now truly reached its farthest limit, and the destruction of the League, at whatever cost of life, was henceforward the only means of coming to terms with human reason and with God.

"At whatever cost!" said they, looking doubtfully from be-

hind a curtain through the open window. What they saw was
the church and the thronged portal, the street packed with people, all dumb, all pale with hunger, kneeling from weakness, or
standing vacant-eyed; and the only sound was the voice of the
preacher — a roar. " The King will abolish the Mass and destroy
you all. Good people, remember your salvation! " The man of
lies, Boucher, had for years flung them forth in his cunning
tirades, and he carried them to their limit, even beyond the
abyss; he snarled and bellowed from his pulpit. Those beneath
him recoiled against the throng behind, who tottered and
moaned in their deadly fear and weakness. Some were crushed
and trodden down, almost without a sound save for that faint
moaning and the roaring of the preacher. Brisson and Nemours
ended their vain talk. They were, of course, overheard. Monks
with a murderous mob forced their way in, crying for the whole
Parliament to be hanged. The Duke had to order his men to
fire.

But, after the worthy Boucher's abuse of the King and human
reason, his hearers departed as hungry as before, first in a broad
flow of human bodies, then in slower streamlets, followed by a
few stragglers like runnels that cannot find the main water-
course. These trickled in misery and weariness into the sur-
rounding streets. A woman sank exhausted against a house wall.
Oh, joy! Her boy had caught sight of a rat in the gutter, partly
open and partly covered, that ran down the middle of the street.
The boy clambered into it, crawled under the flagstones, and
wound himself out of the tunnel grasping the creature. " Something to eat, Mother! " At that moment two landsknechts came
up, one a giant, the other a little fellow with a peaked nose. He
grabbed the boy and tried to seize the rat, but the boy shrieked
and would not let it go. Then the huge landsknechts picked up
the boy, grasped him by the back of his jerkin, and holding the
child in his fist like a parcel from a shop, he stamped round the
corner of the next street. His sallow friend, who had one sunken
eye, glanced back once, and they had gone.

The few people in the alley stood rooted in terror, and in the
stillness the wailing of the child was heard for a little while. His

mother made as though to run after him, but staggered, and stumbled against another woman who just then came out of a house. Then came the mother's shriek, a shriek of horror and despair, and she fell to the pavement and lay motionless; the woman from the house stepped over her. Two old folks in a dark corner whispered: " This isn't the first time. The dame yonder knows only too well what the landsknechts will do with that boy. Her own son died, but no one saw him dead, and since then they have lived on salted food." Their quavering voices faded, the old creatures crept away, and the woman from the house passed by. She was almost a lady, she gathered up her dress lest it should drag in the mud. In her stony face the eyes glared crazily into a void.

A Struggle of Conscience

But next day the King let three thousand persons out of the city, that they might not die of hunger. His exalted ally, Elizabeth of England, heard of it and was very displeased. He had to send his special envoy, Philippe Mornay, to pacify her; and he did so gladly, for he was not sorry to get Mornay away for a while. He was to represent to the Queen that the death of a few poor French folk would not have induced the Spanish party to surrender Paris, so long as they themselves were still supplied. Moreover, he allowed the population to make brief forays by night, to harvest the grain in the fields under the walls. Bread suddenly reappeared in the bakers' shops, wherefore the people blessed the King. The monks and the city guard replied by spreading deeper terror and the news that the King was merely providing bread because of his great need for Spanish gold. His army was dissolving, and the troops of their rightful lord, Don Philip, were on the march. Praise be to God, the paltry heretic was lost. His grandest dream, to see the capital of his kingdom perish, would not be fulfilled.

Henri heard all this and was horror-struck. The monstrous doings that went on behind those walls and reached his ears were, alas, no new thing; his conscience told him so, and as time passed, his conscience grew ever more insistent. This was unworthy conflict. He was fighting unarmed men, the citizens of his own capital. Men broken by exhaustion and half-demented, they were even transgressing against nature, — while he ate and slept in safety.

Wherein his conscience had not told the whole tale, as he well knew. He was also in the midst of an intrigue with the lovely Abbess of a nunnery, and he actually transferred his quarters to another monastic house. And Henri's conscience reminded him, after a night of pleasure, that these nuns gave themselves to him as Judith did to Holofernes. At first they were but lambs on the slaughter-bench, but in the end they turned to raving furies as they saw the fires of damnation, and they would kill him if they could. There lay a curse and a blight upon heresy, thought the Protestant King, but wore, as before, a curl round his ear in the fashion of his fellows. Marshal Biron bantered him on his " change of creed," the name he gave to the diversion Henri sought with several holy ladies. The King sent for the old man and for the first time made clear that he meant to abjure his religion and adopt the other.

The resolve was wrung from him by remorse, and misery over the deeds that he had really committed, though in some measure against his will. That no old veteran could ever understand — though indeed Biron was well acquainted with all the darknesses and depths in the character of the debonair monarch. Their own disputes, before these two had found each other and embraced, had indeed been of a sort to try and test them both, as Biron never forgot. Erect and lean, swaying slightly from the wine he drank at all hours of the day, without ever beclouding his wits, a death's-head with a hanging moustache — there stood Marshal Biron, pondering and giving utterance, no one would have guessed with what affection for his master and how full of doubt. " Sire, shall I make this known? "

Henri nodded; he could not find his voice. Then he whispered: " Yes — but as though you were lying."

To which Biron retorted: " Vain it is to try to guess the truth. I do not know it myself. For Your Majesty has, as a Huguenot, defended your faith and your claim to the throne for more than twenty years; even against myself, who was your enemy and the enemy of Admiral Coligny, whom we Papists brought to such a dreadful death. I have forgotten nothing that happened in those days. And you, Sire? "

It was kindly but weightily spoken, and the King listened. Here was a Catholic who meant to warn him; and Henri asked himself whether he should really abjure the religion of the Queen his mother. He felt himself peering into a livid glare of light, from which someone marked and watched him — and who that was, only his sense of guilt could tell. He was dazzled, the glare was the inner light of conscience. And the figures of his mother and the Lord Admiral rose before his vision.

Pale and greatly shaken, he stiffened, controlled his voice, and repeated his command. At the last moment he turned in the doorway and cried to the Marshal: " But don't tell my Protestants. Not my Protestants."

He knew that they would, of course, hear of it. And he could predict the attitude of every one of his old friends. Glad he was that he had sent the austere Mornay to England. By the time the rumour reached that country it would be an idle legend, and though Queen Elizabeth might well conceive suspicion, Mornay would talk her out of it. His face indeed was absent, but there were others and enough to show him stern or melancholy countenances. Roquelaure, so eager for distinction, and Turenne, the man of the future, these were strong enough to speak their minds and to look askance at a perjured King. Agrippa made as though he had no inkling of what was going forward, but did in truth intend to take his King unawares. " Sire," he began, " I am in a tribulation of conscience."

" You, Agrippa? "

" I. Who else? A friend in Paris has betrayed to me the names of certain conspirators and has even sent me their letters that I may see what they are plotting against Your Majesty's life."

" Give them to me."

" To you? Why, Sire, the Spanish Ambassador will pay me more than you, if I let him know the business is discovered. But although I am always much set upon money, as you are aware, I would never seek it by dealings with the enemies of the Religion and my King."

"You prefer to wait until the murderers have got me? Or what price do you offer?"

Agrippa had never looked so formidable as at that moment. In a minute he seemed to have grown three inches.

"None. Care has been taken that when these people come into your presence you shall not know them."

"Then I will not believe that I was ever in danger."

"As you please, Sire," said Agrippa boldly and with his usual touch of humour. Soon afterwards it came about that certain Spanish lords, by direction of Don Philip, offered an Infanta in marriage to the King of France. Henri, in his anxiety for peace with his subjects, made haste to receive the envoys. Only the first of them was brought to him, and his hands were held, the left one by another, the right by Agrippa, who made as though the gesture were an undesigning courtesy — but gripped the man's wrist fast. Henri understood. He promptly dismissed the pretended agent, nor did he ask what became of him and his fellows. He offered no reward to Agrippa d'Aubigné for saving his life, still less did he thank him for the lesson that a man may be unselfish, honest, and resolutely loyal to his own cause.

He believed that disloyalty was a charge upon himself from God, since it was his destiny to save the kingdom. He gave honour to God — thus Henri justified his disloyalty, a none too easy matter before an all-knowing Deity. He obeyed Him against the memory of his mother and the Admiral, of all the champions of conscience, against the creed of the pastors, and heedless of a million victims of the religious wars. Neither old friends nor party nor the beloved cities in which worship was allowed, nor even La Rochelle, could be regarded now. No comradeship with those of his own faith, no psalm in battle; nothing could stand against the call of the kingdom. For that was more than a creed or a purpose, more even than fame; here were human creatures like himself; so he told himself, and really felt, that he was saved. Human creatures — but some of them, beyond those walls that he could see with his own eyes, sinned against nature. Thus it befell them, so soon as there was no king to hold them to their duty as men. That he would do, and that alone would justify him before the face of God and man.

"We will receive the two infidels," said he, by which he meant the Cardinal of Paris and the Archbishop of Lyon. He called them infidels to confirm his faith in the kingdom, of which such creatures take little account. With more than a thousand noblemen he betook himself one August day to the cloister outside the beleaguered city, where their emissaries waited on him. They were gentlemen of weight and dignity and had as yet suffered no privation, nor had any of their suite. They bowed before the King, but not obsequiously; the beleaguered city had no need to do so, in the person of her envoys. The King could not greet them with equal ceremony, the press around him was too great. And he said: "Do not be surprised to see me so beset. It is worse in battle."

He might well think that these men's sole purpose was to gain time until Mayenne could get fresh troops from Flanders and relieve Paris. Their parleys with the King might placate the starving folk of Paris, who might otherwise be tempted to an outbreak. The two Bishops were for their part convinced that the starvation of a few thousand common folk was as indifferent to him as to themselves. It was merely a question whether his popularity would allow him to admit as much. The most sagacious course seemed on both sides an exact observance of the formalities, wherefore the King asked the envoys for their written credentials, which they gave him. Therein was written that the Lords Cardinal and Archbishop were to approach the "King of Navarre" and beg him to consent to a general pacification of the kingdom; and then the Duke of Mayenne, that he too might give his mind to the matter. Vain words, and an insult to the royal rank.

Whereat Henri pointed out that it was no business of a "King of Navarre" to pacify Paris and France. However, he wanted to see his kingdom in peace and quiet and cared not to dispute a title. He said he would give a finger for so much, and indeed he offered two. One finger was worth a battle to him, but he promised two for a general peace. The two ghostly diplomats found him apt in dissimulation, and he rose in their esteem. "But," he cried, to their increased amazement, "Paris will wait in vain for peace so long as terror and starvation reign within her walls. We want no bodiless words of peace. I love my city of Paris. She is my eldest daughter." Therewith he unmasked their embassy of peace; but not everyone whose nakedness was now plain observed it.

He had lain a prisoner in Paris, that was all, said the two clerics to themselves. He called himself father of the people, but let him once suffer defeat and he would find himself behind bars again, whence he would never come out alive. And when he went on to compare himself with the true mother before Solomon and said he would sooner abandon Paris than win it through violence and death, their admiration was not unmingled with amusement, and they exchanged a meaning glance. Then they set about capping his dextrous deceit. They pretended to be doubtful of his military strength and the extent of his victories; they foreboded a turn in his fortunes. If Paris surrendered before the establishment of a general peace, Mayenne and the King of Spain would recover it again, and their vengeance would be terrible. Then they saw what they had never seen before.

A soldier upon whom the grace of majesty descended before their very eyes. They no longer understood who was here speaking and from what an eminence. He swore an oath, then paused in horror at his own words, but once again he swore — and by the living God. "We'll beat them," came an answering clamour from his noblemen, and their outburst was far more effective than a practised unison. "We'll beat them. It is truly sworn! No dishonour, while God lives!" The envoys realized in amazement that he had taken his stand in conflict with their world; against the crippled ruler of the earth, Philip, the inhuman dominion of Habsburg, a living majesty had raised its claim. They must confront it and believe. In life most things happen at a venture — such as the daily experience of high-placed, sceptical gentlemen, who regard every man of power as a betrayer and accept him as such. A shudder ran through their limbs, and before their eyes the earthly picture quivered, as they envisaged true majesty. Majesty — a feeble word for what was a plainly overmastering grace from God — how vague and unconvinced is the common attitude to God and grace! Two Princes of the Church had never considered the matter until faced with a soldier upon whom the grace of majesty descended before their very eyes.

Thenceforward Henri had his enemies in his hand during that parley. When the moment of high vocation had passed, he made lavish use of his advantage. He no longer treated the pair seriously, but demanded the surrender of Paris within a week, as though it were a trifle. ("Majesty may never long endure, we would not wear it out; grace, too, is a rare visitor; moreover, we are too well disposed to our good people to use greatness to force them to their knees.")

"You have a week, good friends. If you would prefer to put off the surrender until supplies are quite exhausted, do so; that will mean a hangman's breakfast for you, and then the rope."

"No King of France could be so merciless to his capital, nor any Christian to two servants of God."

"Then wait and see."

"It is to be feared that we two shall again be sent to you, but next time with ropes round our necks."

"Then surrender the city at once."

"If the Spaniards and the sixteen hear of it, they will hang us."

"Then wait for Mayenne and fresh troops from Flanders."

"Your Majesty might defeat them in the end, and we should the more surely be hanged."

"Then plead for surrender."

"Sire, you would forget our services and hand us over to the vengeance of the people."

"Then let them starve."

"You are falsely informed, Sire; no one is starving as yet."

"Then I bid you prosper. The cemeteries are not yet exhausted, plenty of children are left untended, and mothers fall down in fainting-fits."

Thereto they ventured no answer, but bowed their heads; there was no more spirit left in them. Their ground had slipped from under them, they felt they had let themselves be outwitted by the King. He had played a question-and-answer game with them, after the fashion of the famous scene in Rabelais, who used to be a mere buffoon. Their dignity was gone and they were utterly bewildered. The King gave them no time to recover; on the contrary, he dealt them the finishing blow. His last words were not quickly nor lightly spoken, but with the solemnity of a judge.

" Monsieur de Lyon," said he to the Archbishop, " a little while ago you fell into a press of people on St. Michael's bridge. Some of them flung themselves before your horse and cried for bread or death. Did not an old man speak to you? "

" I do not remember," stammered Monsieur de Lyon, and his head swam, as it probably would do on Judgment Day.

" He did so speak, and he said that these cries of despair were a last reminder from God."

At this secret revelation by the King, a faintness came upon Monsieur de Lyon, as upon a humble mother when she sees her child carried off for some dreadful purpose. His retinue supported him, and the Cardinal stood pale and haggard at his side. The King called for wine to hearten them, and while they drank it he mounted his horse. As he rode away, he told the nearest of his noblemen who it was that had warned the Archbishop on the bridge. Master Ambroise Paré, a surgeon and eighty-five years old, had used his last strength to speak upon the bridge, and now he lay dying. " In old days he was with the murdered Coligny," said King Henri, then set his lips fast and spoke no more.

His companions were silent, there was no sound save the dull clatter of hoofs. Henri was thinking of old Huguenots. As one of them, and still the same, so rode he here.

AN ARTIST

From his camp some officers came to meet him. Farnese was on the march. He was already in Meaux. The King laughed contemptuously, for Meaux was too near; he would have had the news before; moreover, his friends the Archbishop and the Cardinal would certainly have had it too and would not have let him fool them until they fell down in a faint. He shrugged his shoulders and rode on, to where two men were exchanging high words by the roadside. Monsieur de la Noue had reined in his horse with his iron hand. Monsieur de Rosny sat askew on his, for his heroic wounds would not let him sit otherwise; one arm was in a sling.

" Softly, gentlemen," said the King.

" Sire, Farnese," said La Noue.

" Sire," said Rosny, " it is a ruse. He cannot be at Meaux."

" Sire," cried the older man, " whom do you believe, this nincompoop or me? Farnese is so cunning that he sometimes even spreads the truth."

Rosny, crosswise on his saddle, diamonds in his hat, but his face composed and cold, turned his back on his guileless elder, and drew up beside the King. " Mere gossip," said he contemptuously. Upon which de la Noue burst out:

" Young man, ride thither in those fine clothes of yours. You'll please the Duke so much that he'll take you prisoner."

" Sir," rejoined Rosny, " I have one arm, and so have you; let us fight."

" I must watch this," said the King, but rather absently. Only the older man looked cheerful. His face had flushed dark red under his white thatch of hair, and the angry face lit up with a boyish laugh.

" I was a prisoner for five years among the Spaniards, and a sore time it was. Sire, in my jail I wrote upon religion and the art of war, and only thus I kept my courage. But the art of war that I described was that of Farnese. He is an artist, never forget it, Sire! "

" Our King is no artist, but a soldier, which stands for more," observed Rosny. His maimed condition as well as his haughty air lent him a sort of frozen dignity. The Breton Huguenot swung his limbs, including the iron arm, with all the more vivacity.

" What I know is the knowledge of twelve years in Flanders, in command of Protestant armies. Before the Spaniards took me, I captured any town I chose. But after the Duke of Parma came — not one."

The King, lost in his thoughts, rode on, and evening fell. Next day came news that the army of the League, with Mayenne, and the Spanish reinforcements under Farnese had met at Meaux. In the King's council of war La Noue urged a firm stand before Paris, while Biron, also an old man, demanded an advance. " We must attack. We have always attacked."

" Sire," said La Noue, " Your Majesty is unrivalled in battle. But you have never met with an enemy who evades battle and gets all he wants by art. I, Sire, know Farnese."

Rosny was on the point of another outburst against this boorish Captain in his leather doublet; but the Vicomte de Turenne, not less noble and handsome than Rosny, restrained him: the youth's fiery ambition had sharpened his judgment of a situation and even of his fellow-men. Marshal Biron was able to explain without interruption that the Royal army, extended all round Paris, could not fail to offer weak points. The enemy would force them and get provisions into the city. Whereupon La Noue:

" But in so doing he must cross a river or go through a wood. That is our moment."

" Attack! " repeated Biron. " March on the enemy when he is far away and not expecting you; that is war."

" Farnese knows your kind of war," cried La Noue. Slowly and with an air from which all the gaiety had gone he added: " But you do not know his war."

" Mere superstition," remarked that alert young Captain, Turenne, while Rosny smiled a chilly smile, and Biron blew out his nostrils. The King questioned all the others, and as they observed that he wanted to attack, the majority voted an advance.

Now at the outset the famed Farnese, Duke of Parma, stirred his gallant adversaries to something very near contempt. Would the commander of such a host entrench himself behind a swamp? The advancing Royalists merely observed the swamp because it blocked their way. They did not see the hill behind, which masked the disaster that was to come.

The Royalists held all the communications with Paris, especially the river Marne and Lagny, on which Farnese might well have schemed to make a covert raid. Meantime he entrenched himself behind his swamp, as though he feared nothing so much as the attack of the new Captain facing him — but he kept that new Captain waiting for his battle, a day, and then a week. The King had a fine array of noblemen, who found the delay tedious, and one by one they rode off with their companies. As for the capital, though they had to beleaguer it for a year, it must have fallen in the end, and filled all their pockets. The elusive Farnese behind his trenches and among his wagon barricades promised no profit; noblemen whose sole concern was plunder made their excuses until further notice. Men like Rosny stood fast, partly from a sense of honour and also because they thought that Spanish baggage must surely contain gold pistoles. A day would come when he would slit those sacks and cram his saddle-bags.

Henri had to admit himself baffled and mystified by his famous adversary. The King sent a trumpeter to taunt the Dukes to venture from their lair. The Italian answered coolly that he had not come so far to ask advice from the enemy. The King grew irritable, but he did not get his battle; he did not even get a sight of Farnese's face. Daily Henri rode out of Lagny, which was covered by his army, though the river was his main line of defence — made his way round the swamp and waited for Farnese.

Days passed and he could never get a glimpse of him. But, more humiliating still, his scouts reported that Farnese was dreaded by his men, and not a soldier deserted. Guard was mounted with iron precision. In the silence of the night, especially, the voices of the reliefs could be heard, in several tongues, but all in unison. With them had come an iron discipline, which had brought them down from Flanders in only twenty days;

every evening they had entrenched their camp, like Cæsar's legionaries. Under other generals these same troops would have been no more than a polyglot horde, mostly Walloons and Italians, with a sprinkling of Spaniards, ravaging the land like wild beasts; but under Parma they were a veritable Roman army.

Henri did not sleep, for he knew that yonder lay his adversary awake, devising to destroy his fame. Such were his orders from Don Philip. Henri must be on his guard. In vain he tried to pierce the darkness. Not a light in Farnese's quarters, though he never slept. Henri half-believed that Farnese could see in the dark and had his eye on his opponent. He was said to be a sick man, and old; indeed, he might be a shadow and a demon, and not a living man at all. On a damp and moonless night a man shivers readily, especially when his thoughts are hovering towards the unknown. Henri swung sharply round, something had touched his shoulder. For an instant he looked into a face — a face caught unawares, which, as it vanished, left an impress on the dark and stagnant air, which reeked of swamp and decay.

With a burst of laughter Henri turned and went. The echo of his laughter seemed to mock him, but he remembered in time that the renowned strategist had not worsted the Hollanders, as had gradually become known. His affairs had gone ill in Holland. Moreover he himself looked with disfavour on a campaign in France; he was only here by Don Philip's orders. Can a man command to order, and win victories for others? Parma was himself a ruling prince, but forgot his dukedom in the service of the King of Spain — who might well be paralysed, for he merely sat, and dreamed, and issued orders for the conquest of foreign kingdoms to a sick man like himself, campaigning in a foreign land. What would be the end?

On the morning after that night of many questions, Parma began to provide the answers; he drew up his army for battle: only, indeed, the army of the League, but he had exchanged their helmets and banners for his own. It was a September day, the fight was hot, and the King's Frenchmen thought they had at last encountered the fabulous Spaniards, before whom the world trembled, but not they! As the weapons crossed, behold, both sides spoke French. Once engaged, they hewed all the more savagely at these supposed Spaniards with familiar faces. Meantime Farnese withdrew his centre from the battle unremarked. He had not even confided in the fat Mayenne, who was laying about him in the van. Behind that modest hill, which had figured more largely in his plans than the swamp and his entrenchments, he threw his troops across the Marne by a bridge of boats — silently and secretly, and under iron discipline. And the battle was so hot that the manœuvre was unnoticed by the combatants. Of the two, Mayenne and Henri, the latter first grasped what had happened. Lagny was taken, or almost taken, from the farther side, and as Mayenne too, at last enlightened, was bombarding it from the near side of the river, the Royalists fell back, and the battle was lost.

Paris was then revictualled by water, while the King attempted a few sharp forays and even tried to escalade his capital. Farnese said of him: " I expected to find a King. I found a hussar." He cast yet more contempt upon the Duke of Mayenne, of the great House of Guise, by letting him plunge so bravely into what his own manœuvre turned into a meaningless encounter. Still, for all his anger, Mayenne could not but be glad that Farnese had left three regiments behind him. When all was duly completed, the great man started on his return march to Flanders. The King promptly sat down before Paris once more, which was a matter of no moment to the strategist.

He certainly conceived the King as an overrated mediocrity, who only needed to be put in his place. As an enemy he was about a match for Mayenne. *Vale et me ama.*

WE WANT TO LIVE

For two full days afterwards Henri was in truth a beaten man. This affair was more disastrous now than in earlier days, after so much patient fighting, some brilliant victories, and in the face of the rising estimation of the world. The capture of the capital postponed, though the provinces had been stripped of troops for just that purpose. Moreover, there was no money; for those two days no bread was baked; even the King's shirts were in rags. Of the company the King then kept, the less said the better.

Totus mundus exercet histrionem; we are all comedians, and when a man's affairs go awry, he soon finds himself amid a rabble of hearty friends, blown thither upon every breeze. A dispossessed German archbishop, turned Protestant from wanton pride — whom did such a man recall? " We too are minded to betray our religion. D'O is a rascal, but he is rich; he shall invite us and entertain our pimps."

On the evening of Ivry the Treasurer had made a gross remark — degrading it was and not to be forgotten. Henri had not forgotten it and had shunned the speaker. Not, indeed, of set purpose; such avoidance is natural when our inner being stands on the defensive, not merely against a stranger, but in truth against our own self. What is a word? 'Tis ill to recognize it as though it had been known already and merely kept concealed.

The Treasurer was now taken back into favour. A man of money is a friend, even though, like a certain Gascon captain, misfortunes in love have deprived him of his nose. The King frequented adventurers, whom many viewed with horror.

Yes. And he allowed them about him, to use them as tests of himself, his health, and his powers of resistance. Hearken to what is happening in Paris, where the citizens are now but maniac impersonations of themselves. In the end each man's own folly carries him along and justifies his life. But men of nobler stamp find it the more impossible, and indeed repellent, to live continually at the peak of folly. Familiar with adventurers up to the point when we ourself appear to be one! Even today a bullet may find its mark, and this shabby little King shall be put away in earth; never to have ploughed up this land with the hoofs of his horses, never to have possessed it as his kingdom. In Paris they hanged the President of the High Court on a charge of conspiring for his King and against Spain.

A decisive deed, which severs city and kingdom more surely than the strongest walls, when he who embodies the law is put to death. Hence the enemies of President Brisson had recourse to all manner of subterfuges. They canvassed signatures for the death of one unnamed, and not till later was he revealed as the supreme magistrate of France. They appealed to the Spanish commanders, demanded indulgence for their deed from the frocked professors at the Sorbonne, and set preachers like Boucher to harangue the people. In the grey of dawn Brisson was lured into the street and hurried to prison with two of his assessors; there their enemies hanged the three of them from a beam and watched them by lantern-light until the three bodies seemed limp enough and their faces looked as they were meant to look. Then they brought their three charges, duly trussed and habited, to the Place de Grève and hanged them on the common gallows.

The great jurist had never conceived that lawlessness could reach such a pitch; there existed a legal code, the earliest in the land, and he was its author. But the activities of the mind not merely set a man at variance with evil reality; they dispossess it until it grows incredible. For the populace, far otherwise. They are hugely exalted when the supreme magistrate so strangely suffers the most degrading death of all. The ultimate brutality that commonly subjects the human spirit is the violation of justice. As it was morning, the square filled up, and the enemy of the dead man, standing beneath the feet of the pendant corpse, began to proclaim the treachery of Brisson; he had planned to deliver Paris to the King, who would have visited his wrath upon the city, and each and all of them would have met an evil end. People of Paris, you are saved; there hangs Brisson! And he hangs upon a gallows in his shirt, and with a black and bloated face. Can that be the President of the Royal Parliament, one of the noblest ornaments of this poor land?

None moved, the mob was benumbed by what they saw, and each fresh arrival stopped as though paralysed. From the corners of the square the suborned accomplices of the assassins cried out that the conspirators were rich, that their houses and all that was in them should be given to the people. None stirred. Plunder was not an affair of every day, here was an occasion to be seized; but the people crept away to their homes. Not until they were some distance from the place of execution did they raise their voices. Then one of the Sixteen heard a man say that the King of France had won his cause with that morning's work, if he did but abjure his false religion. At this, the man, a tailor, was somewhat aghast; and he proclaimed in a fury that he would cut the throats of all the Sixteen, save only one.

The King, in the company of his adventurers, heard every word from Paris, but pretended ignorance and let the adventurers talk — not from curiosity. He knew what was in such men's minds, and what would be their advice. Abjure, at once, and the capital will open its gates. Such people are crammed with their own experiences, occasions missed and blunders made. They grew more eloquent than ever in court and camp; and as they had been the King's friends for two whole days, their warnings were not unheeded. Henri's hearing was acute. In the hubbub of a great hall, and apparently absorbed in his own amusement, he could distinguish distant conversations, several at the same time. A group of younger men, hidden from the King, but recognizable from their fresh voices, were listening to words of wisdom from these hardened men of the world. The ruffianly d'O was scarifying the horrors of poverty. "No man should be as poor as the King," observed Rosny. Henri, who burst out laughing at this, caught every word. After Rosny, he heard his keen young Captain, Turenne, agreeing with Captain Alexis: "And keep out of trouble," announced that noseless creature.

Old Biron and de la Noue were conferring in low tones; nor did they raise their voices, being now of one opinion. Only one thing remained for the King to do, after his humiliation by Farnese, and that was to make an end. The end that Paris itself offered him at that hour; they could not mean another, although shame forbade both men to name their thought; and had the word been uttered in their presence, they would have burst into a fury, Biron no less than the Protestant La Noue. As soldiers, they did not favour any peace, since war was their livelihood. Most of all, they disliked laying down their arms after defeat. None the less, they spoke of what the occasion offered, though they did not name it; but Henri heard and understood.

He heard his Huguenot, Agrippa, raise his voice. Agrippa

d'Aubigné was disputing with the German Archbishop whose
conversion to Protestantism had cost him his throne, and since
then conceived the Mass as the sole safeguard of thrones; wherefore he was very urgent in favour of Mass. Henri broke away
from his circle, made his way across to Agrippa, and opened his
mouth to say something. What he would have said was: " I will
not "; Agrippa saw very clearly what was coming. Then a nobleman called Chicot touched the King's arm. Chicot could say
what others dared not, for which reason he was called the King's
Fool, and with a sort of ironic good sense he had assumed that
office. The King, too, behaved as though he had really conferred
it, and let the so-called Fool speak truths he would not himself
have admitted. And what was both new and true it was the
Fool's privilege to be the first to utter. Chicot nudged the King,
cut him short, and said for all to hear:

" Friend, you have a queasy look. Take a holy-water clyster."

A man whose calling is that of fool, should surely rouse a laugh.
But the bystanders said nothing, and the silence held the room
until it grew burdensome. The thronged company suddenly noticed they could no longer breathe; windows were flung open to
the evening; and as they all pressed towards them, Henri and his
old friend Agrippa found themselves isolated in the middle of the
room. Both were pale, as they noticed by the light of the tapers
that then appeared. And both were silent, each stricken by the
feeling that the last word had been uttered.

It had been Agrippa's habit to compose abusive verses when
in his opinion the King had treated him ungratefully. He was a
man of high temper and ready speech and had never shrunk from
telling his King a harsh truth. He risked what would be ill received, and was rewarded with disfavour. But not this time; it
was plain that the King was in sore distress. Agrippa dropped
his eyes and said:

" You have fought a long fight and a good one."

" The end is not yet," retorted Henri.

Agrippa's sole answer was to raise his eyes.

" Agrippa," said Henri in a voice of authority, " we will call
upon the Lord our God."

" I call upon you, Sire, and beg for my discharge at last."

" It was for that du Bartas also died," said Henri, half to himself. " We know each other; and we want to live." Whereupon they left the company.

They mounted their horses, and afar in the open country they came upon watchfires, tents, the encampments of an army; no one about the King, not even the alert d'Aubigné, had a notion of what had been going forward. Henri had been raising a new army, heedless of the one that had dissolved; he had written countless secret letters, sent out envoys, and from far away he had heartened his noblemen with words of which even Agrippa, a poet, had not the mastery. That he had done without a spoken word, while to all appearance he was frequenting his adventurers and preparing for his apostasy. " Sire," said Agrippa aloud, " I do not want my discharge, after all."

The King made no sign that he had heard; he was busy issuing orders regarding the approaching march on Rouen. If Paris could not be captured this time, then the capital of Normandy should be taken from the League forthwith, and Mayenne, and Farnese too, should be drawn northwards, to battlefields well known to one at least. Agrippa d'Aubigné, as he rode round the camp in the wake of this amazing King of his, grasped the plan and savoured its shrewdness. Suddenly he was dumbfounded to hear the King call to one of his pastors: " Monsieur Damours, lead the men in prayer."

This same pastor had, by the King's command, struck up the Psalm at Arques, and so, on the edge of ruin, brought victory over the mighty army of the League and deliverance to the champions of freedom and of conscience. Once more they were at his side. From tents and watchfires Huguenots thronged round the King, the older men to the fore; their faces, like their King's, were weather-beaten, and there were scars upon their bodies, as on his; that was all they needed to know. They had fought for him, and would fight for him again, and now they would pray at his side.

Agrippa d'Aubigné, beset by hoarse, devout voices, tried to join in with them, but his own inner voice overmastered the words he would have uttered. "A pious betrayal, Sire. You are deceiving your old champions of freedom and of conscience. But your purpose is ready and resolved. You will alter nothing, as God wills not otherwise. Lord, Thy will be done. If my King is to betray the faith and his own word, I keep both, to God and to him." In this spirit Agrippa, too, prayed at last and set his mind at peace.

Two Campaigners

The King sat down before the city of Rouen, and its capture threatened to cut off supplies from Paris. At last Mayenne marched to its relief. The leader of the League had in the meantime brought Paris half-way back to reason by hanging and by shooting, scarce before the blind fury that possessed the city had driven it into the arms of Spain. He had indeed to summon the Spanish commander from Flanders; without Farnese he could no longer hope to destroy the King. His formidable ally would have taken the city of Rouen as eagerly as the King himself; on which account Mayenne had to use every sort of shift to keep him at a distance from Rouen. The King, always set upon a battle, could certainly be lured to meet them on ground of their own choosing. But the King was now acquainted with the strategist Farnese and evaded open encounter, with the purpose of displaying arts more after his own taste. So he approached with only a body of light cavalry, nine hundred horsemen in all; and none understood his plan.

On the way, it was reported that the Spaniards were advancing with drums and trumpets, a mighty army of eighteen thousand infantry and seven thousand cavalry, in close array, the cavalry in the centre, baggage on the flanks, while the lighter squadrons swung back and forward like the pinions of a mighty bird. The advance of Farnese over the rolling wolds was a noble spectacle for an adept in the arts of war. It appeared in view of the King as he and his horsemen stood covered by the walls of Aumale; but, eager to see more, he rode forward ahead of his escort.

The great armament had suddenly halted, under the spell of

an apparition; and Henri, beyond all his hopes, at last saw that apparition in the light of day: an old, withered, boylike face, beardless, peevish, and weary. Yonder he sat, a shrunken figure — for sorrow always shortens a man's stature — in a cart, at the head of his splendid army — and his feet were thrust in slippers. Thus he rumbled on two wheels up and down the ranks, master of all he saw. A wave of his hand, and beneath his eye, or on the uttermost flank, every manœuvre was fulfilled, as though between painted scenes, with stage machinery controlling evolutions that seemed to be commanded by gods on fiery clouds — true triumphs of human artifice. It was a magnificent performance; and the spectator, as he ventured farther and farther into the open, could not take his eyes off what gave him such delight.

Clearly he could descry them — the withered boylike face and the slippered feet. In the light breeze that followed him Henri thought he could sniff a miasma of disease. He wondered whether the soldiers caught it too. Healthy men must suspect something sinister in one who is always carried or driven and goes unarmed. Were no murderers sent against him? No. Enough that none have made the attempt. Frail he is, but unassailable. Litters and carriages carry him carefully through Europe, that he may win victories for the Ruler of the World. But he wins them coldly and without joy. He uses his talent in a spirit of renunciation, and moves on, while he allows his soldiery to burn and murder as a respite from harsh discipline. When the trumpet sounds they must stay their hands, or they are hanged. An apparition beyond all reckoning, he is feared in all his bodily frailty and his joylessness. In him the many-tongued subject peoples of the World Dominion recognize the image of themselves.

Henri, King of France, was exposed on the open plain, with but a scanty escort behind him, who discussed in undertones how they had best warn him; but he was in no mind to tear himself away. He stood bending forward, and scarce breathed. He would never see that sight again; indeed, he would take care that it should never return. Alexander, Duke of Parma, shunned his lovely land, his jewel of a city, all the statues and the paintings;

he left them all for a campaign that was no concern of his and which he thought senseless and foolhardy; but he could not resist the practice of his art. The passage of the river at Lagny and the magical revictualling of Paris — a masterpiece. And here, with his great stage machine, he was planning yet another marvellous surprise, yet another masterpiece of strategy.

Rosny's clear, calm voice broke in upon the King and reminded him of how matters really stood. " Sire! Your servants here love you more than their lives. You must not expose yours any longer."

" What — afraid? " asked the King, which rather took his gentlemen aback. However, Rosny reminded him on their behalf that with nine hundred men he could not attack a large army in elaborate battle array. He had never thought to do so; but in a strange partiality for his adversary, he twitted them that Farnese was the first enemy they had feared. They swore that all they valued was his life. He yielded, for Parma's horsemen were already on him. He and his nine hundred had to fight for their lives, and many of them fell. The King was slightly wounded, he only escaped because his great adversary would not believe it was he; so much of a hussar, and so little of a king.

But Farnese was to become acquainted with this King before he departed, not long afterwards, to die. It came about that Henri beset him with marches and countermarches on a peninsula between the Seine and the sea, which had been his purpose from the outset, the fight at Aumale merely serving to mask his plan. Then it happened: the artist and the army, his magnificent instrument, caught and held. There were no provisions on the peninsula, and a Dutch fleet was on its way to the aid of the King. Farnese, already wounded, seemed lost. What did he do? Exactly what he had done at Lagny. At that point the Seine was as broad as a lake, but he crossed it on a bridge of boats one night, without a sound. When the Royalists awoke, and the prisoned enemy had vanished, they yelled with rage. Henri laughed and admitted the ruse was excellent. His elusive foe left behind a message that showed that he at last took another view of the King of France; and it plainly foreboded death.

" This King wears out more boots than slippers."

It was later heard that Farnese had entered Paris; but there he dealt with his friends as promptly as with his enemies. " My task ends here," he was reported to have said, to interrupt a vacant silence. He had in truth achieved several prodigious feats, unruffled by the changing luck of war. An artist who, once his work was done, left behind what he cared nothing for, — the land and the people — and amid rolling drums and blaring trumpets carried his fading fame beyond the horizon.

Henri's task was by no means ended. He would have to be immortal before that came to pass; so interminable must be the fight for what he meant to make his own — the hearts of his subjects.

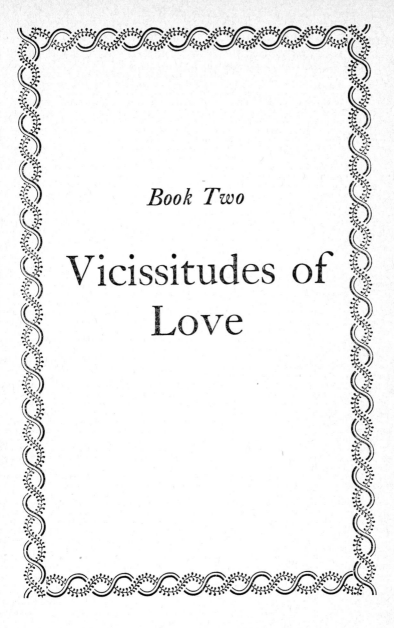

Book Two

Vicissitudes of Love

Show Her to Me

THE KING was hunting in the woods of Compiègne; on that day he pursued the stag almost within the confines of Picardy. There they lost the scent, the King and his Master of the Horse, the Duke of Bellegarde. The field was long since out of sight, and the two companions were resting in a clearing. The King had sat down on a fallen tree-trunk. Rays of sunlight filtered through the now fading autumn foliage and flecked it with gold, shedding a mild radiance on the two seated figures, one of forty and one of thirty years.

"If only we had something to eat!" said the King. To his astonishment the Master of the Horse promptly produced what the King had but dreamed of, set it all out upon the tree-trunk, and they ate and drank their fill. While eating, the King pondered. As Bellegarde had brought provisions in his saddle-bag, his purpose must have been to leave the hunt and disappear — whither?

"Where did you mean to go, Feuillemorte?" asked the King abruptly, and with a quizzical look awaited an answer that did not come.

"You look even yellower here than usual, Feuillemorte; 'tis the effect of all these withered leaves. You are in fact a personable fellow, and only thirty. Oh, to be thirty again! In those

days they were so willing, and they were always there. Look
yonder between those two oaks. Can't you envisage a feminine
form scarce venturing to step out of the darkness? In those days
they came at once."

"Sire," said Bellegarde, "would you like to see my mistress?"

"Who? Where?"

"She is very beautiful. The castle is not far away."

"What is her name?"

"Cœuvres."

Quickly asked, promptly answered, and the King at once knew
who was meant. "Cœuvres. Then she is a d'Estrées."

"Gabrielle," said the young man, and his heart lilted with the
name. "Her name is Gabrielle, and she is ravishing. She is
twenty, her hair is pure gold, brighter than the sunlight on these
leaves. Her eyes are coloured like the sky, and I sometimes think
they alone make the day beautiful. Her eyebrows are brown, and
arched in twin delicate and noble curves."

"She'll shave them off," interposed the King, whereat the
lover started and fell silent. Such a notion had not come into
his mind.

"Show her to me. Today you are pledged to her. But next
time take me with you."

"Sire, I will do so now." Bellegarde leapt up, he could not
wait to show the King his lovely mistress. On the way they spoke
of the family, and the King remembered.

"Your beauty's father is called Antoine and would have been
Governor of La Fère had he not been turned out by the League.
And the mother? Surely she ran away?"

"With the Marquis d'Alègre, years ago. Before she went, she
is said to have tried to sell her daughter. But what does that
prove? You yourself knew your predecessor's court, Sire."

"It left a good deal to be desired in the matter of morals. But
your Gabrielle was too young to be sold."

"Sixteen, and as yet half grown. Even so I noticed her at once.
But fortunately I did not get her until she was already ripe."

"Ah. And her sister"; the King was searching his memory;
"what was her name?"

" There are six sisters. But Your Majesty means the eldest, Diana. Her first lover was the Duke of Epernon."

The King had almost said: " And all six, with the eldest, must have lain with a regiment, between them." He called to mind that together they had been known as the Seven Deadly Sins. But he observed:

" You have indeed become acquainted with an agreeable family, Feuillemorte. Will you marry your Gabrielle? "

The Duke of Bellegarde answered with pride: " One of her ancestresses on the mother's side was honoured by Francis I, Clement VI, and Charles V. There loved her in succession a King, a Pope, and an Emperor."

But the King had taken his mind off the gallant ladies from whom his follower's beloved claimed descent. The name of the Duke of Epernon had fallen from Bellegarde's lips, a name burdened with old conflicts, by no means yet composed. All the cares of his kingdom came upon the King; he let his horse drop to a walk despite his companion's impatience and talked of his enemies. They had divided the kingdom among them, and each in his own province set up as an independent prince, owing no obedience to the heretic King. Even Epernon, who had begun as one of the late King's boy favourites. " Bellegarde," he said at last, " you are a Catholic and my friend, tell me whether I must take this perilous leap."

The other understood, and answered: " Sire, you certainly need not change your religion. We serve you as you are."

" If that were only true," murmured the King.

" And you shall see my lady," cried his companion in high good humour. The King looked up. Beyond a wooded valley and a rippling stream, over hills and undulations of rich autumn foliage, above the tree-tops and against the blue of heaven, shimmered the castle. Thus do castles often look from far away, aery and insubstantial (before we come to know them), and their roofs aglitter. What awaits us? Turreted and bastioned, with guns peering from the ramparts, and roses climbing up the walls. What awaited them here? Henri's gnawing anxiety about his enemies, his dread of apostasy, made him sensitive to first impressions. He stopped, said that it was late, and made as though to turn back. Bellegarde became imploring, eager to win his master's commendation for his incomparable possession. The King was told of wine-dark lips, and pearls that glittered from between them; cheeks like lilies and roses, with the lilies shining through, and a body no less white; a bosom of marble, the arms of a goddess, and the legs of a nymph.

The King yielded, and they rode on.

The castle was guarded by ramparts and a drawbridge; a main block and two projecting wings, each with its little pierced turret. The central building was of two storeys, with a steep roof, open colonnade, huge doorway, and carved window-frames. Originally a crude fortress, the castle had been elegantly rebuilt; and there were climbing roses everywhere, from which the last petals were fluttering down.

The King waited outside while his companion entered. At the far end of the vestibule rose the two arms of a curved staircase. The Duke of Bellegarde passed under it into a room filled with green light from the garden beyond. He reappeared in the company of a dark-haired young lady in a yellow gown embroidered with wreathed roses. Lightly she stepped ahead of the Duke, curtsied to the King, and from that modest attitude looked roguishly up at him. Her slitted eyes hinted to her lord that he need not take the lovely creature's modesty too seriously; nor did he so. He promptly said:

" You are indeed so ravishing, dear lady, that you must be the charmer on whose account my Master of the Horse comes hither so frequently. My expectations were not too high."

" Well spoken, Sire; pray continue. In the meantime your Master of the Horse is looking for my sister." Whereupon she drew back into the vestibule. The King followed.

" You are Diana! " he cried, with an air of astonishment. " So much the better. You are free. We shall understand each other." To which she, in a sharp staccato, said:

" I am never quite free. But he that wishes to understand me must be experienced. Do you know how many women he must have had? Twenty-eight."

It was common report that the King had had just so many mistresses, not including fleeting encounters. She knew it and was twitting him.

"Excellent," he observed, and thought of offering the girl a rendezvous. But at that same moment a figure appeared at the head of the staircase.

Her foot hovered on the topmost step. She wore a green velvet gown, stretched over a swaying hoop. From above, the reflection of the falling dusk shimmered on her golden hair and the pearls interwoven in its coils. The King stepped forward, stopped, and his arms dropped to his sides. Oh, the unimagined magic of that descending form! She moved like a fairy, like a queen, thought the King, as though he had never known ugly queens; but he felt like a King in a fairy-tale. And yet, as fairy and as queen, she moved with easy childish nonchalance. One of her hands lay at her pearl necklace, the other slid down the balustrade — as when a lissom body droops and falls, each step a miracle of ease and grace, poise and dignity, all in one. The King had never seen the like.

He stood in the shadow; she did not know it, or she was not looking for him. She had missed Bellegarde, who had dashed too quickly up the wrong arm of the staircase; she laughed at him and turned her head with naïve vivacity. Forgetting where she was, she sprang up two steps and would have run into her lover's arms. At a sign from him she stopped, and continued her radiant progress. The King did not wait for her, he had stepped slowly backwards, and when she reached the bottom of the stair, he found himself outside the doorway.

From the very centre point of his being a sob burst upwards, and when it reached his throat, it choked his speech. When Gabrielle d'Estrées was presented to him, he was dumb. The Master of the Horse dropped the girl's hand and recoiled. He knew what he had done. The King could not speak; he seemed stricken and shattered — horror-struck, Bellegarde could not but think, and he looked at his lady's face; had it changed into a Medusa's head? No, she was still a girl like any other, though lovelier indeed, as Bellegarde knew best of all. His pride of ownership did not prevent his thinking that the impression she had made upon the King was exaggerated, apart from the fact that it was dangerous.

Gabrielle drooped her brown eyelashes, which were long and shadowed her shining cheeks. Not a look nor a smile could suggest to the King that her modest demeanour was feigned. Here was a woman that neither wished to please him nor stir his curiosity — as if a white and fair-haired goddess could be so demure. Was she conscious of it? Then he was indifferent to her. The King sighed; he begged the divine apparition not to constrain herself on his behalf, and made a movement towards his Master of the Horse, who took the girl's hand and led her a few steps farther, where petals were still fluttering down from the roses by the wall.

" Sire," said Diana, " you will now be blind to all my charms, but I am a good sister."

He asked hurriedly whether, besides the two of them, there were others at home. She answered no; her father had ridden out, and her aunt was paying a visit in the coach. Her aunt? He lifted his eyebrows. Madame de Sourdis, she said, and no more was needed; he was well acquainted with his kingdom. Madame de Sourdis, sister of Gabrielle's fugitive mother, and herself a woman of gallantry; betraying Monsieur de Sourdis with the late King's deposed Chancellor, Monsieur de Cheverny. Monsieur de Sourdis, formerly Governor of Chartres, in the same case as Monsieur d'Estrées: without a place. All of them were without places, they would want a great deal of money. The affair would be a costly one, thought the King, but did not dwell on the point. Why struggle against the inevitable?

While Diana went on talking, he stared, with set eyes as in battle, across at Gabrielle, and his lips moved; he felt in the depths of his being that this was she.

" This is she, and I must needs be forty before she comes. They compare her with marble, they speak of purple or of coral, of the sun and the stars. Empty echoes; who can give a name to what is nameless, save only I? Who but I can possess the infinite? Goddess or fairy, what is she? Queen I will not call her.

All my life long I have sought, and never found, and this is she."

Even when talking to Bellegarde she kept her air of modesty, or was it merely coldness? The expression in her eyes was baffling; there was a promise in them, but what they promised was uncertain. " She does not love Feuillemorte," affirmed Henri, despite his tormenting jealousy. " But did she notice me? Her eyes are still downcast. Now she bends her face over a rose; I shall never forget the turn and droop of that fair head. She lifts her face — in a moment her eyes will be upon me. Ah, no. Not again."

In two long strides he was before her and said gladly: " The rose, mademoiselle."

" Would you have it? " asked Gabrielle d'Estrées courteously, but with a dimly haughty air; Henri observed it, and agreed that haughtiness suited her. He kissed the rose she handed him, and the petals dropped as he did so. Another gesture from the King dismissed Bellegarde; and Henri said eagerly:

" What do you think of me? "

That she had known some while before, for all her vague and poetical expression when she looked at him. But she answered:

" It would be more usual to say what you think of me."

" Have I not done so? " cried Henri.

He had forgotten that he had been speechless, and thought she must have understood.

" Charming Gabrielle," murmured the King to himself.

" Who told you so? Your eyes are not upon me," she answered calmly.

" I have already seen too much," he burst out — then he laughed lightly and began to pay court to her, as indeed she expected. He was charming, he was bold, utterly the gallant King of eight-and-twenty mistresses; he upheld his reputation. She held him off, but not without a touch of provocation, for courtesy's sake, and because it is pleasant when a man does not belie his fame. That was his sole success, and he knew it but too well. He felt duly abashed, but talked on and suddenly found himself asking after her mother. Her perfect face grew chill, indeed, as marble, and she replied that her mother was absent. " At Issoire, with the Marquis d'Alègre," he added, since he had mentioned her, and in faint requital for Gabrielle's chill demeanour. At that same moment he realized that she must needs withdraw, and only did not do so because he was the King. But a look measured him from head to foot and filled him with sudden weariness. What she had seen as her eyes travelled over his person he followed, feature by feature, in his mind. A pendulous nose, he told himself more than once, and each time with more emphasis, as though that had been the worst. But there was more.

He looked round for Bellegarde, anxious to compare his own weathered countenance with that of his friend, so handsome, so much taller, and what teeth he had! In his youth, as King of Navarre, Henri had had his teeth gilded; that led, and always leads, to much trouble later on.

Diana looked at the King, and she said: " Sire, you would like to rest? A room stands ready for the night. There are excellent carp in our pool for your supper."

" Give me bread and butter; I'll kiss the hand that brings it me here outside the door, before I take my leave. I will enter Monsieur d'Estrées's house only in his company."

All this was addressed to Gabrielle, and she it was who went in to fetch what he had asked. The King sighed, in something like relief, whereat Bellegarde and Diana were much astonished.

Henri had hoped that Gabrielle would mount the stair and once again come down it. But she went into one of the lower rooms and had soon returned. The King ate his bread and butter standing, while he talked and laughed, and asked about the harvest and the local gossip. It was thus he would have passed the time with any of his subjects, the bakers at Mans, and the Knight of the Turkey. Then he and his Master of the Horse prepared to mount. But he took his foot out of the stirrup, stepped up to Gabrielle d'Estrées, and spoke in a hurried whisper; his eyes were filled with fire and life, she had never met his like, and he meant to leave a memory behind him. " I shall come again," he said, " dear love." He mounted and rode off, without a glance behind him.

When the horsemen had disappeared among the trees, Diana asked her sister what the King had said to her in secret. Gabrielle repeated it. "What!" cried Diana. "And it leaves you so unmoved? Conceive what this means! No more and no less than fortune. We shall all grow rich and powerful."

"For a light word that he spoke at parting."

"But spoken to you; whether or not you are worth it, to you he said it, and no other woman will hear the like from him so soon, although at least eight-and-twenty have heard it before. We are neither of us fools, and both of us marked him as he took the bait."

"With his rotten yellow teeth," added Gabrielle.

"Do you dare to say such a thing of a King?" said Diana, choking with indignation.

"Oh, spare me," pleaded Gabrielle. "After all, he is old."

"I'm sorry for you," said her sister. "A man not yet forty — and a seasoned soldier. And such a firm, straight figure!"

"His skin looks as though it had been smoked, and his face is seamed with wrinkles," observed the adored one.

"When a man spends his life campaigning, he has little time to trim his beard."

"His grey beard," added Gabrielle.

Her sister cried out in a fury: "And his neck was ill washed, if you want to know."

"Do you think I did not notice?" drawled Gabrielle.

Diana was now quite beside herself. "For that very reason I would have lain with him this night. Only a great conqueror and a famous man can permit himself such lapses."

"I am for more ordinary habits. The homage of a King of France is indifferent to me, when he wears a threadbare doublet and a shabby hat."

Whereupon Gabrielle departed. Diana called after her, in a voice that rose into almost a shriek:

"You are thinking of that smooth-faced, scented nincompoop of yours!"

And Gabrielle said, over her shoulder:

"You remind me. The King smells most unpleasantly."

A Ride by Night

While the King and his nobleman were riding over the hills among the yellowing trees, the sky was red with the evening light. Then the forest rose up black before them. The King halted his horse and looked behind him at the castle, poised above the tree-tops. An afterglow from the sinking day lit the roofs with gentle radiance. Not long ago they had flashed and glittered, and had promised — what? He had been afraid. That was reasonable enough; indeed, he never felt otherwise when riding into battle. But this time, he felt, he was to be worsted and taken prisoner.

What in early years is divined by the light of instinct is soon forgotten in the folly of experience. " My part," thought Henri, " will this time be patience. Let us endure and close our eyes, we can do no other; scarred as we are by experience, we cannot please at first encounter. That alone decides. Before all that was to befall me, before all the terror and the toil, as a youth of seventeen, I knew the gardener's daughter, Fleurette. It is dawn and the dew is shining on the grass. I have taken her and loved her, our night was full of rapture, I still hold her hand, the spring mirrors both our faces; and as quickly as the image in the water, love also had dissolved, I was already waving to her from afar, and my horsemen had carried me away. And now — the dark forest."

He rode into it. Bellegarde was far ahead of him, and Henri, quite alone, let his horse go forward at a walk. " I shall have to lay long siege to her," said he, " and sieges are usually raised when enough time and men have been lost. Not this one, friend; here is a frontier of your freedom, and you must rather bleed to death." He shivered, reined in his horse, and peered into the darkness, to which his eyes were gradually growing accustomed. So grave a matter, and its aim was happiness! But as the summons had come, happiness did indeed appear; it set his heart throbbing, lightened his head, and he told himself that age was a delusion and could only possess us by our consent. He would be happy, he would be seventeen again; " and the promise of

happiness is today called Gabrielle. Take it! Here's no place for
doubt or modesty; shake off your weariness and fight! Remember the King of Navarre, a petty monarch who faced a sea of
perils." But he had not been worsted nor would he be worsted
now.

As he stood up in his stirrups to clear his lungs, he caught sight
of a motionless rider in the distance, at the end of a long forest track, overhung by branches; but between the foliage and
the shadow, far away and very small, Henri could descry that
mounted statue. This was the man she loved. " 'Tis true, and I
bow before the truth. But if he loved her, he would promptly slit
my throat. Will he not? Then I am the stronger, being King.
He is handsome and he is young; kill me, Feuillemorte, or you
will lose your lady. She will not always think me old and ugly, I'll
take care of that, Feuillemorte. My beard is grey, but that makes
no matter, for I myself am as young as any man. She will learn,
however much it costs me; and though I must give and give
again, and sue and plead and supplicate, in the end she will not
love you any more, Feuillemorte; she will love me."

He rode up to the silent horseman, and leaned out of his
saddle. " Bellegarde! Wake up! What do you mean to do? "

" Sire, to accompany you, unless you wish to be alone."

Henri was amazed to hear a calm and courteous voice.
(" What! Did the storm not touch him, was it only I that was
so shaken? I'll break his complacency at least.")

" I am growing old," said the King as they rode on. " It is to
be marked from the way in which women have latterly encountered me. One, if you can believe me, had me to sit at a table
laid for twenty absent guests, while she crept out of the house
and drove away. That shows a man his place, and so it was today.
You can be content. Are you content? " repeated the King, as
no answer came. A confession of jealousy. The King had triumphed.

" It was your own wish, Feuillemorte. You insisted I should
see your lady, and would have shown her to me in her bath. She
is truly white and rosy, as you said. More white than rosy, indeed. Never have I looked on anything so white, so shining, and

never in one glance alone did I compass such a vision of joy. What a pity I am old! "

The words were spoken with regret (if not with deep design). Bellegarde, as he listened, felt the more certain of his happiness, which was a reality and no mere vision. " Indeed I am happy," cried Bellegarde, his face upturned to the silent tree-tops. And without a pause he went on in an undertone:

" I have the loveliest lady in the world, I am Master of the Horse in France, thirty years old, not ill-looking, and the evening is delightful. I have the honour to be riding beside the King. Sire, you would like to rob me of my lovely lady, which would be the highest honour for your nobleman. But Gabrielle d'Estrées loves me, and you would be betrayed."

" You will be forgotten," said Henri in the same low tone.

" I am her first," said Bellegarde. " Even at the court of the late King, when she was sixteen, we fell in love. The King made us dance together, both wearing the same colours. Glad I am that we then resisted our desires. I had laid no finger on her, but she was mine, and not for the Cardinal of Guise nor the Duke of Longueville. The flight of the King from Paris parted us for three years, and by mere accident I found her here again; but are there such accidents? "

Too consequential, thought Henri, and longed to interpose. Much too long and consequential; but he said nothing. As the forest darkened, Bellegarde did but plunge with more abandonment into the silent rapture of his happiness.

" I was told she was in Cœuvres. I rode there — she was standing in the hall. A look, and it was decided. She had waited for me three years long, I was still her first. The aunt was on the watch, I paid her, and the door of her room was not locked that night. The staircase led up into a pierced turret on the side wing — and there I slept with her that night." Bellegarde stopped, sobered by the last words, fell silent, and his lips no doubt were set.

" Is that all? " asked Henri, rather taken aback, for it was surely entertaining to pay the aunt and sleep with the niece.

" I have said too much," said Gabrielle's lover. So Henri felt;

he was ashamed to have listened to it all. His intended victim's confidences put him out of countenance. For he had already forgotten what, in the moment of clear vision, he had foreseen that enterprise would cost him — humiliations of every sort, deliberate blindness, and decencies defied.

The riders came to a clearing — the one, indeed, where their adventure had begun; it lay flooded in moonlight. Each suddenly noticed that his companion had grown pale and grave; then Bellegarde, in that deep solitude, fell to talking like a courtier.

" Sire," said he, " pray do not ask me to boast of my youth. A happy King is young at forty. I perhaps am so for the last time today."

" You are uncommonly yellow, Feuillemorte. The moonlight does not favour your colour. Health counts as well as youth. You should take a cure, Feuillemorte."

CHARMING GABRIELLE

Wherever Henri travelled and sojourned, he had to keep an eye open for enemies, now and always. One day a peasant made his way between two enemy forces. With a straw mattress on his head he tramped four miles through the forest, reached the castle of Cœuvres, crossed the bridge into a courtyard — when a maid cried out to him. " Stop, fool! The kitchen is at the back! " Something was thrust into her hand, the man whispered in her ear, she gaped and turned and went. Out of the house came Gabrielle d'Estrées.

She saw before her a stocky peasant, grey of beard, with a lined and blackened face, like all his kind. " What do you want? "

" I bring a message for you, mademoiselle, from a lord who will not be named."

" Speak, man, or go." She herself had just turned to go when she caught the fire and intelligence in the man's eyes. Was that a peasant? Where had she seen those eyes before? Surely she had marked them then!

" Sire! " she cried, started back, and said in a low voice: " How dreadful you look! "

" I had announced myself."

" In such a guise! Do I not deserve that you should come in silk and velvet, and with an escort? "

Henri laughed into his grey and dusty beard. Ah, he had been too old for her! This peasant was older than a king can ever be. He had won his way so far. Yet a little while, and when he came in grand array, she would find him handsomer than Feuillemorte.

Gabrielle eyed the house uneasily; the windows were still empty. " Come, I will show you the carp pond."

She ran, and he strode after her, until they were both behind the house. Henri laughed into his beard. Already she was vain of her royal suitor, never would she show him to her family as a grimy peasant. He went on.

Behind the buildings the garden sloped steeply down, and so was admirably concealed from observation. A broad flight of steps strewn with yellowed leaves led through a tangle of foliage to the pool below. In two or three sudden leaps Henri was at the bottom. There he stood, a stiff straight figure, no longer a stocky peasant, and waited for Gabrielle to walk down, as on the first occasion, when she had set down her foot and trodden on his heart.

At the top she paused, then placed her foot on the first step. One of her hands lay at her pearl necklace, the other slid down the balustrade. Her long brown eyelashes were lowered. She moved. The miracle of ease and grace, poise and dignity, was again presented. His heart throbbed, the tears welled into his eyes. This, he felt, was a picture that would never fade. When she approached, the drooping eyelids still veiled her eyes. But when the blue eyes opened, they held all their magical uncertainty. Did she know, or did she not, what she was doing?

Henri asked no questions. He gazed at her hair and at her face. The sifted light from a cloudy sky lent a radiance, a limpid grace, to her golden hair, and a suave, bewitching whiteness to her skin; he shook his head.

" Sire, Your Majesty is displeased with your servant," said Gabrielle d'Estrées, with elaborate humility, and bent her knee in half a curtsy. Henri shot out a hand to raise her, and grasped her arm. For the first time he felt her skin.

Henri felt her skin and remembered two experiences, which he would never have dared confess to her. The first: a balustrade of delicate old marble, warmed by the sun, at Nérac in his native South. He stroked it and he felt at home. The second: a horse of youthful days, whose vivid, rippling hide he caressed in the ecstasy of possession.

"Be careful, Sire, your hands are dirty."

He took his hand away; it left a black mark behind. Henri laid his lips to the place, but that she would not allow; she had her handkerchief. But when it touched his face, it too was stained, like the arm. "Really!" she cried, with an ungracious laugh; but he, for one moment, was lost in a world of infinite adoration. Her skin beneath his lips, her skin that he was kissing, tasted like the flowers and the ferns in his native mountains. Such too was the taste of the sun and the eternal sea — hot and bitter; he loved creation in its toil and sweat. In it all things were contained, even — and here he muttered: "God forgive me!" — even God Himself.

Then he marked her ungracious smile, and he too laughed, a soft low laugh, whereby he recovered her good graces. And they went on laughing for no reason, like two children, until Gabrielle laid her hand upon his lips. As she did so, she flung a glance round — with that entrancing little tilt of the head — as though their odd behaviour might have been observed. She merely meant that he should realize the secrecy of their encounter, as indeed he understood. So he asked her confidentially about her Aunt de Sourdis, and what her likings were — whether for jewels, silk, or money.

"A place for Monsieur de Cheverny, I should think," said Gabrielle coolly. "And one for Monsieur de Sourdis," she continued, as the thought came into her mind. Then she paused for a moment, but added quietly: "I would also a place for Monsieur d'Estrées, who has been in a shocking ill humour of late. As for myself, I don't know which I like best — jewels, silk, or money."

Henri assured her that next time he would come duly provided. But if he were to appoint the three gentlemen in question to governorships, he would have to make some conquests first, of cities, and broad lands — and of a certain sleeping-chamber, towards which he waved a hand.

"The staircase leads into a pierced turret on the side wing. . . . There I slept with her," he said abruptly, and the voice was that of his Master of the Horse. Gabrielle recognized it and bit her lips until they hid her little glittering teeth. Henri, with still sceptic eyes, watched Gabrielle; she was as lovely as the day, a first eternal day. Not till that instant had he marked the delicate curve of her nose; and what eyelashes had ever been so long and richly brown? The slim high curves of the twin brows! Shave them off indeed! — perish the thought.

Gabrielle d'Estrées dismissed him across the fields behind the castle, to avoid encounters. And as he again slipped in peasant guise through the enemy lines, his mind was set, not on the allurements of Cœuvres, but solely on the prospect of taking Rouen. The League had sent a captain to command that lovely city — a man, indeed, whose wits had been stricken years before on the night of Saint Bartholomew and who was now quarrelling with the citizens instead of fortifying and provisioning the place. The King would have had to expend the utmost of his strength on the taking of Rouen, but he knew it and had proclaimed his purpose. When he resolved upon another plan, questions were asked; nor was it long before the answer was discovered in the Houses of d'Estrées and de Sourdis and in her that was their crowning glory. Then the King rode openly and with a splendid retinue to Cœuvres.

On the very first occasion all awaited him in full muster, for they had been duly summoned: Madame de Sourdis in a stiff hooped frock, Messieurs d'Estrées, de Sourdis, de Cheverny, and six daughters, of whom only Diana and Gabrielle remained. The younger ones knew that grave matters were on hand, looked roguish, and romped away.

Madame de Sourdis accepted with much gravity the bag which the King produced from beneath his short red cloak. It was a small leathern sack; she emptied it into her hand, and for the first time her face lit up as she eyed the promising little heap of jewels. She took them as a royal pledge that still larger ones would follow — in due time, as she confidently observed. During this opening transaction the lady faced the King alone, in the centre of the great hall that led from the ground floor into the garden; there looked down from the walls busts of many a Marshal of that House, the weapons they had carried, and the banners they had taken, elaborately arranged.

The King began to wonder where all this would lead. Rosny had reluctantly lent him these few sapphires and gold topazes. Here was a terrible woman, with a truly basilisk eye. Shrunken and withered — the very pattern of the female poisoner. A bird-like face — and whiter than any face he had ever seen, he reflected with some horror; it was only too clear that all the women of this family were thus endowed; and what made one desirable, in others spoke of poison and of death.

The lord of that castle had a bald pate, which flushed red at every surge of feeling. He was an honest old gentleman, and much given to hunting. Sourdis was short, broad-beamed, and quite devoid of shame, despite a mask of geniality. Cheverny, the deposed Chancellor, looked all the taller. He overtopped the company and here counted for a personable man, though elsewhere his sallow, parchment-like skin would have been ill viewed. He was, nevertheless, the most elaborately dressed, which could be accounted for by his relations with the lady of the castle.

Henri took in the three noblemen at a glance. His experience of men was wide and sound. But the women? Time would show. They always wear a mask at first; and what we see is partly what they mean we should see, and partly what we imagine. Gabrielle stood hand in hand with her sister Diana. A family group, modest and delightful. Henri had almost forgotten that here was a desired woman, incomparable in the splendour of her loveliness, the goal of life, the very embodiment of love. Surely we hold it in our hand until the last moment, and can at will draw back.

All of this was known to a woman like Madame de Sourdis.

With a sweep of her hand across the great panniers of her gorgeous gown, she motioned to the pair to stand apart. Gabrielle dropped Diana's hand and went to Henri. At first he said nothing, he had seen a new vision of his love; so would it rise upon him every day, as punctual as the sun. Draw back — never!

In the meantime the hall was becoming crowded. The door stood open and the outer door as well; and through the vestibule the coaches could be seen in endless succession. Lords and ladies from all the neighbouring castles had come in their most magnificent attire, as to a betrothal; and they thronged the walls, whispering excitedly as they watched what the King was doing. He raised the hand of the lovely d'Estrées nearly to the level of her lips and slipped a ring upon her finger — not indeed a ring that would have much delighted any of the ladies there. A narrow hoop adorned with a few roses, such as a younger son might well have presented to a poor stepdaughter. This done, the hostess waved a staff to the lackeys as a signal for refreshments. Syrups, almond milk, sweetmeats, and Turkish honey made their solemn entry, and tables loaded with pasties and wine were set out under the eye of a portly cook, in response to the curt motions of Madame de Sourdis's staff, which she brandished in the fashion of a fairy. She turned her head just as Gabrielle did — but what was so entrancing in Gabrielle was in her absurd and merely roused disgust. Such opposites are never far apart.

Lured by the lavish feast, the guests forgot their diffidence and jostled for places. The more distinguished induced the King's gentlemen to present them and assured him of their loyalty, which was needful enough, as it was not long since they had stood in arms against him. Although this was plainly to his profit, he merely observed that all good Frenchmen recognized and served him; then he left them standing and talked only with the Duke of Longueville. He was Gabrielle's other suitor; she had hovered — perhaps she was still hesitant — between him and Feuillemorte. So it seemed from their expressions. Longueville wore his hair bleached, and his face was girlish, as had been the fashion at the late King's court. But he was brave, and once when in a lady's company he had, though clad only in a shirt, cut down the intrusive husband. The King made him tell the story, and Gabrielle d'Estrées withdrew in dudgeon. She could well plead that she had been carried away by the throng as it surged through the hall, struggling for a glimpse of the King or for something to eat. Jostling figures, the haze and reek of a great assembly, nodding plumes, and here and there the odd appearance of a neck poised on a starched ruff that seemed to float bodiless through the room.

The King himself, carried with the throng, soon found himself at the far end of the hall, which was kept free by a ring of sturdy retainers. There the hostess waited with raised staff, as though her magic had conjured the King thither. He was placed at a table by himself. D'Estrées, de Sourdis, and de Cheverny served him standing; the first with wine and melons, the second with a fat carp, and the third with game pasty stuffed with truffles. The King was suddenly seized with violent hunger, but he first commanded that Gabrielle d'Estrées should be seated at his side. She was not to be found. Her father bent over the King as he filled his glass, and said with honest anger, as his bald pate flushed: " Sire, my house is no better than a brothel. If I were to go through the bedchambers of this castle at night, to avenge the honour of the family, there would be no survivors. But 'tis not to my purpose that it should die out. My sole comfort is the adulterous pair at Issoire."

He was referring to his wife and the Marquis d'Alègre. The King asked the old gentleman what he meant. Monsieur d'Estrées answered that in the city where he was Governor, his extortions to satisfy the insatiable Madame d'Estrées had made him detested; and the end would certainly be disaster. Then came the carp. Monsieur de Sourdis, who served the King, spoke of no family troubles despite the sprouting horns so clearly visible on his brow. No, his sole care was for the city and domain of Chartres. There he had once been in authority, and there too his friend Cheverny had been Governor, before they were both driven out by increasing lawlessness and the collapse of the royal power. In the carp's opinion — for Monsieur de Sourdis closely resembled one — the capture, not of Rouen, but

of Chartres was much the most urgent matter; with which verdict the erstwhile Chancellor, who replaced the carp and laid
before the King a truffled venison pie, heartily agreed. This lantern-jawed official was not merely proficient at his table duties,
he knew the royal mind and inclinations, and what he said and
did was well considered.

" Sire," he observed in a tone of grave insistence, " you could
force your city of Rouen to surrender, and thus once for all secure your province of Normandy. But it would be a bloody victory. Your Majesty yourself has said that it vexed your soul to
see your subjects lying on the battlefield, and where you won,
there too you lost. But a high officer of State, well known there-
abouts, might well induce the burghers of Chartres to submit to
your authority." He knew where the King's inclinations lay, and
he had a dignified utterance.

It was now the turn of Madame de Sourdis; at a wave of her
staff a huge covered dish was carried forward, and when the silver
lid was lifted the roguish creature came forth in the guise of a
living Cupid, one finger at the corner of her mouth, roses in her
hair, and a quiver stuffed with arrows. While the room grew
clamorous with admiration of the lovely archeress, Madame de
Sourdis, red-haired and topped by her twin feathers, one red,
one yellow, raised her staff before the King and said: " Shall I
lower it? Chartres for Monsieur de Sourdis, and for Monsieur
de Cheverny the royal seal."

Scarce a flicker stirred the King's eyelids, but Madame de
Sourdis saw it. She lowered her staff, and there beside the King,
and very close to him, sat the charming Gabrielle.

Valley of Jehosaphat

To the east of the city of Jerusalem, where it stands over
against the open Mediterranean and the not far distant Dead
Sea, lies the Valley of Jehosaphat. It is, in fact, the low ground
between the circle of the city wall and the Mount of Olives. We
know the land, we know the valley, and all too well the Garden
of Gethsemane. The truly devout will be buried nowhere but

in the Valley of Jehosaphat, for there the trumpet of resurrection and of judgment will be first heard when the day comes and it is sounded forth. But among the trees of this garden, on this very soil, our Lord was tempted. Judas meant to betray Him, as indeed He knew, for His own weakness had taught Him how prone were men to fall away from God. He did not want to die, and in the Garden of Gethsemane, with drops of anguish on His brow, He spoke to God: " O my Father, if it be possible, let this cup pass from Me; nevertheless, not as I will, but as Thou wilt."

Valley of Jehosaphat was the name given to the Royal camp before Chartres, and when one day the King, covered with mire, was clambering out of the trenches, whom did he see approaching on a litter? Henri ran like a boy to help Gabrielle alight; in doing so he had almost forgotten the Lady de Sourdis; both, escorted by the King, made their way into the Valley of Jehosaphat. Gabrielle wore her green velvet gown, which went so well with her fair golden hair. She tripped through the mire in her little red morocco shoes, but on her face there was a smile of victory. A rambling old tavern was set in order for the King's lady; she made no attempt to withhold herself, but that very night she received an ardent and devoted lover.

She did so because her more experienced Aunt de Sourdis told her it would profit her and that the King was a man to pay after the event, which would indeed serve only to intensify his passion. The astute old lady proved to have judged rightly, and the first to profit by the affair was Dame Sourdis herself, as her old friend Cheverny received the seals from the King and was appointed Chancellor. Misfortune long drawn out makes for unbelief. When that gaunt official, a creature of old Catherine de Medici, who had planned the Night of Saint Bartholomew, came into the presence of the Protestant King, his brow was damp with sweat, for he thought that all this would prove no better than a farce and that he would soon be privily removed; such would have been the view in his own day.

No one was in the King's immediate company, excepting only his First Chamberlain, d'Armagnac, a grey-haired man who had gone everywhere with his master for many years, to prison and to freedom, through mortal peril and through his days of glory. He had saved his King's life, got him a crust of bread at need, and guarded him from harm, so far as it threatened him from men. He never warned him against women, for he himself, like his master, found no evil in women, save unloveliness. D'Armagnac actually admired Dame Sourdis for her red hair and her bold blue eyes, which compelled the admiration of a cavalier from the South. Hence his favour had been won for Monsieur de Cheverny, and he was concerned that Dame Sourdis's friend should be well received by the King. At a curt gesture from Henri, d'Armagnac took the seals and the keys from the table and handed them to the King with all the elaboration of a public ceremony. Henri could not but respond; he embraced the Chancellor, paid him due compliments, and forgave him his old transgressions. " Now," said the King over his shoulder, " the Chancellor will not aim these two pistols — by which I mean the seals — at me, but at my enemies."

Cheverny, brazen-faced as he was, stood aghast. From the far end of the room came much muttering and whispering and, if ears did not deceive, the clash of weapons. Protestant gentlemen they were, and it was not only this performance that had roused their wrath: they disliked the presence of two ladies in the camp of Jehosaphat. It galled them to think that on their account the important city of Rouen had not been taken, and time was being thrown away before Chartres. They also feared yet worse disaster from the King's new passion, for they had no longer any confidence in his religion.

Having escaped the perils of that encounter, Monsieur de Cheverny remained for a while quite bewildered; his friend Dame Sourdis made clear to him who wielded power in Jehosaphat. Not, indeed, the pastors. But the pair agreed that Gabrielle should have none but Protestants in her service. She herself admitted it was best. For the rest, she danced. Every evening there was feasting and dancing in Jehosaphat; it was a truly festal siege. Then, when all had gone to bed, the King rode out on picket with a hundred horsemen. His night was brief,

the sun found him at his labours, and in the daytime he hunted
— all this because the presence of his lady robbed him of his
rest, as none had ever done before, and stirred his strength and
energy beyond all earlier experience. And he grew the more impatient when the beleaguered city would not fall. Gabrielle, as
he well knew, had followed worldly counsel, not her own heart,
when she yielded.

Henri swore that this should not continue, for women act
from many different motives; with them, calculation does not
preclude feeling. Forty years had taught him that. At twenty
he would scarce have had dealings with a lady encumbered by a
horde of greedy kinsfolk. He would never have troubled to appear before her first as a little old peasant, to whom she had said:
" How dreadful you look! " then in Royal array, and then as a
soldier, imperious, resourceful, and alert. But at last she should
see the conqueror. To him her heart would certainly succumb,
for women dream of men that conquer, and for such they readily
forget a young Master of the Horse. Then she would be his, and
the battle over.

Chartres fell at last, for the Royalists had driven their trenches
up to the very walls. They carried one outwork after another,
then the citadel and the city, and in this fashion Henri also mastered Gabrielle, who did not love him even yet, when she shared
a room with him in the tavern of the Iron Cross. The sight of
his unwearied energy carried an outwork of her heart, and he had
reason to believe that he would penetrate the innermost citadel
when he took possession of Chartres. And that was on the 20th
of April, a glorious day — pealing bells, streets beflagged, children strewing flowers, chanting priests, the Mayor with the keys,
and four magistrates carrying a canopy, from beneath which the
King, erect upon his horse, surveyed his city, which, in the very
hour of conquest, cheered his entry.

The solemn reception took place in a famous church of pil-
grimage, and there, for all to see, sat the radiant lady whom he
loved, with all her retinue; the King displayed his majesty before
her, and a side glance or two convinced him that her heart was
melted. Suddenly, and oddly, she blushed and bit her lip, and

a quizzical look came into her eyes. Then, by ill luck, the King
descried a figure lurking behind her in the shadow; someone he
had not encountered for a long while and whose name he never
spoke. And there he skulked. Henri, in his first fury, beckoned
to all his Protestants; they forced a passage for him, and he hurried to sermon in a certain house of ill repute. True it was that
his pastor had been assigned no other resort in which to serve his
God; a common haunt of actors, pimps, and thieves. The King
preferred it to the company of decent people; but there was so
much indignation that he did well to leave Chartres.

Before doing so he composed his quarrel with Gabrielle, who
swore that his eyes had deceived him, that the nobleman in
question could not possibly have been in the church or she must
have known! This was her best plea, and he was minded to accept it, though its weakness was all too plain. What told him
that she had not known? Not that errant, limpid look in her
blue eyes, for that said: Beware! No matter, he acquiesced, just
because she was still not solely his, and the battle for her must
continue.

She retired to Cœuvres, where he visited her, and Monsieur
d'Estrées announced that his visits affected the honour of his
house. Both spoke as man to man. " How did you yourself describe your house? "

" As a brothel," growled the old gentleman. " Common noblemen had abused it. There was wanting but a King, and him
we have."

" Friend, you had better have come with your daughter to
Chartres. You could have kept your eyes open; and you would
now have been Governor of Chartres. Monsieur de Sourdis is
Governor in your stead, but he is disliked for being so ugly, and
he has taken to peculation — there's more of the pike than the
carp about him now. I need good honest men, my friend."

" Sire, I long to serve the King, if I may likewise preserve the
purity of my house."

" There will be time," said the King. " Will you begin in my
company? "

" I will," replied Monsieur d'Estrées, and his bald pate flushed.

The King rode away without having seen his beloved, and as he rode he pondered on the Queen of England's offer: three or four thousand soldiers, with pay for two months, and a small fleet — if he set about besieging Rouen in good earnest. That was her condition, natural enough from an old woman who lived solely for power; other salvation had she none. The King spurred his horse into a gallop, leaving his astonished escort far behind, and rejoicing in his lithe limbs; far away in England sat an old grey woman.

Elizabeth, now in the late fifties, had executed favourites from mere apprehension of their power and had treated her Catholics no otherwise. Henri had never sacrificed a woman, and indeed he had often spared his would-be murderers. He had beaten no Armada, certainly; he had dealt the World Power no such blow. And though Elizabeth was near sixty, her people did not see her age; she appeared before them on a palfrey in the guise of a mighty Queen, as comely as she had ever been. Elizabeth knew one will and one alone; nothing could break it, neither love nor mercy. And Henri reflected that the title " Great " would befit him not at all.

His horse had dropped into a walk. No, " Great " he could not be called. But how much more time does a man of forty design to lose before he sets about his business? He was, as he well knew, in no hurry to deal with Rouen, he wanted to pro-vide for Monsieur d'Estrées first. Which he promptly did. He took the town of Noyon and installed Gabrielle's father as its Governor. That good honest man then felt impervious to dis-honour. His daughter had confided to him that her purpose was to be Queen.

Her retinue was Protestant. She gave money to the pastors for their heresy and was herself already suspected of practising it. As the summer wore on, the King began to give her such large presents that enough was left for higher matters than her per-sonal adornment. On the advice of her Aunt de Sourdis, she approached the Consistorium and asked whether they were pre-pared to dissolve the King's marriage. If not, the emissaries pointed out, it was to be feared that the King would abjure his religion. He would thereby at once get possession of his capital and therewith power enough to induce the Pope to agree to whatever he wanted — nay, more, to whatever Dame Sourdis and her lantern-jawed satellite suggested. For Henri in his passion was oblivious of the world that summer. An uneasy condition of affairs.

He was active enough, as always, in daily business; but he was almost unheeding of what lay further ahead, and as most of the decisions had been taken, he let them stand. Is there a man proof against respites, distractions, and indulgences? Perhaps not, but a man certain of his cause should thus gain resolution for the next leap. With women this is not so; their hearts may be fatal to their calculations. The House of Sourdis made skilful use of their choice instrument, but she was not above feminine weaknesses. At Cœuvres, where none now lived save her retainers, she received Bellegarde.

From Noyon the English envoy wrote to his mistress that the King could not tear himself thence owing to his passion for the Governor's daughter. More than once she had vanished from the town, and the King had no need to inquire after her, all was carried to his ear: the first time, where she went, and the second time, what she did there. On her third excursion he himself followed her from a distance and unseen, for it was night. The hoofs of his horse had been bandaged. Came a patch of moonlight, he halted in the shadow. She was driving a squat, low-hung cart, drawn by a ram, and her pleated cloak trailed along the ground behind her. With throbbing heart he watched the vision move through the white glare, and when she turned the corner of the forest track, he rode across country until he came up with her again.

He reached Cœuvres from the fields at the rear, tethered his horse, and crept into the dreaming summer garden, so lush with leafage that no lurker could need to fear discovery. But Henri smelt out his enemy. His senses were so sharpened by jealousy that in that dank and stagnant air, among all the exhalations of the teeming earth, he could scent a man. Thrust but one bush aside and you will expose a malignant face! Meantime Bellegarde did not stir, he stood as still as Henri, while his lady glided down the stairway to the pool.

Not a sound stirred the night. The leaf that she had touched in passing still rustled as she stopped and peered down into the darkness. The long steps lay half in shadowed blackness and half in harsh white light. There was silver in the folds of her cloak; and the hand that held it at her throat was set in silver. A great hat, her protector on unlawful ways, shaded her face to her chin, which gleamed white beneath it. O pale betrayal! O woman in the night, magical and treacherous both! Tears welled into Henri's eyes and blinded him, he leapt from behind the bushes, took three steps at one stride, and had her in his arms before she could escape. He laid his head on her shoulder and said between his teeth: "Would you run away, dear love — from me?"

She tried to control herself, but her voice still quavered. "But you took me so utterly by surprise, my lord!"

He paused before he answered, listening. Her face, as he could see, was drawn and tense. "Surely we know each other to the bone, sweetheart," said he in a romantic tone that took its colour from the night and their uneasy hearts. "Does not the magic mirror of our fond foresight show us both where each of us may be, and what each of us is doing?"

"Yes — yes, indeed it is so, my lord" — but she did not hear her words. Her ear was set to catch the crackling of a twig; it grew fainter and then ceased. She breathed a sigh of relief.

Henri knew as well as she who had then departed. "Sweet sigh! Enchanting pallor! Deny no more that you are here on my account. We could not fail to come together. Are we not one of the eternal pairs of lovers? Around them the world may fall to ruin, it is all unheeded — Héloïse and Abélard, Helen and Paris."

She was terrified that he might conceive the notion that his part was now not Paris but Menelaus. This brought a smile to her face; she shot an ironic glance at him from under her large hat and said: "I am cold, let us go."

He took her finger-tips and led her lightly up the garden steps, across the sleeping courtyard, and to the little pierced turrets on the left. Not until she reached her room did Gabrielle recover consciousness of her surroundings, and as there was nothing to be done, she quickly threw off all her garments and slipped into bed. Beneath it, on the floor, lay her other visitor — as a sensible lady could hardly be expected to foresee. Only a man himself possessed by passion could understand his rival's rash impulse and guess that he would not resist it; he carefully surveyed the room as he entered. The bed stood in the full moonlight.

Henri lay down beside Gabrielle, and she took him affectionately into her lovely arms. As she reached them out to him, he observed for the first time that they were slightly too short. And what most infuriated him was that his rival could also see that defect. After love-making they felt hungry and opened a box of sweetmeats which Henri had brought. Both stuffed their mouths full and said nothing. Meantime Gabrielle was aware of a sound that was not the chewing of her companion. In her alarm she stopped eating and stiffened. " Take some more," said he. " Are there ghosts in your turret? Don't mind their groans, I have a naked weapon ready to hand."

" O my dear lord, 'tis terrible. Night after night I have had to sleep with the maidservants at the back of the castle, when this groaning began." This time she felt no desire to laugh.

Henri said: " I wonder if it may be the ghost of Feuillemorte. It is long since I have seen him, he may be dead. However, ghost or man, we all must live," he said, and threw some sweetmeats under the bed.

Both waited — and from beneath the bed came a sound of grinding teeth, which suggested wrath rather than satisfaction.

" Let us fly! " begged Gabrielle, trembling and clutching him in her arms.

" How can I if you will not let me out of bed? "

" Take me with you — I'm afraid. Open the door, I'll throw your clothes out to you."

She climbed across him and seized him by the arm. " Don't look under the bed! " she implored in terror-struck tones. " That would be fatal."

"Ghosts are not my worst enemies." The agony that now struck at his heart made his speech indistinct. "I'm very ready to believe in ghosts. What I may not believe and will not know is the past, that for you was flesh and blood, and still perhaps lives in your thoughts."

"For God's sake, let us fly!"

"I know all about you: Feuillemorte, Longueville, and what came before them. When the late King was sick of you, he sold you to the Levantine money-lender Zamet."

He could have added to the tale, though he believed in none of it; it was torment that forced his speech. But she fell at his feet, clasped his knees, and held them until he got out of the bed, and even so remained crouching on the floor so that her body prevented his seeing beneath it. He dressed without a glance at the bed. Then he put her cloak about her shoulders and carried her down the winding staircase, back across the court-yard, through the garden, and into the open fields, where his horse was waiting. He set her before him on the saddle. In the silence of the night, and above the pad of muffled hoofs on the soft earth, Gabrielle caught some whispered words: " No mat-ter. I know. Temptation, trial, and a heavy hour. But I'll win you yet, sweetheart."

CATHERINE ONCE MORE

The garden at Cœuvres was sunk in summer, and Henri, so to say, in his love, a condition in which no man sees farther than he sets his foot. But this tangle of emotion cleared as the sea-sons turned, and the King pursued his affairs again with even more energy than before, several at once, and with the clearest vision, despite shocks that might have made him lose his head. A blow from blue heaven was his beloved sister's sudden scheme to abandon and betray him and get her adored Soissons crowned king; instead of brother Henri, she herself and her good spouse would be upon the throne. When Henri heard of this, he hit out in all directions. He threatened death to all who had a finger in the business. He commanded his sister to appear at his campaigning court; if she did not come, he would have her fetched.

He would have her brought by force from their old home, Béarn, where she had been plotting secretly against him, not merely in the matter of her marriage to her cousin Soissons. Then there had been attempts to murder her own brother, as she must admit. What sort of doings were these, as between a brother and sister grown up in company and linked together at perilous passages when there had been no handhold anywhere? When all was said, whom had the children of Queen Jeanne save each other? Amazing as it was, Henri here forgot Gabrielle d'Estrées, the cause of so much delusion and confusion, but what did that signify beside his little Catherine's conspiracy?

He named her as he had done in childhood and clapped his hands to his forehead. He kept his room while her coach rolled daily nearer, but at last he could endure no longer and dashed forth to meet her. Yonder she must be — behind that little cloud of dust, all that was left of his earliest life, and if it vanished he would indeed be self-estranged. The dust-cloud opened, the coach halted. No one stirred; the escort of noblemen reined in their horses and watched the King step up to the carriage door.

" Madame, will you please to alight," he said in formal tones, and not until then did she appear. A farmstead stood among the fields not far away. They left all their attendants behind them on the highroad and made their way thither. " How grim you look, sister! " said Henri; " and I am so truly glad to see you."

It was kindly spoken and meant to cheer; not in the least as he had meant to speak. No answer came, but his sister turned her face towards him, and that was enough: he was shocked by what he saw. The searching light of the wide beclouded heaven revealed a careworn face, stricken by sorrows. The limpid girlish bloom — which for him would never fade — marred, but only on the surface, like a rose dimmed by showers; but only on the surface. He soothed his conscience, which had struck him at first sight of her. " Old? — absurd! Age cannot touch us." But

age caught and gripped him in that moment: they were growing old.

Suddenly he admitted his own guilt, though he had just been
pondering on hers. He ought to have had her married long
before, and why not to Soissons? How long does the time for
happiness endure? She had fought against herself because he
was a Catholic. Now he was soon to become a Catholic himself. Why torture ourselves? We are all comedians. *Totus
mundus* — And the parts we are called upon to play are mostly
farce.

They could see into the farmhouse, which was deserted. Henri
wiped the bench outside the door so that Catherine could sit on
it. He himself sat on the table, a massy plank set upon unhewn
balks fixed in the soil, and swung his legs.

" Why torture ourselves? " he repeated aloud. To speak of
treachery would have been most unsuitable, and indeed quite
false, as is sometimes recognized. " Sister," he began, " do you
know that it was mainly from fear of you that I never dared
abandon our religion? But for that, how easy it would all have
been. Never could I have thought that you would do so yourself
and aspire to be a Catholic queen."

He spoke lightly and kindly, almost gaily; he must make her
smile, even through her tears. In vain: her face remained set
and rigid. " Brother, you have often disappointed me," said
she when at last she had to speak.

His retort was prompt. " I know. And yet I had the best intentions when at a good hour I proposed to our cousin the alliance with our family."

"You did so to get his support; and when he no longer had
a party to help him to the throne, you broke your word," she
said sternly; her rising temper heartened her to speak her mind
and speak it without mercy. She was the only living creature
who could reach his inner self, otherwise he would have never
discovered that he had indeed broken his word. It had not lain
upon his conscience hitherto; merely incidental, like Soissons
and all his business. The real peril had been the House of Lor-

raine, and the real peril still was the House of Habsburg. The worthy cousin could be diverted by a light word: "You shall have my sister." Well, it had been spoken. At that time the Catholic gentlemen had been especially urgent that Henri should make an end and abjure or they threatened to put that cousin on the throne. An utter trifle, repeated Henri to himself; how otherwise could it so wholly have passed out of his mind? Now it reappears as treachery. Treachery indeed!

His sister nodded; she had read his thoughts. "Always your own advantage," she said — now no longer stern, but grave. "You are quite heedless of the happiness of others, and yet you are a kindly man, or what is called humane. But, alas, forgetful."

"Things are so easily forgotten," he murmured. "Help me, dear sister," he pleaded, well aware that an appeal for help would be more effective than for forgiveness.

"What do you mean?" she asked, knowing what he would reply; for the same thought was in both their minds — the assembly of the States General in Paris.

He went on contemptuously: "My beaten friend Mayenne is making a mighty fluster and sending messengers all over France to summon the States General, that the kingdom may decide between me and Philip of Spain. They are not content to lose battles."

"The Count of Soissons," said she, "may well be chosen, a Bourbon like yourself, but a Catholic already."

"Then I'll abjure before they do it, God help me!"

"Brother!" she cried in horror. She leapt up from her bench, and limping all too clearly now in her agitation, she hurried along the low wall of the farm to where a peach hung from a trellis; she picked it and brought it back to her brother. He kissed the hand from which he took it.

"In spite of all," said he, "we remain what we are."

"You surely do." She assumed the austere, aloof expression of feminine fastidiousness that always came into her face when talking of his love-affairs; and indeed it was thus that she viewed her own delinquencies. "Once more you have a mistress who can twist you as she pleases. You will not abjure our religion to please the States General," she insisted, though in this she was somewhat less than fair. " No. But let Mademoiselle d'Estrées lift one finger, and you would betray our beloved mother and the Admiral, and all of us, as we observe."

" Gabrielle herself is a Protestant," he replied, to save himself an explanation, for after all she did consort with Protestants.

Catherine grimaced. " An intriguer, who makes you many enemies. I am quite sure she wanted you to arrest me, and that it was at her instance I was summoned." She looked with indignation at the squalid farmyard and the scattered poultry.

" She has never so much as mentioned the matter," he retorted vehemently. " She is a sensible woman, and devoted to my interests. You have behaved most treacherously to me, and your lover has left the army without leave."

His outburst promptly calmed her, and he would have said no more. " Go on! " said she.

" And what is more, your marriage would put me in peril of my life — is that enough? If you have children, then there will be no end to the murderers on my track, so all men tell me. And the knife is my terror. God grant me death in battle."

" Beloved brother! "

She stepped towards him and clasped him in her arms; he bowed his forehead on her shoulder. Her eyes were dry, the Princess of Bourbon wept less readily than her royal brother; nor had she his imagination, and the mortal peril that he feared from her marriage she regarded as a figment of her enemies. But the sorrow of that hour pierced the more deeply into her heart; he, with his tear-blinded eyes, saw no mark of it on that age-stricken face.

She then reminded him of something that had happened long ago, just before the end of his captivity in the Louvre; indeed, it was just at the turn of events before his flight. He had come upon his sister Catherine in an empty hall, in the company of his double; the same face and figure, but what gave life and truth to both was the fact that the man was dressed exactly like Henri, and his sister was leaning on him just as she used to lean upon her brother in old days.

" I had dressed him up to look more like you than he really did," said she. And a now middle-aged Princess sitting in a farm-yard added: " Pray eat that peach; I know you are longing to." He did so, sunk in meditation on the interplay of currents beneath the flow of daily life.

He threw away the peach stone, and said, still sunk in thought: " How otherwise could I have threatened death to those who might try to part us? It is not my habit to make such threats — and I would not — even to hold the throne, only for your sake."

Then brother and sister finished in the old familiar fashion a conversation that had reached its end, though leaving many doubts unsolved. Unconsciously they turned their hands palms upward, noticed what they had done and smiled; then the brother led his sister back across the fields.

Then Henri, as though he might be overheard from the road, whispered into Catherine's ear. " Believe nothing, Catherine, of what I next shall do or say."

" You will not make her — Queen? "

This was the momentous question which she had come from so far to ask; he evaded it, but in a fashion that made his meaning clear.

" You are the first."

The Princess bade her people turn her coach. The King stood silent, and they did so despite the general surprise at having travelled so far for so paltry an encounter. The Princess with her ladies and with her Negress, Melanie, climbed into it; the King shouted to the coachman to drive hard. Then he spurred his horse up to the coach, leaned forward, grasped the Princess's hand, and so rode onwards for a while. Then, at the entrance to a wood, the road narrowed, and the King had to rein back. There he halted, watching the coach as it diminished into the distance, nor did he turn until it disappeared in its cloud of dust.

Agrippa Once More

In such a press of affairs a man might easily have lost his head. The assembly of the States General in Paris, an agreeable medley of crazy sectaries, and the besotted agents of a World Power now decrepit, but avid of her neighbour's territory until the very end. The great lords postured before an audience that was in fact the starving populace. Oh, for a lawful king to divide the bread of France among them, and how they would have worked to earn it! "The parts that we are called upon to play are mostly farce." Thus spoke an old friend of the King of France, now famous, called Montaigne. Never did the King forget he had proclaimed himself no sceptic. No, there are manifestations of the world that sicken us of indecision and destroy the quality of mercy. We must assail and master, even at the cost of blood, what the outer world is too prone to pardon, at least for a while. If not, we shall, for reasons of State, violate and abjure our very selves. God knows what may be the end. But we may deem it His command: we must not shrink, the abyss will soon be yawning at our feet; let us leap while there's yet space to take that mortal leap.

Time then presses. What does Henri do? He sends for his old friend d'Aubigné, his preacher, sword in hand, his valiant better self; psalms for ever on his lips, head erect, smiling the confident smile of those whose faith is firm. " I," the little man would say, " stand high in favour and cannot be spared from the business of the State "; but in his heart he sadly recognized that the last time had come — the last time when he would speak to his King face to face. Henri would soon take that mortal leap, and his old friends would be left behind, his friends of battle and of poverty and of the Religion.

Bluff Agrippa used his privilege of speaking to the King; he spoke what was in his mind, starting as usual with the fact that he was in need of money. Moreover, he had, as was well known, saved the King's life five or six times over. " Sire, your finances are controlled by a rascally adventurer, and 'tis this very d'O who importunes you to become a Catholic. Now pray what will be the end of that! "

Agrippa thought: " If it is to be, then there is no word that I can say. What a horrible abyss between what is and what is not yet. Now stands the King with bowed head. Now he speaks."

Henri: " *Totus mundus exercet histrionem.*"

Agrippa: " The Pope's new son will not do him credit, I see that clearly. But why desert and turn against you those whose courage and loyalty was sure? "

Henri: " Is it an act of reason? — that is the sole question. Rosny has so advised me."

Agrippa: " But he has china-blue eyes and a skin that looks painted. He would not care if you went down to hell."

Henri: " And what of Mornay? Mornay, the very pattern of virtue. We have discussed these matters. Both are against the doctrine of purgatory; and I would deny it against any priest, depend on that. But at the Last Supper I have always held that we drink the Lord's veritable blood."

Agrippa: " Discussion is good and profitable to the soul, so long as the soul desires the truth. Mornay is an honest man and believes you such. You can easily deceive him and suggest a council — theologians of both creeds, assembled to investigate the true faith. But if the true faith be not the profitable faith, there is little sense in a council."

Henri: " Not so. More than one pastor has admitted that the soul can find salvation as well in one creed as the other."

Agrippa: " Though the flesh of such pastors is weak, their spirit is certainly not willing."

Henri: " I am much concerned for my salvation."

Agrippa: " Sire, I believe it. I do now implore you to recognize where your own salvation lies. We are not all of cold and iron intelligence like Rosny. Nor are we all as innocent as your Ambassador, Mornay. But one of your best captains, Turenne, asked why we should not betray the King; the first act of betrayal is his own."

Again the King bowed his head once more, as Agrippa observed.

Henri: " Betrayal. A mere word."

He thought of his conversation with his sister. Those who live heart to heart betray each other, see what they have done, and know that that betrayal was fated from the beginning. Suddenly the name of Pastor Damours reached his ears.

Agrippa: " Gabriel Damours. At Arques, when you were lost, he struck up the psalm and you were saved. At Ivry he led the prayers, and you won the battle. But now a time has come when he thunders against you from the pulpit. There's many a poisonous reptile might hiss at you and do no harm. But that harsh voice speaks truth, and the guilty man, from whom the faithful turn their eyes away, shall be stricken as with poison."

It was true. The pastor had written to the King: " Listen to the voice of Gabriel Damours, not of a certain Gabrielle! "

Henri: " Which is my guiltiest deed? "

But Agrippa would not answer — whether from modesty, or because he scarce presumed to pronounce final judgment. The whore of Babylon, as Pastor Damours had privately described her, though not, in avoidance of scandal, before his congregation. What disasters would the d'Estrées bring upon the King? She betrayed him, as he very likely knew. And her father was a thief; disgrace could scarce go further. . . .

Agrippa: " My soul is sorrowful unto death. Great were the days of persecution and honourable exile. The little province in the South, when the throne was far away, and when you had no money for a wrestling match, you favoured me with some pious observation that entertained your court at no expense. The star above our hut in those days was the Princess, your sister."

Henri: " I always suspected there was something between you."

Agrippa: " She set my verse to music, and she sang it. She lent melody to my poor words and made nosegays of my humble spring flowers."

Henri: " Dear Agrippa! "

Agrippa: " Though my voice fails me, I'll confess I saw her once again. You sent the Princess away privily and promptly, but I was waiting behind the hedge."

Henri: " Conceal nothing — what did she say? "

Agrippa: " She said that the Salic Law prevailed in the House of Navarre, and bestowed all upon the male heir — except the quality of steadfastness."

The words struck at the King's heart, and his arms dropped

at his sides. Then he clasped his hands convulsively, and muttered:

" Pray God for me! "

A Mysterious Husband

So Agrippa did pray, and so did many in those days, each in his own heart, for they thought him beset by perils; to the soul especially, but bodily dangers also. Deliverance did indeed come; or a prospect of deliverance. Monsieur d'Estrées gave his daughter in marriage.

Her adventure at Cœuvres — the King in the bed and the Master of the Horse beneath it — had come to his ears. Bellegarde could not keep silent. Moreover, the jealous admirer avenged his humiliation by paying his addresses to Mademoiselle de Guise, of the House of Lorraine; but that House still aspired to the throne, and the Duke of Mayenne was no less than ever at war with the King. Hence Feuillemorte disappeared — both from the trenches before Rouen, and from the King's armed peregrinations through France. Old d'Estrées took advantage of their absence to marry Gabrielle to Monsieur de Liancourt — a man of paltry presence, whom he had himself discovered. Nor had he much intelligence or character, but he had begotten four children, of whom two were living. Gabrielle's father took occasion to point out the futility of her love-affairs, whereas with her future husband she was certain to become a mother. This was, indeed, Monsieur d'Estrées' particular concern. Moreover, the chosen husband was a wealthy widower of thirty-six, his castle was near at hand, and he came of reasonably good family.

Gabrielle, with death in her heart, was haughtily obdurate, but her resistance from the outset was half-hearted. Her handsome lover seemed to have abandoned her, nor did she expect help from her exalted lord, else she would have summoned him. Indeed, it gave her pleasure to think that both the exalted lord and the young admirer would be exceedingly enraged. Monsieur d'Estrées had some trouble with the rather timorous son-in-law, who was terror-stricken at the thought of rivalry with the King over a still recent conquest. Apart from which, Mademoiselle d'Estrées' beauty was more than he could compass. His desire for her was too violent; and this, combined with his shyness, must lead to disillusion. He knew himself for what he was, though indeed his want of self-esteem endowed him with a sense of spiritual superiority. Such was Monsieur de Liancourt; and being such, he took to his bed as the marriage day approached and shammed sickness. The Governor of Noyon had to send a company of soldiers to fetch him to his wedding. It was a trying affair for everyone, save for that worthy old nobleman d'Estrées, who was heartily conscious of his rectitude; that, for him, was an unwonted experience. Madame de Sourdis had tearfully abandoned her ambitions for the family. But she accepted the vicissitudes of fortune.

When, three days after the wedding, she took occasion to make the journey from Chartres and announced herself at the Castle of Liancourt, what came to Dame Sourdis's ears? Or, rather, she herself put it decorously into her niece's mouth and then neatly extracted a confession. Even then it was none too clear what exactly had happened; but the fact remained beyond dispute; Monsieur and Madame de Liancourt slept apart. At this news, the girl's indignant parent galloped the whole way to the castle — but was met with embarrassed faces and could get neither a yes nor a no. Not until she was alone with him did his daughter admit that the marriage had not really been consummated, and that after her experiences with Monsieur de Liancourt there was little hope of its ever being so. The old gentleman, his bald pate purple with wrath, rushed in upon this undutiful son-in-law. Father of four children — how dared he offer such an insult? Monsieur de Liancourt excused himself by explaining that he had in the meantime received an unlucky kick from a horse. " Then you should not have married! " snarled the old gentleman.

" I did not; you compelled me," replied the harassed husband gently. He passed indeed for a shy man, but he could at times assume an air of such vacant self-absorption that none could tell whether they were dealing with a monster of cunning, an idiot, or something barely of this world. Monsieur d'Estrées's courage suddenly failed him and he fled the castle.

The news that reached the King's ears brought him immediately afterwards to Noyon. He learned not only of his sudden deprivation of his Gabrielle, but also of her mother's frightful end. Issoire lies deep in the Auvergne country; always regardless of her duty, Madame d'Estrées had not been able to bring herself to leave the Marquis d'Alègre alone, even at the cost of missing her daughter's wedding. Far better had she gone to it. The ageing woman wanted all that was left to her of love, but in regard to money she was also very insistent with her lover. The Governor of Issoire had to grind the faces of the people to satisfy his lady's demands. Both were at last hated with a hatred that grew near to murder — and it happened. The deed was done on a June night by twelve men, among them being three butchers. They overwhelmed the guards, burst into the sleeping-chamber, and butchered the pair. The Marquis had defended himself stoutly, but they were both thrown naked on to the dungheap.

Said the King to the Governor of Noyon: "That fellow at Issoire came to a dreadful end." "And so did his concubine," observed Monsieur d'Estrées, nodding like someone whose just expectations are fulfilled. The King could not fail to feel himself beset by the supplications of his friends: here, he might have heard them urge, was his opportunity. His mistress's mother had gone her way before and reached her end. Surely nothing could prevent the daughter following her mother; this was precisely what the King now undertook. Gabrielle was now under the protection of a husband; Henri was merely glad it was not Feuillemorte, who would have given him more trouble. He went to his loved lady, he pledged himself to whatever she might choose, but she must come away with him, and she must live with him; he could not bear life otherwise. Nor could she, confessed Gabrielle at last, and sobbed upon his chest, and she may actually have wept, though Henri did not see her tears. In any case she wailed out the name of Monsieur de Liancourt, and yet another word, that made his heart stand still. "Is that true?" he asked.

Gabrielle nodded. But she whimpered that she meant to stay with her husband in spite of his shortcoming. "My poor mother's death was a dreadful warning to me. I fear Monsieur de Liancourt because I do not understand him. What he says has no meaning, and what he does is more than I can guess. He shuts himself in his room. I have tried to look through the key-hole, but he covers it."

"We will soon find out," said Henri, and marched in bellicose mood to the master of the castle — but in him he found no adversary. The door stood open, a dim-featured personage bowed; apparently aloof from all mundane affairs, except in the matter of his dress, which was embroidered in silver, and his ruff was starched and spotless. His breeches and doublet fitted with a precision that seemed oddly conspicuous on so paltry a figure. Groping for a hold on some reality, Henri asked this elegant nobleman where he got his stuffs and how much he paid for them. And while Liancourt was answering, he cried:

"Is it true you are no man?"

"I was one once," said Monsieur de Liancourt, and looked as though he had been. He said in all formality, with interjected bows and pauses: "I am so at times, Sire. And I decide for myself when it is fitting that I should be so."

This could be a flat insult, or possibly a measure of deference to his wife's royal lover; but it seemed impossible to pin the fellow down to a statement or a fact. Henri went on, in an almost pleading tone:

"And that kick you spoke of?"

"I was certainly kicked by a horse. The verdict of the faculty on the kick and its consequences may be variously interpreted." An observation that left the King open-mouthed.

Henri began to feel disquieted. The man's face was too vacant, his discretion too elusive, and his assurance too horribly like that of a sleep-walker or a ghost. The creature admitted nothing, wanted nothing; it merely took shape and appeared, in a truly dim embodiment. Henri could bear it no longer. He crashed his fist upon the table and cried: " The truth! " His fury was indeed aimed not only at the apparition, but even more at Gabrielle, who had probably lied to him and lay with the fellow every night. He strode up and down the room, collapsed on a chair, and bit his knuckles to the bone.

" By your life — the truth! "

" Sire, your servant awaits your orders."

At this point the infuriated Henri recognized that reality speaks with the voice of authority. He might have thought of this before, but mastered himself in a moment and pronounced his judgment.

" You will give up Madame de Liancourt to me. You will, in compensation, be appointed Chamberlain. Gabrielle will receive from me, as a contribution to your joint property in matrimony, Assy — the castle, woods, fields and pastures."

" I ask for nothing," said the husband. " I obey."

" Gabrielle will continue to bear your name. I may create her Duchess of Assy later on. When she dies, your daughters will inherit — Sir! " he roared at Liancourt, who appeared to have gone to sleep standing. The King proceeded:

" In return for which, you will — lest worse befall you — confirm our contention that Mademoiselle d'Estrées married you under compulsion, and you never fulfilled your duties in marriage, whether owing to a kick from a horse or some privy disease. Do you understand? "

Monsieur de Liancourt understood, as indeed Henri now realized, despite the man's strange torpor, into which this largess, these threats of death, these turns of fortune, merely plunged him deeper. Henri marched out and slammed the door.

The occupant of the room sat rigid for a while with his head on his knees. When he at last got up, he bolted the door and covered up the keyhole. He took out of a chest a large leather-bound book stamped with the arms of the House of Amerval de Liancourt and began to write. He had for some time past set down the events of his life, and now he set down the last. With great exactness he described the King, what he had said, and his agitation as he paced the room. Intentionally or no, the figure and demeanour of the King were so truly rendered that the writer could see them on his page. Of his lovely spouse he had long since made a speaking portrait. He concluded his narrative with a pronouncement to posterity, headed in bold script: " A weighty and veracious statement by Nicolas d'Amerval, Lord of Liancourt, to be read after his decease and to be preserved for all time.

" I, Nicolas d'Amerval, Lord of Liancourt and other places, in full understanding, and certain of my death, but uncertain of its hour — " he embodied this ultimate message in the solemn form of a testament; then he added that he had been the victim of injustice, lies, and violence. He was not incapable, nor unskilled at the fleshly labour of procreation — this he stated before God. If he were to admit the contrary in a process of divorce, it would be done from obedience to the King and in fear of his life.

Pastor La Faye

Gabrielle went straight to Henri. He sent his noblemen to bring her to his campaigning court, and both were happy. The lady was delighted to have escaped from her spectral castle, where dreadful things were done behind closed doors. He was delighted to be loved; her radiant, ravishing body remained calm in self-surrender, which was no surprise to that tempestuous lover. But what a change was here: in former days a cheerless submission to his desires, and now such utter acquiescence and affection! Henri thought the victory was his, and he who stands upon a peak feels free. It was, to all appearance, a matter for his pleasure whether he stayed with Gabrielle or not. The end was so far away that time scarce came into question; though a man knows from experience often repeated how long, or rather how short a while, such matters endure.

Not so Henri. This was beyond all experience, and was to fill his mind and heart as none of the rest had done. There was not space enough for him and all he was to do in the years that remained to her until her death, the greatest death of all before his own. She now gave herself in friendly fashion, but no more; for she was frank and would not feign. But what she did not yet feel he would make her feel; he would strive and he would win her tenderness, her ardour, her ambition, her devoted loyalty. He always came upon a new discovery; upon each step of these relations he entered a new world. Indeed, as King and man he changed as often as she, through him, became another woman. He would belie and shame himself that she might love him; abjure his religion and win the kingdom. He would be a conqueror, the shield of the weak, the hope of Europe — he would grow great. Soon indeed would come satiety; all these things were destined and would come to pass in due succession. And in the end the great King's mistress would pronounce the final judgment: she would die, and it would be his lot to become a dreamer and a seer. Meantime the people of his age would look askance at him and all he did. They turned from him as he, in solitude, mounted higher and beyond their ken. Nothing of this was known to Henri when he summoned Madame de Liancourt to his camp and court and was happy in her company.

Here indeed she pleased everybody and made no enemy of man or woman. The women marked her and admitted there was nothing lewd in her speech or demeanour. She behaved with girlish modesty towards every lady of higher birth or riper age. Not by intrigue and misdealing, but by favour of the King, she held her rank; and it seemed foolish to grudge her what she so had won. The men of the court were plain soldiers, men like bluff Crillon and bold Harambure. "One-eye" his friend and master called him. "Tomorrow there's a fight, One-eye. Take care of it, I want no blind commanders!" The older Huguenots of that court were men of chaste life, and herein unlike the King. The younger took him for a pattern in all matters; but for both sorts of Protestants, and for his Papist followers, Henri was the hero, to whom only admiration could do justice, and only love could wholly understand.

All of this the lovely d'Estrées came to realize as she was drawn unresisting into the atmosphere that surrounded the King. Here he assumed a personality far beyond the lover, to which she had to adapt herself; and even the conqueror of Chartres, whose glory had so won her vanity, was but dimly seen. All these men would at any moment have offered up their lives for what he was, and every woman would have sacrificed her son. And each and all of them, men and women too, would have thought it well done, for the King stood for what was best in them, their own completed being, their faith and future. Gabrielle, a calm, collected character, by no means given to extravagance, watched them in silence and with faint amusement — but soon learned where her prospects lay, and how she must behave. And if her heart was not exactly touched, her mind was changed.

She was the quietest person at the court. There was little that revealed her rank save her aloofness, or, as it seemed to many, her indifference. Her admirer Monsieur d'Armagnac, First Chamberlain to the King, called her the Angel of the North. None except Henri understood her magic as did d'Armagnac. Angel of the North, echoed the other Gascons, and gazed ecstatically into her bright baffling eyes. The noblemen of the North called her so in the spirit of their master, with less irony and much complaisance. At length Agrippa d'Aubigné, crabbed as he was, admitted that the lovely lady d'Estrées practised no unlawful wiles.

Exposed to such a glare, Gabrielle made scarce an error, and certainly not the fatal one. People wondered whether she would mention the name of Bellegarde. Whatever her demeanour, and whether she did so or not, she surely could not but take harm. At last she did mention her former lover, but all such predictions were frustrated. Young Givry, about the same age as the Master of the Horse, and no less handsome, paid elegant and respectful court to her; and through her to the King. " Monsieur de Givry," said she to him one day, within hearing of several others, " there are words that the King will never forget — words that have become famous here at court; you told the King he reigned in brave men's hearts, and only cowards would desert him. These were your words, and true indeed they are. Monsieur de Bellegarde is no coward, and the King will soon see him in his place once more."

That was all. No mention of Mademoiselle de Guise — whereby she made clear that she desired no talk of love-affairs;

nothing counted but loyalty to the King. That was neatly done — and with all the air of candour and simplicity. Scandal had been forestalled — or had it not? The open claim to stand, blameless, where she stood seemed to many beyond warrant. The pastors at the court were constantly harping on the position; the King and Madame de Liancourt, both married — a double adultery, in defiance of the world and of religion. The pastors raised their voices and cried " Jezebel "; the prelates were silent. " Jezebel," said the pastors, as though the wife of the Jewish King Ahab, who perverted him to the worship of her native Baal, could be compared with the Catholic charmer of the King of France. Jezebel had indeed been denounced by the prophet Elijah; and in the end the dogs ate her, excepting only her skull, her feet, and the palms of her hands, as that prophet had duly foretold. None the less, the pastors were harsh, and therefore unwise. They alarmed the lady and defeated her goodwill.

From the priests of her own Church the King's mistress received nothing but kindness and courtesy; not indeed in hopes of a high marriage, which was still outside all reckoning. It was not yet clear whether the Lady d'Estrées had actually parted from her husband, and priestly diplomats, always prone to a wise passivity, were not likely to touch the King's marriage. Even his change of faith, so much the centre point of events, and imminent as it sometimes seemed, was never mentioned in the conversations of the prelates with the King's mistress. Which meant a hint to Gabrielle, and she understood it. Her secret hours with Henri heard no whispered allusion to his conversion. Meantime she dismissed her Protestant retinue — quite quietly, on the advice of her Aunt Sourdis, who marked the passage of events.

Pastor La Faye was a kindly old gentleman who in old days had dandled Henri on his knees. He it was who spoke to the King. He could do so because he was unhampered by pious zeal and the pedantry of virtue. He admitted that a man could save his soul in either creed. " I must soon appear before God. But were I a Catholic, and called to Him from Mass, instead of from sermon, as is my hope, the Lord in the radiant vault of heaven would not take much account of where I was."

The pastor sat while the King paced up and down the room. " Speak on, Pastor. Unlike Gabriel Damours, you brandish no flaming sword."

" Sire, this is an evil choice. Do not offend your comrades in the faith by suffering yourself to be torn out of the womb of the Church."

" If I took your advice," replied the King; " there would soon be neither King nor Kingdom."

The old pastor passed a hand over his face. " Worldly talk," he observed without emphasis, as though it were a matter of very small account. " The King conceives himself threatened by the knife if he remains in the faith. But if he abjures it, neither our freedom of conscience nor our lives will ever again be safe."

" 'Tis your own safety also that is in your mind," cried Henri, and added in a flush of mortification: " I seek peace for all my subjects, and peace of soul for myself."

" Peace of soul," repeated the pastor. Then with slow dignity he continued: " So we speak — but so does not speak the world. Sire, after your apostasy you will lose your carefree spirit, you will no longer stand, frank and fearless, before the people, who have loved you; and the Lord, too, loved you for their sake; you were kindly because you did no wrong, and cheerful while you were not guilty of betrayal. Afterwards — Sire, afterwards you shall cease to be our hope."

True or false — probably both; but his words were weighted with pastoral authority, and the King blanched, which so shocked the old gentleman that he whispered hurriedly: " But you can no otherwise."

He was about to rise, in order to show that the voice was now no longer of the Religion but of a common man. The King bade him remain seated, while he himself strode up and down the room. " Go on! " he said, more to himself than to La Faye. " Have I developed other faults and other virtues? "

" No," said La Faye, " they are still the same, but they take another meaning as the years pass."

The King: " And am I never again to be happy? "

The pastor, wagging his head: " You call yourself happy. But

from God there came to you in older days an unremorseful happiness. Soon you will suffer much wrong, and yourself do yet
worse wrong — for the sake of your beloved mistress."

"My beloved mistress," repeated Henri, for so in fact he called
her. "That she should do me hurt!"

"Sire, be on the watch, for these things are fated. Go in
peace."

What was the meaning of it all? The King was sickened at
the old man's riddles and reproaches; he went out into the streets
of his city of Noyon. There he came upon a tumultuous throng
that fell back at the appearance of the King, and out of it appeared no other than Monsieur d'Estrées, Governor of the city,
but since his daughter's exaltation Governor also of the province.
He tore himself out of the clutches of some persons who tried
to hold him back.

"My Lord Governor," said Henri sternly, "who permits himself to lay hands upon you?" Guards appeared, and the mob
turned to fly. Monsieur d'Estrées's clothes were torn, and strange
objects were seen protruding from his pockets: a child's bonnet,
a pair of baby's shoes, a watch, a wooden hobby-horse most hand-
somely varnished.

"I bought the horse," said Monsieur d'Estrées.

"But he did not buy my bonnet," said a shopwoman. "Nor
my baby's shoes," added a mechanic. Another asked him in a
genial but derisive tone to pay for his toys. The King stared in
painful expectation at his Governor, who gibbered unintelligibly,
but the deep flush on his red pate betrayed him. His hat lay
trampled on the ground, and a prosperous-looking burgher bent
suddenly and picked something out of it — a ring. Not an imitation, a real stone. "From the case that Monsieur d'Estrées
bade me show him," said the dealer.

"There is nothing missing," said the King. "I had wagered
the Lord Governor that he would not be able to pick up all these
things unobserved. I have lost and will pay you."

So saying, he strode away.

THE KING'S SERVANT

Thereupon he left the city promptly and without farewell; Armagnac always kept baggage ready and horses saddled. Henri's purpose was to put a distance between himself and the d'Estrées family, to continue the war, and ride his ways unhampered. But because he so yearned for Gabrielle, and because he could not but be ashamed of her, he risked his life in the trenches before Rouen. The Queen of England was seriously angry with him for so doing, as he learned from Mornay's letters. Several Catholic noblemen warned him in the meantime that they could wait no longer for his conversion. Mayenne gave them a last respite in which to pass over to the majority party. They had the time until the States General met. And that assembly would surely choose none but a Catholic king. In the midst of all these harassments, Henri espied a litter swaying down the Dieppe road. He knew at once who was inside it, and his heart leapt, but not from joy and fierce desire, as when the litter had arrived in the Valley of Jehosaphat. Much had passed since then.

He went into his lodging and there awaited her. Gabrielle, silent and alone, entered the room. " Sire, you humiliate me," said she — without pleading or reproach, and in all her unruffled beauty; which tormented him, like the loss of something treasured. In that perfect face he marked traits that made it yet more perfect; this while both were silent, dreading the conversation yet to come. A hint of a double chin was what Henri saw. A tiny dimple, visible only in a certain light, but how incomparable! " I am ready, madam, to give you satisfaction," he heard himself say, formally, as to a stranger. But she remained unperturbed.

" How could you conceive so false a view of the affair? " she said with a shake of her head. " You must protect my father and myself against the people of Noyon, who have ceased to show us due respect."

" That was scarce to be expected," said he curtly — but he waved her towards a chair. She sat and eyed him all the more severely. " The fault is yours and yours alone. Why did you not promptly punish the insolent mob who brought these charges against Monsieur d'Estrées in your presence? "

" Because they were justified. The things were hanging out of all the slits in my Governor's clothes. I felt as if I had stolen them myself."

" Nonsense! 'Tis a trifling weakness of his, and of late it may have increased. We were used to it; but from mere forgetfulness I forgot to warn you. How often has my Aunt de Sourdis gone round to the shopmen and explained what had happened. Be-sides, the things were usually valueless."

" The ring was not valueless," said he, and eyed with amaze-ment the marvellous hand resting on the chair-arm and the glit-tering stone upon it. She was wearing the ring!

" Upon my soul! " said he, though his tone was really one of admiration. " But, madam, pray explain to me what my Gov-ernor wanted with children's toys."

She looked at him, and her expression changed. Her face, glowing with frank wrath at the thought of insult, softened into a kind of tenderness. Nor was the change assumed.

" Gabrielle! " cried Henri in a hoarse undertone, and his lifted arms dropped. " Why the toys? " he whispered.

" Ready for our child," she said — bowed her head and softly stretched out her opened hands. Humbly and certain of her power, she expected to be kissed and thanked.

At their next encounter her demands were more considerable: the King was to appoint Monsieur d'Estrées Grand Master of Artillery. He owed her father some reparation, she insisted. Why not this? She did not explain. Henri tried to take the mat-ter lightly. " What does Monsieur d'Estrées understand about the use of gunpowder? It was he who blew up the Grey Tower."

Baron Rosny had blown it up, while the King was besieging Dreux. Rosny, who was a skilled mathematician, was also ac-quainted with the arts of mining and gunnery. " Monsieur de Rosny's mine " was, before Dreux, a common expression of mockery for the elaborate and pedantic preparations that went on for six days and nights until the massive walls of the Grey Tower were packed with four hundred pounds of powder. The court, with all the ladies, gathered to witness the explosion and made very merry when the sole result was a cloud of smoke, a dull report, and then, for seven and a half minutes — nothing. Rosny's pompous presumption seemed to have met its due penalty — when the tower suddenly split from top to bottom and, with a frightful crash, collapsed. No one had conceived of such a possibility, least of all the besieged. Many had been standing on the tower, and perished. The few survivors were each given a crown by the King. Rosny would have liked to be Governor, but saw himself again set aside, first because he was " of the Religion." His enemy, the fat ruffian d'O, could moreover promise the King a portion of the public money, so much as he could spare from his own peculations. So he was, of course, appointed Governor.

But the Grand Mastership of Artillery was still vacant, and Henri meant to give it to his excellent Rosny. He meant it for a reward when the honest fellow returned from the city and fortress of Rouen, whither his King had sent him, with instructions to negotiate the price of surrender.

" Dear love! " said Henri to Gabrielle d'Estrées. " Beloved mistress," he pleaded, " grant me this one wish. Choose whatever you please for Monsieur d'Estrées, except only the Grand Mastership."

" No," she answered. " I and my father would be held in contempt by the whole court if you did not give us this satisfaction."

Her condition perhaps explained her obstinacy. Henri extricated himself for the moment with a vague promise and at once sent an urgent letter to Rosny enjoining him to make haste. He was not to let the business fail over a matter of money, and whatever happened he must get the gates opened for the King. Gabrielle might forget all about the Grand Mastership if she drove through a triumphal arch into the capital of the Dukedom of Normandy.

At the moment matters so stood that the King's envoy was in sore need of the letter. Indeed, without that letter the King might easily have lost his city of Rouen, and Rosny his life.

For two whole days Rosny strove manfully over the price with

Monsieur de Villars, who commanded in Rouen for Mayenne and the League; he combated all the Governor's conditions and maintained that the Royal Treasury could not meet them. Meantime delegates from the League and the King of Spain offered untold gold to Villars, upon any condition. Rosny, a man of common sense, very much a Northerner, could not get over the notion that it would have been much better to have blown up the towers and bombarded the city rather than squander good money. On the other hand, Rosny, later to be Duke of Sully, was extremely set upon his dignity and inclined on that account to a good deal of display. He would have succumbed to the ministrations of his Governor, who lodged him in the best tavern in the town, deputed his own retainers to wait on him, sent him his secretary, and received him in his mistress's house. So far all would have gone well. Meantime Villars, a frank, straightforward man, produced his conditions, which were such as might have been expected in view of the lavish offers of the other side. In the end a lengthy list had been drawn up: offices and dignities, fortresses, abbeys, a million and twice a hundred thousand for the payment of his debts, a year's revenue in addition, and then more abbeys. It was beyond the compass of any memory, and Monsieur de Villars, as an orderly man, had written everything down, and read it out.

Rosny did not answer at once, for he thought to himself that this was highway robbery. Hence the excellent entertainment and the reception at the mistress's house. And if he refused any item, Villars would sell himself to Spain. And rightly, had it not been for the Royalist cannon. He would show how gunpowder can be smuggled into towers. And in the end Villars would hang.

Thereupon, with bland blue eyes and unexpressive countenance, he began his very modest counter-proposals, but the Governor interrupted him; there was still something he had forgotten. For at least six miles out of Rouen Protestant worship must be prohibited — this to a heretic and the envoy of a heretic King. As a result, the conversation grew more heated and could lead to nothing more that day. None the less a preliminary pact was made, but merely because Rosny was so fond of documents and signatures; and without a document, however trivial, he never retired from any transaction. By courier he informed the King of the monstrous stipulations. But before instructions could arrive, Monsieur de Villars got into his head that the unsuspecting Rosny was his intending murderer. His visitor was impersonating Rosny; some adventurer had devised the plan of seizing the person of the Governor and extorting ransom. Enough; when they met once more, the Governor, with bulging eyes, thought of nothing but hanging and strangling. Rosny had indeed bethought him of the prospect on the first occasion, though his demeanour had not betrayed what was in his mind. And now his sound sense told him that only a violent scene might help him and avert the worst. So he more than promptly countered the Governor's fury, and even called that nobleman an infamous traitor; whereat Villars was so astounded that he could barely speak.

" I — a traitor? You are beside yourself, sir."

" 'Tis you that are so in speaking of some murder plot, of which I have never even heard; your purpose is to break faith, for you have set your name to our pact."

These stern words recalled Monsieur de Villars half-way to himself, so that when his lady entered he said: " Pray do not shout, madam, I'll shout no more." None the less his sobered mood, which was mainly due to astonishment, would scarce have lasted. The Monsieur de Rosny's innocence sorely needed tangible proof, or it might yet go ill with him. At that very moment one of his servants brought him the King's letter, with Henri's instructions in the matter of the Governor's monstrous demands. But the lady of Liancourt's demands were the immediate inspiration of that letter; otherwise it might not have arrived so opportunely. Indeed, it may well have been that Rosny had already received it at his lodging. The effect of its delivery here during that high encounter was so notable that on later reflection it could hardly be conceived as an accident. The Governor's mistress promptly expressed her scepticism.

The King accepted all the terms save only the ban on religious worship, which he did not mention, and Monsieur de Villars likewise passed over the point; he was, however, to be appointed Grand Admiral. He promptly made amends to the envoy for having mistaken him for his intending murderer. One of the real murderer's agents had fortunately been taken. The Governor sent for him, noosed a rope round his neck with his own hands, and the retainers hanged him from the window then and there. This done, all that remained was to celebrate so fortunate an issue. " A pox on the League," cried the Governor, in bluff military fashion from the window, where the pendent figure had already attracted the attention of the mob. And he added: " Shout: ' Long live the King! ' " This they did, and their voices echoed as far as the quays, where the ships fired off their cannon. Salvoes were fired from the fortress walls, and not a church bell but pealed in celebration. A thanksgiving service in the Church of Notre Dame, with Rosny in the front row of seats; reception by the city corporations, and the presentation to the King's envoy of a magnificent service of silver-gilt plate; wherewith Rosny left the city.

When he had lain wounded under a pear-tree during the battle of Ivry, there also he had won a victory, and indeed made some rich prisoners, for the man was a favourite of fortune. This time, by his own efforts,.and with but little aid from fortune, he had secured for the King one of the most notable cities of the realm. And the King's faithful servant was indeed expectant of reward. He appeared, he was embraced, and he made a moving speech. The silver-gilt service belonged to the King; as a matter of principle he accepted presents from no man. Whereupon the King bestowed the plate on him, and three thousand gold crowns into the bargain. So far so good. But when Rosny asked for the Grand Mastership of Artillery, the King again embraced him and appointed him Governor of the town of Mantes. Rosny lost his self-control and roundly accused the King of ingratitude. Thereupon the King, with his old habit of jesting upon serious subjects — which had never been to Rosny's taste: " I have long been called ungrateful. But get someone to tell you the latest news from court."

Rosny had soon discovered the whole story. He shut himself

up for an hour and then went to Madame de Liancourt. She at once divined that he had come about the Grand Mastership, although there was nothing to reveal as much in his unfailingly dignified demeanour. He was wearing a great deal of jewellery. " Madam, I have asked for the honour of being present at your levée. The King uses my services; it may be that you will one day have need of them."

To which Gabrielle thoughtlessly replied: " I thank you. But when the King is in the field, he receives my letters through Monsieur de Varenne." This was a former cook, who now charged himself with the delivery of love letters. Rosny paled; his face was still high-coloured, but his colour grew a little fainter. Gabrielle was aware that something had miscarried, but omitted to excuse herself at once, and all her efforts afterwards were vain. Had her Aunt de Sourdis been at hand, she would have been better advised and might still have avoided making this man an enemy for life. Instead of which, the moment she observed her blunder, the unlucky creature hardened her heart and stared haughtily at Monsieur de Rosny, so that her woman stopped brushing her hair, and a long silence fell.

At last Monsieur de Rosny knelt down on a stool and replaced one of the lady's slippers, which she had kicked off in her agitation. Gabrielle watched him impatiently and reflected that even so he could not become Grand Master of Artillery, for Monsieur d'Estrées held that office. The injured man made no sign; he uttered some compliment on the smallness of her foot and took his leave. Scarce had he left the room when Gabrielle's heart turned over with fear: she had not offered him her congratulations, she had not even remembered his exploit in the matter of Rouen. He was now certainly on his way to the King. " Run! Fetch him back! " she cried to her woman. In vain; Rosny did not come. He asked himself why he hated this lovely woman from his very soul. And he had not yet discovered the true reason: their likeness to each other. Both fair of hair and from the North, high-coloured, and of cool understanding. Bound to the King, a man of quick laughter and quick tears, by their own advantage; but slowly something grew up within both of them that went beyond the experience of their being — a feeling: only the man from the South can teach them in that fashion. Each was soon demanding more; not merely from a complaisant King, but from a devoted lover. Two jealous people, loving the same person, and eager to do each other hurt — this until the very end.

The King had already betaken himself to Saint-Denis, where he was afterwards to abjure his creed. In this matter he was not yet quite resolved; his mind still wavered, though so much was made manifest that the last decision might well have been taken without so much deliberation. Meantime he held council with clerics, lent his ear to the proceedings of the assembly of the States General in Paris, waited half-heartedly for happenings that might turn his purpose, tried to parley with himself and even to come to terms with his God. In his uneasy forebodings he yearned more than ever for the company of his beloved. When, on this occasion, he left her behind in another city, he was still innocent of certain experiences that were soon to be his; thereby, indeed, it was established that the two were inseparable. The King could conceive of no better emissary to bring his beloved safely to him than his brave Rosny. The devotion of a good servant is not shaken by disillusion. He cannot fail to love Gabrielle, since he sets his salvation upon Henri. So Henri thought.

Rosny at once provided for the journey. Let him not reflect for whom the task was undertaken, nor what was to be the centre point of that decorous cavalcade. Whether she were his enemy or no, he was disposed for a measured progress through the land and a ceremonious entry. He rode ahead with his retinue, then came a gap of a hundred paces; then two mules drawing the litter of the King's mistress. Again an interval. Then a coach with four horses, for her women. Far in the rear, twelve baggage animals. It was an admirable and imposing spectacle, bespeaking, like all the Baron's undertakings, his sense of propriety and good order. Unluckily all men are not, like Rosny, sensible men and aware of their responsibility. At a steep declivity in the road, the driver of the four-horsed coach got down to relieve a need of nature. A skittish mule, despite the baggage on its back, galloped up to the coach horses, with all its bells jingling, and burst into a bray not less formidable than that of Silenus' ass in the Valley of Bathos. The four horses bolted; as was inevitable, the heavy coach crashed into the light litter, toppled it to the foot of the slope, and with it what was most precious in the kingdom. "Stop! Stop!" came a volley of shouts, but such was the general consternation that no one raised a hand. Meantime the pole broke, the coach came to a stand-still, the horses dashed on alone, and were caught by Monsieur de Rosny's escort ahead.

The lady had escaped so great a peril that the horseman could not reach her quick enough. Terror stifled his speech, he could only make gestures of devotion; and he burst into hoarse cries of joy as soon as he found his voice. The lady was in a fury, and she was also deeply flushed. No one had hitherto seen her other-wise than with a lily shimmer in her cheeks that far outshone her roses. This was observed by the horseman with secret satisfac-tion, for he recalled several of the King's mistresses whom Henri had abandoned because of their proclivity to red blotches on their faces, which he could not endure. It would indeed be twenty years before that fate descended upon one so young; no matter. Rosny felt in good humour and would simply have con-tinued the journey. Not so the lady; someone must feel her an-ger, and if it could not be Rosny himself, then he should thrash the coachman with his own hand for his untimely need of na-ture. The King's servant did so, and a little later he delivered the lovely traveller to his master, now in all the glory of her lilies. "We were green with horror at the accident," he told the im-patient lover. "But Madame de Liancourt turned a lovelier colour than ever. Sire, you should have been there to see."

POOR ESTHER

For the time being, the pair shared the same lodging in the old abbey, which caused the preacher Boucher to bellow with fury before all Paris. His success indeed was no longer at its height. His hearers were not trampled to death in the thronged church, there were fewer attacks of falling sickness; this was mainly due to the breakdown of the assembly of the States General. It was at last observed that the various claimants to the throne of France were all of them precarious, but outside the gates of the capital waited the true King; he needed but to abjure his faith and he could enter the city forthwith. And he proved his wisdom in that he made no further attempt to force an entrance. The gates stood open, the peasants brought their provisions, and the citizens of Paris ventured out. They were now fully fed and so had plucked up courage; even their long-forgotten curiosity returned; he who listens with a rumbling belly to the lies of Boucher at last forgets to use his eyes and sense.

They thronged in masses to Saint-Denis, but a few solitary inquisitives made their way to the old abbey; or at most two friends, who thought to find safety in each other's company. After all, there was very good reason to think that this personage was Antichrist himself, for how otherwise could an excommunicated heretic have maintained himself so long against the entire League, the Spanish armies, Philip's gold, and the Papal ban. Two little burghers crept that day into the cloister garden, sought a hiding-place, and there established themselves with the provisions they had brought. Ha! there was the monster, as punctual as if they had raised the Devil, except that he was not preceded by a cloud of sulphur. He had not even his bodyguard with him, he wore no armour and carried no weapon; nor was he clad like a king. They were promptly discovered, though he ought not to have been able to see them through a hedge. There must be something uncanny about the man. " Sire! We have no evil intentions."

" Nor have I."

" We swear that we never believed you are Antichrist."

" I should think you blockheads if you had. There is time for us to become better acquainted. The three of us have to live together for a long while."

He beckoned them out of their lair, and in a trice they lay before him on their knees. He laughed good-humouredly at their consternation and suddenly asked gravely about the sufferings of the siege; and when they mentioned a certain flour which had been got from graveyards, as they now hardly cared to believe, the King closed his eyes and turned pale.

In time to come they talked about this encounter to a large number of curious persons, who were less interested in what the King said than in his expression and demeanour. And whether he were a kindly man or no.

" He is a melancholy man," observed the one who had looked most narrowly into his face. The other protested.

" How can you tell? He was jesting all the time. And yet, to be sure — " And the other, who conceived the King as a man of light humour, faltered and was silent.

" And yet, to be sure — " said the other, who had conceived the King as a gloomy man, in an equally hesitant tone.

" He is tall." Here they were both agreed. " A fine upstanding man, very affable and so plain-spoken that we were taken aback, that we — "

" Shook hands with him," interposed the second. The first man fell ruefully silent. He had almost revealed that they had prostrated themselves before the King.

In his cloister garden the King received a visit from Pastor La Faye, who was leading a veiled woman by the hand. " We entered unobserved," were the old man's first words. Henri was mystified; he looked from the pastor to the woman, but her veil was impenetrable. " Unobserved — and unexpected," he remarked curtly; he was on the way to Gabrielle.

" Sire, and my dear son," said the old man. " God forgets nothing, and when we are least prepared, He brings our deeds before our eyes. And the doer may not disavow them."

Henri understood. He must have known this woman, but where and at what time he could not tell. In vain he looked for some mark on her uncovered hand. No ring; but the fingers were swollen and toughened by toil. He cast about for names in his mind, in much anxiety lest he might be spied upon, and longed to turn round to the windows of the house.

" She is of our creed," said La Faye as he unveiled her. It was

Esther, of La Rochelle; Henri had loved her as well as twenty others, and perhaps better than ten of them — who now could tell? Meantime he was on his way to Gabrielle.

" Madame de Boislambert, I perceive. Madam, the moment is ill chosen, I have business." And he thought: " Gabrielle — she will certainly get to hear of all this! "

" Look closer, Sire," said the white-haired pastor, very sternly. " Those of the Religion do not flee from their consciences."

" Who spoke of such things? " Henri feigned anger, but as he spoke, his anger rose. " I am in no mind to run away, but I have business and permit no intruders. Not even you, Pastor."

" Sire, look closer," repeated the pastor. At that moment something within Henri fell away from him, and his impulses of desire and anger faded. Before him, now indeed unveiled, stood an old, sick, and distressful creature — who had once entranced him as a man and inspired his energies. He would not have got so far, nor ever to the open gates of his capital, if all these women had not inspired and entranced him. Esther! Had she come to this! (" La Rochelle, the fortress by the sea, strong refuge of the Huguenots, we had marched thence into many a battle as champions of conscience. No need of those lightning looks, Pastor: we are agreed. It is the right moment.")

" Madam, what would you? " asked Henri.

And he thought: " The moment for the Huguenot Esther to appear in her misery before me is very surely this one. I am to abjure the Religion, and in requital I am happy with Jezebel, who perverted King Ahab to the god Baal; and in time to come she will be eaten by the dogs. O beauty, so swiftly punished, our ingratitude blackens thee; toil and trouble have indeed blackened the face of Esther of La Rochelle."

At this point he would in fact have fled had she not spoken.

" Sire," she said in a hoarse and quavering voice, " your child is dead. I get no more payments from your Treasury. I have been cast out by my own people, I am alone and starving. Have pity! "

She tried to curtsy, and in her weakness nearly fell. It was not Henri but old La Faye who held her up. His eyes flashed, and

Henri flung him a gloomy look in response. Then he went. At the end he nodded to the pastor in token of a promise that what was needed should be done. And as he made his way along the corridors, his step slackened and he pondered. What had he done, and what could be his recompense? Here was the most shameful instance of his heartlessness. Fleeting tears welled up into his eyes, while he made his way to his next woman. That was his reputation, all knew it, he himself was the last to notice how he stood.

He was amazed at what had befallen him. He had left victims in his path. By all precepts and his own true consciousness, he should have acted differently, as he knew the troubles of life very well from his own, and had always stood in need of resolution, both in the school of unhappiness and on his passage to the throne. But victims are the guerdon of uprightness. Henri again remembered Esther, because he had no money with which to make her the allowance he intended; he would have to deprive his beloved mistress of just that sum. This he conceived to be out of the question, and indeed he was afraid to suggest it, as she would certainly make no sacrifice. He had only to recall the vision of her lovely hand on the arm of the chair, and on it the gleaming jewel which Monsieur d'Estrées had stolen.

Sunk in perturbation, he entered her room with unwontedly soft tread. From the anteroom he could see through the open door; there sat the lovely creature at her dressing-table, writing. A woman should not be writing, except to her lord. What other letter could be wholly unsuspicious? Henri now moved noiselessly, and not because he was absorbed in thought. At last he peered over the writer's shoulder, without her noticing him, though they were both facing a small round mirror. Henri read: "Madam, you are in distress."

He recoiled, realizing at once to whom the letter was addressed, but in tense anxiety he followed the circling of the pen, which rasped as it moved, or the sound of his breathing might well have been heard. The pen indited, in a large crude script: "Madam, that is our destiny, when we have put our faith in fine words. We must be prudent or we shall justly perish. I do not pity you, for your conduct is base, and your appearance here in the garden dishonours my sex. I will give you money to depart. The father of your dead child might easily forget." The pen proceeded, but Henri had read enough. The mirror was clouded by his breath, and she saw no face in it when she suddenly looked up. He promptly retreated backwards from the room, convinced she was aware of his presence and that what she had written was less for the woman than for him.

He departed for several days; indeed, he contemplated breaking with Gabrielle. She was arrogant and burdensome. Through the letter she had conveyed to him that she would never forgive him if he helped the woman. In truth he did not dare. His business in several cities should serve to make him forget his lady's caprices. He forgot her caprices, but not her; and in his great longing for Gabrielle, not a thought was left for a poor unfortunate. On the third day he learned that his beloved had received the Duke of Bellegarde.

He fell into a frantic passion, which, at the outset, was very like the fever that in his youth had seized upon him and flung him prostrate after any extraordinary strain — the collapse of a resolute nature when the void opens; hence that passion. At forty years he must no longer be taken unawares. With his own hand he must close the open rift in the purpose of his life, as, at that safe age, a man may do. To horse, and woe to the traitors! He left his escort behind and moaned his lamentation and his vengeance into the rushing wind. He must be up and doing — he spurned the prostrations of despair; but punishment must fall upon them both. In pitch darkness he galloped through a wood; his beast fell, and he found himself sitting on a pile of withered leaves. " Monsieur de Praslin! " he cried, as his noblemen appeared.

Into that proffered ear he uttered orders that he never could have thought to give. Bellegarde should die. " Carry it out! You shall answer for it with your head." Praslin had no love for the Master of the Horse and would gladly have killed him in a duel, but he did not believe the King. Henri did not deal in assassination, he had never had a personal enemy put to death, and he would not begin with Feuillemorte. "Sire," replied Praslin coolly, "we will wait until daylight."

"You think I am out of my senses," stormed the King. "I want done what I have ordered you to do. And not only Bellegarde. You are not to kill him alone, if you come upon them both together."

"I hear badly in the dark," said Monsieur de Praslin. "Sire, you are known everywhere for your kind heart, you are the Prince of a new humanity, and a master of that kind of doubt so favoured by philosophers."

"I am so no longer," retorted Henri harshly. "Both shall die — the woman most of all, and first." And his voice rose into a shriek as he added: "I cannot look at it"; he veiled his eyes against the visions that came before his mind.

The witness of that dark hour strode on ahead, that he might see no more of it. At last the King swung himself into the saddle. When they reached Saint-Denis, the sky was grey with dawn. Henri dashed up the steps and demanded admittance, but he had to wait awhile outside, and through that blank portal he could recognize, as though he had been within, all the preparations for a hurried departure. Anguish came upon him, those within could be suffering no more sorely. At last the castle gates were opened, his lady stood before him — restored to him once more; for he suddenly realized that he had given her up for lost. The blood surged into his heart at the thought that he had her back. She was dressed as though for a journey, a woman fully clad in the greying dawn, opposite a window that was then flung open with a crash; and then came the sound of a leap into the garden.

"Pray explain, madam."

She looked him in the eyes and answered coolly:

"Someone who had fallen out of favour with you and asked my intercession."

"He leapt out of the window. Let him be stopped."

She barred the way. "Sire, your enemies of the League made proposals to him; but he did not reveal them."

"A pest upon the League! Madam, how comes it that you are

dressed and that your bed is in disorder? Intercession — in the grey of dawn and beside a disordered bed!"

She confronted him in her broad hooped gown. "What you fear did not happen," said she with complete composure.

He stamped his foot; this encounter was too temperate for his taste. "Defend yourself! You do not yet know that I am come to expel you from this place."

She looked earnestly into his eyes, with the expression of one who watches for the marks of rising fever. "Sit down," said she — and herself did so, thus exposing the disordered bed. Then she spoke.

"Sire, this is not the first time you have insulted me. You treated Monsieur d'Estrées with contempt. And you degraded me when you received that woman in the garden. You went without bidding me farewell, and I omitted the folly of answering the letter of a more loyal friend. He appeared before dawn, which you should consider a mark of delicacy. Would you have preferred that we should be observed by the awakened house?"

With an effort he listened to the end, clutching the arms of the chair lest he might leap out of it. Then he drew it towards her and spoke, word by word, into her face:

"He was to fetch you away; that is why you are so dressed. You meant to go; you meant to marry the man."

"With your permission," she replied — her face uplifted, but not moving it from his.

"That I will never give," he murmured. "The mother of my child," he added abruptly and aloud. At the word she blinked her eyelids twice, but made no other sign; a silence fell. Both knee to knee, and almost chin to chin; and a breathless pause. A shiver shook him, then his mouth and throat suddenly felt parched, he could not swallow; he went to the table and drank a glass of water. Whereupon he left the room without another glance at her.

Madame de Liancourt waited no longer, she had her baggage packed. She was not sure whether she had lost the game. Her best course seemed to be a visit to her Aunt de Sourdis. Dame Sourdis had said: "Whatever may happen, never plead, and

never on any account express gratitude." Gabrielle could hear
the old lady's voice from afar, as she gave vague orders to the
maids about her baggage. She had indeed no depth of mind, and
it was from want of forethought that she committed her momentous blunders, as with Monsieur de Rosny. But this time
it was enough that she recalled the principle impressed upon
her — never to plead, and never to express gratitude, but always
merely to wait until the enemy gave an opening. And she
thought: " He has no one. No one in the world, for he is about
to make a leap that he is pleased to call the death leap. He is
more certain to lose his party than to win the kingdom. When
we lie together at night, I say but little; he talks to me. It pleases
me to play the innocent."

Here she bade her maids cease packing. Left alone, she put
on her lightest, most transparent dress; of a sudden she was certain that he would come back. His women had mostly betrayed
him, there were too many such tales. He had never before been
jealous, though he was so for the first time now. " That must
be painful for him," she said in an undertone, and, her hands
lying limply in her lap, she was aware of a fleeting impulse of
affection for him who, for her sake, was to become another man
and would with her help enrich his capacity for suffering. She
came near to remorse. She had blinked her eyelids when he
spoke of his child.

He entered, lifted both her hands, and said: " It shall be forgotten."

" You are troubled, Sire," she answered gently — but did not
fail to observe that he had endured an hour of horror. His face
looked pale and weary. Weathered by a hundred campaigns
and strained by years of fighting, a face does not grow weary nor
pale; one must look beneath the skin. And that she did, and was
moved at last.

" Sire, you have the most irresistible way of paying court to
me." So saying, she opened her arms, no longer merely tolerant
and kindly — passionate at last.

When, for both of them, the moment of surrender had passed,
nothing was thereby altered — he, as before, restless and vio-

lent, she unruffled and unsure. " Angel of the North! " he cried
in a voice of desperation. " Swear to me that nothing shall equal
your fidelity, save only mine." But he did not pause. " But how
can you swear this to me now? Twice have you broken faith
already. You look on calmly at my terrible suspicion, while you
forgive another man his open treacheries. Feuillemorte is afraid
of the League, and he has not only paid court to Mademoiselle
de Guise, he is involved with her mother too. You are nothing
to him, and he is not a man of mine."

The jealous man grew frantic in his eagerness to humiliate his
adversary, to subjugate that inviolate heart. "And you could
write to him! After all your promises! You shall never again say:
' I shall do.' Only: ' I do.' Resolve, madam, to have but one
servant."

He groaned aloud, clapped both hands to his forehead, and
dashed from the room. He felt that he could fall no lower.

In the old garden Pastor La Faye was awaiting him. When
Henri saw him, the bond between his misery and his guilt so
struck at his heart that he stopped and stood motionless. The
pastor was ten paces away, under a clump of trees. " Poor Esther
is dead," said he.

Henri bowed his head on his chest and remained so long
speechless that the old man in the shadow of the trees could
bear the silence no longer. He said: " It may well have been
your guiltiest deed, Sire. Poor Esther has reached the throne of
eternal love."

Henri looked up, and above the tree-tops he espied the heights.
" In the Valley of Jehosaphat I for the last time had the choice "
— and he hurried away.

La Faye remained shocked as well as sad. This was blasphemy.
The King must be deranged. He was preparing to abjure the
Religion, but dared to compare himself with the Saviour, when
He was tempted, and withstood.

It was not until later that Pastor La Faye discovered that the
Valley of Jehosaphat had been the name given to the Royal
camp before Chartres, and when one day the King, plastered
with mire, clambered out of the trenches, whom did he see ap-

proaching in a litter? The being created by the Almighty for His inscrutable purposes with the King.

An old Protestant would not have believed that Gabrielle d'Estrées had never urged her lover to change his creed. It was only then that Henri himself knew the truth, in so far as it is to be divined simply in speech and silence. But afterwards he admitted it when a friend questioned him about his conversion: " Sire, who really converted you? "

And the King answered: " My beloved mistress, the charming Gabrielle."

Book Three

The Death Leap

The Mystery of Injustice

PHILIPPE MORNAY had in truth but one English friend left. And as Henri's envoy made his way yet once more across the Channel, on the last and most burdensome of all his missions, the company of those he had known came back into his mind. They were many, in various ranks of life, and some had so long passed out of his ken that he might well have forgotten them. But his first and longest sojourn had been his exile, when he had learned much of what he knew. The people who had taught him survived in his recollection, and many of them there alone. The fugitive Protestant's property had been confiscated, and if he had been caught in his own country he would have ended his life in prison or on the scaffold. A young man, whose poverty did but edge his mind, he frequented every sort of society in London, and, haunted still by apocalyptic visions of Saint Bartholomew's night, he made the most of them and told his tale wherever he might be. The guests at cheap tavern ordinaries listened with blank faces. Whether they took him seriously was more than he could say. In reply to his savage imprecations on the murderers then dominating his country, the horrors which the exile conjured up, the prophecies of retribution in the next world and in this, they merely said: " Do you truly think so? "

One day in that far-off epoch he took his clothes to a tailor to be mended; while the tailor sewed, Mornay talked, and the man's wife brought in some other occupants of the house to listen. It was some time before the exile realized, in the fury of his feelings, that clad in little but his shirt — for the suit he had taken off was the only one he had — he must look an odd sight and was now exposing his soul as well as his person. He fell silent, nor did his audience utter a word until the tailor gave him back his clothes. Then one of the women neighbours brought him a mug of beer and said: " I am sure it all happened thus, but so very far away. And I never heard of a woman drinking blood before."

This had taught young Mornay never again to express his feelings. Deeds so horrible, that cried aloud to God, should surely have roused the world: a hundred miles away, in another Christian realm, they were no more than a tale that is told, which might have been a better one. Thenceforward the exile clung to the knowledge that loses no truth by the passage of frontiers and speaks a common speech. Thereby he would find acceptance. So he pestered all the booksellers of London to publish his theological writings, but in vain. Some were afraid of certain views that were interdicted even in that Protestant land. Others insisted that the author must write in English, not in Latin. But he had some profitable encounters with learned and distinguished persons in the bookshops. Some took a liking to the foreign exile and invited him to their houses for the enjoyment of his disputations, and some engaged him to teach French to their children. One of these was Lord Burghley.

He had sons, the eldest of whom was of the same age as Mornay and a youth of ready mind, by no means indifferent to the Frenchman's vicissitudes. Here, thought the Englishman, were two young men, both of the same faith, both with minds perturbed and eager to serve a higher humanity; both, too, of like origin, save for the unequal value of their rank, for nobility stood for more in England — none the less there was little to choose between them, and fate, with a trifle of goodwill, might well have changed their places. All this the sagacious youth observed, but expressed nothing of his wonderment at his own good fortune. There he sat in safety, while Mornay had had to flee his country. Mornay had been robbed, menaced, and affronted to his very soul. A golden future lay before young Burghley, merely because he was such a one as Mornay, but an Englishman. God save the Queen!

The great man's son paid homage to his star, but he felt too deeply not to understand that he too must bear some guilt for all these squandered foreign lives. It was no concern of common folk. But a man of knowledge is under bond to stand forth for Christendom one and indivisible, lest it be brought to ruin by the practising of evil, which we do nothing to prevent. And he began to think of Christendom as a structure, rising by ever-narrowing stages, of which the topmost vanished from the picture. So vivid was the vision that, though no draughtsman, he promptly sketched out the design. It stood upon pillars, detached but closely clustered, as it were England, France, and the other lands and kingdoms. Suddenly upon that serene structure dashes a fiend with brandished torch. Besotted in his fury, he fires the first of the pillars; the second too is soon ablaze, then others also. A Christian looks on, his hands clasped across his anguished breast, but he does nothing to avert disaster — which, by some strange miracle, does not come to pass. The building still tops the wrecked pillars as though hovering upon air; and the upper parts of it are still unseen. When the artist showed it to the exile, the latter, after observing it awhile, said:

" Evil is beyond the compass of the mind. Your drawing signifies nothing less than the mystery of evil."

These words perplexed the artist, who bent over the paper as though he were looking at it for the first time. But Mornay — long and weary is the exile's journey and much he learns from it — felt in that moment proud of the wrong that he had suffered, for it was a part of the mystery. And so he always deemed it in his own mind, although in life he championed the right, in which there is no matter for marvel.

Young he was, and in those days he was more disposed for tennis or rowing with his English friend than for learned conversations. The pair lent each other books, and still oftener they shared the same companions of both sexes, each and all in brotherly innocence. O lovely Thames, stream and air and banks steeped in lush, light colours — summer days that turned even a haunted exile into a carefree child. How soon that paradise perished — that light-footed company with their singing and their kisses and their nosegays, a snatched caress in a green glade, and the sound of muted viols behind a hill — alas, how soon it perished! The exile returned, chose the Prince he meant to serve, and travelled upon his affairs to the courts of Europe, but most frequently to England; in all of which there were certainly no youthful delights. Englishmen were now his diplomatic adversaries, nor were they agreeable or easy to handle. Yet every time he saw the chalk cliffs and set foot upon that shore, he heaved a sigh as though he were coming among friends. He had indeed but one friend there, to whom above all others he owed his friendship for that land. A country is beloved for an attitude of mind, a faith, an ancient fame, of which it is far less conscious than he who visits it now and then and lands beneath its cliffs.

Lord Burghley had inherited his father's title and was now High Treasurer of the kingdom. The envoy went to him even before he waited on the King's Ambassador. He came to a house that stood apart against a sky of flying cloud, above a shore scattered with fishermen's huts. Mornay found his friend in a modest apartment, where the Minister was directing the labours of a number of clerks; it was from here that the finances of the country were conducted. At the appearance of the visitor the clerks looked up curiously; he stood facing them until they dropped their eyes again, their curiosity unsatisfied. After a due pause the noble lord observed: "I trust you had a good journey," and led him into his own cabinet. Not until then did they shake each other by the hand and look long into each other's faces. By way of pretext they both said: "You are quite unchanged," but they had done so because it heartened each of them to look into the other's eyes.

"The position is difficult," Burghley began as they sat down on the hard black chairs. Mornay realized that Burghley meant to help him through the interview that was to come. He swallowed with an effort. "But that, for you, is no new thing," Burghley continued.

"I have not lost my courage," Mornay managed to reply.

"Last time you had none too easy a task here, but you brought your business to a good issue in the end."

"Because your Queen is just and firm," proceeded Mornay. He repeated: "Just"; and then added: "Firm." Of whom was he thinking, who was neither? He hurriedly suppressed his unuttered thoughts and said: "My King is still the resolute master I have served for so many years. It is his position that is shaken, not he. Your Queen is displeased because he would not starve out his capital. Nay, worse; a rumour has reached Her Britannic Majesty that my King is proposing to abjure the true religion."

As Burghley fell grimly silent, Mornay asked him in a low tone: "Do you believe it?" Then, raising his voice: "As God is my witness, I am certain it is not true."

"Then you are the right man to convince the Queen," was the reply.

"Will you stand by me, Burghley, as you did before?"

"Friend," said the High Treasurer, trying to speak in the old familiar fashion, "it was a mighty simple matter last time — not to be measured with what faces you now. The Queen had a man in her mind. We were all young."

"Young? It is only two years since."

The Minister paused and pondered. In very truth, two years ago the Queen still loved, still suffered. But he said nothing, and Mornay went on: "Two years make no great matter. A passionate nature like that of your great Queen remains so always, whether the impulse be a man or one incomparably nobler: religion. I have already sweated blood and water over the Earl of Essex — "

Again the Minister was intent upon his own thoughts and let the envoy speak on. Passion, he thought, is easier approached than wisdom. What could he do when the Queen could neither rage nor suffer.

"I have already sweated blood and water over Essex," said Mornay. "And what will come of this affair?"

" Something that will amaze you, my old friend " — the words were on Burghley's lips. But he merely answered: " This time you will talk more and with greater vehemence than Her Majesty. You have nothing to fear from the Queen."

" Truly, Burghley? When Essex remained with the troops in France in the face of all the Queen's appeals and orders, preferring to brave her disfavour rather than miss the arrival of the Duke of Parma — the threats and imprecations that burst upon my head! My King had not received Essex personally, nor with proper ceremony. My King had rashly exposed his own life, but, most unforgivable of all, he had let the English troops, and Essex — Essex! — fight in the front line! Not another English soldier should be sent against the Duke of Parma until Essex was back at court. Her Majesty was sick to death of French affairs. After a last outburst of fury, she did not sleep all night, fell ill, and so the matter ended."

" Two years ago," repeated Burghley, with lowered eyes. Then he looked up and said: " Remember, Mornay, you are speaking of the past. You got the regiments in the end, though not until you had gone and Essex had come back. We two, Mornay, were able to prevail in some measure on the Queen, because we — not of set purpose, but because it is in the hearts of men like us to do so — we took no heed of that which makes all women alike. You, Mornay, are well favoured by the Queen."

" Still? I had heard that something was reported against me in my absence."

" A foolish trifle," said Burghley; and he laughed as he rose, well pleased that this oppressive colloquy was ending on a lighter issue. " When you were besieging Paris, someone at table with you derided the Queen's faulty French. She is too generous to bear malice, and you will be received as is your due. You are the trusted friend of England and its ruler."

All in all, this had been an encouraging encounter. It was surely a good omen that as early as the third day the Queen summoned the special envoy to her presence. She sent a state coach to the Ambassador's house, and Monsieur de Beauvoir la Nolle accompanied Mornay, escorted by an English guard of honour.

At the moment when the two gentlemen entered the presence chamber the Queen appeared through a door at the farther end. Her numerous retinue fell back against the wall on either side. But for the array of cavaliers and ladies, Mornay would have been unaware that Her Britannic Majesty was there in person, though indeed the length of the great chamber lay between them. She seemed to him shorter than he remembered her before. That long-limbed form seemed less rigid, and she no longer wore her hair in a high headdress, as had been her habit. Indeed, Elizabeth was actually wearing a coif.

So much Mornay observed as he entered; then, traversing the room with eyes obsequiously downcast, three paces away from her he stopped, looked up, and saw her as she was. The Queen was no longer painted, except for some blue and black patches round the eyes, designed to soften their harsh set look, like a falcon's steely, lidless glare. All her features had sharpened since last time, and they bore signs of age. Or rather age had been allowed to lay its touch upon her — indeed, this weakening of the great lady's will was what struck Mornay, who had all his life conceived of Elizabeth of England as the fleshly embodiment of power established and unassailable. But for her long rule and her indomitable youth, freedom of conscience in Europe would have had short shrift; and whence would have come the aid and comfort that had heartened the King of Navarre, afterwards of France, in his darkest hours? Mornay suddenly marked a wisp of grey hair straying from beneath her coif. He paled, and it was with an effort that he set himself to address the Queen.

The speech was no more than a ceremonial display, as was everything that passed that day. The Queen listened standing to the solemn homage of the King of France, presented by his special envoy, first in Latin and then in English. When the time came for her to reply, she mounted four stairs to her raised seat, but not with the light step of a year or two ago. She moved slowly — perhaps deliberately so. It was then that Mornay began to be sceptical. The change was too visible and too abrupt; moreover, her purposely dragging gait moved one of the cavaliers to offer her his hand: it was the Earl of Essex. Elizabeth did not even glance at him, she barely touched his hand, but suddenly her regal airs returned. Enthroned, her close-fitting stomacher erect and rigid, sat the Queen, clad in the dark grey silk that she had worn for many years. Her favourite, who looked no more than six-and-twenty summers, though his smooth face belied his age, stood in a nonchalant, boyish attitude, with a look of disarray that did not hide his elegance — and one leg lightly poised. Thus he had helped the old lady to her chair, and thus he stood now she was seated. It should be known — foreigners were present to see and report the matter — that he was more of a personage at court than the Queen admitted. He was master; against his charms the Queen had no other counsel than that of quickly growing old. All this was uttered in his mere aspect. His devotion was a mask, and even his undeniable grace was a counterfeit of what it seemed. Charming now, he would soon degenerate unless his patroness took care. That slim leg would be set firmly on the ground: and the great Queen would do well to watch a heady youth who might cease to be her plaything and from mere wantonness become her terror and her bane.

Mornay detested the favourite and was delighted at what then occurred. The Admiral, the Marshal of the Court, and all the officers mainly concerned in the ceremony stood round the royal chair in a half-circle, while Essex behaved as though they were mainly a background for himself and he were exhibiting the Queen. He beckoned to his uncle Leighton, who in his turn whispered to a second gentleman, and a third produced a written scroll — not at all readily, as could be observed; they were affronted. But Essex coolly snapped his fingers to hurry them, took the document, which was the Queen's ceremonial reply, and he it was that gave it her. He alone of that assemblage seemed to possess authority when, with a kind of careless deference, he was seen to hand the unrolled parchment to the monarch. In an instant a curt gesture of the Queen, who had begun to speak, had flung it to the floor. The favourite, now ousted from the picture, made a grimace that slowly darkened into wrath. Then he noiselessly slipped out of observation behind his uncle.

Her Majesty's voice was clear and imperious as ever, it carried beyond the pillars and tapestries, and the ladies stood openmouthed; for such force may be absorbed with the intake of the breath. Elizabeth described the King of France as the sole Prince of Christendom who stood sword in hand against Spain — whereat she rose and plainly awaited the applauding murmurs of her court. Thereupon with a few gracious words she dismissed the two envoys. As they bowed they noticed the roll of written parchment lying on the floor untouched. They withdrew, keeping their eyes fixed upon the Queen during their departure, and Mornay, who was on the watch, observed that Elizabeth stepped sideways from the dais and so trod upon the parchment.

Only five days passed before the Queen sent a privy summons to Mornay. He came on foot and found Elizabeth alone, by a book-strewn table. The diplomat took advantage of this fact; he extolled the good fortune of a monarchy that was not a camp and set no double sentries at its gates, but stood safely on its own just institutions. Elizabeth, who had greeted him with courtesy, drooped her head so deeply that after his first few words she could gaze up at him and ask him with a mute look what in truth he meant. She was well guarded, whether he met her soldiers in the corridors or not; that of course he knew. His purpose merely was to open the matter of his visit and announce that his master, the King of France, was heralding an age of domestic peace, such as England owed to her great Queen. Hence he hoped that no offence would be seen if his master's dealings seemed strange and hesitant at times. This was, by his intention, to lead up to the rumours of a change of faith. The Queen ignored it all.

" I have often had to complain of the King of France," she said in the ringing, cadenced tones that she used with such effect. Then to his astonishment she added: " He should have used the force I sent him to take Rouen; that was why I sent it."

Mornay remembered that only two years ago she had behaved like a damned and demented soul because her Essex could not be extricated from Rouen. Here sat a woman who had made her renunciation. She was wearing no coif, her white hair was unconcealed, and beneath it still a glimpse of red tresses, now covered with a weft of white, like the glitter of hidden gold.

"He could have starved Paris out," she went on, but less emphatically than she had spoken about Rouen. Mornay was ready with explanations: a King must spare the lives of his fellow-countrymen, even when in revolt. He and they must live a common life together under the providence of God.

She eyed him once more — how much of this was hypocrisy? Then she remarked simply: "I commend your master."

The envoy bowed acknowledgment. And the change of faith? he thought. Speaking more familiarly than before, she explained what it was that she commended.

"Your master is a King. He prefers to buy his cities rather than bombard them into ruins. Therefore he employs hucksters like this fellow Rosny."

"A faithful servant," objected Mornay to the more specific charge. Elizabeth nodded.

"He is indeed one of the earlier friends. A King makes new ones. He lets the old ones drop" — with a wave of the hand — "when they have served their purpose."

Gladly would Mornay have asked whether the new ones might also be rogues and traitors. But he did not speak.

"He may survive without the change of faith." At last! The envoy's heart began to throb. Elizabeth kept her lips open, she was listening into the distance. "There will be much blood shed," she said in an undertone, with a shrug of her shoulders. "The age of peace is not yet at hand. After each of his battles the powers will consider whether he should then be recognized. 'Vederemo,' said the Pope. But the allies of the King of France would at last have had enough and lose hope as well as patience." A sudden sharp glance into the envoy's eyes.

He realized that this was his moment, but he did not know how to begin. He had expected a torrent of reproaches, but Elizabeth seemed unperturbed by the fatal rumour; she spoke as though it were true and behaved as though she wished it so. Mornay did not believe her. The great Protestant could neither give up hope nor patience because her ally held fast to the Religion. She was not made so, her suspicion fell on others. Could she be hiding her known passion for the true faith under a mask of age and renunciation? This would explain the turn of their conversation. The moment pressed; he must not blunder. He must not admit that the King might renounce his faith. She was testing him, to make him speak with candour. That he would do, and could do without peril. His King would not recant.

When Mornay had thus stiffened his courage, all in the drawing of a breath, his deep-set craft came back to him, and all his inner strength. So he began quietly to recount the achievements of the new faith, and of human liberation; they were identical, and for that very reason Protestantism was laying hold upon the world. Venice, the oldest republic, had offered her commendations to the King of France, she was watching him and what he did, being in a mind to separate from Rome. The Pope himself had actually observed: "We shall see," because he could no longer maintain the ban of the Church upon a sovereign backed by half Europe. "He is the only prince who stands sword in hand against Spain." Mornay carefully repeated Elizabeth's own words. "And Spain may yet raise armies in her hour of doom, her dissolution may lie heavy on the world; but what can she avail in the end? My King is not only the one hero and prince who wields the sword; here are the nations of Europe, and a movement for human freedom. Setbacks will but speed it onwards, defeats will bring it increase. My King fights and stands on firm ground; that is the will of God in history."

The Queen listened and was silent. There was an intent, almost girlish expression on her face; she drooped her head over the table and sat with her chin on her level hand. The thought flashed through Mornay's mind: Had she merely caught the art behind the self-betrayal of that speech? He could not linger on the reflection. He must drive home what he had said and banish the Queen's doubts — but how? — for all the true facts had been spoken. He had set them forth as they should stand, if so be that his master held to the faith. Impossible! — as Mornay recognized; he could go no further, for Henri would not hold to it. He would recant. This unassailable conviction now first came to the unlucky Mornay on the matter; and it came to him by virtue of his own words, under the Queen of England's chilly eyes.

He took his hands from his chair, held them uplifted for a moment, and turned his eyes away. Suddenly his resolve was taken; he stood up, laid his right hand against his chest, and said in quiet tones: " I confess it. My King will abjure the Religion. He dares to take the death leap, as he calls it."

And Elizabeth's silence signified: " We understand each other. But why not sooner? " And Mornay answered her:

" Because it is a fact, and so appears; but it is none the less untrue. Twenty years of war for conscience' sake are not less real and ineffaceable. He cannot with his heart recant."

And the movement of her shoulders said: " Without it, then." Mornay, speaking more intently:

" Five times he has changed his creed. Three times from black necessity; this will be the fourth time for that reason, nor will it be the last. That I can testify and that I know. To gain the power that should be his, my King must needs fight for our freedom or he would have achieved nothing. I trust Your Majesty may think of this day, and of a humble servant who has offered you good counsel. I beg you not to take my master's recantation in good earnest, and not to withdraw from him your aid and your regard." Mornay drew a deep breath to nerve himself for what still needed to be said, though it had not entered his mind until that instant.

" The King of France means to establish a national Church; both creeds united, and the Pope banished from our faith." Then, having grasped and compassed the whole matter, he ended gravely with the old, old words:

" *Imminet schisma in Gallia.*"

Elizabeth eyed him, nodded approval, and her sole answer was that zeal had bestowed on him what nature had denied: the gift of eloquence.

" *Si natura negat, facit indignatio versum,*" said she. What she meant was that she did not believe a word, and Mornay must be demented if he thought she would. But she spoke kindly, and what she then said was meant to recall him to his senses.

" I commend your words, my friend, touching the fight for freedom. How else could he have achieved his greatness? And after his recantation he will still fight and beat the Catholic Majesty of Spain. I am sure of it, and I will stand his ally. But regarding a separate Church — " And her voice suddenly hardened: " Monsieur Duplessis, where have you spent the last ten years? "

He saw that he had shot his bolt and lost; he could only add, as a good Christian: " God's glory is of no less account than the King's service."

At this, Elizabeth's face suddenly grew lined and old. " Such opinions will soon drive you into exile again," she said in a quavering, almost tearful voice. " You are gifted with the power to imagine and persuade. You did your utmost with me, but I am an old Queen and know the world. Your master will cherish you Protestants, for I am told he is a kindly man; but withstand him in good earnest, and he'll have your heads. I dealt so with my Catholics, though I did not cherish them. The will of God fulfils itself in varying ways. He'll have your heads," repeated the old lady in a sorrowful tone; and had she not spoken so, that terrible presence and that ringing voice would have been beyond all bearing. Even now Mornay was tempted to dash out of the room.

Then she added, as though at a sudden thought for Mornay: " But you shall come to no harm; I'll speak a word for you in season. You have served me as you have served your King; and I never forget. But I shall not welcome you again as his envoy."

She was speaking more naturally, and her face had softened. " He made a Protestant victory impossible when he took his new mistress." She waved aside Mornay's protest. " A Queen knows these things. Who will now conspire against his Catholic victory? Mistresses are apt at conspiracy." She sat stiff and rigid, her hands gripping the knobbed chair-arms, and in her eyes the steel-blue, lidless falcon-glare. Then she leapt to her feet, stepped quickly forward, flung back her head, and said in voice that rose nearly to a shriek:

"Did you see him?"

Mornay stiffened, as at the sight of something monstrous. "I know him," she cried. "I have begun to know him now. When we dragged him out of Rouen, we should have left him there. Fool that I was!"

She strode up to Mornay and bent over him. "You understood the meaning of that pantomime — with him to the fore, making a display of me, his Queen! Then learn the look of danger. Your King speaks of a death leap. I will not take that leap." The shriek turned to a wail. "The King will have to destroy what he loves most. Tell him so. Be sure you warn him, he must be beforehand with traitors. He must read the end of them in their own eyes before they know it themselves."

The woman was now weeping undisguisedly; she flung herself full length across some silken cushions on a coffer — a monstrous, stricken thing in agony. Mornay felt that he ought not to look at her, but he made no motion. It was the Queen. He trembled, perhaps in horror and perhaps in awe. Beneath a mask of age and renunciation she had indeed concealed her passions, whatever they might be. Not indeed a passion for the faith, but for all that concerned her power and her kingdom — so the pious Mornay told himself, refusing to contemplate the worst of all. None the less, before his inner vision stood a black scaffold, and he could see who mounted it.

He waited with averted face. When at last he turned his head, Elizabeth was sitting at her table of books; she had opened one of them, and her lips were moving. Then she noticed him and said:

"Your thoughts were straying, master envoy. Meantime I was reading Latin, not French, for my French is faulty, as you know. You have surely had a vision of dark times, and they may well be near at hand. An exile once more in the years when the soul needs peace. But I like you well and I offer you refuge."

This was Mornay's dismissal, and he could return to his Thames-side inn. It was not in his mind to visit anyone — not the Ambassador, and still less Lord Burghley. His room aped the splendour of a castle, but it was a tawdry, empty splendour, in which the unhappy man saw a pattern of himself. Henceforward he was a whited sepulchre. If only he had had the courage of his new condition. He had indeed entered the Queen's presence like a man among living men; it was she who had made him understand that he was cast out among the dead. He remembered that he had upon occasion trafficked in politics by pretending that his master would recant, but conceived himself as merely using a ruse. Now it had turned to truth, and he himself was the gull. He stood with bowed shoulders at the window; beneath him the glittering river rippled past. Once there had been summer days — the Thames, stream and air and banks steeped in lush light colours, days that turned even a haunted exile into a carefree child. Summer days.

Mornay was not the man to linger over such sentiments, nor did he yield to despair. For the following week he kept his room, on the pretext that he was ill, but indited a learned and most persuasive document upon the necessity of a Gallican State Church. If he could have assembled the Council of Pastors and Prelates and the King in his room at that very hour, he was sure that he could have prevailed. But the work was done, the room desolate and empty; so Mornay kindled a fire and burnt the document. Then he waited on the Ambassador, Beauvoir, gave him a plain account of his failure with the Queen, and touched on what had also happened at the audience; she would declare herself if she were pressed. Beauvoir must arrange yet one more audience: Mornay would now be strong enough, she would protest to the King against his recantation. She would restrain him from an ill-judged act — Mornay laid stress on this, and Beauvoir agreed, although he was averse to any interference from the Queen of England and regarded Monsieur de Mornay as a theologian rather than a practical statesman, despite his worldly arguments. However, Elizabeth replied that she was not at leisure, she hoped that she would soon see Monsieur Duplessis-Mornay again, and her Admiral would place a Royal ship at his disposal for his journey home.

Before the vessel was ready to weigh anchor, Mornay went to take leave of his one English friend. This time the High Treasurer admitted him by a small privy door, not leading into the clerks' room. Mornay stepped through it and made his way into the black-panelled cabinet. On the table, between two glasses, stood a bottle of *clairet*, the King of France's daily wine. " We drink to his happiness and prosperity," said Burghley, and they did so standing.

They sat awhile in silence. " Now you know how matters stand," said the noble lord, making a wry face, as though the wine had been sour. " Your King has, as he has always had, an ally against Spain."

Against the Religion too, they both thought. And against the right. Such is the world, they thought. No kingdom remains pure from error and repentance. Mornay spoke very slowly, savouring his words. " The King ventures on his death leap with great self-denial, more than we could ever show. And where shall I find words in which to praise your great Queen's wisdom? Her Majesty is marvellously eloquent upon the subject of good and evil."

" Marvellously so," repeated Burghley. His eyes began to twinkle, and he raised his forefinger as though past echoes of such eloquence came back into his mind. " I see," said he, in his usual simple tone. " You failed. Pardon me, my good friend, that I did not foretell to you the issue. I know how wise the Queen is, and I know too that it is harder dealing with wisdom than with passions, and she has conquered hers."

Mornay did not reply — nor did he mention Elizabeth's self-betrayal; he dismissed it from his mind. After a pause he said:

" This shall make no odds between the King and myself. I know my duty, and will do it the more heartily after he recants, for he will then be in worse peril than before."

Burghley laid a hand on his arm. " You too will have to recant."

" No! " shouted Mornay — recovered himself at once, and continued in an undertone; whether he spoke in humility or defiance, Burghley could not tell. " Who am I that I should presume to disavow the truth? I am amazed that kings do so, and the universe still stands."

"Drink a glass while I look for something," said Burghley. He got up and pressed a sliding panel in the wall. Some moments passed, then he produced a paper and spread it out on the table: it was yellow with age and torn at the folds. It still depicted the ancient structure of Christendom, rising by ever-narrowing stages, of which the topmost vanished from the picture. Both men surveyed it in silence — the mysterious fiend dashing in with brandished torch, the pillars aflame, the anguished, helpless Christian near at hand, the building still standing above its wrecked supports as though hovering upon air. At last Burghley spoke:

"The mystery of evil, so they called that drawing. How much we knew in those days — before we actually knew it!"

"And all we still hope for, in despite of hope," said Mornay.

His friend gave him the paper; he smoothed it into its tattered creases and put it away. "Farewell, Philippe," said his friend.

There was not a tear in either man's eyes, their faces were harder than before. But contrary to habit they embraced.

The Vanquished

His Catholic Majesty was receiving absolution on his knees. The confessor laid his open hand on the thinning locks of that bent head, then helped the King to rise. "Draw the curtain!" said Don Philip curtly to the priest, as though he were speaking to a lackey. In that moment he was cleansed of his sins and acknowledged no spiritual superior. Until they come creeping back again, thought the priest, to whose experience the Catholic Majesty was a man like other men. However, he obeyed, drew back the curtain from the window, and extinguished a last lingering taper. It was fixed against the wall above the table, backed by a silver shield that threw its reflection down upon the outspread papers. There had been many tapers when the night began, but they had gone out one by one above that sleepless head.

The faint grey light of a spring dawn glimmered into the room.

The priest marked the King's red eyelids and suggested opening the window. "Wait until I bid you," growled the ageing monarch. "I am in no hurry for the day!" He sat and closed his eyes. "No hurry for the din and turmoil, and least of all for the lewd desires of men." He was clad in black, with but little white about his person; his garments were creased, and his hands stained with dust and ink. His chin sagged askew on the limp ruff, as his head drooped forward and he sank at last into an uneasy slumber. As the King began to snore, the priest glanced up and down the desolate street. At the corner could be espied the corpse of a horse, forgotten there since yesterday or since the week before, with only its upturned belly visible. As the sun rose, the flies would come. The houses, colourless in the bleak twilight, stood aloof in a closed semicircle round the royal castle, wearing an even meaner and more submissive air across that unpeopled void; no lurking shadows now round those crouching habitations, only the castle towering up to the first light of day.

Far below, beneath the window, could be seen a beggar-boy, dragging an enormously fat woman, as ragged as the boy, but three times his age. Both had clearly spent the night on a stone bench between the pillars of the palace; now they were picking over the refuse, to get the titbits before the others came. When the lad espied something eatable, he clouted the crone and she bustled towards it. He was master. The priest thought scornfully of worldly masters, especially of the one now snoring at his back. But the sleeper started up, at once recovered his senses, and said: "Enough. The world knows no rest. There could never be any true rest for this world."

"Not even in the square beneath your room," agreed the priest. "Rest and peace are with God alone. It is the King's mission to punish men for their vain desires — and give them a good clout behind," this last remark vanished between his teeth.

"My mission," repeated the King. "Why, then, do I not succeed — and, as the days pass, less and less? The Empire and its iron peace, more than once was I near to spreading it over Christendom. But a rebel always rises up and thwarts me. Why does God allow an insolent captain — "

" A heretic," corrected the priest. " He may not dispense with heretics, their downfall adds continually to His glory."

" And to my troubles. My sleeplessness, my maladies, and all the temptations of the soul. This barbarous earth is an unwholesome dwelling-place. A day without revolt and heresy and I should at last be ripe for peace everlasting."

" Amen," said the Father.

" Instead of which I lose battles, and an insolent captain wins them. What profit is there in my Catholic Majesty? In Paris they choose him King of France. A kingdom is slipping from my grasp, the key to my whole Empire, the last that I must add to my father the Emperor's domains; then the world would be subjected and redeemed."

" It is beyond your powers. You should be more humble."

Don Philip's voice suddenly grew shrill. " Is that captain humble? He recants, he enters the bosom of the Church, and soon he will be King of France. And you allow this. The French bishops are gathered about him at this hour, they instruct him in the faith, he will but laugh at them and profess what they please. Then he will enter Paris — with his mistress; a rebel, heretic, and libertine, and you allow it."

" You gave only eighty thousand talers to buy France."

" I did much more than that. I caused Pope Clement to decree that no priest should come near him. And now they are all thronging round him, only too ready to favour this pagan, this philosopher, who is standing out for his own terms. And I am cheated of a kingdom because you betray the faith."

" Say rather that you lacked resolve to win it." The priest thrust his head forward. " Why were you not yourself in Paris at the Infanta's side, to proclaim her Queen of France? This captain is there and answers for himself. And you think to win a kingdom sitting at a table! Why, you have lost heart already, and it is a shaky table." He grasped and shook it, and when the King half rose from his chair, the priest waved him back. " The question is not whether the Church does her duty by you; that is presumption. The question is whether you are doing your duty by the Church; and that will be considered in Rome."

At these words the King recoiled and sank back into his chair; the priest towered up before him like a black-clad giant. Don Philip's face contracted at the blow, eyes and nose and mouth dwindled into a patch of wrinkled skin. All that was left of his crushed face was a scanty beard, a narrow forehead, shining faintly in the grey of dawn, and a few wisps of colourless hair straggling over the egg-shaped skull.

Then, as the moments passed, fear was mastered. Don Philip turned his chair with its back to the window, so that the priest had to walk round it. "Duty," said the King, reflected, and then said once more: "Duty — that has been my whole life. Let Rome consider what she will, nothing can alter that." The priest, not troubling to answer, blinked at the growing light, while the face that was King Philip's reappeared, and what a face was that! — arrogant, inhuman, and remote, with all the feline cunning of the hours of mastery. He had no need to raise his voice; his subjects from his uttermost domains would have understood him from mere terror.

"I ruled the empire of the world here, from this table; what need have I to use my limbs? Before my mind alone has the earth bowed down, and a waft of my will has moulded it like clay. There are foolish captains who ride up and down, men without vision, men trammelled by their sluggard minds. This captain is one of them; but I — I move with the speed of angels."

The priest made no movement. "So far," he thought, "'tis well enough. Soon he will grow bemused and end with a tirade of abuse."

"I am pure, too, as the angels are. Like the unembodied spirits, I abstain from flesh, and this by the force of my own mind, like all else that I have done. You have made me pray and confess my sins; I could the more easily have taken flesh into my arms, as does this captain, for you would have given me absolution. It needed no favour from the Lord on high to make me one of His elect. All this was achieved by my mind and will — and thus I ruled the empire of the world without yielding to the lust for human flesh. It has never yielded to my touch, nor wafted its fragrance on me, nor moistened with desire in my

arms. Soft flesh is for the enjoyment of this captain, for the
kingdom of heaven is not, nor ever will be, his."

" What matter," thought the priest in silence, " as flesh comes
thus into your speech and haunts your every thought? "

" At last the blow will fall and fling him into uttermost hell."
Don Philip no longer masked his fervour, he spoke in a sort of
chant, with upturned eyes. " The hands of God will soon be
outstretched to set me beside His throne — that great throne
with rounded pillars whence comes all the splendour, not from
the Lord Himself; He abides in shadow, as I do here. But that
splendour falls on flesh — the immaterial flesh of angels. They
are clad in female forms of wondrous beauty and outstretch
them to the touch, though not with any mortal motion, nor
any such traffic with the flesh as is the usage of this captain."

The priest conceived that his moment was at hand. He said
in a markedly indulgent tone: " What do you know of heaven,
Don Philip? Your deeds have brought no favour from Heaven
upon your Empire, which lies sorely stricken. Between you, who
are wholly and entirely upon the hither side, and eternal salvation, stands the Church; forget it not."

At this a set, despairing look came upon Don Philip's face.
He tried to protest that he was speaking as a Christian who had
just confessed and was for the moment without sin. That made
no impression on the priest, who grew more peremptory still.

" Sins of thought. What you have confessed, and are so continually confessing, are sins of thought, and in them you are
belly-deep. You would be sanctified. That depends on me alone.
My word will undo your deeds and wipe out your thoughts."

" Do you believe that? " asked Don Philip, now in utter bewilderment, as the priest could tell from his pale eyes.

" Sleep," he said imperiously, " and take care not to dream.
Alas, the licentiousness of the King of France is the cause of
your temptations; I have long known it. Sleep; I will plead for
you, and you shall awaken without sin, until the next time."

Don Philip closed his eyes, but upon his own breast there was
no rest for that uneasy head; it should have lain and found forgetfulness upon another's; upon that soft and fragrant flesh for

which his being so craved. Don Philip was troubled lest the priest, on guard before him, might divine his every sin of thought, and even see it as it was. For some while he feigned to be asleep. When he made the motions of awakening, no priest was in the room. Don Philip rose with an effort, shuffled to the window, opened the shutter, and peered out.

The sunlight had reached the depths, and the ground beneath the castle walls was flooded with radiance. On the far side of the roadway the houses lay dark and shuttered. The deep furrows in the unpaved square, the potholes choked with refuse, stood out harshly in the clear light, and dust swirled past in the dawn breeze. Some beggar-boys dashed round the corner; Don Philip withdrew his head, thinking himself observed. No, a litter turned into the square, a silken couch set upon two wheels, drawn by three mules, and shaded by a gold-embroidered canopy. The driver, who was walking at the side, vainly slashed his whip at the rabble of boys who grabbed at the harness, flung themselves before the mules in a struggling heap, and came near to wrecking the whole equipage. The lackey dropped his whip, and a tirewoman flung money among the yelling horde. Then the lady rose from her cushions.

A sumptuous and opulent lady, but not a lady of the court, Don Philip was well assured of that. She looked about her, perhaps for help, perhaps to see if she were observed; but no one was about at such an hour. Only Don Philip, peering out from behind his curtain. A luxuriant beauty, her bosom framed in black silk and bared to view. Indeed, she put out a bare leg from her litter, to get a better view of her tormentors. But Don Philip felt that her intention was that she herself should be seen, and seen by him — though this could scarce be so. The hour was too early, a person of this kind did not leave her bed in the doubtful expectation that an elderly potentate would be peering round his curtain after a sleepless night. He was deluded by his bad conscience, and the evil that he did in thought held him at the window.

" Who," he asked himself, " am I? Nations must row in my galleys. And I? A prisoner — without joy, without flesh. Ten paces through yonder little doorway into the chapel, and there I stand before the Lord, untrammelled by any other presence. What this priest will never learn is that the Lord has speech with me, as with an equal. Wherefore, indeed, He gives me my dismissal at my own table." And he said aloud: "I am a prisoner, I, Philip, next unto God."

"Blaspheme not," said the Father. "Next unto God, and a prisoner — who ever heard the like?" He spoke in a voice of harsh contempt.

"Silence!" hissed the King between his teeth. He barely glanced over his shoulder, now not in the least perturbed at this sudden apparition of the grim and towering figure. And Don Philip said imperiously to his accustomed taskmaster: "Who is that woman?"

The priest, after but one look, answered: "Everyone knows her. The most notorious harlot in the city. I am her confessor. And I would have you know that I have through her discovered conspiracies against your safety."

"Fetch her."

"For what purpose? She has lately confessed, there will be nothing new."

"On your life, you shall go and bring her."

The priest had understood, and his disgust was written on his face in a look that passed from pious horror into plain contempt, and yet was touched with a sort of kindliness. "I should bring you a grievous sin," said he in a matter-of-fact tone. "Moreover there would be witnesses, for there are some in the palace who have already risen. Wait until tonight."

Philip merely looked at him, with the result that the priest backed towards the door. "I must consult my superiors. Your purpose may be venial, as your sins of thought are getting the upper hand." So saying, he left the room. Don Philip paced up and down before the window like a sentry; every time he turned he made sure that the litter was still there and that Madam Flesh had still one foot upon the ground. Madam was now, like a true-bred harlot, hurling the filthiest abuse at the rabble for breaking one of the reins, while the driver tried to reharness the mule. Don Philip swung sharply round with no shuffling of his feet this time, and at every turn his anger and his fear increased. The litter and the lady would be gone before the cursed priest arrived. Then, as he strode back and forth, he was aware of a movement in the room, a shadow on the wall. It was the nobleman who brought him his chocolate; his orders were to be as silent and invisible as a shadow. Don Philip, now beside himself, roared:

" Drink it yourself! "

The nobleman was so dumbfounded that the cup clattered in his hand. He had received the cup from a chamberlain, who took it from a page, who had it from a lackey, and he from another of his kind, all having received the salver from the imposing cook, to whom it had been handed by a long succession of kitchen-men, at the far end of which was some scullion who had boiled the chocolate. The unlucky nobleman thought with all the speed of fear. On its way through all these hands the chocolate had cooled, but it might also have been poisoned by a hand unknown. The King knew it, conceived him guilty, and therefore bade him drink. He drank, and promptly fell down in a faint. Don Philip did not heed him, for the priest had at last reached Madam Flesh.

The Father knew how to be expeditious. In five bare words he made the matter clear to the illustrious harlot; she, with great presence of mind, refused, and the price was promptly raised. She was on her way to early Mass (she said), for good reasons of her own; she would not be stopped, her salvation counted for more than an old gentleman's caprice. Don Philip guessed what was going forward. He struck his bell, which did not awaken the unconscious nobleman; but a secretary was waiting outside, and the clatter of the bell brought him running in. " Go down at once. Double the Father's offer."

The figure was already so outrageous as to take the priest's breath away. " But what a recommendation it will be! Think how you can raise your prices, daughter! " But she insisted on going to early Mass; and why she was going she knew only too well. When the secretary dashed up, she laughed at his offer.

" Old pig," said she, and for the first time looked up at the King's window. Don Philip quivered to his marrow. He forgot to draw back, and the sovereign and the harlot took each other's measure. Her eyes flashed through a lace veil, his strained through a haze of madness and of torment.

The woman got into her litter, which was ready to move, and she waved it forward. She snapped out an answer over her shoulder to the priest and the secretary. Don Philip, in one single leap, dashed at his nobleman who was rising feebly from the floor. " Stop her! Only stop her, and she may have all she asks."

With that, the deed was irrevocable, thought the harlot as she turned and went with the three envoys. She had protested that she wanted to go to Mass, and that for a very good reason. She had given her warning. On the previous day she had observed suspicious symptoms and had gone out at the most secret hour to pray that the disease might be averted. She had been prevented from praying, so the disease must come. And a few days later it became apparent that Don Philip, the Ruler of the World, was infected.

MEDITATION

The momentous crises of life are not reached by such a man as Henri as the result of long reckoning or of sudden resolve. He sets himself in the due direction as yet unconscious of it, or, knowing it, he is incredulous of the goal. He is led on the way he means to go, there are times when he divines the ordeal before him; but it lies so far ahead. He has started on that journey, he can scarce turn back, it is a doubtful enterprise which he can hardly look to see fulfilled — when, behold, he is at that journey's end. It was a dream. Not for one moment had Henri conceived himself a dreamer — he who was so constantly in action. Strokes and counter-strokes, all that a man must do to win a kingdom and hold the heart of a woman adored, victories and defeats — how can a man dream in the midst of deeds? Battles, sieges, and pacts, cities conquered, cities bought, and so too with men: cajoled, outwitted, paid, or overmastered. When his enemy

Mayenne tried to seduce his Catholics, he countered by persuading his adversaries to meet him in council, until they admitted that their only reason for withholding allegiance from the King was his religion. Whereupon he of course made known to the assemblage — through an Archbishop, in fact — that all was well, for he would change it.

That promise he had often made, and many mistrusted him, as was no matter for surprise. Still, in Paris they chose neither the little Soissons, who could scarce have expected to be chosen, nor the Infanta, since the Spanish party was discredited by its atrocities. They chose the rightful King, whether he abjured heresy or not. It was assumed that he would abjure, whereby many misgivings would be set at rest. If he fobbed them off afterwards, the guilt was no one's, not even his. Many came to recognize that he had a conscience, and the right to one. Men grow tolerant when they have suffered long enough from their own obstinacy. Those who thought themselves best informed curtly denied that he would recant. " The man from Béarn will never change his creed for profit," said an ambassador. And Henri liked the saying, though he then stood upon the verge.

The bishops and prelates gathered round him, instructed him in the faith of the majority, or, rather, they met or tried to meet his arguments, for Protestant Jeanne's son was no mean adversary in theology. Three days before the event he had so long foreseen, he was still contending vehemently against the doctrine of purgatory, which he called a sorry jest: did these gentlemen take it seriously? He packed them off with their Form of Recantation, and they went, to reappear later with another. But the Papal Legate had forbidden them even to approach the heretic. Henri for his part announced, and caused it to be recorded, that whatever he did, he was answerable solely to his conscience, and if his conscience said him nay, not for four kingdoms like his own would he desert the faith in which he had been bred. When he had uttered these words, and the cowled secretaries had taken them down, a great silence fell.

Not upon the assemblage, where there was more argument and much discussion and debate. That silence laid hold upon the soul of Queen Jeanne's son. Never in his life had the sound of the outer world been thus stilled, never had he stood so utterly alone. For the first time he observed that he was dreaming. He had merely seemed to act, his will and his impulse had been but a muttering in sleep. What was happening within him he did not understand. He struggled in vain for the word that would scatter the delusion. He had become the denizen of a dream. One word, and he would know many things, even who he was.

That night Gabrielle wept. At her side lay Henri, watching her in silence. It was the first time that she had used their nightly companionship to implore him to recant. Neither by day nor in the privacy of the bedchamber had she intruded upon matters of creed. She knew instinctively that herein her body and his love could not turn the scale, or they would do so without words uttered and tears shed. Besides, tears did not come to her with ease. The charming Gabrielle was not tearful. She had no gift for pleading, she disliked expressing gratitude, and seldom betrayed emotion. Meantime her Aunt de Sourdis had appeared, and told her with much insistence how matters stood. The King was wayward and uncertain, he argued with the prelates and appealed to his conscience; why? — when a man had resolved upon a step, and had in fact already taken it.

"Not a step," replied Gabrielle. "He calls it a leap, and he lately wrote to me: ' On Sunday I shall take the death leap.' "

She said this in a quavering tone. The wily old lady sensed at once that sentiment was invading this business, to the disfavour of practical good sense. So she passed over all such lesser considerations, such as the interests of religion, the condition of the kingdom, or even the risk to a Christian woman's soul when she lives with a heretic. She took her stand on serious arguments, and said: " Would you have your father turned out of Noyon? And Monsieur de Sourdis from Chartres? And is Monsieur de Cheverny to surrender the seals, all on account of your obstinacy? The King will lose the game and have to flee from his enemies, like the rest of us, and the fault will be yours. But I am still here. What? If you had a heart for your besotted cuckold, would you refuse to do the one thing that would make him recant? "

" And what is that? " asked Gabrielle, not without alarm.

" Withhold your body. Then he will do his duty. And I am come here to set you in the way that you should go! "

" I don't believe it," said Gabrielle. That damped the old lady's eloquence.

" Gabrielle, you are sorely changed."

She made a show of dabbing a kerchief on her painted eyes.

" Pray think of us all, and the poverty and persecution that we know too well and that now threaten us once more; my dear child, think, if not of us, at least of yourself. Only his conversion to the true Church can safeguard your future. He will get a divorce, he will marry — and raise you to the throne. All this still stands today in your power, and you know how power looks; just as you do, deep-bosomed and with rounded limbs. If you let it slip today, this very night or tomorrow fortune will have fled beyond your reach. Then you will have brought him ill fortune; and in ill fortune he will live and die. If you feel for him in this little matter of recantation, surely you will spare him what will be far worse. At every turn ill fortune will be yours. And in ill fortune, my beloved child, believe me, in ill fortune no woman can keep a man, and Henri least of all."

But Gabrielle's fears had vanished. She smiled a slow smile and shook her head. She was secure; and she would hold him. At this Dame Sourdis fell into a fury; she stamped, she raved, she poured forth a torrent of shrill abuse.

" Too stupid for a whore! " was the end of it. " And we depend on such a creature as this." Wherewith she raised her hand. Gabrielle caught it before it fell.

" Aunt Sourdis," she said, in a strangely unruffled tone, " I was touched by one thing that you said. So I will shed tears tonight."

" I am very glad to hear it." The old lady was already pacified. " And you will withhold your body from him too? "

To that question Gabrielle made no reply; she opened the door to admit her ladies.

When, that night, she lay sobbing with her head pillowed on her lovely arms, Henri did not ask the reason; and, as Gabrielle noticed, despite her lamentations, he was no longer looking at her and her parade of grief, but was staring at the carved canopy of the bedstead, on which the reflection from the taper on the night-table flickered to and fro. Gabrielle was baffled; it would be very hard to prevail upon the King as she had promised. She sobbed more bitterly and begged him in God's name to recant; he had given his word, and if he did not he was lost. Did he hear her? His expression was that of one listening to something he could not understand. Suddenly she ceased moaning, fell silent, and her heart spoke. Its voice was scarce above a whisper.

" We are going to have a son."

She forgot that she had blinked twice, as though caught in a guilty act, when he had called her the mother of his child, and since then he had made no mention of the matter. In that night hour it came upon her that he was indeed its father, nor did she ever again doubt that he was so. For in that hour she began to love him; and she did so because she felt for him and because he was beyond her understanding. But he had marked the soft utterance of her heart; he laid his cheek to hers, she clasped him in her arms, and one of her tears, a real tear, trickled into his mouth. Thus, for a while, they lay.

She closed her eyes and let sleep come; but she felt that he was still lying as before, guarding his secret. And she said, already half asleep:

" My dear lord, what do you see above you? "

And he murmured, between his deep-drawn breaths: " I would not see, I would hear, and I am waiting for a word. It is no use to think, only to listen. When the silence within me is deepest, comes the sound of a viol, I know not whence. Deep, dark tones, rightly cadenced for that word. But the word does not come. It is very strange."

When Gabrielle awoke, he had gone; he was back with his prelates, who were instructing him in the faith, this for the last time; no more questioning nor hesitation. So today, a Saturday, they kept him five hours at one sitting, the last of all, and he too had no thought of curtailing it; rather, he feared the finish of the orations, for that day they were little else.

In another room of the old Abbey of Saint-Denis during these momentous hours the King's mistress and his sister were sitting together. The Princess Catherine had come just like Dame de Sourdis, and with the same dispositions; but the intent of them was different. Her brother was to recant that he might achieve greatness. She hoped he would be forgiven, though she was not too hopeful; she did not know whether, in God's estimation, a kingdom ranked before a soul. Therefore she felt deeply for her brother; he was the head of their House, which was fated to rule and must pay the price; but that, pray God, should not be his salvation. At need, thought Catherine, she would herself have recanted, to mount the throne with her poor Soissons. She would have been damned, but her brother saved. And now he was to be a great King; Soissons had never been of much account, none knew that better than she did. She had never seriously meant to play her brother false — only to save him from disaster.

Her journey thither had indeed been in some measure a flight from Soissons, who had blamed her because he had not been chosen king. He thought she had worked against him and for her brother; they had parted on bad terms, as they often did, but their quarrels did not last. They had lost too many good occasions to want to sacrifice their companionship itself. They would, as before, be reconciled, though Catherine none the less felt occasional gusts of fear. She sat beside her brother's mistress, brooding, more upon him than on her own account. Gabrielle too; and if nothing else, the foreboding that came from each to the other by a mere waft of feeling had set them both at one. There was much else also to incline them thus, and most of all: Catherine knew that a child was on the way.

When the women spoke, it was in a whisper, but they were mostly silent, as befitted that tense, oppressive hour in the old Abbey.

" They have been pressing him for a long while now. Can he have signed? " asked the sister.

" All is ready for tomorrow. To me he says neither yes nor no; he listens, looks upwards, and is secret," answered the mistress. There was a long pause before she went on in an undertone:

" I wish that he might have been spared it all! Especially now — " this almost inaudibly — " when I am expecting a child. When he expects me to bear him a son."

The sister understood from Gabrielle's mere breathing, or guessed her meaning from the way she passed her hands over her body. She embraced Gabrielle and said into her ear: " We are of the same family. I too await your child."

That was the utterance that had been in Gabrielle's mind since her lord's sister had been in her company. She was accepted; a stranger no more. Strange indeed now seemed to her the calculations of her Aunt Sourdis. If she was to be Queen, and Queen indeed, then it would come by ordinance of nature, through her body, and because the King's sister, who was stroking it with questing fingers, was henceforward her sister too.

Catherine went softly back to her seat. The lovely face, as she could see, was marked by weariness and sorrow, but she was fruitful. Her own face was withering unfulfilled and would never bloom again, not even in another and smaller one, for she would never have a child. It was hard not to be jealous. That light-hearted brother of hers — well, this time he knew his own mind and would hold to it; there was no chance in that quarter. (" Ah, my dear, but Queen? You will never be Queen; wait, I know him. He will put you off until it is too late.")

Meantime the Princess's eyes were straying round the meagrely furnished room. Only one treasure: a picture of the Virgin lavishly set with variegated jewels. At Catherine's yet unuttered question, Gabrielle blushed and turned away; so Catherine did not ask it. (" Very well, my dear. They bribed you with presents to prevail on him at last — with tears, I suppose, and all manner of heart-breaking lamentations, by night, in the act of love.")

Scarce had the thought crossed her mind when Catherine covered her eyes and said: " Forgive me. What he is about to do is no fault of yours. The fault is in the circumstances that each and all beset him, and the people that each and all betray him. I also have done so in my time, I also."

She had for the first time raised her voice, for it was her conscience that spoke. " My poor brother! " Here the door opened — not flung gaily back, as was usual when her brother entered. But it was he.

When he looked up, for he had been staring blankly before him, and was aware of the two creatures whom he loved the most, he grew promptly boisterous and gallant. He kissed them, twirled his sister round, knelt before Gabrielle, caressed her, and laughed. But they marked his impatience to be gone, and in truth he was not really in their company. He fell to mimicking his prelates and bishops, their voices and their persons. It was to be feared that His Lordship of Bourges might at any moment sprout wings and start for heaven. The women watched him with faces quite unmoved. Suddenly he broke off, turned his ear to the window, listened, waited, and went out.

" How he has changed! " said Catherine, deeply shocked. But Gabrielle bowed her head for shame that he had been sad in her company.

Henri went down into the old garden; it was, for him, the recreation hour. He compared it with those in the Collegium Navarra, when he had been a little schoolboy and had played between lessons with two friends now dead. Suddenly he found himself at the spot where poor Esther had been brought to him by Pastor La Faye. Between Henri then and Henri now there were long years of innocence, of guilt, of knowledge, and of ignorance. He stopped and caught a conversation behind a hedge. It was carried on in whispers, like every other on that tense and lowering day.

A voice: " He will put his old friends to death. How can he help it? "

Another: " Later — perhaps. If he has not forgotten in the meanwhile. We know him to be ungrateful. His new friends have yet to find him out."

A third: " So easily moved to tears, so light, and so forgetful — but which of us does not love him? "

A fourth: " Not the man he is now. But the man who sailed into harbour in that little ship."

Henri was moving on when the first voice began again: " Every man among us must look to his own safety."

" Nonsense, Turenne," said Henri, as he appeared. " I am your man, and I think to remain so. You shall convince yourselves of that when the time comes."

He laid hold of Agrippa d'Aubigné from among the rest, stepped aside with him, and said into his ear: " For your sake I risk my salvation." This with wide eyes and burning eyelids; not lightly nor forgetfully, nor with any sign of tears. Agrippa was shaken by pity; how could this man fail to win affection?

None the less, Agrippa was the only one whose heart went out to him; as was then made plain, though the older, pleasanter days had encompassed Henri with much easy friendship. But the warmth of that one heart set him aglow before he sauntered on, to be alone, after his habit, and to catch what he might hear. Once past the hedge he turned towards Philippe Mornay, his envoy, who had arrived with weighty news and had not yet been received by the King.

" Monsieur Duplessis, that little ship — you helped me to sail it into harbour; but could you choose it? It is another harbour now."

He soon reached the far end of the garden, where birds were twittering, but, alas, not birds alone. Over the low wall two heads were bobbing up and down, each trying to convince the other of the most innocent intentions. " Pray be our friend, Monsieur de Rosny," fluted Madame de Sourdis. " You are really so already, for you need us as much as we need you."

" It is even so and not otherwise, honoured madam " — whereat Rosny dived and Madame de Sourdis emerged.

" The Grand Mastership of Artillery is a small matter now," she said in a tone of roguish assurance. " For one snipe that flies away you shall shoot ten."

" If only you do not take wing," sighed the Baron, and sank out of sight once more.

" The King will get a divorce and marry Madame de Liancourt. Advise him well, and you are well advised. You rogue! " tittered the lady, and submerged. In her place appeared the cavalier, with that smooth face of his which could utter anything with unruffled dignity.

" I have laid the plan with him already, my good lady. He is only recanting that he may make his mistress Queen. Once the stroke is played, all will promptly become Protestants — the King, the Queen, and even you, dear lady."

At this the Sourdis remained for a while below, and when she reappeared once more, her eyes were hard. She had understood that he was mocking her. " You will be sorry for this," she hissed. Her gown positively whistled through the air as she whisked round. A door slammed. Rosny, his face still unperturbed, went on into the garden; there on a bench sat the King. Henri allowed his astute and faithful servant to approach before he asked in a hoarse undertone:

" And your true opinion now, in this last hour? "

" Sire, if the Catholic faith is understood and received in the right sense, it might be of great advantage."

" You said that long ago. Nothing else? "

" The next world." Rosny paused. " For that I can give no warrant." And his smooth face puckered slowly into a laugh. But before the laugh broke, the King was up and away. And what Rosny found remarkable, he sang. It was growing dark beneath the trees, and like a child he sang in the darkness.

Lights had in the meantime been lit in the refectory of the old Abbey, and their reflection shone into the garden. As the King came into the shafted beams, he ceased his strange singing, some conversations in the half-storey above the hall ceased, and the lawyers whom he had summoned to his presence trooped through the open windows to await him.

Henri ran up the steps. The vestibule beyond the illuminated doorway was all the darker, and Henri was invisible as he stood there and looked at the desolate hall; so small an assemblage made the space seem larger and more empty than it was. " My men," thought Henri — and thus indeed they looked. Presidents and councillors in threadbare raiment, with deep shadows under eyes that still glittered with fever and the privations of mortal perils long endured, officers of the law, like those before them and those yet to come, they had steadfastly resisted force in the name of law. Justice is indeed not law. It may be a dextrous evasion of the law and its pronouncements. " Not a single Protestant among them," thought Henri; " and yet they fought for the kingdom no less than my warriors of Coutras, Arques, and Ivry, and without their battles mine would have been in vain. They took the side of the persecuted against the men of power, and stood to arms against the mighty robbers. Thus I too conceived my part, and I have won back plundered lands for thousands upon thousands of my peasants, every one of them: that was my kingdom. Yours is law; thus you conceive your part in the world of men."

He stepped forward, his hat upon his head, nor did they remove their shabby hats; and he said to them: " My learned brethren:

" We have ridden through the land and swung the sword, my learned brethren. And because we were men of our hands, we now stand here, and the door of our capital is opened to us. The Parliament of Paris has unbarred it for me; your President Brisson's awful death was the first sign and the last warning."

The King took off his hat and bowed, and the men of his Parliament did likewise. After a pause for memories unuttered, the First President of Rouen, Claude Groulart, spoke; though a Catholic like the rest, he was solely concerned that the King should not abjure his creed, were it against his conscience. And Henri answered:

" I have at all times sought only my salvation, and always prayed to the Divine Majesty that I might be given grace to find it. The Divine Majesty revealed to me that as a consequence of the abominations committed in Paris by others — though I myself must answer for them — my salvation is bound up with the establishment of law, which is the fullest measure of humanity that I know."

This delighted the men of law, and they shouted: " Long live the King! "

Henri now no longer stood aloof, he mixed freely among them

and explained familiarly to more than one what trouble he had had with the Divine Majesty before his recantation was approved. He did not speak of a death leap, though the thought was present in his mind. All this had befallen him beneath the walls of his capital, a city filled with horror. There he came truly into God's presence. It is written: " Thou shalt not kill "; and this law was so human that it might well be from God.

" Likewise a King who respects his fellow-men and their lives as well," interposed a voice. He himself made light of his own part and assured them he had been mainly moved by the instruction from the prelates and, praise be to the Holy Ghost, he was beginning to acquire a taste for their teachings and their arguments. Whereupon he led his men of Parliament to a table set out at the back of the hall and offered them other than spiritual fruits: piles of melons and figs, dishes of meats, and flagons of wine. It was long since they had enjoyed such things; they ate with gusto, and by the time anyone felt disposed to look up, Henri was gone.

He lay down without eating and promptly went to sleep. When he awoke, it was morning, and Pastor La Faye was at his bedside. Henri bade him sit down, embraced the old man, and asked him once again whether it was true that the qualities of man could change their meaning as time passed, according to what La Faye had maintained. It was indeed so, replied the pastor.

" His faith too? " Henri went on. " May it now signify what is false, having once been the true faith? "

" Sire, you will be forgiven. Go to the cathedral with a joyful heart, that our Lord and our God may also rejoice."

Henri sat up, he laid his head against that withered breast that so yearned to comfort him. And thus, in the arms of his ancient friend, he said:

" My reasons for recanting are entirely worldly. There are three. First, I am afraid of the knife. Second, I would marry my dear lady. Third, I want to possess my capital in peace. Now give me quittance."

"Your torment has been great; I give you quittance," said Pastor La Faye, and departed.

The First Chamberlain d'Armagnac clothed the King entirely in white — like a boy for confirmation, thought Henri to himself. He stood up a man renewed; it would scarce be believed that this was the fifth occasion. A God had long since ceased to attend the ceremony. The Devil, if he existed —

"I wonder you did not take a bath beforehand," Armagnac reminded him.

"I shall need it more afterwards," replied Henri. And from his tone that astute retainer gathered that he had better go.

Henri was alone, but he could not understand for what purpose he had wanted to be so. Where was Gabrielle? In silent agreement she was that day sharing a room with Catherine. All had left him; but he would soon be escorted by a glittering throng, through crowds of his people gathered to watch him abjure his faith. Not merely abjure the man that he had been, but make his peace with the majority and take their colour. What was he? A sack crammed with dust, like the rest. Until yesterday he had striven and disputed with the prelates over words. God had not listened; He was wearied by all matters of faith and cared no more for one creed than the other. He deemed our fervour childish, and our purity He rejected as mere pride. Henri's Protestants did not know Him, for He had never led them by that thorny path, and they presumed to speak of treachery when a man followed life and listened to his voice of reason.

Meantime he was not called upon to think; over his festal garments of white silk, embroidered with gold to the tips of his toes, he hung his black cloak, put on his black hat, and bent his black plume so that it nodded as he moved. Suddenly he heard the strains of a viola, the very same that seemed to reach his ears when he had stood and listened during those tumultuous days; and the word he sought remained unuttered; nothing but those ghostly cadences. The sound grew louder, as though it were no longer a fantasy but real music; Henri understood that all was now ready and in order; the thoughts that had possessed his mind, and the garments of white and gold and black that arrayed his person. Daily, in his fears and doubts, in exaltation and abasement, he had meditated on how the soul constructs her creations from calculation and from dream. For these he risked his soul's salvation! Thus he groaned, until he remembered the trump card — that his salvation was the re-establishment of law. He sang in the darkness, because he had been made afraid of the other world. But he knew that men were born to seek the truth, not to possess it, which only the Power on the other side can do. It was for him to rule on this side; here and now was his terror of the knife. A vile confession, but he made it. Did he love Gabrielle the more, or did he fear the knife the more? But he also conceived of inhumanity as the most abominable of crimes, and nothing, not even woman, did he reverence like reason.

All this sped, effortless and in a flash, through his liberated spirit, because he had known and weighed it all before, and in what moods of darkness and oppression he could barely call to mind. Indeed, he thought that pure enchantment, like music, had rapt him to some white and golden realm of bliss — but the melody grew rounder and richer, although it was not rendered in very accomplished fashion. Who could it be, if not Agrippa? Henri stepped out upon the balcony, and behind the nearest bush he spied the hand that drew the bow. He laughed and beckoned, and Agrippa showed himself in his everyday doublet; he wore no festal garb and did not mean to go to the ceremony. He would not be present when Henri abjured the Religion; but he was playing to the King, on that ecstatic instrument known as the *viola d'amore*.

At first Henri's chin quivered faintly, for was he not easily moved to tears? But he noticed in time that the excellent Agrippa was making merry in all innocence and affection. So Henri winked, and the other did likewise; down yonder the old friend, with homage born of irony and kindness; above him the white-clad candidate for confirmation, with his grey beard and weathered skin. In the end they both gave up the effort to be dignified; Henri aped a stately lady listening to a serenade, Agrippa fiddled frantically and began to whistle an accompaniment; but the moment had passed. The cathedral bells rang out in a shattering peal. Both started; Agrippa disappeared behind the bushes; the King with one leap was back in the room, smoothed down his clothes, passed a hand over his plume to make sure it was duly nodding — and the door opened. They had come to fetch him.

THE ALLIANCE

The great day, as ever God made, was the 25th of July 1593; it could be no other than a day of blue sky and very hot. The people of Paris had been forewarned and had dressed up in their best clothes, such as they had been able to keep through the times of tribulation. They carried armfuls of flowers and baskets laden with all manner of provisions. The entire Sunday was to be spent at Saint-Denis for the King's recantation and reception into the Church, which would be a spectacle worth seeing, but a long one; in any case the sacred hour of dinner was likely to be missed. However, so rare an event was well worth it. Afterwards they would camp out on the meadows. The baskets were stowed away so that nothing might be stolen, and all looked forward to a joyful day.

The flowers were strewn upon the streets, in the pathway of the King. He was to be clad in white, so rumour had discovered and proclaimed. His white silk shoes should be crimsoned by crushed roses. The women were sure he was a handsome prince, and he should walk ankle-deep in rose-leaves; so they pushed and jostled across the causeway, and several were knocked down. This troubled the victims less than the guards, who first shouted warnings, which were inaudible above the pealing of the bells and the atmosphere of excitement. So the soldiers had to resort to force and with rough good humour succeeded in pushing back the crowd to each side of the street. At that moment the procession appeared.

What did the King observe as he walked along the narrow alleyway between the packed throngs on either side? Gay-coloured fabrics hanging from the windows, the roadway strewn with flowers, and children still flinging roses over the heads of the guards. The people wore the white scarves of the Royal party, and on all faces — some lantern-jawed and pious, others bubbling with excitement at what they were to see — there was an air of contentment. There were few that did not cry: " Long live the King! " The deeper voices of the bells echoed the shouts; but how poor a jubilation compared with the mighty event which had that day come to pass! And yet — surely — from near at hand, the faces were still marked with fear.

Five years, thought the King, five years of terror and misery and riot were behind those faces. Had he done no more than stage this festival for them, it would have been almost enough. But there should be better things to come; how could he fulfil so many and such eager hopes? His head felt near to sinking under the burden of man's incapacity, for how could he make them happy or even satisfy them all? But he had to hold it high, that they might stand in expectation of the glory and the power, his and theirs.

The crowd saw him escorted by princes and lords, high officers of State, noblemen, and a throng of lawyers. Of his own family there were few, though the Count of Soissons had consented to appear. In the van and in the rear marched bodyguards and Switzers, with silent drums. Twelve trumpeters held trumpets to their lips, but blew no blast because of the pealing bells and in token of the sanctity of the event. Of all this the mob was well aware, and, indeed, the mob always knows very well what is going forward — when it lends a hand to savagery and riot, and when it plays its part in some great and noble ceremony. The people were delighted with their King's magnificent garb, his erect figure, and his soldierly carriage. But the high arched brows looked sad, and the eyes were too wide open; forty years old or a little more, and so grey-haired already. Hard it was to say how much remorse, how much misery of their own, had struck at the hearts of these agelong enemies of the King — it was indeed at

long last that they had come to do him honour, and now stood
there, a welcoming throng. Here it was that among the shouts of
salutation a few voices were sorrowfully stilled. A few knees
strove to bend — but scarce could do so in the press of people.

An old crone, who certainly had seen many things, said in a
voice that was heard by those about her as well as by the King,
who was then passing: " He is a handsome man. His nose· is
larger than the noses of most kings." A remark that raised more
laughter than was its due. The King would have liked to stop,
and his drawn brows relaxed. Once again he was tempted to
pause when several onlookers in threadbare leather doublets eyed
him·— or rather his hat — in steady silence. He remembered
that he had worn it last at Ivry. The older men came from even
earlier days, they had seen it at Coutras. He sought their eyes,
they looked into his, and he watched them until others hid them
from his sight.

Outside the cathedral, before Henri set foot on the lowest stair,
a strange faintness came upon him. He had to grope with his
foot; even the crowds faded, faces and voices grew dim and
slipped into the distance. It lasted but the space of one step,
then all was as before, except that Henri, as he mounted, saw the
fleeting vision of a giant, who stood and blinked to hide the glitter in his eyes. So vividly did he see it that he missed the lowest
step; but thereafter he was wholly set on the part he had to play.

He strode through the great portal. After five or six paces he
found himself confronted by the Archbishop of Bourges, arrayed
in white damask and seated on a ceremonial chair surrounded by
the prelates. The Archbishop asked who he was, and His Majesty
answered: " The King." The said Monsieur de Bourges, who
had lost the porcine look aforementioned, was dignity itself as
he surveyed the King, and his utterance was the very expression
of spiritual power: " What do you desire? " " I desire," returned
His Majesty, " to be received into the bosom of the Catholic,
Apostolic, Roman Church." " Do you truly desire this? " asked
Monsieur de Bourges. Whereupon His Majesty made answer:
" I do, with all my heart." And kneeling upon a cushion, which
the Cardinal de Perron slipped beneath his knees, the King once

more made his profession of faith — nor did he forget to pronounce against heresy of any sort; and he swore to destroy all
heretics.

All this was heard in silence, and the profession of his new
faith, which the King had written out in his own hand, was even
handed by him to the Archbishop, who received it seated; then
at last the Archbishop deigned to stand. For one fleeting moment as he rose, he seemed to the onlookers hesitant and at a
loss; and what made him so was the ominous look in His Majesty's wide eyes, those same eyes that at Ivry had held a squadron
of enemy lancers spellbound until help came up. But here there
would be no such aid, here he was in their hands. So the Archbishop rose to his feet. Without taking the mitre from his head,
he sprinkled the King with holy water, bade him kiss the cross,
and gave him absolution and the blessing.

Both Monsieur de Bourges and Henri knew very well the order
of events, but it was a matter of much difficulty to make way
through the church to the choir; the throng surged across the
nave, clambered up the vaulting, and crawled through every
opening in the great stained windows. In the choir Henri merely
had to repeat his oath; but he did so with some show of impatience and haste. Then they moved behind the high altar, and
during the singing of the *Te Deum* Henri made his confession.
Such was his reception into the Church. In plain fact, Monsieur
de Bourges wheezed audibly, and Henri closed his eyes. Did she
know he had caught a fleeting glimpse of her behind a pillar?
Lovelier than the women of paradise, as rich in promise as the
night — would that the joyous night had come! There was a
special reason for that yearning: as he made his way through the
throng he had heard an utterance let fall by one of the procession.
If his own people spoke so, what did Monsieur de Bourges think?
The man was a lawyer and with his fellows had escorted his
master in solemn procession. And now that the King had taken
his death leap, here was a man muttering calamity. His neighbour, in the turmoil of the crowd, had not heard the words. Only
Henri, always a man of his ears, caught them: they were a
prophecy, dark and dreadful.

Thereafter he heard Mass, celebrated by the Archbishop of Bourges; a faldstool had been prepared for the King, of red silk embroidered with gold lilies, topped by a canopy of gold brocade. The King received communion. Then came the awkward task of re-forming the procession in the same order as before, for the return to the Abbey, where a banquet was to be held. The King's escort had in the interval been scattered, and it was some time before most of them could be extricated from the throng. Among his noblemen Henri missed Chicot, known as the Fool — and indeed he would just then have gladly had him at his side, for Chicot brought luck. Ha! what was that? A scuffle and a hubbub under the vaulted roof, among a knot of men each struggling to be first to slide off a carven dragon's head projecting from a pillar, to which they were all clinging in a confusion of arms and legs. Someone took a flying leap — ha, Chicot!

He plunged and crashed, flinging people to the right and left, but landed astraddle the neck of a huge man lying prostrate on all fours. As though in terror, he clutched at the man's curly hair until he forced the pock-marked face round and upwards — Henri recognized it, but a little while ago he had seen that familiar blink. There was the man, convulsed with rage, and seemingly with pain too, though Chicot was but tugging at his hair. He made no effort to heave himself up, rider and all, though he was a powerful fellow. Indeed he was apparently too much hurt to crawl, though what had hurt him was not clear; but as Henri emerged from the great west door he could still hear the fellow bellowing behind him. Still wondering, he led the great procession through the thronging crowd, which the guards now made no effort to restrain. The drummers and trumpeters, oblivious now of the pealing bells, set up a rival clangour.

There was a halt at a corner where a tortuous alleyway opened into the street. Hundreds had jostled forward to get a sight of the King's face, but none succeeded save an old, old woman; no one pushed her back, and she suddenly found herself sundered from the mob, face to face with the King, not knowing how she had got there. He took both her hands, and she kissed him with lips that grew soft to kiss her King. Thereupon the King said to the old crone: "Daughter," said he, "daughter, that was a good kiss, and I'll remember it." He caught some flowers flung at him, gathered them into a bunch, tied it with a ribbon that someone handed him, and slipped the nosegay into the old lady's bosom, which sent the mob nearly frantic with delight.

For a while Henri turned his face to left and right, so that they might see it and be assured of his goodwill. At that moment he stepped into the alley and saw, what none else saw, though he gave no sign of it — Chicot leading his man away. He held his prisoner's arms fast behind his back, and the man, three times the stronger, made no resistance, but limped along hunching his shoulders. Chicot, tall and gaunt and square-set, towered above him. He had lost his hat, his hair stood up wildly over his high bare forehead; and as he kept his eye fixed upon his prisoner, his hooked nose, his narrow cheekbones, and his truculently tilted beard stood out in sharp outline. Outside a small squat house at a turn in the alley, a hammered sign, from which hung a dried garland, marked a tavern, which would then be quite empty, as the townsfolk and all strangers were accompanying the King along the route to the banquet. Chicot and his giant had but to enter and discuss their affair in the deserted parlour; and he could imagine what would happen.

Henri was hungry, as they all were; indeed, their delight in the splendid festival of reconciliation with the King doubled their appetite and his also, not to mention that he was secretly relieved and thankful at what he had seen in the little alley. In the refectory of the old Abbey his first act was to shout: "Let all men enter!" The guards withdrew their halberds from the door, and the hall was suddenly as packed with people as the cathedral, and in the press a table and all the food on it was overset. Fortunately they were all in a good humour, and a mob that has just become possessed of a King is careful to do no damage. They would sooner tread on each other's toes than smash a dish. Moreover all the King's gentlemen were most zealous in their courtesies — not under orders from the King; many of them made place for a common man at table and conversed with him.

Most were merely concerned to see the King, as being a King

of note, who had much engaged their minds before they saw him face to face. Yonder he sat at the end of the hall, alone on a raised dais. His appetite was excellent, as was plain for all to see; and these were the meditations of a certain peaceful burgher: "He has made good provision for us; the times are gone when, on his account, we ate flour out of the cemeteries. He does not look like a man to have pressed us so hard as that. He is not what we were told he would be by the Paris preachers, a beast out of the Apocalypse, nor even a common wolf. I, the peaceful burgher — for despite the licence of the times I was always just a peaceful burgher — I shall bear witness in the future that he looks like you and me. Never again shall I crawl behind bushes in his garden to spy on him, as I once did, kneeling in the mud until I was so purblind that I couldn't tell whether he was tall or short, nor whether his humour was good or bad. Now I look at him fairly and full in the face. Ah, they are beginning to troop out into the fields to eat their dinners, there will be room in the hall, and I could wish him a good appetite. But I will not venture. What is it that deters me? Is it his splendid dress — his grey beard, and his lifted brows? No; the reason is that he has invited everyone, sick men and beggars too. I would not care to see them in my house. What a man!"

With such reflections the little burgher discreetly trotted out to join the others in the fields. The company sat long at table. More than once Henri raised his glass to his eyes before he set it to his lips; then they all turned and pledged him — including the man of Parliament, whom Henri had in mind and meant to single out. He was a lawyer after his own heart, with heavy-lidded, shining eyes, sunken temples, and hair completely white, and a grave beard that masked an ironic mouth. It was not long since he had been starving, though that had not quenched his irony. He had lain in prison, doubting every act not truly tested and based on the inborn rights of mortal men — haphazard acts determined only by power and by weakness and impelled by anger. He compared his own ill star with that of maltreated children crippled for life, when the State is so oblivious of justice that it does not yet realize that these are its own maimed limbs.

Henri loved the man, or he would have paid little heed to what he had heard, for much is heard that makes no matter, especially by ears as acute as his. In the cathedral, when Henri had just recanted, he had passed the man by. As he did so, the man whispered to his neighbour, who, in all the turmoil, did not catch the dreadful words, but Henri heard them. He set down his glass again, beckoned, and the lawyer came up to the King's seat. " Friend and comrade," began Henri.

" When you lay on damp straw — and, if the Royal cause had not won, you might easily have been hanged out of the window — confess that your pulse beat fast. You had ceased to be the sceptic that you wished to be; such was your mood that you would have quartered and beheaded your enemies and burnt them at the stake, assuming that in that same moment you had been master, and your enemies at your mercy."

" Sire, it is so. Truth to tell, except for brief hours of reason, those were indeed my feelings while in prison. But when I came out I was calm once more and no longer wanted to kill any man."

Henri leaned nearer to him and said: " Would you be now so much the master that you not only could not kill, but could join hands with those who were your enemies by a mere pedantry of faith? "

" Sire, I would have done as you have done."

Henri paled and said: " Now I realize the horror of what you said by a pillar in the cathedral to a man in a green cloak."

" Sire, I should still remember what I said without the reminder of the green cloak. Pray God it may be wrong. I grieve you should have heard it."

" Is it as you said? Then all your law would be in vain. You are poor judges if a man must be punished because he tried to act less guiltily and so end a conflict."

" There is no word of punishment," said the other — just so loud that the revellers at the table would not overhear. " It was a monstrous crime I feared."

" For which I was ripe," said Henri.

The lawyer could consider himself dismissed. He turned with

a deprecating air to leave a last apology; and he expressed it in the words of Montaigne, the humanist.

"A man of good life may hold false opinions, and the truth may fall from the lips of a rascal who disbelieves in it."

Henri watched him go. "Of course; we know all that from our friend Montaigne. It is precisely the wisdom that my ailing but tough old friend gathers from all of us and returns to us perfected. All the more horrible is what I heard him say in the crowd, all the more horrible and evil."

Therewith he promptly bethought him of his fool. What in the meantime had become of Chicot and his victim? He had better find out which had disposed of the other. Henri half thought of sending soldiers to that tumbledown tavern in the byway. But he did not, for several reasons, not least from self-respect. In one way or another it must have come to light that he had been afraid. But he got up unexpectedly; his guests would otherwise have sat at table for hours.

Back to the cathedral once more, for, by way of spiritual conclusion to the banquet, there was to be a sermon from Monsieur de Bourges, and Evensong followed promptly on his last Amen. His Majesty listened to it all with great gravity. Then he mounted his horse, but only to offer up a prayer of thanksgiving in another church some distance away. When he returned to Saint-Denis, it was night, and bonfires had been lit; people who had emptied their baskets and drained their raptures to the dregs that day were now dancing round huge blazing torches, the nimbler hopping on one leg; and the sober onlooker could scarce fail to see that there was no more sense in that rejoicing. They had hailed their King that morning because, for love of them, he was treading a very thorny path, and for the righting of old wrongs had made their cause his own.

Now night had fallen, they received him in another and uproarious fashion, which was little to his liking; moreover he was wearied from that day, more utterly so than if he had been fighting a battle from dawn to dusk. He reined in his horse and wondered what had been happening in that tavern. Of all that, they knew nothing. They were dancing round the flames. Reeling, yelling fools! He hoped some of them would get soundly scorched. Well, he would ride to the tavern. If he found it empty, then that would be the end of that, as well as of this day, and he was bitterly tired.

The old Abbey lay in darkness, for none expected him. Not his dear lady, though she was certainly awake and listening. But she did not call him, nor did she want him in her room. Alone, until the sun came, they dared make no other venture, for each by instinct knew whether the other's hour was burdensome or light. But he now called for his bath, and his First Chamberlain, Monsieur d'Armagnac, at once sent all the lackeys hot-foot for water. The sound of hurrying footsteps in the darkness roused certain persons from their beds, among them Protestants, and these were over-hasty in their judgment, conceiving that the King was washing himself clean of sin, after hearing so magnificent a Mass!

It was not so.

The Story of a Plot

Chicot, tall and gaunt and hatless, held the fellow's arms fast against his back, while he stumbled along with his huge shoulders bent. As they made their way in this fashion along the tortuous alley, otherwise deserted — not one bedridden ancient was so much as peering out of a window — it was by no means clear which of the pair was in control of the other. Chicot seemed to be supporting his companion lest he should collapse from some mysterious weakness — unless it was that he had caught a criminal and was bringing him to a place of safety. Only one of them knew the way; not the King's Fool, but the other man. He knew that alley; he had suddenly hobbled into it, groaning as he went, and he had the tavern, too, in mind, while Chicot was utterly astray. For him the main thing was that they were out of the throng and could bring no scandal on the great procession. The populace were intent upon the solemn hour of dinner. Here came no fragrance of baked meats; the day was hot, but the darkness of that alley grew danker and more fetid at every step they took. Over it brooded a very miasma of evil; the first house reeked of avarice, the next of lechery, while the last stood steeped in the horror of murder undiscovered.

The man was near to fainting, or he so pretended. Indeed, a pool of blood was gathering beneath his feet; and whence that blood had come, Chicot knew. He was still waiting until a patrol came by, when he would hand over to the soldiery the intending murderer of his King. But none came; he could no longer hold his gigantic victim, who slipped from his grasp against the protruding wall of a tumbledown house. Chicot had to prop him against it, or they would have both crashed sideways to the ground, with the man this time on top. Chicot could not call him by name, having no notion who he was except that he was clearly a discharged soldier. The King's Fool whistled for help. The landlord then showed his face, and a not ungenial face, as promptly as if he had been waiting behind the door. " Two of you, eh? " said he, speaking without thought; which gave the fool much to think of in a hurry.

First the landlord must help him with his capture, and together they managed to drag the huge creature inside the house. They had scarce laid him on the bench when he fainted in good earnest. The landlord, being short and fat, was now out of breath, but Chicot promptly answered: " Yes, two of us; he recognized me as an old Leaguer. We were both in the infantry of Mayenne, who never managed to catch the man of Béarn alive or dead. We did the deed today, after Mass."

" If that is so, then you should be by now invisible," said the landlord, who looked at the unconscious man, cocked his other eye at Chicot, and liked the looks of neither. " He was told as sure as heaven that the moment he had struck, he would become invisible. And here he is, very plain to see, and you too, which is even worse. Why were the two of you in it? Why did he trust you? That's not like La Barre. I know the fellow."

" So do I," said Chicot in the hearty tone he commonly assumed when he mocked people with what they would later recognize as truth. " I have known my old friend La Barre longer than you have. Why, at this very moment he is wearing a jerkin of mine that used to fit me when I had a belly as large as his. But I got a tapeworm in my innards and kept on losing flesh, so I gave the jerkin to old La Barre; I could not give him the tapeworm, despite our sworn friendship."

These details reassured the landlord; he accepted them as some sort of evidence. " But why are you both still visible? " he asked, more from curiosity than suspicion.

" Because," said Chicot, " we were only partly successful."

" Then the King is not dead? Praise be to Jesus Christ," blurted out the little landlord; and he plumped down on a bench with a gasp of relief.

" You coward," cried Chicot, towering over him, " to say so pitiful a thing! You plan an assassination, then cower all day behind bolted doors and curtained windows, telling your beads " — he pointed to a rosary lying on the table. " And praying that the deed may miscarry and both of us be caught. Isn't that what you prayed for, hey? "

And the fat landlord answered: " I did pray that it might be done, and then that it might not. And now it is half done. And I can only half see you," he groaned. For apart from the effects of fear, in that genial countenance the eyes were almost engulfed in fat.

" Only half of us is here," said Chicot, with a hint of warning in his still unruffled tones. " If the King dies of the seven wounds we dealt him, I and La Barre will vanish and be no more seen. You will be left behind, and deservedly, for those plaguey prayers of yours. They'll take you and put you to the question, and they'll sit you on red-hot iron, and I dare say they'll mistake your backside for your face."

Here the landlord fell forward, howling, and roused the unconscious man, who moved his head. Chicot, unluckily for him, did not notice this, and he went on describing to the fat host what happens when a man is quartered: the cracking and the rending of the joints, while with his own eyes he sees his limbs wrenched from him by the straining horses; and certain hairy little devils standing by to seize the gobbets of quivering flesh and plunge them into brine. All this Chicot recounted to the now frenzied little landlord; but the man on the bench listened and lay motionless.

When the landlord's lamentations subsided in despair, Chicot asked him gravely whether he would like to get his neck out of the noose. That, said the landlord, was the only thing he could pray for now; henceforward he would have no more traffic with mortal sin, of which he had much still burdening his soul.

" Well," said Chicot, " I take it that you value yourself more highly than the man on the bench."

" To be sure," said the landlord.

" Then all is well," observed Chicot, " and the two of us, though of course we stabbed the King no less than he did, may this time save our skins at the expense of our friend La Barre and his existence on this earth, which indeed has gone on long enough. Run out and fetch the watch; we'll give the man up, and bolt."

But the landlord protested mildly that this, as they were placed, would hardly do, though he was not one to boggle at a good deed more or less, and La Barre was a proper gallows-bird. " But we are birds of the same feather, and they'll not believe our lies, they'll take us too."

" Oh, I know how to lie," observed Chicot. " I shall explain that I was in the cathedral when the King recanted, and marked a man I had never seen before. He had the very look of a King's murderer, and he was always fending off the throng from his right side; from which I guessed that he must have slipped his knife between his trunk-hose and his shirt. When I had worked my way up to him, I could see the outline of the knife; it was an ell long, pointed and edged on both sides, which made his jaw twitch at every touch. So I thought I had better take a hand. I climbed a pillar on to a projecting dragon-head, to which several people were already clinging. My friend was only a little way off, and as the King passed, and my friend was already fumbling in his hose — I leapt and landed on his neck. He crashed to the floor with a yell and split his hip. So I saved the King, as may God save him in good time. I caught the murderer, and, finding no patrol, I brought him here. Now, gossip, will the judges believe that story? "

" Your lies would take in any man," agreed the landlord. But when Chicot again bade him run and fetch the soldiers, he scratched his head and admitted that he did not like the plan. He was in favour of settling the affair then and there, without any intrusion from outside. " We had much better cut his throat and put him in the brine-tub. I've a large cask in the shed yonder, plenty large enough; there's a mass of salt junk to be had from a man of that size."

" I am not of your opinion," said Chicot, with much gravity. " My preference is for quartering, a traditional and orderly procedure, whereas the Church, I believe, does not hold with pickling corpses." He could never resist a gibe at the Church. " Indeed, I fancy we might suffer more from it than our friend yonder — though his folly certainly merits such an end."

The pair discussed the question with much earnestness, each standing to his own opinion; but unlike the Fool, who remained unruffled, the landlord grew highly excited at the notion of wasting so much good salt meat. However, at last he sighed and yielded. " Very well. You helped to stab the King, and you know how to lie. I will fetch the soldiers."

No sooner had the landlord gone, than the unconscious man thrust his head backward so that the mop of flaxen hair dangled over the edge of the bench and he could peer across at Chicot. " Hey, master," said he feebly.

" Well, friend? " replied Chicot, though he was much startled.

" You have sent the landlord for the soldiers," said La Barre; " now help me out of this. We both stabbed the King."

" What? " cried Chicot, quite dumbfounded. " We stabbed the King? " But La Barre continued:

" I have been asleep and dreaming. Pull the knife out, master. I have lost so much blood that I can't remember what happened when we stabbed the King."

But, bewildered as he was, he had recognized Chicot from his voice, and the cunning giant would gladly have drawn the King's own Fool into his murderous plot had there been the slightest prospect of himself escaping the executioner. " I ought to have had you put in brine," Chicot flung at him between his teeth. He fell to pacing round the room, while the other watched him from the corners of his eyes. Knowledge of a crime like this was an enduring peril unless he promptly disclosed the whole matter and like a true and worthy citizen gave evidence that would bring the criminal to the wheel and gallows. How did his King regard him? As his faithful Fool? Or as a hired assassin? Either alternative was possible; in times like those a man fell readily under suspicion. He must act at once, get this fellow's story out of him, and judge him, if he would himself evade the judgment.

So much resolved, the Fool drew the knife out, the double-edged knife wherewith La Barre had meant to stab the King; but it had split his own hip, and when it was removed, a great gout of blood spurted on to the floor. The giant, unused to pain and blood-baths of this kind, was on the point of fainting once again, but Chicot clouted him on the ears until he recovered himself, then bound up the wounds with the giant's own shirt, which he dipped in diluted vinegar, propped him up, gave him a cup of wine — and ordered him to tell his story.

" 'Tis a long one." — " Make it short." — " The landlord will soon be here with the soldiers." — " He'll be too bemused to come back yet awhile." — " Why? " — " They'll tell him that nothing really happened to the King." — " Did nothing happen to him? " At this point Chicot lost patience.

" Fellow! Here I have your knife. I'll not come near you. You are bandaged, and the wine may have put some blood back in your veins. But from this safe corner I shall throw the knife, at your bare neck — and stab you, as you would have stabbed the King, over the heads of the crowd. For that is how you meant to kill the King."

" You know too much," said La Barre. " I give in, and I'll tell my story."

" Take care and tell no lies! I am a servant of His Majesty, and if your lips lie, I shall hear your vitals shout the truth aloud."

At this, La Barre fell off the bench in such terror that Chicot reflected that he was behaving more like a Fool than a judge; and he forgot to start questioning his victim until the latter observed, unasked, that his name was Peter Barrière, commonly known as La Barre.

"And by profession a King's murderer. You could not have advanced so far in any other, for the name will be written on the page of history."

"I am no man's murderer," cried La Barre. "It was others made me so. I was a shipman on the Loire and at two-and-twenty as innocent as on the day I was born at Orléans."

"Who robbed you of that innocence?"

"A recruiting-sergeant bribed me to enlist under the Queen of Navarre, but I, by ill luck, fell in love with one of her women."

"I respect ill luck," observed Chicot gravely. "But first, as touching Madame Marguerite de Valois, whom you call the Queen of Navarre. She plotted against her husband's person and throne, so she is kept a prisoner in a castle; but she suborns the like of you, to help her escape and plot against us once again. Against me too, an officer of His Majesty. Since you entered the service of the Lady of Valois, you have really lent yourself to a plot against my person."

"I fancy you are talking like a fool!" growled La Barre; and Chicot thought so too. When he talked plain sense, like a nobleman, men laughed, because he was known as the King's Fool. And now, when gravity was called for, he must needs act the buffoon. And he was cursing himself heartily, when La Barre brought him back to the matter in hand.

"It all came from my unlucky passion for the lady, who was utterly taken up by day and night with the gay doings of the court. If I lay upon her bosom, we always seemed to roll into the pond, or the floor of the hayloft gave way, or ghosts appeared in our room. But it was just the courtiers' playfulness, and the lady took care that I should love in vain."

"A most self-sacrificing fidelity," said Chicot with approval. "Thereupon you of course resolved to kill the King."

"Gently," said the other. "The notion came to me in dreams. The Queen commanded me, while I was asleep, to help her husband, the King of France, into another world; then she would leave me in peace with my girl in this one; she even promised her a dowry."

"Did you merely dream this? Think — surely the Queen did give you that very order?" He spoke in deep earnest; all the mockery had faded from his voice. And La Barre answered:

"She did not: I went in to her when she was alone and told her of my purpose. Then the Queen began to weep, turned to the wall, and implored me not to think of such a deed. Soon afterwards she dismissed me from her service, and I left the castle."

Chicot, whose heart was throbbing, made no reply. How could he report this to the King? The King's own wife had sent the murderer forth instead of clapping him in her deepest dungeon.

In his agitation he came out of his corner and fell to pacing back and forth, brandishing the murderer's stiletto. Every time he passed, La Barre recoiled, but he watched Chicot with blinking, glittering eyes. Chicot paid no heed, possessed by the horror he had heard. He had meant to give his evidence like a true and worthy citizen, and now his position was more perilous than ever. Suddenly the fellow made a grab at the knife and was within an inch of seizing it. Chicot sprang backwards to the door of the dark shed, stretched out an arm, and opened it. "Inside with you!" he cried. But the other begged most pitifully not to be shut into the dark abode of the brine-barrel. He had still much to confess.

As his judge wavered, La Barre began about a priest at Lyon who had urged him to kill the King and had also promised that when the deed was done he should become invisible. This same priest had also sent him to a Grand Vicar of the Archbishop, to whom he had disburdened his heart, but received no answer. But no answer may yet convey an answer. All the more so as a Capucin also had encouraged him in his purpose, and a famous Italian monk had actually given him the same advice. In brief, the intending murderer of the King had confided in so many ecclesiastics that half the clergy in Lyon must have been merely waiting for his attempt. The King's Fool stood open-mouthed:

could his master have so many mortal enemies in his faithful city of Lyon? Meantime La Barre, now in full flow, and with an occasional blink at the fateful shed, spoke of his journey to Paris; and Chicot said no more. He knew how cordially the preachers of Paris regarded the King.

The reason for which one notorious priest had approved the murder of the King struck vilely on his ear: it was urged that the King, whether he went to Mass or no, could in no case be a Catholic, and the priest would never believe him one. " What now? " thought the Fool. " After recantation they might well have held their hands. They stab at any price."

" But why did you not stab the King before I caught you? " he asked. The answer was that a revulsion had come upon the murderer; he felt himself drawn backwards, by a rope that seemed to be slung round the middle of his body. Chicot sank into a reverie; he even forgot where he was. The silence in the room deepened, until a whispering began, which Chicot did not hear; it gradually grew louder, and the sound was as of someone speaking outside the curtained window. " La Barre, have you got him? "

" No," said La Barre to the window.

" Then we will get him."

" How many are you? "

" Five."

" Why, friends, how do you come to be here? " asked La Barre once more.

" The landlord fetched us instead of the soldiers."

" Wait," said La Barre. " I will speak with the officer, he may give himself and the knife up of his own free will. Well? " he asked the now dumbfounded Chicot, and stepped threateningly towards him. Chicot, realizing that he must keep the knife at all costs, leapt backwards into the shed; another leap; but at the third he found no floor beneath his feet and fell.

He expected to be plunged into an abyss where he could neither see nor hear. Nothing of the kind. Chicot promptly emerged, backside upwards, from a heap of muck, but still brandishing his knife. Then he listened. Only one voice reached him, that of the man Barrière, commonly called La Barre, asking him whether all was well. " Come down here," answered Chicot, " you and your five fellows, one at a time, and I'll cut the heads off each of you."

" There's no head here but mine," said the murderer, " and that I mean to put in a safe place at once. My head, and my loquacious belly. You cozened me into believing that you would get the truth out of my vitals, and I was terrified. Well, it is the voice from my vitals that tipped you into the cesspool. And there you shall stay; farewell. I'll come up with that wandering landlord somewhere and speak to him seriously about this business of pickling corpses."

La Barre was gone; first his voice, and then his footstep. In the pitch darkness Chicot plunged about in search of some sort of foothold to help him to clamber out. Once back in the room, he sank on the bench and lay with head flung back. There was no hurry; dusk began to fall.

A BATH

King Henri sat in the water so hastily fetched by the lackeys and the maids. It was heated on the furnace, and then poured from kettles into the cavity in the centre of the bathroom. It was a low-roofed, narrow room, with a tiled tank approached by steps, on the last but one of which the King lay naked, soaking in the water, which was kept in motion by his First Chamberlain, Monsieur d'Armagnac, who stirred it with branches and now and again scattered a shower of drops upon his master's head. For so damp an occupation d'Armagnac had taken off most of his clothes; he was wearing little but an apron about his middle. Henri recited to him a translation of some verses by Martial which they often quoted to each other.

" A slave, girt with an apron of black hide, stands to serve you when you take your bath."

The First Chamberlain countered with the same verses in the Latin; it had always amused him and the King to recall that the poet was not describing a man, but a Roman lady being mas-

saged in her bath by slaves. D'Armagnac was usually greeted
with a lively jest from his master, but was not much surprised
when no jest came that night, for Henri was absorbed in dreams;
nay, worse than that, by the looks of him — he seemed sunk
in gloomy meditation or haunted by some dark premonition.
D'Armagnac silently dipped his branch and scattered a soft
shower over his master's head and chest; at last, when Henri
stretched himself and looked up at the whitewashed beams, the
First Chamberlain laid his branch on the edge of the bath and
stepped against the wall. The space round the sunken tank was
narrow; in one corner stood an iron tripod carrying some lighted
tapers, and on the opposite side, behind the King, his clothes
lay on a chair. Their thick gold embroidery held them unright;
the breeches and the doublet sat there like the figure of a headless, neckless man.

Henri thought of those leaping, scorching bonfires, evil and
devouring, into which the mob thrust whom they could; he
would be a proper victim. They were ready traitors, there was
no relying on their pacts. One Mass was useless. He would always have to conquer men anew, as had always been his fate.
By a pillar in the cathedral he had heard words said that put
fear into his heart, they were so terrible. What was Chicot doing? The words were proved true before ever they were uttered.
A blinking giant would have gladly made them so. The knife!
That lawyer had said: " Now he is ripe." Where could Chicot
be? Not that Chicot could bring much help now. Henri had
taken the death leap at last.

He lay full length upon the steps under the rippling water,
and sleep came upon him. Monsieur d'Armagnac stood motionless and watched his old comrade's limbs relax. He reflected that
they both were growing old. It was no help to pretend indifference, though that was the way in which a man must face the
years. The First Chamberlain, girt with his leather apron, left
the bathroom barefooted, carefully locked the door, and stood
on guard outside it. From time to time he peered through the
keyhole; once he laid his ear to it; the sleeper had said audibly:
" Where can Chicot be? "

But when the man so named did in fact appear at the end of the passage, Monsieur d'Armagnac stood even more squarely in the doorway. He at once felt that there would be trouble were Chicot admitted to the King in his bath. And as that nobleman approached, he thought of yet more reasons for keeping him outside. Monsieur d'Armagnac folded his arms and stiffened, as he used to do when a young man. But Chicot said:

"Fear nothing, sir. I shall not intrude."

"You may not do so, sir. You stink like a goat, and you are drunk."

"You are more like a goat, sir, with your hide apron and your hairy thighs. As touching my odour, I caught it from a loathsome cesspool into which I was made to jump by a belly-talker. As to my condition, when I got out again, being much shattered by my untoward adventure, I not unnaturally took an excess of wine; I did not feel able to report the matter to His Majesty unless I were tipsy."

"You shall not enter," repeated Monsieur d'Armagnac, gravely, but merely for form's sake. From the bathroom came the sound of splashing water, the King had awakened. Chicot went on in a flat, metallic voice. He was wholly sober and had nicely calculated what was suited for the King to hear, what he should suppress or soften or suggest.

"'Sire!' I should say, if the King could hear me," he cried in a high, clear tone, "'Sire, your murderer, or the man who meant to be so, was a soldier who had never had a hand in any evil. It was love that led him astray. He was a lover, and he could not endure to be continually abused by his beloved, to amuse a licentious court. Which was that court?'" Chicot himself put the question, as no one else did. "The scene of my story is the castle of the illustrious lady known as the Queen of Navarre. A place where anything may happen."

He paused and drew breath. From within came more sounds of splashing, as though the bather were tumbling in his bath. But Chicot waited vainly for any protest or command. "Idleness is the root of all evil," he said at last. "Love is the sole pastime in that castle. Behold a poor soldier who tries to ruffle with the rest. He would kill the King! The illustrious lady of course claps him in her deepest dungeon."

" Hey! I'll have no lies! " came a voice from the bathroom.

" Nay, but she wept," said Chicot in a humble and remorseful tone. " She wept bitterly, and dismissed the soldier — "

" And sent me no warning," sighed Henri in his brick tank.

" How could she? " cried Chicot — this was imagination, but he thought the plea was plausible. " Monks, priests, and prelates pestered her unmercifully; indeed, the poor lady's life was threatened; she was watched and her letters intercepted; she could send no message, though in her own chamber she wept bitterly."

Here a sudden sob burst from Monsieur d'Armagnac. The Queen of Navarre, of whom Chicot had spoken as of a character in a romance, was for the First Chamberlain the living comrade of those nights of murder, of the school of unhappiness now long past, and all the troubles of life, which he himself had faced at his master's side for so many, many years. The face that then was hers had glowed with the fire of sense and yet mirrored the cool radiance of a star; she slipped out of bed and up the steps of a throne; and her name was Margot. She had been worshipped by all — and they were many — who loved human beauty and human understanding — one of them was Armagnac, to whom she had given her incomparable hand. " Our Margot," he thought, and he felt the weight of years; " and now she hates us unto death." Unmanned by his emotion, he left his post. The rising tears half-choked him, and as he strode down the passage in his apron, his breath came and went in shattering gasps.

But in the bathroom all was silent. There sat one who was easily moved to tears, and therefore the less trusted. Why was he not weeping now? Chicot nodded to himself, and strands of tousled hair nodded over his high smooth forehead. He could have peered through the keyhole, but he did not. The man within was alone, unobserved, a naked man at the mercy of a knife; and an incomparable hand, once beloved beyond all others, had not been raised to hold it back. The possessor of that knife was one of those who hopped round bonfires, and with every one of them he had now made his peace. For their sake he had heard a solemn Mass, for them he had dared the leap of death. Be it so. Let the blow fall — so thought he, sitting in his cell.

" Chicot! "

A long while had passed. The man outside no longer listened, he was sunk in dreams. At the sound of his name, he started and dashed into the bathroom. " Bar the door! " cried the naked King. " How many were concerned in the plot? " he asked softly.

Chicot recounted them exactly, he had no more thought of palliation. His hard Fool's mind had seen the vision of murder, and he meant to make it plain. There might be a murderers' den round any corner, like that whence he had come. Now dens of murderers are matters for jest; and the soldier who talked with his belly and expected to be made invisible when the deed was done, and the landlord too, were comical enough, but there was that in the atmosphere of the room that hardened both men's faces. Not purposely, but from the habit of his calling, the Fool made a merry tale of his dispute with the landlord as to whether the man should be quartered or put in brine. The ruffian with the gashed hip, the result of an injudicious lust for murder; the belly-talk, the five companions, and the cesspool — a very merry tale, but those two faces grew yet harder. The ruffian had fled, he was powerless, his fate was set. He would have another knife sharpened on both edges; again he would lie in wait for the King, and he would be taken; for he was now known. His tale was told.

Chicot had finished and was silent; and the King was silent too. Suddenly he looked up. " Tell me one thing. La Barre was never near enough to stab me. How would he have done it? "

Chicot slipped the knife out of his trunk-hose, from the very place where the murderer had hidden it, and flung it — quicker than eye could follow. The King turned his head; behind him his white silk suit sat in the chair, as though it were himself, headless and neckless; and where the neck would have been, the knife quivered in the wall, a whole ell of it, in the centre of the neck that was not there. " Well aimed," said Henri. " You deserve a hundred crowns for that throw — if I had them by me at the moment." Naked as he was, he laughed. Once more he looked round at the knife and laughed aloud. Chicot from courtesy twitched his lips, as though to indicate: " I am Your Majesty's Fool. Even in jest I am still serious."

Then it came into Henri's mind to say: " By a pillar in the cathedral stood yet another man, who spoke in secret to his neighbour, but I heard. It was my man of law, and what he said was: ' Ah, now he is lost. Now he is what he has never been before: ripe for slaughter.' "

At these words Chicot burst into a trumpet-roar of laughter, for the jest was not his own. Henri laughed too, but not so heartily. To maintain his good humour, he had to keep looking round at the knife, sticking where the neck might have been, but was not.

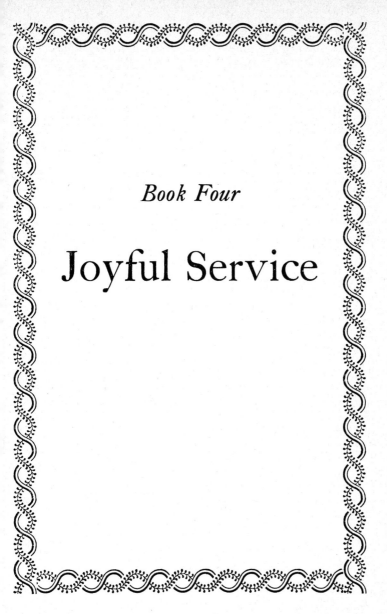

Book Four

Joyful Service

The Anointing

THE HOLY oil with which a King of France was anointed and consecrated was kept in Reims; but that city was still in the hands of the League. Moreover the capital was still held by the enemy. Intent as he was on possessing Paris, it was most necessary that he should first be anointed and crowned. Though he himself took small account of this obligation, it was generally held to be all-important; so search was made for a holy oil. The best that could be found was connected with the tradition of Saint Martin; this decided Henri. He knew every foot of the kingdom for which he had fought so long, and he knew, having himself ridden against them, the patron saint of every place; and it was most commonly Martin. Good, Martin it should be; and the great cathedral of Chartres should take the place of Reims. No good Catholic could belittle the solemn act if the scene of it was Chartres cathedral.

Now Henri well remembered that at Saint-Denis, when he recanted and accepted the true faith, there had been general jubilation, and a concourse of people from Paris, with whom he had made his solemn pact; and among them was a murderer. It was doubtless true that the murderer had been there already; he was scarce to be distinguished from the crowd in which he had been hidden, and which seemed heart and hand devoted to the

King. The merest blunder; men stabbed just as they sang and knelt. Occasions alter, the spirit of men is manifold. The task was to lay hold of good men, as they are called, and confirm them in that goodness. Reasonable beings should never be otherwise than cheerful, self-restrained, and merciful. But a realm must first be established wherein these virtues may reign. All the more needful were these solemn ceremonies that helped to tame unruly hearts. If they were often held, thought Henri, his murderers' hearts might be melted even to tears; though that was uncertain. He could only point the way and go forward. That was the power of the King; indeed, it was power in essence, as he recognized, not for the first time, for thus had his course been laid; and yet, too, he could not hold so high a motive for his recognition of power until the final issue; there was too much to do.

The solemn ceremony at Chartres had to be built up anew; the persons who should have played their part in it, and the emblems that they should have held, all were missing. Crown and sceptre and all the rest had been in rebel hands and were now melted down, broken, dismembered, or merely stolen, as seemed most profitable. The dignitaries who should have been summoned by virtue of their office were either on the enemy's side or in his power, especially the bishops. A few lay lords excused themselves because they distrusted the royal power. Paris remained Spanish — why these solemn ceremonies? But there are always loyal servants to be found, and they promptly set to work on what was needed; such as the two-fingered Hand of Justice on which oaths were sworn, the sword of State, and the woven tapestries, enough of them to cover the walls of a cathedral. All these were made or contrived in haste; other notables replaced the absent, and a rehearsal was held, to ensure that each of them was familiar with his part; and on the morning of the ceremony two noblemen rose at three o'clock: the cathedral had to be prepared.

The King had spent the whole of the foregoing day in hearing sermons explaining the significance of the ceremony, and in confession and prayer. On the morning of February 21st there

escorted him to the ceremony two bishops and several high personages, of whom he in outward aspect was the highest. He
wore a garb that seemed to him fantastic: a voluminous smock
of silvered linen, and beneath it a long shirt of crimson silk. He
looked like a figure from another age, but both his ladies — his
sister and Gabrielle — insisted he should so appear; at the instance, in fact, of Dame Sourdis, whose admirer, the Chancellor
Cheverny, set great store by due observance. The Chancellor
and several other gentlemen of rank followed on foot, among
them the Grand Master of the Horse, the Duke of Bellegarde.
Henri could distinguish his old friend Feuillemorte by his walk
and would gladly have turned and smiled at him, but the mere
thought of his strange attire forbade such familiarity. Once more
he stepped into the cathedral, under the eyes of the watching
throng, preceded up the stone-flagged nave by heralds and much
visible pomp of power, even a constable with unsheathed sword;
then came Henri, quite alone, with a solemnity that no one
wholly understood, least of all himself — was it a splendid spectacle, or was it little better than a pantomime?

The heralds began to cry out names, the old traditional twelve
names, as they had once been borne by the great nobles of the
kingdom. No Duke of Aquitaine answered, for there had long
been none to answer, and indeed had one been there, he would
have been wearing an ancient costume from a masque, like
Henri. But he heard the worthy Soissons, his sister's lover, make
his answer; and thenceforward each one present answered for
one absent. When the Bishop of Chartres, in place of the Archbishop of Reims, anointed the King with the holy oil, which was
not the true oil, the process tickled him, and to stifle a laugh,
he coughed. This in the devoutest of attitudes, with forehead
bowed; but at heart he was with the charming Gabrielle, up
yonder in her gallery — he fancied, at any rate, that the charming Gabrielle viewed the whole display with the same feelings
as himself. She would be thinking of Feuillemorte, and how
Henri had thrown him sweetmeats as he lay beneath their bed.
And Henri looked more ceremonial than ever.

In the meantime the charming Gabrielle, on her high gallery

in the centre of the nave, had no memories of the sort, nor was she in any such humour. Her dear lord had once more taken all the proffered oaths, and especially that against the heretics. In her deepest soul she would never have believed it. She listened to the acclamations. They were beginning a *Te Deum* in his honour, and in that instant she envisaged him as the little old man with the blackened face who came on foot to the castle of Cœuvres, and she had said to him: " Sire, how dreadful you look! " And then trifled with him for a long while, betrayed him sedulously, and would not be his until he proved his greatness when he held his court afield. A singular court it was, that had moved after every turn of war. She had had to hold a balance between pastors and prelates; her aim had been the enrichment of her family. Monsieur d'Estrées was a thief, and she protected him; without doubt it was her loyalty to her family that alienated Monsieur de Rosny. She had worked for the conversion of her heretic, delicately at first and in secret, as she had been told to do; but she still had loved the other and almost run away. Not until near the end, in a night of tears and mysterious visions, did she discover whose child she bore beneath her heart, and who in fact was her dear lord. So had it come to pass that the charming Gabrielle sat above the nave, quivering with joy and pride, her eyes dazzled by the very ecstasy of seeing her lord receive the crown.

Strange how a man can be mistaken. Henri was careful not to look up at his lady; he feared that the desire to laugh would make her cough too. Solemn ceremonies do not gain by repetition, for those who can see below the surface and have an eye for comedy. Henri had exhausted all his gravity in his struggle with his conscience, his arduous meditations, and the effort needed for his death leap. It is done, ask not wherefore. If for power, now that it is at last achieved, there is no illusion in it left. The herald calls the name of a dead man, a live one answers. The Bishop, lately mitred, lifted the ampulla, which was the finest of the regalia on which they had been able to lay hold. Then upon that doubting head the crown was lowered, the crown of France, which should have been a venerable object, but was in fact fresh from the workshop. Such is the spectacle of power. A ray of sunlight flashed upon the sword that Marshal de Matignon held erect before him, which should have been the Constable's sword. In point of fact there was no constable, and Matignon, who made lewd verses with equal skill in Latin and in the native dialect, was no doubt turning a couplet at the very moment when the sword flashed. So much for power.

In the meantime Henri was thinking of another whom he carried in his heart; she who really wielded power over the hearts of men. He disliked this ceremony; he did not see how it could help to tame unruly hearts. He was here conscious of no murderer's presence — which, by so much, was a great relief; perhaps, however, this absence of foreboding meant that the anointing and the crowning and the great day's event made his person invulnerable for a while. The lawyer's bitter phrase had after all been wrong. And as the peril to his life receded, the King grew grave, he recovered the gravity lost over the antics of a Fool in a squalid tavern, or in a bathroom when that same Fool came into it. It was not thus he looked at his faithful Rosny.

During the ceremony Henri had more than once turned towards Rosny, and was startled by what he saw; here was the one man who was sincere. He might have been a figure from the portal of the cathedral; there too he could have held his own as a broad-faced, sculptured image, for ever imperturbable. A Protestant, he listened to the King pledging himself to destroy the heretics; his face remained unmoved. He stood up and played his part though his inner voice told him that the whole thing was buffoonery. That was the expression, for himself alone, of the harsh Huguenot austerity, of his own opinion of that solemn ceremony. But the astute Rosny bade that disturbing voice be silent; and his outward attitude and mien were that of a true and faithful servant of his King. Henri, who was a good judge of men, knew his Rosny; and here, amid all this solemn ceremony, he became certain that Rosny was his man for ever.

Not long afterwards he summoned him to his Council. In due time, and at his own instance, he was created Duke of Sully and became all-powerful in the finances of the kingdom and

Grand Master of an Artillery the like of which had never before been seen; in act and deed the King's right hand — so long as his great King was there, and not a minute longer. To Henri he had pledged himself, and become his man, regardless of an old Huguenot's inner voice. They were to play into each other's hands. Here then, while the solemn ceremonies proceeded, was born a great career, as Henri turned and turned again to look at the Baron, and was more than once startled by what he saw. For he was looking in the face of duty and stony gravity, despite that secret voice that said: Buffoonery. A man of the middle sort, reflected Henri, not to say a middling man. But an admirable example for a King! So Henri thought, for simplicity then seemed to him greatly to be desired. But very hard to come by, save for the Rosnys of this world.

The King left the cathedral more royally than he had come. His gait and carriage had acquired dignity; and he wore his fantastic raiment with conviction. Such a central figure lent impressiveness to the pomp of a procession which had hitherto seemed haphazard by comparison. The mob fell silent as it passed, and knelt. Henri did indeed change his clothes before sitting down to table — and waved d'Armagnac aside when he proffered the white silk suit; he wanted to be comfortable, in everyday garb. In the banqueting hall he sat beneath a canopy, which in no way affected his appetite; alone at his own table, overlooking on his right the table of the lay lords, all busily engaged in filling their bellies; in doing which they were following their King's example. They, after his recantation, were to be otherwise his peers, though he indeed would be the first among them, and together they were France. That was not his view; he thought it presumptuous, and, moreover, rather less than true. He had the doors again opened and let the people in. He feared no throng, only the nobles were offended.

But good humour was soon restored. He told the noblemen who were serving him that Don Philip, the Ruler of the World, had caught the dread disease. There was much amazement at His Catholic Majesty and his strange aberration after such long abstinence. Such a penalty for a single sin! What if every amorous king was visited by so prompt a judgment! Whereupon all of them, to left and right, swung round abruptly towards the table standing crossways to their own and stared at the King beneath his canopy. The King laughed, so they could all laugh too. Their laughter was at the King of Spain and his ludicrous fatality. Many of them took the story for a jest, even if a trifle venturesome; these laughed the longest. There were some great lords, mostly clergy, whose eyes were moist with merriment, and they clapped their lifted hands towards the King in token of approval. How much more often than he of Spain had their King challenged the disease, and never caught it yet! Nay, more: his enemy was now infected. So much luck deserved applause.

Some grew meditative, and their laughter was stilled. A man so lucky was to be feared. A double game at his expense might come to evil issue; and so far as any of the guests still maintained relations with the Spaniards in Paris, now was the time to break them off. The Spaniards would not stay in Paris when their sovereign was laid low. Luck had given the signal, let it not pass unheeded. Someone said aloud that not only the Ruler of the World, but his Empire too had caught the disease, for it was rotting and dropping off him, limb by limb. This was repeated all down the table and canvassed with much vivacity. Meantime faces had grown flushed with wine and food, and voices rose. This masculine banquet had, as a consequence of the news from Spain, assumed the aspect of a carouse, and the King wanted to bring it to an end. Any observant guest could see as much, and such a one was Cardinal du Perron, who had slipped the cushion under Henri's knees when he recanted.

Du Perron handed the King his fingerbowl, bowed, and asked leave to sing a song, which was unwonted for a Prince of the Church, and the company fell silent to listen. The Cardinal sang into the King's ear: a brief and tender little ditty that brought the tears to Henri's eyes. At the upper ends of the two tables only these few words were heard: " Lips of coral, teeth of ivory. Alluring dimpled chin! " At sight of the King's tears, first the guests near by and then those farther off realized to whom the song referred. One after another they rose, until all were standing, paying silent homage to their King's good luck; awhile ago they had merely clapped applause.

The image of his luck was called Gabrielle; of this they were mostly aware, for the banquet had stirred the wits of even the dullards. Others compared the treasure that was his with the uneasy news from Spain. The thoughts of some few went deeper, they noted this transformation in one so unstable, and they saw in this fidelity the resolve to be settled and to possess. And he was destined to great possessions in this world. Valiant he was to the verge of greatness. And that valiance lacked only possession to be greatness indeed. So at least thought all men of sense; and the man of most sense, Monsieur de Rosny, of course conceived greatness as bound up with possession. Hence he here and now decided, against his own instinct and intent, to make his peace with Madame de Liancourt.

The banquet was now over, but in the evening there was another yet to face, the banquet with the ladies. Some went away to sleep off the interval, or diverted themselves with talk. Henri played ball, with long heavy leathern balls, mighty hard to throw after a heavy feast, and where they struck they left at least a bruise behind. A hit on a full belly sent the victim staggering; one of the gentlemen was soon prostrate on the grass, and others fell out exhausted. But Henri had not had enough, and as his noblemen failed him, he shouted to some burghers standing by. Which of them was the best at ball-play, he asked, and to their amazement, he named the very men after a single glance. Those chosen were a butcher, a cooper, two bakers, and a juggler who had unwittingly strayed among his betters; but he was a good deal regarded for his prowess at ball-play. Decent citizens were not commonly disposed to mix with rope-dancers, jugglers, and gallows-birds. But a game makes all men equal, and for the moment the juggler's professional training set him on a level with the rest.

The King, hurling the great balls, first flung one of the bakers out of the game. For near an hour the others endured, until suddenly butcher, cooper, and second baker succumbed; all three turned and hobbled away. "Now!" cried the King to the juggler — and thenceforward they pelted each other with the great balls, which seemed to hurtle back and forward with almost magical speed and lightness. The players darted from place to place like quicksilver, stretched out a hand, and the balls flew into it unbidden, not one, but three and four and five, as airily as soap-bubbles. It was indeed a marvellous display. A throng of people crowded round them, lords temporal and spiritual forgot their digestions, and all stood watching the exploits of King and juggler.

But this amazing display could not be kept up indefinitely, as soon appeared. Reality may not be confused with art. Both players began to sweat; and as the sweat ran into their eyes and nearly made them miss, each at the same moment slipped off his doublet — on a February day towards evening — and they stood in their shirt-sleeves, the King and his opponent. But something more was plain to view. The juggler was wearing a stout shirt, but the King's was split all down the back. It was old and threadbare and unequal to all this violent exercise.

Henri was at first puzzled by the whispering and muttering all round him. He heard murmurs, and now and then a sigh, but at last someone dared to say: " Sire, your shirt is torn." When the words were once uttered, the feeling of pained surprise at once turned into merriment. At first the King himself laughed, though he was also near to flying into a rage. " Armagnac! " he shouted; and when the First Chamberlain appeared: " I thought I had six shirts," said Henri. " There are but three left," replied Armagnac.

" So I am allowed to go about with my back bare: Such is the fate of a King, when he ransoms his cities from the League Governors, who have drained them dry, and then remits their taxes. All the broad lands I conquer I give as free gifts to my peasantry. There's enough for my regalia, but not to buy a shirt."

Then he went — and at the right moment, for the tones of his voice rang in the ears of all the bystanders. It was bravely and nobly spoken. The split shirt had become an oblation to the kingdom, an added radiance to the royal glory. Here was a King indeed. All saw him in their inner vision once more striding through the cathedral, in the fantastic raiment that he wore so regally — and they thought the departing figure in the torn shirt more impressive still.

Henri dressed in his best for the banquet with the ladies, the giver of the feast being his own dear lady Gabrielle. The great hall of the Archbishop's palace at Chartres, lit up by a myriad tapers, glowed with every sheen of gold. Clusters of tapers in glittering candelabra, backed by wall-mirrors or set upon the table, flooded the brilliant throng with a light that flattered and lent distinction to them all. Of the women, there were none but beauties at that table, and men whose years were not a few seemed to have recovered the fresh cheeks and unwrinkled brows of youth. In the gathered glow of all those tapers they looked truly noble and magnificent; they scarce recognized each other in that rich illumination. All the glory and the gold was centred at the table; beyond it the forms of things dissolved, and the rest of the room darkened into a dim haze that hovered beneath the ceiling like cloud vapour in the faint moonlight.

The King and Madame de Liancourt sat facing each other, as master and mistress of the house. On either side of Gabrielle were placed a line of noblemen. Henri had on his left Madame Catherine de Bourbon, his beloved sister; next to her, the Princesses and Duchesses of Conti, Nemours, Rohan, and Retz. On his immediate right, the Princess of Condé, a kinswoman of his House; and next to her the Ladies of Nivernois and Nevers. He repeated these names silently to himself, for they were the great names of his kingdom, and the bearers of them had come as though their presence were a matter of course; but he knew what it had cost to get them there. Of their husbands several still sided with his enemies, if only for appearance' sake, and held some sort of command in Paris, while the wives sat at table with the King. Such company was not brought together without preliminary manœuvres, more intricate than the most elaborate banquet. This lovely scene marked the end of much sweat, much darkness, and much blood. Would that it might truly be the end!

Such were Henri's thoughts as he observed the ladies on either side, each one of whom he loved, and more so than either had any notion. A glance passed from time to time between him and Madame de Liancourt. Sometimes it said: " Well, we have got so far." Sometimes it hinted: " Things might have turned out otherwise." To him and to her the meaning of it was: " I thank you; and I love you."

Henri thought his Gabrielle more beautiful than ever, as he looked at her with pride and with a stirring at the heart. The splendour of her attire was indeed something like a challenge; the ladies could scarcely take their eyes off her. Such gorgeous velvet, of a colour beyond naming, but rich with all the tints of old gold and autumn foliage and spring sunshine; and her arms ringed with heavy bangles in the Spanish fashion. Never had a dress so perfectly matched both daylight and candlelight. And the hoop of diamonds on that golden head, so delicately poised on the crimped ruff, shone with all the more glory on the tresses that rippled from beneath it in a dazzlement of splendour. True it was that this admiration was reluctant; the picture was a lovely one, but their hearts were hostile, and they were not far from wishing that this sun might set.

And yet they could not but be touched as they looked at Gabrielle. Her condition was written on her face that very day in a look that stirred others besides her lord to affection and anxiety. So pale, so drawn, scarce a trace of that dimpled chin of which the poet sang, or of that transparent, pearl-like skin. The eyes alone were larger, and the piteous glow of fever in them moved those onlookers to forget and forgive the milky whiteness of that bosom, and the pendant of beaten gold set with rubies and pearls. The noblemen each side of her were gentle-spoken, but the ladies who leaned across the table and said a heartening word to the expectant mother were more truly sympathetic. Madame Catherine, the King's sister, watched for the moment when the hostess had to give an order, and beckoned for the dishes and the goblets in her stead. One of her more distant neighbours, Monsieur de Rosny, leapt from his chair and hastened, before the lackeys could arrive, to pick up a spoon that had fallen from Gabrielle's quavering hand.

As the feast had become thus transformed from a banquet for the crowned King into an offering of homage to his lady, Henri put aside his meditations and announced to the company that he meant to approach the Pope regarding the dissolution of his marriage, in the intention of marrying Madame de Liancourt. His own tribunal could divorce her from a husband who, as he himself admitted, had been incapacitated by a kick from a horse. The laugh that greeted this he took for general approval — and he went on to say that his dear lady would soon bear the rank and title of Marquise. Not yet content, he raised his glass to the Marquise and looked at her so long and earnestly, with such wide eyes and lifted brows, that everyone realized that she would in time mount higher still. The exaltation of the lovely Gabrielle was not to end until she graced the throne of France at his side. She was to be Queen.

But the general approval did not last. Indeed, he only assumed it while flushed with joy and tenderness. Every one of that company had a clear vision of what a Queen of France should be; not a lady of that land, none of them must have known her, nor ever have had to give her pride of place — a matter that by no means touched the ladies only. From that moment Monsieur de Rosny bore his part in that deep-rooted antagonism that Gabrielle had to face from everyone so long as she lived and could influence the King. Meantime, and in this place, Gabrielle was spared their enmity. She would not live for ever, perhaps she would not live through childbirth, she certainly looked none too well — and so there was a feeling in her favour. Best of all, they knew the King and his promises of marriage. If he had kept them hoodwinked, as he had done until that day, then indeed there would have been matter for concern. But once spoken, already broken. Enough; the lovely d'Estrées was in none too good a case, from any point of view.

So Gabrielle was treated with every mark of sympathy and respect when, following the King's example, the company rose from table. Henri led the Princesses of Bourbon and Condé up to her; and the ladies embraced and kissed. There was not one of them who, when face to face with Gabrielle, would not have told her that she was more ravishing than ever. And sincerely too; they felt neither hostility nor envy, only a kinship with a woman in her condition; and therewithal the kinship of humanity, for at that assemblage in her honour there was present, in some sort, an unseen guest, on whose account they thrilled with fear. And who would not applaud a beauty that seemed as changeless as a work of art! Before a beauty that may well be in league with death, all heads are bowed.

The doors that led to the staircase were then opened. Some noblemen took the candelabra from the lackeys, and each took his stand upon one stair. Before the King and his lady walked the Princesses of the Royal House, and after an interval the other gentlemen and ladies. In the centre of the vestibule Henri led his Gabrielle by her lifted hand, lights were raised on high, and they ascended. A very solemn ceremony, thought Henri, who was feeling young and lucky. The ceremony was interrupted by an incident, which did but heighten its effect. Gabrielle was overcome by faintness; the King had to lay an arm about her and help her to the top. The others remained below; the ascending pair soon passed out of the candlelight into a dim glow, like a moonlit haze of cloud, and vanished as though utterly dissolved.

THE MASKED LADY

Paris was ripe and overripe to receive the King. Not even the Duke of Feria, who still commanded in the city on behalf of His Catholic Majesty, could believe that a Spanish party yet existed. Almost the only obstacles were the defiance of a few irreconcilables and the fears of a larger number who could not hope for pardon. The leaders of the League, including Mayenne, had removed themselves and their property into safety against all events. Not one of the sixteen prefects of the city wards had failed to assure the King of his secret loyalty; the tailor had been but the first, when the King's enemies hanged his highest magistrates. The mob were sick of horrors. Priests who preached of them were no longer popular; indeed, they went in peril of their lives. The populace were now all for forbearance and under-

standing — though rather inclined to violence by way of estab-
lishing their goodwill. Hence many riots, which were indeed put
down, but mostly to save the face of government. There is no
ruler in extremity who would abdicate and flee so long as he had
weapons to his hand — even if only the weapons, and scarce the
arms to wield them. The Spanish commander disposed of more
than four thousand foreign troops, who could hold the walls and
gates at least.

The King could not simply march into the city. He could
deal with those four thousand — but he had to think of his own
people, awaiting their gracious King. He had let them fetch
provisions from without, that they might eat; how therefore
could he now bombard their houses and ravage the capital into
submission? Of course he could not. He had to act up to his
reputation as a popular monarch, and it was only as such that he
could seize power. Henri spent several weeks deliberately encouraging people's notion of him as a man like other men. *Nihil
est tam populare quam bonitas.* He would stray about the countryside while hunting, which provided useful opportunities. At
two o'clock one morning he stopped quite alone before a house
— not, indeed, a robber's den, though it belonged to one of his
Treasury officials, as he was well aware; there was little in his
kingdom that he did not know. The girl who opened the door
did not recognize him; he told her who he was, ate a little butter,
refused a bed, lay down on the hearth, and on awakening next
morning he asked to hear Mass; the priest had to be fetched from
three miles away. Could a King be so homely, and a converted
heretic so good a Catholic?

Many distrusted him, as for instance a pig-dealer, with whom
he sat down at table — again he had lost his way. The company
in the rustic tavern did not observe him, or perhaps pretended
to be dullards; when a King practises guile, the peasant is more
cunning still. However, the pig-dealer, in seeming ignorance that
he was addressing the King, spoke his mind in no measured
terms. Henri could only carry off the affair in the grand manner.
He looked out of the window as some of his gentlemen trotted
up and stopped; they had no doubt been in search of their lost

master. "Think of that, now!" said the villagers. He soon had their hearts, clapped the pig-dealer on the back, gave him a good answer, and the man heard no more of the affair. And those same villagers said afterwards that the citizens of Paris could not know the King or they would open their gates. There's no contending against such agile wits.

It was a masked lady in particular who was taught a lesson in this regard by Henri. She had come expressly from Paris to Saint-Denis, where he then held his court once more; and she reported for his private ear the condition of his cause in Paris, but in so low a tone that the listeners at the open door could not catch one word. Besides the King's own people, there were certain visitors from Paris who had arrived that day as though by chance. Not one person in the adjoining room was wholly deceived by that masked lady. Who could she be? A burgher's wife, friendly to the Royal cause? How much could she know? Moreover, would the King, who fears the knife, interview a veiled visitor in private? Most improbable, surely. Then the King's voice spoke, and in tones that were certainly meant to carry if possible as far as Paris, he told the masked lady she had better inform her good friends inside that he lay there with an army and had no notion of withdrawing until he had entered the city, though not by force. Let them place no faith in the Duke of Mayenne. Their lawful King alone was a man of peace, and he was willing to pay for peace with his capital. He reminded the masked lady that all the other cities which opened their gates to him had prospered. For ten years his citizens of Paris should pay no taxes — indeed, he would ennoble all the city corporations; the friends of his cause should live happily ever after. "Those who have betrayed me, God alone shall judge."

All this he announced to the masked lady, as though he were addressing, not her alone, but a whole people whom he refused to mistrust, whether or no they showed him their true faces. Then he dismissed her, still masked. Swathed in a voluminous cloak, she passed the door and through the waiting gentlemen. They followed her to her carriage. Two of them stood aside, kept their eyes off the carriage, and understood each other without a

single look. One was Agrippa d'Aubigné, the other a certain
Monsieur de Saint-Luc, in the King's service.

In the meanwhile a dusty horseman galloped up, just in time
to see the departure of the masked lady to whom the King had
thus spoken his mind. The man in the leather doublet clearly
thought he deserved the same confidence. He marched into the
house unannounced; in the centre of the empty room stood the
King, no figure now of pride or arrogance; he was staring at
the floor, and he did not raise his head until he heard the tramp
of heavy boots.

"Pastor Damours!" said he. "I might have expected you, at
such a moment."

, "Sire, a wish of your heart shall be fulfilled. A harsh voice
from days long past now speaks to you."

"'Tis the right moment," said Henri.

"Certainly, Sire; a masked personage has just hurried from
your presence. You alone saw your visitor unmasked, and alone
know whether it was the Devil."

"I have no dealings with the Devil. I would rather die — or
lose all my power."

The pastor as he stood clapped his hands on his two thighs.
"Power! You recanted for the sake of power; death is no great
matter now. For power you are playing an elaborate comedy.
People talk of your devices and laugh — I would not have them
speak and laugh so about me."

"Have I had no success, Pastor?"

"You have indeed. You know how to catch your fellow-men.
I would not care to angle for whiting thus."

He slapped his chest, took off his hat, which he had not done
until then, and sang — just as in old days before battle.

> "Let God, the God of battle, rise
>   And scatter His presumptuous foes,
> Let shameful rout their host surprise,
>   Who spitefully their power oppose."

His voice rang through the hall. Damours raised his right arm and took one step forward. Once more into battle, the veteran Huguenots in the van, the dead marching at their side, all chanting in unison; and the psalm, the psalm for the hour of destiny, that struck terror into the enemy and shook his ranks. Victory for the champions of conscience!

> " As smoke in tempest's rage is lost,
>
> Or wax into the furnace cast,
>
> So let their sacrilegious host
>
> Before the wrathful presence waste."

His voice rang through the hall. The King waved a hand and it died away. The pastor lowered his arm, and his chin also sank upon his chest. He had forgotten where he was. Henri too forgot that hour, and both of them fell silent, absorbed in their inward vision of days dead and done, days when consciences were clear.

Then Henri took the man's hand and spoke: " Your hair and beard have whitened, and you see mine. Your face is as hard as ever, and it is also marked with sorrow. I now show my face to you as it really is. Is it a cheerful face? Well, I confess that the seizure of power is at times a game I like to play." He paused, and said once more: " A game it is," and went on more rapidly: " Well, and why not? It is the way to seize power in such a world as this."

" And you are the man to do it," said the old man.

" To every man his allotted task," replied Henri mildly. " I have for that reason listened to you, Pastor Damours."

" You must listen to the anger of the Lord," said the old man vehemently, and the veins in his temples swelled.

" I must indeed," said Henri, as mildly as before; but it was high time for the other to change his tone. He did so, and the throbbing in his temples ceased.

" Your Majesty must forgive poor Gabriel Damours for entering your presence in this fashion."

Henri opened his arms. " Now you are yourself again: Gabriel Damours as I would have him, the fear of God before his eyes, his heart unshaken in his loyalty."

He opened his arms and waited. Here was the moment for all his Protestants. Away with all these slanders — it must and should be true. Kings suffered more than they gained by living in an atmosphere of mistrust. If only old friends might think so, when they had been betrayed and their privileges had gone. But no one leapt into those outstretched arms. Henri let them fall, and added:

" Pastor, what I must do is done for your sake too. You shall receive your rights when I am in power."

" Sire, forgive poor Gabriel Damours; but he does not believe you."

Henri sighed. " Then," he went on in a pleading voice, " let me tell you a merry tale of the masked lady. It is quite true, for I can take no credit for it."

But the Pastor had already backed towards the door. " What do you want? " cried Henri. " Am I to lay my capital in ruins? Am I to convert my people by force to the Religion? Am I to fight and kill like a savage all the days of my life? "

" Sire, pray let poor Gabriel Damours go." His voice no longer rang with reproach, nor thrilled with the divine anger. By no means; he who stood yonder by the door, with half the room between himself and the King, seemed to have dwindled, and not solely because he was so far away; the fire within him had died down.

" I would make my confession to you, Gabriel Damours," said the King across the intervening space.

" Sire, tell the truth to your conscience, not to me." Hard words, but feebly spoken. Henri only understood because he really said as much himself. He turned his face away. When he looked up, he was alone.

Then he took his stand facing the wall and forced himself to confront the truth that this had been his farewell to his Protestants. No last farewell, he would show them what his purpose was and that he had not changed. But none believed him —

none; neither Damours nor any of the rest. And Henri told himself to beware of traitors; none were likelier than his old friends.
With his eyes on the wall, he went over in his mind all who
might prove treacherous. Strange that the image of Mornay appeared, and yet he was sure of Mornay. That pattern of virtue
would surely continue to serve him in perfect uprightness and
duty. But he knew he must not ask Mornay to approve his seizure of power, nor to be one tittle less virtuous for his sake. That
irked the King; he was at ease with treachery and traitors in those
days, and lived in such an atmosphere. He banished the vision
of Mornay's Socratic head and summoned up another.

Not one single friend: he was alone in this satiric business of
seizing power. Satellites he had and boon companions. Masked
ladies brought to audience — it was well that the Pastor did not
ask who the mask was; that ruse should remain for ever unre-
vealed. Who would have thought that she was own daughter to
the Governor of Paris, and he in secret treaty with her father?
Well, whatever might become of other men, Henri had always
thought him honest. Henri disliked Mornay's virtue, and he disliked Brissac's treachery no less. His predecessor had already
been suspected of dealings with Henri. Mayenne removed him
and appointed Count Brissac, solely for his simplicity of mind.
If that man were simple, then Henri felt that he was no deeper
nor more secret than a little child. In truth the man was urging
him to take his capital by guile; a most unpleasant fellow.

All this passed through Henri's mind as he stood glaring at the
wall — though it had been his habit to meditate while striding
up and down with a wind upon his brow. A tap at the door
brought him to himself again. Two cheerful visitors appeared —
not to be encountered in any other mood. The first, his worthy
Agrippa, was clearly brimming with news and scarce able to contain it. Young Monsieur de Saint-Luc could wait; the complacency written on his face was a warrant that he would not object.
He made much of outward form, and the deference to the King
with which he stood aside for Monsieur d'Aubigné was a model
of grace and decorum.

" We are late," said Agrippa, " because we had to send all those

listeners about their business; they would have served no purpose
after the masked lady had gone."

"They would have been unwelcome," said Henri. "Since she
went, I had another visitor — it was a brief and excellent scene,
but not fitted for the eyes of third persons."

Agrippa asked no question about that. "Sire, you cannot guess
who the mask was."

"You had pledged yourself that she was harmless. I am not
curious."

"What if someone told you, Sire, I had been in Paris?"

"You? Impossible."

"As I stand here. To be sure, I was disguised as an old peasant
woman, and passed the gate on a cabbage cart."

"Amazing! And did you see the Governor?"

"He bought my onions in the market — Brissac, his very self.
And we thereby agreed that for the greater security of the royal
person and cause, Madame de Saint-Luc, the Governor's own
daughter, should come and receive your commands. Is that a
surprise?"

"I am quite dumbfounded," said Henri, to whom Brissac himself had announced Madame de Saint-Luc's arrival. Every man
must have a secret from his neighbour. He esteems his part the
more for being complicated. *Totus mundus exercet histrionem*,
why not Henri too? The capture of Paris would not have amused
Agrippa but for his disguise as a peasant crone. The tribulations
of poor Gabriel Damours — these histrionics quite put them
from his head; besides, who could tell what part poor Damours
himself had had in mind? His had been a truly Biblical appearance.

All of this by the way. These reflections did not prevent Henri
from questioning his old friend, and that in so ingenuous a fashion that the young gentleman behind Agrippa bit his lip to keep
himself from laughing. But he did so, more with the intent that
the King should clearly realize: first, that Monsieur de Saint-Luc
was far superior to the man of the older generation, but also that
he was at one with the King in the amiable purpose of sparing
his feelings. Henri disliked the man's air and was moved to say:

" Madame de Saint-Luc was excellently disguised — you would not have known her yourself? "

If the King had expected that the young gentleman would attempt some sly retort, he was grievously mistaken.

" Excellently, Sire," agreed Saint-Luc. " I did not recognize her."

" You are lying," said Henri; " to outdo us " — this with a glance at Agrippa — " were it only in discretion."

" Sire, you are a moralist."

" Today I am," said Henri. " I would therefore know why Monsieur de Brissac plays traitor. You doubtless know your father-in-law from more sides than I; he must have others. At the last court he seemed a simple sort of person who collected pictures. I was in alliance with the late King my predecessor. Brissac could have thrown in his lot with me, but was quite capable of making his own choice. Why go over to the Spaniards if he was to dupe them in the end and betray their cause to me? "

" Your Majesty honours me extremely in acquainting me with what, if turned to wrong account, might greatly hurt your cause."

Here was a sane and honest answer, which put Henri in a more accommodating mood. " Brissac," he remarked, " cannot now go back. He is too deeply committed to me." Then he looked the young man in the eyes and awaited his explanations. The other cleared his throat, looked vaguely about him, and admitted that it was but a chair he needed. " If I am to think, I must sit down."

" I walk about on such occasions. But since it is you that must do the thinking, let us sit," said Henri.

Agrippa too drew up a chair, in much astonishment at all this sudden gravity. Brissac? A most unsoldierly fellow — he pictured his silly air of mystery as he bought vegetables from the disguised peasant woman, haggled, departed and came back, and let fall a whispered word or two each time. It was all a matter for laughter, if indeed it were worth mentioning at all.

" Monsieur de Brissac is a serious case for every moralist," observed young Saint-Luc, with the gravest self-complacency, now that he felt himself on firmer ground. " When he opened the matter of my marriage to his daughter, he led the girl into the room — masked, just as she appeared in your presence. However, I realized that it was not his daughter but someone else. He believes that no one has really any eyes except a connoisseur of pictures like himself."

" Indeed, a serious case," said Henri.

" He has studied many pictures, not to mention books."

" He is a slovenly-looking fellow," observed Agrippa.

" More than that." Saint-Luc made a kind of rending movement with his hands; and as he did so, it was noted that he was still wearing his left glove.

" Monsieur de Brissac collects beautiful things, not simply to hang them on the wall or put them away on shelves; he soaks his mind in images and inspirations. He is what he reads and sees."

" Until there is nothing of his own left," said Henri, who now understood. Saint-Luc went further:

" He does not play traitor. He is a traitor because much practice and the most assiduous art have made him so."

" Does he call himself a humanist too? " asked Agrippa d'Aubigné, leaping from his chair. " We were, and we were men as well. I composed verses as I rode and fought. I had heavenly visions when I stood barefooted, throwing up trenches like an earthworm for the valiant humanist I served."

" That," said Henri, addressing vacancy, " is the proper way. The other may be more diversified, but it shakes a man's character and leaves him without a face." Then turning to Saint-Luc with a short laugh: " 'Tis a good device of Count Brissac to collect pictures and read the classics, since they induce him to surrender my capital and provide me with entertainment too. Does not Feria suspect? "

" How should he? Monsieur de Brissac himself proposed to the Duke of Feria that several gates should be blocked, that the outer walls might be more easily defended. Feria is no soldier; he does not realize that the guards will be withdrawn from the blocked gates, and Your Majesty will force your way in through them; you will understand that they will only be filled with earth."

"That will be discovered before the day."

"No; my astute father-in-law has suborned the Warden of the Merchant Guilds, the petty magistrates, and half the city. Indeed, people ask who is not involved, excepting Feria; he congratulates himself on his Governor's simplicity."

"No doubt everyone knows what he means to make out of this business."

"Monsieur de Brissac expects that Your Majesty will be so gracious as to promote him Marshal of France."

"Does he indeed!" said Henri, but his expression did not change. He repeated the words, as the horrid comedy took possession of his mind. He had been a fighter all his life. He had wielded his own sword, by the strength that was his he had endured — all his life. He had fought all his life for his conscience and the kingdom; and the whole struggle would have been futile but for this amateur of pictures, this vapid traitor. The irony of it all came full upon the King, but he mastered himself, though the blood surged into his face. The laughter that was near his lips would have been too horrible.

He rose and walked to the window. Saint-Luc waited a minute before he tiptoed after him; he understood the impulses of the human soul. Then he took the freedom to speak; but to stress his deference, he spoke with a sort of mincing stammer. The King did indeed despise him, but he did not like to think that that was the intention. Without turning his head he repeated what had come to his ears:

"The good man is having a baldric embroidered, so I hear. The Archangel Gabriel, very neat and ingenious, worked upon white silk. My Marshal proposes to present it to me on the day of my entrance — who can tell why?" he concluded, thinking of the unlikelihood of such a performance.

"Today is the 14th of the month. It will be in a week," lisped Monsieur de Saint-Luc. At these words, Henri swung round.

"You know more than you should, unless you have seen the Governor. Were you in Paris in disguise?"

"By no means. But all the details of the plot are here at Your Majesty's disposal." So saying, the young gentleman drew a paper out of his glove, the left one, which he had kept on. Henri snatched it from him. " Who gave you this? "

" Brissac himself."

" Then he is here."

" He was here — and by permission of the Duke of Feria. He came with two notaries, to transact some urgent family business with me. I left them as soon as I had the paper." This he said without his previous diffidence, nor was there even a tremor of exultation in his tone. A very knowing young man; no need to linger with him now.

" My horse! " shouted Henri from the window.

" Sire, you will never catch him now."

In a flash Henri was outside, in the saddle, and galloping towards Paris. He soon came in sight of a huge jolting coach that filled the whole roadway. He could but ride round through the wood and stop between two trees until it came rumbling towards him. Through the window in the front Henri could see the notaries, three of them. Clad in black with pointed hats, all alike, wizened and old, and so wearied by the efforts of the journey that not one of them seemed likely to notice a horseman by the wayside. Moreover their eyes were closed, their mouths were open, which made them look even more of a pattern than ever. Henri was on the point of shouting out, but did not, and the great spectral coach had nearly lumbered past him when, at the last moment, one of the three notaries raised a hand — the hollowed hand moved slowly, very slowly, forward, towards the nose of him who sat dozing opposite. Ptt! he had that fly. And oh, the joy on that wizened, homely countenance!

A fly caught on an unsuspecting nose; while the King, to whom the catcher of that fly was to yield up his capital, looked on. Now Henri knew enough, and for just that reason he let the coach rumble onwards. He began to wonder seriously whether the man were in his right mind.

What trouble such people took to be so crazily crooked, he reflected as he rode back at a walk. Well, he carried in his memory no little sense very painfully collected on his way through life, beginning with the night of Saint Bartholomew. It was his task to make all this impossible; indeed it was the business of a King. They would go on, they would make it hard for him. Pah! Conceive of catching flies as a sign of recognition, and sending a masked lady as an emissary! Well, he must play his part.

The Seizure of Power

All came about as arranged. Brissac was a model of circumspection. He told the Spaniards to rely on him and keep quite quiet, so that the traitors should not suspect. For there were traitors in the city, and they might easily discover Brissac's purpose to arrest them all. And so the haughty Spaniards, from mere belittlement of danger, let destiny move on.

Henri played admirably into the hands of his coadjutor. He might indeed have taken him prisoner by mistake. About four o'clock on the morning of the 22nd, Brissac nearly fainted because there was no sign of the Royal forces. But this was merely owing to a thick fog, and as soon as Brissac left the outer walls, he too was engulfed in it. Fortunately his son-in-law, Monsieur de Saint-Luc, was in command at that point, so there was no mishap.

The two blocked gates were cleared, and the morning bells began to peal just when the King entered his capital. His noblemen could wait no longer: in full armour they leapt the final barricades. He himself walked with hand on hip, head a little to one side, and all the air of coming home after a few hours' hunting. He had been away for eighteen years.

The first face that met his eyes was the angel face of Brissac. Such purity of feature and of heart is rare, and the faces of mortal men are not commonly so marked. Kneeling on the muddy ground, his blue eyes upturned, Brissac proffered to the King a white baldric. The King promptly girt his own about Brissac's shoulders, embraced him, and hailed him " Marshal."

By way of gratitude, Brissac advised the King to put on his armour. It was agreeable to go about among the populace in a plain doublet, as His Majesty of course wished to do, but one never knew. Henri started: the knife! — he had forgotten it.

No; Brissac was referring to the surging crowds, so easily set in motion in a great city, and so dangerous; even a King may be swept away by them and fall among his enemies.

Henri replied that they should never take him prisoner. Nor indeed did they mean to do so. "No one," he said, "wants to keep a bird like me in a cage." But he yielded, and entered his capital wearing a cuirass beneath his cloak; and in place of the white-plumed hat, so eloquent of peace, an iron helmet. His triumph, already marred by the rain and the deserted streets, was sadly damped by this array.

No one was abroad so early, and there were few faces at the windows; the Royal troops, split up into detachments, dispersed a few stray Spaniards, cut down thirty landsknechts or threw them into the river; and that was almost all. Monsieur de Saint-Luc and his company came upon a stronghold half-heartedly defended by some burghers; but the King met with no resistance. He sent to the Duke of Feria ordering him to forthwith leave the city. A second messenger went to the church of Notre Dame, to announce that the King was on his way.

When the people of Paris awoke and left their beds, though the news sped from house to house, they would not believe that the King was in the city. They were aghast. Their first thought was of pillage and slaughter; and this though many had seen him face to face at Saint-Denis when he recanted, or at his coronation at Chartres, and had sworn him fealty. That stood for little now. A day of pomp and ceremony is well enough; the day of victory was always a day of blood.

Nothing was further from Henri's mind than bloodshed, nor did he reckon with the fears of the populace. The new Marshal, Brissac, sent gendarmes, chosen for their stentorian voices, on gigantic horses, to announce that the King was in possession of the city and proclaim a general amnesty and pardon. The people of Paris were told to remain quietly at home. Whereat they promptly came forth, cheered the white scarves of the French soldiery, and the King's trumpeters, and carried the King himself shoulder-high to the cathedral.

All the bells of Notre Dame were pealing, each in the familiar tone by which it was known and named. Ahead of the King walked a hundred French noblemen, in token that he was King indeed. But in that same ancient church there had but lately been intercessions to Saint Geneviève, to defend her city of Paris against Henri. There were those who recalled them now: the Archpriest, who uttered the appropriate salutations, and the Cardinal, who remained unseen. But the mob had forgotten; not the individuals who made it up, every one of whom remembered many things. But the mob, as though none of this had happened, surged into the cathedral and joined in the ceremony with every sign of glad devotion.

It was now for the King to speak; he closed his mind to all outside the moment; and yet he felt uneasy. Before the event, he had known more clearly how matters would go forward and had envisaged the things to come. He replied to the Archpriest: " I mean to protect my people and lighten their burdens, and in that purpose I will give the last drop of my blood! " He also affirmed his Catholic faith, calling upon God and the Holy Virgin. But there was still a cloud upon his mind. He had the feeling that he was not there, and that all these people were denizens of a dream. The event now seemed trivial. That was because he had been awaiting it too long.

Paris, Paris was his, and acknowledged to be his. In yonder chapel hung a painting depicting him as the Devil. He had noticed it, as was observed, and the picture was taken away. He knelt in the choir and heard Mass. Afterwards, when he stepped out on the great flagged square, for one whole minute the scene faded, and before his inner vision appeared a wooden platform hung with tapestry, which had stood there an unimaginable time ago. Upon it he had been married to the Princess of Valois. He could measure the height of it against the façade of the church. Standing in the sparkling air amidst the flower of the kingdom, he had then looked down through a festal crowd, as though his were to be a delightful life and he a favourite of fortune. And then began the School of Misery; he learned the Pallor of Thought, and became familiar with the Troubles of Life. Now — Paris. And what did that mean? That he would have to toil as hard as ever, be still more upon his guard, turn every mishap to a good issue; and Paris — he would never conquer Paris while he lived.

During that brief moment on the square of Notre Dame, while Henri's eyes were sightless, his soldiers had managed to drive back the crowd beyond the roadway. He was shocked when he turned and saw them. "I can see," said the King, "under what sort of tyranny these poor folk have been living" — and he resolved, now his own long struggle was over, to share it with this people. He commanded that they should be allowed to approach him again. "They are hungry for the sight of a King," said he, thereby signifying all that he had done and suffered for their sake.

He bore himself with a somewhat imposing air, as is inevitable on such days. Early that morning in the half-dark street he had caught a soldier purloining a loaf. The man knew no better. But the King was in his city of Paris. There should be no pillage in his city — though the baker could not have been in the least surprised. In a corner house a man stood at a window with his hat on, staring down insolently at the King. He believed indeed that he had nothing to lose, being in any case proscribed. The King's men were eager to seize the man, but the King would not let them, and there was much murmuring against this abandonment of common usage.

On his way from Notre Dame to the Louvre every shout of welcome stirred the King's heart, though he was repelled and irritated by the blatant folly of a cheering crowd. Thus he made his way through the city at last in his power — and well he knew that he must make his power felt, he had no business to have allowed a handful of citizens here and there to cheer him as he passed, while a thousand times as many, in their kitchens and their shops, went on with their daily lives, and at most said, as they paused for a moment in their tasks: "The King will be in a high humour at entering Paris. But it is a mood that will not last."

In a country town called Eauze, an unimaginable while ago, a young King of Navarre sat at table in the market-place with rich and poor, who had expected him to have them killed for not

opening the gates of their own free will. Meantime he was dining in their company. Through him they made acquaintance
with an attitude of mind that they had never met, called "humanity," and they were utterly taken aback. Men do not change
in the passage of the years, and Henri longed to take his great
city to his heart. Between Eauze and Paris, down the intervening
years, stood a double line of mailed figures: the deeds that he had
done. And so it was that every cheer between Notre Dame and
the Louvre jarred upon the King, although it also stirred his
heart. He was in truth prepared for violence — and violence
there was.

A priest, armed with a partisan, roused the mob against him.
A ruffianly old survivor of Saint Batholomew was knocked over
in a scuffle and broke his wooden leg and his musket. There was
firing at the King's men from the windows. Henri also watched
an effort to build a barricade, and enjoyed the sense of something
actual and real; indeed, he would otherwise have lost his way. He
could tell it from the hostile efforts to bar it, and so safely reached
the Louvre. He sat down to dinner in the long gallery, the banquet was arrayed, all the courtiers and lackeys in their places,
with all the air of having expected him for eighteen years. He
flung care aside and ate with gusto, being careful not to look
about him; he merely repeated his order that the Spaniards must
withdraw by three o'clock, if they valued their lives.

The Duke of Feria, Governor for His Catholic Majesty, was
not yet disposed to yield; he still held some of the outer wards.
But Henri sent him a peremptory message, and Feria, who was
no soldier, submitted. He gave way rather sooner than Philip's
Paris supporters, the men who had drawn, and spent, his eighty
thousand crowns; and with them any allegiance to the Ruler of
the World was at an end. Outside the centre of the city, which
was firmly under the King's control from Notre Dame to the
Louvre — there the dregs of what once had been the League still
seethed. Wild men of every rank and degree, with fearsome,
savage faces, brandishing their weapons — in an hour's time they
would be no more than ludicrous; but here they were still formidable, fighting for a cause already lost.

An unarmed mob met them upon their own ground. Mostly lads, who cried in shrill high voices: " Long live the King! " These were followed by mounted heralds with trumpets, proclaiming peace and amnesty. After them came some magistrates; and before them the last Leaguers laid down their arms. There was nothing left for them to do, for they were met like men and brothers, with outstretched hands. For many, the whole of life was emptied of its purport, they could not shed their habits at a stroke; here all at once was an end to force and fury and the coarser view of life, if a pack of lads and lawyers could, when the hour struck, make plain the courage that lay behind a love of peace. Several of the wild men perished from the shock of the too sudden passage from madness back to sanity.

Of all that happened on that day, which was much, there was one thing only that Henri's heart desired and he meant to witness. He climbed the Porte Saint-Denis and stood at a window. Three o'clock; still no Spaniards. Yes, they come, treading very softly, hat in hand, in silence, and with eyes downcast. These mortals had been the proudest men alive, and they had conceived their Empire, if not their persons, as immortal. They might have lost cities in the past, but never had they marched out of one like this without a fight, merely because their time was past and they had been deserted by their own master.

Rain pelted down upon them, but they held their heads erect; some carts followed them with their baggage, which was scanty, for they had never been thieves. Their many children tripped along beside them, and their dogs padded after them with drooping ears. A woman on a cart cried: " Where is the King? " Long she looked at him, then raised her voice and cried: " Good King, great King, I pray God for your good fortune." Proud Spanish woman! In a closed and shuttered coach drove the Papal Legate. The King waved a hand after it, and wondered why his ironic gesture came to a sudden standstill. The Duke of Feria, a grave, gaunt figure, left his carriage to comply with the formalities imposed upon the vanquished. He bowed with dignity, moving with stiff and measured strides, and had passed Henri before the King could find a word. Spanish soldiers closed ranks round the

Duke's carriage. The remainder of the troops were Neapolitans, German landsknechts, and Walloons, an epitome in little of the World Empire. The commanders of the last companies turned their heads at the King's parting words: " Salute your master, but do not come back." And he added in an undertone to the by-standers: " I wish him a good recovery." Which was greeted with much laughter.

Henri contained his exultation, or it would have burst all de-cency; he doubted his own fortunes. If our life has an aim, we know not what, it is never achieved. He was delighted to find that his feet were wet. The Spaniards would have to make their long march in waterlogged boots. " How was the weather when you rode up from the South and seized my kingdom and occu-pied my capital? I was a child when I first heard that men had enemies, and you were mine. See my grey beard, what a struggle it has been! And it seems so only in recollection; a gallant enemy has kept me cheerful and light-hearted half my life. Today I re-ceive my reward — for a life of tenfold toil, but I have won it. Pass on, and farewell, my gallant enemies! "

His vision clouded, and he stumbled as he made his way down the staircase. Affairs awaited him in the Louvre, and he said: " I am drunk with joy. What say you? " For a while he strode si-lently up and down the gallery; then suddenly he halted, stepped forward stiffly for a pace or two, and swept off his hat with a mag-nificent air. Yes, he was aping the Duke of Feria's last melan-choly salutation, as was noted not without disgust. For the rest of the day he wore the bewildered air of one astray in a strange world. " Chancellor," said he to Dame de Sourdis's friend, " can I believe that I am really here? "

He recovered himself when a few high members of the League hurried to pay their respects, answered curtly and turned his back on them; there was too much haste to claim what each conceived as his deserts. But the King's angry shrug was but one expression of his joy. A few hours later Henri had received certain submis-sions that could not be honestly intended; the elders of the city brought him mead and tapers, together with asseverations of their poverty; and he brought himself to praise the goodness of their hearts. But he promptly sent mounted couriers after the Papal Legate to induce him to return. Whatever the Legate had wanted, were it even a genuflection, from the most faithful son of the Church he could have any sort of pious demonstration and any fantasy of faith professed.

Meantime the priest in the closed and shuttered coach drove on. It was not known that evening in the Louvre whether he had been overtaken by the King's messengers. The castle lay in the centre of the city, and that day the King had seized power. To-morrow the news would echo in the ears of all the world, in those night hours rumour sped along all her highways; on the morrow the minds of all men living would be possessed by the greatness of the King, for the reward of his achievements renewed their splendour. Nothing could withstand his name, he would be the most tremendous figure in the world — but under the falling rain, along those sodden roads, every one of which led to Rome, a closed and shuttered coach rumbled inexorably southwards.

King Henri, in his palace of the Louvre, saw it like a moving insect, very small but very clear. And this crawling object would move faster than Fame, which flies on wings. It would arrive everywhere before the news of that day's doings. Whenever it was reported, at courts or among the people, that the King of France had seized and now held his capital, there would be voices to reply: " Rome will have none of him." Then were his deeds as good as undone, nor was he really in his capital. And he repeated to all whom he received: " This is the day of days "; but he could put no heart into the words.

The spasmodic jerking of the King's shoulder gradually made plain to all that company that they were unwelcome, and one by one they took their leave. Then through all the rooms and cabinets of his palace the King wandered like a man in a dream. Sometimes he would pause and clap his hands to his head as some fresh thought came to him; no, it was always the same. He had let that coach escape; and now he knew, too, why the hand he waved at it had stopped abruptly in mid-air. " Well? " he cried, recoiling at the sight of some strange faces; for he knew they must be birds of ill omen. They told him that a certain pertinacious priest had been murdered in his cloister for advising the monks to recognize the King. Henri pretended to shrug his shoulders over such a trifle.

But the tears came into his eyes. " I am grateful to my enemies," said he to the bearers of the news, " for saving me the trouble of having them arrested." Whereupon they too observed from the King's quick movements that they were not wanted. Henri called one of them back and bade him hasten to the ladies Guise and Montpensier. They were his enemies and were now surely quaking in terror of his vengeance. Let them take comfort and be assured of his friendship — such was his message. At last he was almost alone. " Armagnac, where has everyone gone? " The First Chamberlain emerged from a secluded corner; he began by pacing round the room to make sure that no one was still there. Then he launched into something of a speech — the reason being that for some while he had had his eye upon his master, at every turn of the day's events, and he knew exactly what had gone forward on that day of days.

The Sense of Return

" Sire, the strangers have gone back to their own place, and even your noblemen have left the palace, for several reasons, of which I conceive there are three. First, you did not invite any one of them to stay; on the contrary, you encouraged them to go. Second, you have been in an extremely cheerful mood, with which most of them could not keep pace. The Spaniards, indeed, were the only ones who could stand up to you, and they have therefore departed as plain and determined enemies of Your Majesty. Those, on the other hand, who remain can scarce present themselves as enemies. It is their task at the moment to transform themselves into your good friends and subjects; not merely from fear, which would be natural enough. But secure from all vengeance, and thanks to your unimaginable clemency, Sire, there exists a pack of traitors and murderers — men who have lived by violence and treachery — who are suddenly to step into the background and change their very hearts. Sire, you

surely realize that there's not a man who would do so, even supposing that he could. That is the second reason why these rooms
are empty."

" And the third? " asked Henri, as Armagnac paused and began to busy himself about the room. " There were surely three? "

" There is indeed another," said the nobleman slowly, as he
struck a spark with flint and steel and lit some tapers. " It was
fortunate that the worthy city elders presented you with these
tapers. Now look about you. All this day you have not once
cast your eyes round your palace of the Louvre."

Henri did so and at last noticed that the place was bare of
furniture. In all the vague confusion of his joy he had long since
had the sense that he was not really there. The Louvre it was —
but emptied out; now, by the light of a few tapers which he and
Monsieur d'Armagnac carried along echoing galleries and up and
down the staircases, he saw how his palace had been stripped. In
the chamber of the old Queen Catherine de Medici, known as
Madame Catherine, his first glance fell upon the coffer where
Margot, his Margot, used to crouch, immersed in leather-bound
tomes. But the coffer was a mere mirage of candlelight and
memory, and the reality was now an empty space.

Dead, like most of their former habitants, were these rooms
that had been hers. Here had come, one day long ago, two men
in black, bearing with them a drawing on parchment of an empty
skull, which they spread out on the table; young Henri's mother
had lately died of poison, and the suspect had sat there and faced
him across that table. It had gone, and with it all that had filled
that room. The pictures of the past begin to fade, now that table
and coffer are gone. We pass into another room; there the tall
chimney-piece still stands, supported by the stone figures of Mars
and Ceres, the work of a master named Goujon. The sight of
them recalled a game of cards once played in that room. The
card-table rose out of some spectral cavity, and with it came the
sinister card party. Blood that none could stanch oozed from
beneath the cards, a dark omen for the players; they had indeed
all perished, their blood had vanished like their cards.

Between those departed tapestries Charles IX had stamped

shrieking back and forth; that window, now dismantled of its curtains, he had slammed and barred, to shut out the screams of murder. On the night of Saint Bartholomew Henri had sought release in madness; he feigned a frenzy on that journey through the palace, which had been a journey through the underworld. A huddle of corpses everywhere — some of friends and some of foes. Where — where was Margot? The shattered chairs had gone, and where was that strip of violet and yellow embroidery he remembered as having been thrown over those two young corpses yonder? Had it all happened? A plot demands a setting; and against that empty scene his memories grew dim. " I am overjoyed, and cannot believe that I am really here " — the words circled in his head as he, the lone survivor, carrying his candle before him, wandered more slowly and silently from room to room, until he seemed to be creeping along the walls.

His sole living companion had gone down into the old court-yard, called the well-shaft of the Louvre, to see if he could find anyone in the kitchen, or perhaps discover something that might serve for supper. Now and again he shouted cheerfully from below, for Armagnac was uneasy at his master's condition and only wished he could have brought him a cup of wine. And indeed Henri was near to seeing visions. In the great gallery he was met by a violent gust of air. Within the dim outlines of windows that had not before been opened he could descry a throng of shadowy forms: gentlemen and ladies of a bygone court, jostling each other as they peered at the ravens. A swarm of them fluttered down into the well-shaft of the Louvre; the odour they loved most had brought them there, and as darkness fell they set about their prey.

The spell was broken by Armagnac, who shouted that he thought he could see a span of light ahead. If he were wrong he would send out soldiers from the guard, for he did not intend that his master should spend such an evening sober. " Patience, Sire! " But patience was the feeblest of his master's spiritual forces at that moment. Suddenly he turned, at the approach of shuffling footsteps — they were really beyond hearing, even for ears like his; but one sense warned him; surely the same sense of return that had brought him visions of that perished court. Well, spirits must be faced like living people; let them see they were suspected for what they were, and they grew dangerous. So he lifted his guttering taper high above his head and calmly awaited what might appear.

It was a squat, hunched figure, not unlike that of the new Marshal Brissac; and for an instant Henri thought it was the Marshal. Then the creature came within the dim reflection of the taper and revealed a strange face, a face that seemed no longer of this world. It had a shadowy mask, with hollow eye-sockets, and between strands of white hair a glimpse of sicklier white; a touch of the hand, and it would surely dissolve. And Henri had no wish that this apparition should vanish too. " My name is Olivier," said a quavering voice. Henri noticed that the creature was now more bent than ever and was clearly afraid. Now, fear is the very last emotion that a spirit would display. What could make a spirit tremble? And the creature that had called itself Olivier was trembling now.

" Begone! " cried Henri, not so much in anger as to see what the apparition would do. It promptly answered:

" I may not leave this palace."

" I grieve to hear it," said Henri, curtly as before, still uncertain as to the powers that might have penned a living being within this desolate Louvre. " How long have you been here? "

" An endless time," was breathed forth. " The short, pleasant years of life, and then the endless years of retribution."

" Speak out and speak clearly," added Henri, who began to feel uneasy. " If you have a tale to tell, let it be such as I can understand."

The apparition named Olivier dropped on its knees — almost without a sound; but the movement was not the movement of a ghost; here was a miserable human creature, a head shorter now, who moaned: " Sire, spare my grey hairs. It would profit you nothing to have me hanged. The furniture has gone for ever. I have paid long and heavily for my unfaithful stewardship of the Louvre."

Henri understood, and recovered his self-possession. " So it was you that stripped the place," said he. " Good. You have made away with what is mine; that is a matter with which I will duly deal. Now tell me how it happened, and how such a rascal came to be put in charge of this royal palace."

" I too wonder now," answered the creature from the level of his knees. " But when I was chosen, I was esteemed a decent man, who had managed his own property with prudence. And it was thought that he would be the man to safeguard the Crown of France from damage. I myself would have taken my oath that I was. Sire, I have been no better than a pickthief, and I know how a man falls to thieving."

" Well — ? "

" For several reasons."

" Three, I dare say."

" Three indeed, Sire. How did Your Majesty know? "

With a fresh outburst of groaning, the man raised his upturned hands in supplication. " I am so stricken that toe and knee will no longer support my body, and I am as good as starved. For years past, the fear of hanging has kept me prisoner in the deepest cellars of this desolate castle. I scarce dare to burn a light, lest a glimpse of it be seen, and it is only at night that I crawl out in search of food." So saying, to prove his words, he dropped on hands and knees, looking uncommonly doglike. And from that, his lowest level, he continued:

" But when I first came here, I walked upright like a man, I had a regiment of lackeys, and treasures beyond price were in my charge. Yonder stood a table of pure gold, with ruby-studded feet; on that wall hung a tapestry embroidered with five thousand pearls, depicting the wedding of Samson and Delilah and the revels of Heliogabalus." As he spoke, the former Steward of the Palace shuffled on all fours, and with surprising speed, to the familiar spots; it was clearly long since he had moved in any other fashion.

" Enough! " cried Henri. " Stand up! " Shaking his white mane, like a great poodle, the old creature staggered to his feet. " Fellow," said Henri, and he spoke in a heartening tone, " confess your secrets."

He had a hope that some of the vanished treasures had been stowed by the madman in obscure hiding-places in the palace, and Henri well remembered how he had come upon such refuges when his life here had been so constantly in peril. But the madman suddenly said something quite beyond expectation. " Sire, I came upon you alone, and in the darkness, when I was running from your nobleman, because he had found my light. You had been looking upon old acquaintances in the darkness. The former court had returned. The air was laden with the fragrance of these great lords and their ladies, and with it was mingled the rich odours of the kitchen. The rich furnishings of the rooms and cabinets gleamed in the red glare of huge torches."

" No, no — not all that," muttered Henri; he was taken aback and once more, he was irked to find, rather alarmed by this old creature.

" I saw it all," said the other, with a cackle. " I felt myself all the while under the watchful eyes of unseen presences, who would not always so remain. I had to pay for my knowledge of the past, and for having been a humanist. I ought then to have fled and surrendered my stewardship. But no, I gave feasts, I banqueted in splendour with rich men of my kind, and a throng of parasites, who were welcome enough if they could present some semblance of old courts. And I had at my call many lovely, costly women, jewels of women, and they ate my fortune up."

" That, my good fellow, was to be easily foreseen," interposed Henri.

" But had I stayed one single night alone in the castle," whispered the madman, " those unseen presences who lurked everywhere — indeed, I would suddenly catch sight of a peering face — they would certainly have wrung my neck."

" You could not bear to live here," remarked Henri. " And the second reason? "

" The second reason was the terror of the times. Paris was a sink of licence and disorder while Your Majesty was winning your great victories, and it was just then your pleasure to besiege the city and starve us out. He who has no money left to squander pours forth blood. And of what happened in this place, and at what night-long orgies, I say nothing."

"Enough!" cried Henri once again. "Proceed. So by degrees your needs were such that you had to strip the palace."

The creature bowed so low that its white locks masked its face. "Ah, it was despair as much as wickedness. Sire, permit a learned humanist to tell you that despair makes a man wicked, and wickedness is close kin to despair. I wanted to see the end of all these things, that was my temptation; and even today I am proud of what was done, for the end has been a fitting end for one who was once great and powerful, now that his desire is sated and he has stripped the palace of the Kings of France."

Henri summed up. "First, this was no place for a man of your kind; second, you practised what was not uncommon in your time, you ate the flesh of men; last, your curiosity has reached as far as death. And death you shall now meet."

Here rang out a living voice, that of Monsieur d'Armagnac, who spoke from outside, underneath the window, to which he had climbed half-way up the wall. He had been anxious to discover with whom his master was parleying in the darkness. The stump of candle, stuck to the bare floor, was now flickering to its end. Armagnac had heard a good deal. "Sire," said he, "throw the fellow out, I'll see his business settled."

The creature which had called itself Olivier seemed solely set upon its own concerns. He had paid as little heed to the King's words as to Armagnac's shout. "Now I'll run like a dog," he muttered, as though to himself alone, then actually dropped on his hands and scurried round the room. Whereupon he stood up, as near erect as he could manage, and almost in a man's voice the figure said: "You see? — that is the price I never cease to pay for the brief and pleasant years of life that came before. It was a very gay and gallant fellow who was transformed into a dog. When I was stripping the palace of the King's treasures and selling them, oh, how those lovely ladies snatched the money that I got! They were so proud to think it all came from a palace and loved me for it, bless them!"

" All of them? " asked Henri, full of unwilling sympathy.

" All. And there were not a few; a double number, the second figure fourfold the first."

Suddenly, in that white, flaccid face, the eyes glittered, and then blinked, just as Henri had noticed in the last of his would-be murderers. Moreover he was prepared for the number; it was the computation of his mistresses, of which he had already heard the tale. This was what the madman was about to utter — not so mad, either, that he did not glimpse a chance of saving his skin by implicating the King at the last moment.

"Twenty-eight," muttered the man of many parts, now a cringing dog, but once a gay and gallant fellow, a vampire, a faithless steward, and a ghost. Henri promptly grasped him by the collar, heaved him out of the window, and let him drop. Monsieur d'Armagnac picked up the huddled heap and carried it to its destined place. His solitary footstep receded into the distance.

The last stump of candle had burnt down and guttered out; but the King, who had that day seized power, at this point felt still more in need of the chair that was not there. It had been a weary day, and that last hour had seemed to Henri the weariest of all. He had found this encounter most burdensome and baffling, and yet it still possessed his mind. There had been more point than sense in it, and it was not quite in vain that the madman who had called himself — so pointedly — a humanist had tried to implicate the King in his own ruin. Henri pondered. After all, he had a wife, who alone cost more than the whole tale of his mistresses together. And he owned three shirts. He had remitted all taxes, dues, and contributions from Paris for ten years, whereby it became no easier for him to buy the remainder of his kingdom. He had to encourage trade in place of war, which had hitherto been the most important business of the realm. He did not yet see how each of his subjects, even now and then, could have a chicken in the pot.

He walked to the window, through which the moonlight now glimmered from a rent in the drifting clouds. A task, he reflected, for more than one man. He knew one man who would stand by his side, but only one. What needed doing must be done at once, for he meant that France should be the first kingdom in the West on the day he came to die. He bade himself stand fast, and Rosny too, so long as they were there. And then? He prayed that his dear lady might give him a son, that he might enter into his kingdom. Without her and her body it could never be truly his. These last words he breathed aloud to the moon, in a murmur as soft and intimate as the moon's own beams.

The King, who had that day seized power, fell to pondering on the moon, where his fleeting fancy conceived the charming Gabrielle as denizen. He had indeed lodged her in a discreetly resplendent palace not far away; so near now seemed that gracious star. "The circled candelabra will be glittering in your apartments at that hour, Madame. I stand and listen and breathe your radiance, Marquise."

Such pleasing fantasies were promptly dispelled by the First Chamberlain, who brought tidings that concerned the King in more material fashion. First, he had found a bedchamber for the King, and led the way to it. Henri followed him absently up and down staircases and along passages, paying no heed to where he went; nor was he interested in the doings of his Chamberlain elsewhere. The latter began, as he was drawing off his master's shoes:

"The man Olivier is in chains and under guard."

"He had long been under guard here in the Louvre," observed Henri with a yawn.

Armagnac continued in a faintly reproving tone: "The First President of your Parliament came from his bed to examine the man, who confessed to all his crimes, and several clerks were needed to draw up the indictment. He will be tried at dawn."

"Quick work, indeed. Where is he to hang? And why are you dragging at my shoes in that way?"

"He will hang on the Louvre bridge, that all Paris may see how the King punishes criminals. Sire, I shall have to cut your shoes off. They are thick with mud and have stuck to your feet."

" It was raining hard when the Spaniards marched out. Leave the shoes on my feet to remind me of the Spaniards while I sleep. I shall not sign Olivier's death-warrant."

" Sire, the people will not love you unless that fantastic rascal who sold your furniture hangs on the Louvre bridge."

Armagnac proceeded to slit the sodden leather, and when he had freed his master's feet, he warmed them in his hands. As he did so, he looked up, and Henri saw that this was not the Armagnac of twenty years ago. He would never have said: " Sire, your people will not love you." He paid not the least heed to the matter — first, because he would never have conceived it as in doubt, and second because the bold fighter of those days was never beset by any doubts at all. He was always on the spot when his master was in peril, and the Duke of Guise, the darling of the people, was near to being cloven in twain by Armagnac, of which the latter made no secret when the moment was past; the very thought of it had made the Duke turn pale.

" Friend," said Henri with concern, " what is the matter? "

There was a gentle, almost diffident look upon Armagnac's face.

" In old days you would never have conceived my people's love as depending on whether or no a man was hanged." He was growing old, thought his master, though he did not say so. Old age, he supposed, must sap a man's self-confidence.

" Do you recognize this room? " asked Armagnac suddenly. Henri started and looked about him. A room of moderate size, a battered lath bed with a straw mattress; but, strange to see, above it, against the crumbling ceiling, a ragged canopy. Through all those years it had endured above the place where once the young King of Navarre had lain with his wife in marriage bed, with his forty noblemen around him; but he had left the bed too soon. The night was not over, and it was to be a night of murder until far into the day.

" Why am I here? " asked the King, who had that day seized power. " I do not care to know. Hang your thief upon the bridge that my citizens of Paris may see that the ghosts are banished. I'll have no more of them about me. I mean to live in the Louvre as though it were a new-built palace; there shall be no breath nor memory of the old one left. I have a new people also, and upon the past their lips, like mine, are sealed. The ghost is hanged, away with him. My people shall love me, because I and they shall work together."

Two Toilers

One morning a strange pair visited the workshop of Gérome the tanner, an open building between street and yard, in a much frequented neighbourhood. The shorter man was the King, the taller his faithful servant Rosny, as was promptly discovered by the inhabitants of the street as soon as they appeared. A few soldiers cleared a passage, shouting: " Make way for the King! "

The entertainment began when the King said to the old craftsman: " Well, good fellow, do you want another journeyman? " The tanner, in his astonishment, said: " Yes "; and in a trice the King stood in his shirt-sleeves, which he had rolled up to the elbow, and so set about the task, as he had learned it by watching the master. He was rather clumsy and inclined to let the leather slip away into the waste that ran in a gutter across the yard and into a tank. Several strips of leather were lost before the old tanner noticed. He considered whether he should treat the matter with the respect due to the royal person or as a master tanner would do, but promptly resolved to act as master and not as subject, and he demanded that the damage be made good.

The doorway was thronged with onlookers. The wily trader thought that he would extract as many pistoles from the King as there were hides afloat in the tank. But it was soon brought home to him that the King's tall companion was his better at a bargain. Monsieur de Rosny beat down the sum until it stood at about the value of the leather. The astounded tanner scratched his head, while the people from the street roared with laughter. The King, who had all this while been working without a word, waved a hand for silence; then, as he washed his hands and put on his doublet, he addressed the company.

" Good people, I have here tested myself at a trade, and I will admit that I have worked to little purpose, though the start is always difficult; still, it is not from me that you will learn how leather may well and truly be tanned. But it was my purpose that you should understand why our native leather, once so much esteemed in Europe, has fallen out of use. It is because after this interminable civil war, with all its disorder, in which no man can work, there are few journeymen tanners more skilled than I. My master Gérome employs none, they merely let his hides slip into the waste. Am I right, master? "

" Sire, your words are golden," said the man, now resolved to take the respectful line. " How does Your Majesty know about such humble matters? "

Henri knew about them through his faithful servant, who had discovered them in some fashion of his own. Rosny was a soldier, but his insight into all matters concerning commerce was remarkable; his King resolved to turn it to good use; and hence the visits of that strange pair to the more populous streets. The King winked imperceptibly at his follower; then he turned again to the bystanders.

" Friends," said he, " pray think of the good name of our trade. Do you want bright crowns to put into your stocking, eh? "

They answered yes, but still with hesitation. The King proceeded:

" And you like good food, friends. A chicken in the pot on Sundays."

To this they did agree, and did so heartily; and two poor women cried: " Long live the King! "

" And my people shall have it," he replied. " Have you sons? " he asked. " How old are they? And what do they do? "

He was told that the lads did nothing at all, for trade was ruined.

" No, your sons learn nothing. Where are they? Bring them forth," said the King, and as the boys were of course among the wide-eyed crowd — for a boy will scarce move out of the street where he was born — the King promptly handed them over to the master tanner. In so doing, he laid his hands upon their heads and stroked their hair. At this, and this alone, the two mothers burst into tears. Other women did so likewise, and the scene would have been most edifying had not Rosny and the tanner once more begun to haggle over the prentice money. At last the King's servant paid it out to the old man, so briskly that the jewels on his fingers flashed. The King reminded the tanner that the boys must be provided with white bread and wine; if they were proved incompetent, half the prentice money would be forfeit; the remainder was to be brought back by the tanner to the Louvre.

The King's precision pleased the people even more than his generosity. They fell back as he emerged, and cleared the centre of the street without any pressure from the soldiers. Then, at that nicely calculated spot, a litter swung down the street, with plumes swaying from its painted and enamelled roof, and was set down outside the tanner's house. " Is this the rue de la Ferronnerie? " asked the lady inside it to one of the porters. Monsieur de Rosny was beside the litter in a trice, and he whispered urgently: " No more, madame, for God's sake. It was arranged that this encounter should be an accident."

" Forgive me. My poor head! I forget my part," said Gabrielle; and indeed she looked pale and weary. Monsieur de Rosny spoke her next words himself, to avoid any further mishap. " How marvellous to meet thus in a great city, as though there were but a single street! "

This was Henri's cue, and he duly picked it up. At the same moment the bells from a church near by began their peal of noon. " Madame," said the King, hat in hand, " I was just on my way home, to eat my dinner with you, like all good folk at this hour." Whereat the people murmured their applause at this reverence for their customs. As the porters were lifting the litter, she said hurriedly — regardless once more of her role:

" Sire, that is a strange sign on the house you have just left."

Henri looked round. On the wall above the archway hung the device of a crowned heart pierced with an arrow.

Henri recoiled, he could not tell why; he felt a chill shudder clutch at his heart. Crowned and pierced. Turning to Gabrielle, he said: " Madame, there is a heart for which you prepare the like fate; crowned and pierced."

It was said softly, for her ears alone. He touched the tips of her outstretched fingers and escorted the lady to her litter through the applauding murmurs of the crowd. Rosny followed, and his face was that of a proud and trusted servant of his King. Behind the mask he was laughing at the pantomime. She had to act it — but his opinion of the lovely d'Estrées none the less never altered; he thought her stupid. Still, he was quite ready to ignore her want of wit as well as her more dangerous aspects and for the present to make common cause with her. Those who have created a new realm must stand together, if the rising regime is to breed faith in the people and take firm shape within their minds.

And so they passed on, the litter, the porters, the King, his faithful servant — escorted by a few guards through the populous city of Paris, which not so long ago would not have let them pass unscathed. Rosny listened, street by street, to every word he could catch. Henri pretended to be wholly occupied with Gabrielle; but there was little that he missed. Someone in the crowd shouted: " Who is the lady? " And a rough soldier answered, as he thrust the man back: " The King's whore " — which was by no means meant as an estimation of the lady, he merely used the term he knew. But as the man was one of the King's own guard, the crowd laughed; and before that laughter could grow dangerous, the King laughed too. It could thus do no hurt.

It was the King's purpose that there should be no hurt done to any man. Change from disorder to the reign of law should come to pass almost unnoticed. He was, in fact, convinced in his own heart that in these days the future was at stake, both for himself and for his kingdom; and what was now allowed to get out of hand could never be overtaken. He had been King in name for five years now; which, he thought, explained his store of patience. A sense as of something imminent was on him, as though he were expected, everywhere and all the time, and salvation hung on every minute. Of this he gave no sign, either to the populace, or at his new-furnished court, or at his Privy Council. He was simple, gracious, and good humoured, and for that very reason he was to be laid low by a virulent fever — which was the price he always had to pay after his greatest efforts and the crises of his life, once met and mastered. His body was mixing that malady in secret, while there was yet no mark of it upon him — except for the eye of a meditative observer among the many who were then about his person. He might, at least after a while, have guessed. When His Majesty lay prostrate, at the inevitable moment, murmuring into his huddled blankets what only his sister and the First Chamberlain could hear — Huguenot psalms — then anyone might well have said: " Aha! " So it was. Many strange things were therewith made clear.

His usual companion, Rosny, had no leisure for such observation; and it is very sure that he did not see the approach of a fever from which the King had so long been free. He was wholly absorbed in economy and ballistics, apart from his concern for his own advancement. The Governorship of the city of Nantes was all that he had hitherto achieved. His kind but wary master was by no means disposed to put Protestants into the Council of Finance; the members, all Catholics, had regarded his appointment as the coming upheaval. Not so much from anxiety for the faith, but rather on account of their private exactions. Embezzlement of the revenue was, for the army of finance officials, even the very highest of them, both natural and permissible. But suddenly they became faintly conscious that, at King Henri's advent to power, these usages would be called in question, if not actually threatened.

The King took care that they were warned, first merely in no more than humorous fashion, on the casual occasions that were always ready to his hand. He still frequented the company of common folk, travelled here and there on his affairs, won his subjects' money at ball-play, and put it away in his hat. " It's safe there," he cried; " and no one shall ease me of one stiver, I'll keep it out of the hands of my finance officials." Which was promptly carried to their ears; but they had little fear of the King, who in a cheerful mood often said more than he meant; they scented danger from another quarter.

In a house known as the Arsenal sat one who checked all their incomings. So much they knew. From that secluded house came forth no word, save only the whisper of their spies. The man in his guarded cabinet drew up tall columns of figures, proving how prices had risen while Spanish gold was still pouring into the country. Wages had not followed them; and since the streams of pistoles had dried up, the high prices still remained, which meant a good life for the few who could afford it, but not for the many. Self-murder was common, and the roads became unsafe. This was usually explained by the growing contempt for religion, and open revolt against public order.

But the silent toiler in the house known as the Arsenal investigated other causes, the discovery of which was to many most unwelcome. They would gladly have haled him out of that house, which was but a hundred paces to the Seine; and it would be a deed well done to throw the man and all his calculations on a dark night into the river, so deep that he never reappeared. Unfortunately the expert upon trade and commerce was also an artilleryman of note. His memoranda for the King dealt with industry and agriculture, but also with the improvement of cannon. In the courtyard of his house were posted guns and their gunners, so that he was not easy of approach. He never rode out unguarded, especially when carrying his memoranda to the King. This meant an escort and some ceremony, but he was then seen at his best. Above all, he knew all about the worthy folk who lived on pickings from the State. It was but too clear that he meant to urge his master to the extremest measures.

Not, indeed, directly. No one understood Rosny, although they had all seen him at work. What was he, after all, and why these high pretensions? Anyone could blow up a tower with a huge charge of powder. When a governor was to be bought, he, as intermediary, acquired the city of Rouen without the use of much intelligence; but not the Grand Mastership of Artillery. That was held by the great lady's father, a nincompoop who grew crazier every day. Monsieur de Rosny, as was well known, had never forgiven that depredation. It was notorious that he was on the worst of terms with the great lady; at the bottom of his heart, always assuming that the man with the stone face had a bottom to his heart, he also hated his King, of that there was no doubt. Monsieur de Villeroy had said in confidence that it was so, and thus it was commonly repeated. Monsieur de Rosny hated the King; but he feared, and with justice, for his life if he betrayed him. On the other hand, he was excessively avaricious; promises, and a bribe that could be recovered from him after a premature demise, would, they thought, bring him over to their side. That was really his intention; these memoranda were merely meant for use by the rogue as blackmail.

Monsieur de Villeroy, who so grossly misunderstood Rosny, indeed thought the world was full of rogues; no experience could ever have taught him how it was possible to achieve anything except by roguery. Again and again he had betrayed the King to the League, and the League to the King — without the special arts and dissimulations that had enabled that fly-catching humanist Brissac to stage an elaborate scene and betray no matter whom, merely for the sake of the performance. That was not the method of Monsieur de Villeroy, a much clumsier villain. Henri, who was a good judge of men, at once appointed him to his Finance Council. There Villeroy practised his depredations, and, being fully occupied, did not lend himself to a darker scheme that was mooted in those days: to kidnap the King, remove him to one of the disaffected provinces, and put him up at auction. If the great rebels bid highest, he would die: if he himself did, he might keep his throne.

Henri, knowing all there was to know about Monsieur de Villeroy and his kind, left them to their self-enrichment, though that did not prevent him warning them, always in jesting, genial fashion, even though he no longer let the warning be carried to their ears, but gave it to them himself. Monsieur de Villeroy had a magnificent estate, to which the King paid a visit, unannounced and with just a modest escort of twelve or fifteen gentlemen, and no lackeys nor baggage; and they were hungry. The King went straight into the cowshed, where a worthy woman was at her milking. " O Sire — good master," said she.

" That am I for all who work honestly as you do," said he, and asked for a cup of milk. All the noblemen sat down with the

King at Villeroy's sumptuous table, and nothing was permitted to be served except milk. This did not perturb the wealthy Villeroy. The King was romantic, a lover of nature. " My entertainment would be too costly if we had anything but milk," said he after gulping it down, for he was a ready talker and liked to make the company laugh. Monsieur de Villeroy laughed with the rest. This buffoon was not yet the King who would catch him in the act. No need to think of Louis XI and his executioner. Rosny's columns of figures would merely bore this swaggering cavalryman. The artilleryman would pester the cavalryman into schemes of administration that would set both the people and their betters by the ears. They would certainly cost him his kingdom, as Villeroy announced later, with much approval, in the Finance Council. The new reign could not last; why shorten it? It would owe them all much money before the end.

One day Monsieur de Rosny rode to the Louvre. These were still the first days of the new reign, April weather; a shower of rain fell as he rode. Now, he treasured good clothes; he could not bear that his hat and ruff should be sodden by the rain; and he had in mind, too, the diamonds that adorned these objects, as well as their master's cloak. By the old bridge of Saint-Michel, when the rain was at its worst, Monsieur de Rosny pulled his horse into an archway; his people could well stay outside. There he witnessed what in those days was only too common: a man preparing to jump into the river. His movements were unmistakable; on the deserted bridge he was to be seen by anyone who looked out of the houses on this side and the farther side. But there were none, either because they feared the lashing rain or bcause the event was too familiar. The man took off his shoes, though there was little to take off, they were leathern rags. He flung threadbare doublet into the water, and emerged naked, a poor atomy that to Monsieur de Rosny seemed barely worth the saving. He would, however, have beckoned to his men, but in the meantime the creature had scrambled up and across the parapet and needed but to let himself drop; no one could have reached him in time.

But someone did. From the farther side — in that breathless moment it was hard to see whence — someone seemed to hurtle through the air, such leaps he took, grabbed the suicide's foot, and dragged him back. The man yelled as the rough stone ripped his skin. Bleeding, humiliated, and defiant he stood before his rescuer, raised his fist — then suddenly let it fall and sank to his knees. His rescuer was the King.

Rosny's light-blue eyes were opened wide at this performance. It had annoyed him, for he felt that he should not have been the sole spectator, the river-banks should not have been deserted. A vast assemblage was the proper audience for the rescue of a suicide by his King. Monsieur de Rosny was convinced, or nearly so, that the parts here played had been duly assigned, though the scene had been less well organized than that in the tanner's shop some while before. Moreover the bad weather had driven the public away. However, a few people collected, as the worst of the storm had passed, and there was now no more than a drizzle. Monsieur de Rosny watched the King take off his cloak — no doubt to wrap round the shoulders of the naked man.

Monsieur de Rosny, glancing round him, assured himself that this gesture at least had not gone unremarked; he then felt it to be time that he should take his own place in the transaction. He rode on to the bridge and obsequiously offered his horse to the King; he would never otherwise have thus offered it to the King, and with but an ill grace to Saint Martin, had he known him. Henri burst out laughing and said: " Look at the cloak; is it any better than the doublet that went down-stream? Give the fellow some money. If I have no work for him, I must see he does not starve. Send one of your people with him to the hospital, to make sure they take him in."

This said, he mounted. The scene had been brief, but every word had told. An onlooker that was not stirred must indeed be narrow of heart and mind. The rescued man bowed courteously and said, in a voice that rang pleasantly upon the ear: " Sire, I must die. The like of me are not worth maintaining by Your Majesty, when there's no work in the cloth or leather trades, nor even in the fields. I have been a student of theology, so I shall be able to report in the next world that our King Henri loves and means to help his people."

Therewith he walked off with the soldier, and for the spectators, who had in the meantime swelled into a crowd, he who stood so near to the next world was now the most important personage. The King, but for his rank, had taken second place and now scarce touched the people's hearts. When he put his horse to a trot, they fell back to avoid the scattering slush, but with an air of blank indifference on their faces. So he rode off at an even brisker trot, on Monsieur de Rosny's dapple-grey, with its master half a length behind him on the dismounted soldier's charger. The little cavalcade of six or seven horsemen soon reached the Louvre without attracting much attention. Rosny asked for an audience, and Henri led him into a great empty room looking out on the river and open to the wind and sun, the April sun, now shining in all its radiance.

"This," said Henri, as he paced up and down, "shall be left empty until I get my furnishings from my castle in Pau; I will live with no others. They are the finest I have ever seen in any castle of this kingdom."

Rosny, limited as was the extent of his knowledge, understood, or thought he did. His master wanted to relate his present great position with the much lighter burden of days now past. Did he need encouragement? Was the furniture inherited from his mother's House intended as a visible reminder of his high ascent?

"Sire," said that faithful servant, "all know that a Prince of the Blood is now in power. A King must not go decked with chains and rings like a nobleman without office or honour. But never leave the Louvre without the escort of a few persons who look as I do! Then, if need be, you may wear an old cloak, to bestow it on the naked."

Henri was bewildered by these words, not because they were too boldly spoken, but the intention behind them was mistaken. He had not in fact gone unescorted to the Saint-Michel bridge to rescue a would-be suicide who was waiting for that purpose. By way of answer, he related an experience.

"I was riding alone yesterday along the road to Saint-Germain.

I wanted to see for myself whether work in the fields had ceased, and whether oppression had driven my peasants to highway robbery. I found that it was so, and I was stopped by thieves. Their leader was no peasant, but an apothecary. I asked him whether he was driving his trade on the highway and lying in wait for travellers to dose them with purges. The men burst out laughing, and I almost had them. After I had turned my pockets inside out, they let me go my way."

Whatever may have been Rosny's feeling — whether of horror, indignation, or alarm — he remained quite unruffled. But his silence lasted just too long. When the King, who was still pacing to and fro, swung round and eyed him, it was in something of a flurry that Rosny produced his memorandum.

Henri stood rigid, and there was a strange expression on his face as he looked at the parchments, from which Rosny read and read. When he came to the columns of figures, Henri traced them downwards with his finger — not solely that his eyes and upturned brows might follow them. At last they reached the six thousand workless clothmakers. "You have the total right," said Henri; and as Rosny stopped, tongue-tied:

" It was revealed to me by a man on the Saint-Michel bridge — a theology student, who in his need became a clothmaker, but there fared even worse, for six thousand of them were already starving. The Paris dye-works used to put out six hundred thousand lengths of cloth every year; now they produce no more than a hundred thousand. Have you the figures, Rosny? Ah, here they are. You reckon readily. And I have ready ears, especially when a student, who could get no work as a clothmaker, told me what he knew about this world before taking his plunge into the next. I and you, my friend, are two useful workmen. Our task is to discover how to put these matters right."

" Your Majesty knows," said Rosny, but there was nothing of the courtier in his tone or attitude. " You have a knowledge of affairs, the like of which I cannot boast." However, he did not deter him from setting forth his schemes, first of all in regard to tillage. He insisted that the roads must be cleared of robbers.

" Yes, I assured my apothecary that it would be done."

"Sire, as I have already remarked, what I propose is nothing new. Robbers are also poachers. A few must be hanged as a warning to the peasantry, who kill game on the royal domains."

"And how shall I deal with the noblemen, Monsieur de Rosny, whose horses and hounds trample the peasants' crops?" asked Henri, and cocked his head aside as he waited for the answer.

"Sire, the chase is an ancient privilege of the nobility. Your country noblemen have few others, and they have to provide you with officers."

"We must be just," said Henri; by which he might have been referring to either side. Then, with head erect, he added sternly: "The peasants are ground down under their burdens."

"Look," was Rosny's sole reply; he turned over some sheets and handed one to the King. Henri paled. "I had no clear notion of this," he murmured. "I am shocked."

"Sire, it is nothing new. But it is a new thing for the country to be ruled by a King who is both wise and bold. What he now must do he was not afraid to do in his little kingdom of Navarre in days gone by; and there was war in those days."

"There shall be no more war," said Henri firmly. "I'll make no war upon my subjects. I would liefer buy my provinces, if I had to go begging in England and in Holland. Rouen and Paris cost me money — you know how much, and whether I could have gone on paying in such fashion."

"To be sure" — Rosny nodded; he glanced round the barren room, which made their enterprise seem all the more doubtful and precarious.

Henri threw all misgivings aside. "Whatever may be before us, the burdens on the peasants must be relieved by one third."

Without a word the man of figures pointed to the scheme he had prepared, reducing the taxes on the peasants step by step. Henri read it, and said: "Not quite a third. But scaled down from year to year. I shall not win my rustics' hearts with that."

Yet one more page seemed then to set itself before his eyes. Here were set forth the local dues, which cut one province off from another and strangled trade. The figures here were the most closely packed. Henri slapped his thigh.

"Here is what I did not know. I'll see to it. Monsieur de Rosny, you are the man for me."

These last words were overheard. The door opened, and the beloved lady entered; the faithful servant was annoyed, though he bowed profoundly. But Henri hastened to greet her. His grave and careworn look vanished in a moment, and he led her ceremoniously into the room. "Dear lady," said he, "you were never more welcome."

"Sire, Monsieur de Rosny is the man you need," she repeated. Her writhen smile struck at his heart, though it brought him no less deep a joy.

"He has weighty business with you. I did but want to see your face."

Thereat he replied with gallantry: "Madame, when you appear, every man forgets his business, even Monsieur de Rosny."

"Sire," cried Monsieur de Rosny, "I was about to boast as much, had you given me time. A chair for Madame!" he cried, and promptly fetched one himself. As he came back, he paused, and half turned to go. The King had bent one knee, on the other he had set his lady's foot and was caressing it. But the astute Rosny realized that of this, too, his approval was desired. He placed the chair, and Gabrielle sat down. The King stood, holding her outstretched hand. And, as though nothing had passed, he proceeded:

"That is what I did not know, Monsieur de Rosny. There can be no steady price for corn so long as the provinces are divided by these tolls. I'll abolish them. In one province there's starvation, and in the next the farmer cannot sell his surplus. I'll abolish them all. It is my will that goods should be carried free throughout my kingdom."

Rosny opened his mouth, but Henri held up a hand. "I know; how are they to be carried? you would say. I'll see to that also. On the highroads and the byroads carriers shall ply from dawn till dusk, with a change of horses every twelve or fifteen miles."

He tapped the cover of the document, which Rosny had closed, as though it were now no longer needed.

" It stands written there," said he heartily.

" Sire, it does, but on a later page, which you have not yet read. Your mind is winged; by clerk's pen crawls."

" What do you think of us, madame? " asked Henri. Gabrielle laid a finger of her lovely hand against her cheek and was silent.

" There's work here for ten years. God knows whether we shall see the end of it," said he, and to the surprise of the other two, he crossed himself. " But we will make a start," he cried cheerfully. " This very day, if we had the first few thousand crowns needed."

" Sire, the condition of your finances can be mended," said Monsieur de Rosny in a tone of calm assurance. Henri and Gabrielle both waited for him to go on.

" If Your Majesty has no money, nor even a sufficiency of shirts, the reason lies in the general disorder and irregularity of every sort, incessant waste and embezzlement, and the senseless squandering of revenue." As he continued, his manner gradually lost its wonted calm. " These abuses have slowly wrecked the commerce of your kingdom, and the administration of your Treasury; they have gone from petty fraud, to the shameless bestowal of the public revenues on powerful persons, whom I can name, and mean to name, and they are here explicitly written down." He rapped the cover of his document. " And I will not rest until they have paid the penalty."

Here Gabrielle as well as Henri observed his eyes, which had grown dark and stormy. The oddly neat, fresh colouring of his face was now suffused by an uprush of emotion that they had never seen in him before. This was a Rosny whom they did not know, but who might well be the real man. Fear came upon Gabrielle; from this Rosny she could expect no forgiveness. Henri was amazed as he eyed his faithful servant. He realized, as he had never done before, the full force of loyalty and faith, and understood that in this human heart they commanded no casual allegiance. They were in fact a passion. The stone knight whom

Henri had taken down from the façade of a cathedral now had come to life, and in good earnest. Why, the man was near to raving. This prodigious honesty might cost him his life; that was his own affair. But, thought Henri, it might do his King more damage than all the robbers put together. Beware the man of stone!

"My friend," said Henri, "I am familiar with your loyalty and faith, more so than with all your calculations, and I shall make great use of them in my own and my kingdom's service. You have a task that will last you all the days of your life. You will never get as much money from my Treasury as sticks and stays there."

"I shall," said Rosny respectfully, now quite calm again; he had recovered his unclouded eyes and girlish cheeks.

"How?"

"I'll stake my head on it."

He explained no further, but the other two believed him.

"Very well," said Henri. "What have you first in mind, and at whom to you mean to strike."

"There are many," said Rosny, "and just those who believe themselves justified in what they do; the worst abuses are committed in the name of justice. The salt tax is farmed out. Scarce a quarter of it reaches the Treasury. All the rest goes to enrich a few lords and ladies. They have divided the spoils, which even so are not fairly shared. Sire, believe me or not, one of them is the Intendant General of your Finances, Monsieur d'O."

"Just an O, and nothing more," said Henri, with an enigmatic smile and a glance at Gabrielle. "An old young man, all belly, or rather he was all belly. It will have been drained dry by now."

"Have you not heard, Monsieur de Rosny?" said Gabrielle. "He is dying."

No; this was news to the man of the Arsenal. His days were spent in calculations. But he did not linger over his surprise, he promptly added:

"Let us sequestrate his property the moment he is dead. When such men die, their satellites desert them."

"That will be considered," said Henri, who was resolved to

consider it for some while. "Take care, Monsieur de Rosny,
that we be not too eager to do the work of others, and Death's
work too."

At this the carven statue from the cathedral, the man from
the Arsenal, said no more. Henri let the silence endure. It was
Gabrielle's crystal tones that broke it.

" Sire," said Gabrielle d'Estrées, " I ask a favour. In place of
him about to die, appoint Monsieur de Rosny."

She said no more, but waited. Monsieur de Rosny was not
her friend, as she knew to her regret. But the King had called
him his own man; and at the beginning of the new regime those
who bore the weight of it must stand together. They were as
yet but three, the three in that bare room. The woman's eyes
said plainly to the servant of the King: " We need each other.
Help me, as I'll help you."

Rosny, quite unmoved, thought: " Nonsense! You, my pretty
lady, will never become Queen. But I shall work and achieve
my purpose, however many years ahead."

Henri uttered nothing — but said a great deal. He took his
beloved lady's hand and kissed it.

Fever

The day began devoutly. Henri heard Mass in a church behind the Louvre, the bell of which boomed louder than any in
Paris. It had boomed bravely once, when Admiral Coligny —
but enough! The King was praying earnestly, when it was whispered to him that Cardinal Pellevé was dead. He had been
President of the Estates Assembly and very active in the cause of
Spain. Since the King had seized power he had lain prostrate
in a frenzy; he had written: " The man must be trapped and
taken like a beast! " And now he was dead. Before the King
left the church, he commanded that prayers should be offered
for the Cardinal. He was near to adding: " And for the soul of
the Lord Ad— " But not even in his mind did he finish that
name.

On the short journey back, his gentlemen took the freedom to reproach him with his mildness and indulgence. A man should take vengeance on his enemies; it was commonly expected, and he who failed to avenge himself was observed, and held in slight esteem. The King had banished a hundred and forty persons, some from the kingdom, but many only from the capital. Not a single execution — how could he thus inspire respect or fear? Monsieur de Turenne, a powerful Protestant and probable heir to the Dukedom of Bourbon, a border domain in the east, warned Henri earnestly against traitors; and with good reason, for he himself was later to betray the King, with several others. Henri answered him, and his Catholics also:

" If you, and all your like, repeated your Paternoster honestly every day, you would not speak so. I confess that all my victories come from God; I do not deserve them; but as He forgives me, so must I forgive the errors of my people, and be more gracious and forbearing to them than before."

The day began devoutly. Moreover, it was a Sunday, bright with the first sunshine of spring. All work had ceased, except only in the Arsenal. Henri sent to his cousin the Duchess of Montpensier to announce that he would wait upon her. It was then eight o'clock; he would come at ten. Not that his intention had at first been wholly edifying. He had, at times, thought of the Fury of the League with a rather malicious amusement; she too was probably crying out that he ought to be trapped like a beast. But she confined her tirades to her house. She could no longer display herself upon her balcony to an admiring horde and incite them to murder the King. She could not use her charms to tempt a villainous little monk to stab the King in the belly. Henri had not forgotten her machinations against the late King.

He foresaw that his visit would be unpopular, and the gentlemen who were to escort him were not informed until the last moment. The King himself was, in fact, a little uneasy; his friend the late King would have shuddered at such an encounter. However, he thought it both charitable and wise to visit the Fury. The House of Guise would never now ascend the throne, and should therefore, like the rest of his subjects, be treated with indulgence and conciliation. But what drew him irresistibly was his mood of malicious amusement. The former Fury in her impotence, and terrified, of course, although on the eve of his visit he had conveyed to her that there was nothing to fear, must indeed be a comical spectacle. This decided him to go, and on that very day. He would give himself a Sunday entertainment, but he meant it should be edifying.

The Duchess, though Henri did not know, had in the meantime become half-witted — not openly so, not before the world, nor to those who still frequented her. For them she was the great lady she had always been; but even before the King entered Paris, there were few who were willing to risk suspicion by consorting with her, and since then none came at all. They disavowed the new master's enemy and would not be found in her company when she was arrested, which, sooner or later, was to be expected. Some snatched at their victims, others savoured their revenge. No, only those in high favour with the new regime could permit themselves such company.

When the Duchess of Montpensier was told that the King would be with her at ten o'clock, the hour was half past eight. The surprising message had been some time on the way. Madame de Montpensier promptly summoned Madame de Nemours, on whom she felt she could depend. Madame de Nemours was in high favour, she was one of the ladies in whom the King took special pride. Old Catherine de Medici used to call her little prisoner King Wren. Meantime he had grown so great that he had gathered round himself a court of noble ladies. He stood in sore need of them, thought his enemy. He had no queen, and his mistress scorned him and betrayed him. The upstart would not dare to lay a hand on Madame de Nemours, who would come and give her countenance. Nor, thought the Duchess, would he in fact dare to lay hands upon her either.

This was her last lucid thought. In her dressing-room she suddenly shrieked for Ambroise Paré, the physician, long since dead. He had once bled her when she lay unconscious for three hours in a frenzy of a hatred that was not wholly hatred and racked her for that reason. " Navarre " — for so she called the King, that she

might not call him " France," while her dazed emotions cried
out " Henri " — had had the Prior of her little monk torn to
pieces by horses, thus avenging the King his predecessor. " Is he
there? " she had asked the surgeon when she wakened; she was
still bemused, but there was that in her tone, and in her face,
that made the old man recoil. So now her women cowered in the
corners of the room as she leapt up and called upon the dead.

Madame de Montpensier's madness was not quite out of her
control. She did not commonly confide either in a doctor or in
her women. She was alone and desolate; the Duke, being in the
King's service, avoided her; and the tale of her years was what
none could guess. But the man who could stir her to the frenzy
that so warmed her heart was approaching her that day. She
dashed about the room, her raven locks, now flecked with white,
flying behind her, and her hands clutched to her bared breasts.
She was tall, well set, and strong. She paused for an instant at
one corner; the woman cowering there dropped feebly to the
floor; all round the room these shivering creatures peered out
from beneath the furniture, as though at a storm from hell, waiting all the while like damned souls.

The distracted Fury conjured up the dead, whom in her madness she could now see about her: the monk, the Prior, both of
them bound upon staves for all eternity, while wild horses tore
their limbs asunder. And in her crazy joy she hailed them:
" Henri," which roused her to yet more frightful paroxysms.
She suffered the torments she inflicted, and without a tremor
she submitted to her own dismemberment, as often comes to
pass in dreams; though this was a waking dream. When the
vision had passed, she found herself on a chair again, exhausted,
shivering with cold, and pleading to be stabbed through the
heart, wailing the name of him who was to deal that blow. Her
women brought her smelling-salts; and then she remembered
that she had dreamed what she had often dreamed before. The
dream of the dreamer's violent execution is often repeated. Of
what came with it and lay behind it she wisely made no mention.

She bade her women dress her hair, and was so impatient that
she struck one of them who was not deft enough. A page who

stood waiting at the door ran off in terror; but the Duchess had noticed him and so learned that Madame de Nemours had arrived. " Enough," said she; " no more paint. I would not appear younger than my years." Her years should be written on her face; it was her best safeguard, not only against imprisonment, but probably against fresh outbreaks. On her way down, she realized that she must take Madame de Nemours into her confidence if she were to be forearmed. In fact she began by telling her the dream of her execution, which had returned to her that very day.

Madame de Nemours was curious, especially because Madame de Montpensier seemed to her much broken down of late. She inquired the obscurer details of the dream and whether the King played a part in it. This the Duchess obstinately denied, but her friend, looking into her eyes, did not believe a word. " He dies with you, when you dream. Tell him so. He believes in omens, and for his own sake he will want you to live a long while." But she thought how horrible it was that this woman should still have her mind set on murder, being herself in terror for her life. The King must be warned. At that moment the clock struck ten, and in the anteroom, two rooms away, they could hear his noblemen's arrival.

There the King left them behind, and hastened on alone, past the tall windows, in a shimmer of sunlight; and his reversed reflection moved with him along the floor. There at the far end of the rooms sat the two women facing him; he laid one hand on his hip and thrust his hat back with the other, to get a better view of them. His sleeves as well as his trunk-hose were widely puffed at the tops, which gave him a slim appearance. Shoulders thrown back, and a ripple of muscle as he walked — here was a sturdy, almost boyish figure; he entered with confident air and greeted his kinswoman as though he had returned from a brief absence. Before the ladies could rise, he had sat down beside them, and was soon deep in cheerful talk. There was a flicker of irony in the corners of his eyes; it was indeed the plainest mark of age about him, for there was sadness in that irony.

He asked solicitously if the ladies were very surprised to see him in Paris, and further whether they had been robbed of any possessions. No? They would, indeed, learn from any merchant that everyone had paid for what he had, even the rabble of camp-followers who had come in with the soldiery. " What say you to that, cousin? "

" Sire," Madame de Montpensier replied, "you are a great and gracious King." (" And this man kills me in my dreams," she thought, with disillusion in her heart, promising herself that she would never dream again.) He thought she was afraid, and teased her a little. Did she really pray for vengeance on Monsieur de Brissac, for surrendering the capital? Whereat she assured him that she wished that it had been surrendered by her own brother Mayenne. He laughed, and said he would have had to wait too long for that.

In all this interplay of talk she felt that power was passing into her, and her pride rose up against him the more familiar he became. Either he knew nothing of what a woman does and of what she dreams — he was acquainted only with acts of State, all unworthy of the passion that she had squandered, and regretted — or he was bent on her destruction, and he must not be suffered to tease her any more. " Sire," said she coldly, " a conqueror never fulfils expectations."

He did not stop to think. " Otherwise a scaffold would stand before every house," he cried, and was quite taken aback by his own vehemence.

The Duchess sank back upon her chair with eyes closed. Henri stepped back a pace, then farther, and would have taken his leave. Madame de Nemours laid a hand upon his arm. " Can you not see that she is old and ill? " she whispered. Suddenly she seized his hand.

" But you are pale and your hand is burning. You yourself are not well either."

" I am not well," he repeated. " But I can never bring myself to remember that I have enemies elsewhere than on the battle-field."

Madame de Nemours said in a motherly tone, like a matron admiring an athlete: " It is your enemies that have made you great."

Then he swore his own particular oath that none could understand. " If every man," he cried, " would examine his own heart, he would there find enough to fight. Let me be left to my own task, I have no leisure to be always on the watch for murderers."

But he bethought him that he had not come to talk like this. He raised a shaking hand to his temple and looked at Madame de Montpensier; she had recovered from her faintness, and her great black eyes were set on him. " Dear cousin," Henri began in a familiar tone, " I am feverish and would beg for a little refreshment. Just a spoonful of conserve."

The Duchess rose without a word and walked to the door. He tried to stop her. " Sire," said Madame de Nemours, " she will not return, she will send her excuses."

But she did return, accompanied by a lackey bearing a dish of apricots; dipped a spoon into it and raised it to her mouth. Henri gripped her hand. " Aunt, pray be careful! " In his alarm he called her Aunt, which in fact she was.

" What? " she answered. " Have I not done enough to be suspected? "

" No one suspects you," said he, swallowing a mouthful. Madame de Nemours stumbled against him in an effort to upset the dish. She thought the fruit might have been poisoned, and paled as she watched the King gulp it down. He wondered if the Fury had put anything into it. Well, she had been ready to take some herself. Too late now. He was in no mood to be afraid. And he went on eating.

" Ah! " said Madame de Montpensier abruptly, " I see why you have such faithful servants." The words were followed by a choking sob. Henri, feeling more cheerful, bade farewell to the two ladies; they had given him a warm hour; and he invited his cousin to the Louvre. When he made his solemn entry into his capital, she must be present. Madame de Nemours asked him when that would be. " When my dear lady has presented me with a son," he said over his shoulder. His face was strangely flushed.

One of the ladies said to the other: " The child is really his."

" There was doubt about it," observed the other.

At midday he scarcely ate, which was quite against his habit; and then he prepared to ride out. Bellegarde was to accompany him, and, among others, a Monsieur de Lionne, handsome, young, and a general favourite for his graceful manners. Monsieur de Lionne possessed the art of so captivating people that they were delighted with themselves, especially women. They felt how much understanding and charm he lavished on them, not merely to give them pleasure, but to make them happy. A truly gallant gentleman, he was never known to do anyone a hurt.

Henri was glad of his company, mainly because he wanted the Grand Master of the Horse, his old crony Feuillemorte, to realize at every turn that there were others more popular than he and that his best time would soon be past. The fact was that Henri still feared his rival in the favours of the charming Gabrielle — despite her devotion, which he did not wholly trust, and her condition, which only made her the more feminine.

They rode through the village of Boulogne; the gentlemen had broken off buds of lilac blossom and, leaning down from their saddles, bestowed them on the village maids, who laughed but refused to be lifted on to the horses. Only one took the spray of unopened blossom, laughed no more, and climbed up beside Monsieur de Lionne. " Feuillemorte! " cried Henri. " See what a handsome man can do before his skin turns yellow! "

" Sire, I have long since forgotten those days," said Bellegarde as they rode out into the open countryside. Here stood a cluster of straw-thatched huts; and before one of them sat a Sunday assemblage of rustics, gathered round a long table of two planks on three upright posts. Glasses were empty, but voices were raised. They were singing, nor did they stop when the gentlemen dismounted. " Hey, fellows! " shouted the King's Grand Master of the Horse. " Come and walk our horses up and down."

They looked round, and several answered gruffly. " We are at home here," said one.

And another: " Until your tax-collectors take the roofs from off our heads."

The King sat unobserved among the group. He swore his own particular oath, which was known about the countryside; some of them looked at him. " Don't let them," he cried, " or they'll have my own roof off me in the end." All were silent; they clasped their gnarled hands together, fist in palm, and their backs and shoulders were the very expression of dumb endurance. Beneath the stained sheepskins of the older men could be seen the shapes of bodies marred by years and years of cramping, straining toil and a grinding monotony of attitude and movement.

Those who had not turned their heads towards the King peered at him now and again from the corners of their eyes and then looked down at their restless hands. And all these rolling eyes and wagging heads gave them the air of a collection of grotesques, or visions of a fevered dream. The King stood up and sought shade under a walnut-tree. Several of his noblemen, among them Monsieur de Bellegarde, joined him, thinking the situation looked a little menacing. Monsieur de Lionne saved it, if indeed it needed to be saved.

He came out of a copse near by in the company of the pretty girl who had climbed on to his horse. They had been together in the copse, so much was plain; but Monsieur de Lionne was leading the young peasant girl by her lifted fingers, as though she had been a lady of the court; and thus, with a meaning smile on both their faces, they approached the table and the youngest man of the assemblage. This youth was still as straight and sturdy as any nobleman, though without the litheness that comes from sword- and ball-play; his movements were heavier and a little awkward. His defects appeared when he made a dash at Monsieur de Lionne, who, with a sudden display of iron strength, stopped him without an effort. But he did so with perfect gracefulness and courtesy. He doffed his hat to the peasant lad, who had tumbled backwards on to the bench, and said he had the honour to bring him back his damsel, for he could not bear that any woman should risk an unpleasant encounter on the highway.

All the rustics nodded approval. To the young man, who was

still showing his teeth with rage, Monsieur de Lionne suggested a friendly bout of fisticuffs, and started some preliminary sparring in the air, with a quite irresistible display of gaiety and good humour. This raised a round of laughter; and Monsieur de Lionne improved the occasion by embracing the young peasant, which the lad suffered him to do. It was only his awkwardness that prevented him from doing what was expected and returning the embrace.

Said Henri to his Grand Master of the Horse: " Feuillemorte, in spite of all I like you best. That is the first quite blameless man I have ever seen. And as I look at him, I feel afraid."

A peasant, who seemed well on in years, dragged his stiff limbs from the bench and stood up to address the King. His shoulders were bowed, his arms and his gnarled hands hung down before him, and he had the gloomy visage of a man of sixty who had never been glad to be alive. " How old are you? " said the King to the peasant.

"Lord," replied the man, " I asked one of your people how old you were; we are of like age exactly."

"In another matter too we are alike," said the King. " The toil and trouble of our lives is written on our faces."

The peasant was silent, and blinked before he answered: " That is true."

He pondered, was about to speak, but paused. The King gave him time; with wide eyes and brows uplifted he waited.

"Follow me, Sire," said the peasant. " Only as far as the brook."

Monsieur de Bellegarde stepped after them, but at a sign from the King he stopped; Henri walked on alone. The peasant led him to a place on the bank where the stream was smooth as a mirror. The King bent down; his face was burning and he longed to plunge it into the water. Meantime it began to swell, and seemed to be swelling visibly in the reflection, though the King guessed that this was an illusion and that the inflammation had attacked him some while before. Upon the peasant's face there was now a deep and meaning look. " Sire," he said, " ride back at once to your castle. You shall live or die as God may decide."

" Better for me and for you that I should live," said Henri, with an effort at a laugh. But his face remained rigid; and of all the experiences of the day that was the worst. At the same moment a sound of snoring came upon his ears, as of a man snoring from a full belly, which annoyed the King yet more. " What is it? "

" That," explained the peasant, " is the man who eats for six."

Henri did not understand. For the first time he saw a cheerful smile upon the peasant's face. " What! " said he. " You are glad of a man who eats for six, when you yourself have not enough for one? "

By way of answer the man pointed to a grassy mound; behind it rose and fell a mighty belly. The peasant strode across and shook the snorer. " Hey! " he cried. " Hey, you old glutton! Up! The King wants to look at you! "

It was some time before the man appeared. He was a monstrous sight, with vast limbs and a face like an ogre's. There was scarce an inch of forehead between the thick brows and the skull. Mouth and cheeks held space for pounds and pounds of food, and the eyes were closed with fat. The great mass of flesh quivered with lethargy.

" Is it true? " asked the King. " Can you eat for six? " The reply was a grunt.

" He can," said the peasant. " He has devoured all that he possessed, and now we keep him in food. He will eat for six at once. Come, gossip, show the King what you can do."

The mass set itself in motion, and the grassy sward shook under his mighty strides. The peasants at the long table received him joyfully; some of them even started singing again. But when they heard that the man was ready to eat for six once more, they hurried away to collect such provisions as they had in their huts. In a trice the long planks were loaded with hams and bacon and eggs, and the empty glasses vanished behind capacious jugs. Thereupon the gaunt and toilworn figures gathered round the mass of flesh and thrust him into place at the table. But at a sign from the King the gentlemen drove the boors away, and Henri faced the glutton.

"And so you devour my peasants. You can eat for six, they say. Do you also work for six?"

The glutton grunted out that he certainly worked, so far as his age and strength permitted. Digestion was a heavy but needful task for a man who had to eat for six.

The King made another sign, and several of his gentlemen set about the mountain of flesh with their riding whips and lashed him round and round that village green. And he could run when he had to, the great creature. The peasants yelled with laughter, but the King was grimly earnest. His face now deeply flushed and swollen, he told them angrily that his kingdom did not suffice to fill the bellies of such guzzlers. "If I had many such as you," he shouted to the great creature, as he lumbered past under a shower of blows, "I would hang you all. Such ruffians would soon starve my kingdom out."

In his fury a sudden chill came upon him; he began to shiver, which he thought must be due to the rising mist. Before he mounted, he bade the peasants eat the table clear themselves; but he knew by their faces that they would do nothing of the kind. They would give all they grudged themselves to that devouring monster, who was their pride. The King spurred his horse and galloped off. "Do you feel cold, Feuillemorte?"

"Sire, our feet are numbed by the wet grass."

Most of the gentlemen could not catch their horses at once, and it was not until some while after the King and the Grand Master of the Horse that they rode off. Last of all was Monsieur de Lionne. He waited until all the others had gone. From the cover of the copse he peered round at the peasants; they were still agape at the King's suggestion that they should eat the food themselves. Monsieur de Lionne lifted the same girl on to his saddle again, and he led his horse for a while, that it might step lightly and with scarce a sound.

Once back in the Louvre, Henri had to admit that he was ill. His vision was blurred, and he knew that he would ramble if he tried to talk. So he took to his bed, the doctors did what was needful, and the strain and agitation passed over into lethargy.

When it was night, Bellegarde hurried into the room and blurted out frantically:

" Sire! Monsieur de Lionne — "

" A much too blameless man," whispered Henri. " He makes me afraid."

" With justice, Sire. A little way off the highroad he slit a girl's belly and put his feet into the open body to warm them."

" A fit end to such a day," muttered Henri. He had no longer strength to express his indignation. And he added with an effort:

" Let him be handed over to my magistrates and publicly quartered."

" Sire! A nobleman! " cried Bellegarde, somewhat over-loudly for a sick-chamber, raising his hands in horror.

" Are you not one? " said Henri in a toneless voice, but with wide-open eyes. Bellegarde could not face them and vanished in the silence.

A little later the sick man received a visit from his sister, Madame Catherine de Bourbon. She had been roused, as the doctors had reported that her brother's condition was dangerous. When she saw his face, she burst into tears, for he did not know her. But the First Chamberlain, Monsieur d'Armagnac, pointed at his master from the foot end of the bed; Henri's lips were moving. She bent down, guessed rather than heard, and softly joined in the psalm. The day ended as it had begun, devoutly.

The Love of a Nation

The malady was mastered much more quickly than had been foreseen — in seven and a half days, in fact — for it had been no more than the body's token to the spirit that a turning-point had come and an hour of destiny was at hand. Then, after a month in which to collect his strength, Henri had to take the field again at once. A Spanish army had marched out of the Low Countries, this time under the command of Count Mansfeld; but the real leader of these invasions was still Mayenne, of the House of Guise, and he had upon his side most of those who thought as he did. The King was in Paris; and what struck the mind of everyone was the fact that he was in possession of his capital. City and province, one after another, submitted simply on that account, and many governors did so for cash down. Remained the great nobles, who made too much profit out of the weakness of the realm and the distresses of the King and of his people. They were not to be overborne. To their great content the King was still excluded from communion. Until the Pope recognized him, which was not likely to be soon, resistance to him was a work of merit.

The King laid siege to the fortress of Laon, and at the same time he fought pitched battles against the invading army sent by that now tainted monarch Don Philip. They came, and would come again, until ruin overtook them at last. Courage, then! Never had Henri showed himself so vigorous. Amid all his toils and perils he wrote the liveliest letters to the charming Gabrielle, such as she had never had from him before. She even became suspicious that he loved her just as fondly from a distance; and she grew jealous of his yearning for her, and of her pictured presentation in his heart. The son, whose birth was imminent, had already been christened Cæsar, for he was a child of war, and indeed of other turbulent events. His father, in his camp, already bore him in his arms, while his mother was still awaiting her hour. These letters brought him so vividly before her that no thought of disaster so much as entered her mind. Thus she bore him his son, Cæsar.

When the good news reached him — it was a lovely day in June — Henri had been clambering all night over the hills round Laon, looking for a place whence he could attack the fortress; he washed the mire from his hands and feet and rode to his farm in the forest. This he had known from boyhood; it was one of the outlying domains belonging to his little native land, Navarre. There, in days gone by, he had eaten strawberries and cream, and he wanted to savour them again, for he carried a boy's happiness in his heart. Cæsar — Cæsar — his heart leapt for joy.

After his midday rest he had, as in boyhood, climbed a plum-tree, and there they found him. Not far away other kinds of plums were flying through the air. Enemy cavalry had been

sighted and might well set a most distasteful dish before him.
To horse — to horse! When he arrived before Laon, he was just
in time to see his old comrade Marshal Biron fall. There he lay;
a lean and rugged figure he had always been, but now flaccid and
defenceless, for death was very near. Henri had an unerring eye
for it when a soldier fell; he knew at once if the last enemy was
to be repelled or not. He lifted Biron's head and shoulders from
the earth that was so soon to cover him. They looked each other
in the eyes, in a last grave salutation of farewell. ("We were
enemies; hence the bond between us since that day. Do not
forget me; you cannot forget me." "Nor you, in the place
whither you are to be called." "No; we shall not see each other
more; for with what should we see, now that these eyes are
crumbling into dust?") Henri watched them intently until they
stiffened and broke.

On one and the same day he had acquired Cæsar and lost
Biron. Grievous were the turns and changes of life, which must
be withstood and endured. The sons must now come forth into
their fathers' places and bring their master aid and comfort.
Biron had left a son with the army; the King sent for him.

"Marshal Biron," said he to the son — from which the latter
grasped that he was to take his father's place. He had expected
no less, though he thanked the King obsequiously; and at the
sight of Henri's tears, he burst into assiduous lamentations. Tall
and muscular he was, rugged like his father, but not lean. The
King was to learn his loyalty later on. At the moment he was
weeping in a fashion that scarce befitted a strong man of thirty-
three — until the King, who began to be disgusted, enlarged on
his future duties as Marshal of France. Thereupon Biron the
younger promptly came down to business. He supported his
claims with every reason that he could readily conceive. "You
have enemies," he bade the King reflect; "I am strong enough
to crush a man to death. What if I were against you! Sire, you
may well speak of good fortune!" Were these the words of a
rough soldier? Or was the soldier craftier than he seemed?

To the King they expressed no more than the pride of a hearty
nature in its fullness of blood and body. When Biron went on

to speak of his powerful kindred, the King indeed conceived this
as a warning. It was his mission and his purpose to break up the
great families and factions and strip them of their power, in the
interest of the people and the kingdom; though this was not
known to Biron the younger. Henri looked at him; the bullet
head with its thatch of bristly hair reminded him of the peasant
that ate for six, an acquaintance that he had made while his fever
was upon him; but, despite its dark brutality, it was the head of
a nobleman, and the son of an old comrade. Henri's heart went
out to the father as he embraced the son and promised him all
he asked.

In July the fortress of Laon submitted to the King, because it
could do no otherwise; but Amiens and several other cities had
awaited the occasion and submitted also. The Spaniards, or what
were called such, were again routed, and the King returned to
his capital and to the arms of the charming Gabrielle. Near her
bed stood a cradle, at the sight of which the King's heart stood
still. The King had indeed pictured his son in his mind's eye;
here he saw him in the flesh — with a cry of blank astonishment,
the father reached hurriedly for a chair; he felt quite overcome —
by joy, of course. And, rightly considered, also because this
strong and healthy youngster was his own, and was to secure his
future and his survival beyond his allotted span, both of which
had hitherto been unsecured. It was this thought that so moved
the King.

As he bent over the cradle, he thought of the toilsome life that
lay behind him, without vision of the future — a life that could
at any moment have been ended by one bullet. Now all was
changed. " Henceforth we are two." He said this over to himself, and at last said it aloud, while the mother eyed him patiently;
his joy was born of her, for all that his joy so outran her understanding. And as he muttered to himself: " A hearty child; now
I am safe," and said but little more, there flashed before his mind
a panorama of his life, especially of his early years. The Queen,
his mother, had hardened him in boyhood. He himself, the son
of a sick woman, had been a far from hearty child; she had inured
him against the weather. This had stood him in good stead when

he had to lie on bare earth in his agelong struggle against his enemies, with his kingdom often as the stake of a battle. Fights and sieges, blood and mire — of what account were they now? " They pass; I stand. And you, my son? "

In the face of his own experience, the father resolved that this lusty offspring of his should have an easy life; no battling against enemies, but peace and joy, a kingdom established and a loyal people. He, Henri, would make it so, and therewith win his people's love. He lifted the child from the cradle, kissed it, and gave it to its mother to kiss. The first and urgent matter was her divorce from Monsieur de Liancourt; then his from the Princesse de Valois. The Pope must consent. What if the King of France and the conqueror of Spain threatened to turn Protestant once more?

The Pope raises his ban, and with his own hand administers communion to the King's envoy. He dissolves the King's marriage, unites him to his beloved lady, and enjoins obedience on all the faithful. All this lay in an uncertain future, but here, in the King's mind, it had as good as happened. For the King had a son and bore him in his arms; much would be thus more readily achieved. Oh, the joy and ecstasy of the night that followed! — never again did he find it in the arms of the charming Gabrielle.

But the charming Gabrielle must first recover. A petition was addressed to the ecclesiastical court at Amiens, to which she and Monsieur de Liancourt were amenable. There the matter was left, until her beauty should be wholly restored and she made her entry with the King. He must now take possession of his capital, no longer secretly and at an early hour of dawn, but with proper pomp and ceremonial. He felt no inclination to make a show and a spectacle of what he had struggled so bitterly to win. But his dear lady was to make her entrance with him; hence all these eager preparations, as the court did not fail to observe.

There was no protest, and scarce a whisper in the court and in the city; both were silenced by the King's bold stroke. So he meant to show himself in his mistress's company to his nobles and his people. Other courts and nations should be made aware that the King had given his lady a share in his triumph and had

determined to call her to his side. The lovely d'Estrées had taken
the first step towards the throne when she bore the King a son.
It was recalled that for fifty years past no King of France
had proved his manhood. The second step — well, the lovely
d'Estrées had already raised her foot to take that too. Truly, they
must be very, very cautious, and concert their plans, or they
would indeed find themselves with a Queen of their own blood
and race.

Such was the general feeling, and it was shared by all — even
by Gabrielle herself. She felt uneasy, especially on the day before the entry, which her beloved lord had fixed for September
the 15th. On the 14th her Aunt de Sourdis took care to leave
her very little alone. Dame Sourdis dressed her with her own
hands in her attire for the morrow — robe and jewels so splendid
and magnificent that none but a princess had ever worn the like.

" No woman of our station was ever so arrayed," said her aunt.
The niece answered: " I am afraid." And a great jewelled ornament dropped from her fingers.

" Silly goose," said the aunt.

She was rather irritable, for, strange as it might seem, Dame
Sourdis found herself pregnant again; perhaps by her sallow
friend Cheverny, but there were others that came into question.
The fact was, she begrudged her niece this regal apparel. As she
stood beside Gabrielle and looked into the long mirror, she
thought her own skin was far more brilliant, and conceived it
gleaming against the black silk robe. Richly embroidered, it was
cunningly draped over the broad flat panniers that tipped and
swayed enchantingly and gave most alluring glimpses of the
lovely limbs beneath. The lady was convinced that hers also
would have graced this masterpiece no less. Through the broad
slashed opening in front shimmered a skirt of heavy silver brocade, sewn with intertwining rows of pearls and great jewelled
stars. The aunt gave her niece a hearty slap on the neck. She
was only the first of many who would tomorrow flush with desire
or grow pale with envy.

She tried to make Gabrielle more nervous than the lovely
creature was already. " You should have looked a little frail

when the time came, my beauty," said she. " Such splendours
are not to be offered up to curious eyes. It is dangerous, not only
for you, but for us all. Monsieur de Rosny will reckon up the
expense of this performance. The King's horses have been sent
back, for want of fodder. Think on that — and look on this! "

Gabrielle saw through Madame de Sourdis. Despite her distress of mind, she said confidently: " I and Monsieur de Rosny
understand each other very well indeed. He helps me, and I help
him." And although her aunt persisted in her warnings, Gabrielle resolved that she would that very evening induce the King
to appoint Monsieur de Rosny to the Treasury.

That same evening, however, the King and Gabrielle slipped
out privily and got into a coach, the very names of the travellers
being kept a secret. They went no farther than Saint-Germain.
As they arrived, the old castle stood up black in the fires of sunset. The previous court had once lived here, and that same
vision of dark conflagration had met the eyes of a small boy; he
had travelled thither with his mother Jeanne from a very distant
land. Thence was to start the great procession on the morrow
into the capital. " Your hand, madame; we are at home. And
everywhere we set our foot we shall be at home."

This he said as they alighted from the coach, for he was well
aware that she felt uneasy. It was the first royal castle in which
she was to sleep. She was indeed uneasy; she shared the common
view that she was being overbold. The common view of kingship is based on superstition; it was, and would ever be, a griev-
ance against Henri that his was different. He tried to soothe her
and laid his two hands round the lovely, girlish brow of her who
had borne him his son. But Gabrielle closed her eyes, she trembled yet more violently, and with eyes still closed she begged
that he would leave her alone that night.

From this he might have learned much; but then he made his
solemn entry and all seemed well. It was evening; the light from
the torches flickered through the narrow streets, over the thronging crowds, and up to the decorated houses. People were still
clinging to gables and beams; from below and from above came
shouts of " Long live the King! Long live the King! " and there

he was, on his dapple-grey, in a doublet of grey silk, stiff with gold embroidery. This time he wore his white-plumed hat, for there was peace; nation and King were united.

He now had the entire garrisons of Mantes and Saint-Denis around him and before him, together with the city fathers and the justices, who might well serve as hostages; so peace there must needs be, and — Long live the King! In other days a cheering crowd had surged round another horse on which sat a fair-haired horseman, in silver armour, with nothing in his heart but death. Slaughter, treason, years of fanatic disorder, until the hero of that city fell at last, murdered. "Let us think no more of him who was Duke of Guise; our people's love this day would seem a little tepid by comparison, and might make us sad. We serve with an uplifted heart; for the service that would win a people's love must surely be so given."

In place of a murderous favourite of the masses, here, before the public gaze, passes the loveliest woman that this world will ever see. Her litter came first, before the King, his troops and noblemen, and the city councillors and dignitaries — a short space ahead, drawn by two mules in red harness, and escorted by a company of musketeers. The red damask curtains were thrown back; all who wished could look their fill on that shy, appealing smile. "She is not proud," said some. "She has borne the King a son. How can she be the hell-cat against whom we have been warned?" And others answered: "She is far too richly clothed. Look at the women's faces. What must she be to face all bitter envy?" "But she does so," came the answer, "by the King's will. She is his glory, his pride, and his honour."

Such was the talk among the jurists of his Parliament, while he and the whole procession filed onwards to the cathedral of Notre Dame. He had a word for all who cheered him and for all who pushed forward to get a sight of him and his lady. His white-plumed hat was oftener in his hand than on his head. Three very lovely women in mourning stood at a window; to them he bowed profoundly. His humanists, awaiting him in the paved forecourt of the cathedral, said: "Well, he led us to victory, and our time has come." But they noticed that they had in

the meanwhile grown grey, as had their King. And they added:
"Power and possession come late, that they may be the better
used." Thereupon they sallied out to meet him, more than a
hundred of them, in red robes.

After the *Te Deum* the same procession was again formed,
but did not draw such a throng of spectators as before; it was
eight o'clock, and high time to get back to supper. The King
reached the Louvre almost alone. The crowd had all drifted
homewards. When he sat down to his own supper, he shivered.
The old palace was very cold. His dear lady's presence might
have brought some warmth into it. But after a public ceremony,
the first in which Gabrielle had taken part, they could scarcely
spend the evening together. Was she, too, shivering in her
house? Both of them were lonely; what might she be thinking
of that solemn entry under the eyes of the Paris populace?

He wished they could be talking over the events of the day:
had all gone well, and if not, why not? She was as quick as he
at divining the minds of those about her. It was their gift to feel
in their very backs what their people thought — just there, indeed, when they had passed and the cheering had died down.
Henri reflected: well, he had done what in him lay; his horse had
duly curvetted when he greeted the three mourning women. He
had not sat his horse like a Spanish potentate, nor had he ridden
like a cavalry captain. The three women had responded very
graciously. But surely the sight of his dear lady must have moved
them all to tears of joy, women as well as men.

"Was she not lovely?" he said softly to himself, without looking round to see which of his noblemen was serving him. It was
in fact brave Crillon, a man scarred by a thousand fights, and one
of his most devoted followers. He had distinguished himself before Laon and had asked in recompense that he might fill the
King's glass that evening. This he did, and answered:

"Yes, Sire, she was too lovely."

Henri turned his head. "Brave Crillon, sit down beside me."

The other gentlemen took this as a hint to withdraw. "Now
tell me, what have you against her?"

"Sire, I worship her," replied the soldier promptly. "Because

I serve you, I honour her whom you love, and trouble my head no further. But the people, being what they are, objected to the kerchief in her hand; it must have cost twenty crowns to embroider it. But what if it cost a hundred! She is my King's beloved."

" A glass with me, brave Crillon. And what else? "

" Sire, many things; and mostly nonsense."

" Out with it."

" I am but an old soldier, I go about among the people unobserved, and I hear them say that you have increased your lady's allowance from four to five hundred talers a month and bought her an estate, while you yourself are deeply in debt. It makes no odds to me. Where there are soldiers, there will be usurers. To provide Your Majesty with money, you have Gondi and Zamet, foreign rogues who bleed you — so the people say. Hence you have to tax your own people, so they say. And tax them unjustly, so they maintain."

And Henri said — this time not for the ears of Crillon, whose glass he had filled and refilled several times:

" Poor folk! So they are still angry with me. They cannot see that I make life no harder for them. I do my best to help them. But they'll love me when I have put in hand the plans of my schemer in the Arsenal."

The soldier caught the word " Arsenal " and growled. " He of the Arsenal is held to be the worst of all. How can a soldier deal with matters of finance? "

" Is that all? " said Henri to his comrade in arms. The scars on Crillon's forehead and cheeks reddened — not from the wine he had drunk, for he could stand far more than that; on the contrary, it helped him to utter what would have otherwise stuck in his throat.

" Sire," said brave Crillon, " if you had but remained a Huguenot! "

" You, at least, liked me as a heretic." Henri clapped him on the shoulder and laughed.

" For my part, you might be the Grand Turk if you pleased." The soldier went on in an embarrassed undertone: " I think you neither traitor nor hypocrite; but the priests in their pulpits call you so, and the monks, who go in and out of every house. The people mostly believe that you have no religion at all."

In a still lower tone Henri muttered over his glass:

" I often think so myself. How can I tell? "

" The opinion is," pursued brave Crillon, " that you were converted solely for your advantage, to get the Pope's recognition. And he is to dissolve your marriage, that you may marry your lady."

Here Henri rapped out an oath. " And I shall do it."

" Yes. If he consents. And we must see you humiliate yourself before the Pope. Our King was not wont to bow to any man."

Henri: " He is God's representative."

Brave Crillon: " And who is God? A God of monks, who go about whispering that you are Antichrist; that your fate has long awaited you and will overtake you in the end."

Henri: " Is that what is said? "

He knew very well that it was, but had not believed that the time was ripe for a faithful servant to report the matter.

Then the old warrior burst out savagely:

" Sire! Divorced or not, you should have married your lady and made a solemn entry with your Queen. If the people want to see Antichrist, show them Antichrist. Never fear; they would have cowered. And thus, not the King, but the Pope of Rome would have been humbled, once and for all, and would have done your will, he and his priests and monks, and the whole rabble of them all. Amen."

" Brave Crillon, it is time we went to bed," said Henri decisively.

AN EXECUTION

The King discovered the plans of an architect since dead, and thereby enlarged his palace of the Louvre while he lived in it. Gradually he collected two thousand workmen, who filled the whole building with their uproar. He was often away on a journey while the works proceeded, these journeys being, in fact, campaigns.

He covered the southern garden front with ornamental traceries of H and G interwined. He also began the great gallery from the Louvre to the Tuileries, and enriched the end façade. As the years went on he was to carry the outer wall of the palace past the wing named after the Goddess Flora and back again to the Tuileries façade. By the time it was all done, his life would also be at its term. And so, all his days, he lived in an atmosphere of incompletion and unrest, of zestful labours, and anxiety over what it was all to cost.

He began on his own dwelling, but it was not long before much else, and the very realm itself, were being reconstructed. And this was closely marked, and with uncertain feelings. What profits the community always breeds the mistrust that far outruns gratitude. When a few persons must lose something — their excess of power, money, property, or influence — the process of change always figures as a public calamity. There are those who make sure of that. The great lords, displaced by this monarch from their privileges, had of course, each and all of them, hordes of dependants. Every one of these lived at the charges of the people, like the hulking creature whom Henri had seen while the fever was upon him, the man who ate for six, while the starving peasants knew no otherwise.

Rosny, who was to become Duke of Sully at long last — the King had been in no hurry, for this cathedral image had been his best servant and made him the most enemies — Monsieur de Rosny, then, was finally put in charge of the Treasury. It was Gabrielle d'Estrées who got him appointed, as the King himself made known to Monsieur de Rosny. Hence a certain indulgence and an averted eye on the Treasurer's part in respect of the financial needs of his loyal mistress and her numerous family.

The Royal Treasurer, Monsieur de Rosny, as he had promised, set about his task with all his might. At his instance, the King allowed him to inspect all the finance offices throughout the kingdom — despite the protests of the older members of the Treasury Board. Hence much malignancy, and the first establishment of real control. There was not an office which Rosny did not force to disgorge, after exposing all manner of peculation and stopping the brutal waste of revenue — this, when need be, by force. For the Royal Counsellor came with armed escort and could promptly retransform himself into a soldier. Moreover, he was a Protestant, and obstinately remained so, thus enabling all the stripped plunderers to cry out that the Religion was in danger. This was dinned into the countryfolk on every side. They ploughed their land once more, but did not pay over their earnings to the appointed officers, which (they were told) was a sin. They fed their flocks, as they had not done for many a year, without fear of seizures and sales; and the roads were free, all customs dues had been abolished. The Provincial Court, which had imposed such dues, was now no more. All of this was due to force, and force applied by two heretics. Let them take heed for their salvation!

This they did, and actually rose in revolt; against the evidence of their own eyes they believed themselves yet worse oppressed. Such is the power of rumour, trickling incessantly through the minds of men, like runnels through the fields. And rumour had it that, under cover of the professed heretic Rosny, another, half-converted and now called King, was planning to destroy the Religion and was in fact Antichrist.

King Henri laughed. He was no better off either, and were he a peasant, he would assuredly revolt. However, he was pressed by many well-intentioned persons to keep Rosny in hand. He was even secretly tempted to pension him off; but he thought of the man's steadfastness, which he himself so sorely lacked; with advancing age it grew more rigid, and as time passed, more dangerous. However, he lavished rewards on Rosny because he took no bribes. These noble plunderers' money Rosny despised on principle; but he gladly let his master compensate him for his honesty. Those little bags that were the guerdon of his faithful service he collected as calmly as in days gone by, when conquered towns were still sacked and he drew his share. He had some reverses and advised his King to hang a great lord, instead of using peaceful means to remove him from his province. " Blockhead! " said Henri promptly. " It would cost me much more to make war on one of my subjects than to buy him."

Doubt and suspicion — these were the harvest that the King reaped, apart from the cash results of Rosny's journeys. It was much the same over the shops in the Louvre. On the level of the street he installed shops, in which craftsmen as well as artists worked, for he made no distinction between them. He wanted his own people and travellers from other lands to see with good advantage how the industries of his country were beginning to thrive. And he began to lay out the Place Royale in his capital: long colonnades round a great central pool, for the display of the King's especial pride, the silk industry, which he had created and did his utmost to encourage.

But his Place Royale was first used by those that came after him, and only for display of outmoded pageantry, not in the service of industry. So the scheme failed, because the King's utmost energy did not suffice for all the tasks that he had to accomplish single-handed within the short time that was to be his. Moreover, the citizens distrusted these innovations, as did the countryfolk; and they, too, concluded from them that the King must be an opponent of the Religion. Burghers and their families visited the upturned sites, which they had long regarded as their own peculiar property. What they saw displeased them; they stood about in little groups and muttered that the King could be no true Catholic. It was well known to be an ordinance of God that dwellers in cities should work in cramped conditions. Airy spaces, colonnades girdling a pool of water — these were for the gentry. There let them hold their wrestling matches and their jousts, as they had always done with Heaven's approval.

And it would be so again, no doubt of that. King Henri had aroused scandal enough with the shops that he had actually installed and fitted up in the Louvre. The clatter of craft-work, the serving of customers, the bustling throng in working clothes — all this under the same roof as Majesty! How could such abominations be permitted? True, the King was building. True, his first step had been to get the gardener Lenôtre to lay out vast flower-beds, and avenues of tall clipped hedges. He squandered on outlandish trees all the revenues that his Treasurer, Rosny, extracted from his people; on stone-pines and orange-bushes and sycamores; then he enclosed that garden and walked alone among his green pavilions. That indeed was regal. What they did not like was his habit of haunting shops and interfering in the common course of life. There must inevitably be incidents; a King must not be involved in such matters, least of all a King whose position was so very insecure.

One day, in a stonemason's shop, a woman had a fit. Many saw it; the seizure came upon her at the sight of a cross upheld by a carved stone image of a saint. The devil that had entered into her could not endure it and struggled to come forth. A priest was summoned, uttered over the poor possessed creature all the exorcisms enjoined upon such occasions, and the evil spirit would have certainly been expelled. The woman fell into frightful paroxysms, and her shrieks were the shrieks of demons. Came the King with his guard. " What is this? " he cried, and slapped the devil smartly in the face. All saw it: the blow brought forth a fearful face from hell, foaming at the lips, and the woman nearly choked. Meanwhile a doctor appeared, summoned by the King. He slit the veins of the writhing creature, as though such a thing were lawful. He half unclothed her, swathed her head and shoulders in towels dipped in cold water. At that moment a procession happened to pass, carrying the Host, and although the woman could see nothing from her wrappings of damp linen, she howled more horribly than ever.

The King had not done well. He left the shop amid the hostile silence of the crowd. Fortunately he was escorted by his guard. The maltreatment of the maniac, who did, indeed, get up and go her ways, was not forgiven for some while. Such a cure was most improper. The shops in the Louvre, the Place Royale, and much else, the bridges that combined the various parts of Paris into a single city — all this, too, was most improper. The King pardoned everyone — he pardoned his enemies of the League, who would have had him hanged, the great lords, whom he could have hanged, instead of coming to terms with them. He let the peasants go, although their distress had lately driven them to banditry; nor was anything done to the Protestants, his former companions in the faith. There had been no execution in Paris since the entry of this King, and that did not please the people at all. As yet.

One day, however, on the Place de Grève, the familiar preparations, so beloved of the populace, were put in hand; the executioner's men set up the scaffold, they greased the wheel, to make it turn more smoothly while the headsman broke the condemned man's limbs. And, that nothing might be lacking, four black horses stood by to tear him asunder. The houses, broader above than below, looked down curiously from their gables to see what might be going to happen. The excited populace stood with eyes and noses peering out from beneath their tall felt hats and square fringed hair. They had not yet believed it true, though they could hear the tolling of the execution bell. But the improbable did happen: a nobleman appeared, surrounded by an escort of soldiers.

He walked on unhindered, for a free passage opened out before him as the crowd fell back. He walked gracefully, with not too hurried nor too slow a step, and he held his handsome, youthful head erect. The women looked long at him, and he met their eyes with a soft appealing gaze that seemed incredible from a man facing such a death, who had done what he had done. The women on whom his eyes fell felt a throbbing at their hearts — they knew not whether from horror, or grief at his fate. Two buxom women in their middle years began a vociferous protest, and others promptly raised their voices. So likely a youth must not be twisted on the wheel; nor could one so engaging have committed any crime, least of all the abominations for which he was to be quartered.

Some few men were cursed by their wives as cowards, and there was much hoarse muttering against the court and the King himself. Then a ripple stirred the crowd, which began to surge and thrust towards the scaffold. Those in front and beside it might almost have wrested Monsieur de Lionne from the soldiers, before he could be delivered to the headsman. The soldiers kept them off only because the headsman was on his knees in prayer. It was believed that the instrument of retribution re-coiled from it himself; a messenger from the King would soon appear with an order of release. Instead of which the execu-tioner's men seized the victim, and at that moment a young peasant was suddenly seen standing on the steps of the platform, who spoke amid an awed silence and in a voice that quavered with hatred and fury: " It was my betrothed. He put his feet into her open body."

At this several women screamed, in the same tone as the now busily pealing bell. They had known this, but would not believe it as they watched the young man's graceful movements. But now he could move no longer, he was bound fast, his arms out-stretched behind his head, his legs from the knees downwards dangling over the greased wheel — and there were other witnesses that followed the young peasant. It was now whispered among the crowd, in accents of fear and horror and wrath, that the youth had often committed the same abomination, more especially on his own domain. Only from dread of his position and influence had he never been formally arraigned. The officials were too fear-ful to proceed, and the peasants were paralysed by their agelong slavery.

Was it conceivable? Was the face of justice changed? The crowd craned their necks and peered into the distance: no mes-senger of rescue yet — the executioner swung the wheel and brandished his iron staff. Then a sigh swept over the whole square. And in that sigh the vast array of people on the Place de Grève in Paris disburdened their united hearts. So it had really happened; a gentleman was put to death according to the com-mon law for thieves and murderers. Not beheaded with a sword like his equals, nor as penalty for an attempt against His Majesty. But broken on the wheel and quartered in retribution for his crimes against poor people. A man who had been muttering at his wife's behest flushed fiery red and cried out frantically: " Long live the King! "

The voice of the people, this time in his favour, did not reach Henri in that hour. He paced the green pavilions of his enclosed garden, racked by the hope that the people had understood. The pealing of the little bell betokened the beginning of the execution; he stopped and wiped his brow. And this or something like it was in his mind: "There are madmen of all kinds. Some whose reason has been wrecked by hate, and others by love. They kill for things of this world and the next, for heaven, which they hope to reach, and for women whom they desire. Heaven and women — both give us life, and on account of both we kill. Many become prophets, like the preachers who write to me and foretell my death. Many make magic on a wax bust of me, thinking to kill me by such means. I recall my fever, my Aunt Montpensier, and the man who ate for six; I remember Monsieur d'Estrées, who stole from mere foolery, or Brissac, the catcher of flies, Parma, the General without a purpose, and Mayenne, who could never learn a lesson; what, too, of my cool, complacent Rosny, who respects money as he does his own honour? — God help me, I have to deal with madmen. Their empty claims, their treacherous deeds, their thirst for blood, and I must endure much more of it all before I die. If they get me in the end — if they get me, then they will see what they have never seen, for they never knew how mad they were."

The Poor Sinners' Bell tolled a last time and was silent. Henri bent his head and prayed fervently for Monsieur de Lionne. "Be merciful to him, O Lord. He loved women overmuch." But in his own mind he clasped not merely the knees of the Lord, but those of his dear lady: she must preserve him from excess, from shame and humiliation. An ever-present menace, for man's reason sways pitifully between bottomless abysses. With you is peace; with you is refuge.

BESIDE THE CRADLE

The Jesuits wanted to provide him with a confessor, but he put them off. None the less he felt that they would grow more dangerous to him the longer he evaded them. But he could not carry humiliation any further; that would disgust Frenchmen of both creeds. To play the faithful son and poor petitioner of Rome, and still to be spurned — which, thought Henri, was no more than he deserved, and he cursed to think so, but only Monsieur d'Armagnac heard those curses. He scarce dared to miss a Mass, however urgent was his business. He tried to excuse himself. " I am working for the public weal instead of hearing Mass. But I approach God elsewhere, as I think " — but the pretext was barely admitted by the prelates, who were the most accommodating of the kind.

The fresh and vigorous cohorts of the Jesuits admitted nothing and forgot nothing. The court loathed them, and the Parliament of Paris indicted them, because these Fathers did not, as was then customary in Europe, regard the majesty of Kings as divine — far from it. Henri, who alone shared their opinion on this matter, secured a very clement judgment to that suit, which by no means placated the Fathers. They conceived clemency and toleration on the part of their enemies as a crime, and even as the only one they must not commit. The case of the King of France was canvassed by them in his own country, as in Spain. Their polemical books were enlarged by several chapters in those days — but the conclusion and the ultimate exhortation was invariably that tyrants must be murdered.

His own spiritual forces, his Huguenots, Henri kept in reserve, whether or not he might need them in the future. In the Louvre there were hidden certain packed coffers — to be kept ready to hand until the end of that reign. With God's grace, neither the coffers nor the Huguenots would be needed; the latter, indeed, were well disposed to leave the way of it to destiny. A King and father of his people knows no favourites; none may stand near to his heart. Those who have worked for the last hour only in the vineyard shall be rewarded as highly as the first. And indeed Henri dealt with his first comers more strictly than with those who came afterwards.

It was not long before Philippe Mornay heard a voice within him say that he would henceforward be an embarrassment to his King. He had never been allowed to report on his mission to England, as he used to do, in private audience. He handed the King a memorandum assuring him of Elizabeth's unalterable friendship. Shortly afterwards she recalled all her auxiliary troops from France. Then Mornay withdrew in silence to his town of Saumur; he had been its Governor since the previous reign. And he fortified that town beside the Loire. He fell to writing theological works, as his habit was — in his leisure — and from this safe seclusion he sent the King the completed plan for the Gallic State Church. Added thereto were asseverances that he was, as he had always been, the King's devoted servant. He certainly regarded the King's change of faith as a brief darkening of the prospect. But he fortified himself in Saumur and evaded the King's appeals that he should come to Paris. At last he went, his suspicions vanquished by his ancient affection.

Turenne, the other great Protestant, never again of his own will put himself within reach of the King; he had to be secured later by a ruse of the admirable Rosny, who was made a Duke for the achievement. When Turenne inherited the small estate of Bouillon, he did not merely fortify himself, as Mornay had done in Saumur; he played at independence, after the fashion of certain nobles who did likewise elsewhere. King Henri was to encounter Protestant rebels besides those to whom he was so well accustomed. Not a few of the Religion who were too weak to rebel heard how he was said to have insulted one of them. A doctor had become a Catholic. " Ah," jeered the King to some Protestant courtiers, " your Religion must be very sick; the doctors are giving it up."

He jested at their expense and longed that they might guess his deeper meaning; but that they could not. Least of all did they understand that he held them in reserve — not for the battle, which God forfend; he would have been content to leave that in their hands. But Henri's object was to put his old creed on a level with that of the majority, both in public law and in general estimation. This would take time; his first steps were to flatter the Pope, keep the Jesuits at a distance, deal strictly with his friends, and not disdain a jest upon occasion. His aim was clear before him, no other saw it, and he himself could say no word of what it was. When he had at last established " the Religion " in his kingdom and set it wholly free, this would be his quittance, and the climax of his reign. But he must have grown very great before he could achieve it.

The excellent Rosny, what did he know, after all? Or Agrippa, who loved him more than any other man? Rosny had dedicated himself to the State, and hence to the King. He was a man of stone; anyone who stood in the way of the King's advancement must be removed, even the beloved Gabrielle; in that purpose he was rigid, though he would wink an eye upon occasion. Still less was this admirable servant concerned with the destinies of his own brothers in the faith. Each according to his deserts. He himself stood firm, cuirassed in steel; he had himself painted in armour, and hung the portrait in the Arsenal, where he made his calculations and drew his decrees. His own career had been full of knightly adventure; it would have provided matter for a romance — which Rosny would certainly never write; he was busy collecting material for his book on the trade and industry of the kingdom. Away with romance, though Rosny could never have been anything but sedate under the most romantic circumstances.

Agrippa was still romantic, for such was the essence of the man. Monsieur d'Aubigné once came to violent odds with Monsieur de Rosny, after the manner of old friends who are convinced that neither will ever betray the other and so speak their minds when they fall out. " Not a word," proclaimed Agrippa, " against the beautiful and charming lady who so inspires the King. But for this beloved lady, we should never have seen his genius unfold and come to fullness. Nor should we ourselves have made much of life, and you especially, Monsieur de Rosny, would have remained the mediocre officer — that you really are," added Agrippa aside.

" Very well," said Rosny in a cold fury. " Meantime the beloved lady is betraying the King with Monsieur de Bellegarde, and the King's son is his."

" Draw, Sir! " cried the fiery little man. His enemy stared scornfully down at him with blue enamel eyes.

" Before I run you through," observed Monsieur de Rosny,

" pray give me a brief description of the beautiful and charming object of dispute in verse, which will certainly be mediocre — like yourself, as both officer and poet," he too interjected.

Agrippa was too proud to defend his talent. Writing poetry and fighting — one did not talk of such matters. But he said — and so swelled in stature that he seemed now to look down upon the other: " There is someone who has been privily handing lampoons to the King. I would not care to be that man."

" What nonsense is this? " said Rosny, in a tone not of question, but contempt. He had firm ideas of his duties. This ruffling, penniless poet, Agrippa, had never been conscious of any reality; duty, for Rosny, was no more than a firm grasp upon facts.

" Your business," Rosny went on, " is with words, no matter what their sense, if they do but sound agreeably. I think you had better not appear before His Majesty; you have been babbling. By your account, this beloved lady is the cause of the people's distresses. She is, indeed, richer than you. The same charges are made in the lampoons, and a man who knows his duty must give them to the King, instead of jesting behind his back in such fashion."

Agrippa had heard one thing only: " I must not appear before the King? I? "

" Or your days are numbered. He will kill you; he has said it."

Agrippa dashed out, mounted his horse, and rode at a gallop to the Louvre. Henri was just entering the palace.

" Sire! Pray keep your word and kill me."

By way of answer, Henri embraced his old friend. Clasped in each other's arms they hid their tears. The King took him to the house of Gabrielle near by. She herself was not within; Henri took Cæsar from his cradle and laid him in Monsieur d'Aubigné's arms.

" Sire, your very image," said the worthy man, despite the evidence of his eyes, for the child was fat, fair-haired, light-eyed, and took after his mother in every way.

" You see," said Henri. " He is mine, and I shall call him Cæsar."

"A proud name," said Agrippa. "The great Julius Cæsar abolished rank and class within his empire; all men were at a level, far beneath the sovereign. He united the nations round the Middle Sea. That means, for nations, that they obey one single ruler."

"And for that very reason are no longer slaves," said Henri promptly. Then he went on:

"Look at those little shining eyes — so innocent of what is to come. You know what scandal is talked about his parenthood. What shall I do?"

And the excellent Agrippa answered briskly:

"Sir, laugh at the rumours and lampoons; and also at the silly jokes of a poor old fellow whose pension does not meet his needs."

"I'll raise it — yet once more." Henri took Cæsar back into his arms. "But laugh I can and will; why, this very day a preacher denounced me from the pulpit for whispering into my mistress's ear."

"During the sermon?" asked Agrippa; and answered his own question. "The King may do it," he exclaimed. "He should ride through Paris with her, take her on his hunting parties, and be advised by her rather than by a scurvy fellow called Monsieur de Rosny."

Henri: "Leave Rosny alone. The Graces think but little of him; but he stands well with the goddess Minerva, not to mention Mercury. I asked your counsel in trouble that was not brought on me by Gabrielle — far from it!" Came the oath that he had made his own. "It is her Aunt de Sourdis who is poisoning my days just now — God confound her!"

"Why?" asked Agrippa innocently, but with an elfish glitter in his eye.

"Must I tell you? She has taken it into her head to become a mother. What example does not do, she could leave undone no longer."

The excellent Agrippa was moved by pity for his master's quandary. "Say no more, Sire. I know all. The niece will hold the aunt's son at baptism, and you are to stand godfather."

" I have promised on my honour," Henri confessed.

Agrippa: " Declare a war; that will get you out of it."

Henri: " No, but seriously — what do you think?"

Agrippa: " What I think is that I don't know whether you mean to marry Madame d'Estrées, or de Liancourt, or the Marquise de Monceaux, and make her our Queen."

" Henri: " I shall do so."

He strode to the far end of the room, and Agrippa to the opposite end. From there Agrippa ventured: " And Monsieur de Rosny? He is in treaty for three Princesses at once. Will you marry them all, and your lady as well? "

" Let Rosny do as he thinks fit," said Henri over his shoulder. " My hour will come."

Agrippa, still from his distance: " Your beautiful and charming lady is the worthiest to rule us. She is of our kind, though raised above us by your love. So shall it be. I see it in my prophetic spirit. The court and the people will open their eyes very wide when these things come about."

" Give me your hand," said Henri; he had heard what he wanted to hear. He stepped into the centre of the room, where Agrippa met him and stood awhile bent low over his master's hand. He felt ill at ease, his conscience smote him, he doubted his own advice, as also the King's resolve. Henri said under his breath:

" Then I can please the old aunt by standing godfather."

Agrippa raised his head, but did not otherwise move. " That is the least you can do," he murmured in a bantering tone lest he might betray his uneasiness.

A Mystic

The christening of the little Sourdis — or whatever he might be — took place in the old church where a great bell often boomed; and it was a most magnificent affair. The streets were packed with spectators, who found much to astonish them, and much, too, they could not understand. The King made a noble figure as godfather, and his lady, who stood godmother, was al-

most bowed down beneath her weight of jewellery. The greatest
ladies of the kingdom served her as maids of honour, a great
noble carried the salt-cellar, another the ewer, and the infant lay
in the arms of a Marshal's lady. He was fat and large; when the
godmother held him over the font, she nearly dropped him. A
witty court dame observed that what made him so heavy were
the royal seals attached to his behind.

This was a hint that the real father was the Chancellor, Cheverny, the bearer of the ewer. Others named the child's own
uncle as its begetter, who was no other than the officiating
Bishop. Good folks, what a state of affairs! The court took the
matter lightly; but mere observers were less inclined to jest. Outside, on the street, there was evil talk, and all of it centred on the
King.

"The sovereign — God hath set him over us, we bow down
before him, and he who has kissed the royal knees dares put no
food between his lips that day. The awe of majesty is inherent
in the person of the ruler. Everyone knew that — did he not
know it too? He engaged his sacred person in abominable affairs
of this kind. Himself, alas, an adulterer, with the adulteress
whom he meant to make his consort, he held strange bastards
over the font. And he actually caressed his mistress as he did so "
— those inside the church saw it all; but outside, where his demeanour could not be actually seen, the performance was regarded as utter profanation of a sacrament and of the King's
majesty.

A young man, soberly and decently clad in black, babbled dis-
tractedly as he stood among the crowd. He was unconscious of
doing so, and when he sometimes caught the sound of his own
voice, he cast furtive looks around him. His face was grey and
blotched, there were pallid crescents underneath his eyes, and
his eyelashes were quivering. "Aha!" said he to himself. "Fear
not. Commit the sin of the flesh during the sacred office. I can
see you, though I stand without; and I know how it is done.
King, you will not confess it; I, too, keep my secret, and carry in
my poor soul, wherever I go or stand, eternal damnation."

"Now you have betrayed yourself," whispered a voice behind

him. The man swung round as he heard that menacing voice, and peered into the crowd; but he could not meet the eyes that held his own.

"At last," he groaned. "I could have borne it no longer; take me away with you."

"Follow me," said the Unknown. But he did not lead that sober-looking citizen to any guard-post; he took him to the convent by the church where that unholy baptism was taking place. They were admitted, the door clanged behind them, the chain clashed, and they entered an empty room. The Unknown secured the door. The window was set high in the wall, and barred. Dusk was falling, and the pallid youth was so placed that the fading daylight outlined his face and hands against the darkness. The Unknown gave him but a single sign, and the tormented creature began to speak, twisting his fingers as he told his tale.

"My name is Jean Chastel. My father, Pierre Chastel, is a cloth-merchant, with a shop opposite the court-house. I was educated by the Jesuits, and am now a law student. I have led a vile life, from boyhood upwards; otherwise I am not known." He shuddered and then groaned.

Sternly his interrogator answered: "Poor worm! You pride yourself on hiding your abominable sins. You twitch and writhe and turn up your eyes and gasp, in foul enjoyment of what you are and have been. God made you, and we will now see for what purpose. You have never confessed the abominations of which you boast, thinking that your teachers have never heard of them."

"Alas! They have not," muttered the other hoarsely. None the less, he had a foreboding that judgment was to be pronounced. It was this fear that had driven him from one unnatural act to the next. Never had he confessed, and his wickedness was now more than he could bear.

"I have never confessed," he whispered. "In the act of confession I have always concealed the mortal sin. Too late; no priest will now absolve me; the Holy Wafer will never pass my lips. Were I a murderer, I would make an attempt on the King!"

" Your Fathers the Jesuits have already decided on your fate. We know all about you and have taken our decision " — the Unknown, who at that point became known, dropped his voice and once again said: " We know."

The transgressor against nature slipped from his chair, cried aloud as he clasped the other's knees, and in a voice that was less than a whisper he began to unburden his agonized soul into the other's ear. The Jesuit heard him to the end; whereupon, wasting no compassion on the man, he confirmed his fears.

" For a sodomite like you, confession naturally comes too late. You can find no rest, neither here nor there. It may be, however, that Heaven will remit your eternal damnation at the price of a martyr's death upon this earth."

" Were I but a murderer! " wailed the wretched creature.

" You have said so already. A miserable object such as you longs to do what he never does."

The sinner: " How I envy that great lord who put his feet into the girl's slit belly and was torn to pieces! He redeemed himself."

The Jesuit: " Too trifling a penalty for such a case as yours. You will go straight into the same pit of hell as a certain other who by his lewdness pollutes the sanctuary and aims his abominable lusts at — at what indeed! He would impose his will on God Himself. He acts in all things as you do. But you are a poor worm, while he is the consecrated vessel of supreme sovereignty — of majesty itself."

The sinner: " None the less I am made after his pattern and he after mine. That, at least, is my privilege."

The Jesuit: " And who shall go hence with him. If he takes the risk; and that is not yet so certain. Born a lecher, he avenges his own nature on other lechers, inflicts a dreadful death on them, and so thinks to sneak into salvation by atoning for his sins in the persons of those like unto himself."

The sinner: " You have told me that I am a man like him. Reverend Father, I see how the matter lies; I must be beforehand with him, and do to him what he purposes to do to me."

The Jesuit: " I did not say so. You have said so."

The sinner: " I'll do it."

The Jesuit: " And earn a martyr's death; poor creature, are you man enough? Indeed, you will otherwise be certain of eternal martyrdom, without choice given."

The sinner: " May I expect God's grace for a week of merit? "

The Jesuit: " Old and hardened sinners have been pardoned for a mere gift of alms, the only one they made in all their lives. But even the most pious and profitable deed may not save a soul once lost. There can be no trafficking with grace, a man must submit himself to it, for good or ill."

The sinner, sobbing: " I submit myself."

The Jesuit: " So far, so good. What remains may not be decided by a humble personage like myself. Is your chosen deed both pious and profitable? "

The sinner: " If he can expiate his offences by my death, how much more easily can I do so by his — since he is the King! "

The Jesuit: " Your expiation is a matter on which the Fathers will not waste their time. They will examine the case and guilt of a King who persecutes the faith, but tolerates heresy."

The sinner: " You say well, Reverend Father, that I am a worm. I take a pride in being so."

Not Yet

On December the 12th the King and the Marquise de Monceaux appeared in the city of Amiens. They came with a small escort and at once waited on the ecclesiastical magistrate, just like an ordinary couple who want to marry and are petitioning for the divorce of one party. They were sent about their business and told to wait until the husband had made his statement of defence. Monsieur de Liancourt had hitherto not responded to the citation. From motives of self-respect he put off the inevitable humiliation, though in truth he had already consented, subject to some personal reservations that he would not waive for very decency. In his coffer lay his solemn written testimony, to be read after his demise and preserved for all time.

On the 17th, when the pair had waited five days, he at last

presented himself at the magistrate's house; he had with him his notary, but the attorney acting for Gabrielle d'Estrées contested the evidence of both. No one else was present, the magistrate's house was barred to all comers. From common knowledge of Monsieur Nicolas d'Amerval de Liancourt, he must have expressed himself with proper decorum. On the other hand, he provided his truculent adversary, who appeared for the Lady d'Estrées, with but few facts to serve his purpose; for Monsieur de Liancourt was a man of no mean intelligence.

The attorney then consulted the woman petitioner and agreed with her and her royal lover that they would no longer base their claim solely on the defendant's impotence. The defendant's first wife had been a step-cousin of Monsieur Jean d'Estrées, father of the woman petitioner. This was a tangible fact, which he could admit with little damage to his honour; it sufficed, however, to invalidate his second marriage.

But the matter did not rest there; the magistrate examined all the evidence in the strictest and most impartial manner, though, despite his conscience, rather more rapidly than usual, owing to the presence of the King. Monsieur de Liancourt was confronted with the female petitioner. He had to answer for the fact he had never been able to cohabit with her, whenever he had made the attempt. He had to listen to the statements of two doctors, a doctor of medicine, and a master surgeon, who produced evidence in their support; though whence they had got it could scarce be understood — hardly by material diagnosis! The man's remote expression, his impenetrable decorum, and his masked self-confidence seemed to lend little weight to any charge of incapacity.

The magistrate turned from the defendant and addressed the plain question to the petitioner:

" Had you, knowing his condition, agreed to live with Monsieur de Liancourt as brother and sister? "

" No," replied Gabrielle.

In the end the marriage was pronounced invalid — the decisive reason being the step-cousin. But there was the uneasy sense that Monsieur de Liancourt had won the day. He took leave of the King with the words: "Sire, I trust I have acted in all matters as you desired." Which might indeed have been intended as plain insolence, though the man bent low in a most obsequious bow, and so remained until the pair had left the room. No one could find an appropriate reply.

Enough; the beloved lady was free, and what was to come need not be forthwith considered. In high good humour the pair hastened back to Paris, where they stopped at Gabrielle's house. She went in to change her dress. The King, booted and covered with dust as he had arrived, was soon the centre of a throng: his cousins Conti and Soissons had brought at least thirty noblemen with them, who were soon joined on their own account by several gentlemen new to the court. They were not known to the door-keeper, but he had orders to admit them, so that anyone who pleased made his way into the small room where the King was sitting.

The King jested gaily with Mathurine the Fool, a buxom young person, no more than slightly touched in her wits, who was a duly acknowledged figure at court. If there is to be an office of fool, then let feminine folly be represented too; and a King, by marking the sallies of a Chicot and a Mathurine, increases his knowledge of his fellow-men. While greeting the gentlemen as they entered, the King kept up an exchange of gallantries with Mathurine, which neither he nor she took seriously, though she, with upturned eyes, pleaded for a kiss. A sudden noise was heard, like a clap on the ear; none could see what was happening in the dark corner where the King sat.

"Curse the crazy wretch, she bites," cried the King. He raised a hand to his lips; in an instant it was covered with blood. A certain Monsieur de Montigny, who had bowed low to kiss the King's knee, started up and saw behind the King an unknown face, pallid and convulsed. "'Tis you or I," shouted Montigny, in a flurry of rage. "One of us has wounded the King." He seized the pallid youth and found at his feet the blood-stained knife. After an attempt at disavowal, he confessed that he had stabbed the King. As a result of the King's horseplay with Mathurine, he had missed Henri's throat and merely grazed his lip. The King said: "Let him go." But the man held out his hands; he was seized and hurried away. He would not reveal who he was; only his age — eighteen.

The King's surgeon promptly sewed up the lip. He would have drawn the needle several more times through the wound, but the King could not endure the pain. The injury left his mouth markedly awry — a defect which was commonly ascribed to his habit of dissembling. The charming Gabrielle dashed into the room just as the operation began. She held her dear lord's head, she kissed him on the eyes, so that he should feel only her and nothing else. When he groaned, she turned her lovely face from side to side and met with none but chilly looks, whereby she realized that, but for a hand's breadth, she would have been left desolate and would have had to go, if indeed she had been allowed to go. She clenched her teeth and was the charming Gabrielle no more.

The King's wound hurt him, but he was not much shaken and said that he would not retire any earlier for such a trifle. Indeed, he went to the cathedral and attended a service of thanksgiving. The would-be murderer was condemned and executed three days later, without revealing his accomplices, though he was put to the question. They were known, however, and the Royal Parliament had one of its former professors hanged. All members of the Society of Jesus were banished from the kingdom.

Such firmness at last induced the Pope to yield; and shortly afterwards he received the King of France into the bosom of the Church, which the survivors of the League had done their utmost to prevent. During their brief respite they all took up arms — Mayenne, Nemours, Epernon, Joyeuse, and Mercœur, powerful noblemen, each in his own province. They summoned the Spaniards from the Netherlands; for the last time King Henri had to encounter revolt and civil war — but judgment had been pronounced on them, and their time had passed away. None the less, the King, despite his firm resolves, lost heart for a while; joyful service? — he had no feeling for it left.

Twenty years of joyful service, begun as a petty King of Navarre; battle, and victory, the seizure of power, the leap of death, and years and years of toil; all of it now seemed futile. He had achieved nothing, neither peace nor his people's love, and no true grasp of power. He was not shaken when another attempt was made upon his life; but he grew anxious and weary — he who had never known weariness. The signs of it were remarked. A lady of the court permitted herself to observe that she had never seen her gay lord in such a mood. Was he discontented? Whereat he rapped out his favourite oath and relieved himself in words — against the people; not by any means against the forces that egged them on to what they did. Of them he must say nothing, even in the presence of that innocent lady. Ungrateful people — who think of nothing but attacks upon their King!

A very gloomy day was the 5th of the new year: great processions, the King following in his coach, the horses walking in step as though at a funeral. Wherefore? Not on his account. They have not got him — not yet. Somewhere in the serried throng a bitter voice cried: " Why, he might be driving in the execution cart to the Place de Grève." There are words at which a man may, as he chooses, laugh or weep. Henri did not move a muscle of his face; he sat like a very criminal, clad in black, with plastered lip. That bitter nameless voice seemed in a measure justified. Was he really on his way to execution?

When he alighted outside the church, his people cheered and his gentlemen offered their congratulations. Henri muttered: " Pah! 'Tis but a street crowd. My greatest enemies would do as much and more." It was indeed a gloomy day. Others followed it, and yet others after them. What a man is and means to be gradually wins the mastery, enriched indeed and burdened with experience. A wise character is not disposed again to blink the fact that unreason and evil exist in the world, from which they are not to be expelled by the most honourable efforts. On the contrary, a wise character tests itself and learns, and merely grows more adaptable to the movement of existence.

Henri recovered his humour — it had been his since boyhood and was still unchanged. Except that he had gained experience on another level of life, and in the light of it viewed the world.

In particular, he did not always behave in accordance with the rules of majesty; he had none of the pomp and mystery of sovereignty. In this regard, the common folk, by means of which they were themselves unconscious, came to an understanding with their ruler. Many a man knew what liberties he could take, provided he chose his hour aright. One day when Henri was at the Fair, there appeared out of one of the booths a buffoon in his own likeness, and dressed as he had been on a certain day: in black, with a patch of plaster on his lip. Suddenly, by a clever twist of feature, the hangdog countenance was transfigured, and the fellow, in his guise of royalty, began to shout ribald jokes, amid the laughter of the bystanders.

There was nothing that Henri could or cared to do. He disposed of the man with a present of money and went his way; again he understood more clearly why he had missed his people's love, like a jouster who fails to pierce the ring. The love of his people was not made so easy of achievement. They claimed of earthly majesty what they claimed of the divine: the ways of a King, as those of God, must be stern, incalculable, but always dignified. Sovereignty in the guise of homeliness was neither understood nor pardoned; it had to be warranted in due time by a greatness and glory that had never before been seen. In the end, perhaps not until after it, he was to win his people's love. But not yet. Not yet would he be murdered, and not yet loved.

His old friend Agrippa said to him after the last attempt on his life: " Sire, you had first renounced the Religion with your lips; this time the knife struck you on the mouth. Woe upon you, had you renounced it in your heart." Whereat the King nodded. In those days he again met the jurist who had uttered that ill-omened speech at Saint-Denis, long before it had been fulfilled by a murderous plot against his life. The man had shunned another encounter and now looked away. The King reassured him by a mild, friendly salutation, nor did he mention their previous meeting; it was only as they parted that he said with some emphasis: " *Nihil tam populare quam bonitas.*" The man looked at him wide-eyed, in admiration.

Thus were the harsh and precipitous passages of life made smooth, and the mind encountered them without fear — or almost without fear. Not that Henri would have greeted an unguarded mob that chanced to gather round him with quite the same feelings as before. " I am glad to see so many of my people," he would observe. " But I must become accustomed to them first." The young Duke of Guise, also, he was delighted to receive, and glad to pardon. The youth had realized what the old Duke could never see: that the time for resistance was past and the claims of his House were out of date. He came to the Louvre and offered the King his submission, and therewith a renunciation by the House of Lorraine of any claim to the French Crown. His father had been the resplendent hero of the League; he had won the people's love. The King said to the Duke of Guise, who stood embarrassed in his presence:

" Enough. We are neither of us men of words. You are with us now, and you shall prosper. I take your father's place." He embraced his foremost enemy and promptly used the advantage by declaring war on Spain.

Philip, once ruler of the world, was defeated by Henri. It was his first acknowledged victory over the World Power. For many a long year the Spaniards had always fought under the cloak of the enemy within his border; there had never been an open declaration of war and an invasion of the kingdom. Henri at last had his old and hated enemy confronting him unmasked. The inner enemy had now dwindled into a feeble contingent of auxiliaries, and was beaten in the company of Spain — this in the venturesome and perilous fashion in which Henri still fought and won his battles. He himself plunged into the fray. With no more than a hundred horsemen he drove a superior force headlong before him and broke them up. He was still the old Henri, the " King of Navarre," as though he were still young. And indeed the very act brought back his youth. All could see it; and with throbbing hearts and open mouths they listened to the voice of *Fama:* " Our King is still young, he is the greatest in the world, there is none like him, and he is ours. In him we have been reconciled. Neither parties nor leagues and not even the faith can part us now. We fight no longer as men harried and distracted. We fight the battles of a nation."

This was the exuberance of the moment, as Henri well knew. Even in the intoxication of battle he kept before his mind what a nation was, and was well aware that his people did not love him. Not yet. Battles are days of festival, though somewhat perilous ones, and victories are a notable encroachment on the truth. Much toil and labour was to reveal the truth about him at last. After a storm of success, life seemed so smooth and so responsive. The last great nobles, or almost the last, submitted, including the corpulent Mayenne. His corpulence had become pitiable: it irked Henri to think that such enemies are never overcome until they can rouse no feeling but that of pity. Henri received them at Monceaux, the estate of the Marquise — with music, plays, banquets, and every honour. He watched Mayenne make three bows, with two adjutants to support his belly. Henri would not permit him to kneel. Only in the park did he stride out until his fat companion began to gasp; that was his sole revenge. "Your hand, cousin — let us now be friends." And he bade Rosny revive him with two bottles of wine.

As was not unexpected, the Parliament would make no grant of money to the King. The nation was too impoverished. But for twenty years long it had never been too impoverished to wage civil war. Here stood the King, who had saved the nation from itself, even more than from the enemy. "I speak," said the King to his Parliament, "from my heart. The French, I know, do not love what they see before their eyes. When you no longer see me, you will love me."

He spoke without sadness or bitterness, but in his most familiar tone; and what he meant them to understand was this: "Love me or love me not. I serve you, and I serve you joyfully."

Book Five

The Conqueror

Fireworks

Two small toy-like cannon were firing harmlessly at the blue heaven. Tiny wreaths of smoke floated over the park and soon vanished in the soft air. The ladies on the broad stairway of the castle laughed as they aired their charms, resting a white arm on a red cushion, fanning themselves, and turning their heads with practised grace towards the cavaliers who sat one step above them. When the gentleman was slim enough, he bent a knee and so remained behind his lady, as long as the performance lasted.

At the signal-shots from the two mortars, all the hedges and arbours and green avenues were suddenly populated by shepherds, shepherdesses, and rustic deities, while invisible musicians played solemn pastoral melodies. The figures of the masque, though intended to present the primeval life of nature, moved and stepped and turned with all the intricate rhythm of a dance; even the little faun butted the shepherdess in time to the music, and her shrieks were set to a melody on the oboes.

It was a pretty performance and lasted a full hour, for every incident had to be repeated. The lady of the castle, in the centre of the front row, clapped her hands, and her lovely face flushed with pleasure. The King, at her side, cried: "Encore!" And so the masque was played once more. In the end the shepherds, in pink and yellow silk, remained the victors, each over a silvan deity wrapped in a counterfeit leopard-skin of lace, whom he laid gracefully upon his back. Then he lifted the vanquished maiden from the ground, held her by his outstretched hand, and circled round and round on tiptoe with his lovely prey. Nothing could be seen but silvery dust, topped by the whirling, sunlit limbs of the shepherdess. Her partner blazed beneath her like a flame. Six pairs, six of these moving flames and burning clouds, spun round and round until a louder outburst of applause hinted to the dancers that they might stop.

Then each man set his lady on the ground, and all twelve, hand in hand, bowed to their noble audience and smiled, as though the whole performance had cost them no effort; but in truth they could hardly stand upright or see. The youngest dancer's wreath of narcissus slipped down over her nose, and she could not straighten it. Gabrielle hurried forward before anyone could stop her — set the little creature's wreath to rights and kissed her flushed face.

The King led his dear lady back to her place, and a faint mutter of applause greeted the indecorous impulse, which the audience would otherwise have disapproved. The shepherds and shepherdesses then departed, and the silvan gods rounded off the performance with ludicrous goat-capers. First they leapt over each other, then over the lower hedges, then over the highest, until all had vanished into the rustling foliage. Then came a burst of melody from the hidden musicians, and to its rhythm the company moved into the castle and took their places at the tables laid out round the great banqueting hall. The King had a small table apart for himself and the Marquise. Her guests sat at the larger one, which had been arranged in the shape of a gallows, as several noblemen did not fail to indicate to fat Mayenne. But his hunger, if nothing else, made him unreceptive of a jest. At his side the blonde hostess's dark-haired sister took the head of the table.

Diane d'Estrées, now wife of the Marshal de Balagny, had had but poor fortune of late. The city of Cambrai, where her husband was Governor, had been surprised and taken by the Spaniards. Now, Cambrai lies in Artois, almost in Flanders; sometimes it was in the King's authority and sometimes not. His fame did not suffer when he lost Cambrai; he was still the conqueror of the Spaniards. The world heard only of his victories and nothing at all of Cambrai. He was a great King, the greatest after Don Philip's Catholic Majesty, whose decline and decay was the work of the King of France; this for the whole of Europe, which would have it so and must be left in that conviction. Pin-pricks were better not regarded, their futility was realized by even the vanquished party. He might disturb such celebrations as those held that day, but he could do no more. In that kingdom he would never again appear as though it were his own. " It is mine," thought Henri; " I have paid for it."

These thoughts were in his mind while he figured at the feast; he savoured the dishes, whispered gallantries into his mistress's shapely ear, raised his glass to Mayenne, his humbled enemy. He called on a certain nobleman of the court, Monsieur de Sigongne, to describe the allegorical piece that he had devised and rehearsed with his company of players; the characters were from the ancient myths, but it was designed for the glory of the King of France.

It was to be performed that very evening in the hall, in addition to a grand ballet on the morrow. The guests, the hostess, and the King no less, were all eager for it; they delighted in agreeable spectacles and things of pleasant import. The reality, alas, was far from cheerful and had to be confronted in good earnest. Days came and passed on which Henri merely wished to be left in peace; he was weary of danger, though never of amusement.

At table it was reported that Calais had fallen. Not a city which had, for a time, been as good as given up; but Calais, one of the keys of the kingdom. A silence fell upon the assemblage. Some were too surprised to speak, some were silenced by the shock or by the privy thoughts that came into their minds, and some, who put on a gloomy air, were glad. Aha! The Cardinal of Austria, at the head of a German army, had dealt that blow at Calais unobserved — Calais, the city and sea-fortress confronting England. How would this affect the kingdom and the new reign? He now had Spain once more upon his coast; and

beyond the Channel the Queen had disavowed her one-time
friend the renegade Protestant. The feasting here must end. A
Marquise, whose rank and name should be very different — her
venal lap should no longer receive the revenues wrung from us by
the accursed Rosny. The guilt lay upon the King, and he must
pay for it.

Such thoughts were never far away; the fall of Calais brought
them to men's lips, and some covered their mouths with their
hands. They looked inquiringly at Mayenne. Mayenne had
been assiduously filling his belly and wished he could have removed himself and his belly from that assemblage. The news
came at an unpleasant moment; just as his digestion had begun,
he had to consider whether he had not blundered by making his
submission too soon. He did not think so — first on account of
his digestion, and further because he could not bear to think that
his defeat had been in vain. He disliked the Cardinal of Austria,
as he had often observed. Mayenne was the first to break the
silence; he muttered into his glass, which lent a sort of hollow
echo to his words: " A bag of bones like that — he'll do no good."
Therewith he tilted his glass and drained it.

It was the speech of one who knew — he had proved in his own
person whether it was possible to get the better of this King. So
all who had been listening to Mayenne looked towards the King.
Henri was prepared; his good humour, which was sometimes
lacking when he thought himself unheeded, did not fail him
now. He said across the gallows-shaped table: " Well, Calais is
gone. No matter. I have suffered worse things in war. Now it is
the enemy's turn, but ours will soon come back. God has never
forsaken me, when I besought Him from my heart. And now
let us honour the memory of the dead — and then consider our
requital, which we'll take with interest and compound interest."

Such were his words. But he remained seated for a while,
though he flung a word or a brief order to some few of the company. At the word " interest," all eyes promptly fell on Monsieur de Rosny, provider of money to the King. His set countenance looked truly formidable; each of that company wondered
silently how much the fall of Calais would cost him in the end.

In his usual cold voice, without a glance at anyone, Rosny said:
"The Cardinal of Austria did not take Calais at once. He got Cambrai first."

The Marquise's sister started up and would have answered angrily. Monsieur de Rosny's stony demeanour made that impossible; indeed, the unlucky Diane could do no other than stare at her plate, as did all the rest, or they would otherwise have too plainly revealed what was in their minds: the mistress's family, and she herself, must answer for this disaster. They enriched themselves, and delivered up the cities of the kingdom to the enemy.

Meanwhile something for which the King had sent was put into his hands — a portrait of the Queen of England. He turned it this way and that until all could see whom it represented: a sixty-year-old woman, rigid and unwearied. Her cities were not lost while she feasted and watched ballets. The King raised the picture to his lips and kissed it, as all thought. In truth it did not touch his mouth, but from behind the frame, which covered his eyes, he sought those of his companion. Gabrielle realized that he wanted to reassure her, but this time she would not listen to his protestations, whether whispered or mirrored in his eyes. She had grown pale. There were enemies about her. In that hour even her dear lord could not protect her against their hatred. And so, in the sight of all, she laid her lifted hands together, as she did when at prayer in her own chamber. She bent over the picture — and not the great Elizabeth, only the wood that framed her counterfeited image, received Gabrielle's submissive kiss.

Despite all, Monsieur de Sigongne was able to present his ingenious play that evening. It was received with profound admiration, as it could hardly fail to be. The hero was a king, so victorious and intelligent and handsome that the god Mars could do no less than bestow upon him Venus, who promised to bear him brave and noble sons. At the supper that followed were served the small oysters that the King especially liked, and he pretended to enjoy them. At least he did not need to talk — he could reflect that for a while he had better maintain the guise of weariness and nonchalance. The war was not at an end, he knew that now, even supposing that his name and fame had blinded him to that fact. A double danger threatened him if he reconquered Calais from the sea, which was his next task; and the Queen of England would certainly send him help. But it was equally probable that she would never let Calais go. So he merely had the choice of whether he preferred the stubborn power of England on his coast, or Spain striking her last feeble blows.

On the other hand, it came upon the King that here was really a new enemy who stood within his frontiers. The Cardinal of Austria, his German princes, and his troops: the old enemy, with another face. Habsburg had several; the World Empire was a hydra. When he had cut off one head, there were ten more to hiss at him. He must destroy the whole monster. He must challenge the Roman Emperor, the universal monarchy, and all her provinces; even Spain was merely one of them; Philip, the Ruler of the World, was under orders; and there were many others. He alone, as present events portended, confronted the entire hydra, which bore the name of Christendom.

The prospect shook him. Only a few moments earlier he had not realized what he would have to face. Now it appeared plainly before his mind, and for the first time. A great calamity had come upon him; that was his first reflection. He confronted what was to be his last mission, and it went beyond his strength.

He rose from the table, withdrawing into a dark corner where none could see his fear nor suspect what now beset him. But his companion laid an anxious hand upon his arm. He looked at her and saw that his fear was shared by his companion — who could not measure it nor suspect its cause. None the less she suffered with him; she had gradually become a piece of himself through her blood and senses, and would remain so until her end. So he drew her to his side and they vanished together into the darkness of the garden.

They mounted the broad terrace outside their bedchamber, where they could be heard by no one. And Gabrielle whispered: " My beloved lord, we have enemies. To help you conquer the Cardinal of Austria, I will sell all that I possess and put the price of it in your war-chest."

"My dear love," replied Henri, "you are my incomparable possession. Let us forget these enemies; there might well be too many of them if we thought of them by name."

A mysterious utterance, which Gabrielle neither understood nor questioned; both stood silent, as though the time had come for endearments. But Henri's preoccupation had put them sadly out of mind. He tried to banish his obsession, but the effort set him pondering on his accepted mission. Above his strength or not, he had accepted it.

He reflected: from his youth upward, all his toils and conflicts had been brought on him by Spain, no matter whom he fought, what bullets whistled round his ears, how many cities he stormed, and how many enemies he conciliated; until, at the end, he had become master of his kingdom. It had cost him half his life and more. Now he wanted rest, and time for the works of peace. Surely the Pyrenees were high enough, no need to pile Pelion upon Ossa. After him, let the new enemy arise, or new heads grow upon the ancient monster. He had had his share — and he broke out in his familiar oath, which reached her ears.

Gabrielle too was stirred by this inner colloquy, of which she had indeed no notion. "Sire," said she, "am I really your evil genius? Calais falls and I am hated. Monsieur de Rosny conceives the guilt is mine."

"My dear love," said Henri, his mouth very close to hers, while his breath came and went in angry gasps, "Monsieur de Rosny shall atone by returning to the Arsenal tomorrow, where he belongs. We will stay and spend the day at your dairy farm among your forty sleek cows, and picnic on the grass. In your honour all the ladies shall appear in rustic clothes. You are the centre of my life and joy."

"My dear lord," she said, "I am again expecting a child from you."

Herewith she closed her eyes, although it was dark; but she could feel his heart leap for joy. His fierce breathing she could no longer hear, his lips met hers, and the deep silence of their embrace was measured by their throbbing pulses.

Then from the garden below came a crack and a hiss, a fiery

streamer shot up into the sky, curved and dropped, and, with a scatter of sparks, went out. Hark to the babble of voices from those strolling in the dim garden or on the terrace or peering from the windows into darkness outside!

All knew, of course, what would follow. After the first fore-runner, the rockets would go up in clusters, and it was so; as the company walked to and fro, the heavens were seared with flaming fountains, rays, sheaves, and globes, which flashed and burst into a shower of blue and red and white. Against a bank of foliage, a wheel leapt into light and poured forth silvery rain, shedding so unearthly a radiance that the garden seemed to rise out of the darkness and hover in the void, a very abode for fairies. And be-hold — the swan! Above that glittering domain floated a swan; it shimmered, moved its wings, and came to rest — and then vanished with that wondrous cry that swans are fabled to utter when they die.

Suddenly, darkness as before, and the onlookers rubbed their eyes. Fireworks, nothing more; and there was much laughter among the onlookers at their own easy bewilderment. But while the performance lasted, strange thoughts were set astir in many a mind — thoughts that soared up to an inner heaven that was marvellous to look upon. Henri had a vision of his whole heaven aflame. With a joy that he had never known, and in full accept-ance, he grasped that mission that had daunted him awhile ago. He would fulfil it and destroy the empire of darkness.

It was they or he; they were still intent upon his destruction. But with his destruction they meant to compass a yet greater one, and destroy freedom, reason, and humanity. Their universal monarchy and world sovereignty had mastered many limbs of Christendom, and a monster would come of them, with a mis-shapen body and many poisonous heads. His cause was to help the nations live, and live by reason, not travail within the swollen belly of the Universal Power, which had engulfed them. It was his mission to save so many of them as still had the choice, and follow in the footsteps of the Son of Man.

Came a spurt of silver from the wheel, and the swan floated overhead. No matter, thought Henri. Nothing was certain; why look forward to Calvary? They should not get him; they had not mastered France. He would, in God's name, found a free League of the kingdoms and republics that had escaped and could still stand against Habsburg.

Outside, the sparks were scattering before darkness fell once more. What was Habsburg, after all? thought Henri. An Emperor dominated, like his peoples, by the monks. In addition, the tainted monarch beyond the mountains, who had talked loudest of all. Well, Henri made no war upon their persons and their country; properly speaking, there was no globe that would show where their country lay. It lay in the domain of Evil. His realm began at the frontier where people can use their understanding and are no longer wholly slaves. By God, he would win that fight!

The first words he said thereafter to Gabrielle, were these: "Truly, madame, my Rosny is an admirable mediocrity!"

A free league of kingdoms and republics was a notion that never entered the head of that faithful servant, though fiery rays tore through the air, and swans floated in the darkness.

"So the fall of Calais is not my fault?" asked Gabrielle. And he said:

"Calais, the Cardinal of Austria, yourself, and I — what are causes and effects? One might get a notion of them while the fireworks lasted, but no longer." He spoke wearily.

"Let us go in," said she; and he escorted his beloved lady into the room they shared, the finest in the house. He shook his head as he saw the bed for the first time. Its mattresses were covered with white silk, and the pillows embroidered with a design of H and G intertwined. Folded across the lower end lay the coverlet, of crimson damask threaded with gold. From the canopy hung curtains of yellow Genoese velvet. Such a bed had never received that impoverished King before. His lady noticed his hesitation.

"My lord, you think as I do, that we should sell everything to fill your war-chest."

"Alas, I have had dreams far more hazardous," replied Henri. "I took them for the true meaning of things, so long as the fire-

works lasted. Indeed, I made my way into a very exalted sphere
— and I scarce know how I strayed there. We are here below,
and must always do what lies nearest to our hand; and what lies
nearest to me now is — that I love you."

SUCCESS

The next matter of concern was, as usual, to raise money; and
this time the crisis produced something like a panic. Any day
their fate might come upon them, and on behalf of Spain, though
at her last gasp, the Roman Empire would move in all its might.
Enemy armies that the kingdom had never seen, barbaric tribes
from eastern Europe, curved sabres, small wild horses, men with
yellow skins and slanting eyes — all this would trample down the
fields of France and burn her cities. No one could foresee that
terror nor picture it, except the King alone. And at night the
horror came upon him in colours all too crude; that was because
he bore his anxiety alone. These anxieties were kept from his
people, and his Paris Parliament, then engaged in grumbling at
the expense of the Marquise's ballets — and even from Rosny,
who found the King was growing hysterical.

When the King quoted figures, they were seldom correct; this
was a subject which, in Rosny's view, he should have avoided.
Eight finance counsellors, excluding Rosny, no longer disposed
of a million and a half crowns, as the King imagined; Rosny saw
to that. But he could scarcely raise funds for war by depriving
eight people of their pilfered gains. Moreover, Rosny liked to
believe that the principle of order was gaining on the world, and
within the compass that was his he laboured soberly to that end.
Still less did the men of Parliament, whose affairs had at last been
brought to a settlement, share the King's notions. Curved sabres,
small wild horses, men with yellow skins and slanting eyes — that
could never happen here. Civilization reigned in France.

And who was it that by much toil and labour made you think
that it so reigned? Thus might the King have replied to his
friends the jurists. But he was silent — he did not want to intensify the danger by speaking his mind, and no others shared his

nightmares. In the company of his beloved lady he betook himself to Rouen; she was bidden to come with him, for he had several matters in mind. After an entry into the city, which aroused no great enthusiasm, he waited for a purpose of his own; he was to make an address that he had long meditated, to the Estates of his province of Normandy. The Assembly was held in the Chapter House of the Abbey of Saint-Ouen, a very sacred place; for a King who there challenged the judgment of such a body, and that for the first time, must risk no failure.

Before he appeared, the assembly had gathered in full strength, and the members could observe how fully each estate was represented: nine bishops, nineteen nobles, and no less than thirty-two burghers, including craftsmen and peasants. Not a large body, but constituted as none of the sort had been before, by the express order of the King, when he first appeared in the presence of his people's deputies. Cautiously, in true Norman fashion, they talked of him and his ways, which were new and strange to them, so far as they had yet had dealings with each other. He had been a heretic and a dubious adventurer from the South when he laid fierce siege to their city, though he had bought it in the end; that they approved as a sagacious and praiseworthy proceeding. On the other hand, as touching his personal demeanour, it by no means befitted their conception of the dignity and reserve that a sovereign should display; quite apart from what is called majesty, which in him was wholly absent. Should a King bring his mistress with him when he received the submission of the sedate and rain-swept city of Rouen, and now of all times, when he made his ceremonial entry? The Marquise had not been offered the customary bread and wine, though she had taken the best lodging in the Abbey. To each according to his desert. Moreover, since the arrival of the pair the streets had been lit, though only by express command, and in their view the money for this purpose had much better have been saved.

Rise, rise — the King! He entered, escorted, with such pomp as he could muster, by twelve gentlemen, chosen for their thews and stature; and the Papal Legate was also present. Sit down under the canopy, my little man from nowhere, now grown so great; you will need a skill that we misdoubt you have not, to overcome our mistrust of your light-hearted ways. But how is this? The majesty so lacking — here it is, displayed forthwith. He stood on a dais to address them, used the words of every day, and spoke quite naturally — but tone and speech were instinct with majesty itself. Of a sort, indeed, to which they were unaccustomed. Not that it seemed to come from other climes, but from a man whose like they had never seen; and he, as was well known, did not always use it. But he had it.

Henri carried a few sheets of paper, loosely disposed like a hand of cards, so that a casual glance would promptly catch the word he sought. The script was large; he had taken care to write out the sentences himself, that there might be no omission and no mistake. He now talked as though the words he used were of no moment, so exactly had he tested them beforehand. He said: " If I wished to shine as an orator " — and he most manifestly shone. " I am ambitious to bear two glorious titles. I would be known as the deliverer and restorer of this State."

At first he ascribed all achievements to his faithful officers, to his high-hearted nobles; then, suddenly, he stepped into the foreground. " I saved France from ruin; let us preserve it from the fresh destruction that now threatens! " Whereby he appealed to all there represented, the main body of the labouring classes. They were to help him, not merely by their obedience; he needed their confidence and asked their counsel. This was noteworthy and new. His beloved subjects he also called them, and said that he had not summoned them, as his predecessors had done, to approve everything he had already decided. " I have assembled you to receive your advice, to trust in it and to follow it; in brief, to place myself in your hands and under your tutelage."

What a word! The noisy breathing of the assemblage at the word " tutelage " was provided for in the manuscript by several empty lines. A glance by the speaker at the last of the sheets and its scrawling script; then the King spoke with all his reserves of power and majesty.

" Such a desire seldom comes to kings, to greybeards, and to

conquerors. All things will come easily to one who loves you as
I do, and would be known as your deliverer."

He sat down, waved them to their seats, and let some minutes
pass, leaning loosely in his chair, as though he had made no great
professions, but had merely spoken plainly to plain people.
Down below they were putting their heads together, until one
cleared his throat, got up, and began to speak; though the secretaries understood but little of what he said. The peasant spoke
the country dialect; moreover, his embarrassment was as great as
his excitement. He promised the King that for his part he would
give a penny out of every pound, and that as often as he sold a
head of cattle or a sack of corn. Others, who saw further and
could express themselves more fluently, added what they could
do. No one on that account believed that much money would
be forthcoming; otherwise, such as were rich would have to sacrifice half their fortunes. He who possessed little, but yet something, made no such demand upon his betters. But so much had
been achieved. They had seen the King in homely guise, and in
his majesty. They mistrusted him no more.

He came down from the dais and disappeared at the back, so
quickly that the onlookers did not know whither and how, which
thus added a touch of mystery to the impression he had made.
They indeed mistrusted him no more — not all of them, and at
least not for the present. There was something strange about
him still, and it may be that this had actually served his turn.
The Normans stood cautiously discussing their opinions of the
King after what had passed, gathered in little groups, rather undecided, not disinclined to listen to those who must surely be
better acquainted with this unusual King. Those were his own
people, whom he had brought with him for the occasion; several
of them specially chosen, to tell the Normans what they needed
to know. Upon these he could rely; less upon the others, who
had remained behind of their own free will.

Henri, behind his curtain, whispered to Gabrielle:
" How did I speak? "
" Nobly. No one can speak as you can. But why " tutelage "?

You brought the word in well, the tears came into my eyes. But would you really have them thus, rather than your subjects? "

He cursed under his breath at her want of understanding, took her hand and laid it on his sword. " With this at my side," said he.

Then he bade her sit quietly in her chair, in view of her condition, while he himself listened at the curtain. At first he caught voices from the Third Estate, slow, lumbering speech, but without a hint of mockery or protest. The dialect did not prevent his grasping the sense of what was said. If the enemy invaded France again, they might equally be Spaniards, Germans, or even Englishmen; and these men preferred their own King. They had not wanted a commander, and they certainly did not want war. But if the worst came, they would stand by their King, who, from all appearance, was their man — he had already made good laws, and had asked them to say how much they themselves thought they should pay in taxes. " If it is too little, he can send his guards to fetch more," said a farmer, who had rightly interpreted the phrase about tutelage.

A burgher observed that appearances were mostly to be trusted, and he personally could tell from the look of every customer whether he would pay. A dishonourable man was either too accommodating or too offhand. Everything the King said had been backed by the right expression.

This commercial view was confirmed by one of the jurists. Whether he were the President of the Parliament of Paris or what he was, Henri from behind his curtain could not tell, but he heard a great deal. " On a man's face everything is visible, both his joys and his fears," said the President, turning towards the commonalty, that they might profit by his observation.

For the benefit of the Norman lords, bishops, and noblemen, he repeated in the words of Juvenal:

" *Deprendas animi tormenta.*"

But one of the lords from near Rouen answered very cautiously: If it were agreed that the art of the tragic actor could make his face reflect any feelings that he pleased, the Greeks would not, as was well known, have esteemed him any the less.

" Curse the fellow," muttered Henri; " he takes me for an actor."

The craftsmen and the farmers reassured him again; they specially esteemed the fact that he had been successful. " The last time he came among us he was out at elbows. And now look at all his pomp and glory. He makes money; we shall do well under such a King."

A shiver of awe went through the company, and the Marshal de Matignon, whom Henri had sent for to support him, saw his opportunity.

" Good people," said the Marshal, " what you and many, many others rightly reverence in the King is something without compare, which never appears save through a special bestowal by God. And that is majesty."

The less they grasped this mystery, the more effect it had upon them. Their increasing inclination to shake off their hard rusticity was encouraged by the word " majesty," for they had marked something of the sort in the King, though they could not give a name to it. They had gradually shed their suspicions, and when Matignon went on to tell them that the King had never spoken so openly and familiarly to anyone, then these northern men at last found their tongues. They talked all at once, they praised each other's courage and readiness to give up what they possessed, not merely a penny from a pound, but half a pound and more. They set their lips to talk of a " great man " and of " majesty "; and some were found to speak of him as " beloved by his people."

Henri, behind his curtain, listened eagerly; in all the confusion of voices, those last words did not escape him. They first made him start and bow his head. Then he raised himself to his full height, and said: " I have them." In his own mind he added: " For the time." And he prayed to God that this spirit might endure until it had spread to his other provinces, which would be easier to win. He knew why he had begun here. His whole people and kingdom must be roused and ready when those small wild horses and curved sabres stormed out of the east.

In the hall the Secretary of State, Monsieur de Villeroy, smote his fist upon the table where the protocols were being prepared. He announced that all the commonalty attendant there that day had been ennobled by His Majesty. At this a profound silence fell, which was not broken until a countryman, no doubt quite overcome, observed rather boorishly, and in the loudest tones: " His Majesty must forgive us, but common blood cannot be dyed blue " — an observation that was greeted with a general burst of laughter.

Those least impressed by the quality of majesty and its resonant success were naturally enough his own gentlemen whom he had brought with him, and especially the ecclesiastics. One of the two Cardinals reminded the other of a verse of Horace: " He leaves aside what he could have in any case, and concerns himself with those who do not want him."

" *Transvolat in medio posita, et fugentia captat* " — the Cardinal repeated the line in the purest Italian pronunciation. The other's Latin was coloured by a French accent.

" *Nil adeo magnum —* "

He hurriedly rendered the lines from Lucretius in his native tongue:

> " Naught is so great and honoured at the outset
>
> That men do not reject it in the end."

The two scholars blinked at each other, with one eye upon the Papal Legate; he had indeed come there in the plain expectation of seeing the King put down once for all. Now he himself had been put down, and he was much distressed; but his memory of the classics was not a whit inferior to that of the two others.

" What eye," said he, " can have bewitched my little lambs, I know not " — thus rendering the line from Virgil: " *Nescio quis teneros oculus mihi fascinat agnos.*"

Thereupon, shaking at the knees, the Legate left the apartment. Then the assemblage broke up.

A Norman lord said, in the doorway, to one of the more exalted jurists: " An old quotation comes into my mind too. *Fortis imaginatio generat casum.* He who holds a matter vividly before his mind turns it into a reality."

And the jurist answered, still in the doorway: "My lord, you have truly understood our King's character." As they were the last across the threshold, Henri heard them clearly. He craned his head out from behind the curtain to watch them go, and marked that the Norman had the long straight back and fresh complexion of his own Rosny. Well, he could not expect them all to be figures from a cathedral porch. There must be lesser degrees of solidity and stony strength. "Rosny," he told himself, "is the Norman at his best, he has cast in his lot with me, and that will weigh with them as long as I endure." "I have them," he said aloud; "even these."

"Dear lady!" he cried; a few long strides brought him to her and he clasped her in his arms, her fair golden head, the roses and lilies of her cheeks, and the eyes as grey as Norman seas. "To win you I would have served still longer," he said, speaking close into her lovely lips. And she heard him with such joy, such pride, that she laughed; indeed, she laughed at him. And he held her very gently because she was near her time.

Two Women Friends

A week later the King's beloved gave birth to a girl. Henri thought her very pretty, and had her solemnly baptized as a child of France. She was christened Catherine-Henriette, after the King himself and his sister. Madame, the sister of the King, could not hold her godchild at the ceremony, being a Protestant. But she had the right of sitting by the mother's bedside, as Gabrielle's best friend at court; indeed, Gabrielle found no others.

Madame, the sister of the King, dilated to the mother on the beauties of her little daughter; and did so with almost pious fervour, for physical perfection portended Heaven's favour to the new-born infant, and a happy life on earth. Her own life, although she was known as Madame, sister of the King, offered no more hopes of happiness; but Catherine was inclined to ascribe her ill fortune to her lameness. She never betrayed her feelings, she was royally courteous to all comers, and there was still much girlish grace in her now ageing face. Gabrielle alone knew her as she was, for Catherine regarded her with an ardour that amounted to devotion. This woman bore beautiful and healthy children to her brother, a boy and now a girl. She was a chosen vessel, graced by Heaven. At her bedside sat Madame, sister of the King, not in token of kindness or goodwill, but to do her honour.

She passed from the baby's perfections to a description of the gorgeous pillow on which it had been carried in the Church of Saint-Ouen. Ladies and gentlemen of the court, splendidly arrayed, had passed the child of France from hand to hand, such as were so privileged. The pillow was draped with a train of silver brocade trimmed with tailed ermine, six ells long, and the honour of carrying it was bestowed on Mademoiselle de Guise.

"They all hate me," whispered Gabrielle. She was still too weak to dissemble her uneasiness. And therewithal she felt that her lord's sister might well be told the truth. "Madame," she whispered, "will our lord marry me?"

"Do not doubt it," said Catherine, kneeling down and stroking the young mother's left hand, the hand by which her brother was to lead this woman to the altar. "You have friends; I am one."

"Have I another?" asked Gabrielle, half sitting up in her astonishment.

"The Princess of Orange wishes, as do I, that the King should marry a woman fitted to be his Queen."

"Am I so fitted? Does a stern and pious lady who in her distant Netherlands hears nothing but ill against me, truly think so?"

Madame stood up, to lend emphasis to what she was about to say:

"The Princess of Orange is of my Religion. We Protestants believe in the freedom of the conscience and the choice of hearts. The King my brother has won the only heart that he desires to keep, and will keep until the end — and he found it in his kingdom."

More she would not say at present; she left the room soon

afterwards, and forbade Gabrielle's women to go in to her, telling
them that she needed rest.

Gabrielle lay and fell to pondering on all these matters, so far
as her head, as yet still drained of blood, would serve her. Freedom of conscience — she did not understand the phrase, except
that it told in her favour. Two Protestant Princesses, and no one
else, stood by her; it was their wish that the Queen of France
should be a lady of that land. Not a daughter of some other royal
house, an infanta, an archduchess, or a princess; not money nor
kinship, on which Monsieur de Rosny was so intent as he
searched all Europe for the alliance that should most profit the
King.

Gabrielle heard of this after the event. The cold calculations
of the faithful Rosny, the hatred of those who despised her and
her origin — she was only too well aware of what, unfortunately,
was common knowledge. Only the King's love and the " choice
of hearts " served to soften and disguise these harsh and cruel
facts. She feared the Infantas, but not until lately had she heard
the warning of her inner voice — since her lord had been awaiting
the curved sabres from the east. Yes, but for his fears, hers would
not have spoken; now, through her children, she was of his flesh
and of his blood. She had borne a second child to her lord, when
danger seemed at a standstill; she prayed that it might not now
advance upon her; but in her heart she knew that it must come.

Gabrielle turned her face from the light, to ease her thinking.
She had two friends, both of the Religion. About the King there
were no Protestants save Monsieur de Rosny, who hated her.
What was to happen? What did Madame mean? No answer,
not now — and would there ever be? " Sleep, and dream of what
you will wear at your wedding."

Gabrielle had been trapped in a game of conflicting forces,
knowing nothing of the issues; she merely felt that there was
something ominous about that game. The balls were flying for
too high a stake, which might indeed be herself. The players
aimed and caught and missed; the last player retrieved the balls
and marched off with the stake. The King played so skilfully he

must surely win. And, after all, he had taken that leap of death whereby so much had been decided. What of the game for Gabrielle? She had gone to sleep and was dreaming of her wedding dress.

The Cardinal of Austria

Henri, Gabrielle, and the court left Rouen and went back to Paris when Carnival began. That Carnival was a notably boisterous affair; therein appeared the first consequence of the great game at Rouen which the King had won. Paris stood aloof no longer. The nobility and even the respectable burghers there deigned to share the amusements of the mob, because they thought that the King had a weakness for the common people and their doings. Gentlemen and ladies disported themselves in the market-place and in the packed streets, cavaliers dived into the throng of criers, students, and porters, though in days gone by they would have had such people cudgelled by their lackeys at the first sign of insolence. Now they joined in the turmoil and the horseplay, not a few of them were soundly buffeted, and an advocate, of whom such exploits might have been least expected, lost his hat in a low tavern.

The ladies forgot their breeding; under cover of the tumult they made their way into the booths where abortions were exhibited. Nay, more, they made the acquaintance of public women of the baser sort. It was put about that one lady went into a harlot's house, disguised of course in a mask, which, even in extremity, was never taken off. Gabrielle, who heard the story, turned her back on the lady at her next reception, although she was usually courtesy itself. It did her no good; nothing could make her popular, neither her assiduous decorum nor that single gesture of impatience.

During that Carnival a quatrain was composed upon the King, the Marquise d'Estrées, and the Cardinal of Austria, who had taken Calais, and all Paris chanted it:

> *Bold Henri bids the Spaniard stand,*
> *And marches out to war:*

But — *he is running from a parson*
And clinging to a whore.

Gabrielle thought of the good friendly town of Rouen, where they would never have made such verses, or repeated them. She tried to prevent this, and even paid a few sturdy fellows to take what steps were possible. In vain; one evening when she and Henri were alone, he betrayed the fact that he knew the verses. And during their tenderest endearments he repeated them.

By way of answer, Gabrielle thrust him indignantly away from her. She asked him earnestly to give up play; even ball-play, well as he played it, and much as she liked watching him, cost a great deal of money; but especially cards, which would get him into the hands of the usurers. She knew whom she had first in mind: a man called Zamet. His house was equally a gaming-hell, a money-lender's, and brothel; and the King frequented it.

She thought best to accompany him, at least to the famous Saint-Germain fair, taking several ladies with her, including her Aunt de Sourdis and Madame de Sagonne. The latter was a gossip; Gabrielle was sure that everything would promptly reach the ears of the court. So she made the King bargain for a ring, for which the Portuguese vender asked a fabulous price; and Gabrielle renounced it. But her self-sacrifice profited her as little as her austerity. Unfriendly talebearers are never at a loss for tales to tell.

On Shrove Tuesday a great ball was given by Madame in honour of Gabrielle. The Tuileries, where Catherine lived, was ablaze with light, every room and nook and corner. Gathered round the King's sister and his beloved were all the ladies of the court, in the same dress of sea-green silk; sea-green because it was the blonde Gabrielle's own colour, and the silk came from the King's workshops. All wore masks; and to distinguish one from another, a man had to know the lady's figure, or have agreed upon signs.

From a hidden gallery came soft and solemn music; there were to be none but ceremonial dances, and some of the younger women began to whisper that the evening would be tedious. It was observed that the gentlemen were late in coming, and then that they all came at once. They made a strange entry, some on their haunches, flinging out their feet before them, and so lurching noisily round the room. Others walked upright between the dancers, their height increased by hidden stilts and astrologers' peaked caps. They carried wooden bowls and knives and rattled them as they went. Their long robes betokened that they were meant to be magicians, while the squatting dancers were equipped with all the implements of barber-surgeons. They even produced what looked like leeches from their pockets.

The ladies at first stared wide-eyed, as their lords circled elaborately round the room, not solely disguised by masks and fantastic noses. The magicians and the barbers, some hopping on their haunches, the others towering above them in their zodiacal hats, not men from the world of men, but mechanic figures in a pantomime jerking past like clockwork toys — the ladies looked on in alarm. Were these the men they knew? they asked, while the masqueraders revolved. Then some began to titter, and at last many burst into open laughter. Two or three laughed themselves into hysterics, flung themselves over a chair, and shrieked.

Their demeanour, and indeed the whole affair, attracted all the palace retainers. Even the porters and soldiers who kept an eye on inquisitive loiterers below left their posts, each assuming that another would take his place. That other thought likewise, and so at last they were all in the royal apartments. They jostled along a gallery towards some open doors whence they could stare into the hall. Then came the loiterers, on whom there was no one now to keep an eye, and all the approaches were packed with onlookers. The soldiers, who had no business there either, took no steps to drive out the populace, and the moving throng was gradually thrust forwards into the hall where the barber ballet was proceeding. The lords and ladies had often enough found their way down to the street; the street was now returning their visits.

Among the street people was a real barber, though disguised in a bulbous cardboard nose. The nose, and his profession, conferred on him, as he thought, the right to dance in the barber

ballet. He squatted like the other barbers, clattered his implements (which were genuine), and tried to fling out his feet in
appropriate fashion. But he had not learned the art of it, so he
overturned the dancer before him and fell into the arms of the
one behind. The fall of the barber in front brought down a magician, his stilts slipped from under him, and he crashed full length
on several of the squatting dancers. Then the next magician
tottered. The sense of terror and excitement grew almost un-
bearable, and mob as well as ladies burst into shouts and yells.

Meantime the real barber lay in the arms of the sham one, and
the latter recognized that the other was what he seemed to be.

" Fellow," he said, " would you earn a crown? "

" Would I not! " said the other.

" You see that green person behind the glass door. You are to
shave her head — shave it completely bald, just as such girls are
shaved by the city watch," said the sham barber. And the real
one answered:

" But she might be a lady. That is dangerous work, it will cost
you a gold piece."

" Very well, a gold piece," said the sham barber, producing
one. " The person is wearing a wig, you are only to make a show
of shaving her. 'Tis but a jest. Be ready when the moment
comes."

By this time the figures of the disordered ballet had disen-
tangled themselves, the barbers stood upon their feet, and the
magicians had thrown away their stilts. The ladies were much
concerned lest their lords might have taken harm in the mishap.
Each sought her own, and the ladies were quickest at recognition. In the tumult Gabrielle d'Estrées seized the King's arm,
having long since marked him as the fourth of the seven magicians. " Sire, let us go! My dear lord, think of Jean Chastel and
his knife."

Therewith she drew him into one of the neighbouring cabinets
and promptly blew out all the tapers within reach. Not once did
she let go her lord's hand, but stood between him and any onlookers. Then she whispered:

" This was folly! "

" Dear lady, I had no part in the performance. I wanted to appear as a magician, that was all. The barber came on his own account. The ballet of the magicians and the barbers, though carefully rehearsed, was never meant to be danced here, I do beg you to believe." And Henri kissed her lovely chin, leaving some shreds of mask on her curving lips.

In the meantime a strange stillness had come over the hall. The pair looked round them, but could not discover what had happened. A disguised and comically bleating voice fell upon their ears. " Soldiers, obey me! I am a gentleman of the court. Arrest that green lady, she has run away from me and stolen my jewels."

A hoarse voice replied: " The girl did well; she has repaid herself and me. You still owe me the price of her, you old skinflint."

The green lady in question, burst into a volley of abuse; and from the hoarseness of her voice it could be recognized as genuine. The speech of the mob can be imitated, but not its voice. Then followed some antics between a girl of the streets and two gentlemen whom the King and his lady recognized from the manner of their talk.

" That is Monsieur de Roquelaure," said Henri.

" That is Monsieur de Varenne," said Gabrielle. And she added in a lower tone: " How dreadful! "

For she guessed, before the King realized it, that the interlude was meant as an insult. Monsieur de Roquelaure, who was of an age with the King, had been a companion of his youth, and still indulged in the freedoms of old days.

" He does not hate me," thought the King. " He is a Protestant. But he loves a jest — and for the sake of a sorry jest he is here betraying me to my enemies, whether consciously or not."

" The pair of fools! " cried Henri, and was on the point of dashing out. Gabrielle held him back.

" What can have come to Roquelaure? " said he. " And to Varenne? He was once go-between for you and me; and so, from a cook, he became a rich man. And now he acts go-between as though he never were one. God help me, I think these people are all mad."

"Less mad than you think," muttered Gabrielle, leaning heavily against him. And through the mask he could see that her eyes were veiled with tears. "My lovely one," he murmured, "my dear heart." In the face of her lamentations he felt helpless. Yonder scene was meant in jest; it was unwise to be serious about trivial matters, though they be not quite so trivial as they looked.

"There is a secret door out of this cabinet," whispered Gabrielle eagerly. "If only one knew the place in the wall! Let us get out of here, my lord!"

But the knob was easily found by those who did not know it. Henri, as he tapped the panelling, moved gradually towards the door and was several times on the point of bursting in upon those antics; for he realized the malignant insolence intended. Two soldiers of the guard had also taken part, and while the pimp set himself in a posture of defence, the pretended courtier shouted for a barber and his scissors. The girl struggled and screamed raucously. In brief, it was high time — high time indeed, for every word uttered was more pointedly aimed at the King and his lady.

He looked round at Gabrielle; she was groping feverishly at the wall. But she no longer looked to escape by the secret passage. He must protect her, and so he would with all his might. Let him but get among them and show himself with face unmasked.

That he would have done, but that another came first; also disguised as a magician, he was about the measure of the King, with the same quick movements, and the brawlers, open-mouthed, recognized his grip as he flung them apart. He seized the barber, knocked the knife out of his fingers, and hurled him to the floor. Varenne, the pimp, was dismissed with a kick, and the two soldiers fled without more ado. Left alone was Monsieur de Roquelaure, still bleating like a goat. But his face grew blank when the new performer took off his mask.

It was the Count of Soissons, which was a surprise for most of the company. He had a good deal of the appearance of his royal cousin, and was not unlike him in the face; but it was a face without wit or dignity; grim and ferocious in that moment, and flushed from forehead to throat.

When Henri's worthy cousin had routed all the green lady's enemies, he took her finger-tips, as though he were escorting a court lady, and might have indulged in more buffoonery but for the fact that the girl was drunk. Unluckily these villains had brought her in without heeding her condition. Her outburst of fury, and the consciousness that all eyes were upon her, made matters worse — she turned and butted into Soissons's belly, though he was posing as her cavalier. The barber, in his efforts to shave her, had loosened her wig, which fell off, and the girl was seen to be completely bald. She herself only remarked it by the burst of laughter from the court and populace. She stood rigid, looked savagely about her, and, finding herself isolated and alone, with a wild yell vanished into the crowd.

It was a sight that distressed and disgusted the onlookers, whether they were of the court or from the street. Only the King could relieve this sense of outrage, and he did. In the company of Gabrielle d'Estrées, his beloved lady, he came forth from one of the neighbouring cabinets; they were hand in hand, and unmasked.

"You have witnessed an interlude played by my orders. I thank the charming lady who played the drunken, shaven girl; she is, in fact, quite sober and has lovely hair. I take pleasure in presenting her with this jewel."

This speech put the populace in high good humour, and the court breathed again. Monsieur de Roquelaure, suddenly enlightened, approached the King and would have fallen on his knees. His Majesty stopped him and congratulated him on his ingenious interlude.

"And now withdraw, my friend, and shut the door behind you. Madame is tired from laughing and needs a rest."

After a while someone ventured to open the door of the cabinet. The King and Gabrielle d'Estrées had gone, none knew how.

He accompanied her to her house, near the Louvre.

"Sire, do not leave me. I am alone."

Henri: "Dear lady, we shall soon be united for ever."

Gabrielle: " You do not think of what you say. You are telling yourself that I am hated. You have seen it for yourself."

Henri: " And I? We are great people, and therefore defenceless. The greater we grow, the more defenceless we are."

Gabrielle: " Have we no friends? "

Henri: " They spoil our cause, as my cousin Soissons spoiled that comic interlude."

Gabrielle: " Dear lord, that comic interlude does not end this day."

She buried her head in a cushion, that she might not hear her own words. Thus she waited until he was gone.

In his solitary Louvre he went to bed. It was eleven o'clock, he had left the ball early. He was not yet quite asleep when Monsieur d'Armagnac came into the room.

" Sire! Amiens."

Armagnac choked at the word, and could say no more. Henri had leapt out of bed. The fortress of Amiens surprised and taken, forty cannon lost; and nothing, not even a river, barred the way to Paris. The enemy could march on the capital.

" He is lost," said Henri, who was in his nightshirt. And his First Chamberlain tremblingly asked who.

" The Cardinal of Austria."

SHOEMAKER ZAMET

Rosny in his Arsenal was awakened and summoned to the King, who was pacing restlessly up and down his little room, behind the cabinet where the birds were kept. The burning tapers did not deceive them, they still slept huddled on their perches. The King was silent; with bowed head he shuffled to and fro in his slippers, and his bed-gown dragged behind him. Several of his noblemen stood stock-still against the walls. Not a word, not a sound. Monsieur de Rosny, as he entered, smelt disaster.

" Ha, friend! Bad news! " cried the King in a voice that was almost a shout.

When the faithful servant learned that the city of Amiens and the fortress were taken, he could not understand. " Who has done this? How has it happened?"

" The Spaniards. In open daylight," said the King. " And such things happen because the towns will not admit my garri-sons. Now I must go to war again — at once; I must move at dawn. Against the Spaniards," he repeated, that none might guess what he in truth feared and foresaw: that he would have to face the Holy Roman Empire.

An intellect like his thinks correctly, but too fast; for this was what he thought: " The German princes, whose faith was once mine, will not now stand by me"; in this he was right. " This time my whole destiny is at stake." It was so, but it had always been so. " The Cardinal of Austria, a General of the Holy Ro-man Empire." True, and more of them would march against him yet. But the Empire itself will not move until more than twenty years are past. You will not be there, Henri. Your part in the guidance of destiny will be the winning of those years. After you, the greatest war of all, and desolation. You will keep it from the kingdom, though you are not there in person. Your shadow keeps it at a distance, because you thought correctly, though indeed too fast. Ah well, a man seldom thinks ahead and acts here and now.

Rosny, the perfect servant, thought and acted exclusively in the present, which was a good thing. If his master had spoken to him about the Roman Empire, Rosny would have privily said: " Nonsense!" though his face remained as stone. The King merely demanded money and cannon, for Amiens. And he had come to the right man; Rosny had already provided for the sec-ond item. As to money, which comes first, the position was not so good. In that hour it should have been to hand but for all the outgoings: relief to the peasants, loans for craftwork, and the purchase price of many towns.

The urgency of the hour moved Rosny to speak his mind. How much had been squandered on the King's building, his fes-tivities, his passion for play? If only they had the money lavished on his dear lady! Three tables would not hold it. He had scarce ended when she herself stood in the room. The news had been brought to her while she lay sleepless and tormented. She had put on that evening's dress, including the mask, and hurried to her lord, to share this heavy hour with him, and looking for protection.

Henri took her hand, and with her face still masked he led her up to Monsieur de Rosny; she bowed her head gracefully, and Henri said: " Here is the lovely lady in sea-green who will provide the money for the war." He bade Armagnac dress him in the magician's costume, he put on his mask, and they went out, accompanied, besides the guards, by a number of the guests at Madame's ball. The night was far advanced, but the streets were full and noisy. Henri had never seen so many beggars; his plight sharpened his vision, the confine between glory and ruin had dwindled suddenly into a razor-edge.

The King made his way on foot, that the populace should see him and discredit the rumours of disaster; and the nocturnal procession thus reached the rue de la Cerisaie and a blank wall — behind which there might well have been nothing at all. But each and all of them knew that secluded garden, that silent house; the King too had long since made no secret of his visits to Shoemaker Zamet. The iron gates swung open, lackeys with torches dashed through the garden, lined the approach, and lit it with a flickering glare. It was a garden in the Italian manner, more pillars than trees, more stone than grass, with temples in place of arbours, built to look like crumbling ruins. The low façade of the house was entirely encrusted with ornament, a single jewel of many-coloured marbles. The master of that house, not less magnificently arrayed, awaited the King at the foot of the small outer staircase, and saluted His Majesty in such a fashion that all his outspread fingers swept the flagstones.

The Marquise walked between the King and the shoemaker, who was now a rich money-lender, and only in recollection of his origin was he still called shoemaker; and three great persons entered the small, heated rooms. All three had various designs upon each other. The rooms were not merely heated; their subdued illumination and soft magnificence was a solace to the eye. The nose, too, was flattered by invisible sprays of perfume. In

Zamet's house all men smelled good, but most delicious of all were the fragrant odours from a magnificent open kitchen, where the furnaces crackled and white-clad cooks toiled for all to see.

The trio, of which each had business with the other, slowly went the round. Two wore masks, no one was called on to recognize them, and at the little tables the feasting and the play went on without a break. Henri discovered a free place among the *prime*-players. He liked *prime* almost more than he liked *brelan*; wherefore the crafty Zamet, a Florentine, or Levantine — no one knew what he was — had guided the King's footsteps thither, and the empty chair had been provided.

"Zamet," said Henri, in his impatience to sit in that chair, "Madame the Marquise will grant you the honour of a private conversation."

"I can scarce support such honour," stammered the little foreigner, his eyes bulging out of a face that was broader than it was long; his hips were those of a woman.

"Then try to imagine yourself a gentleman," said Henri. He was about to turn away, but pointed to several of his escort. "I have brought barbers with me — though you are the only proper latherer here. But take notice: I am no mean magician."

So saying, he hurried to his place at the table. Zamet looked the lovely mask straight in the eyes; there was an empty space around them, and he coldly asked: "How much?"

"Sebastian, I admire you," cooed Gabrielle in a whisper; she laughed a pearly laugh and bent her head backwards, disclosing a glimpse of her ravishing chin. Seeing that the bait had taken, she promptly changed her tone.

"Five sacks of gold," she said imperiously, in a voice that rang like a bell lightly struck, and bent over the little man, who recoiled — merely because she was Gabrielle, the mistress of the King of France. He really felt as though he were being crushed beneath one of his marble slabs. And in his terror he called her Highness.

"Your Highness must first permit me to get my breath." He gasped the words from his short thick neck and began to retreat. She snapped her fan together and whispered:

" I have secret news. The King has beaten the Spaniards."

Then she herself turned her back.

Gabrielle chose a table where the guests were supping. After all her excitements she suddenly felt very hungry. None of the other masks recognized her, or they pretended not to do so. Gabrielle talked as they did and drank a glass of wine, for she well knew that the hottest fight was yet to come. Someone behind her whispered:

" Come! "

Gabrielle glanced over her shoulder and waited to see who it was.

" Sagonne," whispered the mask in the sea-green dress worn by all the ladies of the court. Gabrielle followed her to a door, behind which the lighting was even more subdued; the room seemed empty. She did not cross the threshold. Her companion said in a quick, mysterious voice:

" Do not enter."

She said it as though it were a matter of course that Gabrielle should be on her guard.

" People like him may be wholly trusted. How otherwise should a shoemaker grow so rich? He made soft Italian shoes for the late King, whose feet were so sensitive that he could wear no others. Then he lent money to the noblemen, at high interest, and there was no one at the court who was not in his debt. In the end the late King had nothing left, but Zamet disposed of all the treasures of the kingdom abroad. Only what we women took from him remained in the country. Shoemaker Zamet has a weakness for women, Madame."

" Sagonne," said Gabrielle, interrupting her, " spare your breath and give me Zamet's message."

The lady stammered, then she decided to utter an indignant shriek. But Gabrielle was quicker than the shriek, and La Sagonne could only hurry after her as she disappeared. Gabrielle was careful that Henri should see her approach. All the onlookers at his table could observe his high good humour, for there were piles of gold in front of him, while his fellow-players wore the unmistakable air of losers. When he saw his dear lady approaching, he closed his left eye beneath his mask. He had noticed the incident with Sagonne. Gabrielle stopped at a deliberate distance, where her lord could still hear what Sagonne was about to say. The Shoemaker's go-between would speak softly and rely on the buzz of voices to drown what she said. But there was one with so fine an ear that he could catch whatever concerned himself. Gabrielle knew of Henri's gift, and that nothing would escape him.

Madame de Sagonne, a fragile, sharp-nosed little lady, masked, but with her thin lips uncovered, came up panting, though her agitation was as like as not assumed. "Highness," she gasped, perhaps in imitation of the Shoemaker.

"Highness, for the five sacks that he lends to the King, he wants ten repaid. I protested, I screamed like a parrot, did you not hear me scream?"

"Your voice was weak, madam," said Gabrielle. "Half a sack was certainly meant for you."

"And a sack for you," hissed Sagonne. She was not the usual patient type of woman, set solely upon money. Zamet should have chosen a more hardened agent.

"The King would thus lose fifty thousand crowns. No!"

Sagonne had recovered her discretion. "You are rich" — she lightly bent her knee and went on in a tone of eager homage: "You can offer our lord and sovereign even more than your beauty. But believe me, I do my part too. I have beaten down the Shoemaker's demand from ten sacks to seven."

"That would do — almost," said Gabrielle.

"Nay, but that is not all," said Sagonne from behind her fan. "Someone called him away. When he came back, he knew that Amiens had fallen, and was panting with rage; it will now quite certainly be ten sacks, and probably twelve tomorrow."

Gabrielle was abashed to learn how matters stood. She paused somewhat overlong before she could say what next was in her mind. This Henri noticed, and he understood her stricken silence; the tears trickled down from beneath his mask as he swept up the gold pieces and pushed them on to his pile.

Then with a self-command that overjoyed him, Gabrielle said:

" Sagonne, your pardon. You have this time acted as my friend. Pray now tell Monsieur Sebastian Zamet that I would speak with him. I will even go into that ill-lit room."

" But he will not," replied the other. " He fears you more than the King. What he offers must be accepted or the affair is at an end."

" Do what I say."

Gabrielle's tone admitted of no dispute. Madame de Sagonne led the way, though irresolutely and halting once or twice. Her demeanour warned Henri that danger was at hand. He actually beckoned to his old comrade Roquelaure, and Monsieur de Roquelaure lent his ear in most obsequious fashion. He hoped that he might now redeem his indiscretion in the matter of the interlude at the ball.

Having received his orders, he slipped quietly into that suspect chamber, hiding behind the closed wing of the door; the other wing stood open. Gabrielle, who made a sign to Madame de Sagonne, was about to enter; but in the very doorway someone called her back: none other than the master of the house himself. He asked the Marquise to remain there, among the hum and clatter of the company; if nevertheless they were observed, a man of his sort could not be suspected of sharing any secrets with the King's beloved. And he leaned against the closed wing of the door, behind which stood Monsieur de Roquelaure. Someone else might catch the cunning Zamet, the King never would.

And Gabrielle spoke:

" Sebastian Zamet, I see that I was wrong. You are more than a money-lender, whose origin and business cannot be covered by any artifice of rank. So I will tell you the truth. Yes, the King is in a difficulty. He has lost Amiens. But he will win the war. I know what I say, and would not otherwise be ready, as I am, to pledge you all I possess."

As he stood silent and wide-eyed in admiration, she began once more.

" I have my news from the war, such as you cannot have. Therefore I give you Monceaux, the castle and the domain, which will one day be a dukedom, as pledge and security for five sacks of gold."

Zamet had already reflected and made up his mind. This woman understood her business, that was certain. A soft heart could have helped no woman to restore a decayed and discredited family; and she herself — what would be her future? The word "dukedom" moved him as none other could have done. He marvelled at the cold assurance of the woman, and conceived her as his equal, or indeed his better. This impression, deluded as it was, diverted his mind from the usual precautions. What message had she received from the war? Upon what grounds did she adventure her whole estate on the highly doubtful victory of the King?

She staked upon him because she loved him. Had his defeat been much more certain, what was solely certain was her love. Long since had she returned to her lord, and in fuller measure, what he had bestowed upon her from his heart; Monceaux too, castle and domain, was his. And the understanding of this matter was beyond the compass of a Zamet. Monsieur de Roquelaure, behind the door, noted every word to report them for his King.

Zamet said to Gabrielle d'Estrées:

"Your property is not worth five sacks of gold, but I will lend six. Not to you, I do not want your pledge. I give them to the King, believing in his greatness. After the victory he will remember this."

"He will indeed," Gabrielle assured him. And she tapped the Shoemaker's hand with her fan, which thrilled him with gratification, and he stood entranced, watching her depart. The money that he lent involved him in the destinies of men. And often, to his profit, he meditated on them.

At one of the card-tables she stopped, and lost, three times; and Zamet felt a chill shiver come upon him that he could barely master. When she reached the King, he took her mask off, and his own, and said: "Behold us"; whereupon he embraced and kissed his lady before all that company. His fellow-players, who had lost all they had to him, sat before the pile of gold like waxen puppets, but Henri overturned that glittering heap; the coins clinked pleasantly as they rolled across the table, and he said:

"Gentlemen, share it all between you. I won most of it by trickery; I am quite sure you marked it, and made no sign because you knew me, although you should not have known me. But if I had lost, perhaps it would have brought us ill fortune. You must know " — and here he raised his voice — "that in scarce two hours' time, I shall be leading you all to battle."

Thereat the whole company leapt to their feet and cried: "Long live the King!"

The King seldom left a company without a last jest. The butt of it was now to be Monsieur de Varenne, once a cook, then a go-between for lovers, and last of all a nobleman; and he was mainly responsible for the droll performance that had been intended to annoy the beloved lady. "A white apron and cap for Monsieur de Varenne," cried the King. "He shall make me an omelet."

The furnace was soon roaring and crackling in the open kitchen, where the cooking was done for all to see. Monsieur de Varenne, arrayed in white, with a cap as tall as himself, was preparing an omelet. It was no common one; indeed, he conceived it on the spur of the moment, for his honour was at stake. He shredded some orange peel into the mixture, added ginger, dashed a few drops of various strong waters into the pan — a flame shot up and fell, and the rich fragrance ravished all the onlookers. They besieged the kitchen; but the most ecstatic admirers of the master were the cooks themselves, the head cook and his assistants. They accompanied Monsieur de Varenne in procession as he bore the golden dish on five finger-tips to the King's table.

Monsieur de Varenne dropped on his knee, all the cooks kneeled behind him, the King took the dish from his hand, tasted the omelet, and pronounced it excellent. At this the whole company clapped their hands. Monsieur de Varenne stood up; he had recovered his fame. Some said to him: "Sir, such a thing may well miscarry. But the King would have praised you none the less. He is fond of his jest, but he never humiliates a man." Which, after all that had happened, was Varenne's opinion also.

The King and the Marquise left Shoemaker Zamet's Italian house. He took leave of his guests in such fashion that his ten finger-tips swept the flagstones of his garden — while his servants brandished their torches, and pillars and ruined temples flickered to and fro from light to darkness. In the street the horses waited, with the litter. Henri rode beside it, thrust his head between the curtains, and said:

"Dear lady, there will be no more rest for me, but you must sleep. I shall take you to my sister Catherine and leave you a hundred guards for your protection."

"A thousand were too few; my beloved lord, do not go without me. I am not safe here."

It was dark, but he held her hand and felt by the touch of it how sorely she was afraid.

"It shall be as you will," he said. "It is my will too." He heard her sigh of relief. "My heart," said he, into the darkness of the litter. Then came her voice:

"No one shall know where I am. I will travel very quietly ahead of you."

"The future Queen must not go in hiding," he replied. "You shall travel under the escort of two regiments, and with you shall travel the six sacks, which I owe to you alone."

In that same hour Shoemaker Zamet had the last fevered gamesters ushered out by his servants. The house was empty at last, and with his own hands he locked his domestics into their quarters; then he went down into his deepest cellar, to which he alone knew the approach. Six heavy sacks he dragged, one after the other, into the upper world, holding the lantern with his teeth. He had weak shoulders and broad hips, and on the winding stairways of his three cellars he several times collapsed; but he got the sacks up at last.

Then he sat down on one sack, soaked in sweat, and not without fear for his life. His conversation with the great lady had been observed. Before the King's men came to fetch the sacks, robbers might seize them, after murdering him first. He had put out every light except his lantern, which he concealed behind his back, and he secured the outer door with chains as well as iron staves. During the agonizing wait, thoughts came into his mind — and they were not thoughts of satisfaction at his chivalrous behaviour, for he was utterly without faith in the King. " He will not win," said Shoemaker Zamet to himself.

"And he must not win." Zamet told himself he was making a gross blunder. The Florentine Ambassador, with whom he was much involved, would report to his government that he had betrayed the Spanish cause. Which would not be true, for he was really serving it. He must serve Habsburg, in whose domains his money lay. These Frenchmen would soon discover the might of Habsburg and of his money. Why had he let himself be overborne into behaving like a gentleman? A man must not expect to keep clean hands in business, or he'll do none at all. " Almighty God, bring this affair to a good end! "

The minutes passed, they seemed like hours, and Shoemaker Zamet fell to prayer.

A shouted password cut short his babble: the King's men had come.

DANGEROUS AFFAIRS

The regiments that marched ahead of the main body of the army northwards were commanded by Marshal Biron the younger. A man without much fine feeling, he behaved in exemplary fashion to the King's beloved. He was stupid, and from mere crassness was destined to commit crimes. He was not a mean man, he was the son of a father who had been a law unto himself, and Biron the younger would have turned his troops against the King had he thought fit. But he would never have failed to respect and guard Madame d'Estrées.

Cannon in the van, then infantry, and within their ranks an iron chest on wheels, containing six sacks of gold. More cavalry, and in their midst a second treasure, a travelling coach. More infantry and another detachment of bombardiers — in such order the column marched on the first day towards Pontoise. Biron wanted to march through the night; it was for the sake of his precious charge that he bivouacked, so he declared, or pretended. Towards evening he would ride up to her coach from time to time to ask how she fared. She, too, would gladly have slept in her coach and travelled through the night. But a tent was pitched for her.

Dawn revealed that the head of the column had been detached, under orders to march rapidly out of the Île de France into the province of Picardy. Gabrielle had overslept, as none of her women awakened her. She was much alarmed when she called for the Marshal and a letter was brought to her in his stead. It was couched in gallant terms and explained that to his great regret and annoyance it could no longer be his privilege to escort the lovely lady any farther. Unfortunately he had to collect the garrisons along the road and attach them to the army. But she might have perfect confidence in the loyalty of her troops. Every man would let himself be hacked in pieces in defence of the King's most precious treasure. And in conclusion Marshal Biron begged that the gracious lady would not hurry, but take her time. Several gentlemen would be soon joining her; though, in the company of her new escort, he prayed that she would still be mindful of her devoted Biron.

She inquired in vain who was expected with the army. Recking little of the Marshal's clumsy compliment, she conceived no good could come of staying where she was. While she lay asleep, the King might well have galloped after her, in the darkness of the night and alone, to overtake her sooner; but as the lights of the camp were hidden by a copse, he might have galloped past. When he was not with her, she feared those lurking enemies who meant to trap her in the end. She was too familiar with hatred; she needed only to close her eyes and she saw their faces: and on them her death was written. But there was yet time and to spare; she must master these forebodings. None the less, after leaving Paris she was a different woman. Thenceforward her marriage portion was fear, never quite dispelled, and sometimes threatening to overwhelm her; only with the King's hand in her own could Gabrielle feel at ease and safe.

She gave orders to break camp, allowed no halt for the night, but after a meal and a brief rest the march continued. Thus by the following evening she and her escort had made their way from the river Oise to the river Somme, where lay Amiens, and the Royal army. But, alas, the King was not there; he had turned aside and left her alone. After days of terrible disquiet he wrote to her that he had attempted a raid on Arras and failed; but he must attack before the enemy could do so, and he meant, too, to shake their nerve by appearing to be everywhere at once.

This shamed her sorely. Her lord was in high humour, when, for him, his kingdom was at stake; for her, nothing but her own paltry life. She resolved to play the Queen and be calm. In that same hour appeared the gentlemen announced by Marshal Biron. They were great lords, especially the Duke of Bouillon and his friend de la Trémoïlle, both Protestants. Their first step was to wait upon Gabrielle d'Estrées. Both believed that she too was of the Religion. They were of that opinion because they knew that the court hated Gabrielle, and her friend was Madame, the King's sister.

The tent was pitched in the centre of the camp, on a hill near the river. The Protestant Prince had brought his own regiment and posted it round the hill, as Marshal Biron learned too late. The outer covering of the tent was of leather, the interior was hung with yellow and silver brocade. Above it waved the King's banner, lilies upon a white ground. The King's lady would not recline on cushions, she took the tallest chair and so received her visitors.

Turenne, now Duke of Bouillon, had grown portly since those early days when he had accompanied the young King of Navarre on his flight after his long captivity in the Louvre and on that first wild cavalcade through the kingdom that Henri was later on to win. At that time Henri was rallying his first followers — in a forest clearing. It so happened, for a while, that the shadows from the sky were cast across the foreground and the farther slopes, while in the midst, lit by a broad shaft of sunlight, stood Henri; and he beckoned each of them in turn to speak with him. With each and all he stood for a while alone and embraced him or clapped him on the shoulders or took his arm.

These were the first. Had he had foreknowledge, he would have seen the future written upon every face and would have been as much alarmed as horrified.

Turenne, now Duke of Bouillon, then a mere coxcomb, had knelt down before his King of Navarre, if it could be called kneeling, to touch the ground for a moment and then leap into the air from mere lightness of heart. Here into this tent came a man of imposing person and haughty countenance, accustomed to look down on others kneeling. He serves no longer; he is himself a ruler and sides with the King of France only so far as may aid his designs; his associates are such as he may choose. Shoemaker Zamet has not become Duke of Bouillon by inheritance; the distinction must be maintained. Nor can Shoemaker Zamet boast of the same immovable self-confidence. Still, small people grow into great ones.

Turenne, and de la Trémoïlle behind him, bowed as befitted them before the future Queen of France. Not content with this, the Duke of Bouillon made plain with a nod and a look of understanding that he thought well of her and regarded her as almost as adept at self-advancement as himself. Or as Shoemaker Zamet, thought Gabrielle, who had taken a dislike to the pair of them. Monsieur de la Trémoïlle said outright what his friend had merely hinted.

" Madam, your family should have witnessed this: the King's banner above your tent! 'Tis glory indeed! What a pity your lady mother did not live to witness it! "

A crude, ill-mannered speech, but forgiven to Monsieur de la Trémoïlle because he was absurd. This without any effort on his part; he moved no muscle of his face. His height and leanness, his crooked nose, his vast beard, his smouldering close-set eyes, all this bespoke a grim and sombre personality. He had but to open his mouth and any such impression vanished. He spoke, not with the deep, tremendous voice expected, but with the nasal twitter of a tumbler at a fair. The shape of his mouth and a defect in his nose prevented Monsieur de la Trémoïlle from speaking like a man of his rank. He made a virtue of necessity and behaved accordingly.

Gabrielle, with her experience of men, understood how dextrously the man's voice could be used for dissimulation and infamy of every sort. This did not prevent her laughing at Monsieur de la Trémoïlle whenever he opened his mouth.

" But let us not forget: we desire to wait upon our most exalted lord," said de la Trémoïlle, whereby he made the motions of climbing, for the personage in question lived high above their heads.

Gabrielle laughed condescendingly; the jest was little to her taste, and with every word would probably grow less so. But for her fears, she would gladly have made merry, as she used to do — how long ago!

Monsieur de Turenne reassured her by extolling the King. Wherever the King passed through upon his journey, he roused the courage of the population, strengthened their resistance, and secured the towns against the enemy. Wherefore he was naturally detained from time to time. The Marquise must be patient with him. " So must we all," he added, by which he referred to many things; among others, to Gabrielle's marriage, and her coronation. She understood his meaning look and faced it. As she waved her hand a second time in invitation, the haughty prince deigned to seat himself, on a chair lower than the seat of the future Queen.

" I will stand," said Monsieur de la Trémoïlle. " Indeed, I could not bear to sit while my lord and sovereign is so ill at ease that he must lie abed."

" Is the King ill? " She should not have betrayed herself, but she sat up rigid in alarm, gripping both arms of her chair. The others, realizing that Gabrielle had no news, exchanged a glance, and Monsieur de la Trémoïlle observed in squeaking tones:

" His kidneys. They are congested, and not to be relieved without pain." The absurd creature turned to face the wall as though he too were about to relieve his own. " Oh, dear me," he groaned. " No use. And indeed that organ was made for nobler purposes." The dismal jester swung round and squeaked into the lady's face: " In that matter the King is no mean performer, as is generally known."

"It is even so," she answered coolly. "And the other organ is in excellent good case. You, sir, are lying."

"We will hope so," said Turenne, replying for his friend, who merely peered down his crooked nose. "Rumour, no doubt, speaks falsely. On the other hand, we are reminded that a King's maladies may stand in the way of his weightiest decisions."

Gabrielle listened and waited. "Often and often has he promised the throne to his dear lady," said Turenne with emphasis. "In that I can scarce be wrong. But not oftener than he has promised our rights and freedom to us Protestants, and he has not kept his word, neither to us nor to you, madam."

"I trust him," said Gabrielle. "Trust the King, he will keep his word when the time comes."

Turenne: "The time has come. He wants to recover Amiens and rid himself of a very noxious enemy. A Prince like myself rules in virtue of his own sovereignty, and I have allies beyond the frontier who are of my religion. I can get reinforcements for the King, or not, and I shall decide as seems due to myself and the Religion."

Gabrielle: "To yourself, I fancy."

Turenne: "Madam, do you understand your own advantage so ill as you pretend? If you would help our Religion, help yourself first."

Gabrielle: "What do you want of me?"

Turenne: "That you should speak privately to the King and persuade him to issue an edict whereby the Protestants are to have equal treatment with the Catholics throughout the kingdom. They are to be allowed to hold their worship everywhere, and Mass is still to be forbidden in their fortified cities."

Gabrielle: "He never promised that."

Turenne: "But he will now act as necessity dictates."

Gabrielle: "He will not, for necessity wears your aspect and bears your name, Monsieur de Bouillon."

Turenne: "Today, or never, I will have the King acknowledge my sovereignty, and my domains shall be independent of his power. This is the day."

" If you have but this day, my friend," thought Gabrielle, " I have many " — but she then and there resolved to dissemble and let the others make their move.

" Well and good," said she. " And now for myself. Where do I stand in the reckoning? "

He nodded graciously. " We are beginning to understand each other. Madame, you would ascend the throne of France. There are many who would kill you first."

And Gabrielle answered sharply: " None of my enemies is stronger than the King's good fortune. Here before Amiens the fortune of war will decide my cause."

" We decide that fortune."

Turenne looked at the lovely creature as though he were seriously considering her fate.

" You are turning in a circle, madam," and he wagged his head to and fro as he eyed her. " I grieve for you. You must not misconceive your party any longer, they are the Protestants. You have friends who are ready to put a hand beneath your foot and swing you into the saddle."

Which Monsieur de la Trémoïlle promptly proceeded to do. He knelt, gently clasped one of Gabrielle's feet and laid it on the outstretched flat of his hand. She suffered him to do it, and for the moment she forgot her intention to remain unruffled.

" Is that true? " she asked eagerly.

The bearded buffoon lifted her foot from the palm of his hand on to the tips of his fingers. Thence he let it drop on to his bowed head, which was almost wholly bald.

The haughty Turenne pointed a finger and merely observed: " As you see, madam."

She pretended to be flattered and convinced, but realized that these friends were dangerous. She begged Monsieur de la Trémoïlle to rise from his uncomfortable attitude. He had expressed his opinion quite beyond mistake.

" The Protestants are to help me up, and I them. If I am overthrown, the blow strikes them too, and more than one head may fall." She pointed to the bald pate.

This took them both aback, and they were silent; they had not looked so far ahead. But it was an intimation on which they must reflect.

" Our alliance contains dangers for both of us," she said. " Come now, we are betraying the King."

" He is betraying us and you," said Turenne, and rose to his feet. With a nonchalant salutation he half turned to go; then he approached nearer to Gabrielle than before and said, behind an uplifted hand, like Shoemaker Zamet:

" Madam, we take our risk. At what price do you estimate your own? I would set it at ten thousand pounds a year. You will get this pension from the Protestant party, and a wealthy Prince will stand security for punctual payment."

Gabrielle did not at once see how to evade this proposal. Trémoïlle helped her. He aped a cheap-jack at a fair, and indeed his voice was well suited to the part. " First bid, eightpence half-penny; any more offers, gentlemen? "

" You must bid higher than that," said Gabrielle decisively. And she dismissed the pair with an imperious wave of her hand, turned away, and called her women.

At the bottom of the hill Turenne rallied his regiment before departing.

" You are right to leave nothing here," snorted Monsieur de la Trémoïlle through his amazing nose.

" She will not say a word to that cuckold of hers. I have a notion that she loves him, as much as Penelope did Ulysses."

" I have a notion that she is as set upon money as Monsieur de Rosny," said Monsieur de Turenne.

Both turned and looked up at the tent topped by the Royal banner.

THEY WRITE

When he was about to arrive, his lady went to meet him on horseback. While still in the saddle they embraced. But in her talk, as they rode back, there were no words of endearment.

" Sire," Gabrielle began, " you must know that the Duke of

Bouillon and other Protestant lords will either fight for you or abandon you, according as you may act."

"They want more power, under the common pretext that their Religion needs more freedom. Be not afraid, my treasure! I am resolved to free the Religion, but these intriguers, who want more power for themselves — I'll clap them into jail."

"Sire, be on your guard, against those of the Religion and against me. They are my party and will force you to make me your Queen."

He looked at her wide-eyed in admiration and amazement. So she rejected her party and relied on him alone, and her lovely face spoke clearly of her shame and agitation.

"What then, my treasure?"

She was silent until they reached the camp. Once in her tent, she confessed:

"Sire, my beloved lord, I was to pledge myself against you for money."

"What offer did they make?" he asked; and when she told him, he advised her to accept. When the exchequer is empty, anything is welcome.

But she dragged forth a sack, set it on the highest chair in the tent, and led her lord before it.

"I have mortgaged all I have. Shoemaker Zamet gave me this sack. I am worth no more. For what I am, I am yours until death, my lord."

This was her confession; he had never before received one like it. Just as she was sinking to the ground, he clasped her in his arms. He pushed on to the floor the sack, which jingled as it fell, and lifted Gabrielle into its place.

Rosny also brought money to carry on the war, though in somewhat different fashion. Every month, so long as the siege of Amiens and the campaign continued, Monsieur de Rosny appeared with one of those elaborate escorts he affected, having collected another hundred and fifty thousand crowns; from members of the Parliament, rich noblemen, prosperous burghers, and especially the tax-farmers. These he threatened with an investigation of their affairs by a Chamber of Justice, and they complied at once. The imposing procession, with a strong detachment to guard the treasure, could then move off — cannon, infantry, more cannon, Monsieur de Rosny in a square of streaming banners, cannon in front of him, the chest behind him, and he, the master, over all. He wore light armour, and round his neck a lady's lace cravat, and his golden scarf was caught over the shoulder by a large and glittering brooch.

He told the King of the attempts to bribe him. He himself was armed against them, others less so. Even the beloved lady's aunt, Madame de Sourdis, had accepted jewellery from a Treasury agent, who had also been insolent enough to slip into Madame de Rosny's hand a diamond worth six thousand crowns. He would never dare to do that again. He had taught that villain a prompt lesson. Quite apart from money, Henri owed everything to his faithful servant, and without him could scarce have survived. Monsieur de Rosny made contracts with slaughterers and kept twenty thousand men in rations. Monsieur de Rosny established well-equipped ambulances with the armies, which had never been seen before, and saved countless lives.

To clip his pride a little, Henri had to remind this incomparable servant that the King himself would not be alive but for the act of a simple soldier. His countryman, a Gascon, who had somehow come among the defenders of the fortress, had shouted from the walls: "Hey! Miller of Barbaste!" So he was often called in his native land. "Take care! The cat's going to kitten!" yelled the Gascon in his own speech, which only Henri understood. Whereby he realized that he was standing on a mine, which would have blown him to pieces had he not leapt aside.

As he was alive and sat a horse, he took Amiens at last, after three months' siege, not reckoning his journeys to Paris, where he had to talk like thunder and lightning to put heart into his capital. The Cardinal — Archduke Albrecht of Austria — was first defeated, then Amiens fell. He was defeated and driven out of the kingdom, never to set eyes on it again — this through the inherited art of a commander who had learned, like Parma, to evade the more hazardous encounters. He wore down the enemy

in trenches and redoubts by means of mines and countermines.
But when reinforcements for the Cardinal came from the Netherlands, he was already weakened, he let himself be defeated and
withdrew. The help sent was meagre. Why was it so? Henri
had, awhile ago, conceived the entire Roman Empire arrayed
against him; but that hour was passed.

Nothing had happened except that he had recaptured one of
his cities and inflicted a defeat on old Don Philip; it would be
the last, the old potentate now wanted to make peace. Peace —
for six-and-twenty years it had barely held, or not at all; it was
and was not, or it was broken. But now it should be inscribed
upon paper and made inviolable, even by the mightiest armies.
It would be sealed; and the honour of Kings would flow into that
burning wax. And it would be sworn, in the name of God.

But what is to be sacred and inviolate calls for due procedure.
Until the envoys with their commissions and their mandates
were on their way and the negotiations could begin, King Henri
awaited them in much uneasiness of mind. Would Habsburg
really abandon his ancient adversary Philip, long enough and too
long the ruler of the world? In the meantime he received reports
on the progress of the envoys hour by hour, and every day he
acted so that his victory should be the decisive and undisputed
fact.

While still in his camp before Amiens he appointed Rosny
Grand Master of the Artillery — not without pressure put on
him by the best of all his servants. His services left the King no
choice, nor his acid expression when he pointed out that he was
still without rank and office: Intendant-General of Finance,
without the title, while the Grand Master of Artillery was Monsieur Jean d'Estrées, a useless old gentleman, but the father of
the King's mistress. She was delighted when the King bought
the Grand Mastership from her father. It was a great sum, and
all went into the pockets of the family; that provided the best of
servants with fresh matter for reproach against Gabrielle. She
had hoped to mollify him. No, her complaisance made Monsieur de Rosny even more hostile, and opposition on her part
would have done the same.

But the King, while still before Amiens, created his beloved Duchess of Beaufort. That was the ratification of his victory, and a public testimony that there was but one step now between his beloved and the throne. His happiness was high; hers was not unclouded. Perils continued to gather round her; she felt the touch of evil hands. She could not pass a day without the King, and yet she would not confess her fears. He had his time of joy, of swift and easy ascent towards greatness and possession. And yet the poor lovely creature knew but too well there were those that looked on him askance. He was on his guard, as she was, and picked his way with care. But true it was that he had won; no one could prevail against him now.

Henri wrote: " Brave Crillon, hang yourself for not having been here near me last Monday, on the finest occasion that has ever been seen, and which, perhaps, will ever be seen again! The Cardinal came to see us in great fury and has gone off in great shame. I shall not stay in Amiens, as I have a matter in hand."

Gabrielle wrote: " Madame, my true friend: Your dear brother, my beloved lord, is the mightiest King on earth. If it so be that his capital misconceives me, and I am named by a certain name at court, believe me, I do not deserve the insult. Madame, I shall ever do my utmost to reconcile the King with the Duke of Soissons, with whom he has fallen out. Our friend was ill advised when he took away his troops from the Royal army and withdrew before the battle, together with the Duke of Bouillon, who is a bad Protestant. Otherwise he would be loyal, as you are. And now, Madame, tell me if you please: How do you mean to receive me, and are you my true friend? "

Catherine wrote — but nearly dropped her pen in horror. She had almost written: " Duchesse d'Ordure," the name by which Gabrielle was commonly known, and the people thought it witty. Gabrielle was not hated equally by all. Some merely repeated what seemed amusing or was in the fashion. Others saw no reason to draw enmity upon themselves by upholding an unpopular cause. The more prudent avoided the offensive title. Madame de Sagonne contented herself with making a wry face when the talk turned on Gabrielle; but only for a moment.

There was no attempt as yet to hound her down. Indeed, the more sagacious foresaw a fresh honour for the beloved lady very soon. She would take half the last step, but not the whole of it. Better not set people by the ears too soon!

Catherine wrote: " Madam, Duchess of Beaufort, my dear friend: I am so delighted with you that I can scarce await your return to kiss you on both cheeks. You have so dealt with my dear brother the King, and so advised him, as I should have done myself. You make no boast of it, but I know how you treated Monsieur de Bouillon. I know too that just after that unworthy Protestant departed he summoned another and a better one. I speak of Monsieur de Mornay; his new favour with our sovereign is your work. Dearest, you do not know it. For you are pure in heart, and when you serve the Religion, you do not reckon your advantage. But you must do two things: you must pray and you must keep an eye to your advantage. I would have you know that the Princess of Orange is here, living quietly in my house. She has been through so much trouble and strife that I regret my errors in her presence, though they were part of me and I could not help them. I have not seen the Count of Soissons for a while past; he is sorely grieved to have left the King with his troops before Amiens. We are weak. But Madame d'Orange, who is a devout and resolute lady, calls my friend Gabrielle a good and virtuous Christian."

The King wrote: " Monsieur du Plessis: The King of Spain wants to make peace with me, and he does well. I defeated him with twenty thousand of my troops, four thousand of which were Englishmen, thanks to the good will of their Queen, Elizabeth. But it was fortunate that I had someone, Monsieur de Mornay, who possessed her confidence as he did mine and could bring us together once more. In token of my confidence I now send you into my province of Brittany, that you may persuade Monsieur de Mercœur to treat with me. He cannot last long, his people are deserting him. He can now get money from me for surrendering my province; but not after my peace with Spain — I shall then come with the army. Show your art, you were always my diplomatist — you even guessed what I thought about the Religion, and how I was very soon to act. When someone stabbed me in the lip, you took it as a warning. Let us believe it so, especially as it proved not to be the only one; but though I try to think and act as a reasonable man should, certain happenings do seem to give the lie to reason. When I rode into my city of Amiens, I passed a gallows by the roadside, and on it hung the body of a man long since executed. But, in my honour, he had been clad in a white shirt. A mouldering corpse arrayed for the Day of Resurrection. I kept my countenance. Not so Marshal Biron; strong as he is, he was fairly overcome by the sight of that hanged man. He had to pull his horse in beside a house, where he leaned from the saddle against the wall and fainted."

The Protestant

Mornay himself had been resurrected, and some recoiled from him, as did Biron from the body in the clean shirt. Mercœur, the last of the House of Lorraine, which still held the power in a part of the kingdom, surrendered it; first because he could no otherwise, for though he talked menacingly of Spanish landings on the coast, he well knew that he would await them in vain. But Mercœur, when confronted with Mornay, was to throw away his power sooner than he need have done. As yet, the royal envoy had not reached the castle, Mercœur was hourly awaiting him. Mornay had transformed little Navarre into a great King — in so far as Henri had not done so by his own efforts. But that was what a Lorraine was ill disposed to admit. He much preferred to ascribe the achievement to Mornay's extraordinary gifts. He had managed to placate the Queen of England after her angry abandonment of her disloyal companion in the faith — what arts would he now use to conjure back the vanished company of the dead? But a little while, and Admiral de Coligny, the victims of Saint Bartholomew, and the fallen Huguenots of the ancient battles would rise out of their graves. And why not? — for the survivors had been equally engulfed, and the fortunes of the Protestants had seemed to be destroyed for ever.

But now he had summoned Mornay, and that was the begin-

ning. The converted heretic was no doubt intent upon bestow-
ing rights upon the Protestants, the like of which they had never
so much as claimed before his day. And who could say him nay?
— he was the conqueror of Spain. First he would set heresy on
high, and then grant a peace to His Catholic Majesty.

The Duke of Mercœur conceived all this as plainly monstrous,
in contravention of all good order and sacred privileges, and also
as more or less inexplicable, if not devilish. A King overthrows
many things in his course of conquest. Venerable institutions —
he sweeps them on one side; great families, and even the House
of Lorraine, he passes over; over Guise, the favourite of the people, over fat Mayenne, and now over Mercœur, on this distant
headland where he had dwelt so long that he had come to think
himself eternal, like the ocean and the power that ruled the
world. But that power was now seen to be transitory; he grew
doubtful of himself; maybe the ocean, too, would soon withdraw and leave that castle high and dry.

But the waves still surged and thundered round the rocks on
which the castle stood, and poured through iron gratings into its
deepest dungeons. The master of that castle opened the window; he liked the uproar of his sea; it should remind him of what
he was when the Protestant with his royal escort entered that
room. The Duke had made his preparations; to match the envoy's escort, just so many of his own people should march in
through the doors on both sides of the room. He was master of
that sea, and a man in authority, and own brother to Montpensier, the Fury. At that moment he noticed his chamberlain making signs to him from without, and the door slowly closed. Mercœur swung round; in the room stood one person only, the
Protestant.

Mornay stood calmly observant while the great lord, though
against the light, blinked at him. Mercœur soon recovered his
composure, surveyed his visitor, and beckoned him to approach.
Mornay waited until the Duke was seated; then he moved the
proffered chair in such a fashion that he would not face the light.
The Duke was compelled to follow him, so that neither had the
advantage of position. But Mercœur reflected that the dash of

waves might well fluster his visitor and put him at a disadvantage. He let the Protestant speak awhile; he placed his hand to his ear, and Mornay promptly stopped.

He waited. The window was not shut. Mornay eyed Mercoeur, and Mercoeur eyed his visitor. A man who had spent his life about the courts of Europe, a man before whom, in a memorable hour, the great Queen had showed herself a woman, was not likely to be so daunted. A man who feared God would fear little else! His forehead had broadened as the growth of hair receded; it was now larger than his face, but still quite unwrinkled; the glory of heaven was mirrored on its smooth expanse. The God of Monsieur du Plessis de Mornay did not love lined foreheads. A thatch of hair was combed across his head, and two locks were wound about his ears, according to the custom of the older Protestants in their great days. King Henri used to wear them thus.

The man was clothed in black and white plumage like all these ravens. A distinguished figure, withal. Choice stuffs, slashed doublet, cut low at the neck — and surely a cross worked into the velvet, black on black, in rich but delicate embroidery; but unmistakably a cross. How deal with such a man? Insolent these people were, but, alas, there were situations that forbade even a prince to chastise their insolence. As for instance by dropping them through the floor of that apartment into the dungeon below. The tide would in the meantime have filled it up to the neck of a man upright, thought the Duke amid the desolate booming of the sea that had made him what he was.

He wished he knew whether the Protestant was smiling. Brow and eyes set in gravity inviolable; all the more disturbing was that thin wrinkle down the cheek, which perhaps carried with it a suspicious smile. The wrinkle ran from the nose, the tip of which was red, down to the grey tuft on the chin, which was exactly adjusted to the gap in the white ruff. He wished he knew whether the redness of the nose was due to catarrh or wine; and especially whether the Protestant was smiling. There was something magical behind that menace. The Duke of Mercoeur felt utterly exposed; he was deluded by certain superstitious notions of the spiritual gifts of the Protestants. There was something uncanny about them all. And this man was known as their Pope.

As the window was not shut, Monsieur de Mornay began his speech again from the beginning. He merely thought that his baffled adversary was making matters as difficult for him as he could. A practised speaker, after many successes in the stormy councils of his co-religionists, could of course, by his mere act, carry his voice without an effort against the uproar of the sea. Monsieur de Mercœur soon realized that, though with but little interest. Whether sooner or later, he would have to yield and resign his authority; the only issue was the price. But something else disquieted him more.

" Have you not a God of your own? " asked the great nobleman who had grown old upon this sea-girt headland.

To which Mornay answered equably:

" My God is the only living God."

" Does He reveal Himself? " asked Mercœur.

" It is He that supports me now and always," said Mornay. He spoke soberly and without a hint of challenge, for he had never conquered otherwise than by the truth; by it he had never failed to conquer, even the mightiest enemy that did not possess it. The last of the House of Lorraine, who was still a man of might, lifted to him an unbelieving face; this troubled Mornay and distressed him for the unbeliever's sake. Wherefore he produced arguments from his own theological writings; never had he spoken at such length before. In the end he passed from eternal to temporal matters. The civil war in France had from the start been an opportunity for ambitious foreigners, not to mention a temptation for half-Frenchmen — such as the House of Lorraine, he implied, and Mercœur understood him, though no name was uttered. This flung him into a sudden fury, which would not have been so violent had it not been roused by his superstitious fear of the Protestant. "To the dungeon with him! " urged the furious voice within, while he presented an unruffled countenance. But he was very near to touching the hidden mechanism that would open the trapdoor.

Mornay, in the simplicity of his heart, believed he had made a deep impression on the enemy of the Religion and the King, in matters both spiritual and secular, to the glory of God and for the good of public order. Monsieur de Mercœur's face had changed; all the unrest and secret bitterness had faded out of it, and the great noble looked at him in such frank and kindly fashion, Mornay thought; while Mercœur, in his evil heart, was savouring his agonizing death by slow drowning in the flooded dungeon.

But there was one thing of which he wanted to be certain first.

"Does your God still work miracles? Have miracles ceased with the Bible, or does He continue them among you?"

"The goodness of the Lord endureth for ever," said the Protestant. For the first time in that room he bowed his head, by way of consolation to a penitent.

At this, the Duke's face darkened. The fellow might well escape out of the dungeon. An angel might swing back the grating, he reflected, and he took his hand from the mechanism. Moreover, though Monsieur de Mercœur did not mark this at once, Mornay had, in all innocence, so shifted his chair that the Duke had had to move after him, and would, at that moment, have dropped through the floor together with his victim.

That day they talked no more; and in the days that followed, the Duke of Mercœur raised more difficulties than he had contemplated. He took heart again. The town of Vervins lay on the farther side of the kingdom, in the Dukedom of Guise, where the House of Lorraine had its origins. At Vervins it seemed that the Spaniards had finally admitted defeat and proclaimed under hand and seal that this kingdom would never be theirs in the centuries to come, nor could be, with the will of God. Mercœur was well served with news, which convinced him that the House of Habsburg was more distinguished for diplomacy than generalship.

Thereupon he fell into a fury with himself because one afternoon he had let himself be daunted by the Protestant Mornay — really, in fact, by the heretic Henri — and had not then ventured to drown his visitor. The man was an emissary from his master,

and, moreover, had perhaps been entrusted with yet higher powers. Higher powers! That remained to be seen. At Vervins, at
least, the Protestant God was not yet made manifest, nor had
He revealed His purposes, thought the Duke of Mercœur in
those days. But he ought to have drowned that Protestant; to
this conviction he obstinately came back, for the solitary turmoil of the elements had made him what he was.

Towards the end of October, Mornay found himself at Angers.
Marshal Brissac, humanist and catcher of flies, had summoned
several noblemen to that town that they might approve the dispositions he had made against the imminent arrival of the King.
Henri was about to journey into his province of Brittany by way
of Saumur and Angers. The Governor of Saumur was Monsieur
de Mornay, the Marshal commanded a Royal garrison at Angers.
All the more shocking was what befell the Royal Governor in the
King's city of Angers, almost under the eyes of the Marshal, who
was related to the author of the deed.

A certain Monsieur de Saint-Phal fell in with Monsieur de
Mornay, Governor of Saumur; in the open street of Angers, while
Mornay was talking to a magistrate. He had with him an equerry,
his majordomo, but no escort other than a secretary and a page.
Saint-Phal was guarded by ten armed men, whom he at first kept
out of sight. He complained to the Governor of Saumur in the
matter of certain intercepted letters, which the Governor had
had opened. The complaint was provocative, but Mornay made
a temperate reply. He had opened the letters, as they had been
found upon a suspected person; but when he came upon the
signature of Monsieur de Saint-Phal, he had sent them on. He
then expressed some surprise, for the event was five months old.

This plain statement had no effect upon the other, who grew
the more truculent and refused any explanation. "Very well,"
said Mornay, in the end. "I am accountable to none but the
King. You, sir, may at any time make the matter an affair of
honour."

Saint-Phal, as though this had been the expected cue, drew a
stick from beneath his cloak, and his ten armed men appeared,
under cover of whom the assailant was able to mount his horse

and escape. Mornay, a man advanced in years, was struck down by a blow on the head.

A wave of excitement swept over the western provinces. No one believed in any personal quarrel between the two gentlemen. The so-called Pope of the Huguenots was to be put out of the fight by a premeditated attack; then the King would scarce venture on his journey and would refrain from giving the Protestants their constitution. Otherwise all was in readiness for a settlement; at their church councils and political assemblies the Religion and the party had prescribed their conditions to the King; they were extreme, and Mornay had induced the King to accept them. The blow on the head came at the eleventh hour, that the realm might be spared this outrage by the party of revolt.

On their side, those that shared the victim's faith told each other that there must be no more concessions, they had made too many hitherto. Remained to them only their strong places and a fresh conflict. So matters stood when Mornay, still sorely stricken, received a letter from the King, in which the King said that he felt the injury in his own person, both as King and as Mornay's friend. "As King, I will see that justice is done to us. Were I but a friend, I would draw my sword."

They were words of indignation and impatience scarce now to be restrained. Life steps quickly forward; but just as a visible height stands up to justify this life and this realm, the movement suddenly halts, as at Vervins and in Brittany; and peace with those of the Religion recedes yet further, in consequence of a broken head.

Marshal Brissac received an order to deliver up his brother-in-law, Saint-Phal, to the Police Lieutenant of the King — "promptly, and without pretext for procrastination, for what has happened struck me to the heart; it touches my authority and the Royal service."

None knew that better than Brissac, catcher of flies; and he approached the sick Mornay's couch with a fervour of satisfaction the like of which he had seldom known.

"Our master suffers more than you, my honoured friend," said Brissac with the face of an apostle painted by an adept. One could almost see the saintly beard, and he kept his eyes upturned like a martyr's to the clouds.

"I offer myself," he said piously, "for imprisonment, that your wrong may be avenged and the King's will done. Better my own sacrifice than to stand by helpless."

"You are not helpless," said Mornay. "You are a hypocrite. You hid your kinsman from the King. He has taken refuge in one of Monsieur de Mercœur's towns. There's an intriguer for you, though he will not last long and is scarce worth your pains."

"What am I?" asked Brissac, and shuddered with horror. "You do not believe such a thing. Look at me and dare to repeat your words."

Mornay did not repeat them, his contempt overcame his anger. Brissac in the meantime managed to grow as pale as a dying man; his eyes rolled upwards, and the crown of thorns appeared about his head. Mornay eyed the performance with disgust. And Brissac thought: "Why not impersonate a devil out of hell, tip this Protestant raven off his branch, and kill him?" Should he? It was not without difficulty that he suppressed the temptation.

"Why heed so lost a creature?" said Mornay to his soul. For a hypocrite, and a man of many faces, he regarded as beyond redemption. Since the assault upon himself, he had also changed his view of Monsieur de Mercœur. Yes, he was always too hasty in his judgments, because he regarded his equals as amenable to reason, now even more than in his youth, for so the years weaken our confrontation of the world. None the less he felt that the great Duke was nearer to God's image than the meaningless nonentity who stood there grimacing by his couch.

Mornay effaced the nonentity from his mind and went on as though he were addressing an automaton. He named the conditions under which he would forget his injuries: a satisfaction in so ceremonial a form that it would leap to the eyes of everyone. Monsieur de Saint-Phal was to kneel before him. At this, Marshal Brissac forgot himself and cried, in an impulse that did him some credit:

" God bless my soul, sir! I would recommend you to wait upon him, and he will offer you his excuses, if not in this unusual fashion. Pray who may you be, after all? "

" The King's deputy — we await the King here, and he will know where to find a man like Saint-Phal and punish him."

" I doubt it," observed Brissac. " Do not forget that, but for me, he would never have marched into his capital."

For what remained to be said, Mornay turned to the wall, no longer to his adversary. He saw now how right the King was to insist on due obedience and service to the Crown, and on the honour of a nobleman. For the rest, let Marshal Brissac protract the matter as he could. In the end Saint-Phal would find himself under lock and key. Mornay swore to that.

Brissac departed without another word; the obduracy of a Protestant is more formidable than his religious zeal. A broken head aroused nothing less than the " Anger of the Lord." Well, they would be given a lesson. Mornay should be led by the nose and made ridiculous. All the better if the King were likewise involved. He would hesitate, and postpone the Edict.

CONVERSATIONS

The difficulties were indeed burdensome. Mornay had scarce left his room when he had to explain to his Church, and convince his own heart, that, before God, he asked no more from the King than he could grant without damage to his interests. " And what if he dies? " asked one Pastor Béraud, who came to Saumur to wait on the Governor at the instance of the Church Assembly.

Mornay bowed his head, looked up, and answered quietly:

" So long as he lives, the Edict as he intends it will suffice."

After that he said no more upon the matter, but thought: " Let the dead bury their dead. It is meet that the living should think us obstinately set upon our faith and upon our honour." He knew too well what it had cost to bring about that hour of life. Let the dead bury their dead. When Mornay cited these words from Holy Writ, he meant them in all piety, and also as an utterance of statesmanship.

He made his way to Paris with Madame de Mornay. Both were received forthwith, Madame de Mornay in the house of the King's sister, where two other ladies appeared with her, the Duchess of Beaufort and the Princess of Orange. The King gave audience to Monsieur de Mornay, although he was expecting the Papal Legate.

When Henri saw his Philippe Mornay enter the room, he could not at once embrace him, as his impulse was; this was a figure that he did not know. Only suffering, not the passage of the years, can transform a man's face in this fashion.

" Philippe," said Henri, " I will listen to every plaint that you may make. You have been abominably used, and I, too, in your person. Let it be some consolation that the day at last has come when I can establish the Religion in its rights."

" Sire," said Mornay in a feeble voice, " I am quite sure that you will keep your word and bestow upon the Religion the same freedom and rights that it possessed now nearly a generation ago."

" I cannot restore you more than you lost by Saint Bartholomew's night," said Henri; and Philippe replied:

" I know."

Both made a gesture of renunciation. After a pause the diplomat respectfully proposed that his co-religionists should, as they desired, be granted six members on the Edict Council of the Parliament. " Which gives you no majority on a Council of sixteen," Henri interposed.

" Therefore we suggest that Your Majesty should appoint the ten Catholics yourself. Sire, our trust is in you alone."

" Not in your fortresses, nor yet in the Edict? "

" In you and in none other."

Henri asked no more questions; he embraced his old friend; indeed, he had never clasped him so long and warmly in his arms. And in his ear he said:

" We must live for ever."

And in the other ear, after kissing Mornay upon both cheeks, the King said:

" Otherwise, after our time my Edict will become no more than a blank sheet of paper."

" We cannot know what is to be," said Mornay simply. " In my zeal for the Religion I had forgot that our deeds scarce outlive us. We ask and ask and are never sated, and would establish freedom of conscience as an eternal law. But it perishes with us, and our successors must win it anew. So wills the Lord of human destinies."

" What did he do to you? " asked Henri. He took a step back and eyed the man before him; he had looked unfamiliar as he entered the room. Mornay suddenly grew vigorous and insistent:

" Sire, he struck me on the head, and the blow is not yet avenged."

Henri: " It shall be avenged, upon my word."

Mornay: " It irks me that you let time pass and my enemies deride me."

Henri: " Friend, the delay over the Edict has vexed you less than your broken head."

Mornay: " Sire, the blow touched my honour."

Henri: " You were knocked down, but the Religion stands."

Mornay: " Without honour there can be no advantage. Though nothing remains of what we shall have done, we shall have done it in all honour; and through it our name will live."

No answer. Henri reflected how often this man had lied and intrigued on his behalf — in all innocence, and yet as was needful in this world. One may go, and the other not. " I reached the height I aimed at with that inner constancy that is my honour. The straight way would be more than honour, it would be a miracle. I evade my murderers, and I forget a broken head. Revenge — is a heavy charge upon what will be afterwards called greatness. Revenge — "

" Monsieur de Mornay, you are a nobleman, and your nobility outruns your wisdom. I see it well. Have you not understood that our vengeance can humiliate none other so sorely as ourselves? "

To which Mornay, a pius Protestant, replied:
" Sire, Monsieur de Saint-Phal must be jailed and must ask my pardon."

" Very well," said Henri. " You shall have your will."

Therewith he dismissed his old comrade, for he heard the rumble of the Legate's coach.

Henri did not go out to receive the Legate, he left the room by the opposite door. Near by there was a view on to the Tuileries and into his sister's windows. The window that he had in mind was but lightly curtained, and he recognized the shadows on it; four of them. " The ladies are aquiver over me," he thought. " They are gathered together, praying that I may stand fast. Never fear, Catherine, this time I am master. Princess of Orange, my hour is at hand, this day there's no murderer in my kingdom that dare raise a knife against me; he could not help turning it on himself."

Striding — nay, almost leaping — back, he reached the room before the Legate. He left the door open behind him; those four shadows should be present at the interview. " Madame de Mornay," he thought, " pray less for me than for your vengeful husband, who will avoid the Papal Legate lest he might, for reasons of State, be tempted to kiss his ring."

Outside, the tramp of the guards was heard, and the door swung open. And Henri thought: " Gabrielle, my dearest lady, look on me. If I withstand this trial, then you too have conquered. Pray with the three Protestants, that you may become Queen."

The Legate stepped into the doorway; but no farther. He waited where he stood for the King to come and kiss his ring. The Legate had come with a large escort, which seemed to float upwards out of the stairway like a lustrous cloud; and, with all the motley array of ecclesiastics and soldiers, and some boys among them, the cloud that accompanied the Legate was a little dazzling. He himself presented the figure of a frail and humble old man, who raised a wavering hand as though it were his wearisome and constant duty. But the King kissed the ring with fervour, whereupon he stepped backwards into the middle of the room. There it was now for him to wait. The escort melted noiselessly away, in the manner of a cloud, and the door, as the Legate noticed with disquiet, was shut. He wished he could look round. Was he really alone with the King?

It is unpleasant and a little unsafe to enter the cell of a condemned man, especially for a vivacious old gentleman, with an insatiable taste for intrigue, but not given to contemplating his own end. Malvezzi, in Brussels, said that the King of France must die. And the Legate reflected that as the door was now shut, there was nothing for it but to move forward with appropriate dignity. This he did, with eyes fixed upon the King, and his heart went out to Henri with every step he took. True, the King was a rebel, a heretic, an incorrigible destroyer of the faith and the divine order, yet his face, in these ordeals, was stamped with dignity and race; no shapely boy nor pious Christian could ever look like that. What a pity! Malvezzi, the Legate in Brussels, had been plotting his death for five years past. That was barbarous, although possibly just, for this King was working for his own overthrow. The other Legate was but pushing at a falling man. He wished he could stop him.

The Legate sat down, and so, but not till then, did the King. The Legate congratulated the King on his victory over the Cardinal of Austria.

" Over Spain," said Henri quickly. " Over Habsburg."

The Legate paused before he said:

" Over Christianity? "

" I am a Christian King," said Henri. " The Pope knows it; the pledges that I offer cost me the fruits of my victory. I make peace, but I could carry the war across the Rhine."

" If you could do so, you would. Only too glad to get peace with your secular enemies, you attack the Church."

" God forbid," exclaimed Henri.

" Pledges! " The Legate raised a warning hand: " You would do well to grant none to your Protestants, and especially not the most vital ones. That will lead you further than you intend, and may be dangerous. You have risen high, you are a conqueror and a great King. Now show your greatness and recognize the limits of your power."

"Solemn words," said Henri, "for much too small a matter. I have let it be understood in Rome that my Protestants will get nothing but a sheet of paper. Indeed, they expect no more, poor souls. The best-informed of them is my brave Mornay, who kissed your ring. I have told him so myself. They know me. Why am I not believed by Rome alone?"

"Because Rome knows you better."

This answer from the Legate followed an oppressive silence. The King got up and began to pace the room with ever slackening strides. At the farther end by the open door he lingered for a moment, to glance at the window in his sister's house. Of the four shadows, three stood quite still, watching the movements of the fourth.

CONFESSIONS

Yonder in that room each of the four women took up the tale in turn, unburdening her heart. They sat round a table, on which lay a book. At the beginning, they were agreed that the King's heavy hour was upon him, and that they must send him their help across the space between. "Let us confess ourselves for what we are. The truth alone can help, both us and him. Let us be truthful. He will feel it, and will do likewise."

Madame de Mornay, as the lowest in rank, was to speak first. She recoiled, said: "I am not worthy," and laid her hand on the book to reassure herself. She was gaunt in person, clad in black, and wore a coif; but a few errant strands of hair betrayed that it had once been red. Her skin was coarse and, at fifty, it was now a lifeless white. The veins on her outstretched hand were blue and swollen. Her eyes were the same watery blue, but such was her self-mastery that they looked beyond the other women into the unseen. If Madame de Mornay had recognized the King across the courtyard, she forgot the fact at once, by the mere exercise of her will.

" I am a Christian," said she, and the four words seemed to come from her very soul. She had an ungracious voice, her face was overlong; it had aged like that of her husband, but was still unwrinkled, and the moving lips looked dry and harsh. All this the three women did not fail to mark; and yet the voice of a soul unburdening itself, with all its weaknesses and transgressions, rang in their ears with a grave melody all its own.

" I am not so much a Christian through my faith as by reason of my sins. I was vain, and my piety was worldly; it was false, like the curls I wore. When the pastors forbade me to wear them, I was angry, instead of thanking Him who sent me their counsel. The affliction that He put upon me " — she avoided the name of the Lord — " in truth, affliction made me no better either. We are irreclaimable; we are destined to sin much or little, not at all or to our eternal damnation."

She cast down her eyes; but as she had done so involuntarily, she swiftly glanced at the window opposite.

" I possess a gift for persuasion. At the instance of Monsieur de Mornay I used my influence upon persons whose suspicions he had reason to fear. I had many successes, and they corrupted me. Such talents do corrupt. Who are we, that we should drive others to despair, for the sake of worldly advantage? I know of one prince who lost everything through me and fled into exile. I, who escaped from exile! I was meddling with a power that was minded to deliver me, but not to bring others to destruction. I did not think of this, while the palpitations at my heart grew worse, and no mountain waters that I drank or bathed in could bring me relief. For it was the warning of my conscience, as I at last understood, when I fell into a very abyss of fear."

The moving shadow yonder was the King. Madame de Mornay saw, and was grieved to see, how he squandered his great qualities, for we do so all the time — whereas we should be frank and honest, at the risk of mortal peril. Monsieur de Mornay's skill at handling men made him first proud, then actually revengeful. He, at least, is saved by the virtue that abides secluded in his mind, and cannot be tainted by worldly dealings. Act he may and does; but he reflects likewise. He was the first layman to write upon religion. In his books he combats all that this world implies, in allegiance to his fellow-men, and to Him who sees us all; he spends hours at his table, writing; there is he free, and there he brings forth the best that is in him.

She opened the book beneath her hand. " Tractate on the Eucharist," she said.

" What! " cried the Princess of Orange. She had been silent long enough, although she had not been wearied. She was never wearied, either in company or alone.

" So that is the Tractate! All Europe has been waiting for it. Here is the book; why has it not come into our hands? "

" Is it true," asked Madame, the King's sister, " that this book so discredits the Mass that the Pope himself will refuse to say it? "

" Mass will continue to be said," replied the other Protestant, but gave no further explanation. Then turning to the Princess of Orange:

" Madame d'Orange," said she to the buxom little woman with round eyes, grey hair, and girlish skin, " you are the most truly Christian of us all. You are so enwrapped in virtue that my last avowal cannot reach you, though in your great goodness you had been willing to receive it. This book must not be known before the King has issued the Edict. The Edict first; for, after the book, we shall get no more. The book will do us wrong; to admit the truth, we shall suffer for it."

" No," said the Princess. And she added lightly to her pale and anguished companion: " We are fortunate in that the truth helps us alone. Whatsoever may fall away and perish, we remain. For we are gathered here that we may stand by the King, as we are and confess ourselves to be, and he hears us yonder with an inward ear. In proof of which his beloved is with us, and shall be Queen."

Her bright eyes rested upon Gabrielle, who blushed and broke into a faint, deep sob. She felt desolate among these Protestants, and yet they were all the friends she had. Much of what they said she had not understood. Self-examination and confession were beyond her compass and they frightened her. And yet, under the look that Madame d'Orange now gave her, she pleaded softly that she would try, for she had matters to confess.

" My dear child, first dry your eyes. Our eyes must be dry when we confess." The Princess interposed less by what she said than by her smile. It was a firm and understanding smile that went straight to the heart. Gabrielle thought Madame d'Orange angelic. Only beings of another origin than ours could smile with such understanding. A quick impulse seized her, and she bent to kiss the Princess of Orange's hand, but before she could do so, the Princess laid a protecting arm round her shoulder; and she signed to the sister of the King to speak.

THE LEGATE'S SPEECH

Henri again looked at the Legate and left the word to him. (" Does Rome know me better than I know myself? ") And the Legate spoke. The voice that came from his meagre person was soft and full. His withered countenance had long been accustomed to remain impenetrable; the man's quick changes of expression had never blunted his natural force. Moreover, his eyes spoke too. There was little recognition in them, but rather a sort of avid vitality, which to certain kinds of men seemed shameless, and not a little shocking. But he was the Legate of the Pope.

The King flung in a brief word or two, which made no difference to what the Legate said. Protestations and assurances. " The most loyal son of the Holy Father. . . . Only a sheet of paper. . . . Peace of the world. . . . Secure establishment of Christendom." The Legate was unimpressed and made his warning all the plainer.

" You give rise to the suspicion that throughout Europe you mean to attach Protestantism to your cause. And not for the advantage of a creed, but for your own glory. It was over such a matter that the Roman Empire perished, and now Holy Church must fall that you may become master of the world. As this cannot lie in the scheme of things, and you know it, be warned. Let there be no reasons for that suspicion."

At a protest from the King:

" Who started that suspicion? Why, truly, hitherto it is I and I alone, a priest, who understands how to be silent. Others hate you, without any clear notion of why they do so. I do not, as you are well aware; I do not hate you. I am concerned for you. I have but to cite your own confession. One day you stood on the top of the Saint-Denis gate and watched the Spaniards withdraw — not as vanquished enemies. Many of the victors climbed up to points of vantage to gloat upon that sight. But you exulted until you were near to fainting at the breach you had made in the order of the world. You speak of your kingdom: I know that words are always right, there are always bold men to bear a hand when there is a chance of degrading what has done good service. Your kingdom is like none other, you are transforming it into a nation — without the ranks and orders that in essence know no frontiers, but have for centuries spread over all Christendom. You make men equal, and you call the result freedom. I was in Rouen with you when you held an assembly of the Estates of your province of Normandy, but you gave the majority to the lowest Estate. Them you suborned, by offering them the power that is yours, in return for money; all of which is called freedom. By the same token, an unruly and isolated kingdom is all the more lightly called your kingdom."

Protests from the King. He too had friends in the world. He loved his people, and they loved him. His peasants must not be slaves, nor must his industries be idle. He had encountered, not order, but its opposite: decay.

The Legate: " Decay is a temporal matter and does not affect the eternal order. What imperils you is public distrust. Here is a King who breaks, like a foreign element, into the ancient communion of universal monarchy. That universal entity mistrusts him. Peace — he will neither be able to keep it, nor will he be suffered to do so. The example of freedom and of self-government is most pernicious. It is an example that must be avoided or it will spread ruin everywhere. Friends — the only friends you have are those who may not fear your example, or you would have none at all. Some are republicans, and others Protestants, and many are both. You rely on Holland and on Switzerland.

The unlucky Venetians are your admirers. In England an old Queen prolonged her life beyond the human term for your sake. And you yourself? "

" And I myself? " repeated Henri.

The Legate: " After your departure, which may be near at hand, no more will be heard of the Edict that you have hitherto but promised to your Protestants. Even in this last hour I shall hope that you are not in earnest: For — your — own — sake."

" For my own sake," repeated Henri.

" It is for you that I am afraid."

A meaning silence fell, and the pair looked into each other's eyes. And Henri thought: " This priest, who consorts with boys, knows much, but not enough.

" The time of my murderers is past," he said nonchalantly.

A pleading look came over the Legate's face. " Look at me," he said; " I am not a friend to death, like many that I know."

And Henri said:

" Today you will not find my would-be murderers among my people."

" Not today," repeated the Legate.

" Let us talk of this in ten years' time."

That was an injudicious observation; the Legate was old and did not care to be reminded of that fact. At this point the conversation ended.

They stood, and some while was spent in compliments from the Legate, assurances by the King, and all the formalities of farewell, the King attending his visitor to the door, thence back into the room, and so once more towards the door, Henri again proffering his escort. It was noteworthy that the Legate most modestly refused to allow the King to accompany him so far. Now that the weightier and more perilous matters had been dismissed, the Legate took occasion to indulge in a little banter, or what, from the way he spoke, might pass for such.

" You are in need of money, as is understandable enough. A King who would make all men equal does best to make them all rich. Most unfortunately the money forces are on the side of the universal monarchy. Here you have but very inferior financiers, such as this man Zamet. He is an agent of the House of Medici, did you know? Though there is little that you do not know."

"What is to be done? " said the King, very ready to drop his guard now that the encounter was at an end. " I have two ways of getting my hands into the Grand Duke of Tuscany's exchequer; by alliance, or by war."

He knew in fact that there was a third way; and the Legate proceeded to mention it, with an air of mystery.

" The Grand Duke of Tuscany is not only a great banker; he has a niece — with all the noble qualities of the Princesses of the House of Medici."

" I know," retorted Henri. " The noblest of them all kept me a prisoner here for many a year, and not a day passed that she did not eye me like a haunch of beef, to see if I were tender."

" Tut, tut, Your Majesty! " and such was the Legate's astonishment that he barely smiled. " A great King likened to a joint of beef? Dear me! — not a matter to be mentioned. But what you call imprisonment may sometimes be fetters of roses."

The Legate had his hand on the door, having, rather surprisingly, reached it first; and he departed before any further outburst of courtesies. His motley escort wafted the little old gentleman out of sight in an instant.

And the King thought: " All in all, the conversation pleased me better than my old friend Mornay's discourses on virtue."

The Legate in his cloud thought: " The man is a martyr. Gladly would I write a new legend of the saints. What was it that always marked our martyrs and our saints? The fear of death, without which no man can be a martyr. But what makes a man a saint is this, and only this — the impossible, the foul, abominable, infamous idea that attacks the universal order and would overthrow it. Good health to those who will not be there, as I shall not be; nor will he.

Henri closed the door with his own hand; for a while he paced to and fro and wandered into the room near by that looked across to the window and the four shadows. Hitherto he had not been aware of them; he found himself reflecting that the Legate had for some time accompanied him everywhere. Had he been secretly present at the fireworks when a dream of his had soared upwards with the rockets? Why, he had forgotten it himself; but the old man knew of it.

He laughed to himself. The shrewd priest was none the less deluded. "You see too deep, you are too suspicious. I have no mind to overthrow Pope and Emperor, and especially not for my convictions. These high thoughts are found on heights that I do not attempt to scale. You find your way alone, while I stay here below and do what must be done. And next of all I must marry my beloved and make her my Queen."

Suddenly he clapped his hands to his sides. Oh, the crazy things that a man had to do before he could get into his marriage bed! The Edict — because her party was Protestant. "But before that, contrariwise, came the leap of death, for then we hoped to conciliate the Church and win the love of our Catholic subjects. But nothing was observable, except the knife that never found its mark."

As he was alone — which he now seldom was — he flung himself face downwards on the floor and groaned, that he might not shriek with laughter. Buffoon, be tragical! Tragedian, make yourself ridiculous! All for a woman! World history in a bedroom. But it was something new to admit as much.

And yet, admitted, it was no longer true. Have a care; Gabrielle is here much brought into question. She put heart into the King, she had borne him over obstacles, such as the death leap and the Edict; and on the way there had been battles, men to be conciliated, much use of force and cunning, not to mention a great deal of honest toil. Had she died in childhood, how would matters stand? There would still remain the kingdom, and this man — who laughs no more, but clasps his face in his two hands. Lies prostrate on the floor, and must suffer sorely, because, for the first time in his life, he has his doubts of love. Ah, had it not been for love! He lay quite still, and on his neck sat a malignant cripple, a thousand years old, who forced his head down with a vast broad gripping hand. Ah, had it not been for love!

Henri shuddered so violently that the ancient creature lost his balance. Henri sprang to his feet. And he cried to the unseen incubus that had slipped off his back:

"Not a Medici!"

He had spoken with such violence that the door opened, and his people appeared.

"The whole court," he said, "is to go over to the house of Madame, the sister of the King, and there wait upon the Duchess of Beaufort."

GABRIELLE CONFESSES

From the table at which sat the four Protestant ladies, Madame, the King's sister, now lifted up her voice:

"I know little of sin, though I live outside wedlock. God is well aware why He permits it. I defy the world before it judges me, and I leave the rest to Him. It has been His will that I should abide by the Religion; no matter what may come. I am abused by him I love, in ways that touch the soul — and also in other ways."

Here Catherine blushed, and eyed the others to see what was in their minds. And they thought no harm. If Madame, the King's sister, had gone on to tell how the Count of Soissons betrayed her, or beat her, or threw her out of bed, these devout women would not have been perturbed. For loyalty in faith is in some sense a counterpart of humble constancy in love. That now ageing, girlish face claimed neither sympathy nor admiration. Knowing nothing of sin, it knew self-sacrifice. Catherine spoke again, and said in her crystal tones:

"The King my brother wants me to marry another. He conceives me unhappy. Let him give us the Edict! That would compensate for much, and not least for my unhappiness. And if yet more were needed to make the balance good, let him set the Duchess of Beaufort beside him; she will bear him lovely children. I want the King to marry her, and I want the Edict — now I have said my say."

Madame, the King's sister, signed to the lady whom she had

just named. Gabrielle had been restored by what her good friend had said.

Gabrielle: " Madame, the King's sister, has spoken truly: I shall bear lovely children to our lord — and many children. I aim at the throne, so I must needs hate anyone who thwarts me, and I especially hate the Queen of Navarre. And yet I could more easily forgive her, if she plotted against my life instead of that of my beloved lord. For truth's sake, I would uncover the worst of my heart; but behind it all is my love for the King."

This touched them all. Catherine bent down a glowing face to Gabrielle, the Princess of Orange stroked her shoulder, poor Mornay lifted her clasped hands. Gabrielle bade them wait until she had finished:

" You do not know what it means to be wicked and worthless. A future Queen should not tell you of these things. For the honour of my lord I will keep silent. But there is a pride, an ambition, and a purpose that are both false and vain. Had it not been for love — so you Protestants say. You in this room have surely never understood the meaning of those words: Had it not been for love. One who does know shudders at her past; it belonged to a stranger whose spirit was distraught. I never possessed my life in all its fullness until I met with one for whom I would gladly die. I have won his heart, and I am for ever his, no matter — believe me — whether he grows greater still or whether he makes me his Queen."

" The time is at hand," said the Princess of Orange. But Gabrielle went on:

" Madame d'Orange, you need not fear that I shall show overmuch Christian resignation. I am resolved to attain my end, and I have not forgotten the lessons of my past. I'll give the court good reason to call me evil names."

Duchess of Ordure, thought the ladies. And, oddly enough, they did not conceive the title as a term of abuse. From her who now seemed so suddenly aloof came the voice of majesty; she spoke out of the King's own rib, she was his very flesh and blood. No one now laid a glowing face to hers, or thrilled at the vision of her beauty.

The Princess of Orange began, not waiting to be bidden:

" I go through life unaltered; that is a great defect in my nature. We ought to be burdened with faults that we must cure
by our wits and by our will. I had no faults of which to rid myself, neither ambition nor arrogance nor selfish purpose. The
poor widow of Monsieur de Téligny became the wife of William
of Orange, who might have married any rich princess. He chose
the poorest, when his enemies were already at his heels. His son
by his first marriage, Maurice, held Holland in succession to his
father. Unlike William, he did not want to see his country free,
he meant to rule it, after throwing off the Spanish yoke. I am
for Barneveldt, for justice and freedom, against my stepson
Maurice, and against my own advantage, for my only boy would
thus be heir to the throne. And all this would cost me nothing;
there lies the blunder. I do not struggle, I make my way by a
certain cheerful obstinacy, for which I get false credit as a virtue."

And she turned her cold clear eyes on the Duchess of Beaufort.

" Ignorance of the dark places of the soul marks, I think, indifference; and those who never err are not much regarded by
our Lord in heaven. I despise death, but that, I am sure, will not
be counted in my favour. I do not die because I love, but because of that same Christian obstinacy that is my heritage. I was
the favourite daughter of my father, Admiral Coligny."

The name was her last word. As she uttered it, the small,
buxom Princess half rose out of her chair. The other three rose
with her, and last of all Gabrielle. A nobleman whose entrance
she had not observed suddenly appeared before her and bowed.
She had scarcely expected this person in particular, and still less
that he would so sacrifice his pride. It was Monsieur de Rosny,
and he said:

" Madam, the King is on his way hither. It is his command
that we should wait upon you. The court is already assembled
and beseeches you to appear."

With Monsieur de Rosny at their head to marshal them, the
ladies walked two by two towards the great audience chamber;
and the buzz and clamour of the world about them soon dispelled the deeper mood in which they had revealed their inmost

hearts. Gabrielle paused and had almost turned and fled before the outburst of homage; it was the first time she had been so greeted by the whole court. They clapped their hands and cheered and bowed and curtsied; then with shuffling feet and rustling garments they pressed back to make way for her approach; a hundred and more, thronging against the walls, she isolated in their midst. And in a shiver of fear at this ominous ovation she clutched Madame d'Orange's arm. Madame, the King's sister, stepped up to the left of her.

Madame de Mornay had fled. Outside, she said to the King, who was mounting the stairway:

" Sire! The Duchess needs your help. Oh, make haste! May you be in time, for I think your lady is in danger of her life! "

Henri began to run. Having reached the door of the hall, he saw — no angry throng besetting his beloved lady; he saw her making a triumphant progress. His heart throbbed with joy as he greeted Gabrielle's victory and his own.

The great galleried hall, with a number of cabinets all round it, had — how long ago! — been the scene of the Ballet of the Magicians and the Barbers; and of that interlude when he and she had had to seek some refuge against the insults they could not stop; how glad they had been to escape through the secret passage! Those had been perilous moments for both. Since then — he had gone steadily upwards, and so had she. At last he had won a real victory over Spain, and he had even held his own against a Legate of the Pope. Now, now he knew himself strong enough to announce his Edict. And this day was her day — the day of his beloved lady. He had half a mind to compel the priest to marry them on the spot and to proclaim her his Queen.

His mind was afire with expectancy. To others came the same thoughts in less vehement fashion. Two ladies, at a little distance from the throng, were whispering together.

The Princess of Conti: " How pale she is! Madame d'Orange should hold her more firmly. I fear she may fall down."

The Princess of Condé, of the House of Bourbon: " There's more to fear than that. If only my cousin's luck holds! He must needs be a great man for such a marriage."

The Princess of Conti: " Is he not great enough already to challenge us all now? His precious whore displays herself to the whole court, with a Protestant lady on either side of her. I believe she is a Protestant herself, or she would understand what threatens her and faint sometimes for very fear of it."

The Princess of Condé: " Truly she is pale; but her pallor may come from pride, not fear. If there is one pure woman at the court, it is Madame d'Orange. She speaks well of Gabrielle d'Estrées, her new-found virtue, and the steadfast love that is to make her worthy of becoming Queen."

" All the worse for her own safety," said the first lady grimly, and the second lady agreed.

Then followed much hand-clapping and wild applause — while a certain gentleman who had but lately appeared at court stood upon a chair and peered over the shoulders of the throng. " I must be mistaken," said this Monsieur de Bassompierre to those about him. " What I now see cannot be reality, or someone will not live long."

Came a voice from below:

" Whom have you in mind? "

" 'Tis clear enough," said the gentleman on the chair. " The King must live. I grieve for this lovely lady, but the knife must otherwise be turned on him."

Said Madame de Sagonne:

" You have not been long among us, my poor friend, and do not realize that our immediate future is cast under the constellation of Venus."

The Ministers Villeroy and Rosny were also caught in the throng. Each had gradually been edged against the wall, and there they met.

" A notable sight, my friend."

" It is indeed."

" It would be well — would it not? — that we should have seen nothing of the matter," said the Foreign Minister, whom the Minister of Finance knew to be a traitor. And Rosny answered:

" It is scarce worth remark. Nor need the court of Madrid be informed of it. The affair will have no consequences. The King himself will forget it all as soon as he needs money again. His Grand Treasurer or his mistress — only the fools of this court could doubt which of the two will prevail. There need be no talk of murder or of death, a money-box strikes harder than an axe."

Thereupon Monsieur de Rosny allowed himself to be jostled away from Monsieur de Villeroy, whom he knew to be a traitor. His words, however much or little he believed in them himself, were spoken with the intention of assuring Gabrielle's safety. He did not like her, nor was he a kindly man. But he had a sense of dignity and honoured the vital forces that had so striven to bring forth that great reign, which he conceived in three embodiments: The King, himself, and the Duchess of Beaufort. But the woman should never go beyond that rank and title; he would take good care of that.

Gabrielle stood up, and she faced the court and her own glory for what seemed an eternity, though it was but a few minutes by the clock. She sighed when her dear lord took her hand and led her through the hall. The crowd began to move, the broken ranks were formed again, and all stood eager for a word of recognition when the King should pass. They watched the King's lips, and, no less intently, the rich lips of his lady, who, with poised fingers touching his, walked a step or two ahead. He, behind the broad flat panniers of her dress, seemed to be displaying her to that company as his jewel and his treasure, and doing so with zest; and, indeed, there was an imperious air about him in that moment, as they all observed.

So Gabrielle encountered none but submissive looks. The colour came back into her cheeks, and she herself, instead of the King, spoke to the bystanders on either side. It was the touch of her finger-tips upon his that steadied her and told her what to say. She did pass the first few courtiers in silence; but before Monsieur de Sancy, Captain of the Swiss, she paused.

"Monsieur de Sancy, the King and I have decided to go into Brittany. I give you my permission to accompany us."

This she said to several others, especially to Monsieur de Bouillon, who had thought it well to ignore his defection before

Amiens. Therefore he bowed respectfully when the lady he had tried to bribe commanded rather than invited his presence on this journey.

Towards the end of her progress Gabrielle came face to face with Monsieur de Rosny. Both tall and fair, their skin and eyes of kindred colouring, they might have passed for brother and sister. But only in outward aspect, and the spectators did not view them so, for there was little in common between the charming d'Estrées and a grim figure hewn from stone. And the pair themselves felt no kinship. Gabrielle held up her head and spoke more haughtily than to the rest:

" You will have to leave your Arsenal and travel in my escort, Monsieur de Rosny."

His face flushed deeply, he gasped, and then he answered:

" I await my master's command."

"The Duchess asks you to attend her," said Henri, and his finger-tips warned her to repeat his words.

She did so. But it was too late.

A Treaty of Marriage

The King's journey into Brittany proved a peaceful progress, although he took with him ten thousand infantry, apart from horses and guns. This escort, which was indeed considerable for an ordinary visit, had been urged upon him by his Grand Master of Artillery. Henri had listened while he said, what he himself knew but hated to admit, that without the threat of force he could not even now have won his province. Another matter, too, he had not foreseen: the necessity for speed. Monsieur de Rosny insisted, and with good reason, that the Duke of Mercœur would only abandon his shifts and subterfuges if he found himself caught unprepared.

That was the reason Rosny gave. The one he did not give concerned the King's beloved, who could not travel on the day appointed; the expected child had exhausted her of late. So Monsieur de Rosny did not travel in her train, as she had intended. He rode away, and she was left behind, prostrate. Three days later she set out. When Gabrielle had reached Angers by easy stages, Henri with his great array was already far ahead. Wherever he approached, the cities of his province of Brittany opened their gates to him; and from all over that sea-girt peninsula the noblemen made haste to offer a welcome to their King. Monsieur de Mercœur in his craggy lair had grown too confident in the might of the unharnessed sea. King Henri haled him out of his wind-swept fortress. It was spring, and the storms were raging with more than common fury; that wild lord of storms had to be content to sit upon dry land, where his power soon ebbed away from him, and he had to sign the treaty.

It was no special treaty providing for the abdication of his sovereignty. It was rather the return of a great province to the King's authority, though, as it were by chance, connected with another pact that was to prove of yet greater import: a contract of marriage. The daughter of the Duke and Duchess of Mercœur was to marry Cæsar Vendôme, son of the King of France and the Lady Gabrielle d'Estrées. This ranked as the main event, if not in the eyes of everyone, all the more surely in those of Gabrielle. It was on this account that she had been so set upon this journey. Delays and obstacles exasperated her into behaviour that seemed quite out of character in so placid a beauty.

The Duchess of Mercœur, Marie of Luxembourg, of the House of Penthièvre, was a great lady who thought a d'Estrées far beneath her. Moreover, the boy Cæsar was born of a double adultery, and she scorned the proposed alliance into which she was to enter. A King of France was not a connection that she wanted, when, like this King, he had made his own way to the throne. And who could predict his future and the succession? It would be disputed forthwith if the knife reached its mark at last. A King's bastard for a son-in-law! And Madame de Mercœur, always a ready intriguer, began to plot and plan against this match. Gabrielle resolved to clinch the matter. When the Duchess of Mercœur appeared before Angers, intent upon further procrastination, Gabrielle had all the gates barred. The great lady had to turn back and possess herself in patient humiliation until the King came, and at his instance she was received back into favour. Many people do not realize how precariously they stand until a gate is slammed in their faces.

In the interval Henri had been to Rennes, where the Estates of the province of Brittany were holding their assembly. As he would not see his lady for a few days, he wrote her letters as at the time of their courtship. Indeed, they were very like those he used to send to the Château of Cœuvres, several of which were intercepted by the enemy, who could very easily have caught the little old peasant with the blackened face. And Henri thought: " Seven years gone, and always I and you. Is it then true what you reproach me with and I deny — that you now love the more? That you love me a thousandfold more than I love you? So much at least is certain: your face has bloomed and ripened, like your heart. You would no longer endure to live without me, that I can well believe, for you could not go back to the life you have left behind. But I, my dearest treasure, am in no different case, and am no more free than you. My fortunes rose with yours, with you I entered upon my possessions — I possess nothing that is not in and through you mine. I view my kingdom in the semblance of your womb — which betrayed me often in past days, but now belongs to me. And though your beauty faded, I could not leave you. Time was when I took back my love; very poor I was, who am now rich."

There was nothing of all this in his letters, which were still carried by La Varenne. But he kept the light, brisk style of his former letters, with allusions to the weapons that his lady herself had chosen, with which the contest would very soon be decided. Thus the King wrote when the speeches in the Brittany assembly grew too wearisome — the last province of his kingdom that he made his own.

He said nothing, either, about the strange events that always seemed to break in upon his more rational dealings, and did so now. They would have upset a highly normal and vivacious lady, and a father's encounters with the abnormal might well have marked an unborn child. When his business with the Estates was ended, he stayed for a day and a night at Saumur, the city of his old comrade Philippe Mornay, who in secular matters had always been both sane and lucid. Much brooding upon theological mysteries may have weakened his sense of reality, but he now saw Monsieur de Saint-Phal everywhere.

" What is the matter with you? " Henri asked. And an emaciated, shrunken Mornay answered in a toneless voice:

" He looked in through the window just now. He mocks me and insults me."

" Come hither, friend," said Henri. " You are in your castle, which you fortified. How could he get inside it; and how would he get out? "

" One who is in league with the Devil " — and a far-away look came over the man's twitching face — " heeds no walls nor lifted drawbridges."

" And where could he have gone to ground? " asked Henri.

" There," said Mornay in a whisper, and he promptly laid a trembling forefinger at a particular spot on the large wall-map.

And Henri, merely thinking how to get out quickest, " Make haste," said he. " Let us be after him! "

The wretched man dropped his arms and bowed his head and wailed:

" The Devil warns him when I try to track him down. Sire, I have your word. You must catch this man."

" You have my word," cried Henri, as he dashed through the door.

He mounted, and rode off with escort enough to have captured a whole band of marauders. The horsemen pulled up at the forest edge, where a house in a patch of marshy ground looked like the refuge of Saint-Phal. Meantime the King was lured aside to follow the hoof-marks of a stag and lost sight of his companions. The forest grew so thick that Henri had to dismount, he could not tell from what direction came the huntsmen's answering shouts, and night began to fall.

By chance he fell in with three of his gentlemen in the darkness, one of them being de Thou, President of the High Court. Already getting on in years, he had accompanied the King on his journey to take part in the negotiations with Mercœur. While in pursuit of the stag, he had fallen from his horse and injured his leg. The King decided that he could not leave him alone, despite the President's plea that the King should return to Saumur.

" How can I? We have lost our way," said Henri. Meanwhile one of the others had climbed a tree and reported that he could see a light. When they reached the place, progressing very slowly owing to Monsieur de Thou's injury, there lay a solitary house in a marsh. They made their way to it; the door was unlocked, and all the rooms empty. In the one where the light was burning, there stood a bed prepared.

" Aha," said Bellegarde. " He has been here. He was going to bed when we surprised him, he cannot be far away."

" Then fetch him, Feuillemorte," said Henri, and looked as though he thought it was so.

The Grand Master of the Horse and the third gentleman made a great clatter in that shadowy house, which began to feel uncanny. Then they departed, splashing their way through the swamp. In the meantime the King urged Monsieur de Thou to lie down; but there was not a bed in the place save the one already observed. The President of the High Court refused; the King must have it. However, he was in such pain that he consented to stretch himself out on the very edge of it, though in the King's presence he would not take the shoe off his injured foot. Henri sat in the only chair before the hearth, on which lay a small heap of wood. He kindled some pine cones, lit the fire, and stared into it wide-eyed. Half vacantly he fell to pondering on this journey into his province of Brittany: with the purpose of entering into weighty State negotiations, after much patient and sagacious preparation. And here he was in pursuit of a delusion — and not even a delusion of his own. He would be all the less likely to escape that night from the forest and a desolate house, with its one solitary burning taper. If murderers had broken in on him, he had no support but a sick man and his own sword. How precarious was human reason! All the strange things that had befallen him passed in a vision before his mind; surely they should have been warnings from his uncompleted nature to itself. A man must never shrink from his own knowledge, he must do heartily what in him lies and what is laid upon him. Well, thought Henri, if he had, he would not be sitting here, and would escape yet darker magic in the future.

All this could be learned by staring into the flickering flames. "Tarry no longer, make the one woman your Queen." He saw her name written in the fire, and heard it in the crackling of the flames.

Bellegarde and his friend reappeared, noiselessly this time, for they had bared their legs above the knee, to wade through the swamp. They assured him they had seen Monsieur de Saint-Phal leaping through the rustling undergrowth, until he had at last fallen into a pit. Henri merely asked them to see to the poor President, who had fallen on the bed from sheer exhaustion and was now asleep, undress him, and dispose him comfortably. After so doing, they conducted the King to a room with one door only, the floor of which was strewn with straw. They left the door open, and each leaned against the outer face of each doorpost. Any intruder would have to force his way between them.

Henri promptly fell into a deep sleep. His two guards now and again shifted their legs beneath their cloaks, to make sure that the other was awake. But at last not a limb stirred — until a piercing cry for help shook them from their dreams. They first thought they were still in the forest and had stumbled into Monsieur de Saint-Phal, who was shrieking with terror. Then they remembered Monsieur de Thou.

The old President had suddenly become aware of a lunatic girl in his room. The poor creature had been so sadly abused in the city that she had taken refuge in the deserted house, from which she would indeed have fled had she known that strangers were in occupation. But she did not. She came back as usual, took her wet clothes off in the dark — the taper had long since guttered out — and hung them over the chair by the hearth, in which there was still a faint glow. When her shift was partly dry, she lay down across the bed, at the sleeper's feet, and was soon asleep herself. It was not long before Monsieur de Thou turned over; in doing so he pushed the girl off the bed, and so hurt his injured leg as he did so, that he awoke.

De Thou pulled the bed-curtain and saw a white form moving in the faint glimmer from the window. It could not be a phantasm, for she approached and looked at him. "Who are you?" asked the President. "The Queen of Heaven," replied the presence. The President knew this must be blasphemous nonsense; he was seized by a superstitious terror and shouted for help. The gentlemen came to his rescue and locked the girl into another room.

Henri had slept on and heard nothing of all this until the day was up and the four of them were riding to Saumur. He merely said that in the President's place he would have been terrified, and then fell silent. But he thought of his own self-questioning beside the fire — the fire in which he had read and whose voice he had heard. Not long afterwards, at the Easter celebrations, when the choir began the *Regina Cœli Lætare*, the King stood up and looked about the church for Monsieur de Thou.

Such were the more mysterious happenings, assuming, indeed, that the sense of them was not understood. No mention was made of them in the letters to Gabrielle. Henri, on his way back to her, fell in with the Duchess of Mercœur; never before had he received such homage and such obsequious assurances from so exalted a personage. He felt all the more suspicious, as he did not yet know that his dear mistress had tamed the lady. He invited her to accompany him to Angers. There were many towers in the castle there — the Duchess of Mercœur counted sixteen or more — and she feared that in one or other of them she might be very safely lodged. And the broad circling walls bristled with her enemy's guards.

Before they arrived, the Duchess of Beaufort came forth to meet them, and was all eagerness to embrace the lady; indeed, she invited her into her litter. Henri admired Gabrielle for having so learned to dispose her feelings and hold fast to her purpose. And this lovely lady was yet more esteemed for wisdom and sagacity when at last, on the 31st of March, the all-important treaty was signed: a treaty of State under the guise of a marriage contract.

In the castle of Angers the Royal Notary, Master Guillot, read the deed, and long as it was; the brilliant assemblage listened with all their ears. The Duke and the Duchess of Mercœur bestowed on their daughter Françoise, upon her marriage to Duke Cæsar of Vendôme, a magnificent dowry in money and jewels; all, incidentally, bought out of the vast sum which the Duke of Mercœur received from the King for his province of Brittany.

At this, many of the spectators could contain themselves no longer. They knew the purport of this pact.

" We knew it," said the Cardinal de Joyeuse to the Protestant, Bouillon, " but we did not believe it. The House of Lorraine is giving up the last vestige of its power. Little Navarre is now master of the kingdom."

" But not of my Dukedom of Bouillon," replied the former Monsieur de Turenne, who had inherited the same, and thought to maintain himself against the King — an ambition which was to be the ruin of him.

Master Guillot announced that the governors and magistrates of the province of Brittany would be left in possession of their offices. At this point came a snort of anger — from Monsieur de Rosny, his face, as usual, a mask of stone, but inwardly infuriated. Notorious rascals and traitors were to continue as they were instead of answering for their transgressions; he had been helpless to prevent it. The royal power, as embodied in justice, had been humiliated; and Rosny, who had so striven in its defence, told himself that the King was weak. He who never yielded could not understand that power may yield. A marriage contract as a cover for a treaty — Rosny merely sneered, and ascribed the whole matter to the ambition of a mistress, who had managed to prevail upon the King.

One Monsieur de Bassompierre, a new arrival at the court, asked what Madame, the King's sister, had to do with the affair. She had been summoned to the ceremony, and her consent had been requested. " Ah," said the newcomer, " now all is clear.

The King's purpose is to give the Protestants their Edict. What we now see is the first step to that end."

Suddenly the Notary's voice was still, deep silence fell upon the assemblage; then came the rustle of two dresses, one of lilac silk, the other green, brocaded with silver; Madame, the King's sister, and the Duchess of Beaufort; between them, the King. Thus the three of them proceeded up the room to the table on which the treaty was laid out. Two names were then called, the Duke and Duchess of Mercœur came forward; and others who were also to sign took their places. The group stood isolated upon a dais, and up the steps of it now climbed two children, a boy and a girl, arrayed like their elders. Walking with measured gait, the two little figures stopped and stood in the most dignified of attitudes, and their faces were the gravest in all that company.

Some who had been looking wryly at the performance, broke into smiles. Not a few of the ladies uttered little cries of delight or sighed aloud in something like relief. Henri watched the faces of the two Mercœurs, whom he was stripping of their possessions and their power. Hitherto they had looked like detected criminals; their colour came and went, the man's eyes reddened, and the woman coughed, that she might not weep nor shriek. But when the children took their stand on the dais, the pair's demeanour changed. They grasped their share in this event. Their daughter would be but one step from the throne. The boy would ascend it with her. The King must marry the mother. If he would but marry her at once!

The King signed first and gave the pen to the Duchess of Beaufort. Her hand was trembling, but with joy. All the spectators craned their heads to see. The loveliest hand in the kingdom traced the most exalted signature that had yet been hers. She laid down the pen and waited with throbbing heart. Her dear lord smiled a reassuring smile. Scarcely had Madame, the King's sister, set down her name, when the two Mercœurs hurried to the table. Philip Emmanuel of Lorraine, Duke of Mercœur, Marie of Luxembourg, Duchess of Mercœur: Gabrielle read the names with shining eyes, her joy made her dizzy. Beneath the burden of it she bent her head on the shoulder of her beloved, who kissed her flushed face.

The witnesses passed the goose-quill from one to another, and not the least important was Monsieur Antoine d'Estrées, father of that day's heroine, who had long since shed his blemished reputation. Thereupon, without loss of time, the betrothal of the children was solemnized by the Cardinal de Joyeuse, in the presence of the court and the foreign envoys. But there were none among that company whose hearts were stirred a second time or were diverted from the issue by the sight of children taking part in a ceremony beyond their years. One clause of the contract was most present to their minds. When the Notary had read it out in clear, emphatic tones, they made no sign that they had marked it, or pretended that it was of small account. If, in time to come, one of the future spouses did not wish to consummate the marriage, he or she had simply to denounce it, at a price — and not a high one for wealthy families.

" This means nothing," said the Grand Master of the Horse, Bellegarde, in a tone of astonishment. " It will be fourteen years before they are ripe."

" I fancy my niece, the Duchess of Beaufort, ripened somewhat earlier," retorted a lady at his side.

Bellegarde caught a view of Gabrielle, though he was not looking for her; and, to avoid her eyes, he dropped his own. His heart thrilled with memories. " Look at her," he heard a voice beside him say. A word had cut short his happiness, he thought, though he had years of prosperity ahead of him. Had he not provoked it, there would have been here no King's son to betroth. One word, and youth and happiness are gone.

" What she was destined to be, that she has become," he said softly.

" And we never guessed it," sighed Madame de Sourdis who would herself gladly have forgotten her efforts that Gabrielle's destiny might be fulfilled.

Bellegarde eyed the children. Little Vendôme had developed

too quickly, he was fat and lumpish; Bellegarde did not like the
look of him. But his heart, and his alone, was once more
touched. " Poor lad," he said to himself. This meant nothing.
The end of that song was not yet known.

THE EDICT

The festivities in honour of the great treaty, in which so vast
a company took part, were in one respect a disappointment.
The loveliest of ladies could not be present. Her condition no
longer permitted of any public appearance. As soon as the King
could accompany her, they both set out for the city of Nantes,
and there she bore him his second son, Alexander. After Cæsar,
Alexander, and he was given the title of Monsieur, as though he
were a son of France.

The city and castle of Nantes then for the first time came over
to the Royal party. And as Alexander-Monsieur was born to him
promptly after his arrival, King Henri signed the Edict of Nantes
— in a flush of paternal joy. So it appeared, nor was the matter
called in question. But shortly before that event came the pact
whereby the betrothal of the two children included and glossed
over the recovery of his last province, by a well-considered stroke.
Those who might have protested were silent, they merely asked
themselves: " How long? Now we move into another room and
sign the Edict of Nantes."

" Well," said the Catholic gentlemen to each other, " this is
where the King would have us. We are beaten."

The Cardinal de Joyeuse: " He grants freedom of conscience.
This is his day of fulfilment. Is he now the Huguenot that he
was? Or has he come to believe nothing at all? "

The Constable de Montmorency: " He calls me his godfather.
But he is not the man I knew."

The Cardinal: " In days gone by at Coutras he defeated and
killed my two brothers. I cannot be his friend. I admire his
obstinacy."

The Constable: " Do we desire the greatness of this kingdom?
It was only at the price of freedom of conscience that we made

a conqueror's peace at Vervins. What else his purpose is, I do not know."

The Cardinal: " Freedom of conscience: if we thought solely as Christians and had not to provide for this world, as does our Holy Church, it should be granted. But we must provide for this world if we are to survive."

The Constable: " He means to survive, that is very sure. He calls his Edict unassailable."

The Cardinal: " It is no more and no less so than himself."

Here the Cardinal turned his open hand and held it back upwards. The Constable understood; beneath it lay a man, overthrown.

" We are beaten," said the Catholics, though some only thought it without saying so. " The King has liberated heresy — if only that were all! Your strong places are in Protestant hands. Where are ours? " they asked a Protestant, one of their opponents who in the thronged room had been caught in his adversaries' ranks. Creeds had latterly been ignored. Today the Religions stood sundered.

" You may now hold your services in many Catholic cities, but we may not do so in yours. You are granted all civil rights, you may hold office, you may even become magistrates."

" And you? " retorted Agrippa over several intervening heads. " Who were they who shed their blood for the King? — and if we live, it is small credit to ourselves. I know some who meant to bring this State to ruin, arm in arm with the Spaniards. Our good swords won the King his sovereignty; and who now claims to control the offices of State, and the Treasury? Those who betrayed him, and would betray him again."

The word " betray " was almost shouted by Agrippa. There had been a good deal of recrimination, but voices were not raised; the King was issuing his Edict. But the gentlemen at whom the word was aimed would gladly have taught him a lesson. However, bold Agrippa's short stature saved him, for he was concealed behind the taller Protestants, and they thrust him backwards until he was out of sight.

Among the Protestants, Marshal de Roquelaure said to Monsieur Philippe du Plessis-Mornay: " You look as though you had taken a black draught. Isn't this our joyful day? "

" So we called the day of Coutras," said Mornay. " In those days we were the army of the poor, the army of those persecuted for righteousness' sake."

Roquelaure: " Our King had hollow cheeks, I see him still."

Mornay: " You need but to turn towards him now; his cheeks are still hollow, his battle is not ended." Mornay would have liked to add: " And I am at mortal odds with Monsieur de Saint-Phal. Nay, worse: when my Tractate on the Mass appears, I shall lose the favour of the King." The Marshal interrupted him.

Roquelaure: " The King today fulfils his promised word, but he goes no further. We should have held the first places in the State; we are now given the rights of tolerance, but no warrant that our position will endure. For forty long years we have fought for freedom of conscience! "

Mornay: " It is achieved, and once for all. The King speaks truth." But Mornay thought: " Freedom of conscience is a spiritual possession. Times will come when we can preserve it only in our hearts, and in exile."

Upon the two Protestants a strange silence fell, while thoughts that shun utterance passed across their vision. And Roquelaure said at last:

" In old days, when the kingdom was not his and he was not yet great, he and we broke crusts together, and prayed: ' All the heathen encompass me, but in the name of the Lord will I destroy them.' Who is now destroyed? Indeed, it would be to no purpose. There is little profit in promises redeemed." So, with a rueful air, said Monsieur de Roquelaure, who was known at the court for his love of laughter and light-hearted mockery.

And Philippe Mornay, a self-tormentor, answered — but the two men would not meet each other's eyes:

" One should not grow old. Here is one who grows not old." He turned and faced his master, whom he had chosen in the days of his youth.

King Henri, on the dais, beneath the baldachin, pronounced

his Edict. He had no notary to read it; he recited it from memory, as his will and his good pleasure. His tone was nicely balanced between conciliation and command, and in the sound of
his own voice he might well have forgotten what, as he stood
beneath this baldachin, were the rights that he was in fact re-
storing: no more than half a settlement, mutilated, and delayed
until the eleventh hour. The negotiations and concessions had
been a mockery; and he thought of all the wrangling, the rup-
tures and renewals, the fair speeches that did but mask the evil
intrigues, the bitterness and hatred, the incarnate lust for gain;
much had gone to make that Edict. His twenty years of war as
well. A petty King of Navarre, uncertain of his life and of the
throne of France, he had had this distant day before his eyes.
Another of his usual appearances beneath a baldachin, and the
Edict was a matter of small account; and yet the kingdom was
more than money and possession, more than the common power
over his fellow-men. At last he knew himself strong enough to
say to them: " You are to be free to believe and to think." And
he wished that there had been present to hear him one whose
eyes and ears were already stopped with earth: Monsieur Michel
de Montaigne; they had talked together once by the seashore.
" What do I know? " was his favourite phrase. They had ca-
roused together in a cottage wrecked by cannon, they had
chanted Horace — Montaigne and his most insignificant dis-
ciple, who now stood beneath the baldachin and announced his
Edict. Montaigne would be glad, as he himself was glad.

He was the only one present who felt any satisfaction, as he
did not fail to mark. Neither party was pleased, they merely
accepted what he granted because he was strong enough at last:
freedom of conscience, with all its consequences. From every
side they stared up at him on his dais, as though majesty alone
sufficed to transform the community and there had been no vicissitudes of war and peace before that day. And Henri thought:
" Long labour, dubious success, brief joy." He would be brief
and make an end, before they were overcome by astonishment.
The betrothal of the children, the birth of his son — that is
what they were there to celebrate; from mere joy of father-

hood he was to make them equal, he would strip the nobles of
their provinces and power. Within the State, creeds no longer
parted them, and rank should not divide them soon. " Give
not too close an ear, we will be brief."

" I assign the Protestants of my kingdom to ten districts, of
which each shall govern itself through deputies: two pastors,
four burghers and farmers, four noblemen. Their petitions and
disputes I shall myself decide."

The King had spoken. He took the parchment from the hands
of his Chancellor, old Cheverny, signed it, and saluted the assemblage before turning to depart. " Now they have it," thought
Henri. " They will need much charity and forbearance to grow
used to what they have."

Most of the company merely stared at the King. Some, who
had understood, whispered to each other:

" Four noblemen against six of the Third Estate. He is beginning with the Protestants."

" That means democracy."

" Or despotism."

As Henri passed the doorway, there were cheers of " Long live
the King! "

But he departed, as though the cheers were meant for someone else.

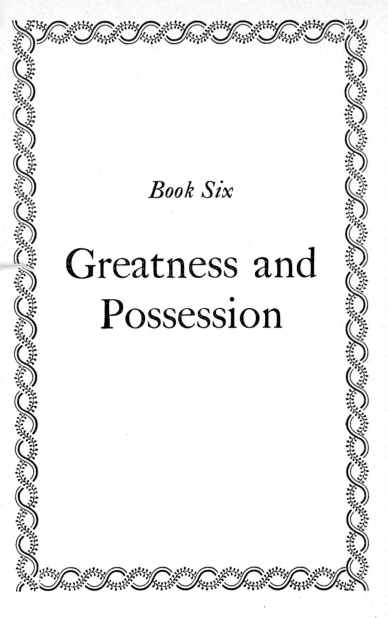

Book Six

Greatness and Possession

On the River

THE WAY homeward was made easy for the King's beloved. He carried her by ship from Nantes to Orléans, a long and very romantic journey. The Loire shone in the soft May sunshine, the light white clouds sailed overhead and passed. The King's ship glided slowly up-stream before a gentle breeze, between the flat, placid banks on either hand. Flower-scattered meadows and fields of corn as far as eye could see, banked on the horizon by a blue line of woodland. In the foreground dark, beetling castles, with roses twining round their towers. And when but one of the four towers had put on a youthful garb of green, its reflection in the water was not of an ancient, river stronghold, but the vision of a dream.

The cities of Angers, Tours, and Blois, one after another, dipped their peaceful shadows in the stream; and the long stretches in between were dotted with villages, hamlets, and cottages. As the ship slid past, the children at their play at once noticed that this was no ordinary vessel. They stood motionless, with empty hands, small pot-bellied figures with grave attentive eyes.

The deck of the ship was roofed with awnings, hung with garlands that trailed in the water, so that the ship seemed to move through floating flowers. The vessel itself was lavishly carved and painted, and the sails curved majestically in the breeze. At the prow, a gilded figure blowing a trumpet, as does the goddess of Fame, perhaps; and as Rumour surely does. In the body of the ship were bedchambers for all the ladies and gentlemen of the court; only the King and the Duchess of Beaufort were lodged on deck. The company took their meals under the canopied pavilions. Here on this lovely river the King no longer dined alone and at a raised table. He sat among the rest, and all disposed themselves as they pleased; a cheerful gentleman beside one little so inclined, and a haughty lady opposite a devout one.

They were all at ease, for this was to be a gay journey, and they realized that to make it so they must be gay themselves. The King's lady was the centre of attention and regard; anyone who addressed her spoke in hushed and cadenced tones, which even bluff Marshal Biron managed to assume for the occasion. Rosny, man of stone, softened as to both ear and eye. His wife went further; she laid such constraint upon herself that she actually became amiable. Madame de Rosny naturally hated Gabrielle more than did her husband, for the hatred was his; and it flourished in her heart. But she made none of his unuttered concessions to Gabrielle; she did not even know of her enemy's good offices, for her husband never mentioned them. His wife's blank hatred heartened him in his own, which was not so blind.

She was his second wife, a rich widow with a very long nose, flickering eyes, sparse eyebrows, a bulging forehead, and a loose, unmeaning mouth. When the elderly dame tried to smile, she looked so forlorn that Gabrielle's heart was touched. The Duchess begged her dear friend Madame, the King's sister, that Madame de Rosny might be given a place between them. It was a day when the passing clouds scattered showers upon the awnings. The peasant women who were working in the fields behind the river-banks had pulled their skirts over their shoulders, and the men covered their heads with sacks before they fled for shelter.

"Duchess," fluted Madame de Rosny, "I am truly happy.

We are all happy to think that you are so. And you see how the country-folk make haste to greet you; they have long since heard of your beauty, virtue, and understanding."

" Surely, madame, the people are running because it has begun to rain? " In vain; the lady's eloquence was not to be stemmed. her blinking eyes saw all she wanted to see, but nothing else.

"Look! — the shepherds and the shepherdesses from your park at Monceaux, just as they are in nature. All as neat and charming as could be. 'Tis a tribute to you," said the treacherous lady.

" Madame," replied Gabrielle simply, " I have to thank you for your kindness. You think as you speak. Well, I would have you know that, when the King compares the poor folk who live here with the rich fields and pastures, the deep woods, and the proud castles, he is not pleased. He hopes his peasants do not fast so often as before his day. But he will not be happy until they all have a chicken in their pot on Sunday."

Aha! So the wily creature put it all upon the King, thought the treacherous lady. Thereupon she pleaded her inexperience in domestic matters, though she was in fact the meanest of housewives, and her dependants lived on starvation diet. Gabrielle knew this very well; and she grew the more fervent in praise of Monsieur de Rosny and his works. The people, and especially the peasantry, could not have thriven but for him. " The King will never let him go," she said, much to her own disfavour. Madame de Rosny recoiled at the words, which she understood to mean that the King's favourite would get rid of his Minister as soon as she could. She must tell her husband; a few more flatteries, and she departed. Her hatred of Gabrielle, which was really his, she had thus laid out at interest, which she now made haste to bring him.

But, to her surprise, Rosny fixed his hard eyes on her and said:

" We have a great King. We have a King whose fortune never fails."

Monsieur de Rosny knew best what he meant by the observation. Not long afterwards a troop of horsemen dashed headlong down the bank to the river, halted at the water-side, and waved their hats. The King ordered the ship to be laid alongside the bank.

"Marshal de Matignon," he shouted, "you bring good news?"

His voice was firm, though he was inwardly at such a stretch that he felt he might drop dead before he heard the news.

Matignon threw up his hat and cried:

"Sire! Peace is signed at Vervins. The Spanish envoys have subscribed to all the terms. They are on their way to Paris, to await Your Majesty. Now there will be peace for ever in this kingdom; our great King has conquered."

The last words were shouted by Matignon across the fields, and many heard them. The people did not yet understand what was afoot, but out of curiosity they left their fields and cottages and came running up. They thronged the landing-stage, they sood on carts, children clambered into the fruit-trees, and the little ones were hoisted on to their fathers' shoulders. All were mute and expectant; they watched the King's lips move, but could hear no word. At last it came:

"Peace! Peace!"

This in a soldier's voice; then he added quietly:

"Children, there is peace."

At his first utterance, some marked the gallant bearing of the King; but when he spoke again, and as a friend might speak, there were others that looked into his eyes. The minutes passed, they watched him, then they knelt — only a few of them at first. When all were on their knees, there stood erect among them a peasant in the flower of his years; and he said:

"Lord! You are our King. If danger comes upon you, call to us."

The King in danger! His companions on the ship smiled at the idea. Gabrielle d'Estrées shivered, and gripped his arm. She would have fallen had he not supported her. "Lord!" cried the tall peasant, and to the ears of many there was menace in his voice: "We'll guard your Queen as surely as yourself!"

At this the company aboard the ship were not a little out of countenance; their faces lengthened, and they stood motionless. But at that moment an offering of white loaves and red wine was opportunely brought. Children presented the gifts to the King, but he shared his with the peasant who had spoken. Each ate half a loaf and drank out of the same goblet.

The ship sailed on, but the good tidings went ahead of it. Whenever human habitations came in view, there were hands outstretched to throw a cable in hopes that it might stop awhile; and the people lined the banks swinging their clasped hands in welcome. As the ship glided by, many other hands flung all the flowers that they could hold upon its deck. The gentlemen caught them and laid them on the ladies' knees. And, to receive these greetings and these flowers, the ship had to put across from bank to bank. At some places trees were pulled down over the boat, and their blossoms scattered on the deck.

At Tours the foreign envoys were waiting; they had come by coach from Nantes quicker than the ship, which seemed to glide so lightly over the waters of the Loire, but was held back by the salutations of the multitudes through which it must cleave its way. The envoys, in so far as they were well disposed, reported that their courts and countries were filled with the King's renown. He had made bold to issue his Edict to his Protestants, which could not prevent His Catholic Majesty's accepting the King's peace on the terms proffered; just because he had first made known his will and proclaimed freedom of conscience. He had felt strong enough to do so, and he was like to be the strongest King on earth, for friend or foe.

The envoys of Holland, Switzerland, the German princes, the Queen of England, and others escorted the King to Tours, with much pomp and rejoicing, as though he had been their own monarch. Much pealing of bells, a ceremonial welcome at the gates, a solemn procession on foot through the cheering populace, and then a banquet in the castle. It was the very castle that had been the late King's last refuge from his enemies. He was then extricated from his distresses by Henri of Navarre, who then also figured as a conqueror — but in the service of his predecessor, who in the end was stabbed to death.

At table, amid the general babble, one Monsieur d'Entragues remarked: "I held his chin up on his deathbed. For whom, I wonder, shall I do that service next?"

The Cardinal of Joyeuse: "A man's conquests are like to be his temptations, as this King knows. He walks warily, in fear of God, and is an admirable Christian. But trust his laugh as little as his tears."

Elsewhere at the table Madame, the King's sister, said: "The King, my brother, has walked in the straight way all his life. Hence his greatness. The Lord does not love timorous men; His favour is given to those that keep a stout heart."

Marshal de Matignon: "It has been a long way; from what looked like ruin to a fame that spans the world. And from the sight of him today one would say he made the journey with small effort, often as I have seen him in a sweat. On the wings of song, say I, for I can turn a verse, both in Latin and in common speech."

"May it endure," growled Turenne, Duke of Bouillon, from a few places farther off.

"Greatness does endure," fluted Madame de Rosny, loud enough for Gabrielle to hear. She bent across to her lord.

"Sire, someone has just said that greatness is an imperishable possession."

"And yet no one marks the brief moments when he did perhaps possess it," said Henri into the lovely Gabrielle's ear. "We may lose all," he added in a whisper, "but not our love."

Dusk was falling, and the company made their way down to the river, to continue their journey on that enchanted ship. At that moment came a posse of armed men, with a prisoner in their midst: Monsieur de Saint-Phal. Aha! Caught at last! Mornay! Where is Mornay?

After a search, he was found lurking on the city wall. For months past he had driven himself all but crazy in his rage to run his enemy to earth, and now he would have none of him. When victim and assailant were confronted, only one of them grew pale and trembled. The other knelt, as though he could do no other, and begged for pardon in the words prescribed. He uttered them with such excessive fervour and such an air of penitence that everyone could tell he was dissembling. There was indeed a suspicion that Monsieur de Saint-Phal was enjoying the affair, and, whoever was tasting vengeance, it was not Philippe Mornay.

Mornay looked round for the King and asked for a word with him alone. They stepped aside, while Saint-Phal still remained kneeling, his fate yet undecided.

"Sire," said Philippe, "I have recovered my reason. I had lost it, as you know. Pray release Monsieur de Saint-Phal and do not throw him into prison."

"Monsieur de Mornay, justice demands that he should go to jail. Both a nobleman and his King were affronted."

"Vengeance is mine, — saith the Lord."

"You should have listened to the Lord before, Philippe."

But as the victim pressed his plea, Henri decided that Philippe should himself raise his would-be assassin from his knees; then justice might be tempered with mercy. And Mornay addressed him: "Sir, stand up, the King pardons you."

"But you yourself," replied Saint-Phal, avidly eyeing his enemy's pallid countenance and reddened nose, "you yourself, sir, cannot possibly pardon me. I can but try to atone for what I did."

"You do not deserve," said Mornay, "that I should help you to your feet. But it is my duty." Whereat he seized the grovelling creature under the arms.

But he resisted and hung on Mornay's arms. They both began to gasp, while the onlookers laughed, or surveyed the scene with horror and disgust.

"I shall go to prison to defy you," gasped Saint-Phal.

"And I," gasped Mornay, "shall pray for you daily, whether you will or not."

At this, the King ordered the armed guard to set the kneeling man upon his feet. This they did with kicks and cuffs, and as they bundled him away it came into his mind that he would not be treated as a nobleman in the Bastille.

Philippe Mornay asked his Majesty's leave to retire to Saumur.

" Monsieur Duplessis," said Henri, " is your Tractate on the Mass still locked up in your library? "

" Sire, it would be my most grievous sin to know the truth and not to utter it."

At this, the King turned his back on him. It was observed that the Protestant was in disfavour, and some few took their leave in much more ease of mind.

THE SONG

The enchanted ship was no longer full when it set sail before a night breeze to Blois and Orléans. Most of the company went away to sleep, but a few stayed on deck with the King and the Duchess of Beaufort. Monsieur de Rosny sent his wife below, as being likely to disturb him in a purpose for which he deigned to linger among these lords and ladies. Marshal de Matignon also remained above, as a lover of romantic nights, and, among one or two more, a page called Guillaume de Sablé. He, a lad of twenty, otherwise of no importance, had on his left cheek a large birthmark, inherited from his mother, which was variously interpreted, as a rose, a fortress, and sometimes as a woman's womb. Gabrielle would have dismissed Guillaume from the court, but Henri asked her not to look at him for the present.

" He is neither handsome nor agreeable," admitted Henri on that occasion. " What else there is about him, I don't know. But I am certain that he is not as other young men. He reminds me of lads who were twenty in the days when I was twenty also. They have mostly forgotten those days, but no matter; there are many more to take our place."

The two gentlemen and the boy had stepped aside. Gabrielle was sitting on a little low chair, like a child's chair, Henri half recumbent at her feet. Sometimes he propped his neck against her knees and gazed up at the stars; sometimes he laid his chin upon her wrist, and the shining worlds revealed her lovely face. She stroked his forehead with her finger-tips, found it flushed, and bade him think only of that perfect hour. The day had been rich in joy, which still echoed in the hearts of both. The echo melted in words, which neither of them knew nor sought:

Oh, the garlands and the laughter as through the night we float,
None but messengers of gladness dare approach our joyous boat.

Henri made answer to the star that shone above his head; and that answer, had he uttered it, would have run thus:

" Toil begets new toil, and that goes on until death. I may not hope to escape that dispensation. The burden is never lifted. Peace is best, but peace endures no longer than a breath. Joy and peace and safety — the tree that snows blossoms on our heads. This journey with you."

" With you," said Gabrielle, for her mind kept step with his and she felt as he did, " with you I would reach our purpose and our end. My dear lord, of that I am confident."

So saying, she kissed him, and he her: a long deep kiss, that was to linger in her mind, and serve her memories of a voyage up the Loire alone with him, and in their hearts the echo:

Oh, the garlands and the laughter as through the night we float,
None but messengers of gladness dare come near this joyous boat.

With his chin upon her knee he looked into her face, and she into his.

" Your greatness, my lord," said Gabrielle, " has from this day won the world's belief, and it can never pass away."

Henri laughed softly at her — and she no less at him. They knew. The water of this river was not the same for one moment of its existence. Was it there at all? Had it not flowed past, while they were watching it, into the oblivious sea? Such was his thought — and so she felt too. In both their hearts echoed an unuttered warning that all is brief, and for that very reason it is lovely. Joy and peace and safety, the tree that snows blossoms on our heads. Of our poor naked body, nothing at all remains — shall greatness then remain?

From not far off they heard the ecstatic accents of the Marshal

de Matignon. He was dilating in a high-pitched voice on the
castles by the river, their placid shadows in the sparkling stream.
They themselves, he said, were now but visions of the past; look
— the gateways silent and deserted, no one wanted to own such
places now.

The gentlemen were out of sight, but at that moment a clear,
deliberate voice broke in:

" Do you think so indeed? We shall soon come to the castle
of Sully, which belongs to Monsieur de la Trémoïlle. Ask him
if he means to give it away for nothing. Why, he is demanding
one hundred and twenty-six thousand livres for the castle and the
lands of Sully."

" That was not the point," said Matignon, whose thoughts
were elsewhere.

" It is very much the point," persisted Monsieur de Rosny, and
again rapped out the mighty sum. " Had the price not been so
high, I would have bought Sully, on my honour. In any case, I
could get it cheaper, and in the end for nothing. But that would
mean favouring the Duke of Bouillon, against my honour,
whereas I am the faithful servant of the King. But it would not
enter my mind. There's no castle nor estate for which I would
do that."

He fell silent and let the vision of the castle speak for itself.
Its towers and roofs gradually came into view, rising transfigured
out of the black, massed foliage in salutation to the passing ship.
The Marshal and the Minister, who were out of sight, certainly
returned that salutation, each entranced in his own fashion. In
front, the shining walls plunged down into the water at the angle
of the river and a tributary stream. At the back, the two tallest
towers and the steepest of the high-pitched roofs rose upwards
from a little conjoined island all flooded in the radiance of the
star-scattered sky and mirrored in the glittering river.

" How beautiful! " said Gabrielle.

" And truly worthy of you," said Rosny, stepping forward at
that moment.

" Not of me," said Gabrielle, " but of a very faithful servant.
And, I am sure, the King thinks so, too."

And Henri repeated, as though his mind were set on other things: " Certainly I think so." Then he recalled himself to the present and said in a decisive tone:

"Monsieur de Rosny, you shall be made happy, if this will make you so. We will consider later how we may come by the purchase price."

Rosny trembled with joy — he had not believed that he would succeed with so little effort. He had no light-hearted confidence in his own schemes, though he had sacrificed his sleep and stayed on deck for that very purpose. His impulse was to kiss the King's hand, but Henri had suddenly vanished. Rosny had to offer his thanks, and the tribute of his heart, which for once was really moved, to the King's lady.

Henri had sought the shadow of an awning and stood by the bulwarks, looking across the stream. Astern, the castle of Sully was slowly receding behind its trees; it flashed forth a last time and vanished. He took but little heed of it; the thought in his mind was: " Possession — but when do we possess? A castle and its domain can be burnt out, a kingdom lost; death is always at hand, and will take both from us in his good time." This was a fortunate journey; he had taken possession of the last of his provinces and forced the enemy to make peace. Of yet more account, and harder to achieve, he had proclaimed freedom of conscience, which had been his object all along. He possessed this kingdom as no king ever yet had done, the very earth and essence of it. But what in truth did he possess?

And while he pondered, and sought to answer his self-questionings, there appeared to him unbidden the vanished picture of a youthful Henri of eighteen, who possessed nothing at all. He was riding with his friends, young men of twenty, against Paris; and when he arrived, it was to find his beloved mother Jeanne dead. He himself soon came into the power of the malignant old Queen, who had already planned the night of Saint Bartholomew. When it came to pass, and his friends were murdered, young Henri Navarre became the prisoner of the wicked fairy, and so remained for many years. Had he any premonition of all this when he led his cavalcade against Paris?

They were as devout as they were reckless — that band of adventurers who all thought alike. They led the village girls astray, but among themselves they often talked of the Religion. All were very vehement against those in high places, among whom God is not; He favours the company of those young men, and indeed Jesus in His very person might appear any hour from behind the next cluster of rocks and take command. In the minds of every one of them His wounds were fresh and bleeding. His story was their living present, they knew Him as they knew themselves. " Jesus! " one shouted; it was Philippe Mornay. And he shouted with so full a throat that all pricked up their ears and looked about them, ready to close in round their Lord and cry aloud to Him: " Sire! Last time You were defeated by Your enemies and crucified. This time, with us, You will be victorious. Have at them! "

Henri, in his forty-eighth year, saw that ancient vision once again; the blood surged to his head, he gripped the bulwark of the enchanted ship. He had almost groaned aloud when he remembered that what those young adventurers had striven for, he now possessed. Had he the Lord on his side now? How could he tell? Even in those days he had not believed that Jesus would bestow His company upon them merely because they were Protestants. The others did, and he had loved them for it. Ha! Yonder was one of them.

Henri said this aloud as he caught sight of Guillaume de Sablé, the page. The boy was also standing alone by the bulwarks; he seemed taller; some mysterious influence in him and in that night had added to his stature. He stood among the stars, their light bathed his cheeks and shone on his strange birthmark. His teeth were clenched, and the muscles of his gaunt face were tense. His eyes mirrored the shining worlds and the fever of his spirit.

" Of what are you dreaming? " asked a voice. The page looked, saw no one; but the unseen spoke again:

" You were dreaming that you were Marshal of France. You may be so one day. There is one upon this ship who composes verse. I am sure you think yourself a poet. Try your powers: find words to fit a King who has won and now possesses his heart's desire. When he had to part from her, no war nor victory repaid him for the agony of love. Through war and victory we win a kingdom, but never the star, at which we look and look until we are ourselves extinguished."

The voice out of the darkness ceased, and Guillaume felt he was alone.

Henri sat for a while with Gabrielle. Rosny and Matignon entertained the King and his lady; all were in a gay and frolic mood, and, contrary to his habit, the new lord of Sully laughed. To these four appeared the lad Sablé, a graceful, modest figure, who bowed and awaited the King's command. The King waved to him and said:

" Sing your song! "

Whereupon the unlooked-for guest bowed deeply to the Duchess of Beaufort, and began:

" Begin again," said the King. " The sailors would like to hear you also."

Several of the men who set the sails on that enchanted ship had crept softly forward as they heard the sound of singing, from so fresh and delicate a voice. They stood listening, with awe-struck faces, while the water gurgled past the gliding keel, and Guillaume, whom indeed they would all have been loth to interrupt, sang his song:

> Oh, charming Gabrielle,
> Fame sent me to the wars,
> When stricken to my soul,
> I rode out with God Mars.
>> Oh, day of bitter sorrow,
>> When we must part;
>> Would that I need not live so,
>> Or had no heart!
>
> There needs no call from Amor,
> Since thou dost look on me;
> 'Tis now the greater Captain
> That has me in his fee.
>> Oh, day of bitter sorrow,
>> When we must part;
>> Would that I need not live so,
>> Or had no heart!
>
> I'll win myself a kingdom,
> By battle and by ruse.
> Yours shall be the whole wide earth,
> To rule it as you choose.
>> Oh, day of bitter sorrow,
>> When we must part;
>> Would that I need not live so,
>> Or had no heart!

Fond star of all my dreaming,
In yon far distant sky!
I am sick with love and longing —
Appear! or I must die.

   Oh, day of bitter sorrow,
   When we must part;
   Would that I need not live so,
   Or had no heart!

When Guillaume had ended, a long deep silence fell, save for a stifled sigh, like the sound of water against the gliding keel. At length the Duchess of Beaufort rose; Guillaume de Sablé's birthmark grew pale in the starlight, and might have been a rose, a fortress, or a woman's womb. Gabrielle kissed it.

The sailors scrambled up the yards, and thence fell to singing the new song, as much of it as they could remember. And Guillaume said to the King:

" Sire, it is your song."

" The words were mine, but you turned them into verse," replied Henri, and gave the boy his hand. He threw a glance at the new lord of Sully, who was wearing one of his quizzical expressions. But he did not speak his mind. What do we possess? A song that all will sing.

His face suddenly softened, and a look of solemn piety came over it as he remembered the old psalms that he had often sung, and compared his song to them. He hummed it into Gabrielle's ear as he led her away.

PEACE OR WAR

There was good eating in those days at the court of France. After the victorious peace the King's first concern was to get the fattest geese from his native Béarn. By the aid of banquets and hunting parties and all manner of festivities he wanted to convince himself and the world that no danger threatened: he was

firmly in possession. The world seemed really to believe it. At
many a feast the King displayed his wonted appetite, which he
had lately lost. " In old days I had nothing to eat," he said
among his friends, " and now I care for nothing." The companion of his youth, Marshal Roquelaure, explained his case to
him. " Sire, you were formerly one of the excommunicate. And
they guzzle like the foul fiend." The King knew better.

Secure he might or might not be, he had, for the present,
reached port. Vaster enterprises — they would in truth have
made him saviour of the continent, as many now conceived him,
though he did not so conceive himself. He knew his mission, but
in his wisdom he postponed and set it aside; not from concern
for his own person, for it would have brought him fame, but for
his people's sake, who would have had to bear the burden. Peace!
Peace! — at last.

Lord Cecil and the Prince of Nassau were received in the
Louvre, before the Spanish envoys made their ceremonial entry.
The King hastened to meet them.

" Don Philip is dead."

He took off his hat, flung it on the ground, and bade his allies
do the same. " 'Tis the latest Spanish ceremonial."

Lord Cecil: " Of course the old villain is dead. What could
he do, after you had beaten him — but die."

Prince of Nassau: " For himself there was nothing left. As for
Spain — "

King Henri: " You mean the Universal Monarchy."

Prince of Nassau: " I mean the bandits chained together on
their galley, who thus rule the world."

Lord Cecil: " It is a pleasant thought that those who ravage
and wreck this unlucky continent are at least fettered to the
same chain, and the fall of one brings several others down."

King Henri: " My lords, there is a time for war, and there is
also a time for peace."

Lord Cecil: " I am a true friend of peace."

Prince of Nassau: " Peace, if it is to be peace, must be doubly
favoured, and agreeable to both parties: not to us alone, but also
to the aggressor. He has made a mock of peace. Spanish armies,

Sire, since your famous peace treaty of Vervins, are no longer to be seen in Europe."

Lord Cecil: " No, in their stead we have the so-called Free Companies. I would call them bandits, and hang up every man of them. Pah! They pass as Spaniards; they come from every sort of country, without war declared; no State has sent them, or will so much as own them. A new and astute expedient, most interesting to a British friend of peace."

The Prince of Nassau, forgetting himself, leapt to his feet and cried: " Not for a Hollander! Nor for a German! My country is being ruined and my people destroyed. It is worse than open war, more horrible and more impious. Sire, you must help. You are the only King that wields the sword."

King Henri said nothing.

Lord Cecil: " Nassau, sit down. This must be soberly discussed. The King knows as well as we do what is going on. These bands of thieves, owned apparently by no one, though everyone knows from whom they take orders, are not merely devouring Holland; they have set upon the Germans, Protestants and Catholics alike. Indeed, Catholics and Protestants have already begun to devour each other. That brings certain advantages."

Prince of Nassau: " Advantages! 'Tis an abomination."

Lord Cecil: " 'Tis nothing to the abominations your countrymen will suffer before these ruffians have done. Advantages, I mean to say, for the aggressor. He is responsible for nothing, as we pointed out. Secondly, his fraudulent war will cost him nothing; these companies live as they go. Thirdly, and most important, there is no reason why these ravages should stop. And they will go on so long as the Universal Monarchy thinks to gain by banditry."

Prince of Nassau: " For a hundred years! "

Lord Cecil: " Say fifty years. Long enough to bestialize this continent. I spoke of eating and devouring as a metaphor. But men will soon learn to eat their fellow-men in very fact."

Prince of Nassau: " Sire, all Europe appeals to you; what will you do? "

King Henri: " My lord, will your Queen support me, as she has often done before? "

Lord Cecil rose.

The Prince of Nassau leapt to his feet.

King Henri was already standing.

Lord Cecil: " Her Majesty is ready and willing to back the enterprise with all her forces, by sea and land."

Prince of Nassau: " The States General of the Netherlands will offer what they can."

King Henri: " Then I should indeed be stronger than our enemy; strong enough to stop a war and make my name blessed before God and man. There must be very weighty reasons that would deter me from saving my own soul and winning the estimation of the world. But I cannot go to war, and I would ask you to hear me to the end. I, too, had to listen to the Pope's Legate, when he told me in this very room that I should in the end have to face Catholic Christendom. He told me I was suspected of trying to attach Protestantism everywhere to my cause — not for its own sake, but for my own glory. And I have strengthened those suspicions by my Edict in Nantes."

Lord Cecil and the Prince of Nassau burst into voluble protest.

King Henri: " Gentlemen, my allies! Men of peace and order! The aggressor is now set on his vile work. I found the world vile while I had dealings with it. But I was not discouraged. My wars were in the interests of humanity. It was for humanity that I fought in France, and should so against the bandits."

And Lord Cecil and the Prince of Nassau answered: " Ah! Then you will march. You are the great man of this age. May their Holy Roman Empire and their Holy Church thus end! "

King Henri: " Just what the Legate said, though he added I should become master of the world."

Lord Cecil, stepping back a pace or two and away from the Prince of Nassau: " That was not seriously said. Her Majesty conceives no such outcome of the war."

King Henri: " Nor do I — and I shall not wage that war."

Prince of Nassau, choking down his sobs: " Sire, do you not pity this suffering world? "

King Henri: " Yes. But first I pity my people and my kingdom — scarred by twenty years of war, that will not be healed in the lifetime of the present generation. I am not the master of destiny, and I should be indeed venturesome if I tried to save other lands from the religious war which we have fought and survived. After years of devastation, an age of reason has begun; and I mean that it shall come to fullness. France has open frontiers, our fortifications are neglected, the fleet is in disarray, and several of my provinces have been ruined by the war. If my people are to eat, and populate the land, I must disarm."

Prince of Nassau: " That your Frenchmen may live in ease and comfort, you condemn half Europe to these horrors. Your disarmament relieves the bandits of their last fear."

Lord Cecil: " The peasants and traders here are certainly happier than they were."

King Henri: " To what other end were men created? And if I did not mean to make them so, they would soon be looking for another King. My own fortunes and my sovereignty hang on one or two lost battles. Gentlemen, whatever my own feelings, I shall send my army home."

THEY CALL HIM GREAT

The Spanish envoys made their entry into Paris. They wore a solemn air, as fitted the occasion of a peace so bitterly contested and meant to be eternal. All the greater their astonishment at the unconstraint of the court and of a King who was accounted great. That was not their impression. The King of France first took them into his tennis court, where His Majesty engaged in an obstinate game against Marshal Biron the younger and the Prince of Joinville. Masked ladies looked down from the gallery on the unwearied monarch's strokes and leaps. Don Luis de Velasco, the Admiral of Aragon, Count Arenberg, and the whole Spanish delegation looked for the Duchess of Beaufort under that array of masks and discovered her easily. She was the centre of attention. The King played for her sole approval, as the Spaniards observed; this in the heat of June and a crowded court.

But he also meant to show them he was active and strong, and still young enough to be formidable. That the envoys remembered later, when they dispatched their report. For the moment they were possessed by disgust that the Most Christian King should doff his dignity before them and offer it to a woman. After the game he invited his beloved to unveil her face, for the admiration of the envoys of His Catholic Majesty.

But there was yet worse for them in store. Two days later the King gave a banquet and a ball. At the head of the table, beneath a canopy, sat the Duchess of Beaufort beside the King; and she was served by noble ladies, the noblest being Mademoiselle de Guise. A Lorraine, from the House that in alliance with Spain had lately been so dangerous to the King of France. Here and now a daughter of that House, which Spain had schemed should rule in France, was handing dishes to — a very different sort of lady.

Later on, the King said to the Spaniards:

" You could have beaten me at Amiens. The weak point of my position was just where the Duchess's tent stood."

And Don Francisco de Mendoza answered with due gravity:

" Even to win a victory, we should not have deigned to attack a brothel."

The Spaniards sat stiff and silent, but the King roared with laughter. They realized that he was not to be humiliated. The ball in the evening was opened by Madame, the King's sister, but at her side appeared the Duchess of Beaufort in emerald-green silk, her hair sparkling with a diamond crescent, and she looked supremely beautiful; as even the Spaniards admitted.

None the less, they were further scandalized because at the court of France women came so much into the foreground. At one point the dance was stopped, all the women in their splendid panniered dresses gathered in the centre of the hall, and from among them stepped a youth with a birthmark on his left cheek; the musicians struck up, and he sang. " Charming Gabrielle . . ."

The Spaniards heard that song often and everywhere until the hour of their departure, and in the end they caught themselves humming it too. Shortly after they had gone and all Paris had viewed the King's vanquished enemies, he himself made his public entry. It was the occasion for a display of ceremonial and splendour. King Henri alone rode in leather and black armour, wearing the white plume, as at Ivry. Thus the world knew him; thus it would have him appear. He acquiesced, and assumed the guise of a great King, as the world conceived it.

The strangers from all lands who had gathered for the ceremony were the first to applaud. After some nonchalance at first, a sudden wave of enthusiasm swept over the populace. Near the Louvre he stopped; from the pavements and the windows and the roofs came bursts of cheering that he had never heard before, and was never to hear a second time. He pointed to where, at his feet, stood a litter, which the bearers had set down.

"Yonder is my peace," said he, " and your happiness, which is also mine."

He rode into his palace, but they had understood; they all knew who was in that litter designated by the King as the symbol of better times. "Charming Gabrielle" was chanted in the streets and houses and on the roofs.

During the hour that followed his triumph Henri was never left alone, although he had a sense that there was something he had missed or forgotten. He was awaited by his court and Parliament, the municipalities, his marshals, his Finance Council — and through the press heralds in chain corselets and golden-lilied surcoats made a way for the foreign envoys.

Ambassadors both ordinary and extraordinary had hastened to testify by their presence to the high fortunes of the King of France — not only those whom he knew, but many quite unexpected, and by no means all his friends. Indeed, his enemies had arrived first, and the earliest were not his open enemies; neither Spain nor the Emperor, whose delegations had not yet appeared and, it would seem, had not even been announced. The first and most obsequious were those that hated him in secret. Savoy was always ready to stab him in the back, and as the Duke had one foot in the kingdom, there would have to be a settlement one day. Habsburg possessed obedient satellites in the Italian princes; their agents were on the spot, they were now offering their homage, and later they would report how the King of France carried his good fortune. And the Rhenish lords, both spiritual and secular, bade their observers lavish compliments on the great King.

The admiration of these foreigners came easily, and sounded plausible but for the plain fact that the origin of what they felt was — fear. Their words were eloquent of their alarm that the King's victory was so much more complete than it need have been to maintain their princes' independence as between him and the Emperor. In western Germany they feared the Imperial power, which did not commonly appear, but was sufficiently proclaimed by bandits. They passed for Spanish, being generally disowned. But there was a far more rooted fear of the King of France and his armies which had conquered Spain; they were nearest to the Rhine, and what would keep them back? Far away in the Hofburg, whence he never emerged, sat the black-clad sovereign of the Universal Monarchy; here on the spot, and active everywhere, was the only King who was a soldier.

The envoys of the German Electoral Princes feared the worst from this dissembling Protestant. The main point they thought they could circumvent, if only by an offer that was too plainly fantastic. Despair cannot choose, and the respite must needs be brief. When the point is passed, the page is turned. Several of the Princes had conceived the notion of electing King Henri Roman Emperor — or at least offering to do so, by way of gaining time. One after another, these envoys asked His Majesty for an audience in respect of a very confidential matter which admitted of no delay.

The circumstances were such that no secrecy was possible. A vast throng was surging towards the gallery of the Louvre; all the egresses were blocked by various crafts and corporations eager to get speech with His Majesty. Certain of the humbler delegates from abroad hoped that their opportunity would come; meantime they maintained their places and their persons intact in that struggling throng. The common folk were admitted, by Henri's usual custom. He had given no special orders; his officers acted in accordance with his known wishes — and it was scarce possible to keep an empty space about the King. Several ladies fainted in the press.

The King stood on a level with all those who circled round him, whose faces were so rapidly transformed as they bowed their homage; but after a while they grew monotonous, and their words lost all connection with the established facts. They call him great, he reflected. They persisted in addressing him as the great King, which means nothing, as they knew. What was a victory? He had won no more victories than would serve to maintain his kingdom. Beyond them all, there lay what he must now renounce, the ultimate victory, the liberation of Europe from a world dominion that was barbarizing Europe into banditry. He could not help. War or peace — he had chosen. Greatness was not his destiny.

Unperturbed by these reflections, he gave to all the grave and measured answers that were expected and befitted a great King. He secretly thought that worldly glory was never to be taken wholly seriously and would stand no searching scrutiny. That, indeed, was a belittlement of his fellow-men, to whom, more than to him, glory and greatness were of value. He swung to right and left with the litheness of a tennis-player. He waved a hand, he flung his head back, moved his feet, all with a regal and yet gracious air. No, he had not to reproach himself with any lack of majesty, none thought him less than royal; indeed, they gazed on him with awe. He certainly had not foreseen how vast a company would gather for this celebration of his victory. For his part he represented an impersonated majesty. He resolved to perfect his performance.

They called him great; if they saw him today in camp, covered with the mire of the trenches, and a battle imminent, they would talk otherwise. They evidently did not believe in a heavenly dispensation, since they attributed his success to chance, and for that very reason were eager to prostrate themselves before him. They found it even harder to grasp that reason does sometimes prevail here below, if only for a while. And they actually proposed that a man who had merely used his five senses should be elected Roman Emperor, as though he and they were out of their wits.

" Noble lords, I guess rather than hear your most notable proposal, for there is much noise about us and you have good cause to moderate your voices. You do yourselves honour by trusting my discretion; this is indeed a matter that might strike painfully on the ears of His Apostolic Majesty. I see that you are in an exalted mood, and, moreover, my true friends."

His answers to the spokesmen of the Electoral Princes cast courteous doubt on the mental condition that had inspired such enthusiasm. Their requests for private audiences he ignored, dismissed them, and beckoned to the next comers, who promptly gathered round him. Those who had passed the King found themselves confronting the Duchess of Beaufort. She sat surrounded by the princesses. She had not failed to mark her lord's treatment of his tempters. Not one of the princely agents omitted to ask her for her advocacy; which she had to promise. It was observed that she grew pale, probably in sudden access of joy. Those who thought the great lady still lovelier in her pride longed most earnestly to know what was going on.

But the Duchess beckoned to her friend, brave Crillon. The doors were promptly cleared and a way made from His Majesty to a modest group some distance off, which had hitherto maintained itself in the struggling turmoil. Otherwise they would never have reached the King. He, escorting the Duchess of Beaufort with uplifted hand, advanced towards these Flemings. They were mayors of towns lately surrendered by the Spaniards, petty councillors from villages uprooted by the war, and priests whose pulpits were no longer standing. They forgot to kneel to their deliverer, they had knelt too often.

The King bade them welcome, and they looked at him and at one another — which of them should speak? At last one of them said in a full, slow voice: " Lord, we wish we were Frenchmen and your countrymen."

" You are honourable men," replied the King. " Let that suffice you. Fear not for your safety — you are good men of your hands; nor for your prosperity — you are not afraid of work. Go in peace."

And one of them said: " We have seen a great King."

Said Henri in the ear of his beloved:

" Always that word: these also call me great."

Thereupon he invited her to sup with him at his table.

Greatness from Within

The honour paid to the common folk from Flanders was duly noted. It was ascribed to the Duchess of Beaufort; there were those who said that the King had not in fact escorted her; she it was who was leading him astray. Well, the King could take those territories before the Spaniards had re-established their authority in Flanders; he certainly had the power. It would be natural that the Flemings should be put to harder service than under Spain. Instead of which he treated them as freemen and ate with them at table.

Against this, remember that in his own kingdom the land-owners were forced to build the roads, for which they exacted toll from the peasants. It was actions like this that made so many regard his rule as the vilest tyranny. Not that he himself was the author of these detestable innovations — not a word against His Majesty. But he used a man like Rosny, a man without scruple, who attacked the rich, heedless of any vested rights. There could be no good end to such a system; the Minister had better take care not to extend his depredations to the foreign tax-farmers. The money-powers of the world would take bitter vengeance on this kingdom.

Despite all this talk, Rosny in fact gave his master very sensible and moderate advice. In long nights of calculation he had tabulated the accounts of Zamet, the tax-farmer. When he produced the result for the King to read, Gabrielle was present, which always gave offence to Rosny, though he had never yet revealed how much it rankled in his mind. The King was horrified at the figures and swore to expel the Florentine. But his faithful serv-

ant warned him against acting in sudden wrath. He undertook
to deal more easily, as man to man, with a person like Zamet than
the King could with the European money-powers if he provoked
their enmity.

Gabrielle expressed her surprise that Monsieur de Rosny
should in such a case as this depart from his usual inflexibility
and ask the King not to dismiss a friend.

" I am hated enough already," said Rosny dryly. But Gabrielle
understood: it was not Shoemaker Zamet who was really in question, and moreover he was a good friend of hers. The best of
servants was here thinking mainly of the Grand Duke of Florence and his niece. She was to oust Gabrielle and become Queen
of France. The calculations of this man of stone were inexorable; to flatter him was trouble wasted. No, he was not
hated enough; she too would hate him. But she would not
say so.

The King was loud in admiration of his Minister's wisdom.
" Observe him, madame. He is so wise because he never sleeps.
I too should give up sleep. We ought to be as busy as we once
were in that tanner's shop in the rue de la Ferronnerie."

Rosny, when allowed to go, said to himself that the danger
came, not from His Majesty's powers of sleep, but from the beloved lady; and she must fall. Thenceforward Gabrielle would
wait until she could bring him down. He saw through her and
schemed to make her disliked — he did not fail to suggest that
the Duchess of Beaufort was mainly at fault in all these matters.
It would not be he, but she that was most hated. She was interfering with the money-powers, she was allied with the Protestants, and her ambition was the throne. At this court and at the
courts of Europe, Gabrielle was regarded as egging the King on
to all the measures that threatened property and advantaged
none but malcontents and the lower orders.

She knew it. These humiliations did not reach her lord, they
were practised upon her alone, and with every due precaution.
No one would have dared to insult her openly; scarce half a step
more, and she was Queen. But when noble ladies served her at
table, behind her back they repeated the Spaniard's remark and

mimicked his wooden solemnity. Ladies of the court who saw into the future, were it only by the aid of astrologers, and especially Madame de Sagonne, privily expressed their admiration for the King's rejected wife, who maintained her rank and would by no means consent to the dissolution of her marriage. Never would she yield to such a trollop, as she wrote from the castle where she was kept a prisoner; whence, too, she had sent a murderer against the King.

Madame Marguerite of Valois, once the most famous lover and the very Venus of her age, had in later years kept none of her native qualities except her talent for intrigue; that was an enduring heritage from her crafty Medici mother. Only the year before, she had called Gabrielle d'Estrées her sister and protectress, begged her for gifts, but always artfully avoided setting the King free. This now brought its reward, and she made full use of it. Gabrielle was at her zenith, she still stood firm, and the hatred with which she was encompassed could not avail to shake her. She who had been Margot now in the tedium of her exile took a delight in fanning the flames of hatred, though it could bring small profit to herself. And the deadly outcome of the hatred of a court and the intrigues of a woman was known only too well to the daughter of old Catherine, who had planned the night of Saint Bartholomew; and she gloated on the prospect. Her game was in a measure disinterested, for she herself could in no case become Queen of France, although her astrologers naturally promised that she would. Indeed, she braved the King's vengeance if his beloved lady met with a disastrous end. No matter; Madame Marguerite had come to life again, and felt herself once more at the centre of events when she attacked Gabrielle d'Estrées.

Gabrielle knew it. Not naturally acute, her unusual destiny had endowed her with insight. By the side of this great man, which in truth he was for her alone, while all others merely called him so — by his side, she had a strange experience. She alone could distinguish the several elements that went to make up greatness. Greatness — people uttered the word, but did not know what it denoted. It had its frontal aspect, which appeared upon the field of victory, in the halls where the treaties were signed, and where the great man proclaimed his Edict. Freedom, peace, and the nation — greatness was outwardly expressed in the struggle to maintain them. But Gabrielle knew the outer aspect and the pride of greatness. She had discovered another and a deeper self, appealing and self-distrustful, but even so she did not believe herself wholly acquainted with greatness. By her gift of sympathy she divined how one thing bred another. Sensitiveness to truth may be a quality of character as well as of the mind.

Henri trusted this woman as he trusted no one; in this matter she often found him as innocent as the dove — she had to display the wisdom of the serpent.

She warned him. One evening in their bedroom she began: "My only beloved, there are now many that flatter you on every side. Here came Flemish burghers to assure you that Flanders longs to become French."

Henri pointed to the first of the eight great tapestries that covered the walls of their common bedroom. The first represented Paradise and the Temptation. Henri pointed to it and made the face that she well knew, which meant: "I know what I am about."

"These Flemings meant what they said," said Gabrielle. "There are other foreigners, from farther off, who waste no flowers of speech, but plainly offer to become French. My beloved lord, you have no notion of the world's faith in you. You have striven so hard that you have no eyes for the reward that may be yours, not at the price of effort, but for love."

"You may say it. The emblem of all my struggles is yourself; your possession is my reward."

And she thought: "But on the day of his triumph, when he was all-powerful, he did not marry me. He knew of the letters written by the Queen of Navarre, and abandoned me to her insults." What Gabrielle actually said was:

"You are neglectful."

The word went home. He began to stride up and down the room, he recalled the feeling that had beset him for a whole hour after his victorious entry. He had neglected the chief matter. A neglected opportunity — when did it return? When he embraced Gabrielle, she was pale and cold. He was shocked, and hastily promised that he would make up for this delay; the time was near at hand.

"My power must be unassailable; except for what I have achieved, I am nothing."

Gabrielle regretted that she had thought of her own affairs. Her great man did not know himself; he was often as helpless as a child, she had to protect him. Her suspicions must be alert, in place of his.

"Sire, you are surrounded by spies."

"And not by admirers, as I might well have dreamed."

"You almost believed the envoys of the German princes when they promised to elect you Roman Emperor."

"Almost; not quite. Like the Flemings, they let their feelings master them, and regard me as the deliverer of Europe."

"No. They are traitors. If you had consented — well, the dispatch was already written. Here it is."

Henri paled. He would not look at the paper; in the lovely face of Gabrielle he wanted to read her destiny, and, for the first time, only hers. Here was the being who had shared his perils and wrenched the knife away from his breast. It should not pierce hers; he would make amends, she should be his Queen.

As she looked at him, pale and rueful, she was struck with pity for this great man of hers, whose greatness reached as far as doubt, disquiet, and renunciation. He did not believe in his legend, and would wholly disavow his greatness, except that it was unforgivable. ("But you do not marry me, beloved; there is always something to be done, and then something more, until all you do will have made us so hated that our happiness and even our lives will have been thrown away.")

So she pondered, while Henri asked her to get dressed again. They would go across to Madame, the King's sister.

"I am glad you are fond of her."

That evening there was a Protestant service in Madame's apartments. The pair could hear the singing from without, and

Gabrielle wanted to turn back. But Henri led her in. " You shall see, madame, what it is like."

What happened was that Henri joined in the singing of the Huguenot Psalm lxviii, the chant of his old battles:

> " Let God, the God of battle, rise. . . ."

Madame de Beaufort pressed her hand against his mouth to silence him. Did he think he could do anything he pleased because he was a great man? He knew nothing of his greatness, and abused it.

It also happened that when the ceremony was over, the King, with the Duchess of Beaufort, appeared before the entire court; for when it became known that he was there, the rooms filled with lords and ladies. So the pair faced them, and His Majesty announced his coming marriage with the Duchess of Beaufort, who would be his Queen.

This pronouncement was made to an array of heads most obsequiously bowed. Majesty had spoken. Majesty was sacred — by its essence and its divine mission; much less so were its secular utterances. " To deeds accomplished we must needs submit; but no one is constrained to believe in words yet unfulfilled. We may bow our heads, but we shall do our utmost, all of us, to ensure that Majesty cannot make its promise good. Majesty will not raise a woman who stands level with all the rest, and not even that, above them all. No daughter of the country shall become Queen of France; only a foreign princess, and we all know who. Majesty knows; he himself is really implicated," thought the more ingenious; and those who did not like the look of things thought so too, though they were in a minority.

Majesty would not, in the last resort, make good his word. It would be against the interests of the kingdom — not to mention that the King had never reached that point in his relations with a woman. So the court whispered. And among those bowed heads there was much whispering.

" When he has had enough of one, he is apt to be reckless in his promise of a parting gift," said one lady.

" Very true, madame," replied another. " Moreover, as every-

one can see, the charming Gabrielle is beginning to lose her
charms — just at the very moment when we are all singing her
song."

" Madame, she has had her third child. Her seven beauties,
and among them the famous dimpled chin, show the signs of it.
She is fattening, and the King never liked fat women."

" Pray what is your opinion, sir? " asked another voice. " Can
a great King truly venture on such a marriage? "

" Only a great King could conceive the idea," replied another,
a secret Jesuit.

" Then he has grown too great."

" Say rather that he has made the kingdom too great for him
to remain at the height of his own achievement," retorted the
Jesuit.

" That is why," said a more ingenuous courtier, " he ventures
to take such a woman."

The secret Jesuit: " No; just because there are limits to his
greatness, he will never take her."

None the less, the King had pledged his word. The steps by
which he meant to get his divorce from the Queen of Navarre
were pressed more urgently upon her, as also in Rome. Had he
been free then and there, he would have kept his word; of this
Gabrielle herself was convinced, all through that summer, and
she breathed again. She savoured every lovely day of it, in case
it might be her last. Henri came often to see her at Monceaux,
and — what made her particularly certain of her cause — he did
not come solely as her lord, or to amuse himself with the children. He summoned his ministers thither and discussed business
of State; he paced up and down the park, for his labours had always called for room and air; in his cabinet he reached no decisions. But when he came to sign the decree, he did so side by
side with his beloved lady, laid her hand on the parchment that
it might bring her happiness, and so subscribed his name.

In her park, with his arm slipped through hers, he proclaimed
that throughout his kingdom, subject to the strictest penalties,
no one should be allowed to carry firearms, not even the small
pistols that were then coming into fashion. This was the be-

ginning of public security, with which nobles or adventurers had small concern. All the working classes were on excellent terms with their King.

This singular King insisted that his tribunals should be independent of his court and of the governors of his provinces. The magistrates were henceforward to be irremovable. Yet another matter: he forbade those families whose possessions were too great already to contract rich marriages.

" And that means," said Gabrielle in the faintest whisper — even Monsieur de Rosny was not to hear — " Sire, that means that all your most powerful subjects will desire your death."

" I trust not," said Henri without lowering his voice. " Madame, ask Monsieur de Rosny. He is meditating the richest alliance of all, for his son is to marry into the House of Guise. I give him my permission. My favour is given to all good servants of the State; and this I would have everyone remark."

" He," said Gabrielle, " is your best servant. Never have I opposed what he advised."

" And he knows it," said the King. " He devises some venturesome reform, and I do the rest. You, madame, give me courage to enforce it."

" You have the Minister that you deserve," said Gabrielle, and waited for a due response. But Rosny was silent. Henri's eyes conveyed to her how little he esteemed Rosny the man, in contrast with the Minister. " Not a generous nature, but no matter, dear lady. Enough that he is honest, and, for all his stubbornness, falls in with my ways. I need him."

Henri said as much to her in words when they were alone and could speak freely. It was a lovely summer in the park at Monceaux — though it were her last. Gabrielle gave herself up to the passing hour and listened to her dear lord, unprotesting. She knew a great deal that he missed. Monsieur de Rosny had an understanding with the Florentine Ambassador against her. He had arranged that the Ambassador should introduce his Princess to the King. What could she do? — the King could not dispense with his servant. But still less would he sacrifice his dearest treasure; he would not sell her for a sack of money. Whether

Gabrielle was merely weary or was too happy to feel malevolent, for just that hour her enemy had no cause to fear her.

She heard Henri speak. Rosny was like others about his person: in the last resort he disapproved of Henri. He was bold, but without imagination. He was dreaded by everyone, but what was the good of that? The money that he extracted from these noble bandits would lie fallow in the State Treasury; there was a war treasure accumulating in the Bastille. The people remained poor. Monsieur de Rosny had not observed that only a happy people makes a happy State.

"And a happy King," interposed Gabrielle, very softly, for she was drowsy from the rich warm air, and because she was even then still happy in spite of the exhaustion she could not shake off. The birth of the third child had been more troublesome than that of either of the other two. Henri called to them, and they leapt into his arms: the sedate little Cæsar, and pretty, roguish Catherine-Henriette. Henri fondled them and kissed them and then bade them carry all his kisses to their mother.

He left them for a while, striding out as he always did when his mind was occupied and excited. No one would believe that Cæsar was really his. Rosny, indeed, thought that Bellegarde was the father; at any rate he gave currency to that suspicion. Had he meant his master to hear it? Ah well, every sort of gossip comes round in the end. Gabrielle had heard all about the Medici; they did not talk of it, they knew each other. He for his part had learned that he was regarded as a cuckold.

He vanished into one of the leafy arbours. Half Europe was set upon playing the Medici into his hands. If he took her, he would himself be promptly in the net of the Universal Monarchy. His victory over Spain was to be nullified; hence the eagerness for that alliance. But a powerful impulse came from his faithful servant, who worshipped money. And if he had his will, he would fairly drown his master in a shower of gold.

Here Henri began to think unkindly of his servant — for the first time, and little was to come of it. Industrious, that he certainly was. He sat in the Arsenal and wrote what he himself did not understand. And he carried out schemes that he privately thought ridiculous; his master's orders were enough for him. But for Rosny's labour for him, the Royal artillery would not now be the best in the world. And husbandry — he was as intent upon it as if it had been an interest of his own instead of the indefeasible right of those who are hungry to be fed. He let the King plant the mulberry-trees for his own silkworms, though when his master displayed them in the Royal garden his watery blue eyes fairly goggled out of his head. And when the King ordered that ten thousand trees should be planted in every parish, he obeyed; he wrote, and he wrote.

As he did so, he took his master for a fool, of the kind who have astonishing inspirations that sometimes turn out well. His fortunes were bound up with Henri's; but could he have betrayed his master with impunity, he would not have done so, being naturally too loyal. His was a rare virtue; and to demand more would truly be a mark of folly, said Henri, addressing the walls of his green arbour, with a genial shrug of his shoulders. It was surely right to find the salvation of the kingdom in whatever it might be — industry or seafaring — and to feel the peasant, soldier, craftsman, workman living the lives of fellow-men. He who could do so might come of very noble race and yet be a very ordinary man. Such was Henri, and the longer he lived, the more natural he found himself and his own acts, though falling short of his ambitions.

The people took the same view of him. What seemed to them questionable or odd would soon become habitual and forgotten. When he now went among them, he wanted to see how many were already better clothed and fed; some recognized him, and some did not. In any event they accepted him good-humouredly as a man like themselves, and more he did not ask. How long ago was it that he had said: " When you no longer see me, you will love me "? That was to say too much, or not enough; there was one who loved him.

He went out into the open; his little son had called to him. The little sister was crying wildly; Cæsar controlled himself in manly fashion and said gravely: " Mamma is ill."

Henri ran to her. The lovely head lay averted on her shoulder.

Henri sought her eyes; they were closed, all the colour had ebbed out of her face, and her sleep seemed unnatural. His heart stood still. He took her hand, but it did not respond. He held his parted lips near hers and could feel no breath from them. He flung himself down beside the unconscious figure, and one knee struck the frame of a little picture. He at once knew what had happened and thrust the object out of sight. In the meantime his son appeared with a cup of water, and Gabrielle at last came to herself. After a sigh, and still only half conscious, she said:

" I wish I might never remember what I saw."

" What was it? You have been dreaming," said Henri softly, and then added eagerly: " Tell me your dream, and I will comfort you."

She smiled, recovered her courage, and stroked his head — that head in which, alas, not all the thoughts belonged to her, but sped towards one she could not love.

" If you loved her, you would be more careful," she said to him, with her face very close to his.

He could no longer bring himself to ask whom. " What have I done wrong? " he pleaded. And she answered:

" Nothing, except in my dream. I have sinned, for I saw you leading an ugly woman by the hand with all the grace and courtesy that I know so well. That you would in reality never do."

" What did she look like? " he asked, with more curiosity than he meant to show. This gave Gabrielle completely the upper hand; she kissed his temples and said tenderly:

" No portrait shows you that. A woman must pass judgment on another, were it only in a dream. Her limbs were coarse and heavy, and though not yet twenty, she was beginning to grow fat. The painters leave that out, and they are more skilful than nature at lending a certain youthful charm to any silly, common face, even that of a usurer's daughter."

He could hear the hatred and fear in her voice. He said very softly:

" But should I not have marked all these defects — in your dream? "

" It may be so, my dear lord," replied Gabrielle. " I could

tell that your elaborate courtesy was in fact assumed. In the meantime Shoemaker Zamet appeared."

" So he came into your dream? "

" Not one Zamet, but ten; each shoemaker laden with a heavy sack that nearly crushed him to the ground. I saw all the ten Moorish, flat-nosed faces peering up at me from below."

" What did I do? Did I kick all ten of them? "

" I fear not. I am very much afraid that you led the ugly lady up and down outside an opened door until all ten sacks were through it."

" And then? "

" I did not see the end, for you awoke me."

" Nor shall you ever see it," he exclaimed, and kissed her closed eyelids; this, O charming Gabrielle, is the only way to banish your evil dreams.

GREATNESS IN ACTION

The King returned sooner than the Duchess of Beaufort from their sojourn in the country; and, back in the Louvre, he held a muster of his court. To the noblemen who complained they were being stripped of their property he said roundly that they must not count upon his generosity. They had better go back to their provinces instead of burdening the benches in his ante-room. He had most difficulty with his own countrymen from Gascony. They took the view that since one of them now sat upon the throne, it was they who had put him there. One had held a candle while Henri read a letter from his lady. The Gascon could have read it too, but he turned his head away until he had nearly faced quite round. And in a flush of generosity, as one Gascon to another, Henri had made him a promise which he had not kept. He and his fellows had at last to realize that they could neither bully nor cajole a King who had long been poor and knew the value of money. And if he had forgotten, he would stop and question passers-by in the street until he knew what could be got for a penny, and how that penny was earned.

These were black reproaches: first, that he gave nothing away, and secondly, that he knew too much. The Church deputies, who came to complain about the Edict of Nantes, he answered by recounting their misdeeds — which, be it understood, he attributed, not to them, but to the spirit of the age. But if they would support him, he would restore the Church to the ancient glory it had enjoyed a century before. And they thought: " Was nothing done amiss in those days? " The same thought entered the King's mind also.

He was hard in his dealings with the burghers who forced their way into offices of State for their own emolument. And even harder with the judges who gave their verdicts for the rich. He flatly told those from Bordeaux that in their courts the fattest purse always won the case. And he had particularly loved and honoured his jurists. Since then his kingdom had grown great beyond all expectation — through his own labours. And now, when those who had sacrificed their all grew covetous, and just men grew venal, the guilt really fell upon the King, and hence his wrath. One day, out hunting, he came alone and unknown to a tavern, where there was no food forthcoming for one so shabbily clad. Certain magistrates who were at dinner upstairs told the tapster to put the man out, though he offered to pay his score. He had them fetched down and whipped, a novel proceeding for a King who had been used to take most things lightly and enjoy a laugh.

Among those to whom the King seemed alien, some said he was ungrateful. Others thought his head was turned, in that he was taking everything into his own hands. Why establish cloth- and glass- and mirror-manufactures when he had so sorely burnt his fingers over his silkworms. All this had accounted for a peck of money. Indeed, the superfluous silk had to be distributed among the common folk, and the merest drabs of tavern girls flaunted themselves in silks and satins. One evening the King received a lesson.

He was sitting in his cabinet at cards, for, alas, he was indefatigable at play, although he persistently lost. His thoughts were mostly elsewhere. The room was crowded, and there were many standing behind the King and eyeing his cards. His hand was a bad one and did not justify an exclamation of delight. But he laughed, rapped out his familiar oath — flung down his hand, leapt to his feet, and said:

"I have a craftsman here in the Louvre who can make them without a seam."

What, in God's name, could he mean? They soon discovered. The King set a foot upon his chair, passed a hand down his silk stocking, and, as the bystanders bent down to look, he showed them a completely smooth expanse of web. They could not believe in so much art, and extolled the King as the inventor.

"Who can better it?" said he. "My subjects shall bring forth and be fruitful. Pray, what have you there, Grand Master?"

It was no more than a plum that Rosny produced, and explained to the King that it was a variety long grown on the Loire, near Sully, until it had acquired the fashionable red and yellow bloom and a most incomparable sweetness. The peasants of the district had named it the Rosny plum. But as it was already grown in other parts and its origin had been forgotten, the plum was known as Rouny. "Names are always distorted by the lower orders," said the Grand Master.

"Distorted or not," replied the King, "yours will live among this people through the ages — under the semblance of a plum," he added smartly. Meantime he hurriedly thrust his seamless silk stockings under the table and made as though he were wholly absorbed in the game. It had been a lesson.

It was thought, too, that another of his other imprudent innovations might well have made him suspect. Discharged soldiers plagued the roads until they were thrown into, or sank into, beggary. The sight of his soldiers holding out their hands should more deeply shame a King than if they had plundered his peasants or knocked a pursy burgher on the head in a by-alley. The King insisted that they should work and help him to extend his industries. He had nothing in mind except the welfare of all the active members of the community. But it gave rise to much scandal; the people became turbulent, and the whole relation between rich and poor, and high and humble, was thereby radically altered. The subjection proper to the common folk was

forgotten. The plain rules of conduct laid down by the gentleman of the court for the tradesman's benefit were answered by
the latter with his fist. And when a dozen lackeys were sent to
deal with him, he countered by arraying a dozen sons and ap-
prentices. And as a rich and fragrant odour emerged from the
kitchen, several hungry retainers sat down to dinner with the
clothmaker instead of giving him the drubbing that was his due.
These were the results of an impious inclination to make men
happy, whereas indigence is good for them and keeps them in
discipline and order.

Those who regarded the world order, like the divine order, as
existing for its own sake, and not for the happiness of man, were
actually disposed to regard King Henri's reign as the advent of
Antichrist. Least important of all was the fact that they condemned it for its effects on the community. Not each of them
for all its effects, for some things serve your turn and some serve
mine; we think upon them differently. Others profit no one, but
merely waste money. These worthies looked on with disapproval
while the Place Royale was being built and fitted up for the very
industries in which they were concerned. And they protested
even more vigorously when the King's ships were sent to the
other half of the world — for what purpose? Gold, imaginary
gold from realms so dim that they were still marked white upon
the map; cold, and empty, and beyond all warrant of experience.
" We shall never see that gold, nor will the King."

A certain Monsieur de Bassompierre, inquisitive by nature,
visited a tavern where public affairs were discussed by all manner
of guests. He was not recognized as a gentleman of the court;
he said he was a foreigner. So he was able to hear the true opinions held by honest folk, in addition to remarks from those less
honest. When he had listened for a while, he said: " I have been
in those places marked white on the map."

Invited to approach, he asked if the rumours were true that
the King had chosen the coldest parts of the New World for his
settlers.

This he did not say with a view to disparaging the King in
their eyes, but merely to discover the opinion of the people and

thereby gain credit at court. Moreover he had never set foot in the far Indies, nor even been on shipboard.

The more respectable burghers carefully abstained from the outbursts of indignation to which this gave rise. A windy customer with patched sleeves, who sat drinking sour wine, roundly refused to be shipped off anywhere; he had a wife and six children, he was half starving, he cried, and it was all the King's fault. It would be intolerable that a King's ship should dump him and his on the edge of a desert and then sail cheerfully away.

The inquisitive gentleman persisted in his efforts to find out what these people really thought. There were mines, he said, even in the coldest Indies; he had convinced himself of that by the evidence of his own eyes; and they were brimming with gold. To the sceptical murmurs thus provoked he replied by referring to Spain, which owed her entire power to the treasures of Peru, and but for them would never have laid a hand upon the kingdom of France.

"But our King Henri beat the Spaniards, and the wealth of the Indies, as you call them, was little help to them." So spoke a solid citizen wearing the hide apron of a tanner. "The King favours our honourable craft; that I know from my own experience. He does not send adventurers abroad, to bring back unearned gold."

At the end of the table sat a magistrate's clerk, who had been given a gratuity that morning by one party to a suit and was now engaged in drinking it. His face was naturally red, but his head positively swelled with anger as he roared:

"Better that they should kill the savages oversea than lie and starve upon our doorsteps."

The clerk had in reality no house, which made him all the more ardent in defence of property. His words were hailed with approval. The inquisitive gentleman, who was now satisfied, got up and was about to go. But during the whole of this conversation one who took no part in it was present, sat on a bench against the wall, and there busied himself with a sheet of paper. He now came out into the light, and it was observed that he was old. His well-worn clothing did not seem to have suffered from any bodily exertion, nor his person, which was still erect and firm. There were lines on his face, marked there by learning and by knowledge, but toilers are apt to regard them as the signs of melancholy.

"Monsieur de Bassompierre," said he to the inquisitive gentleman, "since you call yourself a seafarer, I make bold to suppose my name is known to you. I am Marcus Lescarbot."

The other was exceedingly embarrassed, for indeed he had heard of the man. Without thinking any evil, he replied:

"You are one of Admiral Coligny's men."

The people round the table exchanged glances. A Protestant.

"I was," said the newcomer, "among the first Frenchmen who voyaged to New France. Such is the name of the northern coasts of America since we set foot there. It is a land with coasts a thousand miles long, and behind them a whole continent, which we have discovered. In this rough sketch I have drawn the treasures of the earth, the fisheries, the trapping grounds, and the temperature of the seasons. Not much is left white upon my map. I give it to those who do not know that land and have never voyaged to the cold Indies, which are not cold at all."

The man who had called himself Lescarbot laid the paper on the table, though he kept his eyes fixed on the gentleman from the court. While all the guests crowded round the map, Bassompierre said softly:

"Pray embarrass me no longer for having lied. I did so to discover what people were thinking and report to the King, for he ought to know."

"But," said the other, "it would be more important that the people should know what the King thinks."

The courtier answered with an air of respect, and even humility: "No one may boast that he knows that. A great King weighs conflicting arguments more often and carefully than we ever understand. You have been received by His Majesty. Do not deny it," he went on, as the man began to protest, "or I shall catch you in a lie, as you caught me. His Majesty received you, and then his Minister."

" The famous Monsieur de Sully." Marcus Lescarbot uttered this name in quite a different tone — a tone of bitterness, of spiritual hatred, of hostility that went deeper than any personal feeling. Why did he not dissemble? thought Bassompierre. His attitude to Rosny appeared in all its nakedness, and the scholar's face suddenly turned into that of a cannibal.

" He is famous, influential, and without him nothing can be done," observed the gentleman of the court lightly. The old man stood, beset by whirling thoughts; then he turned to the other guests poring over his map. And he spoke of North America with such fire, such fervour, that they could have imagined themselves at a fair, listening open-mouthed to a mountebank crying a universal panacea.

" What would it cost," asked several, " to fit out ships and fetch the gold? And what if the fleet is wrecked? "

" It will not be wrecked," exclaimed the stranger, pale with passion, and therefore yet more suspect. " Think no more of gold. You talk like a crass Minister, who cares for nothing but what glitters. There is no blessing on any treasures save those with which nature rewards our labour. The gold-mine that I know is called bread and wine and fodder. That is money."

His audience pondered. The man's clothes were shabby. He had not yet brought back much fodder from the cold Indies. But someone at the table spoke; it was the tanner, and he said:

" King Henri will never send adventurers into those lands; I have spoken with him, — he bore a hand one day in my workshop, as everybody knows. If you can prove there's profitable work to be done across the seas, he'll listen."

" A glass! " cried Lescarbot the seafarer, once the Admiral's man. " I am still sober. I would drink with the tanner."

He drained his glass at a gulp. Then he sat down and spoke to them all as a man to men.

" The King is ready," he said. " It begins, as in so many other matters, with an ambition of his youth. His Minister may tell him that above the fortieth degree nothing grows nor thrives, but the King will not be deterred. He knows one thing: men thrive there. They are savages, indeed, who do not know the doctrine of salvation; we should be all the more ready to go and save them — at the risk of shipwreck. There are men yonder, and men here, who deserve that we should take that risk on their account. Do you hear me? "

The more eagerly they listened, the more urgently he pressed them. One of the group at the table had clasped his head in his hands and stared wide-eyed at something that was not there. " I hear," he muttered, without moving his lips. In the utter silence Lescarbot went on:

" There are men here who can get no work to do, nor enough to eat — discharged soldiers, and craftsmen unemployed. Some even of our famous cloth-factories are idle."

" True," muttered the guest with his head between his hands.

" There are men yonder who understand no handicraft and till but little ground. And they are heathen, too. For their sake also we should cross the sea. Those yonder and those here — our King will help them both; that is his purpose, if we cross the sea. We, and he with us, when he was still called Navarre and was a Huguenot, asked ourselves, when New France had been discovered: Ought we to seize these lands from their inhabitants? No. We must win their friendship until they are like unto ourselves. It is not our purpose to destroy them as the Spaniards have destroyed their far and alien peoples. We hold to the law of mercy and of pity, according to the word of our Saviour: ' Come to Me all ye that are weary and heavy laden, and I will give you rest. I will comfort you, I will not destroy you '; that is our Lord's intent, and our King's also."

Deep silence fell, and bewilderment came upon those faces — it was always so hard to realize that the law of humanity would indeed be kept and the King would act by it. The guest that held his head between his hands found his eyes veiled with tears, as a long-past scene rose before his inner vision: the bridge in a downpour of rain, the parapet, himself half over it — he had begun to slip and would soon have fallen headlong. Someone dragged him back. A moment before, no one had been in sight; and instead of the void in which he had looked to be engulfed, someone dragged him back to life; covered his nakedness with his own cloak, sent a soldier with him to the hospital, had him cured, gave him work, and transformed the forlorn student of theology into the cloth-worker at that table — one of the resurrected clothmakers in the factories lately opened.

The former suicide felt that he must speak; for the first time he was moved to tell what he knew. It had hitherto seemed to him a matter for some shame, but not of much moment. Suddenly an urgent, crowded world opened out before his inward vision. He stammered, struggled with his agitation, and spoke. He had turned towards the magistrate's clerk, whom he was quite unwittingly addressing. The clerk, a corrupt, gorged rascal, had no notion why he was listening so attentively. Was this a lawsuit, with much money at issue?

Marcus Lescarbot had fulfilled his purpose, and discreetly departed. Close behind him was Monsieur de Bassompierre, determined not to let this very notable personage out of his sight. There was now no more doubt what the King had decided. The Royal Governor for New France had been chosen and would be ceremoniously appointed. The inquisitive gentleman could well divine the next scene in this affair of the colonies as it would be staged with some splendour at the court. The previous one had taken place in a common tavern, but it was the true precursor of the last. And he congratulated himself on having been present at it.

As they made their way out, they were stopped by some musicians crowding into the tavern. Fiddlers, harpers, and a singer; here they found assembled ready listeners — the courtier, the seafaring scholar, the citizens, some honest, some less so, some scalawags, some thieves, and some redeemed from thieving. Then and there they struck up:

" Charming Gabrielle."

Visible Greatness

Henri was arrayed from head to foot in silver armour. He stood before a raised throne, over which was draped his purple mantle. Above him a red canopy, unsupported from below. The smooth, tapering back of the great throne was topped with a golden lily that glimmered faintly against the crimson baldachin. The white walls of the structure, which gave it the semblance of a chapel, mirrored the embodiment of Majesty, high above the throng, though no eye had yet looked on it or its reflection, for all the backs of that company were bowed.

Gabrielle d'Estrées curtsied deep and long. Of all those that paid homage to Majesty, she was nearest to the throne. Before her and behind her, in the centre of that endless gallery, an array of obsequious shoulders and faces made obeisance to the throne. The throne in the centre, and herself nearest to it. As she bent low before the King, she did not forget that in a moment she would mount those steps, escorted by the Grand Master, who would then turn back and remain with the rest below. Gabrielle d'Estrées, and she alone, would be uplifted from the throng, and above her there would be no one but the King. At the King's feet, at the edge of the dais, she would sit, with her dress draped down the steps in token that she was the Queen, but yet not quite the Queen. Behind that bowed brow came the thought: "When? Soon; the next time; now, within an hour — alas, never."

Her dress was of white silk, silvered like the King's armour. The Queen's robes would be of red velvet, the hue of skinless flesh. Gabrielle resolved to have them ready against the event. Her lord, she felt it in her heart, would soon stretch out a hand and raise her to his side. She did not look up; no, Majesty did not move a finger, nor even a finger-tip, to summon her. His eyes looked very far away, beyond that room, the throng of courtiers, and the mob now pouring in through the opened doors. They knelt, they shuffled on their knees up to the shrine of Majesty, throned with mask-like face above that array of bended backs. And Gabrielle, in her thoughts, urged him to keep that mask; she knew the body in that armour, lithe though lightly scarred, still young, but often ailing. She had often tended it, and loved it well.

She was near to forgetting her part. The Constable and the Grand Master took both her hands and led her up the steps to her seat at the edge of the dais. She sank down, draping her dress over the two lower steps. The King shifted his feet, his eyes dilated, but his mask remained unaltered.

The Constable and the Grand Master had returned to their places; which was the signal to the company to rise from their obeisance and break up into the usual groups. Madame, the King's sister, sat on the step below Gabrielle; it was the broadest step, and she did not drape her dress over it. Beneath her, disposing themselves so as not to hide the ladies, stood the Chancellor, the Grand Master, and the Constable. On the left of the royal figure, in its awesome isolation at the top of the empty, forbidding stairway, a number of shabby-looking personages had defiantly taken up their stand; and there, somewhat strangely, they were left undisturbed.

The court then assembled in due precedence, ladies on the one side, gentlemen on the other, both at the distance from the throne prescribed by their rank or service. Princesses, marshals, and presidents, royal princes, with little Vendôme, all in front upon both sides, in the full light, which was caught and diverted by curtains and intensified by ingeniously tilted mirrors, so that the sun-god shone solely on the throne. Beyond its rays, in which the King stood haloed, the human figures in the background faded. Of the more distant, little was visible but a patch of white shoulder, and in one case nothing but a bulbous nose. Colours and outlines dimmed until they dissolved. The front figures were veiled in grey, except in so far as a flicker or a line caught a reflection of the Royal glory. The sun-god shone upon the throne.

In the centre, by agency both human and divine, the disconnected rays were caught and focused upon Majesty made manifest. A dazzling figure, but the blindest of them all was Majesty himself. He raised his brows, he strained his eyes, but beyond his own bedazzled gaze the varying depths of shadow remained impenetrable. He shone upon them, but he could not see them. The faint rustling on the floor of a long dark shaft betokened an assemblage on their knees. And behind his tortured vision Henri found himself wondering why he had decreed this crazy spectacle.

But it was time for Majesty to make a motion and reach out a hand. The Chancellor presented a parchment with a seal attached. Henri took it and gave hurried orders that this magical display should cease. The ingenious mirrors were removed, the curtains drawn back, and the scene began to appear in the light of reality. The King's first look was at an alcove half-way up the long wall, and behind the balcony at an easel that concealed the painter. A youthful face peered out, and the painter nodded. Majesty can be reassured. His likeness has been caught by expert eyes; a sure, quick hand has made good use of the minutes when a King, called great throughout the world, stepped out of that world and assumed the empty guise of Majesty. The painter smiled, under cover of his easel.

The King then spoke. He had unrolled the parchment and held it against one of his silvered cuisses. His other hand pointed to his most distant hearers, who were still upon their knees. At the motion of the King's hand, they rose from the floor, making less noise with their feet than with their shuffling knees. They stood expectant; and the King spoke:

" There are men here who can get no work, nor enough to eat — discharged soldiers and craftsmen unemployed. But in New France there are men who understand no handicraft, and till but little ground, and have never heard of the salvation of souls. For the sake of these men, and of those, we will cross the ocean."

Thenceforward the King addressed himself to the shabby figures that had been so strangely permitted near his throne. True it was that a certain guest in a tavern had uttered these same words before him; and here he was again that day beside the throne, one of those same shabby figures, of whom, indeed, the foremost was an Admiral. No resplendent hero of the seas, but a weather-beaten Admiral; well fitted to carry out the Royal enterprises with endurance both of body and of mind, which he and his comrades would soon most certainly need. Marcus Lescarbot, threadbare and dour, and the little group of seamen with him, all were eager to board a ship and set forth on that perilous voyage through mists and storm. Those who were not wrecked would sight New France.

"But ought we to seize the lands that are called New France from their inhabitants? No. We will win the friendship of these men until they are like unto ourselves. It is not in our minds to destroy these distant peoples. 'I will bring you comfort,' was what the Lord said. He did not threaten to destroy you; and His will is your King's will also."

The words were old, their meaning was divine, as no one could deny, and they came well from a King's lips. Still, the conquest of colonies was a doubtful project that might or might not succeed. What would be the probable end? The wreck of several ships, and a few wrecked men on a desert island. Monsieur de Rosny-Sully dismissed it from his mind as nonsense and looked no longer upon men who would bring no gold back in their pockets.

Marcus Lescarbot, who was facing him, thought of the old Huguenot seamen, and of one who had been Chancellor in Navarre in days gone by. He had been the first to conceive colonies as an obligation upon humanism. From him came the words that both had remembered and now spoke, each from a steadfast heart. He conveyed them to the people, but the King spoke them from his throne. Meantime they had both grown grey. It was a long way to New France, observed a man whose courage wavered. Contemplation of the way already traversed increased the distances that lay ahead.

The King raised the parchment with the seal attached, held it out towards the Admiral, but not so that the Admiral could reach it. And the King announced for all to hear:

"I appoint the Marquis de la Roche as my Viceroy in the lands of Canada, Newfoundland, Labrador — "

He recounted several more names, familiar to the seamen, and latterly heard in public places also, and now to be found inscribed on globes. These were adorned with pictures of seamonsters, gods, nymphs, cannibals, and strange beasts, some terrible and all marvellous. There is a perennial charm in fairy-

tales, and under that influence some of that company were very
ready to believe the King and voyage with his Viceroy into
the unknown. The whole assemblage, with the newcomers now
thronging into the gallery, all pressed forward towards the King.
Their hearts, to be sure, dropped into their hose, not in fear of
the nymphs or the cannibals, but because every step brought
them nearer to the throne.

So the King came down among them. He thrust the mag-
niloquent commission into the Admiral's pocket and kissed him
upon both cheeks. Then he mingled with the future colonists,
who were only too likely to die of scurvy or be cast ashore upon
a desert island. He warned them in measured terms that there
was still time to go home. But none, at such a moment, turned
to go, as the King clapped them all upon the shoulders.

Outside the throng in which he was now moving, his admonitions and heartening words could still be heard. His voice was
gradually drowned in outbursts of applause and joy. The gentlemen of the court eyed one another; they knew their Henri.
A youth would no doubt have told him that he was making the
voyage to see those nymphs, and the King was no doubt descant-
ing on their charms in very lavish fashion. A wave of gaiety
swept over the company. Some grew very venturesome and
crowded round the throne in a superstitious desire to touch it
with their fingers, or even their backsides. And in the hubbub
the King disappeared.

Where was he? In the search for him, the array of courtiers
broke up in confusion. The Duchess of Beaufort had also vanished, and with her, Madame, the King's sister. Beneath her
former seat stood the page alone, still solemnly balancing on his
thigh the King's heavy helmet, an open lion's mouth. He was
questioned, but made no answer. The most inquisitive of the
gentlemen said in his ear: " Young Sablé, speak. He is with the
painter up yonder. I did not look up, but you did. Dolt! Will
it be soon? "

The page clapped the helmet on to the inquisitive gentleman's head so that he could neither hear nor see.

As Henri entered the upper room, he found Peter Paul Rubens

busily dabbing colour on to his black and white drawings, in disconnected patches, just as the sun had projected them on to the real scene, when its rays clove into the assemblage and dissolved all solid forms into alternations of light. The painter had presented the events separately upon the sheets: the King enthroned, the King speaking, appealing to his people, and walking down among the throng. From his point of vantage the painter had seen what had escaped the rest — the King with his seamen and future colonists, talking as a man to men, with his hand on the shoulder of a lad whose eyes were closed in ecstasy. The painter had ignored the merriment, loud as it had been. The men about the King stood in amazement, some of them open-mouthed.

The King himself was truly an inspiring figure, as self-confident as a seaman braving shipwreck; but his lip was writhen by the scar of an old knife-thrust, the brows were drawn as though in pain, and there was a deep wrinkle round the right eye.

" That will never do," said Henri. " But it is the truth. Monsieur Rubens, I shall put this sheet away and shall not lend you my face for any such faithful portrait. The courts of Europe must not know me thus."

" Sire, the courts that employ me get what they want, the outward semblance. It would not be always advisable that I should turn the inside outwards."

Young Rubens spoke with gaiety. It was with a bright and genial eye that he observed this great King; he had the picture of him finished, but purposed to make it so like that it would not be believed.

Henri: " You would represent me as a melancholy man."

Rubens: " Not so, Sire. A favourite of the gods, whom they have treated with some strictness. But beneath those enduring features they have bestowed their own eternal gaiety."

Henri: " I suppose your experience of courts has made you so ready with your tongue. You Flemings are usually slow of speech. Yours is a cheerful trade, Master Painter. You have your way with men, eh? You depict them as they seem to be, but you put into the picture what goes on underneath the skin.

Your forehead is still unwrinkled, and your hair still fair, and you know exactly how all of us are made. I too — when I was young, I was very fond of looking at an anatomical atlas."

The King turned his hand over, in token that his knowledge of the human structure had been of great aid to him in life. Thereupon the pair fell silent. They were standing under a window in the chill light. The room was empty save for the table on which the sketches were spread out. They looked at them one after another.

The door opened for the Duchess of Beaufort and Madame, the King's sister. Rubens made a courtly bow. When the King came in he had poured out wine for Henri and for himself. Henri introduced him.

" This is Monsieur Rubens, who has already come to fame, which exalts painters above princes. But Monsieur Rubens has never dropped a brush, and I could never pick one up."

" Sire," said Madame, " we are longing to see your throne."

The painter, still bowing low, said:

" Madame, you are better acquainted with it than I am. You were sitting beside the King."

" There you have it, Monsieur Rubens," said Henri. " She will not credit her own greatness nor mine until you have made a picture of them."

Gabrielle thrust the drawings aside with the tips of two fingers. She had not failed to notice that when she entered, the painter had turned over one of the sheets and covered it up. He watched her fingers; should she be allowed to find it? It would be wiser to keep it to himself, distort the likenesses, and present it as some classic theme. He would make it five feet high and four broad; just a picture and nothing more.

Gabrielle did not find the picture which the painter had covered up, but she picked out several single figures. First she recognized that long and hollow back even sooner than the stony profile. She trembled, and the drawing dropped from her hand. Henri was quicker than the painter — he seized the sheet and kissed his lady, whispering in her ear:

" You are right. This is a terrible fellow. Try to find your own presentment in one of the more becoming drawings, if such there be."

Madame had, happily, seized and shown the Duchess, to comfort her, a sketch of herself portrayed in all the richness of her contours, the flesh tones lightly indicated, and even the sheen of the silk. There sat the charming Gabrielle, already undeniably of full figure, and all the worthier of the throne; a little lower sat Catherine. But the page! She looked and quivered. He stood on the floor between them, with the great lion's-head helmet balanced on his thigh; and his face was her brother's face when he was young. What could have been the painter's intent? Pray Gabrielle did not notice it! But no — how could she? That time belonged to her alone, none but she knew that face.

After this, Catherine would look at nothing more and said it was time to go. The King took his lady's hand, and they were just departing when Rubens said reluctantly:

"I have something else."

He meant what he had really meant to keep to himself — a picture and nothing more.

"True," said the King. "You have been showing us the various details. Where is the scene as a whole?"

Then Rubens picked up a sheet which he had turned over covered, and held it between his two hands. Madame had seen enough, she wanted to go, she longed to recall her memories in solitude. What lay before her now? She felt a chill come over her, as so often lately, and she guessed that it foreboded an end not far away.

Henri and Gabrielle, still holding each other's fingers, stood rigid, as though spellbound to the spot, and merely stretched out their heads to look.

The throne, a white void, and in the centre the Royal figure almost dissolved in the concentrated glare, but the thousand imponderable rays had taken solid shapes: as angels and cupids — plunging, glittering curves of intertwining limbs, a pictured pæan of immortal exultation. The Royal figure, lightly sketched, stood wide-eyed and oblivious, both of the human shadows below and of the inrushing flood of angels and amoretti. But on the edge of the dais sat a woman stripped of any godlike semblance, and naked. Visible in all its fullness and its bounty was that woman's flesh, and above her stood enthroned the lord of light, dimmed by his own glory.

"A masterly work," said Henri, "but a trifle merciless, for we are quite outshone by our surroundings. You shall paint the picture, and I will often look at it, to humble my pride. Such we are, and no more."

"I did not mean it so," said Rubens in confusion. "I call it Majesty."

Gabrielle, seized, like her lord, by an uneasy desire to do penance and humiliate herself, said: "The woman is stripped of her pride, and therefore she is naked. Not in celebration of that luscious flesh which must one day pass away. I could swear that her knee is moving, and that she means to kneel before embodied greatness."

Her nerves were growing dangerously tense. This woman, at the most menaced passage in her life, transformed that admirable picture into something terrible — and an expression of pure horror came upon her face. Henri had drawn her away, and the painter tried to put the picture out of sight. But she pointed towards it.

"That is my body," she said in a pitiable, broken voice that was not hers. "Someone has studied it unknown to me. He who knows every fold of my flesh can certainly reveal what will be my end; and he is an astrologer."

"Not an astrologer, an anatomist," exclaimed Henri. Too late, Gabrielle flung herself shuddering into his arms. She had seen the living flesh of her likeness dissolve. On the edge of the dais, no longer turned towards the throne, sat a skeleton.

GABRIELLE: LIFE AND DEATH

In the autumn of that year Alexander-Monsieur was christened; and the cost of the festivities was enormous. In the opinion of the court, the King's beloved, since the birth of her two elder children, had overstepped all decency, and it was high time to make an end. One means of doing so was to involve the King's affections once again. This was the course recommended by Madame de Sagonne, and she undertook to choose the object. The beauty selected to suit His Majesty's tastes was of course a new arrival at the court, young as Eve on the first day; and, above all, slim. She did truly please the King, when she danced in the great " Oversea Ballet," almost naked, for she was one of the group of Indians. These were the inhabitants of New France, where it was surely too cold for such generous exposure. Meantime Monsieur de Bassompierre, who had been put in charge of the diversions of the court, was less intent upon matters of geography than on his friend Sagonne.

The King looked pleased enough when, as occasion offered, Mademoiselle d'Entragues passed his seat, and he drew back his feet lest she should trip. Her sole care was to make herself appear as tall and slim as possible as she pirouetted past on her long legs. By this means, too, the dark beauty's eyes glowed down upon him from above, in presentment of the allurements of the Indies, while not neglecting her own. The King smiled into his beard, but he passed the whole evening beside the Duchess of Beaufort.

In the first place he felt tired, indeed almost ill, but he saw reason enough for this in his manifold labours of that year. The end was at hand. Whether or not it would bring an illness, Henri had never believed in his illnesses, and he could no longer learn to take precautions. Though man's nature had been his lifelong study, his own body was continually offering him surprises.

" Sire," whispered Gabrielle, " you are weary of these diversions. I shall not take it amiss if you leave my entertainment and lie down."

Henri understood from this that he must reassure his beloved in the matter of this intrusive young dancer.

" Little Henriette," he began.

" So you know her name," observed Gabrielle.

" I know her father very well," said Henri. " Though I often met him in the field afterwards, I can still see him standing be-

side the murdered King, my predecessor. He stood at the head
of the bed and held the corpse's chin to prevent it falling. He
did once let it drop, in his fury when I appeared. The gentlemen in that room would have much sooner seen me dead upon
that bed. But that chin was a horrible sight."

" Go and rest, my lord, I beg you; it is no matter if people say
that you found my fête tedious."

Gabrielle's concern touched Henri. He answered: " I will do
as you wish, although I feel quite well." He vanished without
taking leave of the company. He told himself that no good could
come to him from Henriette d'Entragues. Beware of the daughter of the man who held the murdered King's chin!

Gabrielle might be ousted by inducing the King to fall in love
with someone else. If this failed, as seemed likely, and the King
remained quietly in possession, so that his lady could not be
dislodged — then some other scheme must be devised.

Monsieur de Fresne, a member of the Finance Council and
a Protestant, was devoted to the Duchess, and in higher places
was her sole support, except for old Cheverny, whose motive was
interested. For he remained Chancellor so long as his friend
Sourdis ruled the King through that fine fat quail her niece.
Such was the general view. How many knew that love is wiser
than self-interest, and Gabrielle no longer listened to Madame
de Sourdis. It was said that adultery had advanced both aunt
and niece, who were now vying with each other in amassing
wealth. Monsieur de Fresne, though he went about his business
in very unobtrusive fashion, was quite undeservedly regarded as
the author of the Edict of Nantes. He was therefore the more
hated, as often happens to smaller men when great issues are
at stake.

This worthy had to reckon up the accounts for the christening
of the little Alexander-Monsieur, and sent them to the Inspector-
General of Finance in the Arsenal, not forgetting to describe the
boy as a child of France. Monsieur de Sully rejected the not
unreasonable claim and substituted a figure far too low — not
even enough to pay the musicians. When they complained, he
promptly had them shown the door. " There is no child of

France," he called out after them. And they repeated the remark to the Duchess of Beaufort.

Then at last the lady and her bitterest enemy showed their faces to each other, in the presence of the King, who had summoned his Minister.

" Now repeat your words! "

" There is no child of France."

" The children of France have a mother, whom you dare to insult, and a father, who will forgive much, but not this."

This being an appeal to Henri, he interposed.

" You may withdraw the cost of the music, Rosny, I will bear it myself. But you must withdraw your words as well."

" Sire, I am a man of plain facts. You have bestowed a title and a rank upon this lady, let that be enough."

" But if I choose, it shall not be enough."

" If, indeed, you choose," admitted Rosny-Sully; his face was now mask-like and ashen grey.

The woman's delicate complexion had also faded. She began to tell the Minister the most terrible truths. Henri did not interfere; he wished himself far away, and in the company of neither. Rosny stood, coldly observant, and let his enemy say her worst.

Gabrielle spoke with an outward calm which did but mark the stress of that inner conflict. She was as good as Queen. The court had recognized her by every sort of homage at the festivities for her son, the child of France. She descended to detail and recounted who had specially humbled themselves to gain her favour. Rosny noted the name of each one, to be dealt with later.

Henri wandered about the room, and by the farthest wall he stood, facing it. His poor lady was giving herself away quite hopelessly; he began to pity her, which was unfortunate. When she insisted that bearers of great names had frequented her anterooms, he for the first time remarked her petty origin. And a look in the King's eye bade Sully not reply.

Gabrielle had suffered too much, and suppressed her sufferings too long. She spoke her mind at last, once and for all. " I make people what they are," she cried, " and the proof is in your own person, Grand Master and Inspector-General. Who made you, sir? Do you believe that it was easy? Consider yourself; were you likely to have pleased the King? How should a man so hidebound serve so alert a master, and how should your dull wits match his winged spirit? You were created to be bogged in your own mediocrity. I dragged you out of it."

There was much truth in this, and before it burst forth from those passionate lips, Henri had expressed such thoughts aloud in Gabrielle's presence. For that very reason he now felt at a disadvantage; it was himself at whom the blows were aimed. Never had he conceived his faithful servant as he was here presented. Thenceforward he was openly in league with that same faithful servant. The distraught creature did not understand — she did not even hear him stamp his foot; Rosny-Sully was now secure, his enemy was working her own destruction, and he let her be. Pray fill the measure full, madame. He stood wide-eyed and silent. The unhappy woman lost her last entrenchment.

"You forget that you crawled to me. You began as my slave."

The word brought a sudden flush of anger, or of shame, into that ashen face.

"Enough, madame! You have permitted yourself just one word too much. It leaves me unscathed, but if am not mistaken, it touches the King. Would my master dismiss me?" asked the cavalier of days gone by. His voice quivered with the memory of countless battles and agonies, when victory was never secure, but now they stood where they did that day.

Henri was sorely at a loss. There were few ordeals he would not sooner have faced than this scene and the evil necessity of choice. He was torn; but he decided he must speak, and speak his mind. As he turned round, his intention was to laugh her back to reason. But as he approached the pair, he surprised himself by saying:

"Dismiss you? I have no notion of such a thing." This to Rosny. And Gabrielle d'Estrées heard him say:

"Give up such a servant for your sake? Madame, you could not wish it if you loved me." The voice was harsh.

Not until he had so spoken did he realize that it had not been in his mind to use such words; they were uttered unawares. He turned and went.

For a minute Monsieur de Rosny tasted his enemy's downfall; her body was quivering, her face waxen-pale, and she scarce realized that his eyes were on her. His fresh complexion, hardly befitting a man of his age, had returned; he left his victim without a word of salutation.

If certain misgivings assailed Rosny later on, he knew how to confront them. The service of the King came first. The King himself had said that such a servant was dearer to him than ten mistresses. Thus and not otherwise had Rosny conceived the King's remark, or had transformed it to mean as much. This version of those unhappy words was the one that he repeated; the whole court soon knew it, and the ambassadors wrote it in their dispatches, which brought all the more support to its author. In good faith he could view the matter thus:

Constant conflict with the King's beloved, who had, however, suddenly become a mistress like any other, wasted time and money to no purpose. The King had now admitted that his love did not reach so far that he would marry her. He — Rosny — had done right and served the King by opening his eyes at last. So Rosny reckoned, and he communicated his conclusion to his wife, the elderly widow, who heard it with high satisfaction.

As a man of conscience, Rosny had to protect not merely the King's service, but his own sense of duty against feminine attack. In his opinion, he had done his duty and needed only to remind his conscience of the woman's threats, had he not interfered. Between the throne and death, both very near, but there was no doubt which would have come first — between them he had opened an alternative: the King's disfavour. Hard for her, no doubt. She might call him cruel, faithless, and ungrateful and she would do so for a while; but later, when she came to live on, safe and secure, in her Château of Monceaux, with a pension from the King, she would recognize who had saved her. He desired no thanks — it was but human duty. She had here and there served his career, and he had repaid her by saving her life. Well and good; the affair was at an end.

Thus conscience expressed itself satisfied, or partly so. But before his beak-nosed wife Rosny did not boast of his benevolence towards Gabrielle d'Estrées. Her nose was so long and so pointed that she might well have discovered the reverse side of benevolence. So elderly a widow had waited a long time; and she triumphed at last without any guilty self-examination.

The Duchess of Beaufort paid a visit to Madame de Sully, who would not receive her. Thereupon the Duchess addressed a friendly complaint to Monsieur de Sully, who did not reply. This behaviour on the part of both would certainly have roused the King had it come to his ears. He would have doubtless felt the insult as aimed at himself. But Gabrielle did not mention it to him. She had enough in hand to deal a blow at the faithful servant when the time came. Still, she feared the counter-blow — not from Rosny, but in the mind of her dear lord; for she had learned her lesson.

Her secret feeling was fear, and it never wholly left her. The King's demeanour did not change; he was more attentive than ever to her slightest wish. He cursed his court and all other courts, the net of circumstance that held him bound, the general conspiracy to nullify his victory over the Spaniards and to render him harmless. Gabrielle understood, and heard what he did not utter — a plea for pardon. So she never engaged him upon her own affairs. She could not have done so without trembling, for since the scene with Rosny she could not, try as she would, control the tremor in her limbs. Her real fear was that her fear might be remarked.

He recounted to her, more confidentially than usual, his personal negotiations with Pope Clement regarding his divorce from the Queen of Navarre. The position of matters was not known even to his Minister. Pope Clement demanded in compensation the recall of the banished Jesuits. The King had replied that if he had two lives, he would gladly give one to His Holiness. She understood: he had only his own life, as also had she; and if he did what they both desired, it would be forfeit. If he made her his Queen, he would have to come to terms with the Jesuits, and that would decree the death of both of them upon their throne. So he pleaded for her pardon. And in the meantime she behaved as though all that mattered was the welfare of the kingdom.

He gave orders for a hunting expedition in honour of the Duchess of Beaufort — not four days after that oft regretted word, at the very thought of which she still trembled. On this expedition he took none but her friends, and especially one who had been converted to her friendship: Roquelaure. All were soldiers, and of them the most loyal were men of simple mind, such as brave Crillon and the one-eyed Harambure. They had with their own hands thrust a would-be assassin of the King out of the saddle, and they had urged the King to marry his good lady. In these men's company the autumn day was fresh and brilliant. They rode far afield, and through a familiar country: their horses' hoofs had thundered over it in battle. The vast forest that reached to the border of Picardy — that day the sunshine flooded through its leafless boughs; but they could have found their way through it in pitch darkness.

"Do you remember, Feuillemorte," said·Henri to his Grand Master of the Horse, Bellegarde, bending across his lady, who was riding between them, "do you remember how dark it was when we came back the first time from the Château of Cœuvres? So dark that you had it in mind to kill me, Feuillemorte. No bad notion from a jealous man. I'll admit that it came into my own mind later, Feuillemorte. Madame, look at him; he, too, is growing grey."

No, she took no heed of the white beard, nor of him with the greying temples. She thrilled at the thought that her lord had kept his young heart for her — for her; and there was a ring of tenderness in his gay voice; the old torment, that he might have lost her or not won her, the long past torment came back and shook him too. "Oh, glorious life!" said Gabrielle.

Strange it was that instead of quickening their pace, as would have been natural with such recollections in their minds, the three set their horses to a walk, so that the gentlemen behind them approached until their voices could be heard. "I have always told him," said one, "to do the deed. Appeal to the people, as he has always done. Get a priest to do the deed, and we have our French Queen. Afterwards — well, wait and see."

It was brave Crillon. The one-eyed Harambure retorted angrily: " And how stands the matter now? The monks are preaching against him again and prophesying the vengeance on his sins. They call on him to do penance that the wrath of Heaven may not fall upon this kingdom. Since the peace, Spain can empty her convents on to us again. The Capucins have appeared with crowns of thorns on their bald heads, and before them came the Guise ladies. Could we have believed all this a little while ago? Or that the King would act so? "

" My one-eyed friend," cried Henri over his shoulder, " you indeed drive the Devil out of men possessed. But I send the doctor to the case, as I always did — and always shall do."

" But there are omens," said another. " Your enemies have taken to counterfeiting omens. And when their turn does come, take care! "

This left Henri without a retort, for he knew that there were omens that could not be counterfeited. It was for him to circumvent what they portended. At that moment he recognized the clearing into which they had turned; here he suggested they should dismount and take their meal. The lackeys arranged some tree-trunks to serve as a table, and set some sawn-off stumps round it. To one only they set a back, and covered it with rugs; thither Henri escorted Gabrielle.

She was wearing a green dress with silver trimming and a hat to match it. The cool sunlight did not set her hair aglitter, as in the festal days when it used to be sparkling with gems. A quieter radiance shed upon one who is still there, though recalling very different days, finds a slow, sure way to the heart. Henri caressed her finger-tips as he served her. Her cheeks were as snow before it melts, with roses budding through it. Oh, glorious life! She had said it awhile ago, but her lord had not listened. Now he marked her talk and pondered, and the company gradually fell silent.

When he gave her his hand to rise, Henri said to Gabrielle: " I may now tell you, madame, that it was from here that I set

out for the Château of Cœuvres with Feuillemorte when I saw
you come down the stairway."

At that moment the Duke of Bellegarde stood nearer to the
King and his lady than all the rest; it was as though he made a
third.

Then it was resolved to begin the chase in good earnest; the
gentlemen and the only lady plunged into the undergrowth on
foot, whereby they went astray and missed each other; shouts and
answering shouts grew fainter, and at last seemed to come from
everywhere and nowhere. The Duchess of Beaufort was lost, although Henri had tried not to leave her side. The Grand Master,
who had made off as though on the trail of a quarry, was no more
seen. The King ordered his gentlemen to beat the forest. He
himself mounted his horse; as he had expected, two horses were
missing.

At first he galloped blindly ahead, over fences and ditches;
over an open grave. Suddenly he encountered Monsieur de
Rosny. Ha! The man who believed that Cæsar was not the
King's son. If challenged, he would deny it, or perhaps he would
not, for he had proved himself right but two days since. Henri
reined his horse in with a jerk. Furious with Rosny for having
been so lately right, he had almost galloped off in a rage. He
wanted to know nothing, nor did he want to figure as a fool. So
he sat motionless while his horse stamped and whinnied; and he
saw a vision of the Château of Cœuvres, as yet out of sight. He
saw through the walls and into a familiar chamber, and it was a
sore effort to look into it, though the vision had come unsought.

The torturing sight that he had thus pictured he now wanted
to see with his own eyes; he was possessed by a violent desire to
be present while the pair of them lay abed. He would lie under
the bed, as the other had once lain, when he tossed him sweetmeats. Seven years since, and they had never ceased to laugh at
him. He had let all the world talk about King Cuckold. Why
had he pretended to be deaf? Because it was not true! he cried,
suddenly without a doubt that he would find the castle empty.
Seven years, and she had become more deeply his than anything
that was so. Their flesh and blood, the children thus created,

the same heart beat in each and all of them. She felt what he did not utter. He knew what was in her mind.

He vowed that if he found the castle empty he would force the priest to marry her to him next day. Thereby one person would find himself checkmated, and that would be the lord of Sully, his Grand Master. No, he shrank before the ordeal, a menacing fate lay waiting, and no man would meet it of his own free will. He turned. In vain. It was intolerable not to know, and reason would be vanquished by passion, by its sudden visions and its fears. Again he turned. He must make up for lost time, but his fears promptly came back; and he rode fast or slow according as fear or desire prevailed.

When he reached the bridge, he thought he was too late in any case, that they had already gone and he had been fooled. As he rode into the courtyard, his horse was greeted by whinnies from two others, in one of the projecting wings of the building, on the left. The little crenellated tower, there the beasts were tethered. The third answered them; alas, the persons in the room above would be sorely disturbed. How would they be discovered?

As he entered, Henri found them otherwise than he expected. Gabrielle was leaning out of the window, her back turned to her companion, who was booted and spurred. On her shoulder Henri noticed some withered leaves, which she had brushed off the branches as she rode through the forest; they certainly would not have remained there had she got out of her clothes. Bellegarde was looking at a great wild bird at his feet, lying with bound claws and frantically flapping its wings. The quarry had covered the Grand Master's hands with dirt, and with such hands he would certainly not have touched a woman.

Although Henri grasped all this at once, he could not control the terrors of the last hour, and they burst forth in fury.

" What does this mean? " he cried as they both eyed him in bewilderment. He too must be appearing to them in an unexpected guise. They scarce imagined that he would writhe like a man in a fit or rail at them like this. So aghast were they that they let him rave until he was exhausted and near to a collapse. Gabrielle had left the window; she approached him with a pleading air, and as his voice quailed after his tirade, she dared to take his hand. How hot and dry it was! And Gabrielle said:

" My lord, indeed, indeed I have done nothing. I thought to await you here and think of old days in your company. The event has turned out ill, and I am sorry I came, though my purpose was good."

He answered, less violently, but with no less anger:

" You lie, madame. I know the truth. You were looking out of the window in the hope it was not I. You would have had time until the evening to laugh at the cuckold more than once."

Bellegarde stood strangely bowed, his face gaunt and drawn. He picked up the captive bird by the feet and made as though to go.

" Answer for yourself, Feuillemorte," cried Henri.

Bellegarde stopped, half turned, and said:

" Sire, I cannot."

" Your accomplice leaves you in the lurch, madame," cried the anguished Henri; until this point he had not believed what he was saying, but he did so now.

Gabrielle shrugged a shoulder helplessly.

" Sire," said Bellegarde, " all that remains for me is to enter the Turkish service. The Grand Sultan kills his people unquestioned. But you shall first understand what manner of man I am. One who is devoted to you, and not from habit only, nor from duty. For long years he has looked into your heart and so admired and loved it that he offered you his life and made you master of his fortunes. I have so thought and acted for a long while, as indeed you know, and it is very certain that the Duchess of Beaufort thinks as I do. Otherwise she would never have permitted me to accompany her to this castle and this room."

Henri looked away and muttered vacantly: " Words, clever words, to play upon the feelings."

Here Gabrielle aptly interposed:

" He says too little. He says I permitted him to accompany me here. No. I invited him."

She did not say why. But her lord had guessed why; he had seen through her from the moment he entered the room. He knew her misery and fear, and he understood her desperate attempt to make him jealous again. She led him backwards into time past, and to those dead days when he had been as fearful as she was now. ("In those days — what would you not have done, dear lord, to keep me. Dearest child, what would you not have done?")

He read in her face — and it was the face into which he had most often looked — he read all that was in her mind, and what she felt, including her pity for what he suffered. In the scene with Rosny he had grieved for her, now she grieved for him. ("We should not give cause for pity, neither I nor you. We are strong. It is well that you reminded me.")

First he embraced Bellegarde and kissed him on both cheeks. When he turned to his beloved, she was panting a little from the strain and glowing with success. She heard his words before he uttered them. As he held her in his arms, he did really say:

"Tomorrow it shall be done. Tomorrow I'll send for the priest. Whether he wills or no, he shall marry us tomorrow."

She repeated: "Tomorrow," her face still radiant, but she wished the priest had been in that room!

Scarcely had they left the Château of Cœuvres than they fell in with the huntsmen and the pack and rode after a stag until darkness fell. When the beast had been caught and disembowelled, and the hounds had eaten and were quiet, the huntsmen stood round the King, who had to lie down and rest; he said it was a bruise on the knee. Suddenly, in the silence of the forest, a second hunt was heard — the baying hounds, and shouts, and horn-blasts, all quite half a mile away; and then, a moment later, the same sounds came from near at hand. Nothing could be seen in the black darkness among the trees.

"Who dares intrude upon my hunt?" asked the King in amazement, and ordered the Count of Soissons to go and see. Soissons plunged into the thicket; there he descried the black outline of a form that appeared and vanished, uttering a word that sounded like "Repent!"

The Count of Soissons came back and said that it was a dreadful voice, which had uttered a word that might have been "repent," but he was not wholly sure. The King did not reply; he sat erect in his saddle and rode beside the Duchess of Beaufort, with the rest of the company close by. And no one mentioned the fact that from the second hunt, which had lately made so great a din, not another sound was heard.

When they reached the next village, the King, without dismounting, asked such few peasants and herdsmen as were still abroad at that hour what they knew about this strange manifestation. Several replied that it was an evil spirit, the forest was his hunting ground, and he was called the Great Hunter. Others told the King that Saint Hubert himself often chose these woods to hunt in, with his invisible horsemen and a pack that was only heard, not seen.

" A saint — that sounds more friendly," observed the King to Gabrielle; but he was not really reassured until the last villager revealed that it was a poacher who pretended to be a demon and thus was able to hunt the King's game with impunity. But now that the King knew, he would no doubt catch him. " I shall certainly do so — the very next time," said Henri, and rode away satisfied, assuring his beloved that they had now got the truth.

Gabrielle said yes, she was sure that was so; but in her heart she thought that no poacher would cry out: " Repent." It was an omen. And so thought most of the gentlemen who were riding so close to her and to the King and who knew what the King thought and did not say. There had been talk of omens, of counterfeited omens, at the beginning of this hunting party. But were they so wholly false when, quite contrary to our character and convictions, we continually encountered them?

It was Monsieur de Roquelaure who started the talk about omens that day; and scarcely had they entered the Louvre when he asked the King to receive him alone. Marshal Roquelaure was now grieved that he had not spoken before. Now it was too late, and the King dismissed him.

" I do not need you. I need a surgeon, and at once."

So saying, he fainted. One of his organs had for some while been congested, and the torment was more than he could endure.

So Roquelaure was not able to say what he had to say — of

which he was afterwards glad, though his conscience smote him.
Too many of the court had been involved in this affair. The
Duchess of Beaufort's enemies had found a couple of mounte-
banks adept at imitating all the sounds of a hunt — the shouts,
the baying of the hounds, and the blasts of the horn, seeming to
come from far or near, at will. In the forest the noise was intensified, and would indeed deceive anyone that heard it. Nothing more was needed but a dark shape in a thicket, and a voice
that cried: " Repent! "

GABRIELLE: IN THE BALANCE

It was no longer a malady begotten in the soul. On those occasions the labouring soul would disburden itself into a fever of
the body. But this time the body gave no support to the soul,
but made matters worse. The surgeon had set to work; every
day he had to aid the refractory organ. Henri bore the discom-
fort well; harder to endure was the realization that his body was
no longer equal to its task. In his fever he said: " If I had two
lives, I would give one to the Holy Father." He said " to the
Holy Father," but his tongue spoke otherwise than his mind
intended; he lay looking for a person who was actually in the
room. In vain the sick man strained his staring eyes to recognize
her; to her he would give one of his two lives. He reached out a
quavering hand towards her, but Gabrielle evaded it.

Her own eyelids were dry and reddened from watching by her
beloved lord, and her fear had reached the point where it grew
frozen. No trembling, and no tears; except when Madame, the
King's sister, knelt and prayed with her. That could not be often,
for Gabrielle feared she might break down if she pleaded with
the Almighty. She herself must stand calm and enduring as the
handmaid of the Almighty and keep this man alive. She undertook the humblest duties, and the loveliest hands in the kingdom
gave help to the recalcitrant member. She spent hour after hour
behind his head, her ear bent low to catch the mumbled words
he could not call to mind, though all were intended for her. His
spirit, straying in bewilderment through dark forests, lost her

image as he tried to seize it. And she, too, seemed to miss and seek him, though he lay there in his agony.

In those days she had the terrible foreboding that they would never meet again with the same frank, free approach that had been theirs. Whatever effort each might make, they were henceforth in some mysterious fashion to be sundered — trees in the mist, the sound of unseen happenings, a scurry of phantoms.

On the night when he for the first time dropped asleep, and slept too noiselessly as it seemed to her, she breathed her breath into his open mouth, until she herself was exhausted. In the morning he awoke cured. Gabrielle's enemies said that, despite her presence at the King's bedside, Heaven had again shown forbearance. But the physician, La Rivière, said that the Duchess had heartened the King's power of resistance, and that was pleasing to the Lord.

Unluckily it was the body alone, and not the soul, that recovered. Henri was still fevered, which made no matter, but he was utterly overborne by melancholy and exhaustion. He had never known such weariness after any of his battles; not even the death leap had left him in such a state. That year had been the height of his achievement, and its reward seemed to be a depression that nothing could lift. All unavailing were the most ingenious stage performances, fairies and dryads flying through the air, magical shapes in mirrors, and a Bird Comedy — all which things amazed and amused the whole court, except the King. Vain were the most alluring ballets — in which the choicest beauties exposed themselves unveiled, hoping that one of them might banish the King's dejection. These ladies, in their eagerness to relieve the King, swayed their delicate bodies to and fro before him, until there was no fold of flesh that still preserved its mystery. Their purposes were excellent, but for the first time in his life he could find no taste for such charms.

" I do not care for these things," he said. " Indeed, I care for nothing," he muttered, and turned away, heedless of the Duchess of Beaufort, whom he had beside him; he behaved as though she were not there. And as he sat with his head in his hand, with no eyes for the spectacle nor ears for the pleasant music, one after another the dancers, the musicians, and the court vanished unregarded by the King. After long abstraction he gradually emerged into reality and found that he was alone. A room empty right up to the great drawn curtain, and behind it strewn the remnants of the spectacle, instruments, machines, a gilded helmet, and a faded wreath. The desolate King flung himself over the other arm of the chair; the chair beside him was empty; indeed, it was overturned. Madame had fled. He could not tell whether he was pleased or sorry to be alone. " I care for nothing any more," he said into vacancy, which returned the echo of his words.

There was commendation afterwards for the Duchess of Beaufort, in that she had seen that her game was played and withdrew from the Louvre to her own house. Only the King's severe illness had allowed her to live with him in the Royal apartments that were never to be hers. It seemed all the more urgent to get her finally out of the way — by extreme measures if that were possible. For she was as much an object of pity as of hate. There were many who regretted in advance what they were prepared to do; and they would go to extremes, if need were. Hitherto there had been no more than the usual abuse; the preachers and the monks grew bolder as they learned of the King's weakness and melancholy, and proclaimed that his life had been spared on this occasion that he might repent. And a vast concourse of people surged into the Louvre, where they pleaded in chorus that the King should save the country and his own soul by dismissing Gabrielle.

She herself received strange visitors, who came on each occasion alone. It was said, though not believed, that the Pope's Legate had been with her. He had secretly entered her house after dark, with one or two attendants only and without a single torch, and had come out again unseen, in spite of watchers posted in the street.

Scarcely less privily came to Gabrielle the earliest of her enemies, Madame de Sagonne. The lady was not received at once;

Gabrielle admitted her only after an hour's probation, in patience and humility. When ushered in, she groped for a chair, and it was with an effort that she spoke.

"Madame, I always desired your interests," she stammered.

"Madame, your wish shall be fulfilled," said Gabrielle with assumed condescension; whereat Sagonne puckered her face into what might be either a burst of tears or a tearful smile. Such a fine-drawn, bird-like face.

"Pray forgive me," she cried shrilly, fluttering her fingers. "I never wanted this to happen."

"What?" asked Gabrielle. "All is well with me, the King has recovered, and he means to marry me. We have no enemy, since you are now my friend."

"Oh, be on your guard, madame! I implore you to be careful of yourself, and I could not plead more urgently for my own life."

As her tiny face turned green and she did actually slip from her chair on to her knees, Gabrielle thought well to speak a few plain words.

"You have talked a great deal, madame. If all that you have said against me for years past now flooded into this room, it would drown us both. But I see that you are now caught in the flood of your own malignancy. Speak; tell me at last, not stories that you have yourself invented, but what you know."

"If I only did know!" Sagonne would have wrung her hands, but they were still fluttering.

"Who means to kill me?" asked Gabrielle.

Sagonne suddenly stiffened and looked at her.

Gabrielle: "Monsieur de Rosny?"

Sagonne: a dumb denial.

Gabrielle: "I should not have believed you had you told me so. The agents of Tuscany — and in what manner?"

Sagonne: "There is much talk and movement here and there, all over Europe, it would seem; so many secret envoys of the courts creep into Paris and disappear again. The love-affairs of the King of France are a matter of concern to the Pope and to the Emperor; but that you know."

Gabrielle: " What have you to tell me that is new? "

Sagonne, almost inaudible: " Zamet. I have heard that the plot was devised in his house."

" At the card-table, of course," said Gabrielle. " Who was there? "

Sagonne made a sign in token that her knowledge and even her strength were now exhausted.

" Avoid that house. You should not ever visit Shoemaker Zamet with the King," she whispered even more mysteriously. " Much less without him."

She made as though to rise and could not — but as her momentary weakness gave Sagonne time to think, she suddenly realized her own position; it was no longer only Gabrielle who had to tremble for her life.

" I have said too much," she gasped in terror. She leapt to her feet, covered her face with her hands, and sobbed: " Now you hold me in your hand."

" No one has any notion you are here," said Gabrielle. But Sagonne:

" Your door is watched day and night. Even the Legate's visit was discovered."

This was said with the astuteness that was hers, and taking her thin fingers from her face, she watched Gabrielle. The Legate had not in fact been observed. But if she could get his visit admitted and confirm the rumour, then she would not have come in vain, and her life would be safe.

But Gabrielle answered: " The Legate? I have not seen him since the summer."

Liar, thought Sagonne. The Duchess d'Ordure should go to her death, she resolved, in belated anger at herself for the blunder she had made. She departed with all the more display of feeling, and remorse, for which this time she gave reasons. She could not have done so at the outset, when it was sincere.

" I have always loved you, madame. It was my affection that so confused me that I had to act as though I hated you."

She then launched on very airy explanations, still with the same distraught air, and as she was speaking, they reached the secret door by which the visitor was to be dismissed. Here Gabrielle said:

"Madame, you may be reassured. The secret of your visit today I shall carry with me to my grave."

At this, Sagonne swallowed; first because her purpose had been recognized, and then at the singular simplicity with which a person so threatened spoke of her grave, in a tone neither of elegy nor of lamentation.

Absorbed in meditations, Sagonne stumbled, and she had to jump over the threshold.

But Gabrielle sent for Monsieur de Frontenac, the King's old comrade; he had the honour to command the small bodyguard. And she said to him bluntly:

"Where is the man at this hour?"

"Two hours from here. But he will enter the city tomorrow evening. Madame, say the word and I'll take him this very night."

"Wait," said Gabrielle. But the soldier protested:

"It is not wise to wait longer. We have not been so hot on the track of any other of the King's assassins. This man has been followed step by step since he crossed the frontier. We could have taken him ten times; a Fleming, unmistakable in any disguise."

"And how would you have convicted him? He must be taken in the courtyard of the Louvre, when the people are assembled; the King will be among them, and I with him."

"Our only proof," objected Frontenac, "will be his long knife. And the turmoil of a crowd offers just the chance to draw it."

"When you arrest him," pursued Gabrielle undeterred, "here is a writing that you must secrete on his person. The Legate in Brussels gave him his orders by word of mouth. But he must have them on him in black and white if the King is to believe that anyone could dare to strike at him."

"No one would believe it," observed the veteran, to his own astonishment. "His Sacred Majesty, conqueror and great King.

But whether or not the King conceives himself inviolable and secure, keep your eyes open, madame."

This was the affair which had occupied Gabrielle to the neglect of her own interests. The King and the Duchess of Beaufort rode, just before midday, across the Louvre bridge — not their usual route, but one of them wanted to see what was afoot, and the other knew. Passing under the archway, they turned into the old courtyard, known as the well-shaft, where lay the offices of the court. People who had business could resort there unhindered by the guards. As the Duchess appeared, some of the mob dashed in her direction, shouting maledictions they had learned by rote. As she turned her horse and left the King alone, they soon fell back, leaving one solitary figure, who was easily caught as he drew his knife five paces from the King.

" Sire," said Monsieur de Frontenac, " this time we owe your life to the Duchess alone." The King's old comrade was in high excitement. A courtier would not have betrayed himself so far. The King dismounted. Pale with anger, he ran towards the guard under the archway, where his beloved, with her clothes torn, was with difficulty protected by the soldiers against her assailants. He ordered the foremost to be hanged.

" Sire," said Gabrielle, " in gratitude for your safety I plead for these men's lives; they have been suborned, your people love you."

Henri did not answer. He wasted no time over words of cheer or thanks. " To horse, madame! " Nor did he lift Gabrielle into the saddle. He trotted beside her over the bridge and through the outer gate. The guards had been ordered to accompany him in full strength, but though they dashed after them, the two riders were soon far ahead; only Monsieur de Frontenac, who was mounted, kept his horse close against the other two and rode with sword drawn.

They did not make straight for the Duchess's house; the King led the way through populous streets, at a still faster pace, heedless of the people — who had to leap off the raised centre of the roadways. The driver of a cart who did not promptly pull aside got a smart blow from the officer, who thundered: "Make way for the King!" The mob saw that the King was pale with passion and wondered what had happened. The women observed the Duchess of Beaufort's torn clothes, and the rumour sped from ear to ear, more swiftly than a King could ride.

Behind him, when he had passed, one said to another: "He is making off with her, because someone tried to kill him for this adultery."

"And she with him," was the prompt retort.

"A paltry end for a King who has been called great."

But, of the women, some said: "He loves her." Others, older, bowed and wrinkled with the struggle for bread, their hands gnarled with toil, said: "You are too petty to understand."

The lads threw out their chests and said: "He will have his will in the end; we should all do as he has done."

A priest repeated at several places: "But the Duchess did more today." So saying, the priest nodded meaningly, and each time disappeared before he could be questioned. The Papal Legate had impressed on him that he must remain unknown.

Such utterances brought no silence, nor any pause for thought. But a mob can change its mood while the uproar is at its height. When the King, his lady, and the officer, instead of riding out of harm's way or summoning help, rode back down the same street, there was no more talk of flight. The crowd surged round them, and one or two actually seized the reins of the two foremost horses, which were now walking; and in such a fashion the people accompanied their King and the lady whom they wanted for their Queen to the great new gateway of the Louvre.

Monsieur de Frontenac had sheathed his weapon when he heard the altered voices, and looked into the eyes of those near by. They were moist and bright, mirroring the chivalrous feeling of a mob. And in a little while chivalry would become indignation, which the King himself did much to rouse by crying: "To the Duchess's house, friends all!"

Again he made a detour. From the doors of the workshops all manner of craftsmen ran out and for a moment stood open-mouthed, wondering if this was some pious celebration. But from the King's anger and the torn dress of the lady at his side they could guess enough. Here were heard the first maledictions against Gabrielle's murderers. When they reached her ears she swayed in the saddle. Henri lifted her down and led her into her house.

From beneath her windows rose sounds of confused shouting, and she thrust her fingers into her ears. If her murderers were abused, they were indeed her murderers. The ignorant mob thought she, and not her lord, was to be the victim. This was the beginning of the end, and amid much that was mysterious, it was the first public clamour that her life was imperilled.

"Your murderers, madame? The fellow meant to murder me; I am used to such attempts."

He sent his guards to clear the court. When he came back, Gabrielle had left the room. He looked for her and came to her locked bedroom, usually hers and his, now locked; nor was the door opened.

"Answer!"

Came sounds of choking, into a handkerchief. Or was she laughing? He hoped she was sobbing. He did not recognize that laughter, which but for the muffling handkerchief would have sounded almost strident.

"One thing I would know," he said through the door. "Who told you of the Fleming's arrival?"

"Guess," she said in her chilliest voice within, and slammed a door.

This she did merely for effect, to induce him to go. As his footsteps receded, she longed to fetch him back again; but she fell on the bed, buried her face in the pillows, and this, and her recollections, brought her beloved so vividly to mind that she began to talk to him.

"Sire, O my good lord, these are very evil days."

Tears came at last. After hours of weeping she found herself on the damp pillow alone. She thought that he too must certainly have locked a door behind him, rejecting all the homage and congratulations — and were he not lying like her, prostrate, he would be striding up and down, stopping now and then to listen, until he caught the tinkle of a little bell, pealing very busily. " Beloved! It is pealing for us both! "

No, he could not hear in his imagination the pealing of the passing-bell. There had been no one like Sagonne to visit him. And the Legate, too — whom had he warned? Not him, at the hour when Malvezzi sent the Fleming forth from Brussels. How came it that the Legate of the Pope, against all natural presumption, wanted to keep the King alive? " I cannot tell," said Gabrielle. She got up and fell into distracted meditation.

There must be something afoot between those two, not rightly known to the King himself. For the Legate had not warned him, but her, and had also enjoined her to say nothing to her lord. It was for him to guess the truth. And that forged letter. He had pulled it out of the murderer's doublet, knew it for a forgery, and therefore the more informing. He would gather that this time much care and courage had gone to the saving of his life. He would no longer ask what they meant by talking of her murderers.

They would no longer ask foolish questions. Alas, how blinded he was by his own greatness! Thus he had stood upon his throne, unseeing, in the radiance of his own majesty. She saved his life from those who aimed at hers. They attacked her on his account, and him on hers. They were to die together, or she was to die alone. Not he without her, that was not intended. They had longed to live the same life, side by side and never parted, but now they were to die two deaths, and they were in competition which should die first.

Her Aunt Sourdis was announced, and was welcome, for Gabrielle was alarmed by her own solitude and on the point of taking refuge where she longed to be, but where she must not go.

Madame de Sourdis embraced her despairing niece, which she seldom did, but joy had set her almost beside herself.

" You saved the King's life. Now he can do no other, we shall mount the throne at once."

Her newly dyed hair was ablaze, and she waved her whitened arms. Keen-eyed as she was, it escaped her for some minutes that her exultation was not shared.

" The people led your horse by the reins. The people are on our side," cried Madame de Sourdis. " The court are beaten," she cried more shrilly still. " The people's will is God's will."

" Not so loud! " pleaded Gabrielle. " He would not be pleased if he could hear you."

" Madame, are you out of your senses? " asked her aunt. " How should he not be glad to owe you his life? "

Gabrielle was silent. She would not indeed have spoken had she herself seen more clearly into the purport of events. She must not put constraint on him, she felt. He had not two lives, though hers was his.

When the excited lady pressed her, Gabrielle at last observed that the King's life had often been saved, and by many others, always assuming that he did not know how to look after it himself. Monsieur de Frontenac had that time caught his second or third murderer. Another rescuer was Monsieur d'Aubigné, as was Chicot, called the Fool. " But my lord rewarded none of them as he did his handmaiden," said Gabrielle d'Estrées, and to Dame Sourdis's amazement she dropped on her knees, faced into a corner of the room, and silently addressed the Virgin on a pedestal.

The aunt grew impatient and departed with mutterings of disgust. If the silly wench had not grown sillier every day, she would have held fast to her Protestants and induced them to raise a revolt in favour of a Queen from the French nobility.

" Madame, most beloved Lady," prayed Gabrielle, " you know my heart, how it was destroyed in the beginning, and you alone can salve my pride. My beloved lord displayed me to the people in my torn clothes, a much greater reward than I deserved. Madame, grant me his life."

A plea for her own life was therein included — not expressly, but Gabrielle was sure she would be understood, and there ended.

GABRIELLE: ABANDONED

Henri let the whole next day pass and did not see her. In the evening she received his letter. " My lovely angel," he wrote from the Louvre, "you believe it is a fine thing to be King, but I am often sadder and more sick at heart than the least of my subjects. The beggar beneath my windows is less to be pitied than I. Some are Catholics, and they say I smell of Huguenotry. The others are Protestants, and they say I betray them and am more Papal than the Pope. I can only say that from my heart I am a Frenchman, and I love you."

In this she read the deep foundations of his melancholy, his fettered will; compared with him, even the beggar was free. And the meaning was that they could not come together. But she was not thereby discouraged. His lamentations gave her confidence and strength.

Suddenly the second murderer appeared. No one had tracked him on his way, he had gone about his business undisturbed — the King himself discovered him and grabbed him by the arm. The King was extremely alert, as he alone realized why these men had been sent against him and that the second would follow close upon the first. Moreover, the first was a Dominican from Flanders; the second, a Capucin, came from Lorraine. Cowled monks, both of them. Spain or Rome, the House of Lorraine or Habsburg, there was no true friendship between them; but on this one matter they were agreed that it would be better that the King of France should die.

The subjects of the Emperor, friend or foe, and irrespective of their faith, were overrun by Spaniards, or those that called themselves such; and they were stripped, spitted, impaled, roasted, and hanged on roadside trees. These were the preliminaries of a vast enterprise, as yet unorganized, and no one called it war; why use so formidable a word? But the attacker, with war still undeclared, occupied the passages of the Rhine in the direction of Cleve.

King Henri's regiments marched forthwith. He had built good roads for them, and it was no mere wooden discipline that inspired his now diminished army; each soldier knew and trusted his King. That was the reason why, whenever the King's troops advanced, the enemy promptly fled. Soldiers cannot endure leaders they despise; they cease to respect themselves, and in a

life of cruelty and licence they look no further than to escape
scatheless.

The attacker calculated that the King's regiments would have
lost their nerve and energy; but he himself must fall. As murder
had failed, war too was given up, if so be that the word had been
mentioned. King Henri was no longer in a condition to depart
to the Rhine himself, though he longed for battle as he had never
done. In the first place, a King of his sort is safer with the armies
than behind all the guards in the Louvre. In battle he could
forget the shame his murderers had brought upon him — as
though he were an uneasy upstart who could always be kept in
fear of his life. He was a Prince of the Blood and would make
them remember the King of Navarre.

Secondly, he had meant to spare the first of the two murderers:
he must not provoke Rome! Now both of them had been condemned together and executed. He was also threatening a suit
against Madame Marguerite of Valois, for adultery. She at once
gave in, and Rome realized that the King was cured of melancholy. Nothing had any effect, neither excommunication nor
fatherly advice, when Henri began to show his spirit once again.
The Royal Parliament had as yet carefully ignored the Edict of
Nantes, which had not come into force. So Henri made his
pronouncement.

He addressed the jurists, between whom and himself there had
been a good deal of regard. " In these days there is preaching of
revolt, and barricades may soon be seen; you, gentlemen of the
Robe, have in the meantime come to fortune; and lie on soft
beds in your own houses instead of in prison and on straw. You
have hence forgotten which side of the barricade is yours, by dispensation and by duty. But if these disquieting indications are
again observed, take warning. You mean little to me, but much
to many. It is long since I played cards with the Duke of Guise,
and drops of blood that could not be stanched oozed from the
cards twice and thrice — was I to be the victim, or were you?
Not I."

Thus he began, but he had summoned them into his cabinet
that they might feel the proximity of power and tremble. " War

against the Religion, that is what you want. Barricades! Mine is on the Rhine; I'll send you there, to walk in your long red robes, each with a musket on his shoulder." This they would not have taken seriously; but he also swore he would fill their offices twice and three times over. Their income would be thus reduced by a half and two thirds, a prospect that touched them more nearly than his threat to behead the agitators.

The Edict was registered by the Parliament. Rome made no protest.

His energy recovered, he married his sister to the Duke of Bar. Madame, the King's sister, a Protestant; the husband to order, a Catholic. Henri sent for the Archbishop of Rouen, who was his own brother — a bastard, but no matter. In the King's cabinet, almost before she knew what had happened, she was married.

The Duke promptly took his leave, nor did it escape the Bishop that his company was no longer wanted. Brother and sister confronted each other alone. And Catherine said:

" Sire, I admire you. How young you have remained! And so prompt in action."

He felt the dark irony, tinged by resignation.

" Madame, it had to be," she heard him say, in a formal tone that he had never used towards her in his life. " In the interest of the throne and my succession. The Count of Soissons must no longer stand in the way of my heir."

His sister's piteous face quivered, she bowed her head, and stole an upward glance at him; stern he was, no doubt, that he might not be less flattering still.

" But," she said, " since you are so prompt to act, you should have made another marriage in this place today."

He said nothing and turned away. She would have left him, but in an instant he was beside her and had clasped her in his arms. They held each other a long while, and neither cared to let the other go. He said nothing, nor asked her any questions. Felt the brother: " Well, we are older. Forgive me what I have had to take from you. It was for my glory that I asked your happiness — and not from any wish to seem decisive. I have let time pass while you grew old, Catherine — you, the living memory of our mother, who looks at me out of your face. So long as you survive, something has not perished."

Felt the sister: "Well, we have each other as in old days, though the end be at hand. Three times has death struck at you, though you have evaded him, both in sickness and in murder, thanks to your experience; now let it be enough. Brother, give up the lovely Gabrielle, who will cost you your life. We have had time enough to face our fates. But you are still young, your inner constancy has stood out against the years, and nothing can really pierce your guard. You cannot wither, you must break. Shall I, weary as I am, still be there when you come to lie in state, with the cross in your folded hands?"

He felt her trembling against his chest. He bent his head back, gazed into her face, and she into his. Dry-eyed, both of them. ("Where are your tears? Where is the time when we quarrelled and were reconciled, when we were kind or cruel, and tears and laughter came so easily?")

The charming Gabrielle began to grow capricious. Though she was not ailing, she shut her door for a whole week; she even barred the secret passage from her house to the Louvre. Henri sent her the page Sablé to ask her commands. Her reply was that she was busy with her astrologers and that they had given her a headache. Young Guillaume dropped on one knee and asked for a word in private. Enough, she said with brisk impatience, and dismissed him. At that time she was absorbed in her soothsayers.

Henri feared the influence of such people. He said: "They go on lying, until in the end they come upon the truth." With such an opinion of them he could scarcely have come into their company; so he asked Madame, his sister, to go instead. She went by the secret passage, knocked at the far end of it until the door was opened, and stepped softly into a room from which came voices. In the light of a single taper sat an astronomer, a woman with a pack of cards, and a third who was reading Gabrielle's hand. The poor beauty had delivered herself up to the three adepts and listened helplessly to their pronouncements, groaning from time to time. A flush of pity came over Catherine. " What will be the end of us? " — words that had been often in her mind of late; and they applied too aptly to the woman whom she had reckoned happy.

The three adepts were each in their appropriate array; but whether in cloak and peaked cap, or masked, or in the sober habiliment of a physician, they could give no clear sign nor picture of what was to come; their message was of doubt and fear, until their victim groaned aloud. The poor soul knew no book but her prayer-book; she recoiled at these heaped folios, and her horoscope revealed nothing except that she would be married only once. Did the stars mean that she had already been married? A marriage that had never been consummated and had been declared invalid? But from the reading of her hand it appeared that she would die young and not fulfil her destiny — if she had another child. She snatched her hand away and closed it convulsively. In vain; at that moment the masked lady swept her cards off the table on to the floor. Gabrielle fled.

She was caught by Madame and led into the farthest room; and Catherine turned the keys in all doors on the way.

" My sweet friend, I am all the more sure you will achieve your end," said Catherine, really wishing that she might.

" My constellations," said Gabrielle in a toneless whisper, " and the lines in my hand, are against it; apart from the cards."

" But the King's will? " interposed her friend.

Gabrielle, almost inaudibly: " It cannot help me now."

Madame, the King's sister: " You are being duped. I respect all the mysteries of heaven, but three soothsayers, each envious of the others, do not tell the same story, unless they have been suborned."

Gabrielle, sobbing bitterly: " But they spoke the truth. The child that is to prevent me from fulfilling my destiny — I bear it in my body."

Then she clutched her friend's shoulder and wailed: " Tell no one! "

Catherine kissed her. " All will go well with you now," she assured her with an affectionate laugh.

Gabrielle did not believe her: " The child is my fate," she said, and was not to be moved. After a while Catherine advised her not to close her doors against young Sablé any longer, but to listen to what he had in mind. He was a bold and loyal lad.

" He can do nothing for me."

" He made your song, sweet Gabrielle. They sing it all over the kingdom. What if he went and brought them here? "

" Whom, and wherefore? To sing that song? Hatred would but shout the louder."

At last Gabrielle promised to do what Madame asked. After her talk with the page, she released him from duty in the King's name, and Guillaume rode in haste homewards to his province of Touraine and the Loire country.

In the meantime Gabrielle would gladly have shut herself into a fortress and summoned help from without, so acute was now her fear, and her anger, too, at the passage of events which reached her ears.

The new Chancellor was her creature; she had replaced old Cheverny, who could be retained no longer in spite of his relations with Dame Sourdis, by a certain Monsieur de Sillery. She had to use all her credit with the King, for by this measure she had at her disposition in his inner Council one man against two: Villeroy and Sully.

The King tried to heal the breach. When Madame told him of his beloved's condition and begged him to comfort her, his feelings overcame him. He made all haste to repeat his vows in her presence — and this time he brought a ring with him. A marvellous ring, which the Bishop of Chartres had put on the King's finger at his coronation, when espousing Henri to France. " Sire, what are you doing? " said Gabrielle. And to her alarm she said more than she should have done. " My stars reveal that your gift will bring me misfortune," she faltered. And Henri answered:

" My dearest love. We could never bring misfortune on each other. My star is also yours, and is called France."

Therewith the ring, so heavy with jewels and with fate, actually slid from his finger on to hers. But she stifled a cry; the ring burned her; she shook her hand, and it dropped to the floor.

Henri saw that she had lost her former strength and resolution. He ascribed this to her condition. His own hesitation —
but why did he hesitate? There was no visible reason except the
finances of his kingdom, the vast sum of money that he owed
the Grand Duke of Tuscany. Who was the right man to take
into his confidence? He sent for Rosny. That admirable servant
was surely too loyal and too sensible not to have forgotten by
now his quarrel with the Duchess of Beaufort. Or if not forgotten, that dispute, futile and repellent as it was, must certainly
have set that cool head thinking. He would be more amenable
than before, not that his heart would have been softened; but
duty demanded of Monsieur de Rosny that he should ease the
King's anxieties instead of making them more burdensome.

Henri, himself not knowing why, approached that interview
almost with shame. Cautiously, and after a few vague observations, he touched upon his plans for marriage, as though they
were not his own, but needful in the interests of the State. The
matter was made more urgent by the Pope himself, who seemed
at last ready to dissolve his first marriage. " If I could have my
way," said Henri, in self-excuse, " my future Queen would
possess all the seven cardinal virtues, together with beauty, dignity, good humour, wit, high birth, fertility, and great domains.
But such a lady is not often born," he said, in hopes of a word
of approbation. But none came.

" Let us consider them together," said Henri — but he had to
go through the list of the princesses, Spanish, German, and of
his own House, alone. Each offered but a few of the seven virtues, and the Protestants did not come into question. The Duke
of Florence was indeed said to possess a very pretty niece, with
a fresh complexion and fair hair. " But she, after all, is of the
race of old Queen Catherine, who did so much hurt to this kingdom and to me."

Henri was through the worst part of the encounter. It was
now the turn of the admirable servant, who truly surprised his
master. He made no objection. In plain conflict with his own

character, he put forward the view that neither wealth nor royal descent was indispensable. The King needed a wife that pleased him and would bear him children. He had better proclaim throughout the kingdom that all fathers of pretty, well-grown daughters of seventeen to twenty years old should bring them to the capital.

Seventeen to twenty — Gabrielle would never be that again. Henri could not but observe that Rosny's assent and compliance were overdone as a warning to his master. He had presented the King's wishes in the semblance of a fairy-tale: fathers who were to bring their daughters from the provinces for selection; the maidens well guarded in a house where the King could feast his eyes on them. And when he had duly inspected them and had made himself acquainted with their most intimate charms, he would then be assured which would bear him the best sons. "Although," added Rosny, thereby passing from the realm of irony and fairy-tale to the pomposity that became him best, "although high personages and eminent princes have begotten very feeble children, as can be shown by many instances." These he recounted on his fingers: first, fabled names from ancient legends; then Persian kings, Roman emperors, omitting none, and finishing with Charlemagne.

Schoolboy knowledge — what a commonplace mind the man had! Henri wondered why he had listened to him.

"Let us not dissemble," he said curtly. "You know whom I mean. But I must not be taken as saying that I intend to marry her." Henri made this proviso to counter any further opposition. "I command you to speak freely and tell me the truth as man to man."

The Minister could do no other than point out plainly to his master that his relations with the Duchess of Beaufort were generally disapproved. Need he repeat it all? The King himself would be ashamed, when no longer immersed in an infatuation. Words which were justified by the freedom with which he had been told to speak. And he went on: "Your succession will be disputed. Why, your own two sons will be at odds about it. The first sprang from a double adultery, the other from a single one. I say nothing of those that you may later get in wedlock; they will regard themselves as your only rightful sons."

Rosny, now called Sully, allowed himself to adopt an indulgent tone that became painfully like patronage.

"I would have you consider this at leisure before I say more."

"You have already said enough," said Henri ungraciously, and dismissed the man.

The King liked to be told what passed for truth. He heard much that was various and interesting, which displayed the minds of men, and was, from one side, always right. It was never the one and veritable truth. How could he tell? And yet from this conversation there remained a sense that his feelings had been hurt, and not because a King had had to endure the assurance that the time would come when he would be ashamed of himself. In the course of a long life a man is ashamed of many deeds and scenes that looked none so ill at the time. If only his dearest treasure were not the object of so many of these so-called truths! He bore a grudge against her in his heart and knew even less than ever how this must end.

Gabrielle, who did know, strove violently against the final issue. In her good times she had calmly watched the approach of destiny, or if she resisted, she was never perturbed. Now there was need of haste, and every evening in their bedchamber she grew more insistent in demanding her right, which she would never otherwise have mentioned: the right to exalt her, which she alone had given to her lord. Charming Gabrielle made nothing of herself; nature and her fortunes had done that. Poor Gabrielle now began to bring her beauty into battle. She reminded the King of the bliss that she had brought him, a bliss that had once been as rich as growing corn.

When, on these evenings, she pointed to her body and praised its present glories, for which he ought to marry her — each time both, in their hearts, were horror-struck. He, at her transformation; she, because she had appealed to the child, which really was evidence against her; of that, the stars and lines in her hand permitted no doubt. If her life was dear to her, all she could now do was to abandon her purpose; she needed no stars to tell her that. Despite her knowledge and her will, she yielded to an evil longing to see the blow fall — and she gasped with fear, because it was against reason and her own self-preservation.

Henri caressed the agonized creature. His own resentment was forgotten, her own sick hatred, if she had hated her beloved in those hours, melted into tears, and they made each other happy. Pleasure, passion, fondness, convinced the beloved and the King himself that here was still the same ring, fused from the pleasures of the senses and the heart. It was a very different ring that had stung her as it slipped from her hand on to his and dropped on to the floor.

They rode out hunting again together. Henri rarely left her side. He sensed her fear, and had vague fears for her himself, against which measures could be taken. Once, as dusk was falling, they were coming back with only two noblemen in attendance, Frontenac and Agrippa d'Aubigné. These four reached the city on the left bank of the river, by the Quai Malaquais, some distance from the old bridges. The work on the new bridge which Henri was building had been held up by all the great doings in France; it had not been started again until that year, and the river had to be crossed by ferry. Yonder was the boat, and a sullen ferryman, who neither looked at his passengers nor recognized them. And the King, who liked to get the truth from everyone, said:

" What do you think of the peace that the King has made? "

The Ferryman: " What do I care about such matters as peace, when taxes are clapped on everything, even on this wretched boat? How is a man to get a living? "

The King: " But has not the King set the taxes in order? "

The Boatman: " The King may mean well, but there's a dame he keeps, who is always needing new clothes and all sorts of flummery; and who pays for that, eh? We do. She might at least be faithful to him, but they say she leads him a pretty dance."

The King burst into a roar of laughter. The Duchess of Beaufort was wearing a great cloak, with a hood that covered her whole face. The boat put in to shore, the two noblemen sprang out and handed the lady out. The King mounted the bank last of all. The boatman as he pushed off shouted after them: " I say it and I mean it! " The man stood, a raw-boned figure, bent over his oar, and did not turn his head. The Duchess said loudly to the King, so that the gentlemen and the ferryman too could hear:

" Let that man be hanged! "

There was only one who was really shocked to hear her speak so, and that was Agrippa d'Aubigné. Henri was familiar with his beloved's now unbalanced temper. Only a little while ago she had baffled the first of his two murderers, at the risk of her own life, and then asked that the man's life might be spared. And he said softly:

" Let the poor devil go. He is soured by misery. I'll see that he pays no more dues on his boat; and he will call down blessings on both of us every day of his life."

A few paces farther on, Gabrielle threw her hood back and said in a voice that hovered between bitterness and pain:

" The man was bribed. The purpose is to show you that I am hated. Sire, when, after the attack upon your sacred person, both our horses were led by the reins, your people did not hate me then. In the courtyard afterwards, and beneath my windows, do you know the shouts that reached my ears? They did not hate me."

" Madame, there is no question of hatred," said Henri. He laid an arm round her, and beneath the loose cloak he could feel her whole body atremble.

" You never made enemies. You were kind, and you made me kinder too. I forgave my old friend Mornay his Tractate against the Mass because you spoke for him. And my Agrippa, when his tongue broke loose — I took him back into favour at your pleading. I love you; be of good courage."

The wind blew cold; Henri drew his cloak more closely about him. Into the kerchief that muffled her whispers she wailed:

" Why am I hated? I do not want to die."

They had reached Gabrielle's house, but she recoiled.

" Sire! " she cried. " My beloved lord! " she cried. " Let us mount once more. You shall see that your people love me."

At this point Agrippa had to break his shocked silence. Was there anyone who did not know what was afoot? Each of them had heard a sound or caught a glimpse. All guessed the truth save only the King.

"Listen to me, Sire," said Agrippa. "Madame, pardon what I have to say."

Henri did not recognize his fighting-cock. This was an Agrippa ill at east and babbling like a criminal caught red-handed.

"You should have seen a throng of people from the country in your capital today. Crowds gathered before the Louvre, crying out that you should know your people's will — that you were to take the risk, and give them a Queen of their own blood."

"Why do I not see my people?" asked Henri. "Whence have they come?" he asked more eagerly.

Agrippa: "From the Loire."

Henri: "I remember. The voyage. And a peasant who cried to me from the shore that they would guard the Queen as surely as myself. I did not send for them. They are not here. What has happened?"

Agrippa: "When they reached the Arsenal and were about to enter the city, Monsieur de Rosny sent troops to turn them back. Their leaders he arrested."

Henri: "The man who promised us his protection? I'll not have it!"

"They were led by someone else," muttered Agrippa — and looked round to see whether anyone was listening. But Frontenac's face remained unmoved; both had known too much, and been silent for too long. Wind, darkness, mystery, and four figures rigid where they stood. Who takes a step, who speaks a word?

Gabrielle: "It was Monsieur de Sablé. I sent him. He was unlucky in having to lead his men past the Arsenal. Sire, punish me, not him."

Henri did not answer. He ordered Frontenac to take the Duchess home. Agrippa accompanied him to the first guard-post, where he stopped. Henri was ahead, but he turned and said:

"I thank you, old friend."

A soldier swung a lantern, and Agrippa recognized on Henri's face all the agonies of conscience. It did not melt his mood. And he spoke in his old insolent tone:

"You thank me too late. Had I only spoken before the hour had struck! At the beginning there were some who were for merely banishing her, so that she could do no more harm. Now there is a vast conspiracy, in which none knows his fellow. But all are in it, and all will be accomplices; even I, and even you."

At this last word, most insolent of all, the stocky little man gave a mocking leap, bent into the attitude of salutation, with legs astraddle and drooping hat. Rightly viewed, it was he who dismissed the King.

Henri shut himself up. He must now calculate the sum, draw a line and write the total, as was someone's habit in the Arsenal. He had the good conscience that is secured by clear reckonings, and he needed none other. He could prove at any time that the peasants were advancing in revolt against the capital, and their leader was very properly jailed for being young and impudent. Alas, the King can be neither, or he would know what to do!

He had dashed through the room, stumbling into two great beakers, which overturned with a lingering metallic clang. Then, as the King groaned aloud, there stepped out of the shadows the tall form of his First Chamberlain, d'Armagnac. "Sire!" he began without leave asked, and in a voice very like the one which the King had lately heard. Agrippa, and now Armagnac, all his old friends had suddenly turned on him.

"What is it?"

"You must know the truth," said d'Armagnac firmly. "Then you will act as a great King should."

"With greatness I am well acquainted," said Henri. "Truth is what is lacking; shall I hear it from your lips?"

"Your physicians know it; your physicians, I say," said the King's veteran comrade, in a somewhat less imperious tone, but there were wry lines about his lips. "They told me."

" Why not me? " asked Henri, with a shrug of his shoulders. " Men like you take things with such solemnity. When I lay ill, they were all gathered about my bed, and my chief physician, La Rivière, told me what he thought it well I should know. Of course, anyone who has examined my habit of body knows something of the truth about me."

" Monsieur La Rivière had not the courage to tell you to your face," said Armagnac in a lower tone, and with eyes downcast.

Henri paled. " Quick! Does it concern the Duchess of Beaufort? "

" Yes." The old man tried to recover his high demeanour, but when he spoke it was in a voice that faltered.

" It seems that she cannot bear another child."

Henri had expected anything but this. " I have begotten it. She carries it within her."

Came the answer: " Her last. Since her illness there must be no more — so thinks Monsieur La Rivière."

The King was silent. Visions, thoughts, resolves whirled through his brain; Armagnac watched them. But as the confusion deepened, he grew the more sure of one, the last, that would not be denied and set a finish to the rest. It had happened, Armagnac saw. His mind was made up, he would never change it now. The woman who had borne his sons, and who must bear no more — he meant to marry her.

The First Chamberlain stepped aside; he knew his master would say nothing, for this was fate, and there was no more to be said on either side. Had he been asked for his advice, Armagnac would have gently suggested that Monsieur La Rivière might be in league with the Duchess of Beaufort. Or if not, he at any rate liked her and wanted to do her a kindness. He was also serving the King, as he understood the matter. And serving him very ill, thought Armagnac with suspicion. He was lying, the King could certainly have children; and the lie came too late. The King was now resolved. But for the same reason as his, the enemies of the Duchess would now set to work.

The old man, who had suddenly aged, with difficulty replaced the beakers that the King had overturned. The King believed in physicians. He did not believe in astrologers, but all the more firmly in physicians. And now they could help no more. Gabrielle was beyond their powers.

Treating of Conscience

The house of Zamet the financier stood silent and discreet, although it lay by the magnificent road that started at the Porte Saint-Antoine. That road of triumphs and processions broadened on the right into King Henri's Place Royale, which was still building. The house opposite turned its back upon the road, and was moreover hidden behind a high wall; to reach this strange abode it was necessary to turn aside down a narrow alley, and thence into a short cul-de-sac. It might be that the iron gate would open; and open it did to a visitor that early morning.

He made his way into a broad courtyard and surveyed the Italianate villa and its grounds with an appreciative eye. All the buildings were low, all the paths and terraces were graceful, airy, and inviting. A man could take his ease there, when the day was pleasant and the garden fragrant with flowers. The house, baths, stables, counting-house, and servants' quarters were agreeably distributed, and all laid out in appropriate fashion — " for, unlike the barbarians, we do not care for grandiose effects," thought the visitor.

He asked the porter whether his master had risen; and the answer was that no one knew. That earliest hour, after all the guests had gone and he had rested for a brief while, his master was accustomed to spend in his bedchamber at his desk, and it was not permitted to disturb him. Except in certain cases, observed the man, with an oddly obsequious air; for the visitor did not look wealthy. None the less he was promptly escorted to the house, though his escort walked on tiptoe. Inside he was received by a majordomo, who laid a finger to his lips in token of discretion; he preceded the mysterious visitor, and after a faint scratching on the wall, he set the invisible mechanism in action.

Sebastian Zamet was not sitting over his accounts, as might have been expected. The mysterious visitor had been somewhat prematurely introduced into the room, and the financier was discovered while still half-way through his prayers. At least, so it appeared, for he hurriedly rose from the floor in his bed-gown. The light of the breaking winter day contended with the glimmer of the candles.

" You have been up a long while. You look wearied," observed Messer Francesco Bonciani, agent of the Grand Duke of Tuscany.

" I was expecting you," said Shoemaker Zamet with a bow, much in the fashion of his majordomo. He had indeed not gone to bed at all; his mind was greatly disturbed, and his sole concern was that this should not be observed. But the political agent had taken his eyes off him and was looking round the luxurious bedchamber. The man had a feeling for beautiful things and took more pleasure in them than in the contemplation of his fellow-men. These he knew, and it was natural that a usurer of humble origin should say his prayers. Who should practise religion if not such people as he?

The visitor's gaze strayed from the carved rosewood bedposts to the damask hangings on the walls.

" There is some difference in this room," he remarked.

" You would like to breakfast," said Zamet quickly. " I will give orders." But before approaching the speaking-tube, he bent across to the candles and blew them out. The corner of the room was thus darkened, and Bonciani all the more promptly discovered the picture. " I knew it," said he.

" What, pray? " asked Zamet, while heartily regretting that he had forgotten to put away the picture. And the unwelcome guest said:

" You did well to blow out the lights. Colours like these shine by their own lustre, like diamonds."

He knew very well that neither precious stones nor mixtures of oil and coloured dust carry their own radiance in themselves. That, however, is the property of wealth. Homage to wealth, whether it be worthy of a powerful mind or not, Bonciani could not forbear to offer. He despised the wealthy and only respected the idea of wealth; that was his justification.

Zamet begged him to seat himself, and piled cushion after cushion into a chair, but Bonciani would not leave the picture. He guessed the painter's name from the qualities of the brush-work, and recognized too that this was a first sketch, which had been worked up afterwards. " It was certainly better in its early state. I would wager that the reproduction on a large scale, which such a barbarian would be sure to undertake, has lost even more of the original charm of inspiration. A genius like this has studied our Italian masters without grasping the main point. With all his efforts he hardly passes beyond the range of the senses. Flesh, high-toned and in abundance; but the realm of true perfection, which is of the spirit, remains closed to him."

" May I beg you to partake? " said Zamet, beside a laden table which had risen noiselessly from the floor.

Bonciani continued:

" None the less, in the beginning it was an inspiration. The King, erect upon his throne, as the embodiment of majesty, and beside him this large and luscious mistress. One could weep that it has been so mishandled. Think what any of our painters would have made of it! "

" He would have made nothing at all," replied Zamet, for the usurer did not like his possession belittled. " Not all artists now have the stuff of great ideas in them. And he managed to sell the large canvas to the King, and the sketch to me. Though indeed I made a higher offer than anyone else in Europe would have done."

Bonciani turned his head.

" I am in a position to pay you double for the account of the Grand Duke."

" My respect for His Highness is such that I would gladly present him with this insignificant object," said Zamet, laying a hand upon his heart, which was throbbing with anxiety. " Though the King would never forgive me if I did," he faltered.

The agent swung round and faced him. Of the man's scruples he took no account; nonchalantly he surveyed the figure before him, the sloping shoulders, the womanish hips, and the face to which the desire for gain had lent a certain firmness; but still a flat, Slav face. Not an inspiring sight, and Bonciani did not linger on it — while Zamet stared with round and bulging eyes at his disquieting guest. He felt that this gaunt but otherwise not unhandsome man in threadbare clothes was about to involve him in extreme embarrassment. The fact that he had been aware of this for some while made matters no easier. Suddenly Zamet burst into abject excuses; the fried oysters had grown cold.

" I will have some more fried."

" No," said Bonciani, " not for me. Though I will eat a few out of respect for your famous kitchen."

He sat down and made a show of breakfasting, but his lips were so sunken that he did not appear to be eating at all. Above the hollow cheeks, eyes and brow were set in a marked outward curve; it was hard to say whether the skull was bald in front or the forehead too high. Bonciani sat rigid, he never bent his head, and when Zamet leaned over his plate, a chill gaze lay mercilessly upon him. His guest was silent and let him chew — a mere reprieve, as the shoemaker well knew. With his mouth still full, he was profuse in his apologies that, as it was Friday, none but fish dishes were available — boned soles with mussels, in an eleborate sauce that was a secret. The King liked it for its tarragon flavour, which reminded him of his native Béarn.

Zamet made haste to fill his visitor's glass a second time, he having emptied his first glass without noticeable result. The sparkling wine should have warmed the blood, but that chill gaze was as chill as ever. Zamet was disgusted with him, a man of mean and meagre habit, whom the Grand Duke kept very ill supplied with money. Rich lords knew whom they must pay; and they need pay little to one who fasts of his own free will and prefers the use of the intellect to any rich possessions. Such men can be used for dangerous work that must be done in darkness, while the Prince's regular ambassador appears in full array, but is not entrusted with his master's weightiest affairs.

" Nothing more? " said Zamet, anxious to dispose of the repast as well as of the early visitor. But he already guessed that his attempt would be in vain. The guest began to talk.

"The only place where food is understood is Zamet's house," said he.

The host breathed again. "So they all say, Monsieur Bonciani, but remember the very moderate fare that is offered at the court."

"I do not go to court," observed the agent, who was steadily approaching his purpose. "I mentioned your kitchen because under certain circumstances even great affairs of State can be cleared up by way of the kitchen."

"Cleared up indeed," thought the financier, and his heart grew heavy, because he knew that fate must now take its course.

"People who say," began Bonciani, "that the life of other people is sacred to them are of two kinds. First, those to whom it really is sacred. These are fools, but they become dangerous when they publicly abuse strong men who act against their conscience or even dare to betray what has been decided and must be done."

This with a frightful look into the bulging eyes that faced him. Then he continued, with the suavity of a printed book:

"The second sort say that their conscience would always prevent their taking life, although they have often done so, and everyone knows it. Our sovereign, the Grand Duke, a wise and just ruler — "

Bonciani paused, and inclined his head in the direction of the door.

"Have no fear," said Zamet, growing gradually resigned to all that was to come, "I have none but French servants, who do not understand our speech."

The book continued:

"It is the duty of a Prince to have no conscience, except the conscience of power. My prince killed his brother and his brother's wife, as everyone knows and no one mentions, for he has thereby given proof of his moral dignity and strength. This is recognized by the mass of common and weak men who would never kill. Average men are so made that they will gladly endure to be ruled by murderers, and there is only apparent contradiction in the fact that they are, moreover, inclined to place faith in the murderer when he asserts his respect for life."

Bonciani emptied his second glass, but his sallow, pallid colour remained unaltered. Zamet had not understood every word of this learned allocution, but all the more clearly did he hear the footfall of destiny.

Raising a long waxen finger, the learned man proceeded:

"Only vast and visible lies are unresistingly believed. When a man has killed thirteen people by poison or the knife, he does not say that he has killed twelve, but that he has killed none at all. That will be accepted without dispute, assuming that he has the power to impose credulity on the people he controls. He must never use compulsion. They believe and are content."

This very philosophic agent was convinced that he was throwing his pearls before swine in expecting a man like Zamet to appreciate these pronouncements. He had in fact no respect for this usurer, as the man ought properly to be called; he had before his mind the idea of wealth, the greatness and stability of which are not determined by man. And yet, though the wealthy be inferior beings, it is unquestioned that their constellation exercises a secret attraction on the strong and splendid works and deeds that they can buy. More exactly conceived, the purchase price of beautiful and vital things is not money; it is rather the villainy of those who can pay for them. Art knows no conscience. Thought is conscienceless. Both live on the existence of a kind of man who, in idea, is without moral constraint, although the individual man of money may, in his weakness, kneel and pray. The conclusion being that a Zamet is necessary, in order that a Bonciani may exist.

While the philosopher thus clarified his views, which he did with singular ease, Zamet gathered all his considerable resources for a desperate attempt — which might not prove so desperate. After all, here was a poor vagabond spy, who could not have got among the great by his mere rascality alone. What profit did he get from these exaggerated convictions?

"Most excellent sir," pleaded Zamet, "I, like you, prize the loveliness of form, and I was entranced by what you said. For-give a man less polished than yourself if he does not reply to you in words. Permit me rather, as I am rich, to show you the treas-ures of my house. There are masterpieces of the goldsmith's art; and the mob of parasites who lounge and spy in my rooms by day and night have not a notion they exist. For you — the choic-est, and not only to look at, but to take away, whatever you shall please."

At this offer, which was meant as a bribe, the secret agent fixed his man with a cold eye. His smooth features, smoother than thought can leave a face, grew wrinkled and contorted — not suddenly, but so slowly that Zamet was for quite a while in doubt what would be the outcome. At last there stood before his very eyes the image of contempt; and contempt the like of which he had never seen before, often as he had met it in his life. Dumbfounded as he was, he could still think with rueful irony: " Sebastian, you are beaten." Thereupon he abandoned all resistance; with a wave of his hand he announced that he, as was indeed intended, was prepared to listen.

As a consequence, Bonciani treated his victim with that out-ward consideration which he had hitherto neglected; the differ-ence between the two men's outlook was unchanged.

" An important affair of State," he said, " is to be brought to a fortunate end by means of a kitchen. The choice has fallen upon you and upon your kitchen, and I congratulate you on the distinction."

" An undeserved favour," muttered the unhappy Zamet.

" The person," said Bonciani, dividing the word into two syl-lables, " who has so often and so gladly dined here, will take her last and final meal in this house."

" I obey. You are not to suppose that I thought to evade this honoured command. But it is my humble opinion, which will be of small import in the eyes of such a man as yourself — that the person in question will not achieve her aim in any case. So why — "

Zamet swallowed a word and went on: " Why set an evil dish before her? "

" A very good dish. A most palatable dish: not, perhaps, to the person that partakes of it, but certainly to the Grand Duke; and the King of France: and the whole of Christendom. The picture that I shall buy from you will soon be famous throughout Europe. That flesh, so insolently exposed by the side of Majesty, will convince the courts and the nations that the only salvation to be expected is when God puts forth His holy hand."

And Zamet gravely wondered that his cook's hand should be esteemed so holy. But perhaps he would be doing a good work? Still, there seemed no small prospect of coming to the wheel and the gallows for it. Well, it was too late now, he must show no more fear. The person to be feared was this visitor. He or his host. And Zamet wondered if he should call his people and have him put out of the way. But it was not a serious idea, and a sharp look from the other banished it.

" I obey," he gabbled. " I am glad to be thought worthy of this deed. But unfortunately I have no means of — shall I say? — attracting the said person."

" She will come of herself at the right hour," was the answer. Here the agent of fate produced a paper and read the news that he had received from the King's confessor, Benoît. Zamet, with his quick, practised eyes, had caught a glimpse of the paper before it was folded up again: it was blank. But even though it had been covered with script, what Bonciani read out had never been written on that paper. Such matters are not set down with names and seals; the pair had pledged their words without witness or proof. That blank paper convinced Zamet; he dismissed his last impulse to contest what had been decided.

As Bonciani flung the circular wrap that served him as a cloak several times about his person and departed, Zamet was still muttering protestations. At last the unbidden guest had gone, and Zamet stood rigid. Then he raised both arms above his head, uttered a deep groan, and tried to kneel — but abandoned the attempt and stood, stunned by the shock he had just received. His conscience spoke: " I, Sebastian Zamet, am to poison the King's mistress. And I shall do it too, because I am as cowardly as a shoemaker, and should otherwise be poisoned too."

In anxiety lest his absence might be noted, he left his bed-chamber and went about his usual business. At the back of his mind he kept on calculating, not merely sums of money. He weighed against each other the Grand Duke Ferdinand and his fearsome philosopher; King Henri and his most treasured possession. Whatever he did or did not do might equally destroy him. God alone could bring salvation, if He really did stretch out His holy hand: He would in that case certainly hold it over poor Zamet. The shoemaker shuddered as the inner voice called him poor, which he had not been for many years.

At this point the feelings of that man of money overmastered him. Though in a timorous whisper, he cried aloud to the Almighty to be merciful. His holy hand scarce needed aid from the money-lender to the court of France, who had there made his fortune and hoped to keep it by the King's good grace. And by favour of the Duchess of Beaufort, he added. She was always wanting money; he would calculate how much she owed him, and whether he could so involve her that she would never be able to meet his claims. Indeed, she must become Queen, to keep the total mounting up!

While he thus pondered, Zamet was sitting in his counting-house; money slid through his fingers, the clerks' pens scratched incessantly, and merchants came and went upon their business. Zamet bent over his money-bags, that no one might see that his eyes were wet. The thought of Gabrielle touched his heart.

Before his inner vision she bent over him once more in all her beauty, as she had really done that night when she asked six sacks of gold for the King's campaign. She had actually displayed her charms in familiar converse with Shoemaker Zamet, at a price. But he had then behaved like a nobleman, she had said so herself. To what end had she ennobled him, if he were now to put something in her soup? She would notice what she had eaten, and surely her last word would be to call him villain. No; he would not do it.

In the evening, in his crowded rooms, amid the music and the noise of the gamesters, Zamet thought otherwise; he was all for Tuscany and Habsburg, the powers with force behind them, and, what a man of business needed — security. Here the noblemen were mere paupers, they importuned him for their gaming debts, and even the Queen would never pay. She even treated him with contempt when he humbly approached with a reckoning, were it only the compound interest due. However, next day Sebastian Zamet drove to the Arsenal, to Monsieur de Sully.

The financier had coaches quite as splendid as the King's, but on this occasion he used a modest carriage belonging to his steward and took a devious way to escape notice. He sat with hands on his knees, feverishly turning over in his mind what he would say to the Minister, and then, without a pause, what the noble lord would reply. Zamet was determined to address him as " my noble lord " that day, although over their frequent business he was accustomed to speak as one man to another. He would say: " My noble lord, your affairs are in extreme peril, as are also mine. For it so happens that our interests in this matter are identical, which was not always so. The events now threatening unite the money-lender and the Minister."

And the Minister would say: " I know. What is happening is common knowledge. But it still consists of rumours. Where are the facts? Where can I intervene, assuming that I wish to do so? "

And Zamet would say: " You certainly will, when you have heard what visitor I received yesterday at break of day; I hope I shall never receive such another. Supposing this disaster happens, how do we then stand? I shall never see my money again, but you? Could anyone, with such a state of insecurity in the kingdom, advise my lord the Grand Duke to lay out any more capital here? You will object that the deed was done by his command. That is a lie of the agent; I know my sovereign. But if it should reach his ears, the main issue to him will be whether the greatest lady at the court may be certain of her life — and he will act accordingly. Will he be likely to send his niece here to suffer the same fate? Most certainly not. My noble lord, your business sagacity will guide your judgment, even though the unhappy lady may have given you cause for less friendly feelings."

Thereupon the Minister would answer with a wave of the hand: " Unfriendly feelings go for nothing. I am responsible.

In my sovereign's capital such questionable incidents must not occur, apart from their financial consequences. Monsieur Zamet, you have shown yourself both wise and bold, since it is clear that you have risked your life to inform me of this conspiracy. The man shall be watched."

Zamet, overcome with gratitude: " My noble lord."

The Minister: " Give me your hand, and call me not noble. I am no more so than you. It is noteworthy how in spite of traffic in money a man may grow steadily more noble. It must be destiny. The King will draw the right conclusion and ennoble you. On your escutcheon there shall be an angel with outspread wings, because you have saved a great lady and this kingdom from disaster."

To such heights did Zamet's imagination soar as he conceived the interview. The carriage having now arrived, the lackey sprang from the backboard and ran up to announce his master, as he had often done before. He came back much more slowly: Monsieur de Sully was not visible.

Had he ridden out? asked Zamet. No. Or had he a visitor? He was alone. Was he then visible for no one? No — that was not the message. It referred actually to Monsieur Zamet.

He did not understand — not yet. The vivid dreams of conscience that had accompanied him thither, still absorbed his mind. There were writing-materials in the carriage. Zamet hurriedly wrote that he was in sole possession of a State secret, and asked for an interview. The lackey ran back again. Suddenly there came a crash from above, someone plunged down the steps and landed at the bottom head first. Zamet asked who had done this, and was told: Monsieur de Sully in person. Then he understood and departed.

Rosny resumed his work as though the interruption had never taken place. But he could not maintain his composure. The man with the long, hollow back left his vast table and stood before a picture of a knight in armour: it was himself. The moment he moved, the knight's eyes followed him and watched him wherever he went. It was a known quality of the picture.

But that day, as he felt those eyes upon him, he flushed until his cheeks burned.

Should he fetch the shoemaker back? He would. Duty demanded that he should listen to the man. How could he face the King if Henri knew he had refused; how could he face him — afterwards? And suppose nothing happened? He was not one to waste any time on gossip. Unsupported gossip; for a man who traffics in matters of this kind takes good care to leave no trace behind him. One must not know such people. He could send soldiers against highway robbers — but he would do nothing to prevent this. He would become an accomplice if he called the informer back. And he refused to be an accomplice.

He would do nothing, he washed his hands of the affair. He had given his warning while there was yet time. He urged both him and her to do penance for their pleasures, which were displeasing in the sight of God. All that contravenes good order and good service is displeasing to Him. The service of the King before all else. It was his mission to maintain the King's service better than he did himself. He had already saved his life. She rewarded him with the King's disfavour, which had, in fact, heartened him to his task. All the worse for one who would not learn her lesson and depart, but wantonly involved herself in the ruin that she knew must come.

Too late, he could not help her. She had caught herself in her own net. She could only extricate herself with her own life. By no complicity of his! The Lord of Heaven saw into his heart. He dutifully submitted to what had been decreed by the Lord of Sabaoth!

This said, Rosny felt his conscience marvellously disburdened. He went back to his vast, littered writing-table, and, as he passed the portrait, boldly returned the knight's pursuing gaze.

THE PARTING

Gabrielle received the great news in a letter of the 24th of February 1599, in which Henri called her his sovereign lady. He had already bestowed many distinguished names upon her, and from the domain of power and rank he had borrowed many sorts of homage for his love. But not this homage; not this name.

She was overjoyed, and her joy made her silent. She did not answer, but felt no impatience, and the week was too short for her to examine every word of his brief letter and weigh its sense. " My lovely angel." It was not so long ago that her temper had been far from heavenly. And lovely — was she, with their fourth child in her womb? Well, her dear lord told her so. " There has never been so faithful a lover as I." That was plain truth, nor was it of set purpose that he was more faithful in the eighth year than in the first. It was the passage of the years that had united them.

Then she thought of time long past, of her own change of heart before she became wholly his possession; and how she had been hard and proud when she was a nobody. Here, at the zenith of her fortune, which was wholly the achievement of love, both his and hers, she took pleasure in curtsying to a poor or sick person when she passed one by.

The seven days passed equably and were, with her child in her womb, and her head filled with dreams, the best days in her life. On the 2nd of March her lord announced to his court that he meant to marry her about a week after Easter. When the day was at last set, Pope Clement had only the interval left for his delays and procrastinations. He passed several days in prayer, and proclaimed a solemn fast for all Rome — this in the middle of Carnival, for he had now to dissolve the marriage of the King of France and permit him to raise a daughter of his people to the throne.

The ring that had fallen to the floor had now been publicly placed by the King on the finger of his Queen. He added lavish wedding presents of gold plate, which did not indeed cost him any more than the ring, for they had been presented to him by the cities of Lyon and Bordeaux. The court did not fail to make this observation, nor others that were calculated to throw doubt on the seriousness of the occasion. But the Carnival, with its general celebrations, diverted the malice that had dogged her

every move; even the rumours and the omens, and the maledictions of the preachers, ceased during that respite.

Gabrielle herself had at the beginning no time to reflect, there
were so many preparations to be made for her great day. She
ordered a wedding dress of flesh-coloured velvet, the colour of
queens. It was embroidered with gold, sewn with silver thread,
and slashed with silk; it cost one thousand eight hundred crowns,
and remained in the workroom of the master who made it until
it was paid for. In her house her own tailor worked at the second dress of ceremony, which proved to be no less costly and
pleased her especially, having an H and G intertwined on the
broad Spanish sleeves. Eight and fifty diamonds, worth eleven
thousand crowns, were to be set in the gold sun-ornament for
the Queen's hair.

Then came the difficult choice of furniture for the Queen's
apartments in the Louvre. The furniture was designed, rejected,
and begun again; and in the end the chairs were like any others,
though covered in crimson silk. But they were the Queen's
chairs, and therefore to be admired; and they were displayed in
the house of Madame de Sourdis until the Queen's apartments
were properly occupied. In the meantime Gabrielle was already
living in the Louvre, but left it the moment after Henri had
gone forth, and by her secret passage.

This was now guarded by her pages, among them being young
Guillaume. One evening when she approached within hearing,
he gave her a strange warning. " Madame," said Monsieur de
Sablé, " when you wander as your habit is through your royal
palace, for God's sake avoid the little staircase in the northern
wing that leads to the uppermost chamber. You may easily come
upon a poisonous spider."

The very next day it happened that she was alone, and, she
knew not how, found her way to the forbidden stair. The throbbing of her heart would have restrained her, but she mounted the
crumbling, dusty steps. The uppermost room stood open, and
beneath the dim dormer window was a very old man bent over
a pile of folios; the secret books once more, from which adepts
could read destiny. Gabrielle stood bent over the threshold, but

moved no farther; she would gladly have evaded destiny, but she did not go. The aged man was only visible in half profile, but she could see that his face was black with wrinkles. He muttered, turned the pages, and scratched signs upon the wall. At length he summed up what he had found. He had a strangely resonant voice.

"Tell no one, Bizacasser. You alone upon earth know the secret of her fate. Not only that the King of France will never marry her; her eyes will never see the light of next Easter Day. But be silent, Bizacasser, a Florentine sage preserves his secret."

It cost Gabrielle an effort to reach the more populous parts of the palace. She had forthwith to receive various persons who wanted to speak with her and by no means expected all the favours that they in fact were granted. She was thinking to herself: "Did he hear me? I stumbled on the stairs; but they were thick with dust."

She refused to be afraid, she would believe no more in such deceivers. The light of next Easter Day — why, it was shining upon her now, and her great time no longer lay in the changes of the stars; it had begun. When she rose in the morning, great ladies handed her her shift; and this would soon be a privilege of duchesses alone. The Princesses of Lorraine were present at her levée. And Mademoiselle de Guise, most devoted of all, arranged her hair. At table the King's bodyguard stood behind her chair. By his order Monsieur de Frontenac took a double escort whenever she went out. What could possibly befall her?

This was her greatest time; her happiest? That had been when he wrote: "There has never been so faithful a lover as I." He had addressed her as "my lovely angel," and had called her his sovereign lady — during the space of one week.

The King now expressed his feelings in acts, which he carried out with promptitude and energy. He assured the future of the mother and the children against all imaginable perils. If he himself vanished from the scene, another should be there with the power to protect them; nor should there be any doubt that this would be to his advantage. Henri cast his eyes upon his Marshal Biron, son of a man whom he had loved, and he had bestowed that affection on the son. He promised him the Constable's sword, and the hand in marriage of Frances, Gabrielle's youngest sister. She was not, indeed, regarded as the daughter of old Monsieur d'Estrées, but as the offspring of her mother's intrigue with the Marquis d'Alègre, which in the event brought about much unpleasantness. Not only that Biron took offence. Antoine d'Estrées would have disowned Frances and stirred up trouble over a long forgotten adultery, had not the King paid.

Biron received new dignities and grants. Gabrielle's brother, a gallant soldier named Hannibal, and devoted to her, was to support the Marshal if there was any question of protecting the Queen or her son Cæsar's rights to the throne. Moreover the King planned a marriage between Hannibal and Mademoiselle de Guise, a now fading beauty and, in view of her past, not desired by princely suitors. But Gabrielle would thus be connected with the House of Lorraine. What more could be done to make her safe? The Royal princesses assured the King that they would support her cause. On her side, too, there was a ruling prince, the Duke of Savoy, who had been thought worthy to give his daughter's hand to the heir of the throne of France. The young Cæsar was indeed betrothed already, but in these changed circumstances a Mademoiselle de Mercœur was too far beneath him in rank. She was cheaply accommodated with the young Condé, an eleven-year-old Prince of the House of Bourbon, the only possible rival, in all human estimation, to the son of Gabrielle. The King even considered whether he should not make a priest of this possible competitor for the succession, a cardinal, and very rich — thus removing any anxiety for Gabrielle and his House.

In the meantime the dark prognostication of the Florentine mage also reached his ears; but it passed him by, leaving no impression. He acted; and if destiny could have been bidden to stand, he had foreseen everything. Two years later Biron was to betray him and die on the scaffold, a greater grief for the King than for the conspirator. And in two months more — where would Gabrielle be?

It was Mademoiselle de Guise who told her about a certain

soothsayer called Bizacasser, while she was plaiting her hair. Gabrielle listened with composure and repeated what Henri had told her about astrologers: they went on lying until they at last came upon the truth. Her fate had nothing in common with a monstrous old man who could not even now keep his lucubrations to himself. Her fate lay plain for all to see upon the strong hand of her lord. She was well guarded, for she was by his side, and wherever he went, she went also.

All this was well enough for the waking hours. But there were dreams. One night as she lay in the great bed of the Kings of France, her lord beside her, and about them all the walls of the Louvre, a vast fire advanced upon her and would have enveloped and consumed her. She awoke, and her cries also awoke the King, who had seen the same fire in his sleep and had been even more terrified by his impotence to help her. They both sat up and embraced. What they said, the comfort that they sought, the fear that shook them, all this was of less account. Behind it lay the horror that so utter an end must come upon them both. So much done, such care taken and provision made — the whole ingenious edifice of peace and security wrecked by a dream.

But in the morning no memory remained of that strange immolation. Henri told his sovereign lady, as he called her once again, that her condition was the cause of her unrest, which had now affected him too; they had better spend Lent in the country. So they journeyed with the whole court to Fontainebleau, where Gabrielle enjoyed those last serene and gracious weeks. Her lord never left her side, and there was no question that they should ever again in life be parted. Just this was what now threatened, but there must be no brooding on disaster; until it makes its entrance, it is forgotten. But then when it appears, it seems the more gigantic.

Father Benoît, a simple priest, had a cure of souls among the common people around Les Halles, before the King took him as his confessor. The King trusted a priest, who was accepted by the people, as being certainly without guile. Such was Father Benoît, and it was on the sole ground of spiritual discipline that he insisted that the King should spend the Holy Week alone, and as part of his penance he must in the meantime send the Duchess of Beaufort away. A man cannot do penance in his mistress's company, and the scandal, which was already widespread, would be much increased. The future Queen must set the example. Father Benoît, from the highest motives, would have her go to Paris and there fulfil her religious duties as publicly as possible.

Henri at first refused. He flatly asked the priest who had put the idea into his mind. The man protested loudly that he paid no heed to men, but was acting in accordance with his spiritual office, which Henri in the end thought was probable. Nor could he remember that Benoît had ever uttered a word to Gabrielle's hurt. He was not against Gabrielle, and he was certainly acting in good faith.

So Benoît thought; later on, after the event, he was to try to salve his conscience and regard his fateful step as uninfluenced. But who was it that told him that the bull appointing him bishop would never be issued — unless he prevented the King from receiving Communion in a state of mortal sin? Who? And how many? Had the Evil One planted this seed in the priest's mind — and what did he look like when he did so? He must have appeared in many elusive shapes, and used such sorcery that he left no trace behind. But one day Father Benoît was gradually to track down the Evil One — later on, after the event. And he was to fall sick from doing so, and beg the King to send him back to his market halls.

When Henri announced the inevitable, Gabrielle's serenity turned to uttermost terror. She had known it. Bizacasser would be right. Father Benoît was in the conspiracy, but her bitterest enemy, Rosny, was in control of everything, even of the stars. This new tone of limitless despair alarmed Henri. She flung herself weeping at his feet. He knelt down, clasped her in his arms, and most tenderly tried to comfort her in this distress that had fallen on them both and must be endured. " O my dear lord! " she wailed, " we shall never see each other again." " Be patient," he replied, " my arm is over you, wherever you may be. Who would dare to touch you? "

And he really thought no one would dare. Moreover, he

ascribed everything to her condition, not only her evil forebodings, but this fearful outburst of hysteria. He, too, found it hard not to rail against this duty so imposed. For the days that remained he saw her as an exhausted creature, all her senses, and especially her eyes, weakened by the weariness of her head, which seemed to be weighed down from morn until eve by an invisible helmet. And he prayed that this his dearest treasure and his sole possession might not be struck down by sickness.

The court was dismissed, each and all to their several parishes, there to do appropriate penance. The pair were left alone with those who were to accompany Gabrielle on her journey and be answerable for her safety to the King. On the 5th of April, Monday in Holy Week, the start was made, the Duchess of Beaufort in her litter, and her lord riding at her side. They rested by the way, and when darkness fell, they tried to dine, but could not. A little farther on they halted for the night, their last night, and the embrace that no longer made them one. Gabrielle turned away her head, aching as it was with the burden of that unseen helmet. She could not sleep; and indeed for some while, despite her exhaustion, she had had no sleep.

Next morning they reached the bank of the Seine, where a long slow-moving barge lay awaiting them, with horses that were to tow that precious burden slowly and smoothly down to Paris. Then followed urgent injunctions from the King to the ladies of the Duchess's household, to the Duke of Montbazon, Captain of his bodyguard, and to Monsieur de Varenne, Intendant of the Royal Posts. They were not to leave the Duchess for one instant; and they swore upon their heads they would not.

In the ultimate minute she clung to him with a strength that was more than hers. "We shall never see each other again — never — never." He very nearly spoke the word of deliverance and went back with her. But the lovely arms relaxed, and he loosed them gently from his neck while he kissed her on the lips. At last she grew resigned to her departure, commended the children to him, and he left the boat. The horses strained at the ropes, and the vessel began to glide down-stream. So long as they could see each other, she waved a beloved hand, while Henri stood with arm outstretched and swung his hat. When she had quite vanished, he dried his eyes; but the beloved image had already dissolved behind a veil of tears.

THE BLACK HEN

Bassompierre, who was a man of sociable habit, promptly produced a pack of cards. If the Duchess did not care for a game, he would do his best to entertain her with his conversation. This, too, failed, and Bassompierre, who continued to behave in a free and even droll fashion, bethought himself that this was a dangerous journey. Inquisitive by nature, he was better informed than most of his fellows. At the next opportunity he left the boat and went back to the King. He had only been deputed to accompany the lady for her entertainment. " Sire," said he, " you must know that Madame is in no way to be diverted from her longing for you, which possesses all her mind. But, above all, she is afraid " — this being a matter on which he had his own opinion, which he did not propose to tell the King. If that fear proved well founded, he — Bassompierre — had not been there. And it was well that this should be made quite clear to the King.

After many tedious hours the melancholy vessel put in at the Arsenal. The Duchess of Beaufort was awaited: her brother, her brother-in-law Marshal Balagny, the Guise ladies, among them the distinguished damsel who had so often plaited her hair, and others, were at the landing-stage. All remarked her sharpened features, her pallor, her reddened eyelids, but they told her how lovely she was looking and received her with much ceremony. The house of her sister, the Maréchale de Balagny, was near at hand; Gabrielle tried to get some rest there. But a number of visitors appeared and thronged the rooms, where Gabrielle wanted to be left alone. She rose. " Whither now? " she asked Monsieur de Varenne.

Now, Monsieur de Varenne was in much the same case as Father Benoît; he gave the best counsel, so far as he knew, and later on was never wholly to understand why it had been the worst. But after the event a little more was revealed to him than

to the unlucky priest. Varenne had always known something of
the agent Bonciani. Not that the man had ever himself bidden
him bring her hither. Intermediaries and go-betweens from a
source unnamed, who made contact with him — such there had
doubtless been, though he had not noticed them. Which went
to show that they were acquaintances of every day and had themselves no notion who had prompted them. When he commended the house to Gabrielle and told her that she would there
find rest and quiet, no face, no voice, came before his mind. The
insidious whispers to which he gave heed in commending the
house had not yet reached his consciousness. That came when
all was over. And Varenne had good grounds for keeping the
truth to himself, assuming that he was ever certain of it.

Gabrielle gave orders to be carried up to the house. Burdened
as she was with sleep, she was agitated and her head was awhirl
with feverish imaginings. This was the forbidden house that she
must not enter. Sagonne had warned her; not with the King, and
still less alone. Her Aunt Sourdis was not in Paris. Her household was scattered, all doing their penances. The King was doing penance; and she was not to be spared a sojourn in that house.
She had never thought to have willingly set foot in it, but she had
no choice and obeyed.

With her in the litter sat Mademoiselle de Guise, wearing
clothes like hers, as though she had been her sister. She had
rather faded features, and as her amorous career was now drawing
to a close, she set all her hopes on her marriage with Hannibal,
the brother of the future Queen. For the rest, she hated Gabrielle, though no more than she hated every woman who still laid
some claim to happiness. She was firmly resolved to accompany
the Duchess of Beaufort everywhere, especially as she was the
only Princess on the spot, and the King would expect it. On the
way she talked gossip and cared nothing that Gabrielle paid no
attention.

There were three persons anxiously awaiting that litter in the
place where it was now expected. The first was the master of
the house himself; the others were two conflicting elements and
hostile spirits. A few days before there had appeared in Zamet's

counting-house a creature whom he would ordinarily have had ejected: his ugliness was sinister, and plainly the expression of a villainous soul. But the old black object whispered a few words that caused the shoemaker to take him promptly into an empty room. When he entered he had been old and crippled; but when he was given a chair to sit on, he did not do like other people, but lay face downwards across the seat and swung himself head foremost under it, without touching the floor. This was done with astonishing agility, and in a trice the man was sitting in the chair, as though nothing had happened.

Zamet realized that his strange visitor was in no wise decrepit; rather, such suppleness of limb seemed to him of devilish origin. Fearsome words were then whispered into his ear. The anguished Zamet did not shrink from pointing to the man's black wrinkles and lumps on his forehead that looked very like horns. It would be impossible to disguise such deep-set marks as these. A face in which the black deed could be read beforehand hardly fitted a man to commit it under the eyes of all. But in regard to this the man reassured Zamet, or rather took his last hope away. He undertook, when the hour struck, to come forth as an angel of light. So saying, he limped away.

The third was the page Guillaume de Sablé; he had kept on the track of Bizacasser since that astrologer's first performances in the upper chamber under the roof of the Louvre. He could then have deprived that noxious enemy of his power to injure, but he had never discovered what in fact the danger was. Guillaume, too, possessed the art of disguise and could slip in and out as noiseless and unnoticed as a mouse. Bizacasser never observed that he was being followed by someone who watched his metamorphoses and was even present in the room of the agent Bonciani when they compounded the poison.

Shortly after Gabrielle's intended assassin had left the shoemaker, the page came in to him — and he, too, whispered no more than a few words, but Zamet shook with terror as he listened. He led the way into the same empty room, carefully locked the door, and clasped his hands over his chest in token of his innocence. Monsieur de Sablé eyed him narrowly and was thenceforward convinced that he had in Zamet no antagonist, but indeed an ally, though a timorous one. The lad possessed the freshness that reaches out to faith in this heart or in that. What man, he thought, who was not black with sin, could hate the lovely Gabrielle?

He asked the tax-farmer whether he was kindly disposed towards Gabrielle, and the latter answered yes, with a face that was damp with sweat. " I have been drawn into this, and it is the sorest trial of my life," he said. " It was not she who worked against me in the matter of the State debt — it was in truth Monsieur de Rosny, who puts everything upon her, because he is her enemy." Zamet clapped his hands to his forehead; he had forgotten that he was speaking to a young nobleman of eighteen years. Thereafter he tried to cover up his meaning, but Guillaume saw and understood.

" She is an adorable lady," he said, " and we will save her."

" Praised be Jesus," cried Zamet. " My lord, do me the favour to see my steward; he will see that you are suitably lodged for the day of this great visit. For the Devil will then be at his work."

" You may be very sure that I am no less a devil," retorted Guillaume. And as Zamet looked at the mole on his cheek, he left his protest unuttered: he too was an adept at disguise. And so they parted, not ill satisfied.

Now the expected day had come; the litter appeared, was set down on the stone pavement in the garden; and Shoemaker Zamet, radiant at the honour thus vouchsafed to him, bowed very low and almost kissed the ground. Monsieur de Montbazon, Captain of the bodyguard, disposed his men in various quarters. The two ladies, with Monsieur de Varenne, were escorted by their host. The lovely staircase and the great hall, where they used to dine and play — how gay the King was just before he set out for the war! How happy they had been! thought Gabrielle, recalling those past hours, in which, indeed, she had been very much afraid. But stay — should she enter the very room in which she had known such fear? An unfounded fear, as it then seemed; but now it appeared to be only too well founded. Her foot quavered; but she went in.

She rested until dinner-time. Mademoiselle de Guise never left her. Monsieur de Varenne posted guards at the door before he allowed himself to go off to his card party. He had found partners as rich as himself, though there were no ladies nor gentlemen of his own rank. The house was thronged with lesser persons in place of the absent courtiers. The news that the Duchess of Beaufort was in Zamet's house spread quickly through the capital. The new rich drove up in their coaches, the poorer nobility made their way on foot, shrinking against the walls to avoid being spattered with mud, and together they filled the financier's house to bursting. The former were glad, for their credit's sake, to lose money in this place, and the others were very ready to win it from them. And they were all equally eager to pay their respects to the future Queen.

Monsieur de Varenne was not to be disturbed, so they pestered the master of the house to admit them to the room. Distracted as Zamet was, this was more than he could endure; and he threatened to have them all ejected if they did not remain quietly at cards. His face was grey, he continually wiped his brow, and his fear for the life of his exalted guest drove him restlessly about the house. He himself saw to the arrival of various matters that had been ordered, among them a basket of poultry, from which a black hen escaped — and suddenly fluttered up the steps; but before it could get among the elegant assemblage, a kitchen boy ran out and caught it. The bird looked all the blacker against the brilliant white of the nimble youth's apparel, spotless as the festal day demanded, and the head of that nimble scullion was the head of an angel. While Zamet was contemplating the mystery, he felt someone touch him from behind.

"That is he," said his steward's voice. "Look carefully, and you will see that the skin of his face is artificial, he has made it from a pig's bladder and painted it those angel colours. Those blond and sunny locks have been stuck one by one on to his pate and sewn into the false skin. They are very cunningly curled round the bosses on his forehead. But anyone who knows the Devil is well aware that he has horns. By good fortune, I can see through him, but he still thinks that I really am your steward."

Zamet swung round upon his heels; another terror had banished the first; here was someone disguised as his own steward. Between the thick beard and the wig he could see two bright eyes in an aged visage. " Sablé," he murmured and groaned, " what will be the end of this? "

Guillaume the page bowed, as though his master had uttered a command. " It is my office to see to the soup and make sure that nothing is mixed with it that should not be." So saying, he departed with dignity, in the guise of the steward.

Zamet realized just in time that he could not follow him through the servants' corridor. He went back into his apartments, where he found the usual scene: a throng of gamesters, drinking and quarrelling over their stakes — it was hard to believe what was really happening that day. A great fire was crackling in the shining, open kitchen, round which was gathered a group of inquisitive people, who tried to seize on the financier from every side. When would the Duchess at last appear? She could surely do no less than dine in public, she owed that to her rank and to the company. A certain Madame de Martigues especially pressed her claim to serve the Duchess of Beaufort at table. There were unluckily no more distinguished members of her sex present, and Zamet had even to be glad that she, a notorious schemer, was available. Scarcely had he promised what she asked when it occurred to him that she might well be the poisoner. He shrieked out: " No! " looked with terror at the astonished faces round him, and plunged into the crowd.

The steward stood in the kitchen with his back to the open wall. He was covered on the side that led into the hall by sundry tall lackeys, who displayed their teeth and muscles to those who were not to be admitted. The model kitchen was full enough of servants, some of whom were lately engaged and unfamiliar; and purveyors were still coming in and out. There was much turmoil and disorder, and the work was a good deal hampered. The steward kept his eye on everything and watched each man's hands and what he did with them, and especially those of the angel-faced scullion. The master cook was continually harrying him to catch the black hen, which kept on getting loose. The youth cursed the creature, which cocked its eye at him and, to avoid being caught, fluttered over his curled pate and then darted under the blazing fire-basket. He was bidden by the master cook to crawl after it; but the black hen could not be found and was thought to have fallen into the fire, when it was suddenly seen glaring malevolently out of a distant corner.

At this, Master Frying-pan lost patience and thwacked his scullion smartly across his delicately coloured cheek; but the blow left no mark behind it, neither red nor blue. But while the youth was chasing the black hen, something passed between the cook and the black hen. Each winked an eye in token of a private understanding. In the meantime the black hen had now turned on the angel-faced scullion and was pursuing him in its turn, with the plain intention of pecking off one of those flaxen curls. It was the steward who grabbed the bird from the lad's back as he fled past.

" You will not wring the black hen's neck, though you may want to," said the calm voice of a man accustomed to power and consideration; then, in a clearer, sharper tone: " I am watching you."

The angel eyed him attentively.

" There will be chicken broth today," he fluted — adding in a snarl: " brewed from a black hen and a white goose." And with a skip and a leap the lad vanished.

Zamet shouted behind the steward's back in a high falsetto: " The Duchess! She deigns to approach, and there is still no soup."

The excitement enabled him to edge through the throng; he reached the ladies just as they were coming out of their room, and, bowing profusely, he escorted them to table. There was one laid for them alone, set in the most conspicuous position, too long and broad for only two guests, exalted though they were. Madame de Beaufort and Mademoiselle de Guise sat at some distance from each other, the intervening space being filled by their spreading skirts, which were alike in cut and colour. Zamet stood opposite his distinguished guests on the other side of the table — or, rather, he did not stand, he bobbed and pirouetted, and waved to his lackeys on the right and left to keep off the crowd. A precious life was in his charge, a life that could not be replaced. He glanced at the table; not a dish nor a knife and fork that he could not see, and not a motion of Dame Martigues's hand could escape his eye.

The wine had been opened by Zamet himself, and he too had wiped the glasses; he filled them, and was relieved when the Princesses drank; nothing had happened to them yet. But he did not like the look of Dame Martigues. She had insisted on serving the Princesses, which, Zamet told himself, he never should have allowed. She was small and thin, and the headdress that increased her height served to compress her face; beneath her paint she had the hard and wizened features of a poisoner. Assuming that Bizacasser were in league with someone here, it could only be with her. The hands with which she took the heaviest plates from the lackeys looked like spiders, but their grip was iron. The sinister creature cut up a melon and prepared it — God preserve us! — could there be something in the juice? Only Mademoiselle de Guise ate a slice. Zamet looked on in agony, but none the less in his thoughts he sacrificed the less important personage. She had held out her plate, and, come what might, Martigues gave her the portion that had been intended for the Duchess. Zamet watched to see the Princess change colour and collapse. There would be this advantage in such a dreadful thing: that it would save Gabrielle. But nothing happened.

She who was to be Queen asked for an orange and peeled it herself — not without examining it with great care. The host's round eyes looked anxiously for a hole in the peel, the tiniest hole, the faintest gash. Ha! — the precious creature put the orange aside, made a wry face, and said:

" It tastes bitter."

Then it was for Zamet to break out. He clapped his hands to his belly and yelled: " Clear the room! " And his lackeys had to usher the whole company of high or low degree into the neighbouring rooms. Zamet brandished both his arms to hasten them. "What, in God's name, has happened? " asked Monsieur de Varenne, who had hitherto been quietly playing cards.

Zamet recovered his composure and muttered ruefully: " The Duchess — ".

" Is not looking well," interposed Varenne. " She is five months gone. Is that the reason for this uproar? "

But Zamet left him, he had made a discovery. While no one was observing the table, and the two high guests sat rigid with astonishment, Madame de Martigues was fingering the Duchess of Beaufort's neck. Not a doubt — she was opening the clasp of the pearl necklace, which slid to the ground. Zamet, on the spot in a flash, struck the thief's hand away with his signet ring, and then sank on to his knees.

" Madame, here is your necklace, it came unfastened."

" I thank you; but has nothing else happened? " asked Gabrielle in a tone of surprise.

" Nothing else. Nothing has happened. Pray be calm. Nothing has happened," he repeated, his moist eyes bulging out of his head. " All is very well. Nothing has happened."

Zamet was in raptures! Gabrielle looked at him as though he were a child, and she knew more, infinitely more, of life than he did. She was very pale and drawn, and her eyelids red.

" Must I now eat soup? " she said. " I would so gladly go and sleep."

At this, Zamet thundered out the word: " Soup " with all the force of his lungs, leapt to his feet and rushed into the kitchen. There he came upon a strange scene: all the cooks, the master cook at their head, and a motley throng of water-carriers, dish-washers, wood-boys, and kitchen-maids, staring at the roof, wide-eyed and open-mouthed. The steward and the scullion were fighting in the air.

The object of their struggle was a glass ball, which flashed in the blaze of the great hearthfire; now one of them had grabbed it, then it could be seen sliding along the other's arm and shoulder, but neither let it fall. To begin with, the steward had snatched it from the scullion when the latter was about to open it over the soup saucepan. The angel-faced youth thrust his head into the steward's belly and recaptured the ball. He made a leap, caught the lower edge of the gallery that ran round the kitchen, and with one heave was over the balustrade. But the steward, despite his ceremonial garb and bushy whiskers, proved no less of an acrobat and promptly swung himself up into the gallery. There they wrestled until the scullion was hurled out into the room. There he seemed to be actually floating in air, until with a contemptuous shout he grabbed a beam under the ceiling, from which hams were usually hung. This he clasped with legs and arms, which did not prevent him launching a kick or two at the steward, who had also taken a flying leap on to the next beam and was edging along it with incredible agility, still intent on laying hold of the ball.

This slid over the scullion's chest or back, according to his position as he wriggled along his beam as vigorously as his foe, each of them now moving so quickly that they really seemed to be soaring through the air, the ball flickering over their twisting limbs and dancing round about them under the ceiling until it hung above the hearth, and the cauldron of soup. Again that contemptuous shout — now was the moment. But the Good Spirit knocked the ball away from the Evil one, just as it opened and its contents were about to fall into the soup. What happened? The ball burst on the tiled floor, and the gaping onlookers turned their faces downwards towards another strange manifestation. Suddenly, from no one could tell where, the black hen appeared just where an enormous grain of corn had fallen, pecked it up and swallowed it. Then it shrieked like a human being (as was afterwards testified), rolled over, quivered, and was dead.

The cooks and the rest suddenly remembered the two demons, but these had vanished, which all thought quite natural, and they crossed themselves. The Evil One had quite openly shot up the blazing chimney after he was recognized. Many noticed him slip off his angel shape and turn into a black bat. The Good Spirit dissolved into a rich fragrance, which imparted a most excellent odour to the soup.

At the entrance to the kitchen, when the scene was over, stood Guillaume the page — but he looked utterly dumbfounded, and now and again he shook his head. Someone touched him on the shoulder — Sebastian Zamet, wearing an extremely sanctimonious air: he led Monsieur de Sablé by the hand to the table of the two exalted guests, Zamet walking on tiptoe all the way.

The Princesses were sitting in the same attitude, their hooped skirts and puffed sleeves diminishing the distance between them. They did not ask why they had been kept waiting. The procession of cooks solemnly approached, headed by the master cook, holding the soup tureen aloft. The golden plates were filled by the host himself, while the cooks knelt; and they remained kneeling until the Duchess of Beaufort had tasted the soup and pronounced it very good. Then Zamet waved them out.

Not till then did Mademoiselle de Guise inquire what had really happened.

" Madame," said Zamet, " there came a black hen. And if my people may be believed, other strange things happened."

Mademoiselle de Guise put down her spoon. Gabrielle went on, but kept her eyes on the page, Guillaume; it was for his sake only that she ate that precious soup. And her eyes permitted him to serve her in his fashion.

" Madame," he replied, " much is being said."

" I know," she said, smiled, and looked at him — and until he was an old man he was to preserve the picture in his mind of how she had looked at him and smiled.

" And much more will be said."

This was her last word to him. As she spoke she glowed with a kind of inner radiance, into which she seemed to dissolve. Afterwards he realized that she had meant her death, and the circumstances of her death, and had offered the living man her thanks, in the guise of one who must soon depart.

THE END OF THE SONG

As she was still alive next morning, she received a visit from Monsieur de Sully. He had stayed in the city on her account, and now convinced himself that she was alive, but could not find words in which to offer his congratulations. It was Gabrielle who spoke, and in most flattering tones; she begged him to believe that she loved and admired him both for himself and for his great services. He listened with complacency and then sent Madame de Sully, that she also might bid her farewell before they both departed to their estates.

Now the wife of a great Minister, who is to remain such, is not at all pleased to wait upon the mistress of the King, who will have her successors; for that was her opinion of the affair. She sat, a stiff, flat-chested figure, beside the sick woman, who shivered inwardly at those chill eyes which so shamelessly estimated what she was worth that day. Madame de Rosny did not give her much longer, on which account she thought any assurances unnecessary. It was Gabrielle who tried to appease her unrelenting visitor. " You must be my best friend," she said.

She must wholly have lost her head, for she added: " I shall always be glad to see you among the company when I rise and when I retire." Whereupon the lady got up, though she was scarcely taller or more sharply outlined standing than seated. She dipped her chin a little as her sole mark of reverence and marched to the door. The lady, who came of the lesser nobility, herself of spotless reputation, and without a stain upon her family, as indeed is more common among Protestants, was so indignant that she sat in her travelling coach as stiff as a broomstick and with her thin lips set and drawn.

Once at home, she did burst forth, and abused her husband for having sent her to wait upon a whore. A disreputable family, an open scandal, and a lost cause; and a decent woman is expected to bow down to such a creature. " She asked me to come and see her go to bed and open her legs. This to me! " she shrieked, quite beside herself with pride and moral indignation. Rosny, not a nervous man, here interposed, for there was no knowing on whom the widow might have cooled her wrath. He promised her that she would see a good game, and well played, provided that the rope did not give way. Though indeed it was not exactly a cord that was before his mind. This silenced his wife; and the valiant knight took advantage of her astonishment to withdraw from the danger zone.

Whether or not Gabrielle had taken the poison, she none the less carried out her religious duties. Her night had been restless, with the usual evil dreams, and then this dreadful woman's visit; however, she went to confession immediately afterwards. The church, dedicated to the lesser Saint Anthony, was near at hand, and Mademoiselle de Guise accompanied the lovely sinner. She assured her from her own experience that women were created to sin from love and need not be anxious about absolution. She was determined to be first among the ladies about the future Queen; her confessions were to encourage Gabrielle to reveal a few of her own adventures. Such knowledge might always serve a purpose.

Gabrielle said nothing — not intentionally, but from weakness and depression. The other's amorous memories were not distasteful to her; this was what was left of the world about her, the last light heart that would speak to her and laugh with her. In the confessional she regretted nothing that she had done, and least of all her faithful love for her dear lord. She did admit that she was grieved at having become an indifferent Christian, but it was now too late to amend. This said, she received absolution and returned to the Shoemaker's villa.

She went out once more on the afternoon of that same Wednesday. The first days of April in that year 1599 were unusually warm, and the vines were blossoming by the roadside. The people ran up as the litter of the future Queen was carried past, escorted by the King's guards under the command of Monsieur de Montbazon, and after it the coach of the Lorraine Princesses. A lovely day in spring, once again the French Queen appeared in public, herself a daughter of France, as were none of those that followed her.

The people knew more, and understood much better, than those who were more nearly concerned. The expected marriage had been often and everywhere discussed. The sight that now was seen forbade all thought of marriage. The robes of marriage and of coronation had been described and were known to all. Here was an intimation of another and a final garment that must be worn by all one day. The Duchess of Beaufort looked grave

— graver than anyone need look in the midst of life. She was weary, and with a weariness from which no one recovers. A look into that litter struck at the heart. A horror in the eyes of all — but no more than half suspected; and scarce had it happened than its significance would be forgotten. Here it passed before many watching eyes.

Gabrielle, as she last appeared, was lovely, no longer in the mere worldly sense, for she bore herself with gravity and modesty — but her loveliness was such as outreaches description. She knew it, and she wished that her lord could see her as she walked through the church. She wanted him to know that place was made for her, whereas her guards had usually had to thrust the mob aside. And those who saw her laid their hands upon their hearts in ready tribute. Ah, he and she were beloved by this people. This she said in her own thoughts, where knowledge and a still buoyant imagination had come into strange conflict. The common claim to live often prevailed over weariness and resignation; and it was to become very insistent at the end.

A dais had been erected for her a little to one side, so that she might not be embarrassed by the throng. The church was full, partly to hear the music and partly because the famous Gabrielle was to appear. Now, while the sacred melodies still spoke of darkness, and our Lord lingered in the grave before He rose again — Mademoiselle de Guise chose that moment to bring herself into notice by some pleasant news: letters from Rome, intimating that the King's divorce would soon be pronounced. But Pope Clement's meaning was not quite what it seemed; he would dissolve the King's marriage, but not so that he could marry his concubine; for the blame for such a scandal would fall upon the Pope. However, he hoped that Providence would release him from his painful dilemma; he prayed daily to that effect, and he did in fact learn of the event on the day and at the hour when it happened: a wholly supernatural occurrence.

By the dim lighting of the church during the gloomy canticles for the entombment of our Lord, Gabrielle deciphered what she was so glad at last to read, though a chill fear was creeping over her body. Then the Guise Princess, in her eagerness to make favour for herself, brought the best news last of all: two messages from the King, which had come in by two couriers in quick succession. They spoke of his longing and affection for her and assured her that his arm was over her wherever she might be. This gave her a sense of warmth and well-being, for the last time in her life. Her companion saw her smile like a child, and rejoiced, for that meant that the game would be an easy one. When the glad, triumphant music of the Resurrection had died away, the two ladies departed, well pleased with themselves and with the world. Except that it had been a little too hot for them in the crowded church, and Gabrielle felt a little faint. When she had entered Zamet's garden, she fell, and promptly lost consciousness.

There was a rush to pick her up and carry her to bed. Her face and every muscle twitched, and eyeballs and eyelids began to quiver. The eyes rolled upwards to the left, and the pupils were seen to be fixed and staring. The much kissed mouth was frightfully distorted, and the jaws were set and locked.

In less than a minute those leaping muscles were relaxed, and limbs and hips, neck and face, were still. The head had fallen back, the face was turned to the left, and the body lay arched and tense above the bed. Her breathing stopped, and she who had just been the greatest lady in France lay with features blue and bloated, a truly hideous sight. Her tongue protruded from her mouth, her teeth had bitten into it, and blood-stained saliva oozed over her cheeks and hair and pillows. It was enough: and the watchers fled from her who had so lately been the greatest lady in France, lest the evil thing might strike them also. At the least they would avoid infection.

Gabrielle came to her senses, looked about her, and saw no one but Monsieur de Varenne, who was eyeing her in helpless horror. He was answerable for her to the King; and his conscience smote him for bringing her to this fateful place.

" Take me out of this house! " shrieked the Duchess of Beaufort; he felt sorely troubled for his own safety, and took care not to send for doctor or priest. He merely obeyed her orders. She demanded to be taken to the house of her aunt, Madame de

Sourdis, and went there in her litter; Varenne lifted her into it, and he alone walked beside her through the streets. She had thought that she would there find her women, together with the great ladies in her service, especially Mademoiselle de Guise. Not a soul; there was no one in her service now, except Varenne, one-time cook and carrier of love letters, now acting as her waiting woman, and he helped her to bed. Her aunt's servants had been sent away while Madame de Sourdis was in the country. Varenne sent an urgent message summoning her back.

Meantime Gabrielle alternated between restlessness and exhaustion. Lying in that empty house, she wept and cried out for her lord. She wanted to go at once to the Louvre, that she might be nearer to him. " I can walk," she wailed, " it is a very little way." Monsieur de Varenne, in his shirt-sleeves, and with an apron about his middle, assured her that she would find it even lonelier there. " What do you want in the Louvre? " he asked, on the point of losing patience. She did not say, although she knew. A gracious weariness made it seem easy for her to die if it might be in her lord's house, in the room that they had shared, where the air was still vivid with their mingled breath.

She went to sleep at last, the night passed quietly, and in the morning she herself thought she looked as usual. Varenne was amazed, and accompanied her without protest across to the Church of Saint-Germain-l'Auxerrois, where she took Communion. It was the Thursday before Easter. Two more days, and then, she hoped, her lord would be with her once again. This time the gratitude in her heart moved her to genuine piety. In the afternoon she felt ill and had to lie down. Before the next paroxysm, she found strength to dispatch a certain nobleman to the King, whom she herself chose as being one whom she could trust. She asked her beloved lord to let her go back to him by boat — thinking, indeed, that he would promptly come to her himself. He would surely not leave her alone in misery, when he read what she had written and guessed the rest.

She watched the man mount, while Varenne added a few words to her letter, intimating that there was no need of such haste. He had been playing cards while she ate suspect food.

He would be punished, and the sooner the King learned what had happened, the heavier would be his punishment. They all knew the King; when all was well, he would forgive. Perhaps even, if the worst befell, he would forgive, because he would be too plunged in grief to be stern to anyone. At last the horseman galloped off; it was four o'clock, and Gabrielle was writhing in pain.

So far as Varenne could understand in his perplexity, this was the kind of condition that preceded childbed. He himself ran to fetch the woman who had already attended the Duchess three times; but he fell in with the page Sablé below, who dashed off in his stead. Guillaume not only fetched Madame Dupuis, but went to Monsieur de la Rivière, to beg him to come at once. Guillaume had understood Monsieur de Varenne in this fashion; in any case, that should be the excuse. However, the physician was absent and did not come until an hour later. By then Madame Dupuis had wholly lost her head, never having seen such a visitation before.

The attack passed off like the first one, except that it was worse. The tearing convulsions were followed by rigidity, together with asphyxia, which distorted the face beyond all description. Madame Dupuis, who in the duties of her calling had always seen Gabrielle with her beauty undimmed — never this discoloured and contorted mask, and hideously rolling eyes — the woman could not endure the sight and stood with her face to the wall. Varenne remained; and during this attack as well as the next, he held the Duchess in his arms.

As he watched her he noticed that the breathing had started again. Her breath came and went in gasps, being of course congested by the fumes of the poison. All was quite natural — this he told himself to calm his mind. Death came in the end, there was nothing devilish about that; indeed, it could scarcely be called unusual, said Monsieur de Varenne, who had been so many things and was now Intendant of Posts and Governor, in close touch with the Jesuits and with other dangerous forces, so why not with death? The death of others first — as for his own, he had not yet envisaged it; his own, if it must needs be contemplated at all, remained on the far horizon of his mind in the guise of a shadowy funeral procession that never started.

His instinct for reality bade him consider the poor sufferer, whom he held in his arms through her worst paroxysms, as having been thus destroyed solely by ill luck. He would have thought it his duty to give her up, as the others had done. But, unfortunately, over against this menacing death stood an equally menacing King, who did not yet know of it. The great danger for Varenne was that the King might hear of the Duchess's death, not from him, but from people who would put the guilt upon Varenne. Hence he had already begun to reflect whether he would not be well advised to send a second messenger after the first, to tell the King that it was now too late.

None the less, he still paid due heed to what he had ceased to conceive of as a human being. It emerged from each of the attacks, and for a space became once more a woman, who looked about her in amazement. What she said was barely to be understood, as she had bitten her tongue right through. But Varenne caught what she meant; he held her up while she wrote to the King, each time a fresh appeal for help. He likewise pretended to send off the messengers, but they none of them arrived, neither the second nor the third. At five o'clock appeared Monsieur La Rivière, First Physician to the King.

His arrival changed the whole aspect of affairs. He bled the sick woman profusely and gave her a clyster of salt water. Meantime Madame Dupuis prepared a warm bath, by his direction, and both put the Duchess into it. These were measures plainly taken against poison, and much alarmed Monsieur de Varenne, who was exposed to every sort of suspicion. His fears, on the other hand, came into conflict with a fresh surmise: the Duchess might not die. This man would save her life. And as there was a chance that she might live, he began to display a sort of feverish assiduity. He felt the temperature of the bath, unabashed by the naked beauty in it; indeed, he praised it very freely. The King would be ravished; she looked lovelier than ever, impossible as that had seemed before. But he also whispered into

Monsieur La Rivière's ear that what he really meant was that the poison was now out of her system.

The physician did not reply. He listened to the sick woman talking — not to hear her words: she was reckoning up the hours to the time when her messengers would reach the King, the first just after dark, but the second and third would meet him on his way to her that night. These were the words, but the doctor specially marked the tone, which sounded wandering and distraught. He watched the movements of the face, now no longer swollen, but sunken and deadly white. And he felt the body under the water. Suddenly he ordered Monsieur de Varenne to leave him alone with the Duchess. The moisture that oozed out of the body darkened the water, but it was not blood.

The physician and the midwife carried the patient back to the bed, there to await what he now knew must come. None the less, he did not cease to tend and watch over her, that life might not be severed before it had utterly run out. That, to his knowledge, would not be for several hours, as the sick woman resisted death with astonishing energy, which came from the thought that her lord was in the saddle and on his way to her.

When the next paroxysm seized her, La Rivière seized the hem of the sheet, thrust it between her teeth, and pressed the tongue against the gums. He did so just in time, or she would have bitten her tongue right off in the violence of the convulsion. And he beckoned to the woman for the ewer just as the vomiting began. Meantime he felt the pulse, now fluttering wildly under the fearful strain, and beyond all computation — for the first time the doctor feared that this life might indeed be cut short before the time. But he went on giving his directions, not for death but for life. He sent Monsieur de Varenne for milk. What was the use of milk, asked Varenne. "Go! Water with a little milk in it."

Monsieur de Varenne left the room and found occasion to fulfil his purpose. He wrote to the King: "Sire, I implore you not to come!"

Then he pondered. "You would see a sight of horror. Sire, the Duchess would never forgive you if she recovers."

Here he got up. Over the still absent word, he contended with his doubts. The physician was tending the Duchess as a person that still belonged to life. He wore a steady, sure expression; a man did not look so when engaged on a futile and imaginary task. Suppose it fell out otherwise, and the word still lacking were later turned into a lie? No matter; his prospects were so bad that they could only be bettered. He would take the risk, for he had no choice. And without sitting down again, Varenne wrote:

"There is no need to come, Sire. The Duchess is dead."

And he sent for the fastest courier.

Madame Dupuis came out for a while to weep. "Is it ended?" asked Varenne eagerly.

In the room were left the physician and she whom men had called the charming Gabrielle. He spoke to her as though she still were so. He said that her slight weakness was connected with the child, and after the delivery she would be quite well again. She moved her head feebly on the pillow, in token of denial, and met his searching look with indifference, as though she did not recognize him. But she had liked and trusted him, and she had called him to the King in preference to the surgeon when the King had been ill. To his question whether she had been well of late, she merely answered that she had eaten an orange that tasted bitter. Then she complained of a violent headache and added that she could not imagine where the King might be.

"Sleep," said he, and she obeyed. But as he stood and watched her, he could see how her will prevented her falling sound asleep, despite her need for oblivion. So he took all measures that he could devise to prevent such a quick succession of attacks. He gave her milk and water at short intervals, which produced a greater flow of black fluid from the kidneys. Madame Dupuis gave eager help, for she marked the effects of what was done, and marvelled at the doctor's skill. But he had now realized that his efforts had failed. The sick woman fell into a restless sleep, and all expression faded from her face. The trembling began, and the breath came in gasps. She opened her eyes, and the watchers noticed that the pupils were enlarged. The doctor tried to stave off the paroxysm by bleeding her once more; but in vain.

When these horrors had come and gone twice more, the sick woman's endurance still held; it was the old woman who gave way. The doctor told her to go and lie down. " It is eight o'clock," he said.

The woman was aghast. " For four hours now she has gone through what would have killed another at the first attack. The child cannot be taken out of her; but is it only a child that she has within her body? " said the woman in a whisper, and made the sign of the cross.

The physician was left alone for the night beside the dying Gabrielle. He stood and watched her. The attacks had exhausted themselves upon her; her they had not exhausted. Here was, no doubt, a dying woman. But no more so than all of us, so long as we are alive. She would be alive tomorrow morning. Tomorrow was Friday, Holy Friday before Easter, Good Friday; that she would live to see it was almost certain; more than that could not be said.

He must widen the opening and take out the child. It would not be a living child, but the mother must be thought of first. Her will was exalted above common nature. After these frightful struggles, and now half asleep, she spoke of her lord — she was with him at last, and she began to babble in her ecstasy. Ah, he must not listen, he must act. A physician's business was to save life.

But suppose his intervention destroyed it? A delivery would in no way counteract the effects of the poison. And she would probably resist them better without such intervention, which could not but be a shock. If Nature would grant thirty minutes of insensibility, he could help her in her healing task. But no: Gabrielle would bleed internally and suffer agonies of pain; and even if he succeeded in preventing that, at the next failure of the breath, in twenty seconds an artery in the brain would burst. She would be paralysed, and die.

The doctor dropped heavily upon a chair and buried his head in his hands. That ecstatic babbling that so wrung his heart

deepened his fears. Whatever he did or did not do, he would
be guilty before Nature, who could do her kindly work, if he
had not failed her; and guilty before men, for they were waiting
to work his ruin.

With shamefast courage he admitted his fear of men. He was
hated as a friend and favourite of the Duchess of Beaufort. It
would be all the more promptly maintained that he had killed
her. He was neither Protestant nor Catholic; he had learned
medicine among the Moors and had been long in Spain; but he
had become highly suspect when, at the instance of the King,
he had restored to their senses those possessed by devils — this
quite lately — and had ventured to assert that they were not so
possessed. The doctor recognized with self-contempt that he
had not tried an artificial delivery, not as being too dangerous
for the sufferer, but too dangerous for himself. He was no more
certain than she was to live beyond Friday.

He made this confession aloud, and as he did so, the soft muttering from the bed was stilled. It was now quite dark, and he
lit some candles; their light fell upon a face now quite transformed. Here lay a living woman, not one who was soon to die.
Her cheeks were rosy and white, of a natural fullness, and her
breath came easily. Mother Nature had here plainly worked one
of her miracles. La Rivière was near to falling backwards in a
fervour of joy, and he flung open a window. At that moment
from below there came a song, and the sound of a young, fresh
voice.

" Charming Gabrielle," Guillaume was singing her song.

Gabrielle opened her eyes, and they were shining. Gabrielle
lifted her head a little from the pillow, she listened and she
smiled. " Fond star . . ." the melody reached her where she lay
on her last bed; and she opened her lips.

> *Fond star of all my dreaming,*
> *In yon far distant sky!*
> *I am sick with love and longing —*
> *Appear! or I shall die.*

"But I come," said Gabrielle, in a clear, sweet voice. "Beloved, I come. Here am I, my lord."

She fell back upon the pillow; but there was yet another verse, and she heard it: the verse of farewell.

> Oh, day of bitter sorrow
> When we must part;
> Would that I need not live so,
> Or had no heart!

The end of the song; and she had heard it.

The Roots of My Heart

Henri received the first of her letters; of her three last only the first reached him. She wanted to come to him and begged to be allowed to come. But she also thought that she was dying — how, then, could she travel? She hoped that he would marry her first for the children's sake. Could she be so ill as this? Varenne in his postscript contradicted her fears: there was no hurry, said Varenne; and he was responsible for her.

"Monsieur de Puypéroux," said Henri to the mounted courier, "who sent you?"

The nobleman answered that the Duchess herself had sent him and would have no other than himself. Was she in possession of her senses? Entirely so. In any danger of her life? Nothing of the sort was to be observed, was the reply. But there was a report that she had fainted.

Henri pondered: After the third child she had been inclined to faint. He had been with her at Monceaux when she did so, from jealousy of the Medici and her picture. It must be the same now. She feared that in her absence he might alter his mind. He would reassure her, but he would have no hasty marriage. She was not going to die — how should she die?

He sent the courier back at once with the message that he would come, and would soon be holding her in his arms. "There has never been so faithful a lover as I am," she might have read, as once before; but on Friday, her last day, her eyes failed. Nor, besides, was she given his letter.

He was uneasy, and even anxious, though against his will. At last he went to sleep, but awoke with a start from evil dreams; then he lay and listened to imagined hoofs. Just before dawn the imagined hoofs became real. Henri, who was dressed, dashed to the door and by the dim light deciphered the message: this one was not from her. Varenne alone wrote; he reported that the doctor could make no headway against the malady, and the Duchess was now very weak. Her life was given up, and her beauty had already gone. And Varenne begged the King to spare himself so terrible a sight.

He did not say that she was dead. At the last moment Varenne had given this more cautious letter to the courier. He had in the end not dared to announce that Gabrielle was dead before she was so. He had caused the false news to reach three other persons, and they would in good faith carry it to the King. Henri, cold with fear, mounted his horse. He galloped headlong. Four miles outside Paris he overtook Puypéroux, who had not hurried. Why not? Henri did not ask. He cursed the man, but of set purpose did not question him, and galloped past. Here by the roadside stood the house of the Chancellor, Bellièvre, and from it Marshal d'Ornano and Monsieur de Bassompierre ran out to meet the King. As Henri saw their horror-struck faces, his heart turned over. They bowed their heads and said: " Sire, the Duchess is dead."

Henri stiffened. He sat in his saddle like a man of stone and forgot where he was and whither he was going. Monsieur de Bellièvre, shocked and astonished to see the King so stricken, broke the silence and told what he himself believed true, describing the terrible condition of her whom he called a corpse; but she was at that moment still living; she still breathed, and called for her lord.

At last tears came to Henri. He dismounted, turned aside, and wept for a long while. Then he said that he wanted to see the Duchess of Beaufort. Whereat the Chancellor firmly pointed out that what he did would be marked and everywhere discussed. Any open expression of grief would be very ill seen. He ran the risk of offending the religious sentiments of his subjects immediately before Easter. Henri was not equal to making any answer; it was with difficulty that he rose to his feet.

The Chancellor's coach drove up, and Henri suffered himself to be taken to a neighbouring abbey. In an access of despair he flung himself upon a monk's bed and there lay in utter prostration, sobbing as the hours went by, all through that Friday, on which Gabrielle still lived and called aloud for him between the terrors of her struggle. Slowly Henri made his way back to Fontainebleau, already in solitude; but she actually lived through the night, so fervently did she expect him. But with her hope, her strength ebbed too. The dawn of Saturday was breaking when she passed.

On the evening of the Friday Varenne had revealed something like the truth to one single person; he wrote to Monsieur de Sully, whom he thought would be disposed to approve what he had done. He admitted his deception of the King and excused it as best he might; in particular, he diverted the suspicion that would have fallen on himself to Zamet. Rosny was too delighted to think of guilt or justice. He awakened his wife, embraced that elderly widow, and said: " My girl, the Duchess will not get up again, so you need not go to her levée. The cord is broken."

At that same hour she did in fact die. At that same hour Pope Clement VIII came forth from his chapel, having plainly received some supernatural enlightenment, long before any letter could have reached Rome; for he said: " God has made provision." Which meant no more than that a number of persons, among them the Pope, would be relieved of a great embarrassment if the Duchess of Beaufort disappeared, and they knew of the measures taken. But the truth of what had happened never reached their ears, for persons whose power is arbitrary never hear the truth. Such was the thought that came into the mind of the physician beside the bed on which the dead woman lay.

He had not been able to escape in time; scarcely had the Duchess breathed her last when the room was full of people —

it was incredible where they could have been lurking and how they had heard of what had happened. All agog, with peering eyes and straining ears, they hurried up and thronged into the room, where they were rewarded by the horrid spectacle that they had sought. The loveliest lady in the kingdom — there she lay, her neck twisted, her eyes upturned, and her face blackened. The first that saw it cried: " The Devil "; and such was the belief, the prevailing belief, among the mass of people who had not enjoyed the sight.

The physician was now caught in the throng and thrust against the bed; and as they were avid of horror, he himself became an object of their superstitious fears, which he did not fail to observe. He realized what threatened him if he did not disavow the dead woman then and there and repudiate, as a physician, any responsibility for her unnatural end. He stretched himself to two inches above his height, aped an angel of judgment, and cried aloud over the array of heads: " *Hic manus Dei.*"

They fell back and made way for him who had seen " God's hand " at work; he could depart. He carried his head high, but he had betrayed the dead woman, the King, and his conscience, and therewith made a resolve which he did not keep, for man is sensible and weak; he resolved that he would never again practise his art.

When Madame de Sourdis got back to her house, she found no one in charge of it — people coming in and out as they pleased. Near the bed she fell down in a faint, but rather for appearances' sake, for she was not a timorous nature. But her collapse did not prevent her catching a female thief. It was Madame de Martigues; she could not get hold of the pearl necklace, but she had drawn the costly rings off the dead woman's fingers and threaded them on her rosary. Sourdis seized upon them and handed the false creature over to the Lieutenant of Police.

During the whole time that passed before Gabrielle was buried, two weeks long, no one was so busy as her aunt. She scarce heeded the circumstances of her end, intent as she was on using it to all possible advantage. She arrayed her niece in the wedding garb of the queens of France, crimson and gold, with an over-robe of white silk. But it was not the niece in person, for what was left of the charming Gabrielle could not be exhibited in public. An artificial figure was laid out on the bed of state in the anteroom of the house, and this received the homage of the court and of the city.

While she herself lay nailed in her coffin and had for ever departed, a coarse image of her was enthroned between six fat candles of white wax. In the coffin the shroud and the blackened face; the image in the golden mantle, the royal crown gleaming on that waxen forehead, and surrounded by eight chanting monks. A mimic corpse, but beside that semblance of loveliness, so hurriedly fashioned, her family kept vigil, and two priests read Mass for her soul. And before the tapestried dais stood kings-of-arms in black corselets of chain mail and tunics embroidered with golden lilies. The Queen, with her lilies, was not lying in her coffin; here she sat giving audience to the world, and twenty thousand people passed before her. Came a Duchess, and a cushion was hastily slipped beneath her knees.

The aunt persisted in this performance for three whole days. For every meal a table was set before the waxen figure, as was the immemorial custom for the queens of France; she was served, and the Court Chaplain said grace. But all this was merely a beginning. The funeral ceremony was still to come; three-and-twenty town criers proclaimed it to the populace, and the names and titles of the High Lady Gabrielle d'Estrées once more echoed through the streets. The church glittered with countless candles; the poor, who had been given mourning clothes and lined the approach, were seventy-five in number. The procession afterwards was headed by the King's guards with the Duke of Montbazon; he had escorted the living woman since her parting from the King; to him belonged the honour of walking beside her coffin. In this ceremony there was no artificial figure taking part. It was she herself. Her three children followed her on foot, ahead of the horsemen and the coaches. The fourth accompanied her inside the coffin.

There was much talk in that procession; only the family and

the head of it, Marshal de Balagny, kept dourly silent, for they stood by the ambiguous phrase of the doctor, about the hand of God. It was said in the procession that the King was rid of her and glad to be so; and later on there was one that said it to his face. Along the streets there were many words of sympathy. True it was that she had died like a dog, without Extreme Unction; but she had received Communion shortly before, so that her end must have been free from sin. The nobility in the procession asserted that they had known all the time that such would be her end. The mob whispered about the punishment of Heaven, which had overtaken her before the Devil could fulfil his bond with her and make her Queen. It was observed both by the court and the city that the King had not himself ventured to take part in her royal funeral. Nor did he have her buried in the Cathedral of Saint-Denis, where lie the tombs of the House of France. There was indeed a second ceremony over the Royal vaults, but she was carried to her last rest at Monceaux.

Henri had shut himself up. For the first week after Gabrielle's death he was seen by none of those usually about his person. Only his Minister Sully appeared at six o'clock in the evening on the Saturday. Gabrielle had in the meantime really died, and her enemy came forth at once. Henri did not yet know that she had been alive while he was weeping for her; and Rosny said nothing on the matter. Henri embraced his faithful servant, who said, in the words of the Psalm: "Let us bow our heads before God's ways" — whereat Henri eyed him fixedly and said no word.

In that moment he realized many things, and especially that he had been right to remain alone with his grief, which no one shared. Indeed, he suddenly looked as though the bitterness was past. His grief was not deep, thought the Minister as he shut the door behind him.

The foreign ambassadors, who had come expressly to Fontainebleau, were not to be refused. Moreover, Henri had to receive a deputation from his Parliament conveying an expression of official sympathy in the exalted language that would have been appropriate to a Queen. Then they again left him to his thoughts;

he stood motionless as they departed. And they marked how motionless he stood, clad all in black, which no King has ever yet worn, even for a real Queen.

At the beginning of the second week he arrayed himself in violet, as is customary for a ruler who has lost a near connection. But he remained shut up for three days longer; only his children were often with him; he could then be heard weeping, which seemed quite natural. It was noticed with disapproval that the ravens came no more.

Mornay, the Protestant, did venture to present himself — as though the Edict of Nantes had not been the real source of the disaster, since it was only then that the unhappy King had been brought to the point when he would have put on the throne a secret agent of the heretics, had God not taken measures to prevent it. Monsieur de Mornay did not come alone; with him was a very aged pastor, whom some still remembered, La Faye by name. These two were received; but the matter of their business with the King remained a secret. Not a sound could be heard through the door, not even by laying an ear to it. And those who tried to pry through the keyhole found it blocked by the key.

After this visit, before he threw open his cabinet and became his usual self, Henri sent for Monsieur La Rivière, First Physician to the King.

As La Rivière entered unannounced, and the gallery was a long one, Henri did not at once look up. He was sitting somewhat stiffly at a table, bent slightly forward. His hand held a pen, but it lay still. When he became aware of a strange presence, a jerk of his head silently indicated to Monsieur La Rivière that he might sit down opposite the King. He did so with an air of embarrassment, and the King began a rather wandering colloquy. This looked very ill, thought the unhappy man, who had managed to save himself by talking about the " hand of God "; but that would be of little service to him here.

Henri's eyes were wide open, and the lids of them inflamed. For a time that seemed to the doctor infinite, those eyes caught and held his own; then Henri said:

" So here we sit."

"My lord! I swear — " burst out the doctor.

"So do I," retorted Henri. "But we must not do so; to swear our innocence would be futile."

And he added softly: "She was not poisoned."

"Do you know that?" La Rivière could not believe his ears. "Your exalted understanding — " he began. But Henri cut him short.

"Never mind my understanding. Let us not speak of mine nor yours. I did not send her to her death. You did not kill her. That is all that we plead in our own favour."

"That is all," agreed La Rivière. "For my part I can only say that I did not dare to try an artificial delivery because she was already too deeply poisoned by her kidneys and her congested liver. She was destroyed, not by a poison that she took, but by one that she herself produced. The child lay outside the organ, in the hollow of the belly, and blocked the kidneys. When we opened the body afterwards, we drew it out in fragments. We of the Faculty can all testify to a natural issue, which our art has hitherto not been able to prevent."

At every "we" La Rivière uttered, he noticed that an eyebrow twitched above those staring eyes. And he realized that he must answer for himself, without help from the Faculty or support from anyone. He who sat before him would deal with him alone.

The physician then made his report, beginning with his first approach to the Duchess's bed. He described all the symptoms that had appeared, one after the other, and had defeated all his efforts in the service of life. The more gruesome the details, the more composedly he told his story — he himself at last was shocked by it; he broke off and excused himself. It was indeed not decent, though scarcely avoidable, to expose the intimacies of a body which had been the most admired in all the kingdom.

"What should I be," said Henri slowly, "had I loved only her skin and not her entrails?"

To this the doctor could find no reply. He watched the change in the face of a man — they called him Majesty. It was plain that he would bring accusations. Majesty can accuse whomsoever he chooses; even Nature? But what Henri said was:

" She might have lived."

" Sire," said the doctor boldly, " not I, but Nature is the healer. But she is at one in being and not-being. My master Hippocrates would say that the Duchess of Beaufort is healed."

" Amen." Henri contorted his lips into a smile. " We are mortal. The only question is at what point she had not yet become so. What did we leave undone, that Nature might have healed her otherwise than by not-being? "

Once more La Rivière trembled inwardly and tried to defend himself. The Duchess had tended the King during his illness without fatigue or complaint. There was no sign of anything amiss, he maintained. Suddenly he flushed — hesitated, and at last recounted the changes in her that should have been observable long since. Dreams? Headaches? Attacks of unconsciousness, and failure of memory and sight — Henri confirmed everything. Thereupon La Rivière admitted that he had been deceived by the excellent issue of her previous pregnancies. The third had given rise to troubles of this kind, though in a lesser degree. It was now certain that since that time her liver had been affected, and this had already marked her for the death she did actually die.

" Did actually die," repeated Henri. And he muttered: " Can a man conceive it? — she is actually dead. Because I saw nothing and would not believe in her fears. Every night I shared them with her, and awoke in fright from a dream, just as she did. From the same dream, both of us." Here he left his seat and fell to pacing up and down the gallery. La Rivière drew back against the wall. Speaking rather to himself than to the desolate man who could hear only the voice of his own recollections, he said, in the words of his master, Hippocrates: " Life is short, and art is long. Opportunity is fleeting, experience deceives, it is hard for us to pass judgment." Whereby La Rivière did his best to mitigate his own responsibility, for his opportunity of watching the Duchess of Beaufort had certainly been fleeting.

But Henri grew more and more burdened by his own guilt as he strode back and forward. He should not have sent her away from him, he should never have let his treasure out of his own hands. He had not hastened to her on the instant when she called to him in her extremity. But, alas, the guilt lay much further back. She should long ago have been his lawful Queen; then she would never have been a prey to all these fears, and she had died of her fear that he had abandoned her. Just as he had once abandoned poor Esther — she who had been conjured up by Pastor La Faye, a shadow, not again to be recognized after long not-being. ("Pastor, there's no hope for me. What shall I do that she too may not vanish and become as though she had not been, like all those now forgotten?"

"Sire, that will not be, for you have learned a hard lesson at last, and are yourself very near the age when men turn away from love."

"I am afraid for my own self, Monsieur La Faye. The dead woman will watch me growing old. What if I prove unworthy of her and of myself?"

"My son, you loved one called Gabrielle. And it was the force of your love for her that made you a great King.")

The last word burst from the depths of him in a hollow sob. The physician by his wall feared to overhear too much, as the King was carrying on imagined conversations in his own mind, fancying himself alone. But Monsieur La Rivière had not been dismissed, and he did not dare to move. Henri stopped by one of the windows and laid his forehead against a pane. Thereupon Monsieur La Rivière very cautiously withdrew.

Outside he was caught in a throng of whispering courtiers, who had been waiting for him to appear. Was the King in a fury? Whom did he hold guilty, and what had each and all of them to fear?

The First Physician gave the adroit and ambiguous reply that was characteristic of the man.

"The King is out of danger, for he has begun to think of his greatness."

And while they were questioning what the words might mean, La Rivière vanished.

Henri, his forehead against the window, was talking to her who could not return to hear.

" With you, and with you alone, should I have become what I ought to have been."

Then he sat down as before, and again read the letter from his sister, the Duchess of Bar. " Would God I could give some of my remaining years, if I might lighten your grief," wrote Catherine.

" Sister, who wast her friend, there would be little help in that." He went on with his interrupted answer. He had already written that he would never cease to long for and lament her until the day he died. None the less, God had sent him into the world, not for his own sake, but for the good of his kingdom. And he added: " The root of my heart is dead and will never grow again."

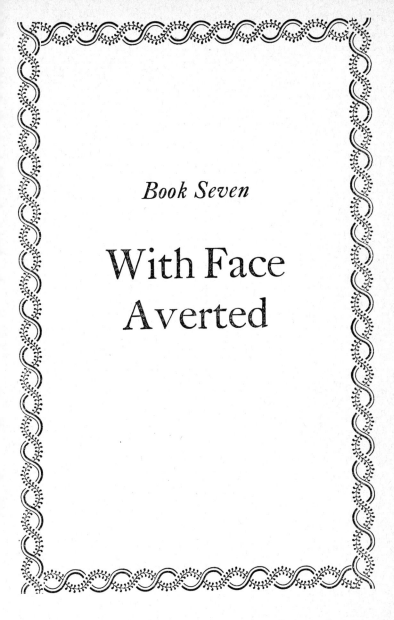

Book Seven

With Face
Averted

The Journey Continues

THE KING and the Grand Master of his Artillery set out for the mountains. They took forty cannon with them to Savoy and were accompanied by fifteen thousand infantry, two thousand horsemen, Marshal Biron, the Count of Soissons, and many other high officers. Brave Crillon commanded the French Guards — here was work for men's hands, which had been sadly lacking of late. By great good luck the Duke of Savoy had not surrendered either the Marquisate of Saluces or the province of Bresse. Hence this expedition to Italy, to seize the two domains without more ado — autumn 1600.

The Duke of Savoy would certainly have kept his treaty if Cæsar, Gabrielle's son, had remained heir to the throne of France and also his son-in-law. But Gabrielle's son was neither now. The King was shortly to marry the Princess of Tuscany by proxy. Immediately after the ceremony the foreign Queen was to take ship for France and bring a great store of money on her galley, the bulwarks of which, so rumour reported, were actually inlaid with countless precious stones. Gabrielle d'Estrées had never owned so many jewels. The King's old comrades in the field had loved her because their master loved her; none the less, facts must not be blinked. A shipload of treasure, and this highly promising campaign — these were not to have been expected in the days of the dead lady, so no one mourned for her, especially in company.

They told themselves that the King had taken comfort. Not merely had he married the foreigner. Four months after the loss of his mistress he took another — no better than the last. Her mother had already stabbed a page. She led the King an uneasy life. He must be glad enough to be rid of the Marquise and to be riding out to war with his old friends.

While the guns were being dragged up the rocky tracks, the commanders admired both the greatness of the King's enterprise and the ease with which it was accomplished. In one single night two towns were taken in two provinces: Bresse fell quickly to Marshal Biron, and Monsieur de Créqui occupied the jewel of Savoy, Montmélian — the town at first, and not the castle, which was immeasurably strong, a mountain fortress unsurpassed. Its turn would come. The cannon now faced another stronghold.

The cannon with their limbers weighed eight thousand pounds; each drawn by three-and-twenty horses, and the great culverins by nineteen. Brave Crillon would sooner have seen an open battlefield instead of this defile between rock and torrent. He liked marching on the enemy at the head of his French Guards; but he was ready to admit that this was the very country for the Grand Master, whose guns worked miracles without the need for fighting. When the army appeared before Chambéry the inhabitants made as though they meant to hold the place. Monsieur de Rosny merely displayed a battery of eight pieces without firing a shot; the gates were opened, and the troops entered. The citizens welcomed them as beings from a nobler world, although the Gods of antiquity must have been rather less encumbered by heavy transport. However, they made plain they could foot it lightly enough if need be, and entertained the townsfolk at a ball.

Said one-eyed Harambure to his friend as they clambered laboriously upwards:

"For whom was that ball given? For Madame de Rosny, in honour of her husband's guns — which are much better-looking than herself? The Marquise is good for nothing, and they say the new Queen cannot speak French. Think of days past, Crillon."

"Do not think of them, Harambure. Past is past. We have buried more than that. She was beautiful, and she was kind."

"Has the King forgotten her?"

"Every day brings its cares. He too is climbing this mountainside."

Here they had to stop; the cavalcade halted — its vast length was invisible in the windings between rock and torrent. The clouds broke in rain, which had long been threatening; and when the storm lifted, there upon a sudden stood a castle high up against the sky. And the Grand Master in the van said to the King:

"Sire, Charbonnières. Let Your Majesty give the order and we'll take it."

"The order is easily given," the King muttered into his beard. Then he went on: "Grand Master, you are soaked to the skin beneath that heavy cloak. Bring up the artillery, and do not forget the balls and powder, and all the equipment on those four-horsed wagons; there's work for three days' rain."

Rosny toiled all day; he fell into a fever and had to be bled. Next morning he mounted his horse, to reconnoitre; the castle on its boss of rock looked unassailable. But, as Rosny knew, there was no part of the earth's crust that was not penetrable somewhere, and he meant to find the weak spot. Brave Crillon was the first to lose patience. "Death and the Devil!" he exclaimed. "Grand Master, are you afraid they will shoot? At you, perhaps, but not at me."

The Grand Master, with ineffably Christian dignity, took his superior officer by the hand and led him out into the open. From above, the musket bullets whistled round their ears, until Crillon confessed he had had enough. "Yes, I see the rascals care neither for the Grand Master's staff nor for my Cross of the Holy Spirit. They might get us in the end. Let us take cover, you are a brave and excellent man," said Crillon, forgetting his fears in his amazement at the Grand Master. He had been accustomed to regard him as no more than a man who transported material of war for other men to use.

The army conceived a new idea of this same Rosny. While the war lasted, Frenchmen became acquainted with what they had often complained of with less reason — an autocratic government. The King had given plenary powers to Rosny that he might win his war. Finances and Artillery, in the hand of the same Minister, lent a force and weight to his actions that spread terror everywhere. Rosny had stopped all payments by the State except for the needs of the war. He compelled the population, on land and on the rivers, to haul the vast supplies of war material nearly to the fighting lines.

Most notable of all, he took a short way with all traitors and weaklings. In his contingent all the officers were new, devoted to him personally, and with a sharp eye for the doings of their commanders. A Marshal and the Governor of a city would, by tradition, have had the right to make personal compact with the enemy. Better not to win too marked a victory, and there would, in the end, have been advantage for the Duke of Savoy as well as Marshal Biron. Savoy counted upon Biron and took no steps to oppose him in the territory of Bresse. But Biron, whether he would or no, had to march from victory to victory; the Grand Master's artillerymen did no otherwise, and they kept a sharp eye on him.

It was a new fashion in war; moreover, it was the King's war and his alone; any man who went his own way was stamped as a traitor and would soon find himself in the grip of the Grand Master. Nor was any plundering or butchery allowed; the inhabitants were spared. The King had said that his enemy was the Duke. The army, thus transformed, admired their King. And from his Minister they likewise learned these new notions. In the end they not merely feared him, but respected him as a great King's servant.

Before the mountain fortress of Charbonnières Rosny made patient dispositions until the guns were at length duly placed. A pitch-dark night, an incessant downpour of rain, four hundred volunteers, to each of whom the Grand Master promised a silver crown. Soaked to the skin, they fled for shelter, and he had to fetch them out in person; some, indeed, were killed. He himself was coated in mud up to the eyes and slept for no more than an hour, but by morning six culverins were in their places. Thereupon the Grand Master found himself at odds with the King, who was in a hurry to see the effect of the fire, before darkness fell. Rosny protested. The guns must first be laid on a log platform and then masked by a screen of foliage. The King lost his temper.

"You want your own way everywhere. Pray remember that I am your master."

Whereat the faithful servant yielded, though sullenly, to teach the King a lesson. The fusillade failed, as was to be foreseen. "I never much cared for shooting at sparrows," said the Grand Master, keeping His Majesty standing in the rain. Next morning the whole mountainside was enveloped in thick fog. Not a glimpse of the fortress; and the King was pleased to deride his Grand Master. But Rosny remained unruffled. When the mist lifted, he laid his guns. One, which he had aimed with his own hand, tore a breach in the wall opposite. The defenders replied, and many of the King's cannoneers fell; he counted ten dead, among them two officers. Henri reminded himself that his Grand Master had been at Ivry, though none would think so. That was very different fighting, and death had seemed nobler on a battlefield. Rosny had been covered with slashes and thrusts, and a very solemn cavalcade had accompanied him home. A remarkable man! He began to feel they were all remarkable — how else did they continue after all the labours and ordeals of the past?

When the castle powder-magazine had been blown up, the garrison capitulated, whereupon the Grand Master made his entry on horseback, and all the inhabitants of the fortress received him on their knees. When they displayed their wounded, and the burnt bodies of the dead, he was moved, and granted them honourable terms. But of the indemnity he demanded he would abate nothing.

The castle stood on the summit of a sweep of terraced rock,

on which there was but scanty vegetation. The King went forth
one day with his Grand Master; and as they talked, he alone had
eyes for the mountain ranges, edged like glass in that clear air.
The Grand Master cared nothing for the prospect, being solely
intent on now taking Montmélian. At the council of war everyone had told him it was impregnable. The King, too, maintained
it was so as they walked along; but with the intention of challenging the Grand Master to excel himself. Meantime the King
looked at the mountains, clear as glass, the bare peaks, the chill
and fleeting colours of early autumn on the distant crags and
precipices. Over the snowfields hung the great blue vault of
heaven. Had the mountains above the King's head been his native Pyrenees, there would have been tawny torrents flashing
down the forest-mantled slopes to blur the still splendour of the
light. But here the air was brisk and fresh and frosty, and outlined with notable precision the target on which the guns were
trained.

It was the Grand Master's habit to be persistently reminding
the King of this or that, and he now bade him remember that
the Duke of Savoy had seen the King's cannon in the Arsenal,
when the pact had not been broken and they were on seemingly
friendly terms. The Duke was at once impressed by such powerful artillery, whereat the Grand Master warned him what he
might expect. " Sir," said he, " I shall use it to take Montmélian." And the hunchbacked Prince stamped on the ground
in fury or in fear.

" Grand Master," said the King, " you ask five weeks in which
to take this fortress. It is the Duke's proudest possession; you
will not have taken it by then. However, you shall have the five
weeks and direct the bombardment. I will be a mere spectator."

Monsieur de Rosny said that the King must not be exposed to
the dangers of the operations; but his real intention was that the
King should not be near enough to interfere. The King understood, and changed the subject. He remarked that this was a
pleasant expedition, provided they could keep out of the way of
bullets; refreshing both to body and to mind, for he was resting

from women, and from those who tried to involve him in such complications.

At this observation, the Grand Master peered sidelong at his master, askance at first, and then with a gathering smile. He was taller than Henri, but he could barely match the pace set by the King, and he began to shuffle along with his hands clasped above his out-thrust hinder parts. The King had always been light on his feet; he leapt down a slope and was back with an autumn flower in his hand before he had finished his remark.

"Grand Master, for the first time among these altitudes I feel that I am near the age when women will cease to trouble or delight me any more. Only one among them all was my joy and my possession. There will never be such another." Never before had he openly spoken of his lost lady. A silence fell.

"Sire," ventured Rosny, "the ship bearing your exalted Queen will bring you both possession and joy. You are merely sick of mistresses, and why this is so you will readily understand when I tell you the story of a King of olden time." The story that he told the King was none other than his own, and he told it to point a moral. Although younger than his master, the future Duke of Sully thought himself a fit instructor for him on all matters, from ballistics to love.

"Six hundred years ago," began the Grand Master, "a famous sovereign in the East lost his most beloved lady." It was sixteen months ago, thought Henri, and marked the purport of the tale.

"The Sultan in his grief swore an oath that he would never again enter his harem. Such a resolve was so foreign to his nature that those near to his person feared for the King's health."

"No," exclaimed Henri. "At Eastern courts there is much trafficking in love. Your King will have been much exposed to such offers."

"Well," answered Rosny dryly, "he did not need much persuasion. He bought a young maid for his harem —"

"Who was a maid no longer," interjected Henri.

"So far as that is an excuse, I let it pass," said the Protestant. "Now, grief and solitude may often drive a man into a frantic pursuit of pleasure. This is what happened to our Sultan, who was by no means content with a single purchase. He bought many women, among whom was even a cousin of his dead lady, perhaps for remembrance' sake. And he actually took his fleeting companions to the very pleasure-house of a certain money-lender, much frequented by his dead lady and himself."

Henri's lips moved. And whether the words were audible or not, Rosny paused. " This Sultan," whispered the King, " knew that he had nothing more to hope from love. He threw himself away, he fell short of his own measure."

The Grand Master did not hear, for he was looking at the mountain landscape for the first time since they had set out for their walk.

" We have forgotten the maiden of eighteen," he observed at last.

" True." Henri was taken aback. " Your Sultan, Grand Master, is forgetful. It may well have come about that, especially when starting on a campaign, his new love slipped out of his mind, for a day or a week. ' Fond star of all my dreaming, in yon far distant sky ' — that song had faded into the past. ' Oh, day of bitter sorrow, when we must part ' — why, he was positively gay! "

The teller of the tale then turned to another character, the Sultan's vexatious Vizier. " Our Sultan had an unpleasant and penurious Vizier. This Minister had been on ill terms with the dead lady on account of the expense that not merely she but her whole family brought upon his master; moreover, she wanted to be Queen. But the new lady was prompt to follow her example. Not merely did her father sell her virtue to the Sultan for a hundred thousand crowns, while the Vizier had to find the money, but what was the Minister's horror when his master showed him a document, signed and sealed, in which marriage was formally promised to the object of his master's desires! He counted three, and then — he tore up that high undertaking."

" Grand Master, you are telling fairy-tales."

The King stopped and looked his companion in the eyes. " You did not dare."

" It would have been useless," retorted Rosny. " You would have written another. You were set on Mademoiselle d'Entragues, and your sole concern was lest you might lose her as you lost her predecessor. There was nothing your servant could do but get you married all the quicker to a rich Princess."

The King made a wry face. " We have not yet received half the dowry we demanded, though I dare say it will suffice to pay for this war. But there is my promise of marriage in the hands of Monsieur d'Entragues, the same who supported the late King's chin on his deathbed. You might have managed matters better, Grand Master."

" It stands written — " protested Rosny. But what stood written was never to be known, for the Grand Master closed his lips and dropped his eyes, which no one had seen him do before. The King walked quicker still. Through the bare garden on the autumn slope they hurried in silence, the Grand Master beside the King, who wondered what stood written. " Love endureth for ever " — certainly not that. He loved Henriette as little as she loved him. He was in haste to get her because time is short when a man is growing old. " The feet of the men that shall carry thee out are before the door ": that stood written.

" Grand Master, out with the truth! I will hear nothing but what is true."

The voice of the King's servant seemed less harsh than usual and betrayed something like a tremor as he answered: " Sire, the sterner truths apply to me alone. I became jealous of your dear lady, in that she loved you and was your possession. Enough that I did my duty towards the King and cannot regret it. Death did the rest. But now you are scrambling over these rocks with me — alone."

A faithful servant, Henri thought, a model servant who, in the race against death, rid him of all the people whom he loved. Who would be the next?

Rosny did not wait to be asked. He named Marshal Biron, whom Henri loved, as a traitor. When Henri protested, he produced evidence. " Your Majesty will deign to visit the scene of his suspicious dealings."

" Grand Master, you want to get me out of here."

" Sire, here and everywhere I would have you conquer. My enemy is he who crosses our path." He spoke in his usual resolute tone. " Take my head. But if you leave it on my shoulders, the heads of those who betray the King shall fall — though they hold a promise signed and sealed, and their thirst for vengeance has prompted them to conspire against my master."

" Grand Master, you regard your own head as the only one that sits safe upon its shoulders. I will not hope that you are right."

Therewith their excursion ended. And Henri told himself that Rosny was always proved right by the event.

RETURN TO TROUBLE

The King visited his Marshal Biron at the scene of his suspicious dealings. First of all, it became obvious at once that Biron was trying to get the King shot by the enemy. The besieged could not possibly guess where the King might be unless they had been informed.

" This is a strange chance — explain it," said Henri, as though he did not know such mischances are not to be explained. But the man's treachery seemed to him even more mysterious.

" Your father loved me, and I him," he said to Biron for the hundredth time; for only the memory of the older man justified his favour to the son. " He began as my enemy and was therefore, when we came together, all the more steadily my friend. Do you think, Marshal, that an unearned friendship should beguile him on whom it is bestowed into hatred and vengeance? "

" That sort of talk is beyond my wits," growled son Biron; he was a thick-skulled, squat man, with a glowering eye, and hours of questioning would have got no more out of him. Henri resolved he would penetrate the man's tough hide and win him by a display of confidence. Truly a traitor can be softened by frankness, and in the end overcome — provided he be not a genuine traitor, but has merely lent himself to treason because, in war, it has become pardonable and even the duty of a man of sense. The leaders set up a state of lawlessness, in which each grasps more power than is his due. And Marshal Biron was not to be fooled out of what he could snatch.

It was to be the Grand Master's business to catch Biron in his own snare. Henri already saw, what Biron was to realize later, that an enemy like Savoy was not worth treason. His fortresses duly fell, and his army evaded battle. Biron abused him as dishonoured, but every man has his own notion of honour.

The first standards taken were sent by Henri to his mistress, Mademoiselle d'Entragues, to comfort her in her distress. Her room had been struck by lightning, and she gave birth to a child, which promptly died. So the promise of marriage was no longer valid, though the family made much ado about it later on, even using threats. Scarcely had she risen from childbed than she went after her elderly lover, and he hurried to meet her. At first she was merely tired and tearful, and the King was distressed at her condition. What should he do? On that very same day, the 19th of October, came news that his marriage had been celebrated in Florence. Henri made ready to apply to Rome for a pronouncement that his new marriage was invalid; on the ground that he was bound by his promise to Mademoiselle d'Entragues. The promise had lapsed, as he well knew.

The young lady soon dried her tears. In possession of the statement for Rome, she first demanded that he should not receive the Florentine when she landed with her shipload of money; or she insisted that she herself should be present as the King's acknowledged mistress. Incredible as it seemed to all present at the scene, the King made no objection. He did not seem conscious of the quandary, if indeed he did not actually provoke it. Bassompierre was in the room, no novice now, and on the best of terms with the new mistress. But he was utterly aghast; even Monsieur de Villeroy flushed at the very notion, and he was less disposed than any man to observe the claims of decorum.

Henriette flounced about the room, while Henri sat. She was even irritated by his kindness and good humour. "So I am to unloose the shoes of a foreign huckster's daughter," she screamed, in the shrill, cracked voice of an adolescent youth.

She waved her long, thin arms until her light shift slipped from her shoulders and exposed her little pointed breasts. " The fat banker's drab shall not come into my presence," she screamed, though this was hardly consistent with her previous demand. The King was always entertained by her tirades; he sat and watched her. Either this exasperated her still more, or she wanted to heighten her effect. She came right up to the King, so that he had to move his foot, and stood poised like a dancer, just as he had seen her on the first occasion.

The charming Gabrielle had then been sitting by his side. Those who wished to part him from her arranged a ballet and exhibited a girl who pirouetted before him on tiptoes so that he had to move his own feet; she so stretched her slim form that she looked down upon him with her fiery, slitted eyes. She did so now. She could now call herself Marquise, though Gabrielle had had to wait much longer for that title, and she was allowed to speak of the Queen as she chose. Henri shrugged his shoulders. He tried to establish tacit contact with the gentlemen present, but they turned their heads away.

Henriette d'Entragues suddenly broke her shrill tirade and spoke with an ominous calm that she thought terrifying; but the King was no less amused than before. He was old, she said sympathetically, and was getting rather hoarse. He had had to buy her, whereas others could have had her for nothing. Here it was she who tried to compel Bassompierre to exchange a glance of understanding — just as vainly as the King. Indeed, that nobleman was edging out of the room. " Stay," said Henri over his shoulder. " Your office keeps you here."

The new Marquise persisted in her honeyed insults. " You never leave that office vacant, Sire. The Duke of Bellegarde held it for your former lady."

The King leapt out of his chair, and his face changed. " That struck you! " cried she, now half beside herself; she pointed her long, thin fingers at him and shrieked out gleefully: " Cuckold! "

At this word she rose on tiptoe and danced a ballet, a miniature two-minute ballet, not moving from beneath the chandelier, but using all her arts: bending her lissom body backward until the hands touched the floor, the long legs still erect, with tense, out-standing muscles. And she had neatly slipped out of her last garments. As her head was invisible behind her, the gentlemen ventured to exchange looks with the King; and what their eyes said was: " A child, who scarce knows what she is saying. Never mind her dances and her antics. A child, with not quite all her wits."

" Madame la Marquise de Verneuil, you surpass yourself, and we shall expect great things of you." Whether he meant to or not, Villeroy, the King's Minister, dropped into the tone of an ageing man stirred by a happy stroke of fortune: sedately pleased, but still mindful of his burdens.

Youth, which here appeared, youth and youth alone made manifest, suddenly twirled her feet and leapt into the air. The leap ended in an obeisance to the King — effortless she dropped into a graceful pose to which she managed to impart a hint of irony. The slitted eyes flashed, and the heaving of her shoulders suggested the adoration of a slave girl for her master. Except that this, as all might see, was no slave girl, nor had she any heart.

The King laughed good-humouredly and threw a cloak over that lithe nakedness. Again in favour, she promptly demanded to sup with the King alone. She waved her hand, and the gentle-men were dismissed.

Outside, said one to the other:

" You should not have slept with her."

" Why not? " returned his companion. " Firstly, I did refuse. Secondly, the King is used to such a thing, and above taking of-fence at it. Thirdly, it was I who introduced her to him. Pray, honour where it is due! But if you mean to warn me she is mad, you have not reflected how difficult it is to satisfy a King whose desires are really dead. Only this young fool can do it — she will keep her place a long while, and while she does, so shall I."

As was morning, so was evening. All times of day passed alike to Henri, so long as this young creature kept him on the alert. She amused him, and she stirred him more than he would have now thought possible. She was a woman of moods, and her charms reminded him of the quickly changing airs. It was a comedy to watch her plaintive pose, drawing tears from her dry eyes. But was her bitterness real? What was the value of the threats that she flung out in a frenzy far too tragic? A turbulent young woman, thought Henri, and encouraged to be so by her family. Since he had lost the companion of his life, he felt so sobered and shaken that he did not dare to wish her back, he even banished her remembrance and forgot her — Henri, what remains?

There remained the lure of women, and of the senses. The old delight was never wholly lost, and the impulse that it brought would last his lifetime. Could his achievement have been different? Could he himself have been otherwise than he was? The forces were working in him; these fragile creatures had the charm that edged his energies. They were many, and there had been yet more as the years passed, each one overmatched by her successor, until with the last and most truly beloved, whatsoever of greatness and possession was to be his came to fullness. This meant dependence on the woman, which was a blunder and could come to no good issue in the end, as the King had many times been warned. Passion helps a man forward while he is young, and the King's youth had exceeded the common span; and even later on, it fructifies his energies. But — the bare patches come.

Nature, balancing her account, ignores the directing self, and futile passion becomes a mimicry of what it was. Bare patches: the ageing lover encounters violent loves that outstrip him and are not worth the effort. How gradually he had had to win his charming Gabrielle, how patient and persistent he had had to be, what abasements he had had to suffer before his passion was satisfied! It was a task as serious as life itself — he knew he must truly touch her heart before she yielded; he did so, and she was wholly his at last. If Henriette d'Entragues, so quickly a Marquise, his shameless, predatory little lady, had a heart at all, he would not trouble to reach it; for this time the indifference was his.

She hated him heartily enough, for she wanted too much at once and did not know what ruses to employ. She hated him for the promise of marriage, for the child that died, and for the Queen now about to land in France. But the neglect with which she was treated envenomed her more than all her grievances. It was to lend a savour to that neglect that she danced naked before those gentlemen. But worst of all — as Henri knew — was his deep-set indifference. He would not serve seven years for Henriette, nor even a day. He was in a much greater haste than that fastidious young person, as is natural: the bare patch. Let it be effaced in the swift passage of things perishable. Oh, to bear fruit once again! " Your energies, Sire, abide their time, you are gathering your supplies and reserves. Fear nothing."

The King passed a few hurried days with his lady, during which she abated nothing of her demands. After every night with him she rose as the future mistress of that court; it should have been merely comic and provided the ladies with a laugh at her expense. But Henriette had a malicious wit. When she got up, she called the King her " Knight of Good Intentions." As this amused him, the ladies and the gentlemen did not discover at whom their secret jests were aimed. That made it difficult for them to maintain the dignity that Madame de Verneuil demanded of them in public. Besides, it was never long before Madame dropped her poses and turned upon the King, her slim claws out-thrust. He had deceived her and betrayed her. He and his Bassompierre were cheating her like a couple of tricksters at a fair. She would soon show him what she meant to do.

Nobody minded and it was indeed a long time before she was feared. The Governor of Orléans, her father, might make himself troublesome to the King, but there were many who were glad of His Majesty's embarrassments. He would not marry this time, the real danger was past; no need to set dark schemes afoot as in the times of the dead lady. Thus Henriette could behave as she pleased. There was in fact some curiosity about the vengeance with which she threatened the King. In the meantime she gave the King pleasure in questionable fashion. It was clear that the King's senses had been perverted. But all delights were welcome.

The only risk she ran was when she abused a dead lady. She

had noticed this, and grew more venturesome. She had not the patience of a clucking hen, she was not a woman with a double chin, and, in her husky but fresh young voice, she actually began to sing: " Charming Gabrielle." At this the King stopped her and exclaimed: " Bassompierre, our horses! I will go back to the Grand Master."

The courtier had the hardihood to order the King's horse only to be saddled. " I," said he, " take the side of Madame de Verneuil. For I observe that Your Majesty has solely that in mind." In fact he ran from one room to another until the enraged couple disappeared into the same bedchamber.

All this was nothing; Henri would surely have to abandon these strange pastimes when the Queen arrived. On November 3rd she landed at Marseille. But the King and his lady still shared a bedchamber at Chambéry. The Queen had brought with her a Papal Legate, charged to negotiate a peace with Savoy; and it was high time. Montmélian would not hold out much longer, and the Duke was hopelessly beaten. Marie de Medici and Cardinal Aldobrandini approached until they were but two days' journey distant, and the existing situation in the pleasant town of Chambéry must now be faced.

The Marquise fell into a fury, she would thrust that promise of marriage under the Cardinal's nose and make him pronounce the Florentine ceremony invalid without more ado. The King should marry her then and there. His patience under this onslaught aroused much surprise. He appealed to the facts, he argued, as though that were likely to serve his purpose, but he uttered no command. Was a subject to be allowed to behave in such frantic fashion? When she was utterly frantic, and by then a little nervous, he suddenly assumed control. More astonishing still, the scene, and the abrupt change of mood, lasted less than fifteen minutes. He took her firmly by the arm and led her to a lavishly appointed yacht that lay rocking on the shining lake. The wild creature was suddenly tamed, and clapped her hands at the prospect of a sail.

Then she burst into tears, as was proper enough at a farewell meeting between two lovers, who must part, though not for long.

Henri had promised to hurry back to her as soon as he could, and she knew he would keep his word. He waved at the yacht as it moved into the distance and vanished, but before that moment his dimmed eyes could no longer see her as she stood and waved. When had this happened before? Whither had he sent another woman, after so many tears and protestations and so many vows and kisses given? It had not been a rushed affair like this, his heart cold and his mind but lightly touched. But then — oh, what sorrow and remorse, and how long it had lingered! — it possessed him still. Hence this fleeting and distorted image of the past.

The Foreign Woman

Marie de Medici disembarked from her ship, the bulwarks of which blazed with precious stones. That one galley did not cast anchor; it had been escorted by three fleets, Tuscan, Papal, and Maltese. The Queen brought seven thousand Italians with her, who were to remain in France, live upon the French, and go about shouting the speech of the foreign Queen.

The greater part of her escort were in a hurry to reach the court. The French gentlemen, who had arrived with the Queen, travelled more slowly, and slowest of all the Duke of Bellegarde, Grand Master of the Horse. The King had sent his Feuillemorte on a confidential mission to Florence and was probably expecting his report with impatience. But Bellegarde did not penetrate the mountains; he conceived it would be time enough to answer questions when the King reached Lyon and had himself seen Marie de Medici.

She proceeded first to the Papal territory of Avignon, where the Jesuits received her in their new style with triumphal arches and flowery addresses of welcome. The city lay within the kingdom and yet outside it. Heretics could here be burnt in effigy, at least, as was done at the theatre in the Queen's presence, sending an agreeable shudder down her back — not solely produced by the performance. Here was the figure seven; these learned fathers had discovered her secret. The number seven had a special influence on the career of a King who, alas, would tolerate no mystery and would set strict limits to the unconscious. Heretics are not burned in his domains; they are more esteemed than Christians. Could this really be the year 1600?

The kingdom is behind the times, and by one person's fault, if the truth must be told. Father Suarez, in the Papal city of Avignon, overcame his natural diffidence, since majesty is plainly sacred. But a prince must be called the more sternly to account if and when he misconceives majesty and the times in which he lives. "We stand for progress and the new age, we are acquainted with its style and taste, whereby the Divine deigns to approach the Temporal " — such were the Jesuit's admonitions to the Queen as she knelt in the confessional.

The first measure to which Majesty must be moved is the recall of the Society of Jesus to the kingdom — this for her own salvation's sake. Again he bade her keep a good heart and stand firm, for he saw before him a woman as imperious as she was narrow-minded, and he knew her for just the needed instrument. She should overcome the champion of free conscience, in so far as he still knew for what he stood. Women weaken the understanding of an ageing man, and this one might well deal the finishing stroke.

The woman herself, when she departed, was more than a little bemused. And when, at her leave-taking, the Fathers expressed the hope that she would have a child, she fell into a state of mystic ecstasy; they might well be satisfied.

Her own two thousand horsemen accompanied her as far as Lyon, where for eight whole days they awaited the King. It was no longer his lady who kept him in Savoy; her place had been taken by the Papal Legate. Scarce had she vanished when her successor peered over the mountains. The first disappointment was that Aldobrandini, a connection of the Medici, who thought to play into the hands of the Duke of Savoy, achieved nothing. The King of France displayed a very youthful determination. There was no exchange of compliments, he had his cannon fired in welcome to this crimson-robed angel of peace. The priests crossed themselves. And, against the echo of the salvoes, the King shouted that he had forty more like this, which were to batter down the fortress of Montmélian, whereafter the Duke must needs come to terms.

The war would have begun again but for an extremely heavy fall of snow. New mountains appeared on all sides, and the besiegers were themselves imprisoned. The Cardinal said that Heaven had decided; against this, in due respect for the faith, the King made no protest, but outrode the prelatical coach to Lyon. He was suddenly in a hurry to see the Queen.

He took a thousand soldiers with him, for he had heard of the splendour maintained by the new Queen and did not wish to be outdone. But his troops were in a shabby condition, their uniforms stained and torn after three months' battling in the mountains. Their King was in his oldest campaigning garb, with boots mud-spattered to the knee. He designed to present the appearance of a victorious army, and he remembered that the finest triumph for a lover had always been victory. He was even prepared to enter her room in boots and spurs.

Outside the house he met some gallant-looking gentlemen, dextrously clad to suggest a sort of martial elegance — not easily imitated. Men are mostly dressed to please or to impress. Henri eyed them and suddenly realized that he had seen them before. There had been many such about the Louvre in times gone by, when he was the captive of old Catherine de Medici. From that same race the new Queen came, and all that she brought with her. Now he knew, and his eagerness abated.

He sent his old retainer La Varenne to her, the trusty messenger of love, now less inquisitive than of old. But even he was astonished when he caught sight of the Queen. She sat at dinner enveloped in furs and wraps, her head swathed in a scarf. The Archbishop's palace, her first lodging in the new country, seemed to her mortally cold; and between the courses she would clutch on a metal ball filled with hot water. She had already drunk a great deal of wine to warm herself, and when La Varenne had managed to convey to her that the King had arrived, which, owing to the difference of language was not easy, the blood surged into her forehead. First she made as though to finish the meat piled upon her plate, which had been several times replenished.

She seemed possessed by a sort of terror, which La Varenne ascribed to the cold or to uneasiness at having been disturbed at dinner. That a great lusty creature of nearly thirty should be afraid of her husband was quite outside his experience, and he would not credit it.

The Queen tried to throw aside her various wraps, but in vain, they had been too tightly swathed about her. She then grew peevish and began to abuse certain absent persons for deserting her. La Varenne did not know the names, except those of two elderly gentlemen who had presumably preferred their beds. It was eight o'clock in the evening. As it was unseemly that a lackey should touch the Queen, La Varenne undertook that duty and put his arm about her — even as he had once held another woman, and tried to ease her, so long as it was uncertain whether she would step down into a grave or up on to a throne. This time his service was rewarded with a hearty box on the ear. He expressed obsequious thanks, and took note that an authentic Queen had now arrived.

Henri waited behind a group of noblemen in a gallery through which she must pass. Here he had his first sight of Marie de Medici, though it could be no more than a fleeting glimpse. She walked rather heavily, he thought, but with dignity; her cheeks, which sagged a little, quivered as she moved. The face was already fleshy, with a long but flattened nose and colourless, vacant eyes. None the less, a woman with a body as yet unfamiliar was passing him on her way to her bedchamber.

" Well," he said to his Grand Master of the Horse, " well, Feuillemorte, old friend, a fine creature, eh? "

This with a touch of scepticism in his tone. Bellegarde gave him but little encouragement. He said that a war-horse, carrying a knight in full armour, could not be compared with " one of those slim little mares whose curvettings so enchant you, Sire," these being his actual words.

" Her feet are sure to be large," said Henri gloomily. " You do not answer? You travelled with her, you must know what her feet are like."

" They are like the rest of her," observed Bellegarde.

The King turned away abruptly, paced the gallery once, and was back again.

" My good friend, I sent you to Italy that you might see many things and I see them through your eyes. But since your return from Florence you have grown very taciturn. Travel usually makes a man talkative. What is it you are keeping back? "

" Sire, the Queen has a foster-sister."

" I know of her from my ambassadors' reports. The Queen keeps *cavalieri serventi* according to the custom of the country. It seems a harmless usage, since the Queen's confessor does not disapprove it. Is that upon your mind? " asked Henri; he began to laugh, broke off, and eyed Bellegarde, who looked away with an air of embarrassment.

" Well? " said the King, this time in a tone that commanded a reply.

" Sire, the Queen has a foster-sister," repeated Bellegarde.

Henri rapped out his ancient oath. " Is that all you learnt upon your journey? A woman that stands guard over another either warns off her lovers or encourages them. Which does she do? "

" Sire, she favours a third course, and a very rare one. Your envoys are discreet in their reports." Bellegarde said no more. The marriage was desired by all, and in no case to be thwarted.

Henri shrugged his shoulders. " The foster-sister has charms, no doubt? Pray set your mind at rest, those of the Queen suffice me. Now knock at her door."

The Duke obeyed, and as he knocked he cried: " Long live the King! " A posse of noblemen gathered in support of their master; the foreign woman must realize that the hour had come. The door was opened, and the King and his gentlemen were about to enter the room. Meantime the Queen, surrounded by her ladies, met him on the threshold; she clasped her gown and sank before him in a deep curtsy.

She was taller than he, and in her diminished attitude he could with dignity embrace her and kiss her on the lips, as a matter of course. To her, the usage was new, and without his help, but still grasping her dress, she rose abruptly to her feet, which he eyed rather longer than was seemly. Then he recovered himself and led her to the fire; the hand in his was quite rigid. He talked a little about the extreme cold and her toilsome journey thither. There was a pause before she answered, and what she finally blurted out, in schoolgirl tones, conveyed no meaning to him; no doubt she had understood just as little of what he had said.

In view of the difference of language and the obstacles to conversation, he decided to make a speech. She need not understand him nor reply, and what he said could be interpreted to her later on. But he gained an interval in which to estimate her charms. He began by excusing himself for keeping her waiting a week. Only a week, alas! he thought; for his second impression confirmed his first: her charms were too developed. It was a fact that her portraits depicted her as ten years younger, before her face set into its present vacant look.

He had kept her waiting, he explained, because he needed time to deal with a brigand. A French Queen would surely long to see French lands freed. As he spoke, he became convinced that she owed her shape and bulk to her mother, Johanna, and the crudity and harshness marked upon her face to her Spanish upbringing; but the lovely city whence she came had bestowed nothing on her save the sounds that issued from her mouth. He would not live with this woman for long. Only the night could save her, and then only if it proved especially auspicious. And this should be put promptly to the test.

He had spoken for barely half a minute, not two minutes had passed since he came in, when he began to feel ravenous. He introduced his suite to her, and she hers to him. More of these elegant gentlemen he had seen outside, each more sharp-edged than the last, despite the elaborate suavity of their demeanour. A dagger may be hilted with chased gold and lie in a velvet sheath. Two were cousins of the Queen, Virginio Orsini and his brother Paolo. Their appearance explained to Henri the foreign custom of *cavalieri serventi*, in which a confessor saw no matter for reproach. He had arrived too late, not eight days, but eight years too late, not now to be recovered.

Henri cursed inwardly, and an ironic expression came over his face; the two Orsini eyed each other, wondering what the King found odd in their appearance. He swore to visit his vengeance on those who had not warned him in due time what he must expect, especially Bellegarde, who had gone to Florence and should have enlightened him. At the same moment he discovered, decorously concealed behind the ladies, the handsomest young man of all. " What is his name? " asked the King, and beckoned to the man, who was handsomer than the cousins, but had hitherto kept out of sight. Here was he who should atone to the King for this infliction, were the King himself with his grey hair and muddied boots not equal to the task.

The Foster-Sister

His name was Concini. As he came forward, bowed with great ceremony, and was clapped on the shoulder by the King, Marie de Medici smiled — for the first time. Her set and pious air turned to one of foolish exultation. She babbled no more; she spoke as though she had actually something to say. These words were not to be ignored; the Duchess of Nemours translated them, for she knew both languages, and also knew a great deal about the persons concerned. The Queen had a foster-sister; the noble lord Concini was husband to this noble lady, Leonora Galigai. The Queen herself began to speak once more; she fell to praising this lady at length and with a vehemence that betrayed fear. And the foolish exultation faded from those now quivering sallow cheeks.

It was noteworthy that the foster-sister remained invisible; only the handsome husband stood and preened himself. The Queen turned her eyes away.

Between the Queen's translated words Madame de Nemours interposed others — her own and intended solely for the King's ear. " Two adventurers under false names. Be on your guard."

Then came the Queen's translated laudation of the lady Galigai's virtue and piety; then again Nemours on her own account: " The dwarf alone is dangerous, since she has all her wits about her. The husband is just a prinking peacock. You had better know from the very first hour, Sire, that your wife stands at others' bidding," said Madame de Nemours, who wanted the King to be forewarned.

That had to suffice. The Queen became more and more uneasy. Encased with her in her voluminous gown, some alien force seemed to swing her to and fro, until the King grew quite alarmed on her account. Then the Queen and her voluminous skirt jerked suddenly to one side, with what was more of a jump than a step, for she was plainly terrified. " Leonora! " screeched Marie de Medici in the voice of a talking bird or of a ventriloquist's dummy. Then, in a whisper, she said: " Leonora " a second time, and pointed downwards.

On the spot where the Queen had been standing, something had remained behind; and the company bent down to get a closer view.

What Henri saw was a shapely little personage in miniature, too symmetrically made to be decently called a dwarf. It was clear that she did not like standing thus exposed to view. Probably she spent her life behind the Queen's skirts, if not underneath them. She had the unhealthy complexion of a creature who lurks in the alcove behind another woman's bed. These enigmas of nature are fated to be destroyed by strange desires and passions. The present one covered its eyes with a veil, but in vain, two coals glowed ominously through the filament of stuff.

Henri recoiled. Here was the foster-sister; this was the last straw, he reflected, with lifted brows and staring eyes. The foster-sister also started back; her impulse, too, was one of flight. Some quick stroke was needed to relieve the tension. Henri tried to kiss the creature on the lips, but she turned her head away and struggled. As soon as he released her, the noble lady fled.

The room was thronged with both parties, the Queen's attendants and the King's suite. The weakly creature forced her way through the press by mere strength of will. The King's people as well as the Queen's were eager to make way for her. Someone put out a leg, but she did not fall over it; she rose on tiptoe until she could nearly look into the man's face. Then he opened the door for her himself. It was brave Crillon.

Henri, to Marie de Medici: "Madame, I would show every courtesy to your foster-sister."

She did not understand his words, but realized his purpose and implored him with outstretched hands to forbear.

It was useless to enter into explanations with the foreign woman. Henri found himself beside Madame de Nemours and said he wanted to see what was behind it all.

"Perhaps a knife, Sire," replied the Duchess.

When he reached the farther end of the room, Henri noticed that no one had followed him. Only the foster-sister's husband, Monsieur Concini, made his elegant bow and invited the King across the threshold. Behind him the door remained open.

Henri found himself in a short and dimly lit corridor, curtained at the opposite end. He shielded his chest with one arm, remembering the warning about the knife, hastened along it, and grasped the curtain before flinging it aside. But the heavy folds resisted him, which was no wonder, as the noble lady was therein enveloped. Her veiled eyes glittered ominously; it was here she had awaited him. She lifted the curtain outside the bedchamber, pointed to the alcove in which stood the Queen's bed, and with a few bold gestures made it clear to him what he must and what he must not do. She did not speak and so seemed more mysterious than ever. The risk of the part she had to play banished her fears, and the creature's gestures left no doubt as to their meaning.

He eyed her steadily, which made her uneasy, for she had a grievous squint. Then he, too, pointed to the bed; and, not speaking in connected words, which would have broken contact between them, he uttered three names, with a pause after each. At the first two, the creature showed signs of jealousy and distress and seemed about to dive under the curtain again. At the third, she recovered herself and tottered slowly backwards towards the beds. Then she clung to that imposing couch and, by her attitude, pronounced a venomous resolve to defend it against all comers.

Henri reappeared sooner than was expected among the Queen's attendants, where everyone, in spite of the opened door, had agreed to ignore what had passed. That mute encounter within had been a matter of moments, and when he was back among the throng, he could have believed it all a dream. He took a deep breath and laughed, and the Queen followed his example. She expressed her pleasure at his gracious treatment of her foster-sister; Madame de Nemours translated, and he made due acknowledgment.

Now feeling that he had done what it was his to do, he went off to dine without more ado. He took Madame de Nemours with him to the door, and when he conceived they would be out of earshot, he told her that he proposed to spend that same night with the Queen and asked the Duchess to prepare her.

In the meantime his hunger had turned to a positive craving for food. " I must have been a very long while in that room," he said to his noblemen. Bassompierre, who was in charge of all these matters, answered: " Sire, not half of a quarter of an hour." Indeed, it had all happened so quickly that time seemed to have stood still.

As he devoured his dinner he told them that they had made no impression on the Queen with all their martial display. " Why didn't you bathe and scent yourselves? What sort of conquerors are these who appear in mud-spattered clothes and are neither young nor handsome? "

They realized that he was speaking for himself, and that he feared his foreign Queen and her foster-sister. So they laughed and promised that the bravest soldier of them all would that night sleep with the she-dwarf. Thereupon Henri answered with unexpected gravity: " When that dwarf appeared, it looked to me as if she had crept out from under the Queen's skirts."

Therewith he visibly sank into meditation; his noblemen dared only talk in whispers. He pondered, envisaging the new arrivals who were henceforward to live under his roof: the sinister foster-sister, her indecently handsome husband, the two cousins and *cavalieri serventi*, all in confidential relation with the foreign woman he had married — for the first time by proxy. At the second wedding he was to lead her with his own hand to the altar, and thereafter his throne would be hers. And here she was — a mass of flesh, dominated by all manner of prejudices, and utterly without goodwill. She had purposely not learned French: he had been told this, Monsieur de Bassompierre had told him so, exulting in his knowledge; she called it the language of heretics.

That promised no good issue, and moreover her villainous company of attendants would roll her back and forward like a cask. It could not be otherwise so long as the foster-sister was with her. She, by reason of her perverted nature, was the strongest of them all. Henri had had a manifold experience of madness; it was to be met with everywhere, as Henri knew; and now madness, under cover of the Queen's skirts, was to mount the throne when she did. The dwarf hated him, she had a treacherous fear of meeting his eye. Henri could break her power. She, with those twin coals, glowing with the fires of an inner hell, shunned every other eye, because it could see through her. The evil eye that she so feared that she wore against it a veil was no other than the eye that saw her for what she was.

The hall of the Bishop's Palace at Lyon, where Henri sat pondering on all these things, was dimly lit. His companions in arms had left vacant places on either side of him; they whispered in the candlelight at the far end of the table and soon fell silent. Bellegarde alone sat by Henri, but he left the King to his meditations; he had pushed the candelabra aside.

The foster-sister's influence over the Queen was through her handsome husband, reflected Henri. For what other purpose did he exist? He himself was not to touch her, and he had better not dare make attempts on the others: the dwarf would poison him. The Medici was to be kept in that condition of foolish exultation which he had noticed in her at once. Concini was merely used to dazzle her; more he could not do, with his vain person and his fantastic name. In the last resort, if the ground beneath his feet seemed insecure, the foster-sister did not exert her power through her handsome husband, but through her own perverted nature. The Queen was afraid of her. When the King kept his ears open, he could catch the quaver in her voice as she mentioned the foster-sister and uttered her fantastic name. The Queen was a poor woman.

Henri came to various conclusions in that dim room, over his emptied glass — whether they were true or false he could not yet know. His reflections ended in a sense of pity for his Queen, her melancholy life, and her domination by this company of masks. His anger had quite vanished; it was not for nothing that he had a grey beard and eyes that saw too much. In the meantime he must set himself to master these people and the situation, and he wondered whether he would succeed. First he must deal with the she-dwarf.

Bellegarde began to think that the King had forgotten him. Henri suddenly bent towards him and said in an undertone:

" Feuillemorte, our friends were right, the bravest of our soldiers must sleep with the dwarf this night."

" Sire, they were boasting," said the Grand Master of the Horse. " None is so brave as that."

Henri tried a sterner tone: " Do you know that I was near to having you arrested, when I realized what these people are like, and what a quandary I have to face because of your neglect? "

" Sire," pleaded Bellegarde, " I know my fault, although it would have been too late and futile to have warned you. In Florence I never caught a glimpse of the foster-sister, she hid behind beds and shunned the light."

" Feuillemorte, you are lying, you knew that the Queen was terrified of her. Madame de Nemours admitted as much to me today; you said nothing. As a penance for your sins you shall sleep with the she-dwarf tonight and master her, you are just the man to do it."

So said Henri, and his faithful Feuillemorte at once grasped his purpose. And he would have thought it excellent had he not been himself concerned. He looked uneasily about him for support — and there indeed was someone who had been listening behind them and was now about to steal away.

" Sire," whispered Bellegarde, " an eavesdropper. Here he is, you could not find a better man."

" Hola! " cried Henri into the darkness. " Come out! "

The culprit did not hurry. But he was indeed the right man, being inquisitive and eager to be everywhere.

" Bassompierre," said Bellegarde, " the King needs for a purpose which you will already have heard just such a man as yourself: young and handsome, ambitious and astute."

" Do you understand? " asked Henri.

" Sire," pleaded the unhappy man, " I am shy with women."

Bellegarde answered; his chief care was that the King should be served. " That is of no consequence; darkness will hide you from your lady's eyes. You shall choose a hiding-place in the room where we were received by the Queen today. There will be no light burning. The foster-sister must in the end leave the Queen's bedroom. Keep your eyes open, as you will not find it difficult to do."

" No need to listen," said Henri himself. " Outside the bedroom door, at the end of a pitch-dark corridor, hangs a curtain. Fold it round you, and as soon as the door opens, put out a leg and the creature will fall into your arms."

" She managed to frighten brave Crillon," protested the unhappy victim.

" You are not merely shy," said Bellegarde, taking up the tale from Henri, " you are afraid. Moreover, you forget the honour that is offered you."

" I esteem it and am penetrated by my own unworthiness. It is to be my privilege to assist, on the wrong side of the door, at the consummation of the King's marriage."

" Do you like small women? " asked Henri.

" She is foster-sister to the Queen," observed the ambitious man. And he could be seen uneasily reflecting how much credit he was like to get out of the affair.

THE ROYAL NUPTIALS

Henri, who had taken a perfumed bath, was on his way to his wedding night in a silken gown and slippers. A number of candelabra were carried before him; behind him walked La Varenne and other noblemen, but the procession was headed by the Duke of Bellegarde.

King Henri pondered as he went his reluctant way, though if he did not do the deed now, he would find even less time for it in the future. Better at once than never. The nuptial bed of royalty is not intended to give pleasure to the sovereign, nor is he ridiculous because he may not be in his first youth. The gentlemen who escorted him through the house had lighted a young King upon the same journey with the same ceremonious look upon their faces; they must have forgotten that he was about to fulfil a function of the flesh, and their minds were solely set upon the high vocation of Majesty. Henri looked round at them to see whether they were really taking this wedding procession seriously, not to mention his bed-gown, which was dragging along the floor. To all appearances they were, or else their faces were inordinately under control. La Varenne, who had provided him with women, countless women and from all ranks of life, was here impersonating a high and dignified officer of the Crown.

Henri did not laugh, he sighed. He walked on, and as he walked, he thought that there was not much to be expected from the approaching encounter. He would win the Queen's love without the aids of art, and would play the Knight of the Good Intention for no reward, he thought, for his insolent young Marquise had called him so for everyone to hear. He would never prevail against that gang of foreigners — by whom he meant Marie's two cousins, and the third, the handsomest of all. Not to mention the foster-sister. The foreign woman would never be wholeheartedly on his side, which would greatly imperil his kingdom — all of which he clearly envisaged on his way to the Queen's bedroom.

And yet all this could be repaired, he realized, if he could implant in himself a real desire for her love. But he had no desire for love, as love. That was finished, finally. Then why consummate this marriage? For the sake of the dowry? Of course not. The heir must be begotten: the heir of Medici blood. But as she had no desire for him, nor he for her, the heir would be wholly hers, not his at all; but he would be the lawful heir.

As he walked on, confronting the future with so clear a vision, he suddenly bumped into a doorpost; it was the door of the room in which the Queen had received him that day. He stopped, to the general surprise, and the whole procession halted. Henri reflected that he had had an heir and had never wondered how much of his blood was his and how much came from his mother. Their blood had been united by the commingling of their hearts, and their feeling for the country and for the kingdom. Everything had been done, every precaution had been taken, that Gabrielle's son should be certain of the throne. And now he himself must dethrone and disinherit him. It was true; he was about to fulfil an act of sovereignty in which there would be no pleasure, or it would be an evil act indeed.

The Duke of Bellegarde ascribed the King's hesitation to their secret understanding with Monsieur de Bassompierre. He whispered to the King not to be uneasy, no one would lift that curtain before due time and find what was concealed in it. Until then their emissary lay hidden elsewhere — " but he is eager for the encounter," said Bellegarde.

" God forbid that we should envy him," replied Henri, with a look that only Feuillemorte could have understood, had he not been here on duty.

Thus encouraged to proceed, the King and his escort traversed the room and the short corridor leading to the Queen's bedchamber; they opened the door when no answer came to repeated scratching and knocking. The reason was plain at once, for all the attendants in the room were beside themselves. The Queen lay like one dead upon her bed and was being chafed with hot towels.

The King was aware of unuttered reproaches for being in too much hurry to consummate the marriage and so frightening the Queen. And truly she was cold all over, as he discovered for himself. At the touch of his hands, she blinked, promptly shut her eyes, and again lay for dead. The foster-sister pushed between the King and the bed and thrust him away, pointing to the indignant faces all about him: the Queen's women, the doctors she had brought with her, and certain handsome cavaliers who had insisted on being admitted. The King promptly marked the three he had in mind.

The looks they gave him brought the blood into his head. His mood of resignation and acquiescence suddenly veered into a fury. Madame de Nemours, who was watching him, expected an outburst. She pointed out to him that the Queen's servants, and especially her ladies, by no means took her part, and that they were much more annoyed with their mistress than disapproving of the King. The Queen on her wedding night was behaving like a virgin of fifteen, which was scarcely appropriate; but she did so with the best intention, to arouse the King's affections — so said Madame de Nemours.

Henri barely listened. The faces of the two cousins and of the elegant Concini plainly irritated him more and more, and Bellegarde, who eagerly awaited the King's command, read it in his glowering eyes. " Long live the King! " he shouted, and the other French gentlemen angrily took up the cry as they fell upon the throng of foreigners and drove them out of the room. This was not easy, as the room was crowded, nor was it done without violence, as the King's noblemen were not popular among the Italians. More than one of the Queen's handsome cavaliers would go about for a while with one eye closed. The ladies shrieked as they were chased through the rooms and corridors. They yielded in the end, and some rewarded their conquerors, while some did not.

When silence at last descended on the house, Henri called the only lackey left to light the Duchess of Nemours back to her room. She turned her head as she departed. " Sire," said she, " good luck with your Queen. But the Duke of Bellegarde should not have made you so many enemies merely that you might be alone with her the sooner."

The same thought came into Henri's mind when all the company had gone. But the deed was done, the seal was set upon the future relations between the parties of the King and of the Queen. They would live side by side in the palace of the Louvre, waiting, hand on hilt, for what might happen. He would forbid duelling, but could he forbid murder? He could see troublous times at hand, thanks to his foreign Queen and her retinue. He thought of his court in the days of another lady, when women were held in respect and men had forgotten how to cheat and brawl.

Times had changed. The year was 1600. It was not the unlucky Feuillemorte who had helped to bring about these changes, it was the King himself and his marriage, which had been unavoidable, together with all its consequences. He had bowed his head as he pondered; suddenly he looked up and cursed himself. The outcome? A Dauphin: for that purpose he was here. Were these the proper thoughts for a wedding night?

The Queen lay rigid still, but this time she was warm. She blinked one eye distinctly and with meaning, either by way of an enticement to Henri or as a warning. Ah, it was a warning, for she moved her head very slightly slantwise towards the narrow alcove behind the bed: something was there that he must see. And Henri peered cautiously across the bed. The foster-sister there stood hidden, her face wrapped in one of the bed-curtains, not knowing she was discovered. But only the she-dwarf could have wedged herself into that narrow gap, and she could not be got out except by force. Henri determined there should be no more violence in that room. The creature might, more than anyone else, wreck his marriage.

She must be removed with due decorum. Outside, an adventure was awaiting her, as Henri suddenly remembered. How was she to be approached? Henri and Marie eyed each other, for the first time in understanding. "Leonora!" said Marie beseechingly. "Dear Leonora!" she cooed. But to that soft appeal came no reply.

Then she said — and these few words were understandable by anyone: "The King has gone. We are alone." But she looked at him imploringly, and with a plainly practised gesture she clasped the ten fingers of her two hands, parted them, and clasped them once again — all in a flash. Henri scarce believed his eyes, especially as hers conveyed a confirmation of her meaning, in case he had not understood. He even lifted a corner of the coverlet. He took the hint and crept in, disappeared, and lay with a pillow pressed down on his chest.

What then took place he could only surmise, for he was not a witness. It would seem that the creature left her lair and looked round for the King; and the Queen, to conceal him yet more surely, flung an arm across him, so that he came near to suffocation under the pillow and the lady's weight.

Then the dwarf began to speak — in such a torrent of fury that each word swallowed up the next, and the sense of it all was lost. But the whole tirade was clearly directed against Marie. She was no doubt accusing her of misplaying her pose of innocence. A Dauphin indeed! She must have made plain that so long as there was no Dauphin, they would have the King in hand. And by " they " she meant herself. And through the blankets and the pillows came a sound that seemed to suggest that the Queen had had her face slapped. Marie, in reply, uttered three words that were clearly audible, and they were: " fever," " thirst," and " lemonade "; and the shrill hoarseness of her voice intensified them into a cry of distress. Marie spread some more of her person on that already loaded pillow, by way of conveying to her husband that she was disposing of Leonora by sending the wretched creature for lemonade.

But the lady Galigai refused to wander about that dark house alone. Her fresh outburst could only mean that it was Marie's own fault if she were lonely and deserted. Why had she let her people be turned out? Was the lady Galigai expected to suffer for a fat and foolish woman who served as a Queen for these heretics and barbarians? A quest for lemonade might prove very perilous, and Marie would have to endure her thirst unquenched.

Marie made one further effort. Came a heavy sigh, and her full weight dropped on the King; once more she contrived to lie prostrate, as though the breath had left her body. The foster-sister greeted this performance with a shrill burst of laughter. The creature's lungs seemed inexhaustible — at least to the anxious ears of the half-stifled King. But at last, as he listened, the sound of that laughter grew fainter and seemed to recede. The burden upon him was lifted. Marie raised the coverlet and very expressively made clear to him what had happened. She struck the edge of her right hand against her left arm, in token that someone had made a very quick departure.

Henri could now see with his own eyes that the other, in her blind fury, had quit the field. He dashed to the door, double-locked it, shot the massive bolt, and looked round. Marie lay ready, naked as she had been born. She received him with the words:

"By order of the Fathers, in fulfilment of my duties to the faith, and because my uncle, the Grand Duke, has so commanded, I am willing to bear you a Dauphin."

It was not until afterwards that he pondered on her meaning, and felt but little gratified so far as he understood her. Here and now her words were of less moment. He had before him a lavishly proportioned human form — and he would certainly have felt no aversion to its exuberant contours in the times when he was indiscriminately greedy of every new experience. But he was not so now, as he realized, in the presence of his foreign wife and her proffered charms. He might have refused them; but should the woman who was willing to bear his Dauphin be the first woman he refused?

Before him, between the dark curtains of the bed, lay a woman whose experience was complete. The fainting-fits of trembling maidenhood had been a pose — though, no doubt, a needful one. Another pose was her unquestioning acquiescence in her husband's will to deal with her as was his duty. Her left hand grasped one of her great breasts, and a fold of flesh hung down over the fingers; the other lay open against a massive flank, so smooth that the observer had never seen the like of it. Daughters of foreign lands are made known to us in many aspects, but they first surprise us by the rich resilience of their limbs and body. The opened hand betokens the very essence of desire, crude and undisguised. The belly quivers, the weight of it tipped sideways, as the body lies and breathes; and the arched hips quiver too. But most significant is that opened hand.

Beauty is born of desire, and there are beauties offered here that do but need an understanding eye. The head lay upturned backwards over the pillow, in what looked like resigned abandonment: a chaste lady, who would prefer not to know what is now to happen. The attitude showed the face foreshortened, to its advantage. It looked thinner; the sagging cheeks were lifted, and seamed by a line that might have been marked there by weariness of body and of life; he could not tell, he must try to understand. Shadows covered the hair — that lustreless, sallow hair — and shadows closed the eyes, which seemed to look more kindly upon the high deed now to be accomplished. Against the sharp edge of shadow the pallid face looked delicately white. The lips were parted, unconsciously, it would seem. They barely stirred, but what they might utter if they did could scarce fail to be understood.

" Here lie I, a stranger, and I have come from far away to you, who are to me a stranger also. We have business together, and that business is not love. You have loved others; are you surprised that I love others too? And I am none the happier for it than are you. If you rid me of all my retinue at one stroke, I should no longer need to fear anyone except yourself. You would be beyond measure hateful to me — though you are so now, since I and my son are to inherit your kingdom. So I beg you the more urgently to do upon me what you have to do. My breasts, my belly, and my hands — they do not deceive. Take them in this curtained darkness, embrace the white, rounded flesh that is my body; I would have you know that full-bodied women are to be the mode of the new century. Come! "

He was prompt. The vision had its effect, and not a half-minute had passed — just so long as was needed by certain others outside the door for what they had to do. At the moment when the royal pair were engrossed in their own affairs, there was heard without a shriek, a fall, the sound of a struggle and of flying feet — all of which was by no means in order. What could be happening? He must go and see. But his lady, being carnally inclined, held him all the more tightly in her arms when the deed was done. She talked, or rather babbled, with her eyes still shut — though most of what she said was meaningless. " Leonora," said a tremulous, girlish voice. Leonora, the foster-sister, must be consigned to hell, if she were not already on her way thither, which was much the same to a mind like that of Marie. She meant to keep him where he was, he was not to expose himself to any perils outside the door until she was wholly certain that she had conceived a Dauphin.

This she had done, she was sure, Heaven had blessed their efforts. The Dauphin and Heaven — these two words revealed to Henri all that he needed to know. Unluckily there was more to be faced than the matter in hand, which was not really a common interest of them both; for the foreign woman hoped to bear a Dauphin to the King, and yet she was his adversary. He would have discovered this in her arms had he not already known it. She sat up and promptly began to talk about the Fathers in Avignon: he must recall them. She had deserved this for her goodwill; and only the Society of Jesus could confront the new age and the present spiritual state of Europe.

She raised her voice because she believed that loud speech must needs be understood and prevail. He did realize the insistence with which a foreign power addressed him and urged its claims upon him — from the marriage bed. So soon as he had achieved his purpose on the body of this woman, she was transformed into an agent of the enemy. No babbling, no wheedling talk. The mask of innocence and of sensuality was put aside. She spoke her mind, made no secret of her ambitions, and plunged into matters that she could neither understand nor compass, with all the arrogant ingenuousness of the foreigner.

Now, upon this earth folly is victorious in the end, as Henri well knew. When he won a victory, he had from each occasion to the next merely won a respite against folly. Had he believed that he could go on doing so for ever? Today indeed he hoped that what he had achieved would last his lifetime. The Jesuits would no doubt return to the kingdom some time, but hitherto he had never admitted that he might recall them himself. His people should not kneel beneath those garish triumphal arches, nor would he have them stupefied by those exuberant orations.

They should not be agreeably awed by those mystic pantomimes, nor strain their scanty wits over the mysteries of the number seven. They should not be besotted by abuse of the intellect, nor inveigled into a love of death, which is contrary to nature. The King was at hand and on the watch. Better, almost, admit into the country their countless writings in justification of tyrannicide. Here stood the King.

Marie de Medici realized this; she was not prepared for it, and she was exceedingly afraid. Suddenly she saw the King standing beside her with his bed-gown flung about his shoulders; and his face looked very ominous. She wondered if she would escape with banishment to a cloister! In her terror, she hovered between two expedients. One was to lie like a corpse once more, this time as cold as ice. She chose the second; she fell to speaking French. She could not really speak the language, but on the voyage to France someone had given her a love romance, from which she might pick up a few turns of speech. Again she dropped into that pleading voice that so ill accorded with her ample person. And she said:

"Adorable youth! Roses grow beneath your feet as you pass by. Even the rock remembers it has a heart when you approach with that air of grace and purity, to which all nature must bow down. The rock — a bewitched maiden, as we know — sheds salt tears. And in your honour, a spring bursts forth that no shepherd has ever seen before."

The King was at a loss. The shepherd did not see the rippling spring, nor the Queen her own absurdity. "Madame," remarked the King, "I recommend you above all to improve your pronunciation. The pursuit will serve to pass the time, and meanwhile you will not talk of matters that do not concern bewitched maidens."

He was at the door, and shot back the bolt. "You must now allow me to go and see what has been happening outside."

It was pitch dark, Henri groped his way down the short passage to the room where the Queen had first received him. Here something stirred, and he thought he heard a gasping sigh. "Who is there?" No answer but a deeper groan. Henri made his way towards it, and at last, by the farthest window, he discovered a figure huddled in a chair and hiding its face.

"Bassompierre! Is that how you have spent the night? Why did you make no sign?"

"For very shame, Sire. I have been stabbed. A man like myself, stabbed by a she-dwarf."

"She is the Queen's foster-sister," Henri reminded him.

Monsieur de Bassompierre admitted that this lent a lustre to the affair. None the less, it had been an unpleasant one. What had happened? He could scarcely say; it had been such a breathless and bewildering encounter, without sense or reason. The intention was that the aspiring nobleman should put a foot out from behind his curtain, and so trip up the creature. Instead she had tripped him up. Had she known that someone was behind those curtains? She tore them apart, and he lost his balance, though he managed to grab one of her heels as she leapt over his prostrate form.

"Well, at least you threw down the Queen's foster-sister."

"Not as I had meant to do. As we lay on the floor I began to protest my passion, and indeed I was prepared for any sacrifice. Meanwhile she was fighting for her honour tooth and nail."

"Brave little dwarf!" observed Henri, secretly regretting that the other foster-sister had defended her chastity with rather less success, so that by now she was in possession of the Dauphin.

"And what happened next? Are you badly wounded?" he asked his unlucky comrade of the night. And Bassompierre sighed.

He explained that he had then picked up his little sweetheart and meant to carry her, still struggling, to where he could do his pleasure on her. But as he had to protect his nose against the lady's teeth, she got a hand free, whipped out some pointed object, and drove it straight at his heart. By good luck he caught the weapon, which merely grazed his shoulder, making no deep wound. Thereupon he had hurled the lady from him, with some abruptness, which he now regretted. She crashed on to the floor, and he could still hear her moaning as she darted away on all fours and was no more seen.

Henri thought it not unlikely that she had been hidden in the room and so had heard everything that was said. But he kept the surmise to himself: Marie de Medici might be standing in the dark passage, listening.

" Is your wound giving you pain? " he asked. " We had better send for a surgeon."

" Spare me the shame, Sire," pleaded Bassompierre. " The house will be roused. Certain defeats are better endured in silence."

" True," agreed Henri. " The dawn will soon break, and then we can go our ways."

So saying, he also sat down, and both waited for the night to end.

Of Treachery

Then followed festivities; and also a fresh attempt on the King's life, which, however, was kept secret. One day the Legate pronounced a solemn blessing on the newly married pair; where-upon Henri would have promptly taken his departure, for the nights with the foreign woman were becoming more than he could bear. But there was still peace to be made with Savoy, and negotiations would be difficult, though the Duke had lost the campaign. He was ready to give up the disputed part of his ter-ritories; but he had it in mind to keep the French province of Bresse. In that contention Henri and his Grand Master espied a villainous trap.

In Savoy there were many heretics and they were persecuted. If the King of France installed a Protestant Governor, he would promptly find himself at odds with the Pope, and otherwise with those of the Religion. His Grand Master had assured him at Lyon that there was a complete understanding between Savoy and Biron.

" Sire, you will see that Biron is incorrigible and beyond all rescue. You have created him Admiral, Marshal, Duke, and Peer. You appointed him Governor of Burgundy, a post always held by a Prince of the Blood. He holds one of our frontiers, and it is his duty to protect it. You know what he has done instead."

" I do not know, because I cannot believe it," returned Henri. " Treachery is against nature."

Sully: " That is not your true opinion. Men, as you know well, are so made that they love treachery for its own sake; they practise it in mere exuberance of mind, or from an impulse of self-destruction."

Henri: " You are an able Grand Master. None the less, I can think of one who never — "

He closed his lips. Even that faithful servant had betrayed Gabrielle d'Estrées — none would ever know why.

Sully, after a brief pause, said in a low tone: " There may be one, but there are certainly not two."

This with a glance from those glassy blue eyes, which said: " You yourself have betrayed your faith, which should have been enough; and many men, and your own word — how many times! Was it always a necessity?

And Henri asked himself whether it had always been so; but could not find the answer. However, he induced the Grand Master to agree that they should wait and subject Marshal Biron to a test. But Sully left a special warning with the King.

" He will demand the town of Bourg-en-Bresse; that will be proof that he is conspiring to admit your enemies to the kingdom."

When Biron finally rode into the city he was accompanied by a great concourse. The whole street wanted to see the famous Captain; and he was well worth seeing, with his bold and ruddy countenance, his huge shoulders and arms — the burliest hind could not have stood against him in a wrestling match. He liked to think that his eyes grew quickly bloodshot like a beast's eyes; there were thirty scars upon his body, he had never lost a battle, and the conquest of Savoy was his alone. Such was the opinion of the people, who mostly confused him with his father and regarded them as one and the same person. Enough that Marshal Biron was the Captain they admired, and the King was not.

The applause in the streets banished his scruples, if he had any, and his fears, which had been genuine enough. The King had evaded the ruse, he took not a foot's breadth of Savoy, but he kept Bresse, a French province. How much did he know of the intended treason? Nothing, Biron believed, after his reception by the populace. Moreover, he also believed that a popular hero would be immune.

With a sinister air he presented himself before the King, who seemed good-humoured and friendly. " That was a handsome tribute to your faithful service," said Henri, pointing out of the window. Biron thrust out his great paunch with a swagger, and retorted:

" The people know me. I could be a Roland to your Charlemagne. But by your treaty of peace, which you made in fear, you threw away what a brave man won. I am sorry for you, Sire," snarled Biron, having so lately been afraid.

Henri ignored the man's arrogance. He showed the Marshal a statuette of the god Mars, modelled to the likeness of the King, with a laurel wreath about its brow. " Cousin, what would my brother of Spain say to this? "

The allusion and the warning both passed over Biron's head. " Pah! " growled the Marshal, " he is not afraid of you."

Henri clapped him on the paunch and laughed.

" A droll youth, but getting fat. Still, I like him."

At this, the face of the deluded man flushed a deeper red. His dull eyes began to roll and glitter. Was it possible, thought Henri, that here might be madness yet again? If the Grand Master knew how soon a weak brain gives way, he would treat treason as a malady. When far advanced, it is beyond the reach of art.

" Cousin," said he, " how much money would be needed to pay your debts? "

Biron: " My creditors! — I must become mightier than Your Majesty before I can satisfy my creditors."

Henri: " A perilous jest, but a good one. A man must make something of himself or what would he be? "

Biron: " Give me Bourg-en-Bresse! "

It was out. The test of treachery had succeeded. Henri eyed him sadly.

Henri: " Why do you want the town? "

Biron: " I conquered it."

Henri, in a sad but now harsher tone: " You had the Grand Master's men behind you, so you marched straight on."

Biron: " Your Grand Master's spies. The King does not trust his Marshal."

The words were uttered in a sullen rage; the man would yield nothing and admit nothing. Henri assumed the tone of Majesty. He stepped back and assured Biron coldly of his confidence. Only thus could he bring the besotted man to his senses. Biron cleared his throat, but replied in a voice that was still quavering and hoarse:

" Sire, temptation is very near at hand. Every great man in your kingdom finds occasion to grow greater at your cost. You are not feared."

" Until too late," muttered Henri, but the words passed unheeded. The traitor eyed him mistrustfully: what did this mean, how much must he confess? At last he mumbled something about the money sent to him from Spain, which failed to fill his ragged pockets. He would never grow rich. " I shall die on the scaffold, or in a poorhouse." Therewith he decided on confession; but he promptly added that the King must pardon him, he had but treated with the other side, he had made no agreement, and it would be better for them both to regard the matter as at an end.

Henri, with a flush of anger: " What threats are these? "

Biron, obsequiously: " Indeed, I ask Your Majesty's gracious pardon."

Henri: " You have my pardon for what I know already."

Biron: " For everything, for what I did or did not do."

Henri: " For what I know — you will do nothing more that calls for pardon."

In an instant he was at his friend's side and laid an arm round his shoulder. " We two," he said into his ear.

Henri: " We two, why should we betray each other? What could be the reward of that betrayal? — since money cannot help you, and when I had gone you would no longer be the man we know as Marshal Biron; they who have just led your horse by the rein would shun you. You would have to fly the country.

You would have to serve my poor brother of Spain, who is not the former Ruler of the World."

Biron, in sudden apprehension: " Take care, Sire! Philip III may be weak, but he can send murderers after you." Scarcely had the word left his lips when he saw the King recoil.

The traitor had touched the King's weak spot — not with any notion of intimidating the King, for he was fearful enough on his own account. But when he saw the King recoil, he recovered his assurance. The King feared neither battle nor beleaguerment, there were scars all over his body, though by no means thirty, but some of Biron's thirty had no real existence. He had often been in danger of his life, and on the last occasion his own Marshal had planned for him to be shot down from the fortress. Had Henri forgotten? Violent death appeared under several guises; only one of them shook his nerve.

Biron, in the harsh and dogged tone he had used at the outset, his eyes expressionless once more: " Take notice that I have warned you. It was with that sole intention that I began negotiations with certain conspirators. I am, and I remain, your loyal Marshal."

Henri: " My wish is to believe you."

Biron: " And to thank me. Give me Bourg-en-Bresse."

Henri: " No."

Biron, as he went: " Sire, remember! I am your loyal Marshal."

Said Henri, when the door was shut: " My friend, I am going to find it very difficult to save you from the block."

He left at once for Paris. His pretext was his beloved Marquise, he wanted to be with his Frenchwoman again after all his nights of duty with the foreign Queen. Meantime he wrote to the Queen, as was her due, letters beginning: " Dear Heart." Henriette was merely addressed as " My Heart," and felt the distinction. She made the usual scenes that entertained him still, though they had long since lost their novelty. She stood for everything that he regarded as French; and this had greatly increased in value since his marriage. Moreover, she was expecting a child by him, as was soon made clear, and Henri was delighted;

his own Dauphin could not have given him more pleasure.

Both women vied with each other in betraying him, and had done so from the very first. The Queen's unfaithfulness disgusted him, but she herself disgusted him apart from that. He did not even receive her when she arrived at the Louvre. It was in the evening, the royal palace lay in darkness, her retinue was belated, and the foreign Queen had to grope her way alone through the dim building, up staircases and through deserted rooms. Such furniture as had been provided for her was shabby and insignificant, and her lodging was mean and unworthy of her rank. She would have spent the night in tears, had so exalted a Princess been permitted to weep. Being what she was, she never forgot that she had then believed that this was not the Louvre at all and she had been subjected to deliberate insult. Another reason for revenge, were another needed.

The Marquise's revenge was more entertaining to the King; it was full of variety and prolific in storms. Henriette would in due time try to carry off her son to Spain; she would kindle the conflict over the succession, and the age-long Spanish enemy would bring succour to the rebels, as he had done in the past. She was in touch with all the conspirators, now, even at this moment, when he was on the track of his old friend Marshal Biron and doing his utmost to save him from the executioner.

She was a light-headed creature; she said what was better left unuttered, and she left letters lying about — all in the hope that her ageing lover would take her seriously. At last she had her will; he demanded a reckoning; he would stand no more of her dancing and her miming and her petty insults. He threatened her with punishment, and she laughed him to scorn. With her face close to his, she said in that husky voice of hers that held him still: " Banish me to a cloister, I am longing to be rid of you. Are you so handsome? Do you think you smell sweet? " Even this she flung at him, and not only when they were alone. Henri used more perfumes than ever, but his wicked Marquise still made scenes after her own fashion.

When he had extracted from her most of what she knew about this far-flung conspiracy, his one desire was to curb her tongue.

" Madame, your perilous secrets must not be published. So long as I alone know them, I will do my utmost to protect you; but take care. The Earl of Essex also believed he was safe because a Queen loved him, and he practised treason as his privilege. In the end my sister of England had to have him beheaded — and has had a pain in her own neck ever since."

The crazy creature drew herself up to her full height and exclaimed contemptuously:

" Yes, but she is a man."

This time the King did not laugh.

That same summer he travelled through the provinces where the chiefs of the conspiracy had their habitations; by this time he knew them all, and more against them than his Grand Master could have proved. Epernon in Metz, Bouillon in Sedan, and even the Governor of Languedoc, his old friend the Constable de Montmorency: all steadfastly protested their loyalty. The King had brought an armed force with him; they knew they were discovered, and their assurances became the more insistent. However, he had not come to hear their lies; it was his policy to make them uneasy, and that he did. He also liked to see traitors with his own eyes, a habit he had acquired in past dealings with his fellow-men. It was his godfather, the Constable, who deepened his understanding, though not the sorrow that burdened his heart.

At this time the Spaniards laid siege to the Flemish town of Ostend; therefore Henri had to put fear into those conspirators. His cousin of England urged that they should help the Netherlands: an aggressive alliance, but Elizabeth's terms were not lavish. Moreover, he could not leave his kingdom at that moment. If he turned his back, his enemies would plunge into their insensate revolt, for they feared no enemy incursion. The King travelled to the coast alone. Alone he mounted the walls of Calais and listened to the rumble of cannon at Ostend; he was beset in mind and galled by his own impotence.

If by long toil and effort he had made this land and people something more than happy — for they lived in toleration of

their various creeds, which was much gained, and they really had
a chicken in the pot on Sundays, or at least more of them did
than before his reign — it was beyond endurance that, here and
now, treason should dash between him and his achievement —
treason, a slavering, cold-blooded beast, one on which he might
well shrink from laying hands. On the walls of Calais, Henri
grasped an iron ring and leaned against the driving storm,
stricken to his very soul because nothing held, nothing could
stave off downfall and ruin. Knowledge was no support — what
did he know? But deeds were as precarious as knowledge. All
that remained was his own courage and endurance, which must
sustain him now from hour to hour.

Yonder in Dover the Queen, his ally, had arrived on that same
day and was waiting for the word he could not speak. Her ships
would have set sail had he ordered his troops to march. No, he
needed those same troops to ward off treason. Elizabeth urged
him to arrest and execute all traitors, and Marshal Biron first of
all. He answered: " She is a learned lady, much practised in conspiracies, and she cures treason in the surgeon's fashion, by the
axe. I am at a disadvantage as compared with her, for I have so
often found that only love, not force, can decide an issue."

But he reminded himself that he loved neither of his two
women, and that was why they betrayed him. He had bought
them, the Queen as well as the Marquise. They betrayed him
to efface their own humiliation. The women who set horns upon
men's heads did so in self-defence, which might be much or little;
but he who does not love them, should let them be. But Biron?
He had loved Biron and would save him even now. It would be
a heavy task, in opposition to the Queen of England and the
Grand Master.

On his return he went to the Arsenal — in no very cheerful
mood; what he had in mind to speak of did little honour either
to his sovereignty or to his name.

Rosny in no way shared his master's surprise at all this treason,
futile treason that could bring no profit to the traitors and would
serve solely to undermine the commonwealth; the end would be

not merely the ruin of a King, but the destruction of a nation and a people. Was this not in conflict with sound sense? Not to mention human obligation.

The faithful servant had his own views. The possessor of power never understands why he is threatened. Rosny provided some very simple explanations. He was surprised at the extent of the King's knowledge. But he laid a finger on the tender spot, he mentioned Monsieur d'Entragues, the Marquise's father. Henri stopped him at once. "You have no proof against him. On the contrary, the Marquise has told me everything she could."

This was what the Minister expected, and he decided to have the houses of both father and daughter searched. Henri believed he had safeguarded his Marquise and now demanded a respite for Biron. "In the first place we cannot touch him, he has an army and some guns."

"We will take his guns away," said the Incorruptible.

"I wish you luck," observed Henri; "it would be easier to arrest the others first."

But the Incorruptible demanded Marshal Biron's head. In the end a cold sweat burst out on Henri's forehead as he fought for his perverted friend.

Said the Incorruptible, calm and clear as ever:

"You know, Sire, that you cannot march your army to Flanders. An armed revolt would break out here behind your back."

"True." Henri had suddenly become as collected as his Minister. "My cousin of England advises me to behead my conspirators; she so dealt with her own favourite, Essex."

"She is quite right," replied the Grand Master. "And the first head to fall must be Biron's."

"His case is decided," said Henri firmly. "He will go as Ambassador to London, to announce my marriage to my cousin of England. He will come back another man."

Rosny doubted this, but he perceived that the King had closed the matter.

Biron did indeed go to England. One day when the Queen was talking to him, she fell to praising his master: King Henri had only one fault, and that was his clemency. "Tell him how traitors should be treated." And from her window she showed the Ambassador a certain object which she had always before her eyes to contemplate: the head of young Essex, whom she had loved. Only the bones were left, but Biron was familiar with skulls, he feared them no more than did Elizabeth herself. She saw from his demeanour that he was impervious to a warning. And she so wrote to the King of France before Biron's return.

During his absence one of his agents had talked, and the traitor was himself betrayed. His fellow-conspirators trusted him no longer after he had figured as the King's Ambassador. They realized that the King knew all and was retaliating: he suddenly deprived them of the town dues, without which not a nobleman was rich enough to stand against the King. They trembled and hastened to the King's camp, without waiting for the King to descend on them. The mighty Duke of Epernon assured Monsieur de Rosny, who was after all only a Minister, that the King had no cause to be holding secret councils, no rebellion was afoot. The Grand Master asked him to tell this to the King himself, which was exactly what they no longer dared to do.

Hatred of the King was especially rife among the Protestant population, for it was reported that the King intended to cease paying for the maintenance of the Protestant fortresses, while he was said to be collecting guns in his Arsenal, with a view to destroying the privileges of both creeds. The most important conspirator was the Protestant Turenne, now Duke of Bouillon, a wealthy prince and unduly impressed by his own importance. He had been poor in old days with Henri, when the King's prospects had looked no better than his own. A comrade of the lean years finds it hard to keep due measure when the fat years come. What, is the starveling of old days to give him orders now? This King is the enemy of every free gentleman in the kingdom, especially those of the Religion, and shows no gratitude to his Protestants for the old battles that they won. All this found credit, because it was proclaimed by those who had possessions, by which most of them were overburdened.

Henri, who received reports from every quarter, watched them turn against him: the Protestants as a body were hostile, even more so than the Catholics, where he at least gained as much as the town dues were worth. Moreover, the Papist communes remembered that he had always put down their oppressors, while his one-time champions of conscience had actually forgotten his Edict. He had in those days been beset by doubt — being in any case disposed to doubt. And now this far-reaching conspiracy, for which he must surely be accountable. After all his achievements, and the successful establishment of a kingdom, why should he be now abandoned by his friends and left in isolation as in his earliest days?

He summoned Rosny to Fontainebleau — though he knew very well that his uneasiness and self-distrust were no matters for his Grand Master. Henri said nothing on the subject, being alone too with his own thoughts. Bouillon and his bearded friend de la Trémoïlle had gone to their estates. Neither d'Epernon nor any other had stood their ground. " I should have told them the truth to their faces." He had not yet mentioned that he regarded all their treason as an imputation to himself.

His faithful servant praised him for his skilful dissimulation. The author of the whole vile business would all the sooner fall into the trap. He meant Biron, of course, for whose blood he was now thirsting. The King was pacing the little garden like a caged animal; Rosny watched him and realized that he must talk to distract his master's mind. The faithful servant was astute, he understood how to wrap up a hint as well as the weightiest decision; he disarmed Henri by analogies from history, or by reports on trivial affairs that are never far away from great events, and in their neighbourhood the great event itself dwindles into triviality.

Marshal Biron had no longer any guns, for the Grand Master had tried a ruse upon him, which had succeeded. He had persuaded the Governor of Burgundy that his guns were worn out. That excellent man had agreed; he sent the old material downstream, and, as arranged, the barge had started for Dijon with the new guns. But unluckily it had lost its way in the night and mist, until it reappeared at the Arsenal, where the Marshal's old guns happened to have just arrived. A good stroke, at which the King could not but laugh.

But Rosny went on with the deepest gravity:

"Sire, your Kingdom is at stake. You must put everything aside, your memories, your feelings, and —"

"And the shame of it," interposed Henri, whereat his servant paused, pondered, but could not grasp the purport of the word.

"Put everything aside," he urged the more insistently. "The example made on the person of your mightiest enemy —"

"Mighty — without guns?" said Henri. "Disarmed and beggared?" he added. "I could very well let him go, there's nothing left for him but flight."

"To Spain." Sully spoke slowly and with emphasis. "Mercy has abandoned him; you have no longer the right to show him mercy."

Henri trembled. A thunderous judgment from on high could not have called him more imperiously back beneath the sway of authority and duty. His relentless Minister was astute enough to leave him alone before the King became aware that his call had come and he must once more obey.

MIDNIGHT

In the little closed garden of the castle of Fontainebleau, a garden where many have been sorely tried, another now holds converse with his conscience. No one may intrude on him, although he is watched by the Queen and by his Minister from the windows, and more than one pair of inquisitive eyes is peering through the hedges.

For several days before Marshal Biron could arrive, Henri accompanied him in spirit. Time and again he bade him turn back and flee; more often he begged him to confess and fall upon his King's neck. On the 13th of July, early in the morning and in that same garden, he thought that Biron would not come; he said so to his retinue, who were massed round all the hedges.

Biron was a powerful man; it was known he had sworn to stab Rosny; why not murder the King as well? But Henri calmed their fears.

This was the first time he had awaited the knife without any sense of fear. Was it that he no longer wanted to live? But he did, and more than ever. Biron — his journey thither, his journey to his own death, so long and toilsome, Henri made it at his side. They had ridden together many a time along the joyous roads of France. He was really thinking of the father, confusing him with his son, just as his people did. Was he to be parted for ever from these old comrades? If they found it safer to join his conquered enemies, what matter? The self-deserter is alone utterly deserted, and it came to Henri's mind that, had none betrayed him, he would have betrayed himself.

He examined his own heart and sought despairingly for what might explain this treason — but there was nothing.

" It was I who brought down anointed Majesty from heaven to earth — for I never believed in my divine right. Nor did I pass each day as though it were a sacred festival. I was not the tyrant whom they would have hated and respected. I was fool enough to take from some their overplus alone, instead of all they had, and fill the poor man's belly on Sunday only. I freed no man from his folly, nor any from his madness. And yet, if I have so failed, I have not brought them freedom. At the end of it all I have to deal in secret with this last attack upon my life. Biron, spare me my own dishonour, it would cry aloud. I can hear it now shrieking about your scaffold."

Came the sound of a scuffle without. Henri promptly thought the dreaded hour had come. But it was a man unknown, who begged so pitifully for an audience with the King that he was at last admitted to the arbour. He fell on his knees and implored His Majesty to spare the life of his nephew, who had been condemned to die. The King had signed the warrant, he knew the circumstances, and they admitted of no respite. But he grew pale as he listened to the lamentations of the prostrate suppliant. A poor youth must mount the scaffold; you, the King, are secretly contending with a traitor that he may set you free.

To the suppliant he said:

" You are doing your duty as uncle, I do mine as King."

Within the next hour he and Biron were face to face. Biron appeared just as expected, his mind still set, as had also been foreseen. A watch was kept without, while the pair paced to and fro between the hedges, the King calm and unruffled, the Marshal in a hot fury at the unjust suspicion, but chiefly because he had been disarmed. From time to time he smote his innocent breast, and railed against the faithless Rosny for betraying him. " Would you have been betrayed by me? " said Henri; whereto the stubborn liar found no answer.

The King embraced him, waved a hand round the empty garden, in token that his guest might confess what lay upon his mind. " I! " cried Biron, and there was a dark frenzy in that cry.

They were seen coming out, one of them in high good humour, but the other breathing heavily and in utter gloom. At table with the whole court, Biron opposite the King, the sole talk was of the siege of Ostend. Henri observed that his brother of Spain, and all the Spanish ministers, must be aghast to see him arraigning his traitors. The war in Flanders would soon be lost for Spain. Biron gulped down his food and remained silent; but his thoughts were easily read. " You know not how you stand," said his flushed face. " You have ceased to be King among your noblemen. Now call on the common folk and see whether they will die for you, as we used to do."

After dinner Henri took the unhappy man into the selfsame garden. As though nothing were yet lost, he wrestled for a soul — which was already dead. " Marshal, try to think; you are — what you are, and here stands your King, Henri. You have no other who will love you. Whatever Savoy may have in hand against you, and your orders from Spain to reveal nothing — forget it all. I'll forget it, too, if you will but speak a few free words."

Free — Biron was so no longer. At Lyon, despite all his anger and arrogance, he may yet have been so. Here he willed his own destiny, though he did not recognize it; he was paralysed and speechless, and his face was already turned towards the scaffold.

Henri counted the quarter-hours and gave him until the fourth, or even the fifth. Suddenly he broke off in the middle of a sentence and hurried into the palace. There he shut himself up with Rosny and the Queen.

The Minister demanded the guilty head for the safety of the State, but had no need to say much; the Queen was much more urgent than himself. Her husband proposing to spare a traitor! It was his affair if he wished to lose his throne, but Marie de Medici did not mean to do so. She knew that the King had once appointed this same Biron, in the event of his own death, guardian of his mistress and his bastard. If he blundered in his choice of the man needed for such confidence, Marie must not suffer for it; her son the Dauphin should grow up under his mother's regency.

The word was out: Regency. Marie knew it in both languages. From time to time she spoke of the matters on which she was most intent, in her own variety of French — not pleasant to the ear, but quite effective. Henri realized that she had made her reckonings and dispositions for the time after his death. He was only temporarily there. And now the friend of his youth, the comrade of his struggles and of the century just ended, must die. It was not pleasant to the ear, the French speech of his foreign wife. He must pay due heed, she said, to order, and to natural law; and a chill began to steal over his body.

Events were moving too quickly for the difficult age that now confronted him. Must he condemn himself to solitude, send his last friends to their death, just before he followed them — was there really no respite? He turned from the foreign woman in disgust. " Monsieur de Rosny? "

" Sire, Marshal Biron can no longer be in any doubt of your purpose; he must be arrested before he escapes."

" Not before midnight," said Henri, and this was the last word.

In the evening there was card-playing. At last the company broke up, but Biron remained with the King, though uninvited. Henri saw that the man had no notion of escape. If he were not wholly beside himself there would come some light into his mind at such an hour; and the King's heart leapt with hope. Once more he appealed to their ancient friendship — but, alas, he was met with dry eyes, and lips tight shut — and midnight struck.

Henri turned away, walked step by step into his cabinet, and lingered while he shut the door. After an agonizing moment he opened it again — Biron was standing motionless, spellbound in his own madness.

"Farewell, Baron Biron" — Henri addressed him by his old name, which brought back twenty years of comradeship in danger and in battle. None heard it now. "Do you understand me?" No.

Marshal Biron was promptly arrested in the antechamber; he blustered at first, as though he took the matter for an ill-timed jest, and then assumed the role of injured innocence — in the Bastille, where a monk once more enjoined him to keep silence, and at his trial, despite all the evidence in his own handwriting, which he was vastly surprised to see; but he furiously denied it all. He had reckoned that the influence of the conspirators and of foreign powers would force the King to let him go. His party was strong and venturesome, the judges feared their vengeance if they condemned Biron. Among them, too, were actually adherents of the old League, which had revived again, as though the heretic had never broken it and the present King had never mounted the throne.

The roads had again become unsafe, the six hundred cousins of the accused had ridden up from Gascony, and there had been many a raid by armed bands. The informer who had provided the written evidence had, though under guard, been assassinated in a Paris street, and his murderers allowed to escape. King Henri had need of all his courage; more courage was needed to bring a traitor to judgment than to face the enemy on the battlefield. The enemy was most formidable so long as he kept at a distance, and by the aid of money, pamphlets, and the passions of the parties on the spot sapped men's minds until the hour came to strike.

Henri went through it all: despite all he had done to bring peace and prosperity to his kingdom, in those days he had to leave his capital — and he had to wait outside it, with one foot in the

stirrup. It was not the traitor but the King that took to flight.
He urgently warned his Minister Sully against letting himself be
caught; if they could get possession of his person, they would
hold him in pledge against Biron. Rosny indeed took every precaution, and must certainly have reflected, in his fashion, that
only a false cause can be founded on crime. Greatness and possession — these are rooted growths, brought openly to fullness,
to be duly tended by a faithful servant. Whatever a Minister
may now have and hold, this is not his kingdom. His greatness is
his master's, and in the worst event his person would be taken.
Henri alone, in those days, with his foot in the stirrup, grasped
the instability of his whole position, the fleeting present, his own
precarious existence — and even so there were fools that looked
beyond it. In those days the interminable twelve strokes of a
certain midnight boomed unceasingly in his inward ear.

Outside the city he received the prisoner's relatives, spoke to
them with kindness and regret, as the servant of justice and of
a necessity of State that he could not alter. He dismissed them
before they could observe what he feared, and what indeed might
happen: the forcible release of his prisoner and open rebellion in
his capital. There had been careful preparation of men's minds.
It was put about that Biron, a good Catholic, was being made to
suffer for his creed. A touching letter was circulated (not written
by Biron), containing all manner of reports to the King's discredit. The good Catholic in his prison did not even know his
Paternoster; rather, he was immersed in astrology, being extremely anxious to live and convinced he would do so. The
King was weak and would in the end yield to his fears. The
judges were beginning to lose their nerve.

Meantime it was not merely in the Parliament that the members were afflicted with catarrh, or invented some pretext that
prevented their appearance. Among the great lords of Biron's
own rank not one was willing to sit in judgment on the prisoner.
There remained the King's jurists of old days at Tours, when
Paris was still under the League; of older days, too, when they
slept on straw in jail and had been very poor. These now left
their soft beds and their pleasant houses; in the face of danger

they became what they had been. They stood fast, and courage revived. If the kingdom was destroyed, they would be the first to go; but these humanists saved it, for they struck hard. They looked to the King; he was imperturbable, and his command was that justice should be satisfied.

It is true that he had many supporters. Time and again Rosny, heavily guarded, rode to his lodging outside the city. Old Elizabeth, his friend, had written him a letter to impress something of her own inexorable spirit on this King. She knew that her cousin of France did not care for the sight of skulls outside his window when he had kissed the flesh upon them in days past. She knew — for she was near her end, and her century would take away, before her time came, the few choice spirits who had played the great game as she had played it.

Biron, however — a full-blooded man, who needed bloodletting — never so much as envisaged death. For the benefit of his guards and all who visited him, he presented an uproarious parody of the foolish doings in court. Scorn and the certainty of victory freed him from all restraint. Until the end he believed he had both power and justice on his side. Power because, while he was here raging in the fullness of his unused strength, the conspirators without must surely achieve their purpose, and Spanish soldiers were on their way to deliver him from prison. But justice was his on three grounds: In the first place, treason is the privilege of the stronger, which he conceived himself to be. Secondly, the King had forgiven him everything at Lyon, excepting indeed what Biron had not been willing to admit. These indeed were sophistries, and could hardly determine the decision of the judges.

The third and best reason was the indefeasible right and duty of the rich and powerful to defend their wealth. The wealth that made them all-powerful was to be used, at the first attack, against the State and the nation, this being the essence of right and duty. In the end the enemy had to be summoned in defence of property. This was not commonly his first concern, but such was the faith of the rich. They are on good terms with their faith and conscience, and at their departure they can still say with

Biron, the traitor: " Gentlemen, here you see a man whom the King is sending to his death for being a good Catholic." He did not know his Lord's Prayer, but he had faith in wealth, and in that faith he died — not without an outburst at the end. He strangled the executioner, and indeed he took him for an impostor. Did the King dare to send the common headsman to a man of his blood and sinew?

King Henri had exactly calculated the price he would have to pay for that scaffold. At the outset he was justified by success. The conspiracy collapsed, the conspirators were terrified. Biron's death, and it alone, frustrated not merely the rebellion but the war, and the ghost of the League vanished as suddenly as it had appeared. On his return to his capital the King was vociferously greeted by a mob of hearty loyalists: he was their father, to whom they owed their peace and life and opportunities. Blessed be the King! But it was a passing mood and was forgotten even before the treasury was full again and all the industries had been restarted.

The conquered had the longer memory. On behalf of their martyr, who had had to mount the scaffold, they had countless Masses said. In the course of the year this conspiracy was followed by several others, which were duly suppressed. Rosny was on the watch, the King would never question his counsel any more, for he had none other he could trust. None the less, these two laid strong hands upon the wealth and power of the kingdom. Biron's last word on the scaffold was: " Because I was a good Catholic." Enough to mark down the King for a violent death, even if he had not been so doomed before. Thenceforward he went about his kingdom in readiness for that hour. A very thriving kingdom, but behind the King of it walked footsteps; he guessed their presence, though he could not hear them. He who looked round saw nothing. All he could do was to live for the day — which was always bright enough, while the heart still beat.

Once, as he rode through the populous rue de la Ferronerie, he came up with an unknown litter moving in the same direction. The horses could not pass it and had to stop; this happened out-

side a house with an open archway, topped by a coat of arms
depicting a crowned heart pierced by an arrow. The King bent
down and tried to peer into the litter, but it vanished in the
throng. His escort wondered why, now that the way was clear,
the King still sat motionless, plunged in thought.

In those days he often used a certain phrase to clinch a statement: " As truly as Biron was a traitor." Soon after the traitor's
execution he visited his Minister in the Arsenal and addressed
him as the Marquis de Sully. Whereat that faithful retainer expressed his thanks, but merely as having received his due; he had
expected to be created Duke and Peer. These had been the
traitor's titles; they had been conferred upon him without service
done, in token of the King's affection. The King's feeling for his
faithful servant was one of admiration rather than love, and an
admiration too absolute not to be a little irksome. In order that
Sully might achieve his destiny and become a great Minister,
Gabrielle d'Estrées had had to die. Biron died, and Sully became
a Marquis. He was later to become a Duke. A man who is always in the right and rids us of all whom we love best is a trying
personage.

The Minister's huge writing-table was littered with papers.
There he sat at his calculations, whereby the kingdom prospered.
Henri turned to his companions. " So much sitting — would you
like to be in his place? I could not endure it."

Then Henri caught sight of a pile of papers and fell silent: he
could see that they were memoirs, and might well have been his
own. The faithful Rosny had no memories that were not his
master's too. As was to be expected, most of the notes dealt with
the growing prosperity of the kingdom, and were headed " Royal
Trade and Industry." The Minister, who in fact wrote everything unaided, in these papers pretended to discuss matters with
his secretaries; they had to remind him every time of all his labours and achievements, as though they had all passed out of his
recollection. And Henri marvelled at his friend's conceit. How
can a man write memoirs when every life contains so much
villainy?

At the same time, whether he would or no, he felt the tears

come into his eyes. He sent all the others out of the room. Alone with Rosny, he embraced him and said:

"Henceforward I shall love you alone."

Days of Mourning

When Her Britannic Majesty closed her eyes in April 1603, a great figure of the past century departed. The age-long ally of the King of France against the Spanish World Power, she had helped him to win his throne and to maintain it. His friendship secured her island against Spanish invasion. The two realms existed by their mutual aid, and for twenty years the two sovereigns had not forgotten each other for a single day. When Elizabeth died, Henri put on no mourning, but he did not forbid it at court, as his order might not have been very readily obeyed. Yet the court did something more, not by order of the King: as though by tacit agreement the dead Queen's name was never mentioned.

The King and the Queen of France lived in their palace of the Louvre, now a truly royal house, and scarce recognizable since it had been so lavishly refitted. It was observed with some misgiving that a special jeweller, Nicolas Roger, had been put in charge of His Majesty's treasures. The Queen had a gold toilet set. Her retinue consisted of four hundred and sixty persons, of whom a hundred and fifty-seven were fed, or " had their mouth at court," as the phrase went. The fifteen hundred court officials of the King almost all received a salary, if only a small one, and each of them had his proper title. There was not room enough for all of them to lodge in the Louvre, and at night the interior and the entrances were guarded by seven hundred soldiers.

Henri slept badly when Elizabeth was dead. His bedchamber was his cabinet, except that a carved and gilded alcove had been constructed at the back of it. On the left of the bed was a door leading to the Queen's bedchamber. Henri had several times locked the door since Elizabeth's death. Here he lay one night, when she had been lying but a few nights in her grave, and thought of her, for in the daytime he was beset by the living, and the mention of her was forbidden. For she had been a heretic;

she had put forth the new religion in the world with incomparable success, quite independently of the King of France, his battles, and his Edict. In the meantime he took his death leap and abjured the faith, at first only for appearance's sake, as Elizabeth had wholly understood, despite her early disapproval. She made no protest when later on he gave out that a discussion between Cardinal du Perron and Monsieur de Mornay had convinced him of the truth of his newly adopted faith. Both equally regarded humanism as their true creed, which is a belief that man is destined here on earth to be reasonable and courageous, free, prosperous, and happy.

She had done much killing, though she disliked shedding blood. So did he, but he had had Biron beheaded. It was right that humanists should stand fast and strike back when enemy forces tried to dam the course of human destiny. His militant Huguenots had defended justice and their own conscience, and he had always done so, as truly as Biron was a traitor. Elizabeth and he had needed to be strong and to exalt the office of King — but not by way of disparaging humanity. They should see and recognize their own earthly greatness symbolized in Majesty.

The night was often past before he had had time to envisage all that was in his mind. Was that the first glimmer of dawn, reflected into his window from the river? When the clocks struck five, the court would be assembled. When they struck six, he and the Queen would hold their levée. None might enter the next room with head covered. All bowed to the King's bed of state, although he was seldom to be found in it. The company were kept at a due distance; even to touch the bed would be an offence against the sacred person. A chamberlain stood on guard beside the bed, and the mere raising of the voice would be regarded with suspicion. Henri was acquainted with other suspects — and there would be more yet to come.

They had never, all this time, learned to respect themselves, and hence they did not respect life. A murder in the capital cost four crowns. He wondered what price had been set upon his own, and whether mourning would be worn for him. He felt drowsy, and his mind began to wander. There was nothing for it but to let them pay homage to his bed as a symbol, to a significance they could not understand. Men's minds were now set upon formalities, which had not been his aim; they were growing subtler, not simpler. He was tired of living in such company — why did he linger? Indeed, he was no longer wholly here, the dead Elizabeth had taken something from him when she went.

Must he awaken? It might be that he would have to come to terms with the Jesuits in the end, as they had already made terms with the present century. But if he called them back, to conciliate the age — Elizabeth in eternity would never hear what he had done. Blessings upon her! A part of himself had passed over in her company. Would they recognize each other on the other side? They had never met upon earth.

Except in her portrait. When he was a boy, little Navarre had been offered to her in marriage, merely as a ruse: his party was to lose its leader and bleed to death in civil war. Later on he had publicly kissed her portrait, that she might hear of it and come to his aid. In the Dutch imbroglio he had then made his peace with Spain regardless of his pact with her. In the end they had lost Ostend, while they vainly waited for each other, she upon the opposite coast; but against the walls he climbed at Calais, the same sea beat. They had missed so much, and never met — and yet how many people had been as near to him as she? Not many had manifested themselves to him as she did — nor he to them. Who but she had been his equal?

He had never asked himself that question when Elizabeth had been alive and there still seemed time for them to meet. The question drifted into his mind as he lay dozing in that morning hour. And the answer followed: " We shall meet in time to come: we do not die. As is made very clear in sleep. We end indeed; but the shadow of our consciousness passes over into other brains, and thence into others again. After centuries have passed, what we stood for will think and act. We do not die with our own century. I and my cousin of England shall know each other for ever."

He started as the clock struck six. As the King gave no signal, the five chamberlains, and the courtiers whose privilege it was to attend his levée, did not appear. A few minutes passed, then the concealed door behind the alcove was softly opened and Monsieur d'Armagnac peered in. He no longer served his master in person, so he was all the more careful to be punctual to the minute. He noticed that his master was completely dressed, and as he stood with his eye to the crack, he saw the King standing at the right-hand door looking into the state apartment.

The room so called was thirty feet long and twenty feet high, with three windows, two of which looked out on to the river, and the third towards the west. The famous ceiling was decorated with royal coats of arms against a rich and elaborate setting of weapons of every description, all carved in oak, walnut, and lime, and overlaid with gold, now growing a little tarnished. The walls were hung with tapestries depicting the legends of antiquity, richly embroidered in gold and silk thread. The furniture was upholstered in old-rose velvet. The bed was raised above the floor level.

The bed of state stood upon a dais, known as the *parquet*, and was surrounded by a gilded barrier. The ladies and the gentlemen filed past it, all on tiptoe, and as they did so, each pivoted backwards in the prescribed act of homage to the closed curtains. Behind them was Majesty, whether present in person or not. The Princesses of Condé and Conti brought up the rear of the procession. When Henri had seen enough and was about to enter, there appeared one last figure, who had been waiting until the court was assembled. She passed with slow solemnity, taking great care to disguise a slight limp. And before her brother's bed of state the Duchess of Bar, Madame, the King's sister, dropped a deep curtsy. " You are making your obeisance, Catherine."

Henri hurriedly closed the door and stood behind it with his eyes covered, but he still saw many things. " Sister, the bed of state came into your mind when we were very young and insignificant. Now you have achieved it, and yet you are not happy. Consider: this bed of state is empty, while a grave — pray curtsy yet again — contains Elizabeth. You, like the others, do not speak her name, but you know that we are alone and must depart. It is scarce to be desired that we should meet again on the other

side, after all that we have inflicted on each other here, and
especially I on you. Could I look on Biron's face again? Or even
on my cousin of England? We should need in the meantime to
have become omniscient, and then there could be no mutual
reproaches."

After a few nights like these, it could be seen that he was suffering. The general agreement to say nothing of the dead lady
was maintained; the King was the first to observe it. He performed his daily duties, most important of which was always to
be where a King must needs be, and do what a King must do.
But his absences of mind were remarked; in the liveliest conversations he stopped and closed his eyes.

One of these absences occurred in the company of two noblemen, Montigny and Sigongne. These had guessed the cause of
them, and thought to gain profit by uttering the forbidden name.
They began by making certain that they were not overheard and
that they could trust each other. Then Montigny said softly
that he shared the King's grief. And Sigongne hinted in an undertone how greatly he had revered Queen Elizabeth. Henri
opened his eyes. In silence he eyed the pair with a chill, forbidding look.

They trembled. The King, who liked to treat all men as his
equals and had just been talking to them in just such fashion,
suddenly retired within himself, behind a mask of cold contempt
— and they hastily withdrew. They had believed that aloofness
of Majesty was a mark of his great office and not of his own
nature. Had he secrets with a person who had departed never to
return? They were amazed at their discovery, but were careful
not to speak of it. The court would certainly have made them
pay for having found out something new about their master,
whom they saw from day to day, thinking there was no more in
him than what they saw.

These same noblemen felt very uneasy when the King summoned them to his garden three days later. Both were troubled
about some possible delinquency in the past. Montigny had
once been nearest at hand when an attack was made upon the
King, whose knee he had at that moment knelt to kiss. Sigongne,

an author of allegorical plays, had enjoyed celebrating the King
in the exalted speech of gods and heroes. But his common talk
had been far from ceremonious, and he had often said unkind
things about the Duchess of Beaufort. Both were typical and
quite ordinary courtiers, such as Henri had in plenty to his hand
when he felt disposed for homely company. It was for that reason that he sent for them today, to attend him in the garden
arbour, which was not overlooked from any window in the
Louvre. He could never have brought himself to say to his
friends and old comrades in arms what he now said to these two
men.

" You are happier than I. For I merely wait for death."

They bowed their heads and stood so. He paced more quickly
to and fro and said how he longed for another rank and calling.
He wished he might live in solitude and find at last the true
peace of the hermit. " The hermit is in need of nothing. Manna
falls, and ravens bring him bread from heaven."

He made his avowal with a deep-drawn sigh, then closed his
lips and did not open them again until he had recovered his self-
mastery. Then he continued: " But such a life is not for princes;
they were not born to live their own lives, but to serve their States
and the nations whom they are appointed to rule."

His hearers were quite taken aback by the King's words;
through all the vicissitudes of his life they had looked on him
as a man of easy heart whose spirits were never dashed. None
knew of the melancholy within him, for though he had more
than once spoken as they had heard him speak, he had never
done so to strange ears. But being anxious not to appear downcast or unduly solemn in the presence of Montigny and Sigongne, he was careful to dismiss them with an appropriate
pronouncement, which they could properly repeat. " Princes
who voyage on this sea have no harbour but the grave, and they
must die while at the helm."

These words lingered in the two men's minds; they reported
what the King had said, for they were amazed at being admitted
to his confidence and could not keep silence. But the phrase
about dying at the helm they were to remember, when the time

came, as a prophecy. The King was a proud man. He ended as he had wished to end.

Henri mourned for Elizabeth until that hour, and then no more.

THE NEW CENTURY

His first act after hearing of her death was to bid Rosny prepare for a journey to England. The friendly disposition of the Queen could not be expected from her successor, still less the firmness of her attitude and her constant watchfulness against the common foe. The King's sorrow gave way to a feeling of disgust, which deepened as James I made his weaknesses more clear. Six weeks later he was known for what he was, just as Rosny was about to depart. On the morning when Henri expected his Minister, came the Queen, Marie de Medici, before the other could arrive. Her intention was to anticipate Monsieur de Rosny's final orders. Her demeanour admitted of no doubt, she appeared before her husband as one to whom he owed a debt, as she had done from the outset, and so continued.

Henri did not let her speak. He had been prepared for some such intervention. Steps had been taken to get matters settled first. The affair had been quietly arranged between himself and Rosny. None the less, the envoy had to choose his suite; there were plenty of noblemen eager to go with him, especially if they could do so at the expense of the State. Marie had long since heard about the project, but had said nothing. She chose the last, decisive day on which to act. Henri promptly picked up a few papers at random from the table and hurriedly enlarged upon the domestic affairs of the kingdom. Meanwhile her expression told him that his evasions were futile. She had never before paid the slightest attention to such matters, perhaps because she could not understand them; but more probably because she held most firmly that the King's position was both dangerous and impious, until he made up his mind to obey the Pope, ally himself with Spain, and recall the Society of Jesus.

As she did not listen, but merely watched for an opportunity to open her own attack, he suddenly asked to see the Dauphin. The child was brought in by his nurse, being now a year and a half old. Henri took him from the woman's arms and sat down with him on the floor. There, on a level with the little face, he eyed it with strange gravity, to the mystification of both nurse and Queen. But they said nothing. " He will see the coming century," thought Henri. And that was his sole thought.

" Boursier," he said to the nurse, " the Dauphin was very weak after his birth. Next to the Queen, it is you to whom he owes his life, for you blew wine into his mouth when his colour had nearly gone."

" Sire," replied the nurse, " had it been another child, I would have done so at once. You bade me, and I dared to do it."

She turned to the Queen. " Our sovereign lord," said she, " was all aquiver until he saw it was indeed a Dauphin. He would not have survived a disappointment. He was beside himself with joy, he let two hundred people into the room, and I had to be very angry, but he said that the child belonged to everyone and they must share his joy."

" Enough of such babble, woman," returned the Queen. A shadow of fear passed swiftly across her face. Her child's sex had indeed decided her own destiny. Had it been a girl, the son born to the Marquise de Verneuil at the same time would certainly have ranked as Dauphin. And Marie de Medici would have had to return by the door through which she had come.

The memory of that past peril soon fled, but Henri noticed it. He embraced and kissed his wife, which she accepted as her due. She had never been immured in her own pride. Henri dandled the Dauphin in his arms. Marie watched them with a look of apprehension. And it at last happened that the father threw the child up too high, and only the nurse, not he, was quick enough to catch it. But it was Marie who first found speech.

" As young as ever, Sire," said she in a fury. " Our merry King very nearly killed the Dauphin." Whereupon she clapped her hands to her hips, looking exactly like a fishwife. It was plain that an outburst could only be averted by dismissing the nurse and child.

"What is your business, madame?" he then said, realizing that she must be faced.

She needed no inducement. She had her rights and her position as mother of the Dauphin, and the King was powerless against her. She needed neither the cover of night nor the intoxication of the senses to set him upon the way that he should go. She made known her will in clear daylight. "You will not send Monsieur de Rosny to England."

The King replied that the matter was decided, and nothing could now be done. The British flagship was just setting sail to meet his envoy.

Whereupon Marie coldly pointed out that his own position was precarious enough; he had little reason to seek the friendship of one weaker than himself. King James would not keep his throne, she was certain of that. This she repeated, with the result that Henri was taken aback and began to listen. " If James is turned out, could you find a better King of England? No. But you could get a Pope elected, with the help of my uncle, the Grand Duke, who has a promise from Clement VIII. It is time to forget your heretical past. Consider your advantage and my own. Your kingdom needs the protection of the Church; and so does your life."

Nothing of all this was new, least of all the uncle, with his alleged power of appointing popes; but what was a Pope, whether a Medici or not? He was the tool of Spain. If Henri submitted, he betrayed his kingdom and put his life yet more certainly in peril.

" You advise me to recall the Jesuits, to prevent their murdering me."

This Marie indignantly denied. The Fathers were, by her account, most benevolently disposed, amiable and modest, and averse to any recriminations. He needed only to make their acquaintance. One or two talks with them and he would no longer doubt where his salvation lay.

Henri tried to laugh, and said, to round off the encounter in friendly fashion: " If they murder no tyrants, I need not fear them. Let them stay where they are."

And yet they both knew, himself and the Queen, that he was always very near the knife. Neither of them said so. But lest he might mistake her meaning, she mentioned Biron, his death and its consequences. It was indeed she who had demanded the traitor's death, but that did not prevent her pointing out to the King how isolated he had become since then. At his own court it was generally believed that he was a victim of remorse, which explained his illness in the previous July. He lost patience and dashed out of the room, exclaiming as he went:

" Bad oysters — that was what made me ill, not remorse; and that is as true as that Biron was a traitor."

There stood Marie de Medici, a lumpish figure with vacant face and foolish eyes; all the more notable was the contrast between her haughty entrance and her subdued demeanour at the end.

" You will know the meaning of remorse if you send Rosny to England against my advice! "

He hurried away, and once in his garden, he drew a deep breath of relief. Here he expected his faithful servant, it was time he heard a word of sense. His purpose was to give the Marquis of Sully his instructions for his visit to the English court. He made no mention of the fact that he relied neither on King James, nor upon his friendship. The age of Elizabeth could never return. He too must adapt himself to this new century. And he only hoped he might succeed without self-betrayal.

Rosny would insist that, after Biron, another old companion, Turenne, Duke of Bouillon, must be put out of the way. This Protestant prince was slandering the King throughout the whole of Protestant Europe; he even alleged that Henri was planning another night of Saint Bartholomew, with the connivance of the Pope. Henri would again confide to Rosny his most pressing anxiety — that his own Protestants had allied themselves with Spain. He had made that answer more than once. Who and what was Spain? In Brussels a woman had been buried alive in honour of the Infanta. Bouillon made no attempt to counter the horror felt throughout the world — and in any case he deserved the other traitor's fate.

Henri knew word for word in advance what his old friend Rosny would say. Both had clear views, though these were not always just nor sufficient. Above all, they acted on a common plan — and while his Protestants fell into a deeper mistrust of the King, his Grand Master was amassing armaments: for what? To save them. Freedom of conscience throughout Europe would in the end have to be defended by force of arms or the kingdom would perish; life must be lived in the spirit and the truth.

These thronging thoughts quickened his pace, and he was actually running when he stopped abruptly. What did the Queen mean about the remorse that would certainly be his? Whence came her knowledge of James and his impending peril? Marie de Medici was not clever; and in the background of his thoughts her husband added: any more than she was agreeable. In the meantime what disquieted him was the extreme contrast between her scanty wits and the hints that she let fall. Whence came that knowledge, or who had taught her the lesson she repeated? On whose account was she giving him this warning? She had no eye for the future. And a plan in hand offers the best foreknowledge of the event.

The Queen's letters must be opened. No easy matter, as the Intendant of Posts was on her side. La Varenne was equally insistent on the recall of the Jesuits. It might be assumed that he urged it as some compensation for his scandalous past; but Bassompierre — a singular convert! But all the others sniffed the wind and so proceeded. Henri was conscious of a conspiracy all about him, which could not be dealt with by the block and axe; for treason is committed in thought, and expressed in an unuttered understanding. Perhaps there was still dissension as to what sort of death he should die. A natural death, as for instance by a surfeit of oysters? Or by the act of God, as manifested by remorse, or the knife?

The Queen had spoken of " her " Dauphin. She reckoned for her regency with a child not yet of age, and a dead man. He did not believe that she desired his disappearance, neither that day nor the next — she was merely preparing for it and offering him a warning in good faith. She had indeed none of her predecessor's ability and craft, nor the vast number of maids of honour through whom old Catherine dominated her court. The ghost of the Medici whose prisoner he had been still walked. The palace of the Louvre was indeed a brothel so far as he could make it so. He was less pleased to think that it was also a powder-magazine. Aha! The Grand Master.

The Marquis de Sully appeared on the outer flight of steps in front of the decorated façade, a gorgeous and imposing figure in the garb he had assumed for the special mission with which his master intended to entrust him. His gait betokened unusual dignity. He was positively strutting, as Henri observed. As a boy, upon an occasion that he would never forget, he had seen the Duke of Alba walking in just such a fashion. It was a gait that, on both occasions, must have been caused by pride and a sedentary life, though Alba was a villain and Rosny the best of men. In the pale, shadowed light of the garden the Minister's eyes blinked, being sensitive from an excess of work. The sunlight flashed on his jewels; he was wearing, as his habit always had been, chains and clasps set with precious stones, and on his hat a costly medallion engraved with a helmeted head of Minerva. His public appearances in this outmoded array of a past century was often greeted with smiles, though behind his back, for he was a very powerful personage.

" It is a fact," thought Henri; " we are growing old. When did it begin? No matter, we have more than one trick left in the bag. If I have to recall the Jesuit Fathers to this kingdom, the issue shall not be quite what they expect."

THE FIGURE BY THE BED

That summer the King heard a preacher whose style was unfamiliar and seemed to him rather questionable, but could not fail to be admired. The enthusiasm of his court, and particularly of the ladies, compelled Henri to take Monsieur de Sales seriously, although his flowing periods seemed to drench the Crucified in fragrant essences and encircled the bowed and bloody head with birds and flowers, so that all its terrors vanished. Yes, it lost the sternness of suffering and became as handsome as the noble ecclesiastic himself, whom the Jesuits had sent to the King of France from Savoy. François de Sales was not of the Order, he was merely preparing for it in tolerably pleasant fashion. He wore a shade over his eyes and had a fair beard. Anyone who heard and saw him could not fail to be impressed, for he knew the value of appearances.

Shortly afterwards the King fell ill; it was the second attack of the same organic collapse. During the first, the Duchess of Beaufort had nursed him back to health, never leaving him by day or night. As he was then upon a journey, he lay abed in the city of Metz, and of his whole court only La Varenne was in his company. It seemed as though it was La Varenne's privilege to attend the sick-beds of exalted personages; in any case he made good use of the occasion. The Jesuits had an establishment in Lorraine; he sent for two of them, Father Ignatius and Father Cotton, who was afterwards to be the King's confessor. The latter was a fool, of the kind whose folly makes them sly, or perhaps the slyness breeds the folly. He burst into lamentations at the sight of the King's condition, and knew no better than to tell the sick man to make his peace with God. He would at least die a natural death and need no longer fear the knife, for which he might offer thanks to Heaven.

At this, Father Ignatius interposed. La Varenne nudged him, but Father Ignatius had already seen his opportunity. Solemnly he promised the King his life if he would reinstate the Order. Otherwise his successors would do so, for the needs of the age demanded it. Henri said nothing, silently agreeing with the Jesuits in so far as Marie de Medici was concerned. But as for the demands of the age, they were more easily controlled than a narrow-minded, headstrong woman. But first he must get well and stand upon his feet.

The challenge and the force of his own will suddenly cleared his head, and the fever sensibly abated. He purposely heaved a feeble sigh before admitting that he was extremely interested in the doctrine of the famous Mariana as to when tyrannicide is justified. " Not that I am afraid," said he. " Attempts have been made upon my life on the most various pretexts. Until recently it was regarded as a crime, or in any case a somewhat drastic stroke of policy. This is the first time that a learned man has elevated it into a sacred right. What may we expect? "

The black figure of the Jesuit beside the bed stiffened to its full height, and he said in a stern but not unkindly tone:

" If someone had stabbed your dead enemy, Don Philip, when you had cause to fear him most, would you have called it a crime? "

" Even so," agreed Henri. " There is someone who will approve our death by violence. Would it be an act of justice, and by whose orders would it be carried out? "

" Not by ours, as you surmise," returned the Jesuit. " The judgment, whether openly or not, is delivered by the nations; their conscience speaks, and the voice of all humanity — we are not here speaking of trained agents."

" Such as yourself, my rascally friend," thought Henri, though he made no reply. Rather, he took occasion to observe that by that account the Jesuits were true humanists. They trained men to recognize good and evil, even in their rulers, and to act accordingly. This was indeed a matter in which the new century had progressed. " We two can come to an understanding, for my conscience does not condemn me as a tyrant."

" Your conscience is prophetic," said Father Ignatius. " Sire, we Fathers of Jesus would willingly be your best friends and look on you as our sole support; we are now being persecuted by the King of Spain, who will soon expel us from his territory."

This clumsy lie first revealed the man, and Henri recognized the Father's face. In years gone by, the young King of Navarre had seen it as the face of a suspect Spaniard who had called himself Loro and had offered to betray a frontier fortress to the King. This earlier embodiment of Father Ignatius had been distinguished by a pronounced squint, which in his present guise passed almost unnoticed. With his gaping nostrils and protuberant forehead this old acquaintance had been a far from prepossessing figure. But in the Jesuit the outward envelope was transfigured by the fire of the spirit. However, this was the man

who had once approached him with murderous intent; so much
was plain to Henri.

In the meantime, though still on his sick-bed, he was now
strong enough to take a hand in the business of his kingdom,
and he began by dwelling on the notable affinities between various sorts of men. La Varenne and Cotton stood in the background, whispering. Their demeanour betrayed a furtive joy that
Ignatius seemed likely to dispose of the King with ease — while
Henri, as well as his new friend, knew exactly what each thought
of the other. The Jesuit thought: " Power, not talk, is what will
win the King, and I will show him power." Henri thought:
" The murderer of those days was put by my noblemen in an
open gallery. Each of them set one leg against the wall, and the
murderer was to address me over that living barrier. But as he
could produce nothing more than vague talk of betrayal, neither
that day nor the next, he was shot."

Father Ignatius began anew:

" The right of tyrannicide is merely a theme for dialectic.
Take notice that the attacks upon your person will diminish
when a decision is taken by a higher authority; by which I mean
our Order."

" I understand," said Henri. " Tyrannicide shall not be a pre-
rogative of other Orders."

" We offer you protection against monks, pulpit orators, and
laymen, in so far as a few of them conceive themselves as inspired, and their insignificant selves as charged with an exalted
mission. That is not our method. We are worldly-minded and
submit all human action, even force, to the control of reason."

" I agree," observed Henri, with something of astonishment.
" Does your Society propose to teach man the correct use of the
intellect? "

The Jesuit answered with another question:

" Has the King ever heard any man commended solely for his
capacity to think? Men are not made to measure. A great man
can never win the wholehearted love of his people, because of
the multitude of opinions held among them, and the most personal of them are the most fantastic."

" There's much truth in that," admitted Henri, but promptly realized that this had been said to catch him, and the cloven hoof appeared at once. " What does your Order demand? "

" The schools. No — no privileges. Our colleges are so good that in the Protestant principalities of Germany many honest folk become Catholics to give their children the advantage of our education. Pray do not think we are prejudiced against secular studies. We teach mathematics, and doctors come to us to learn anatomy."

" I am glad to hear it," said Henri. " And what do you reserve for yourselves? "

" Almost nothing. Latin, if you will. Any discipline, no matter what, gives us occasion to shape your subjects to your service, all alike, in equal and absolute obedience."

Henri: " Do you set my portrait on an altar in your classrooms and burn candles to it? "

The Father: " We avoid exaggerations and take care not to be harshly explicit. To put the matter candidly, we use kingship — willingly or no — as our intermediary, so that men may learn, not to think, but to obey. This for their own salvation."

Henri: " Such salvation is mere conscienceless stupidity."

The Father: " We call it piety and glad subjection."

Henri: " So that you live and carry on your controversies without knowing for what cause."

The Father: " The past century was conscienceless and stupid, in so far as it took such measureless pride in the intellect, in its inventions and discoveries and its great enterprises, none of which guide the mind to truth. The human personality in freedom grows more and more overweening until in the end it lies groaning on a bed of sickness, desolate and decayed."

Henri, quietly: " Suppose I had you arrested and imprisoned in the fortress? "

The Father, bending over the bed of sickness: " I could wish it for myself, for I should be lying imprisoned to the greater glory of God. I would not wish you such a fate. Do not forget that we have not yet been able to extirpate the arbitrary claims of the human intellect. Fanatics obtrude everywhere, even in the best-disciplined Orders. A knife is soon drawn. Sire, it is high time for your own safety that the Society of Jesus should provide you with a confessor."

The old threat — Father Ignatius thought to leave the King alone with it, and turned to go. Henri beckoned to him to remain.

" It is in Germany," he said, " that the Society of Jesus has been most successful. All was peaceful there until those murderous bands began to terrorize the wretched peasants. The suppression of the monasteries was a good deed done. But, alas, it brought no relief to the people, it merely enriched the princes and the nobility, which your order has always favoured."

" The German nobility is our sword," said the Jesuit. He spoke quite simply, without a touch of humility or pride.

" A great war lies before you," said Henri, " and it will be your war. A war against the peoples."

" But in the cause of the rulers and the princes who, at our bidding, are expelling their Protestants, like the Emperor Rudolf. Sire, you are the Most Christian King. You love your people without distinction, even the heretics. You want to give them back their faith and their natural inequality. With our aid you may do this, in all gentleness and tolerance, and without a devastating war."

" Amen," said Henri, rolling his eyeballs upwards, in imitation of a honeyed preacher he had lately heard. And he recalled that semblance of the crucified head, garlanded with birds and flowers. " How is it that my people are so valiant? " he asked with sudden vehemence. " Why do my Frenchmen look upon that head of blood and wounds as a warning to be strong? "

" Take care," observed Father Ignatius; " you must spare yourself." He evaded a reply, because the King had plainly overtaxed his energy. Henri certainly felt very ill; he called for La Varenne, and the two Jesuits left the room. Between two agonizing attacks the King signed the permit admitting the Society of Jesus into the kingdom. Whatever Monsieur de La Varenne afterwards imagined, he had no hand in that decision. Why it was made was not then known even to the figure beside the bed.

WEAKNESS, HASTE, AND FORCE

The condition of affairs was now faced and put to proof. Had an organ of the body failed, it was made to serve once more. When a new traitor rose up to deal his blow, he encountered a wary King, acquainted with every device of treason. There was no more reckoning on the loyalty of women: the stormy d'Entragues, and the cumbrous Medici, what schemes had they in mind? Would his Protestants, who had grown exceedingly embittered, come back once more to him whom they had called Navarre? The great war was to be fomented throughout Europe, as though upon agreement that it must not be deferred. The King of France had recalled his Jesuits, though he meant to guard against the ultimate evil, as he conceived it. But how should he deal with them? And how would they deal with the King of England, who had made them various imprudent promises? The alliance between the two Kings was liable to the sort of explosion that suddenly blows up a fortress. As for what still confronted Henri — the whirlwind of events swept through his years, and they were now numbered, as he began to understand.

His special envoy, the Marquis de Sully, was near to being present at a sea-fight. The English ship to which he had, from courtesy, entrusted his person had briskly bombarded the French fleet, which had landed the envoy's numerous escort at Dover, and as it started on the return voyage, hoisted the lilies of France in salutation; this was regarded as a provocation by the English, these being territorial waters. The incident, unimaginable under Elizabeth, revealed to Rosny the changes which had taken place since her death and awaited him in London.

They were obvious already on the journey from the coast to the capital. The King of England's Chamberlain had indicated by painted signs where the guests were to pass the night, but many citizens had effaced them in the interval. On his arrival in London, the plenipotentiary of the King of France was saluted by the guns on the Tower, the city walls, and the ships. Amid thronging crowds he entered a state coach and drove to the palace of the French Ambassador, Count Beaumont. All doors were closed to his noblemen, who would have had to sleep in the street. It was announced that the gentlemen who had accompanied Marshal Biron on a previous occasion had involved themselves in brawls, and an English citizen had been stabbed. The Marquis promptly gave his young retainers a lecture on decorum. Unfortunately some of them visited a brothel, and once again a man was stabbed.

Rosny was infuriated that he, the most dignified Frenchman of his day, should be involved in such an incident. He threatened to have the young bully put to death, and the Mayor of London had to do his utmost to dissuade him. Moreover, it was only by chance that he himself avoided an egregious blunder. He had intended to present himself to the King in the deepest mourning. Lord Sidney told him, just in time, that he would be the only person wearing black. King James and his court would have been gravely offended, especially the sensitive monarch, formerly only King of Scotland, and now King of England, not by desert, but by inheritance. The name of his great predecessor might not even be mentioned. Sully contemned such pettiness on the part of the survivors; they could not get rid of glory as quickly as they had wished, so they stopped their ears.

It was with the less misgiving that, for his address to the King at Greenwich Palace, he used the luxuriant style that had just come into fashion; even Rosny had had to learn it. He described his master and His Britannic Majesty as veritable paragons of monarchy, combining in themselves all the virtues of the new age and of antiquity. He had never expected his predecessor to listen to this sort of language; conversation with the Queen had been on business, or on learned subjects. He assured the King that his master had been wholly consoled for the grievous loss of Elizabeth by the peaceful ascent to the throne of a successor with a mind and heart of more than human compass. The King of France, who had sent him on this mission, had conceived so high a notion of his brother sovereign's exaltation that the friendship and alliance between them far exceeded his always happy relations with the departed Queen.

Elizabeth had gone, so much was true; all the rest was fantasy.

Rosny went so far as to assert that he wished her feeble-faced successor just as fortunate a reign as his own sovereign. " May your sceptre and your reign ever increase! Only divine aid could lend me eloquence to match my theme." Flattery, however, has limits, and the human measure of it did not suffice to implant confidence and energy in a nervous monarch who mistrusted his own capacity. King James, to lend a closer ear to this heartening eulogy, had stepped down from his throne. When the speech ended, he began to stammer out a reply. He was in no way embarrassed by the envoy, who looked at the floor, out of consideration for this unhappy heir to the Crown of England. But the high officers of this King from Scotland stared at him more blankly as his speech thickened. They had indeed been in the service of the old Queen, and they were disposed, especially Lord Cecil, to make the foreign ruler feel that his succession was an accident, and that he stood alone; he had been brought in from without, and such force as he could muster came from the dead Queen. In their presence he was always under trial, and this made him stammer. So he snatched all the more eagerly at the papers proffered to him by the Marquis de Sully.

They were autograph letters from the King of France. The King of Scotland and England soon became aware that here were no more flowery phrases; the matters in hand were plainly stated, and they were: Holland; troops for use against Spain; and a sum of money. As James glanced through the documents, he was only thankful that he could hold them up to hide his face; yes, his heartfelt gratitude to the envoy and his opportune papers might well have induced James to give his consent to anything. He had indeed promised the opposing party, his obsequious Jesuits, as much as they demanded. But under the eyes of Lord Cecil he was helpless, nor did he find himself his own master later on. However, the handwriting of his cousin of France did encourage him to announce that he had always had a true affection for the person of King Henri, and, indeed, had not forgotten it in Scotland.

Then he abruptly started a discussion on theology, thence passing to the chase and the weather. Rosny, who cared little for the chase, extolled his master's skill in this pursuit, as in all others, thinking thus to lead the conversation round to politics, but with no success. The ceremonial reception remained without result. The envoy therefore asked for a private audience, and most insistently, for he knew that Philip III of Spain had been pressing His Britannic Majesty with offers of an alliance. James I seemed well disposed; he invited the envoy to attend a religious service, whereafter the subject of the chase inevitably came up again, and the rest of the conversation was taken up with the immoderate heat of that summer.

With the French Ambassador, Rosny was admitted to dine at the King's table, as the only two guests. The sovereign was served, to their amazement, on the knee. It was the only form of sovereignty he exercised, thought Rosny. No result again.

On the day following, Rosny was visited by the envoy of the United Netherlands, Barneveldt, who represented to him the desperate condition of his country. Ostend had held out heroically for twenty months against overwhelming Spanish forces and could hold out no longer. The resources of the Dutch — supplies and troops and money — needed to be doubled.

Barneveldt: " For God's sake, send us help! Can't you see that the expulsion of the Spaniards from our provinces will decide the fate of the continent? "

Rosny: " The King of France wished to be assured of the English alliance; he will then march at once."

Barneveldt: " But the great Elizabeth waited in Dover for a signal, and she waited in vain — "

Rosny: " Her days are over. Her successor is served upon the knee at dinner, which is how he rules. My King rules otherwise. But a pious man like you must understand that God Himself permits the darkening of our free will. Even treachery, by His will, walks abroad to thwart good men like ourselves and teach them steadfastness."

Barneveldt: " Do you also understand why England permits the enemies of her religion and her freedom to gather on the opposite coast? "

Rosny: " Doubtless from a desire for peace. Moreover, Spain

is an exhausted power, and its last convulsions are little to be feared. My King, especially, is not to be allowed to hold the opposite coast, and on the continent the two powers, one exhausted and the other very vital, are to balance each other by unceasing war. That is what England calls European peace."

Barneveldt: " Pray tell that to the Councillors of King James, tell his Parliament the truth. Lord Cecil regards himself as a true friend of peace."

Rosny: " Do you think so? King James speaks freely, because he has no power at all, except in so far as he is served at dinner on the knee."

It was this colloquy, in which to all appearance he was explaining the situation to someone else, that first enlightened Rosny. He proceeded daily to inform the British statesmen of everything that it might profit them to know, with his accustomed logic, and an eloquence supported by figures. He was not discouraged by the fact that these gentlemen really wanted no information and listened impatiently to his account of the burdens that a last desperate attack by Spain had imposed upon the King of France. He had to defend all his many frontiers simultaneously by water and by land. Spain and her vassals were everywhere. Since the reign of the Emperor Charles V one single dynasty, in its greed for universal and absolute power, had threatened the nations of Europe and every free country.

It was Rosny's business to say this; it stood in his instructions. At the same time he was prepared for the fact that the tribulations and dissensions of the continent were not much canvassed here and seemed remoter than the affairs of the New World. It was the unique greatness of Elizabeth that she had felt and thought with Europe — though only in her old age; such comprehension was beyond her in youth. Monsieur de Rosny became uneasy when his opponents curtly interrupted his political disquisition and came down to figures once again — this time their own. What of the debts that the King of France had made in this country, in the time of the late Queen? No British soldier should set foot on the continent until those debts were paid to the uttermost farthing.

" God in heaven! " exclaimed Rosny to himself. The friend of peace, Lord Cecil, grew very loud and emphatic. His Majesty of England had no notion of ruining his country on behalf of the States General of Holland. If they could not pay the money, nor yet the King of France, they would all remain good friends, but there would be no alliance, nor any contribution for defence, and still less for attack. " God in heaven! " cried Rosny once more under his breath. If only he could make them see light! Their existence was equally at stake. And they talked of debts. The Society of Jesus had been admitted to England also, Spain was already in the land. And they boggled over debts.

On the broad field of capital and interest he had to deal for days together with His Majesty's Councillors. He maintained that, as a member of the Council of Finance, he was acquainted with the intentions of the King of France. As, in reality, only Rosny himself knew the productive power of the kingdom, he set the yearly payments at a moderate level, that a surplus might be available for war. " If His Britannic Majesty means to impose upon my master all the burdens and sacrifices of the war, which I steadfastly refuse to believe, for I expect better things from King James's wisdom and generosity, then no one can conceive my sovereign as obliged to strip his treasury at such a crisis."

But they did. The Councillors of the King of England insisted that he should do so. The envoy explained their stubbornness by their wish to be firmer than their feeble master: this in recollection of the late Queen, whose policy they had wholly misunderstood. He determined to make the King acquainted with the whole situation, as no one else had initiated him into his great predecessor's principles. Rosny had reckoned on an exceedingly heavy task. But the interview that followed passed off with most unexpected and miraculous ease. King James took the envoy by the hand, led him into his cabinet, locked the doors, and bade him speak his whole mind. And Rosny did so.

He told the whole truth to the hapless monarch. He was not afraid to bring the Queen into the matter — she would have declined to allow old debts to be considered, when in the other scale lay the common interest and pledges of the two kingdoms.

And above and beyond the plainer truths, Monsieur de Rosny set before James's dazzled vision something that gleamed and sparkled, and was called: immortality. He talked for two whole hours; then James himself asked him to outline a treaty there and then. It was not necessary, Rosny had the draft in his pocket. James, with his own royal hand, made some trivial alterations, merely in token of the fact that a new sovereign was exercising his authority — if only for that day and a single hour. Rosny did not delude himself nor overvalue his good fortune. It was enough to have got James on his side beforehand; indeed, the King now summoned his Ministers to listen to his will.

Lords Cecil and Montjoie, the Earls of Northumberland and Southampton, learned from their master's lips that he had fully weighed the arguments of the Marquis de Sully. His decision was, in the matter of foreign policy, to continue in an understanding with the King of France. He had also decided on a close alliance between the two kingdoms against Spain. Silence! No interruptions! These were commands. He offered to the States General of Holland his royal guarantees and assurances. " Now, Mr. Ambassador, are you satisfied with me? "

Rosny kissed the hand that seemed to have all too suddenly strengthened. He expressed his warm gratitude in the choicest language. That was his last speech in England. As the result of all these alarms, an old wound on his mouth reopened, a wound he had received at Ivry: a battle of long ago, but a victory that still endured. Days of violent fever followed, after which he was able to take leave of King James, and was presented with a magnificent gold chain, set with jewels, more permanent than any treaty, and a letter from the King assuring his cousin of France that he had felt deeply gratified by the appointment of the Marquis de Rosny to fulfil this mission. James continued in high good humour.

For his part Rosny distributed some very costly presents: to the King six thoroughbred horses; to the Queen a Venetian mirror, framed in gold and set with diamonds. Even the Secretaries of State, who had done their best to furbish up the treaty, were not forgotten; they received a number of elegant gifts, such as are commonly presented by gallants to their ladies. With this ironical hint, the envoy took his departure. His master awaited him with impatience, and indeed went some way to meet him.

After a stormy crossing and a night in the post coach, Rosny found the King under a clump of trees in the company of de Villeroy, de Bellièvre and Soissons. The first was to convey to Madrid the results of the envoy's mission. The second concealed his misgivings. The third, being the King's cousin, did nothing of the kind. " If Monsieur de Rosny is on such excellent terms with the English," said the Count de Soissons, " he ought to have brought home more than empty promises, assuming that he was given any " — which was an open insult. But the King's cousin could say what he pleased, and Rosny had to swallow it. Henri himself replied. It was easy to find fault, he told his gentlemen, when another man had done what was humanly possible. Nothing more could have been achieved. He himself was satisfied.

In Paris the King and his Grand Master had another colloquy. " What," said Henri, " do you really think? "

" Sire, that it is not a good thing for a foreign King to get his new throne by inheritance and without a fight. I realized that when my many speeches reopened the wound on my mouth — the wound I got at your battle of Ivry."

" Then," asked Henri, " there is no pledge, nor hope of one? "

" We must continue to back reason," said Rosny, " though the conflict be a long one for you, and I know too well that reason moves more slowly than the evil principle, which, being against nature, and therefore weak, is always in a hurry."

" Weak and in a hurry," said Henri under his breath. " And therefore disposed to force."

The next years did actually prove the disposition of weakness towards force. The King of Spain offered the King of France an alliance, with the object of a joint landing in England, the conquest of that country, and the extirpation of all Protestants. Henri reported this offer to King James. In the meantime Ostend fell. Spain lost forty thousand men under the walls of that heroic city. When General Ambrosius Spinola entered it at last in triumph, King James was aghast. The plan of the powers to make a landing on his island was the one thing wanting to complete his terror. Plain as had been the warning given him by King Henri, the wretched man had as little faith in him as in himself. The pact with weakness masquerading still as force, which Henri had refused, was accepted by James. He had always dallied with the French treaty, but he made haste to sign the pact with the King of Spain.

He thought to stem the course of destiny. Against weakness, which is always in a hurry and therefore violent, no restraint avails. Spain, bled white and like a corpse enthroned, was still greedy for conquest and kept no less close a grip upon her later than her earlier victims. Her advance guard and her executioners were already quartered in the country next destined for attack. These were the English Fathers of the Society of Jesus, from whom, under a King like James, no good was to be expected — no mercy, and but little prudence. A far different man was needed. King Henri had likewise admitted them to France; his reason for doing so was known only to his faithful Rosny. To the Parliament of Paris, which had protested, and still protested likewise against the Edict of Nantes — to his lawyers Henri replied: " I am touched by your concern for my person and my State. But I would have you know that the opposition to the Jesuits comes from two sources: the Religion, and the priesthood, in so far as it is ignorant and undisciplined. The Sorbonne knows nothing of the Fathers, it has merely condemned them, with the result that its lecture halls are empty. All the finer minds are now turning towards the Jesuits, and I cannot but respect them."

How well, he went on, had they gauged the spirit of the age, and how great had been their success! They did not inculcate tyrannicide. None of his would-be murderers had been involved with them, least of all Chastel, in spite of his confession. How much did Henri believe of all this? He had admitted to his faithful Rosny that he would sooner have his enemies inside the country than beyond the frontiers — there they became romantic figures, idolized by their devoted disciples in France, who pledged themselves to their service and were only too willing to under-mine the State until it collapsed. Duly admitted, their doings were plain for all to see.

"Their schools are models of their kind, though they are bet-ter at dealing with children of noble families. They have asked me for my heart as a relic for their churches. Love me, for I love you — such is our attitude to each other."

Rosny thought that this might be a subterfuge. This selfless devotion to the little ones had not been shown even by the earliest disciples of our Lord, in those primitive days, and was scarce credible in their late successors.

Henri called his Grand Master an incorrigible Protestant. The Fathers carried with them an atmosphere of melody and fra-grance that suggested a landscape full of birds and flowers. But he added gravely: "I know my enemies. The Fathers of Jesus are agents of the World Power. All I can do is to let them see the weight of my vengeance. Grand Master, drive my cannon through the streets."

A Trafficker in Women

Cannon are not an infallible defence when there is treachery on all sides, creeping abroad in ever new disguises. A woman whom the King needs, and from whom he will not part, becomes an instrument of his enemies. At the beginning his Marquise, to add an edge to her allurement, had lightly played at conspir-acy — and it was with some such purpose in her mind that she danced her sinuous dance for her adorer, shedding her garments one by one. But since the arrival of certain Fathers such antics were sternly suppressed. "Be serious, my lovely one, or careful. You are sooner lost than he. Do you know us for what we are? We bear many names: Spain, Austria, Pope, Emperor, Money, the Society of Jesus — no matter which we use. A Will unnamed addresses you, Madame la Marquise. The judgment of the cen-tury has gone forth against the nations, and therefore against this King. Whether you understand or not, you shall serve our pur-poses."

" O Father, how you frighten me! To me it was no more than dance and mimicry. I did hate him for breaking his promise of marriage; but remember, I have not all my wits about me. People talk about such things, but do not do them. What? I? In all seriousness? I do not understand you, except that otherwise — And suppose I went straight to the King with your abominable proposals. Ah, no. Not a word more, forget what I said last. I want to live. And I obey, that I may live."

Henriette d'Entragues had gone too far. After the fall of Ostend the unnamed World Power drew her utterly into its dark activities, and her whole family as well. And when the conspiracy was discovered, it was known by the name of d'Entragues. The Marshal, a weakling, and his criminal son, d'Auvergne, played a poor part in the trial that followed; Henriette remained unshaken and insisted on her rights. She had the King's promise; her children and none others were legitimate. Kill him? God in heaven! What had she known, then, and what had been her purpose? Her own brother pleaded that the whole responsibility was hers. She wept, but only when unobserved. She addressed her judges and demanded mercy for her father, a rope for her brother, and justice for herself.

It seemed surprising that she should want her brother hanged. Henri, who did not like taking life, saw into the hearts of his fallen enemies. This woman had been, in her good days, more attached to him than she cared to know. As she had confessed this at last, though only to his inward ear, all should be at an end between them there and then. No. He pardoned the father, clapped the son in prison, and sent the dangerous mistress into a convent. If only he had left her there and forgotten her in another's company! That he could not do; no other had her light, contemptuous wit, her darting caprice, her charm in self-abandonment, an audacity that shrank from nothing, yet never lost its poise; no other possessed in such completeness all that Henri conceived as French.

The atonement was enough, and he recalled her, with the most unfortunate effect upon her attitude; she would have preferred desertion than a love so uncontrolled. He did more, he recognized her children. But to what purpose? — "her Dauphin," as she called him, remained excluded from the throne. Monsieur d'Entragues, as the price of his life, had to surrender the written promise of marriage. She hated the man who had humiliated her, and the more favour he now showed her, the more deeply did she hate him. She was given a lodging in the Louvre, and thereafter he had beneath his roof the most malignant influence of all. All others who desired his death had at least their wits about them; not one of them but felt that there was a malady in the air, the plague of conspiracy, and in mere tacit acquiescence they agreed beforehand that a great King must die.

In his palace of the Louvre they all regarded each other with detestation — the Queen, the Marquise, the two cousins of the Queen, and the overweeningly handsome Concini. But his dwarfish wife, the foster-sister, was the most vicious of them all. Every one of them reckoned upon the King's death, though that was no reason for keeping each other alive. It was expected every morning that Madame de Verneuil would be found murdered in her bed. The Queen was furious because the King had the bastards of the Marquise educated with her own children, and also with the children of the charming Gabrielle: he wanted his entire family under his own eye. One day the birth of a new brother was announced to the Dauphin; his father's mistress had had another child. "Th-that is not a brother of m-mine," said the Dauphin, who stammered in his early boyhood.

The Dauphin Louis admired Henri and imitated him in his less pleasing habits, such as pouring wine into his soup and dressing carelessly. He guessed what grown-up persons would scarce expect of so odd a child, and he was filled with a strange ardour that they could not understand. "The King, my father," he would cry. Louis also had his hatreds in those days; most of all he hated his mother's cavaliers, and after them his mother herself — in fleeting fashion, of course, between the kiss upon her hand and the blow that stung his cheek. "Monsieur Sigisbée," he said, as the *cavalieri serventi* of the ladies were called, "take care, Monsieur Sigisbée, not to visit my mother, the

Queen. You will find the King, my father, within." When the handsome gentleman tried to laugh and presumed to stroke the boy's hair, the Dauphin ordered the nearest guard to give him a thrashing. And there was something of a scuffle before the nobleman could escape. The royal parents saw him run as they stepped into the doorway. Henri was delighted at the resplendent Concini's discomfiture.

Marie de Medici repressed, on principle, every sort of self-expression, especially such as seemed likely to be pleasant. Dauphin Louis was promptly reprimanded — though he ought really to have been praised. For his mother detested Concini; she had at last discovered that his handsome person had been exploited to her ridicule by her foster-sister, of whom, however, she had a superstitious dread. Leonora Galigai lived in an upper chamber, alone and unapproachable, although the rumour was that she prowled round the palace by night. She was solely set upon money; she hoarded it and sent it home, in case she ever had to flee the country. And those who should provide her with it were plainly the King's enemies — that conglomeration of people which, for want of any fitting designation, was known as "Spain." But for her foster-sister, thus suborned, Marie could with difficulty have been persuaded into complicity in certain schemes. She would not have listened to Concini if Leonora had not sent him — he would have got no farther than her bed's edge. On the contrary, in her husband's arms she would have forgotten the tasks laid on her when she left her country, she would not for long have worked against him as agent of the World Power, for he begot fine children of her and offered her yet more — his heart.

But hatred had been born and it increased. Up above lived a demented woman, invisible for fear of the evil eye. Below lay side by side a foolish woman, with an evil conscience, and the man whose love she might perhaps have had. He had spoken his mind to Rosny. "She is the mother of my Dauphin, and were she not the Queen, she and she alone should have been my mistress." That could never come about, because of evil conscience and the hatred now fulfilled. Marie would not let her

husband sleep, she wearied him with her detestable *cicisbeo* —
conceited little nincompoop, who was, however, growing fat and
developing a female bosom; apart from all the money he cost
her. "Me also," said Henri. "Banish him," said Marie, in mortal terror lest he might. Her sinister foster-sister would have denounced her to her confessor, or cast a spell of sickness on her.
Poison was not easily administered; every dish had to be publicly tasted by the officers appointed, before Their Majesties ate
of it. None the less, it was not often that the Queen ate with
the King; they had quarrelled too often, and Marie would insist
that she was in peril. Poison? And from the King? They shook
their heads. No one could conceive the agony of conscience that
rose from Marie's vitals and held her by the throat. Through her
nights walked the shadows of her husband's murderers, not
known to her, nor yet unknown. And he sat up in alarm when
she awoke with a shriek.

He often pitied her for having to live at the mercy of her
foster-sister — whose power, however, brought him certain advantages, as countering the influence of the Orsini cousins. As
time went on, neither Virginio nor Paolo ventured into the
Queen's room alone and without attendants; they would have
done so at the peril of their lives. As discarded lovers they led
an inglorious existence at court, though they assumed very menacing airs. It was known that they were afraid of Monsieur
Concini, a neutrally minded gentleman who did not frequent
women, but used them in his dealings. For the Queen he had
political traffickers, who enriched him and his dwarfish ally.
From other ladies he drew regular subsidies, in return for which
he introduced them to the King. The King himself was slow
in payment.

But he discovered a trick that would win Concini to his side.
An empty heart is never mastered, but he was careful to keep
the creature in play suspense and make him even vainer than he
was. When the young man had wheedled a little money out of
the greedy she-dwarf or the King's own wife, he had the im-
pertinence to offer the King a present of some valuable horses,
and the King accepted them. "Sire, you are riding a very no-

ble beast." " Monsieur Concini gave it me." And after horses, women. The Louvre was full of beauties; one slept exactly over the King's cabinet. On one particular night he lay abed behind the gilded barrier, for the Queen had locked herself into her room. Someone scratched softly at the door: Concini. " Sire, you made a motion to the lady up above that she was too respectful to understand. Your faithful servant has enlightened her upon her good fortune, and my experience has overcome her prudishness. A man like myself makes an incomparable doctor in affairs of love. You will of course allow him his due fees." With outstretched hand: " In such measure as the King deems honourable."

Agreed, though no money passed, and they went forth, the King in close converse with the trafficker in women. The lady up above was, after all, on terms with Henri. Madame de Guercheville, maid of honour to the Queen, hated all the intriguers who had established themselves at the court: the Marquise, so utterly malignant, and the sordid pair to whom every affair was solely one of money. She had made a show of bargaining with the contemptible Concini over a night of love; but in fact she wanted a discreet occasion to tell the King all she had found out — the secrets of the Queen and her foster-sister, what schemes the latter had concocted with her handsome husband, or the Queen with her confessor. The King admired Madame de Geurcheville or no Concini could have thrust her into favour. To impress on her that it was he, and his reward had been duly earned, Concini unlocked her door, for no lock could daunt him; he bade the King enter and promptly vanished. Then she talked, while Henri sat upon her bed. He found her clever and devoted to his interests. And when he began to find her desirable as well, she said with a faint quaver in her voice:

" Sire, you have forgotten me. A long while ago I invited you to a table set with many covers, but without any guests. And then, because I knew I would otherwise have listened to you, I left you alone in the empty castle. And on that flight from my heart I wept my heart out. My name is La Roche-Guyon; you have forgotten all about me."

"Not among a thousand!" he cried. "Did I not appoint you maid of honour to the Queen? It was in your person, Antoinette, that I first met virtue. And now you tell me that you wept over me in those old days."

"Sire," said Madame de Guercheville, "the women who refused you are, for that very reason, your most devoted servants."

"It is a dread judgment that you pronounce on me," he replied, but rejoiced to know that in his ill-reputed Louvre there was one virtuous woman. She had made herself look beautiful; her hair shone, there was a sparkle in her eye, and the light glimmered on an uplifted arm. In the yoke of her night-shift two rounded breasts rose and quivered, as though they longed to yield — therein the rarest charm of all. The King held Virtue's hand between the two of his. The tapers shed a gentle radiance on the room. It was a good hour.

But that selfsame hour was an evil one for Marie de Medici. Behind her locked door she had listened to what was going on in Henri's room. The whisperings of the villainous Concini left her in no doubt. But Marie was wrong as to the identity of the lady to whom he paid so prompt a visit. She never thought of the virtuous Guercheville. First she waited awhile, until a profligate pair could not disavow the reason for their meeting. Then the Queen dashed forth, losing one slipper in her hurry, but did not pause to look for it in the darkness — and burst into a room of which the door was open. The Marquise de Verneuil was sitting up in bed, reading. And there was a smile upon her face, for her book, though a large and ponderous tome, was entertaining. The Marquise had propped it against her bent knees, and over them her bright eyes twinkled a greeting at the infuriated lady: she had long since recognized the plumping footsteps, and even heard the slipper fly off the royal foot.

The Queen's aspect was beyond all expectation. Matted hair, eyes that looked yet more crazy in her besotted rage, and the flaccid flesh of an ageing woman in her transparent garments, all embroidered and beflowered like those of an innocent girl. Henriette d'Entragues would truly have exchanged her place with no one.

The Queen, breathing vengeance, or whimpering plaintively, hobbled up and down the room, one foot slippered and one bare. And when finally she had knocked the screen over and found no one behind it, she clapped her hands to her hips and cried: " Where is he? "

" Who? " asked the Marquise sweetly.

The book! His head would surely appear from behind the mighty tome — and Marie dashed upon it. Said Henriette gravely: " Take care. He is in the book, madame, and he will shortly speak."

Marie blinked. She was short-sighted without her spectacles, but at last she made out the title: a Latin Father of the Church. Then came her husband's voice, admirably aped by Henriette.

" Dealings with women defile both the inner and the outer man."

Marie started back. " Why, this is sorcery! " she snarled. " So you're a witch as well as a whore! "

" You fat banker's drab! " retorted Henriette, with an air of calm and confidence, but under cover of the folio she prepared for flight. When Marie struck, she hit the empty cushion. In the alcove between wall and bed the crazy creature danced and jeered. Marie tried to come at her, but the other shot a hand downwards and flourished something that flashed.

" Aha! " cried Marie. " An assassin, too. You have it from your mother, who stabbed a page."

" We stab pages, but not exalted ladies " — and so saying, Henriette put the dagger out of sight. " My mother loved Charles IX before Monsieur d'Entragues married her. She, too, was a witch and a courtesan. My origin is worthy of yours, madame. For we have the same husband, and each of us a Dauphin. Mine is the rightful one."

Then the pursuit began. Marie scrambled clumsily across the bed, the lithe Henriette slipped under it and darted round and round the room. " Here I am, who'll catch me? " she chanted, while Marie gasped for breath. " One — two," counted the younger woman. " Madame, you are beaten."

" Mercy! " panted Marie.

She lay exhausted in a chair. The enemy had covered her nakedness and with submissive reverence now knelt before the Queen and offered her a cup of wine. " Drink this, madame. No one in the whole palace would be less disposed to put something in your cup than I. You frightened me, and I easily lose my head. Let us understand each other. Both you and I have many grievances against the King."

" Tell me what you know," said Marie. " Something is happening to him at this hour. You were sitting awake and waiting."

Terrible forebodings suddenly came upon the unhappy woman. The agony of conscience rose out of her vitals and caught her by the throat. " He has been abducted," she said softly. " At last. And we both worked for this to happen."

" Not I! " shrieked Marie.

" Nor even I. Pray be calm," said Henriette. " But we must have the courage of our secret thoughts — both courtesan and Queen."

Marie was now drooping sideways out of her chair, her head between her arms. Her body quivered violently, then less and less, until it at last was still.

" You may not sleep here," said the boyish voice beside her. " Madame, it will soon be the hour of your public levée. I shall appear and do you reverence, defiled as I am both within and without."

The Queen made her way back leaning on the Marquise's arm. Henriette found the slipper and put it on the royal foot.

BEWILDERMENT

The Intendant of Finance and the Grand Master of Artillery added another office to those he held: that of Foreign Affairs. Monsieur de Villeroy remained Minister, but was not to know that Rosny was charged to watch his doings. This was needful because Villeroy, not precisely a traitor, but merely a friend of the Spanish alliance, had no secrets from the court of Madrid,

nor from the Archduke in Brussels. The King and his faithful
Rosny made ready for war, although they were not set upon any
conquests. The World Power itself desired no otherwise. That
power was breaking down, but though ever more unable to support a war, it vilified the peace — somewhat after the fashion of
those whose greed for land is to the very end unsated, though
they have space and enough in which to live. Hosts of spies
were sent into foreign countries, charged to spread insistent doctrines that were to save the order of society elsewhere; but that
was merely the order of yesterday, and it dissolved in dark deeds
among those same saviours themselves. The contempt for law
and the spurious ideas then rife in Germany were bound to end
in degradation and aggression, and the continent was faced by
an incalculable war.

A King whose heart is set upon his country's interests and con-
tinuing prosperity does not idly await an attacker who attacks
from weakness, and a prospective war that might well be a disaster immeasurably prolonged. He acts at once. A brief stroke
dammed the spreading poison. Jan Willem, Duke of Cleve,
Jülich, and Berg, was without heirs. If he died in the near future, Habsburg would claim his domains; the rights of an Imperial fief would be exacted. But the King of France announced his
decision that the succession should not go to either Austria or
Spain. Such was his first warning, and he accompanied it with
the assurance already given, that he did not want the dukedoms.
He wanted peace as he conceived it, and his advantage was that
the nations, too, conceived it thus. The urgent matter was to
come to terms with them. They were all risking hostages to fortune. It was a fact that they looked towards the King of France
and often judged their own princes by the measure of his renown.
Thus it was that the little Rhenish dukedoms grew into what
they afterwards became.

What of Spain, which stood so very near? In the Spanish
Netherlands there ruled an Archduke and an Infanta, at whom
the nations shuddered. In honour of the Infanta a woman had
been buried alive — no further testimony was needed. Strong

men there were in power of a sort who had not yet discovered human life: they had ignored the whole century of discovery, the most glorious that the West had ever known. Their self-esteem was built on sepulchres into which they were sinking while yet alive. The King had won his war against the Spanish Netherlands before it was declared. But he made plain, as always, his readiness for peace, and tended his kingdom like a garden; he even negotiated a pact between the United Provinces of Holland with their enemy in Brussels. As though there were nothing in the wind, the Princess of Orange visited the court of the Infanta — two ladies of the highest rank in Europe. One regarded rank as a vocation and a sacrifice of self. The other cared solely for ceremonial and fashion, and wore chains of little golden balls filled with essences; she knew nothing of self-sacrifice; indeed, it was in her honour that the woman had been buried alive, and her conscience remained unshaken. Persons of both sorts had hitherto lived side by side at both courts, and the same soil was inhabited by peoples who had nothing in common but their bellies. The King of France secured them a respite, though he made ready for war.

What was his purpose? That was the distrustful question so often asked, but it admitted of no straightforward answer; he worked for peace without, and within his kingdom he had come to an arrangement with his Jesuits; moreover, he retained his Minister Villeroy, whose sympathies were Spanish. But just then a disquieting incident occurred, for Monsieur de Rosny took his new office very seriously. He found reason to suspect one of Villeroy's clerks. The Minister himself was not implicated, it was not desired that he should figure as a traitor. However, he thought it safer that the witness should disappear; the said clerk was shortly afterwards fished out of the Seine, not drowned but strangled. In a few days came the first of January; in the early morning Rosny appeared with his New Year gifts in the Queen's chamber, where Their Majesties still lay abed. In the dim light he offered his compliments and presented, as the custom was, two purses; both were filled with gold and silver counters. The King took the first. As no hand took the second,

Rosny expressly offered it to the Queen: " Madame, here is one for your Majesty."

She did not answer, and Rosny noticed that she had turned her back on him. Said the King angrily: " Let me have it. She is not asleep, she is in a rage. She has been tormenting me all night, and she did not forget to abuse you too." Therewith he led his faithful servant into his cabinet and burst into bitter complaints against Marie, the scenes she made, and all her vexatious qualities. Of course they both knew that her breeding was at fault. What was to be done? Rosny offered his counsel indirectly; he deplored the unmeasured attention paid to the Marquise. She had visited him at the Arsenal, and there paid court to him, anxious to make sure that he would really pay the allowances granted her by the King. She seemed to think that the Lord High Treasurer's sole duty was to satisfy her claims. It was futile to explain to her that the King did not get his money out of his own pockets, but that he and all the rest lived on contributions made by merchants, handworkers, and peasants. " One master is enough for them; they have no notion of supporting a horde of relations, cousins, and mistresses as well." Such were the very words that Rosny used to the Marquise, and he repeated them to the King.

It was a broad hint to Henri: both knew that it was well founded, and yet that nothing could be done. But it did produce some coolness between two men who were, after all, solely dependent on each other. Cotton, the confessor, a Jesuit of the sly and simple type, disquieted the King in the matter of his waning popularity. The fault lay, so Cotton urged, with the inexorable extortioner, who thought solely of amassing money and led the King into the mortal sin of avarice. This shook Henri, who wanted it to be said that his people now lived a happier, not a harder life. He bade the Marquise be silent when she inveighed against the Minister, but an impression did remain. He sharply criticized the administration of the finances; and what he said was the plain truth. The King's business was now conducted honestly, but for that reason the people suffered. It was no matter that the revenues of the State should be well applied when a poor peasant's only cow must needs be seized. A broad hint for Rosny: once more they both knew it was justified, but that nothing could be done.

Cotton sniffed the morning air; he promised his superiors that the King could soon be induced to expel his incorruptible Protestants: then he would be truly isolated and in their hands. Rosny struck back and brought Cotton into ridicule. His astute police thrust a paper on him unawares in which the confessor addressed a number of questions to the Devil; the answers were supposedly given through the mouth of a man possessed. Rosny published the fraud, and amid the resulting merriment the matter that was really in negotiation with the Evil One passed unnoticed. And that was the King's death.

The better to cover up his blunder, Cotton had himself murdered, or rather he himself made a trifling gash on his person, which by the court and the city was accounted against the Protestant Rosny. As soon as this reached Henri's ears, he rushed to the Arsenal and embraced his faithful servant. " Were you murderously disposed, you would not have begun on that fool of a Jesuit." Rosny was not so sure of this, but promptly seized the favourable hour. " Sire," he said impressively, " you and I realize the seriousness that lies behind these absurdities."

Henri: " There is an attempt to set us at odds; that is serious enough."

Rosny: " It is your war they have in mind. They aimed at your Grand Master, not at your Finance Minister."

Henri, rapping out his age-long curse: " I really believed that this time I was enveloped in obscurity."

Rosny: " You are still visible, whether you will or no, and your aspect is unchanged. People are surprised that in your affection for the Society of Jesus you have alienated all your Protestants; King James does not go so far, and he is less trusted. It would be natural to conciliate them."

Henri: " Nonsense, man! Those of the Religion betrayed me with Biron."

Rosny: " Think no more of it, and make haste. Who can foresee how soon a Protestant army will be needed to protect you and your rule? "

Henri: " Must it come to that once more? True it is that the mood of Spain is hardening, and I can feel it here and now. None the less, you are watching Villeroy, and I — the Queen. I cannot speak of the matter, but you know more of it than I."

Rosny, hastily: " Respect seals my mind and lips. I conceive that the King's lady is wholly absorbed by his greatness and intent upon nothing else. Moreover, no person in your household and court is really powerful enough to call in the enemy. The conspirator sits within his walled and gated city. He has troops, and the frontier at the back of him. Sire, upon this I stand firm: the Duke of Bouillon must be destroyed and die."

Henri: " Grand Master, you are on too easy terms with death. Can the Queen be wiser than you are? She loves no heretic; but she would spare this one. Consider whether your plan would serve to conciliate my Protestants. Biron, whom they would not let me save, was not one of them. This man is."

Rosny: " They are the more eager to see the strength of their King displayed, and see that he is still their own Navarre. Sire, little is accomplished by complaisance alone, least of all in dealing with the hard-headed race of Huguenots."

Henri: " It may be so. Were those in La Rochelle of such a mind, and did they admit me willingly to their fortress, I would go to them. I would lay my hands upon the shoulders of my old comrades and remind them of the ancient toils and labours that were theirs and mine, and are still the greatest experiences of our lives."

The Minister took the King's last words as a command, which he promptly obeyed by making all haste to the approaching meeting of Protestant Deputies. " Gentlemen, I announce our master's arrival — as Minister I am but one of you, but I stand very near the King and enjoy his confidence. The King retracts nothing, he has surrendered nothing, neither the common cause, nor the struggle for it — which is never ending," said Rosny weightily, as though he were no longer in the Arsenal with a few hearers, but already in the city of Chatellerault, confronting the Synod.

And Henri repeated the words: " Which is never ending," and laid a finger on his lips. His war, a high and holy war, that would come sooner than the war that meant disaster. We wait, make ready, and are silent.

The Minister had sagaciously induced the King to make him Governor of Poitou; in this province lay the place of assemblage, and also La Rochelle, the fortress on the ocean. On the 15th of July 1605 he set forth, and not alone. The Governor took with him upon his journey fifteen hundred horsemen, for he was determined to tell his companions in the faith several stern truths. The Synod received him with the honours they would have offered to none other but the representative of the King. But Rosny had never believed that they could be traitors. Even if their strong places had been fully fortified, they were still not strong enough, and were only held under the terms of the Edict of Nantes. The Minister bade them calmly defend their fortresses a little longer; that was a matter that concerned them and not the King. In the meantime he desired to hear no more of their grievances, for he knew them, but they did not know his plans. It was more especially his will that they should avoid all negotiations, not only with his foreign enemies, but also with the cities and the persons in the kingdom who were not favourably disposed to the King. These Rosny named by name — though one, whom all had in their minds, was tacitly passed over; but they realized that the hour had come to make common cause with their master and comrade of old days. So they said Yes and Amen to all the demands made upon them by his envoy, their brother in the faith.

None the less, after the assembly they sent the most influential members to wait upon him, and among them Monsieur Philippe de Mornay; but far from obtaining any concessions, he was sharply reprimanded by Rosny. What? Mornay had fortified his city of Saumur in such a fashion that it alone needed eight thousand men to hold it! Plain folly — with no guns to man the works. Suppose the adversary collected all his forces!

There might not be long to wait! The King's most deadly enemies were still concealed, said Rosny. Had he more in mind
than he revealed, and was it not solely Bouillon's notorious conspiracy that had brought him here?

He let them guess. They were merely allowed to know that
their King relied on them in the event of an unnamed danger,
should a poisoned cup be offered them that would paralyse both
land and people; let there be but heard the unforgotten tread
of the Huguenot regiments, then that cup would pass away.
Strange that the inexorable Minister, their brother in the faith,
who merely demanded the surrender of their privileges and their
public rights, and even their security, should have actually fortified their faith in their King. However far they had been parted
by the toils of life, not to mention the King's own derelictions,
they would have him once more among them in the guise they
knew so well. Come, Henri! The fortress of La Rochelle will
admit you; and though you bring a mighty army in your train,
we will open wide the gates and withdraw three hundred ells
from our own walls!

In La Rochelle

September: he came in person, and there was much exultation in his Huguenot domains, though not a few tears were shed
in silence. To get a glimpse of him, the citizens of La Rochelle
climbed up on to roofs and arches and swarmed up the masts of
the ships in the harbour. The bells saluted him with the old
familiar peal. Thus had they rung when he rode into the city,
a fair-haired youth who had just escaped from captivity under
old Catherine. He had then hastened to abjure the creed that
had been forced upon him and adopt that of his birth, before he
confronted his companions in the faith. Today they received
him as he was, with all that a hard life had made of him; for his
hair and beard were white before their time. "The wind of
iniquity has passed over them," he said to his ancient comrades,
as they sat together afterwards in the great city hall — sixteen
tables, with seventeen covers upon each.

The younger generation stared open-mouthed when they saw
that legendary figure in the flesh, lifting his glass, wiping his
mouth, and gazing wide-eyed at his guests. Those same eyes
had held the enemy spellbound at Ivry; his lancers had halted
until ours were on him. On those same eyes were marked the
image of all men in the kingdom, and now of every onlooker
that day. There, too, was the image of the loveliest woman
who had ever lived. She was of the Religion, as he was, too,
in secret, and on that account his lovely Gabrielle had been
poisoned. In his eyes lingered the images of the dead — though
they were not wide enough nor grave enough for all who
still survived in them alone. Those there assembled were
alive because he had fought so hard a battle. Such were the
thoughts of the younger generation, but their awe soon passed
as they grew familiar with that singular face, spoke in un-
embarrassed fashion of their daily affairs, and began to bicker
and to laugh. Now and then one of them leapt up to get a
closer view of the King. Some, yet more daring, kissed his hand,
or even asked him for a word.

Henri and his old companions reckoned up their numbers.
They were in a high humour, gathered in a little group, for the
world had moved on without sweeping them away; none the less,
their talk often turned upon the dead. These had gradually
grown more numerous than that little company, whose hair had
been whitened by the wind of iniquity. The latest death among
those of the Religion was that of Monsieur de la Trémoïlle, a
man who had always been derided, and his memory still provoked a laugh. As a friend of the Duke of Bouillon, he had been
abominated by the King, and had quitted the field none too soon
or he would have been thrown into prison. But the mention of
him was but brief. After their long estrangement the King and
his Protestants had to let many dead men rest.

It was Agrippa d'Aubigné who had special reasons to turn the
talk away from La Trémoïlle. " Are there any dead men? " he
asked. " Or is it merely that they are not here? " Agrippa alleged
that they could communicate with the living from the place of
their abode — indeed, it was undeniable that some of them

came back. On the day his younger brother fell, Agrippa had lain between two comrades on a straw pallet, saying his prayers aloud. At the words " And lead us not into temptation," he was conscious of three raps by an open hand, so clearly heard that his two comrades sat up and looked at him. " Repeat that prayer," said one of them; and as he did so, at the selfsame words there were again three raps from his brother's hand, as was made plain later on, for he found him dead on the battlefield.

" Agrippa," said Henri, " you are a poet. Not everyone, when some loved being dies, is aware of it a mile away, let alone twenty miles." In so saying, Henri was thinking of Gabrielle, on her last day, when she was still alive; but Henri was already mourning her, there had been no three raps to bid him hurry to her bedside.

Agrippa, who in matters supernatural was always on the side of the Almighty: " We were quite sure we had buried a certain Captain Atis with military honours, but he slipped very softly back to bed by night; he was cold; he got in by a window. It is a matter for the theologians," he concluded, rather dashed by the ensuing silence.

Henri was silent not from any awe at the uncanny; on the contrary, he now noticed that he was no longer impressed by stories of omens and of marvels, which had once evoked images in his mind, and even something more than images. He looked at the simple-minded warrior, so fervently set upon a future life, and in his fear of death so ready to credit the most fantastic stories. Agrippa's conscience was at work — that and that only was the explanation of those three raps each time he said: " Lead us not into temptation."

But his old companion in arms would not be put out of countenance; he laughed and said they had their theologian ready to hand in the person of Philippe Mornay. Henri did indeed ask him for his opinion; but as Mornay took no account of phantoms and launched into a discourse on eternal bliss, with all the exactitude and detail of a layman whose knowledge comes from God, Henri barely listened. He sat in thought, his head resting on his hand, amid all the clamour of the banquet.

Here he now sat, among the companions of his crude youth, in the old abode of piety, friends to the right and left of him, and no canopy above his head. It was as though he were contemplating a semblance of what he had been in his earliest days, though he could scarce recognize it from so far away — either its forthright courage or its weakness. We must grow old, before the knife loses its terrors. Today and in this place it first becomes clear that the fear of life has left us too. As for eternal bliss, that has no more meaning now. It is a sad day when a man ceases to be fearful for his life, and loses the hopes that reach to the other side of time. A man grows sad and sober the more work he has done, and he conceives it all as ill-fashioned and incomplete.

With head half turned away he looked through a window at the sea-wall, where he had walked in the times of his mother Jeanne, as a fifteen-year-old boy. It was night, the waves, as now, racing inshore and breaking against the wall; and in their thunder was the voice of a far country, where he was not known, but in the wind he could scent another world — a world that was surely free from hatred and from force, and free from evil. Since then, mariners and colonists sent by the King had actually sailed across those seas, suffered shipwreck, and come near to starving on desert islands. But those who had come back were still as eager as ever. They begged for a new expedition. They were now utterly convinced that this was a high and just endeavour, and they had no fear of failure.

When a man fears nothing, he is bidding farewell to life, as Henri had discovered in his own person. When had his fears begun to fade? He could no longer tell. He merely knew that the fight in which it was his lot to fall was by no means the last, and after him it would spread further than if he had been there. He believed that the war now preparing was a necessity. But if he fell before that war broke out — no matter, his mission was still unfulfilled. And this, while he was yet on service, was an utterance of farewell.

As he thus sat and pondered, the others were troubled by his aspect — without understanding why. " Our King of Navarre," they said, but in silence, for no words passed. " And now we have him back, white-haired." Agrippa d'Aubigné was the first upon whom their eyes next turned. Mornay broke off his discourse on eternity, and Agrippa leaned across to Henri: " Sire, when I look at your face, I grow as bold as I have ever been. Loosen three buttons of your doublet, and have the grace to tell me why you have come to hate me so."

Henri paled, whence all could tell that he would speak his mind. " Did you not betray me? " he asked. " As though Biron were not enough, you engaged yourself with Bouillon. I know your letters to his quacking friend La Trémoïlle. Well, he is dead, henceforward he will quack his treason in another world."

Replied Agrippa: " The late La Trémoïlle was so much weaker than Your Majesty. Sire, I early learned from you to stand by all those who are persecuted and beset."

Henri embraced the simple-minded warrior and said: " Those of the Religion cherish even their betrayers."

And so there was reconcilement between Henri and his Protestants; when the time came they shook hands and parted.

All this while Mornay had sat in silence, except for his disquisition on eternal bliss; which Henri was distressed to observe. He stayed behind alone with Monsieur Duplessis de Mornay in the hall; the guests were departing as dusk fell. In the doorway some lingered for a last glance. It was clear that the most important matter was still to be discussed, for the King sought the embrasure of a window with his ancient counsellor, the first among all Protestants, and commonly known as their Pope. So the last of those two hundred banqueters stepped softly out and noiselessly closed the door.

Henri led Phillippe by the hand to a window, where he stood and eyed that now ageing face, which looked contracted beneath the expanse of forehead. The eyes were clear and steady: " we stand firmly on our feet, in spite of certain shocks, such as the business of Saint-Phal." They were wise eyes, though now touched with the light of evening; no bold ventures were to be expected from the man who now confronted Henri. (" When we were young, my Kingdom of Navarre, a kingdom none too firmly founded, boasted an astute diplomat, whose instinct for the truth endowed him with strength to see through every sort of liar. Those times are past; but it was just then that we most feared the knife, as only those can do who are yet untried, utterly intent upon their task, and know they may yet miss their due occasions.")

"Philippe, have we achieved enough?"

"Sire, you have achieved what was your purpose and your mission. You must surely recognize that more than this is neither demanded nor permitted by our Lord."

"Do you know, Monsieur Duplessis, that a great war is coming to fullness?"

"I am excluded from your Council. Much affliction has taught me to recognize the Lord's ordainments. My body is raw with new and open wounds, and there is another yet to be inflicted."

What was the man whispering in the half-darkness? His forehead was bent and hid his face. Then Mornay raised his head and said in high, clear tones: "Keep the peace for your lifetime. Sire, as soon as your breath is out, you are delivered from your high responsibility, which then returns to God."

"So?" said Henri. "Is that what you mean by immortality? And, Philippe, what of your eternal bliss?"

No answer but a sigh, and Henri would have turned away, but he added:

"You have amazingly enriched your knowledge of God. You say of Him, with some pedantry, that He, as in former days, could fill your heart. We meet once more on earth today, but your mind is solely set on the dialectics of eternity."

"My son fell at the storming of Geldern," said Mornay quietly.

Henri clasped him in his arms. "My poor friend," said he.

Their hands remained clasped for a while as they stood looking into each other's eyes. Mornay was later to write a tract called *Tears*. He seldom wept in earnest, nor did Henri, except for trivial causes. Decisive issues found him armed.

"Your only son," said Henri slowly. And the echo of the words was: Of what use is your faith?

Mornay added in the same simple tone: "I have now no son, and therefore no wife either."

Henri wondered what he could mean. Had Madame de Mornay received the evil news yet?

"She knows nothing," said the stricken man. "The messenger reached me this day. I must take her the news myself, and she will not survive it. Then I shall be parted from the two people that sustained me — and is there to be no meeting elsewhere?"

"You are certain of one in your own mind."

"Not now." This in a more emphatic tone; then he added quietly: "Charlotte will not only leave me, it will have been her wish to go. I do most deeply fear that life is the end of everything, and with it ends the promise of eternal bliss."

"Friend," said Henri, "we have nothing to fear. I know it from this day, and on that account I give thanks for my journey to La Rochelle. At the end a voice will say: 'We do not die' — which simply means that we have done what it lay in us to do."

Mornay took this for the King's last word; a quiver at his heart warned him that it was so. He bowed and took his leave. Before he turned to go, the King said:

"If your prophecy comes true, you must not fail to give me an exact account of Madame de Mornay's death."

GRATITUDE

The King's return journey first showed the advantage of his expedition. The garrison of La Rochelle escorted him to the next Protestant fortress; thence the garrison marched out with him as far as the next halting-place. Noblemen, whatever their faith, rode to meet him from the whole countryside, and for many a mile his carriage moved at a walking pace, such was the press of people. They mingled with his guards and spoke of accompanying him to his capital. He alone realized what was in their minds. They themselves neither knew nor said.

Scarce was Henri back in Paris when the news came of the attempt on King James's life. A store of gunpowder had been found under the palace of Westminster, but was laid bare in time. Otherwise all the assemblage would have been blown to pieces, King, princes, and peers, and the whole of Parliament: the Crown of England would have been wiped out. There was enough powder to have destroyed a great part of the city. It was the foulest deed of the century hitherto; and from it men could tell whence came the doctrines that were unsettling the age — How the ground beneath our feet was undermined, who had amassed what would have blown all to pieces, and introduced it into all the free States now left in Christendom. The tolerance of the free peoples smoothed the way for their enemies, who had accomplices everywhere, and all governments were insecure.

It was promptly agreed that the Society of Jesus had been at work, backed by Spain — a power that had certainly been defeated, but not yet finally, and was still unwearied in intrigue. Spain could never learn reason or moderation and grew more and more inured in guile and crime. That ancient power had raised a new fighting force, soldiers of the spirit, if murder be a spiritual act and a martial virtue. The Jesuit Mariana had taught that the killing of kings was justified. His disciples in England had been industrious, though less so in their books. And yet books are forerunners of overt acts; King Henri was ill advised when he defended the recall of the Fathers, as being guileless and well-intentioned persons.

In France they did indeed surpass themselves in their devotion to the little ones, while elsewhere, after the first shock of fear, a store of powder was cleared away. There was no honeyed talk in England; the Puritan Parliament sat on powder-casks. Had the King of France left them, as King James had done, unwatched? He was to fall out with his Protestants again, and not come straight back from his expedition, which had really been an inspection of his armies, now in readiness. The attempt at Westminster would have been followed by another here. But the Grand Master's cannon rumbled through the capital.

Henri awaited him when the discovery of the gunpowder plot had just been reported to them both. It would have been in the manner of that faithful servant, to have presented himself forthwith, by way of reminding his master who had sent him to La Rochelle, and to whom he should be grateful for the fact that no attempt had been made on his person. The day passed: no Rosny. Henri sent privily to inquire for him at the Arsenal. The Minister was at work as usual. And Henri thought that he expected to be visited by the King, or to be named Duke and Peer of France. A punctual reckoning was among his virtues. But Henri's life had been saved by many men who were not yet Captains. He, too, had often hacked a man out of a mêlée and thought of no reward. Henri knew quite well what in all this was false, or, rather, less than true. Rosny was a very astute man — or, to describe him better, he could take a broad view. What would have happened to France without Henri's Protestants? The man himself was a most obstinate heretic, which is what had put the notion into his mind, and he had on that account enjoyed the episode. None the less, he was never a man of inspirations; he sat, and he reckoned.

But Henri told himself that his faithful Rosny's vision was less keen than in the past. When had it begun to fail? He could not tell; he had not marked the slow change in himself. Rosny had been incorruptible, though insistent upon his due; and he was so still. He was, as he had always been, didactic, vindictive, and inclined to be overbearing, in petty rather than impressive fashion. And yet with all his pettiness how did he contrive to be impressive? And how was it that such greed of grain brought happiness? "A hundred thousand crowns for you, Monsieur de Rosny, if you can answer that! I fancy you are as baffled as I am, Maximilian de Béthune, or, if you prefer my lord Duke of Sully. Titles sound even more grandiloquent when it is time for us to possess our souls in silence."

When the news of the gunpowder plot came in, Henri thought of the man who had come to be his second self, for they were now a pair and must work together. His mind was unperturbed; he had been little moved by the attempt on James of England, and he was wholly unafraid. Not so Marie de Medici. She dashed into her husband's cabinet and burst into such a senseless tirade that she suddenly forgot all her French. " I had warned you. You may now be sorry that you sent Rosny to England to ask for an alliance."

" There was no alliance," replied Henri.

" But you have made one with some other traitors, in La Rochelle. Heretics are your doom, and you are running upon it now. I knew what must happen," she said unguardedly. At this point she fortunately fainted and had to stop. Returning sense brought an unmistakable look into her face: the look of evil conscience. She was still weak, or wished to seem so; and she gasped: " Sire! Remember the wrath of Heaven. The pious Fathers want you to be spared that visitation."

" I am quite sure of that," said Henri, to soothe the distracted creature. But what he meant was that those cellars had not been stacked with powder under any celestial fiat.

When the King was ready to retire — that night in his bed of state, with the room thronged with courtiers who had hastened to appear before a sovereign so manifestly guarded by good fortune — the Grand Master came at last. Henri caught sight of his great figure above the bent backs of the throng and dismissed the company. Then he opened the gilt barrier and led the Grand Master by the hand into his cabinet. " I believe," said he, " that we have business to discuss."

Rosny had brought with him in a portfolio the work on which he had been engaged all day; there was much and various business, though all in some measure relating to the powder plot. The King's ambassadors throughout Europe, including those to the Grand Turk and the Pope, were to receive due instructions as to what they should say in the matter of that plot. These pronouncements were set in measured terms, but they were all intended to confront all eyes and senses with one peril, and especially with the smell of gunpowder, not to speak of sulphur and a cloven hoof.

The ambassadors to the Protestant princes, the republics, and the free cities were alone to speak freely and without ambiguity. The Emperor and the King of Spain, the Archdukes in Brussels, not forgetting the Grand Duke in Florence, and the other money powers of the clay-footed colossus, were all planning war. Their open aim, of which they boasted, was the destruction of free conscience, and they would no longer tolerate free thought nor allow the free States to exist. A proof of this was the attempt upon the Crown of England. Let every man among them mark daily in his Bible, as he read it in the morning, that he was doomed to the same fate. Then followed quotations from Holy Writ, which Rosny put before the Protestant princes for their endorsement.

He pointed out that there was a King in Christendom, and only one, who wielded the sword, and used it not for his own advantage, nor for worldly ends. The nations, already half at war, looked towards him; and the coming war would spread over the whole continent and last for many stricken years. Let all men be warned, and learn their lesson in time. Deliver us from evil! The King's ambassadors were to speak in terms of religion and of war, and speak for the populace to hear, though not neglecting the decorum of diplomatic speech. Henri put the mass of documents on one side, but twice he read through a draft letter to King James.

" Grand Master, you use threats. This is no fashion in which to assure him of my satisfaction at his safety."

" Sire, it will get you the alliance, now or never."

" And to that end he is to put his Jesuits to death, by your desire. That is better left unsaid, for he will not **do** so and would resent the imputation on his weakness."

Rosny was about to reply, but paused and merely said:

" You are right. One King knows another. I was ill advised."

Henri looked at him. Here was an almost humble Rosny. An unexpected guise, especially at such a juncture.

" In certain matters you are wiser than any king," said Henri, speaking with precision. " James, with his Crown, was not alone in his escape from peril."

The Minister stiffened; once more he assumed the semblance

of the stone man on a cathedral façade. But he blushed, as
Henri observed with amazement. Hitherto when Rosny changed
colour, he did so from anger and flushed suddenly. This time
the blood spread under the skin, through which flooded a deep
sunset glow. True it was that Rosny felt abashed because he
had saved his King, and desired no gratitude. These two were
now utterly united. Gratitude would have been out of place.

"We will give thanks for the Lord's mercy," said Henri.
"Each in his own room," he added. "It has been a long day,
you have written a great deal, and I may now lie on my own
couch; your visit has spared me the bed of state."

So saying, he accompanied his friend to the door.

BE NOT AFRAID

Not a good time for traitors. It was the first occasion since
the beginning of this most notable reign when the usual un-
thinking homage was not offered him on days of festival. A
regular majority gathered and followed this most unusual King.
Wherever he went, he found a throng assembled, and many
voices shouted: "To the frontier!" Henri said nothing.

During that year and the next much befell that might well
have saddened him, but good cheer came and whispered in his
ear: "You have at all times acted at the bidding of your country
and your people, otherwise they would not now be shouting:
'To the frontier!' It is for them that you have created the
State; but who created you to be what you are? After God, your
people." So said good cheer in his ear.

Henri never mentioned the war. The general revulsion
against murder, and vengeance on traitors, did show that the
kingdom had begun to realize its isolation as the sole warlike
force confronting the arrayed enemies of the free peoples. And
its prosperity was what made it so generally hated. Tolerance,
moreover, respect for conscience and for life, was very perilous
to oppressors. "Our humanity is far from perfect; none the less,
it is detested by powers in whose domains it is a crime and
where the true worth of the human being has not yet been dis-

covered." But Henri would not strike at once, in retaliation for the insolent attempt that first opened most men's eyes. There were several nations in Europe which would fight for some measure of good living or defend what they had achieved, convinced of France's mission. Hence the appeals to the nations then put forth by the King of France, and continued for four years, of which the fourth was one too many, for it was to be Henri's last.

Rosny was less deliberate; he had continually in view that the army might march the next day. Meanwhile he prepared the public mind, with the King's assent, and therefore with the less scruple. Foreign observers compared the broadsheets that appealed to Europe to support the just cause of the King of France with the placards on the walls of Paris, and recognized their common origin. The placards were disavowed, as were the broadsheets, and removed by the police when all had read them. The attempt on King James provided powder that seemed inexhaustible, and now served to blow a cleavage between the enemies of the King, a diminished minority, and their instigators; and they contained some plain truths from Monsieur de Rosny, always supposing that the voice was his.

Father Cotton wept at confession, by way of inducing the King to reveal his plans against the Church. Henri said he had none. The good Father had proofs of his assiduous obedience. In regard to the Society of Jesus, which the King himself had admitted to the country, he appealed to the very words of Father Ignatius, whom he remembered in the days of his sickness. The figure at his bedside had said that it was not the Order that decides when a King must die, nor any pronouncement from authority and power: the decision comes from the majority of his people and the public conscience.

Well? How stood the public conscience since the attempt upon King James? How does conscience decide? Certain unknown persons, undistinguishable in the vast company of like-thinking people, printed indictments of the Jesuits and their secular allies, which were received with loud and heated applause. " Let it be understood," said Henri, " that I do not agree.

In my view, the Fathers are men of innocent intentions, though it is always possible for a fanatic to find his way into the most disciplined Order. Father Ignatius was of this opinion; that was why he was so much surprised by the events in England. As for myself, I must confess that last night I lay with a woman not my wife."

The King received absolution from the tearful Cotton. In the meantime other printed appeals were put forth, designed to turn the King's majority into a minority. These too were placarded on house walls under cover of darkness; but venomous as were their attacks on Monsieur de Rosny, the insults to the King were particularly gross; the police did not touch the placards. On the selfsame wall appeared one plainly from the Minister, and another of opposite origin. About midday the first was torn down by the city watch. Lampoons upon the King were much enjoyed by the mob.

His enemies did not dare reproach him with warlike intentions, it was too late for that. There were shouts of "To the frontier!" whenever he rode among his people — until he preferred to go about on foot, in shabby clothes, alone and unregarded. Thus he heard much not intended for his ears, but what was well that he should know. All agreed that the King was a great King. Then came talk of what they knew and what they had read, in mutual confirmation: of what the enemy party put about in print, because there was some justice in it, as must be admitted, even by Henri; poor man, he was beset by traitors. In his own house there was the Habsburg woman, who hated everyone, and the King most of all. His palace of the Louvre was full of her lovers, every man of them a traitor; even his mistresses betrayed him, not to speak of the horns they planted on his brow. The Queen's foster-sister was a witch, and rode on a broomstick. He was the centre of a general conspiracy.

And the majority said: "So much the worse. We must compose our differences, even with the Protestants. We certainly do not love the Protestants, who are both selfish and hard, and intolerably arrogant. But he needs them now; we must tolerate the cursed heretics, even at the peril of our own salvation. Behold the kingdom! Our King has made it what it is. Nor is he a man without resources. Bad times for traitors, these. When Henri sent his Grand Master against Bouillon, no one backed him, least of all his fellows in the faith. The Queen and Villeroy and the Spaniards were insistent that his life should be spared. So he was not executed, as Biron was; the occasion admitted of mercy. A Protestant Governor was merely installed in his city of Sedan."

But the minority did not quit the field on that account. They had the wealthier noblemen on their side, and in the face of Christendom, as a whole, they felt themselves as a majority. They again grew virulent, as in the times of the League. Tirades were delivered from the pulpits, and blood was shed in the streets of the capital; a Protestant walked abroad alone in peril of his life. The Guise ladies reappeared; they organized processions of female penitents, barefooted and crowned with thorns, a spectacle too often seen, but one which never failed in its effects, for the sight of wailing women always arouses tears. There were cries for retribution. "How long shall the accursed thing be suffered to live among us?" — the accursed thing being the King. And the question was: How long?

Be not afraid. The King allowed a Protestant temple to be built nearer Paris, only two miles distant instead of the pre-scribed four miles. There were savage outcries, but he laughed. "I pronounce that from today the distance thither is four miles." And he compelled respect for the doubled distance by erecting a gallows half-way to the temple. And so he appeared, to all men's eyes: the Protestant, who in times gone by had starved the city, plundered and burned the outer wards; at last the King had shown his face. None the less, the majority were his, for the kingdom had made progress, and he with them. Indeed, they were joined by some from the minority, and this by the measure of his own severity. Only a tolerance that can be severe convinces waverers. A lust for murder prevailed among his hardened enemies. During these years the King several times escaped assassination.

The Queen at that time was an unhappy woman who did not

understand what so distracted her own mind: she wished him dead, and yet she feared for his life. She stormed at her husband because her children were brought up with his bastards; but she was possessed by all the grievances of her Spanish party, and particularly the alliance with England. Henri had secured it, and henceforward the two powers stood surety for the freedom of Holland. Rosny, back from Sedan, arrived just as Marie had raised her hand against the King. He seized it and said: " Madame, take care."

Those words she was never to forget, Let him keep incessant watch upon his master, who walks in peril. When at last the murdered corpse is carried to the Louvre, and the dead husk laid in the royal cabinet — why was Rosny not on guard? Are we, then, immortal? But that day he gripped Marie's hand and said: " Take care." Henri tried to soothe the distracted woman. " Madame," he said, " this man is the terror of my enemies. To you and to me he is the surest friend. I name him Duke of Sully."

Thus Rosny got his dukedom, and Marie could least of all forgive the occasion of its conferment.

At the next of her great receptions, she kept the Duke of Sully standing and would not let him speak. The Queen herself rose and actually walked a step or two to meet a foreign visitor. He did not look important, but she knew him as the secret agent of the General of the Jesuits. Moreover, Sully also had an eye on him.

The unimportant personage was far from pleased, and whispered into Marie's ear a sharp reprimand that she might well hope no one had heard. " Madame, can you suppose that we could have you treat me with favour and so make the Protestants suspicious? Pray hasten to obey the order I am commanded to bring. A bronze equestrian statue is to be made of the King. This, as a symbol of worldly glory, is to be set up in an open public place, and the sight of it will make him more popular than ever among his people. The statue of a man still living will be plain evidence that our devout daughter has made good provision for the King's fame after death and desires that he shall be immortal."

The words, and their unuttered meaning, opened an abyss that Marie could not plumb; several years were to pass before her mind had thus matured her vision. But she obeyed orders; and in return the General of the Jesuits sent her a Chinese writing-table as a mark of his approval. Months went by, and the statue was ready to be set up in its place; this was to be on the Pont Neuf, built by Henri himself. While the works were in progress at the entrance to the bridge, the secret was well kept, but the time came when the business could no longer be concealed from the King — who at once gave orders that it should be stopped. Marie wept and raged and sulked; and she stayed away from the receptions to the foreign delegations, which were then much involved in the King's plan. He gave way, but on condition that there should be no ceremony and no inscription. The monument was a very faithful presentment of a Roman commander, but unfortunately the face was very like his own.

For two weeks it stood up on its tall pedestal, uninscribed, and beset by thronging crowds. Neither horseman nor coach could penetrate that concourse; and there was much uneasiness about. Men asked what the inscription was to be, being very eager to supply one themselves, some in the language of glorification, others in terms that would blazon their hatred of the King. But they were held off by the King's guards, especially at night. Some adherents of the King mingled with the crowd and swore it was not he. The real King Henri's nose drooped right down over his mouth, and was crooked too. The King was by no means so handsome as that statue.

" No indeed," said the more malicious onlookers; " but he would like to appear so! Such a man would be the pattern of a hero, not the cuckold and worn-out lecher that we know. He would not allow our faith to be persecuted, nor would he be afraid of war." Whereat those otherwise disposed would have had to admit that it was they, and not the King, who had so persistently cried out for war. That they forgot, for the truth is apt to be too burdensome for public disputes, apart from the fact that truth is a dangerous thing. There was more inclination to make the mob laugh at the expense of the Jesuits; the Fathers might preach very learned sermons, full of wit and eloquence, much to the taste of the court, but they were not understood by the common man.

A madman appeared among the throng exactly two weeks after the erection of the monument, and he bayed like a dog at the bronze rider's horse. He had been bellowing the usual abuse at the Jesuits and the King, and now he stood baying at the pedestal, having been pushed to the front by the exultant crowd. The Swiss guards, who could see no harm in this performance, did not intervene. Suddenly he clambered up the pedestal and there stood, first clinging to one of the statue's feet. Then he stood erect beside the armoured rider and cried out that he too was a Huguenot and had come here to call down the anger of the Lord upon the city of Paris.

And he seemed to be doing so to some purpose. His eyes blazed with a baleful glare, his voice rose to a hollow screech, and there he stood, like a raven, poised above the crowd, and his fluttering black cloak added to the semblance. Suddenly he flung out clutching claws at what seemed to be vacancy; but the madman's burning eyes had discovered someone in the throng. He broke off his tirade and burst into maledictions on the King, his friends, his enemies, and the government. The Devil was preaching disguised as a heretic. The guards were Swiss, and in their amazement grasped but little of what he said. Before they could drag the fellow down, he had leapt into the middle of the throng and crawled away between their legs, once more baying like a hound.

At a point where the crowd was thinner he emerged and made a grab at the cloak of one who had just turned to go. His own cloak hung loosely about him and, from behind, none could see that he had drawn a knife and for one long minute held the King under the menace of his uplifted hand. But the King fixed the madman's eyes with such force that his eyelids drooped and closed. No force was needed to seize the man's knife.

At a sign from the King, his hackney was brought. Monsieur de Bassompierre was pale; not so the King. From his saddle he caught sight of two of the Capucin nuns who had walked in procession so excellently disguised as victims of persecution. Bassompierre addressed them politely with the King's request that they should get their confessor to expel the devil out of the demented creature.

Several who had caught the would-be murderer protested violently. A doctor — and if the madness had been feigned, the gallows! So they all shouted, amid the applause of the whole assemblage, while the knife was passed from hand to hand. The King was not the man to conceal an attempt upon his life. He exclaimed from his horse:

" Good friends, you have now learned many things. Now you know that certain devils are cowards, who confess the truth when they are expelled from their victims. This one, as every one of you shall hear, will recant all his lies — I have done no hurt to your faith, I have never wanted war, and — vilest slander of all — I am not a cuckold."

These words were greeted with a mighty burst of laughter; only the bronze commander, who wore the King's face, sat unmoved. The King himself moved away. And the crowd shouted after him: " The devil will confess, be sure of that. If not, he shall answer for it."

The King set spurs to his horse and was soon galloping away along the river-bank.

A REPORT

When Madame de Mornay heard that her only son was dead, Monsieur de Mornay held out both his arms to catch her when she fell. But it was an unneeded gesture, for Madame de Mornay did not flinch. She said: " My friend, I was prepared. It was not for nothing that our son was trained in the handling of weapons. You rightly decided that even as a boy he should not solely study Latin and Greek, but should live an active life, that he might set an example to the age and not be corrupted by it."

She spoke in a toneless voice which her tense will kept steady.

She looked over Monsieur de Mornay's shoulder, for the sight of him would have weakened her resolve. He drew a deep breath and said: " *Utinam feliciori sæculo natus.* And now? The fortunate age — where is it? And our son, who was born for it — where is he? "

She bade him not ask feeble questions; parents like themselves should be thankful that their son's life on earth had been spent and ended to the glory of God. " Our Philippe was in his seven-and-twentieth year." Here her voice did quaver. Monsieur de Mornay led her to the table at which the pair had sat facing each other for so many evenings, every one of them in talk of Philippe de Mornay des Bauves, their son. How when he was thirteen he had been by his father's side at the siege of Rochefort, as a first and needful experience of the calling for which he was destined. At fifteen the Princess of Orange had taken him into her service; Holland offered good opportunities to a young man of the Religion, in matters both military and scholastic. The King had expressed his intention of having the lad about his person. But Mornay thought it was too early for his son to learn the morals of that court.

He himself had been educated in his youth by travel, first as an exile and afterwards as a diplomat. Exile had given him his wife and son. It had also fitted him to devote the five-and-twenty best years of his life to the King's service. His son should enjoy the advantages of a knowledge of Europe, but, he hoped, never know the desolation of one who is unsupported by any State. He too went to England, as his father had once done, though not in poverty and humiliation, nor too well acquainted with the mystery of injustice. His parents, when they sat at table in the evening, were delighted at their son's popularity in high society in London; he was a hardy young nobleman whose knowledge was lightly worn. His father had sent him to the Frankfurt Fair, to learn the practice of trade; he then had visited Saxony and Bohemia, and attended lectures at the famous University of Padua; but from Venice his father recalled him to the Netherlands, there to bear arms for the rights of a nation and freedom of conscience.

It was not the war that robbed the youth of so bright a future, but the theological controversies of his father, who thereby fell into disfavour with the King, and this was visited on the son as well. His career was broken off, and good fortune seemed to have deserted him. The King permitted Monsieur de Bauves to raise a regiment against Savoy, but soon afterwards the enemy made peace. Three years passed; embitterment had broken down the older man, and the younger one was worn out by hope deferred. The King had said: " He is young no longer — he is forty. His years are twenty, and his father's doctrines have clapped another twenty years on to his age." Sick of inactivity, Philippe again volunteered for service in Holland. And there at last he fell.

" In the seven-and-twentieth year of his age," said Madame de Mornay to her husband, who sat facing her. " But not too soon, since God willed it so. A life is always long enough, whether it contain his years or thirty more."

In so saying she had named her own age, and Monsieur de Mornay took note that she showed no more signs of thankfulness. He tried to stir her powers of resistance. " Dearest and best of women, today is a day above all others, today God is putting us to proof, and we have to show whether we believe in and obey Him. This is His doing, and we must be silent."

Whereat Madame de Mornay sank into silence, nor during the next month, before she took to her bed, did she make any mention of God's dealings with her. For appearance' sake she wore a simple and quiet mourning garb. But as her real condition was thus suppressed, it found outlet in bodily pains, which were this time beyond all lenitives. Madame de Mornay had been tormented by them indeed since her youth, after certain dissensions with the ministers of God regarding her own worldly weaknesses. Her palpitations of the heart and the other symptoms of melancholy gradually became inseparable from political affairs and her dealings with all people. A person of station finds it hard to lay down her duties, especially as Madame de Mornay was a woman of authority as well as brains. So in truth she had proved herself during her husband's frequent absences, though he had always been prepared to find her an ailing woman on his return. So much so that Monsieur de Mornay, notwithstanding his trust in God, acquired a faith in medicine. In every corner of France, where he went about a great deal, he knew the abode of every reputed pill-compounder. He had read Paracelsus, and, as was especially enjoined by the famous doctor for cases of the kind, he sent oil of vitriol and coral, and essence of pearls, to his suffering lady at home.

These remedies used to bring her some relief. But for the loss of her son not even the letter from the King in his own hand brought her comfort for a single hour. Of even less avail were the other messages of commiseration to the parents, from Prince Maurice, Villeroy, Rohan, and Bouillon, the ladies de la Trémoïlle, and the Duchess of Zweibrücken. Worst of all, the maternal admonition to her son, urging upon him the example of his father, would never now be read. Monsieur de Mornay had come upon the unhappy woman while her hand was vainly trying to add yet one more word. " I cannot," she said. " I am too much shaken by my pains. But in a place where no bodily ills may follow us I shall find him once again." So speaking, she betrayed herself. She wanted to die and be united with her son. And from the very beginning there was nothing else than this behind her scarcely uttered grief.

This once said, she lay down, never to rise again. Her husband realized that she had now repudiated the obligation of living, of which no one of us can be deprived. He did not dare appeal to her conscience; the sight of a human being longing to go hence, and already oblivious of her companions on earth, is always awesome. The plain woollen curtains of her bed remained closed except for a gap from which her hand hung down, pallid and grey like a snowfall several nights old, but seamed with light-blue veins. That hand revealed all the agonies of body and of soul, even without the tortured woman's groans. Monsieur de Mornay stood like an alien shadow against the bare white wall, on which hung a cross as black as his own garments. In her own room Madame de Mornay had always insisted on plain limewashed walls, like those in a Protestant place of worship. The duties of her station had carried her into many a rich and resplendent room. The inmost of all, where her own self could be unfolded, had no other adornment than the glory of renunciation.

Once she cried out to her husband and asked him anxiously how the doctors had decided: was it true that she must now think only of God? Tenderly he told her she was in peril. But God was all-powerful, and they would pray together that she might live. She understood his meaning and accepted her death as certain. She was visibly glad that it should be so, and at once rallied enough strength to fulfil her last duties. She gave instructions as to how her family was to be informed, and for the legacies destined for each servant. She sent for Pastor Bouchereau, and herself chose passages of Holy Writ for him to read to her, especially the Psalms, though she seldom waited until he had finished: too much remained to be done. She had to speak words of cheer to all the domestics kneeling round her bed. They must be made to understand that she believed in the divine forgiveness, and that she heartily accepted the promises of the Gospel.

But in all her eager piety she grew gradually worse, until an access of fear came upon her, and she cried out for deliverance. Breathless, and tormented by the tumult in her blood, she tore the coif from her head. Over the drawn, sweat-stained face fell a veil of hair, in which some auburn threads still glimmered among the white. It was in the matter of her hair that errors of her life had begun in days gone by, and led her into self-inflicted penalties that gradually grew so outrageous that her friends were shocked and fled her company. The domestics vanished one by one; and the pastor urged Monsieur de Mornay to get a narcotic from the doctor, whom he offered to fetch.

The sick woman caught the words and cried out against the long hours that must pass before she could at last find rest. She had suffered to the limit of her strength; surely it was enough. She had lost all her patience and humility and seemed to hold that a dying woman needed them no more. " I would be alone with God," she said to her husband as he wiped her face. Whereupon Monsieur de Mornay spoke to her steadily by her own name and tried to revive her resolution. " We must not come unwitting into the presence of the Lord," he warned her. " We are to fight for the last hour of our life; He sends us that last hour, and it may be decisive for eternity." At the same time he recalled the danger of death which His Majesty escaped by Heaven's favour, and by virtue of his own persistence. The great King — for five hundred years Christendom had not seen his like — suddenly rid himself of human fears, and thenceforward faced his duties with the ease of one just starting out on life, though with the wisdom brought by years. See how the latter end of life may be decisive for eternity!

Madame de Mornay was so struck by this bold comparison with His Majesty that she began to breathe more easily, and in an instant all her pains were forgotten. She sat up, embraced her husband, and assured him that with him at her side she would endure; she would think no more of deserting her post. " Our son fought until he fell. I will take no narcotics to make my last sleep painless. Go and tell the doctor so, my friend," she said, as the pain flung her back on her pillow.

Monsieur de Mornay did so. While he explained to the member of the Faculty in his library that the sick woman felt relieved without his help, the gasping and the moans came to their ears once more. The doctor got up to go to her, but Monsieur de Mornay barred the way. It was out of the question to explain to the man, whom he knew to be an infidel, why the dying woman would not accept any specific that would made her passing easier. Monsieur de Mornay was on that account regarded with suspicion — this intrusive personage even hurriedly searched the bookshelves, as though there might be something unlawful therein concealed. In point of fact, something of the kind might well have caught his eye: the tractates, which Parliament had condemned and which were partly responsible for the King's disfavour. Monsieur de Mornay in no wise displayed the courage that inspired a dying woman near at hand; he leaned against the dangerous volumes and so thrust them back, but he managed to persuade the doctor to leave the house. He told him that there was an exalted personage in the chamber within, who must not be disturbed.

This sounded credible, for Madame de Mornay appeared to be addressing someone. She spoke haltingly at first, for her tongue was still heavy. " Lord, I know Thee. A feast is preparing. The musicians enter. The guests appear in a blaze of light. The Master of the house approaches."

Her husband peered vainly into the room, which was by now growing dark. He himself did not observe the Master of the house; he felt alone and desolate and could only guess at the answers that followed.

" In Thy house, O Lord, are many mansions. Let me in."

" What hast thou done? "

" For Thy sake I went into exile. I repented of my worldly wisdom, and the warnings of my conscience struck a mortal weakness into my heart."

" Forget not the best."

" I have given my son to Thee. I have defended my husband even against the King."

" Forget not the last."

" Is it this — that I was resolved to endure my torments unrelieved until Thou camest? "

" Thou art accepted. Make thy heart glad at My feast."

Therewith all the dying woman's pains were stilled; she recovered her full breath and began to sing in soft unison with the chorused voices and instruments that reached her ears.

The lonely figure by the wall could hear that all that company was young — even his wife had found her youth once more, to judge by the sounds she uttered. He felt old, and far too weary for that feast; he could not follow when that summons came. His wife cried: " Philippe! " in a clear, fresh voice, with all the soft grace of maidenhood. He had never known her thus, for they had first met as exiles. " Philippe! " she cried exultantly — and he understood: her son was in her arms.

When her voice ceased, he went to her bedside carrying a candle, and what did he see? His young wife, as she had been a very long while ago. Her mind was clear, and she was beautiful beyond belief. She whispered: " It is the hour. Be brave and steadfast, do not yield. Glory comes before the grave."

Her last sigh; and as it left her lips, she herself closed her eyes, which then opened no more. Glory comes before the grave, and after it — nothing. Your Majesty was right to reject the dialectic of eternity. Believe, rather, one who heard and saw; and now, in obedience to a command from his exalted master, sends his report.

Book Eight

The Great Plan

Words to Strangers

THE KING was arrayed with more than common splendour when the Swiss came to renew their alliance. On their way to the capital they had been frequently entertained, and with lavishness and display by Monsieur de Villeroy. In Paris the Regiment of the Guard were drawn up in the streets from the palace to the rue Saint-Honoré. Troops lined the main staircase of the palace, two files on each stair, and the Swiss made their way up it with no little sense of elation. In the great hall of the Louvre they were confronted by a double hedge of Scots; they were to realize that the King of France had foreign troops in his service. The Swiss were not his only friends.

But they were indeed old friends of the fighting days now past, and that friendship had been secured by treaties and profitable trade. And in his latest war against Savoy the King had saved their neighbouring town of Geneva. So the Duke of Montpensier awaited them with a brilliant suite, and the Count of Soissons was also there to offer them a welcome. The Prince of Condé was in the King's anteroom and escorted them to the dais on which the King sat enthroned. His Majesty rose and took off his hat, a black and white hat set with a magnificent diamond clasp, and there were more diamonds on his baldric. The Swiss would have done obeisance to all this indisputable wealth, apart from all else that met their gaze. The King's right hand lay outstretched along his thigh, and as each Switzer kissed it, he laid his left hand on the man's shoulder, which mightily pleased them all.

Their spokesman was an advocate from Bern called Sager. Admiral de Vic acted as interpreter, a seaman being more versed in foreign speech, or at least, from much practice, apter at guessing the sense of what is said. The King made them a short answer, but so gracious that they were all delighted. At the numerous festivities that followed, only the Cardinal of Paris was absent, his excuse being that there were so many heretics among the Swiss, at which the King laughed very heartily. The King had the Church of Notre Dame sumptuously decorated, and the most elaborate Masses were sung in honour of our Lady. Turkish carpets underfoot, and the seats covered with lily-embroidered tapestries — thus the King's allies once more swore their proved loyalty. And through the chanting and the music came the thunder of Monsieur de Rosny's guns at the Arsenal.

In the matter of food and drink the Swiss were treated much more lavishly than any other foreign delegation. The court of France concluded from their aspect that for them no honours could equal the delights of the cellar and the kitchen. These strange cousins, with their crimsoned faces and vast posteriors, looked for all the world like an array of Bacchic deities. So the Swiss were set at the royal table in a single row, according to rank and dignity, each opposite some dignitary of the court. The music of drums and pipes and other instruments enlivened the entertainment, and many healths were drunk — to the King, the Queen, the Dauphin, the alliance, to wish the Queen good fortune in childbed, and more of the same kind.

Their Majesties dined in a room apart, but they afterwards appeared among their guests. The Queen came only to the doorway, merely to see how often these gentlemen raised their glasses. The King drank with them; he looked with wonderment at one Confederate who had to swathe his paunch in stays, and he made another ancient tell him stories about the age-long battles of his distant forebears. This continued for five hours, after which, sated and satisfied, they sought their lodging. And the rumble of the Arsenal cannon accompanied their snores.

Such were the Swiss, loyal friends, and almost fellow-subjects. But Lübeck, a city on the Baltic, head of the mighty Hanseatic League, about this time sent her Burgomaster, Reuter, to the court of France, a Councillor named West, several rich merchants and men versed in law, with an escort of mounted guards, not to mention a concourse of clerks, who followed the coaches in open wagons. Their alleged object was to get certain trading privileges from Spain. These were afterwards approved in Madrid, but mainly as a result of the visit paid by the Hanseatics to the King of France, which had caused great anxiety to various persons interested.

They started at the end of November 1606 and journeyed for many days before they reached Paris, where, on the 19th of January of the following year, they were received by King Henri. The strangers from the north encountered a very different King: not a single jewel on his soberly clad person. Even the splendours of the Louvre were dimmed. There was a guard of honour, but fewer noblemen were present at the reception than members of the Royal Parliament and pastors. The addresses were made in Latin. For such as these there could be no more question of Mass than of music or any sort of revelry. By contrast to their predecessors, their faces were hard and grey, and there was but little flesh upon their heavy bones; their speech was broad, and they were never seen to laugh.

Bearded, garbed in black, wearing enormous ruffs, one of them, the Councillor, with chains of red gold across his chest — these surely must be haughty Spaniards from the far end of the continent? The King walked gravely among them, inquired and noted each man's name and any outward differences. He gave his hand to each of them, in no way expecting it to be kissed. Then a few of them stepped forward and indicated that their leader wished to speak. This was Burgomaster Reuter, and he was not an adept at courtly address. He bluntly said that a terrible war was now threatening Christendom. It would destroy trade, and in particular would lay up the Lübeck fleet; moreover, the Reformed faith would suffer still further persecution. This had already begun, and the trade routes were even now unsafe, both by sea and by land. The Hanseatic League realized that the Imperialists were responsible for all the unrest in the world; they contemned both a reasoned faith in God and the peaceful exchange of goods. In the besotted fervour of ignorance, in denial of the right to free intercourse and free conscience bestowed on us by our Creator, Habsburg was fomenting this infamous war — and this must be the end, said the speaker; for the first time he raised his voice and flung out his chest, so that the gold chains clinked.

The King eyed him fixedly. He knew that the man's due title was Magnificus and that he was the head of a community possessed of much more power than territory. He had travelled from far away and must have some purpose in his mind. When he had finished his speech, what should he be told in answer? And how much? First of all, that Henri did not want war.

The Burgomaster reminded the King of the treaty he had made with the Hansa three years before. At that time their object had been a common defence against piracy, as practised by English freebooters in northern waters. That pest had since been ended by the alliance between the Kings of France and England. It was no longer the existence of these pirates that had induced the cities to send their envoys to the illustrious King, but his Great Plan for the salvation of Christendom, which had most certainly reached their ears. This same Great Plan had been heard of in remotest Europe, though it seldom found mention in the dispatches of diplomats, who may have read of it as a rumour and a dream. " What is this scheme, and what is it conceived should be our part in it? " asked Reuter with blunt candour.

Henri first looked round at the two figures behind him, on the left Admiral de Vic, and Rosny on the right, both with the impassive martial countenances that only relax when a command is given. He made his decision, staring wide-eyed at the stranger's forehead. He was wearing high-heeled shoes for the occasion, but his firm, yet graceful carriage, his level, fearless eyes, also made him seem taller than he was.

The King opened his mouth to speak, and then paused. In the expectant silence he reflected that he had quite well understood the Burgomaster's broad Latin — which was strange, since French Latin sounded wholly different. Suddenly he rapped out his familiar curse: he knew what he would do. He must resort to the Latin dialect of his own Pyrenees, using, where possible, classic turns of phrase, but addressing them wholly in his native speech, which he was sure they would understand. And he began.

" I greet Your Magnificence. I am gratified that so many representatives of your illustrious League have, for friendship's sake, undertaken this laborious journey. I share your sentiments. You recoil from the war that is descending upon Christendom and gradually spreading over this continent. I do not want war."

Here the King paused. At a wave of his hand chairs were brought; but the envoys remained standing none the less, in expectation of the weighty pronouncement that would, it seemed, now follow. And Henri went on in tones that strangely recalled the voice of his mother, Jeanne:

" I do not want war. This war must neither destroy your liberties nor threaten this kingdom. Deliver us from evil, is our prayer, and it will be heard by the Almighty, for we are mighty too. My Admiral de Vic has made my speech known in the lands of the north, so that you know that I am ready and watchful. My envoy de Vic has told you that I do not wield the sword to my own advantage, nor for worldly gain. I am strong, and though war may be waged by others, I do not want war."

Three times, thought Henri, he would tell them the same thing — three times, and that should suffice. " You must know that I have not only a greater army than other powers, and many noble ships, but I am chiefly strong because I am supported everywhere. States and peoples stand by the cause that promises them salvation, and I can maintain the cause. Among all my allies, I would name Holland, a republic like your own, and the Swiss Confederacy, a league like yours."

He omitted the Pope, and indeed he had made terms with other countries, as was scarce likely to remain a secret to these

Protestants; but they also had certain connections which they would not care to mention either. In more resonant tones he spoke of England, Venice, the Netherlands once more, Scandinavia, the Protestant princes of Germany, Bohemia, Hungary. "You see that I have not been idle" — this and what followed he uttered with special urgency, with his eyes set upon the Magnificus and his companions.

"My allies, all together, have even more troops than I; so tremendous an army has never yet been seen in Europe. I say nothing of the number and the power of my guns. My Grant Master, the Duke of Sully, will show you them and my war treasure, all in coined money — larger, I fancy, than any other land can show. All this being intended to make an aggressor pause and keep the peace, which hitherto nothing but plainly superior force could do."

He dropped his voice, feeling suddenly at ease with these strangers, whom he regarded as discreet, sagacious men. And if they did talk, they would but add one more to the fantastic legends that had gathered round his name.

"My Great Plan can be readily understood by wise men like yourselves. Behind it is the reckoning that a peace that merely imposes armament upon us is far too costly a peace. You are merchants, but we too are not unacquainted with book-keeping, that being a matter in which my Duke of Sully is wholly your match. Peace is worth its price, if it be not paid by us alone, but by all the Christian States in unison. I and my allies will convince you all where your advantage and your safety lie: in a League of all the Nations."

It was clear from their expressions that he had taken them utterly aback; he had foreseen their doubts before he spoke. Some shifted uneasily from foot to foot, whispers were heard from here and there, and one man flung himself noisily into a chair. Henri waited for the motions to subside. Then he said in his accustomed tone, but with unusual emphasis:

"If, according to the words of His Magnificence, only war can destroy those who strive for power, then we must be the first to take up arms. But I know a better way, and that is justice. Fifteen States of Christendom shall sit in a Council which will compose your disputes and close our common enterprises against the infidels who threaten eastern Europe. The dynasty that Your Magnificence has found to be so ambitious will welcome the support of the League armies. Moreover, the League shall decide the final frontiers of its States. This is no longer a time to stir up ancient matters and to redistribute the territories of the civilized world as we may think fit, as though it was by chance they came into existence, which is, in fact, true. But that is the work of history, and history has leisure for her purposes. Religious creeds, like States, shall have their frontiers guaranteed. What! Another religious war? I am the one sovereign who knows those wars," cried Henri, in the voice he used before marching into battle; this pæan of an uplifted heart was uttered in the tone of a command.

" I know religious wars. Let no one dare to provoke one in my lifetime! "

" In my lifetime," he heard a whispered voice repeat. It was strange that the man who was so amazed that he had had to sit down now rose, and the three words were uttered in French. But there were tears in his eyes. It was now for Henri to be amazed. But he showed no sign of it; the next few words he spoke in a paternal fashion, as though what he said was a matter of course, a plain dictate of experience and of knowledge. Once he slowly shrugged his shoulders, in token that what should cause surprise was not his Plan, but the fact that the simple truth belonged to him alone, and others had only half understood it hitherto.

" Fifteen Christian realms shall form the League " — this he wanted to impress upon his merchants, for they sailed the seas and could carry the news all over the world, making no commitments before the diplomatic measures that should follow. Would the world believe? No matter. Six hereditary monarchies — he counted them in his mind. Six sovereign States, which elected their rulers, beginning with the Pope and Emperor, and ending with Bohemia and Venice. Among the republics the King of France included, as usual, the Netherlands and Switzerland, but he mentioned a third, which had been forgotten: Italy, with her small allied States. Fifteen Christian realms would compose the League; and as the League would dispose of an armed force with which to punish any aggressor, there would be peace. " Let every State be secure within and without, let freedom of belief, and justice, be safeguarded, and you have a peace worth the price paid."

He ended, and looked away from his audience to let them gather their impressions. He talked to de Vic and Rosny, standing just so far away from the strangers that he could still hear what they were saying. And what they said was this: these were high ideas, and subtle observations, though not then to be realized. Perhaps later — But how late, if there is ever to be a lasting peace? Nations are easily led, and those in high places will always be covetous. They were so themselves, as they must needs admit, and those who blocked their trade routes did so with good reason.

The King asked Monsieur de Vic to interpret, as knowing the Baltic dialects. But someone said: " He would be strong enough to carry his Great Plan through. He has won many wars. He will win another."

" Ha! " exclaimed the King with a laugh, seeing that his purpose had been penetrated. " We must not forget my cannon, which are to open the ears of those fifteen Christian realms. Show the travellers my Arsenal."

Grand Master and Admiral, he took them both by the hand and so took his leave of the strangers. There they had the company they wanted, though let them not take him for a dreamer, with his head among the clouds, nor a wanderer astray in high places; his way was long, and always difficult, but he followed it to the end.

He beckoned to one of the assemblage while the others were departing towards the door. It was the man who had been so overcome by his astonishment and whispered three words in French; it was he, too, who had lately said that the King would be strong enough.

" Councillor West," said the King, " why are there tears in your eyes? "

The man shook his head in token of denial. He cared to know no more — but he kept his eyes downcast a little while too long. When he looked up, he was master of himself again. He bowed his head, this being his only salutation. Then he stepped backwards towards the door, gazing steadfastly at the King. His answer remained unuttered.

DAVID AND GOLIATH

The Swedish Ambassador at the court of France was named Grotius, a scholar of world-wide reputation. King Henri had sent for him before he had been appointed to his office. At certain times it was his habit to shut himself up with Monsieur Grotius, for what purpose no one knew. The court suspected a Protestant conspiracy against Christendom. His other dealings, such as the reception of foreign delegations like that from the Hansa cities, were looked on with the same enmity and mistrust; and the King's armaments were no less suspected by his own court. As for his pronouncement that the Rhenish dukedoms should never come under Habsburg rule, no one used it more treacherously against him than his Minister Villeroy.

Through the length and breadth of Europe the cry went up that he was the aggressor and that he would be the author of the great war to come. The peoples did not say it, nor did they believe it. They were well aware whence came all their miseries — the forced abjurations, and the torments, and the ravishment of their children and their homes. The Germans, upon whom the adversary had first descended, regarded the King of France in the light of a deliverer. He was just in his dealings, and both creeds expected from him a recognition of their right to their own faith and their security. The opinion of the world is created by writers, the issue being in whose interest they write. Practised in proving to a nicety both what is true and what is false, not even what happened beneath their very eyes could have moved them to be honest. Meantime the name of Grotius began to be known; this luminary of international law was to advise the King of France, which did not suggest that there were any infamous schemes afoot. But those gentlemen felt they must take care lest they fall into disrepute.

At the Emperor's court it was said:

" Let him have the Empire. Let him be King of the Romans and leave the Pope nothing but his Bishopric." This they said among themselves, and not to him, to tempt him, as in the past.

A hero armed, who also wields the sword of the spirit, is not to be withstood. The accusations that were to convince all Europe were met with doubts and contradictions. Uncertainty regarding the Great Plan inspired hope as well as fear, and in the same men's minds. At the Emperor's court there was more than a disposition to abandon the Imperial cause, not only since it had begun to weaken. And this was so because certain glowing prospects which no one understood, but which were known as the Great Plan, had so appealed to the King's enemies that they were wavering.

The Elector of Saxony caused a sermon to be preached before him on the evident likeness between King Henri and David, who slew Goliath. In Switzerland a book was published entitled *The Resurrection of Charlemagne*. The citizens of Venice asked every Frenchman they met whether he had seen his King. Nay, more; they were Spaniards who set their hopes on him.

His position at this time seemed to observers strangely like what it had been at the beginning of his career, when rumour was very far from conceiving him as King of Europe; it scarcely called him King of France. And indeed he was not really so then, for his authority barely existed except where his army stood. But the King had behind him the concept of the Kingdom. So, too, today, he had his Great Plan, which seemed promising enough, though it would not be understood. It was simple to assume that his armies would conquer, as they always did. His own Grand Master was wholly convinced of that. He put his master's notions on paper, where they at once became distorted. He alone realized that the King would attack, and the sooner the better; but he had better look after the rest. Whatever schemes he might be concocting with Monsieur Grotius, whatever he might have told those foreign merchants — and all his notions, if somewhat belated, came to Rosny's ears — they were but idle fancies in the end. A King who had achieved so much might devise his little schemes, for all that Rosny cared. There should be due note made of everything, against the time when he might feel in need of goodwill after some setback. And indeed he had it always. Still, the simplest plan would be to attack.

For a quick stroke the Grand Master and the King reckoned on the Netherlands. The war was postponed, and Rosny himself had to admit the derangement of his policy when the States General concluded their separate armistice with Spain. That was the Habsburg counter-stroke as Europe seemed minded to fall into the arms of her deliverer. The King of France had to record a failure — though not among the nations most devoted to him, which were mainly those farthest off. But the powers did not fail to notice that the nearest of all his allies had stood aside before the hour of trial. " Sire, your victory was beyond question," said Rosny. " In my opinion it was secure, even if your other allies had been tempted to behave like the Prince of Orange."

From this the King gathered that he was to expect a fresh turn of events. None came, and in his heart he knew that none would come. His end would be upon the heights that he had reached: he must not linger till his strength gave up. And what after all was that end? The very eagerness that burnt within him. The power of his spirit was such that he faced none that did not know him. Friend or foe, they had all fallen under his influence. But the power of the spirit must not be unduly strained for too long. The moment must not slip. He must bestir himself. Now or never, march out to war, or that war is already lost.

Henri, who usually liked to be on his feet, began to lead a more sedentary life. The room in which he sat was gradually filled by thoughts that came and came again, unsummoned, and then departed. What he hated to admit was that his room was a refuge against his own court, which, being nearer to him than any other court in Europe, was therefore the most sceptical. Here the King was mistrusted, for they knew the man, or they made bold enough to judge him, each according to his own trivial experience of him, which had, however, become common talk and was believed. The King was a hardened gambler, an ageing lecher, and an atheist. He was a prey to instability of mind such as would make any ruler dangerous, particularly one who took nothing seriously. He had been a destroyer from his birth. Had he met his end at twenty on the night of Saint Bartholomew, he would not need to seek it now in a war against all Europe.

He had raised up common folk and put down great ones, and, as the first to disregard traditionary rights, being himself a traitor, was eager to punish others for treason; he had beheaded a Marshal, and plundered principalities. He had had his own statue worshipped by the populace on the Pont Neuf; Protestants were the unfailing abettors of all his derelictions. Conceive of him absent, and peace and tranquillity would at once return. The country was utterly sick of threatening Christendom and appearing as its bane. If only this reign could end! A regency by the Queen was what was needed. Thus would order be restored within the kingdom and without.

Such, at the bidding of authority, were the sermons preached in those days; and, as was natural enough, duly disposed laymen were induced to lend their aid. Speakers thus addressed the mob at the usual street corners — but the people already knew their minds upon this matter. They had their memories of all that King Henri had done, against which words were mere sound and smoke. They shared with him his feeling for the land. These were not men who could be set against the manifest welfare of the kingdom and the public tolerance now enjoyed, which had cost such labour to establish. Save for him, it would not have been achieved, and he had stood by them in that contest. The common people, workmen and street folk, had a secret bond with King Henri, though they were not aware of it every hour. The street-corner orator was by no means deprived of his applause, as happened on one occasion when the King himself was coming back from hunting and found himself enmeshed in a throng.

It was blocking the rue de la Ferronnerie, outside a house on which was a coat of arms displaying the device of a crowned heart pierced by an arrow. The wretched hireling stood bellowing hoarsely on the curbstone, for a certain malady had already attacked his throat. He had lately taken presents from both parties as a law-court clerk, though he had not been dismissed on that account, but because he had caught the pox. Now he squandered in Paris taverns all that he earned by his tirades, though at times his voice entirely failed. Then he thrust his tongue out and gesticulated wildly, until he could manage to croak out a word or two more and revile the King as a lascivious dotard. All this he did at the charges of the Duke of Epernon, the same who now rode at the King's side. He was also accompanied by the Duke of Bellegarde. Behind them came the Queen's coach, surrounded by noblemen; and beside her on the cushions sat the Marquise de Verneuil, for the ladies were now on confidential terms.

D'Epernon had not expected to see anyone at that street corner. Moreover he was hard of hearing and gouty. When he recognized his own ruffian, he knew what was going forward and set spurs to his horse. In vain. The man's voice failed again, but a woman began a song. The King's song, unforgotten, now rang out again, and all joined in. He could not but rein in his horse and wait. " Feuillemorte," he said, " we must have heard this before."

> Oh, charming Gabrielle,
>> Fame sent me to the wars,
> When stricken to my very soul,
>> I rode out with God Mars!

The song was chanted, as though it had been a psalm. The coach, rumbling inexorably forward, soon caught up with the waiting horsemen. The Queen, in a fury, cried to the coachman to drive on. There was no room to draw aside, and the King had to go forward. And he heard, receding into the distance:

> *Oh, day of bitter sorrow,*
>
> *When we must part,*
>
> *Would I need not live so,*
>
> *Or had no heart.*

The King rode fast, and ever faster; except for his Grand Master he left all behind.

"D'Epernon," said the Queen imperiously to the grizzled cavalier who dutifully thrust his head through the window, "arrest as many of that shameless mob as can be caught."

"Ha? Hey?" grunted Epernon; then he understood, and assured Her Majesty that orders to that end had been already given.

Then came the Marquise's turn; she could break any man's heart, as is easily done by a woman who can ring such changes on her voice. "Not that I think of myself; I am used to insults, and tears are my very life. It is what may happen to Your Majesty that troubles me and fills me with such fear. A sovereign who behaves with the cruelty which we have just seen and heard — there is nothing that he might not do. It is a terrible thing to say, but the Queen's life is at stake. Monsieur d'Epernon, see that all lies are punished, and I'll thank you on my knees."

"Ha? Hey"? said the gouty old gentleman. He bent down from the saddle with all the readiness that was naturally his, except that he had, indeed, a murder in mind.

The King's friend and the King's mistress were the chief figures in the conspiracy that followed. D'Epernon was warned; the Grand Master was hard upon his track, he had caught Biron and Turenne and would not be likely to let him go — unless he were struck down first. Such too was the resolve now taken once for all in the evil little head of the youthful Henriette. The fate that was to descend upon Henri lay in the hands of an aged nobleman who felt his last privileges slipping from him, and a woman who had to reproach the King with nothing less. Their remaining task was to persuade the Queen that it must be; she did not yet know what. They must not go too fast or she would, at the moment, take fright and confess to her husband. She must be brought to the point when they could say to her: " He must die." Never fear, that time would come, and a word uttered is a deed done.

The coach was now moving slowly at the bidding of the Queen, who was no longer in a hurry. It was the hour of dinner, the streets were emptying, and a grey dusk was falling on the city. Marie's *cavaliere servente* was talking to her through the other window of the coach — Concini. She hated him because he did not sleep with her; but she loved him when he sat a horse. He was so handsome that her feelings overcame her. She appeared in public as mistress of the jousts in which he contended in her honour. They were no more than tilting matches, truly laughable affairs. The King really did laugh. If he were at all mortified, none heard of it but Rosny.

A lackey so shamelessly fortunate as Concini finds it difficult to impress an air of guilelessness on his supercilious features. He did more as he talked through the window to the Queen; he spoke with sorrow for the King. " His false friends have offered to have me murdered."

Marie began to fear for the safety of her lovers. " If he dares to do that — "

The listener held his breath, in the hope that the word might come with no more effort needed. But she said:

" Then I must be prepared for him to poison me."

No more; only a thought that had long haunted her feeble brain seemed to have settled there insistently at last. She was really too stupid, thought the Marquise on the seat at her side. And d'Epernon, when he had understood, thought that a Medici should have been more easily handled. The indispensable lackey on the other side slipped a flower stalk between his white teeth and smiled.

PATERNAL JOYS

Henri dismounted by the guard-house of the Louvre. As he turned out of the archway, someone stumbled heavily against him; no apology came, but it was dark. Bellegarde, who was at his master's heels, seized the fellow, told him what he was, and asked if he did not know the King. The unknown retorted that he could tell in the dark who must needs be recognized. Whereupon he was flung to the ground, and when he rose, the guards were on him.

In his cabinet Henri found his First Chamberlain. " Look at my left shoulder."

" Sire, there is nothing visible," said Monsieur d'Armagnac. " But if your skin itches, you must crush a certain bug."

" Old palaces like this," replied Henri, " are full of vermin; I'll have them all destroyed."

Armagnac sighed. He told himself without figures of speech that his master was at a disadvantage against these malignant enemies, for he was disarmed by his own nobility of mind. " In our youth we had come within a hair's breadth of striking down the Duke of Guise, as he was in fact struck down later, when he grew too great. Today it is we who are great and allow ourselves a perilous contempt for lesser fry. They will surely take their vengeance. Little folk never feel so outraged as when their moral betters do not deign to retaliate. Meantime we are living in this lowly palace of the Louvre, and not upon the Great Plan, nor in the high places of the mind."

Such were the old man's reflections, without any figures of speech, in so far as they were not indispensable to the matter in hand. Sighing yet once more, he departed, for he observed his master sinking into his own reflections. Henri had simply listened to a song echoing down a street, as in days gone by. The Dauphin was now a tall stripling. The dead lady had been many years asleep. But the brief war and the endless peace, the fifteen realms and the final ordering of Europe — when had he first conceived of all these things? When had he said that this should be his task, and that he meant to overthrow the empire of darkness? There had once been a festival of fireworks in the park at Monceaux. By the side of his beloved he had watched the sputtering wheel of fire, and the swan hovering above it. An inner heaven had then burst forth in flames within him, and he had envisaged a free league of kingdoms and republics. His cause thenceforward was to ensure that the nations should live in the light of living reason, and not dream terror-struck dreams, in the swollen belly of the Universal Power that had devoured them all. That had been the true origin of the Great Plan. Not very realistic; and simple, as is every true enlightenment. Monsieur Grotius was now drafting the scheme, and Rosny reckoning the cost.

At the outset he had set aside the Great Plan, forgotten it, and banished it to regions not of this world. But it had gone forward by its own motion, and changed with the changing times. It was true that in the meantime he had been absorbed in many enterprises, good and bad. He had to do justice and injustice from day to day. What he did was soon done, but its consequences were endless. His dear lady had died. Many others died, or he had had them put to death. As truly as Biron was a traitor, he now lived with barefaced traitors in his own Louvre, which had become uninhabitable. Monsieur Concini was proposing to buy a princely estate at a cost of several millions. Whom should he depute to warn him? He could not bring himself to do it; the peoples and the courts of Europe saw him otherwise than in the role of a man betrayed who merely asked that outward decorum should be observed.

They saw him heavily armed, allied to all the world, and if he allowed his enemies a respite to breathe, it was merely an act of grace. Every day such grace was granted to the Queen. She was in relations with the plotters, although her uncle's successor in Florence was bound to him by treaty. They all had a treaty with him, and they would keep it or break it according as he lived or died. Well, he would live, because the Great Plan was now a reality come to fullness; he had not devised it, nature had brought it forth. He who has allowed himself time in which to ripen can tell what will be in the years to come, though he himself shall have departed a hundred years before. He, by God's aid, would accomplish all this, — but he must wait awhile for the proper hour to strike. He would have Concini warned.

He asked the Duchess of Sully to do it, a lady who seemed assured of respectful obedience from everyone, by reason of her own stern character and the fact that her husband was a man much feared. But it fell out otherwise. Madame de Sully, to avoid scandal, did not approach the Queen's admirer; she addressed herself to the Queen, and with the utmost delicacy: Her Majesty must not endanger her reputation. There followed an outburst of rage on the part of the cavalier or *cicisbeo*. Not that he was in any concern for the lady; he summoned her to the Louvre, as though the place were already his. In the Queen's presence he burst into the most unseemly abuse of that austere Protestant lady. He called her a foolish old frump and accused her of designs upon himself. She could tell her King that no one gave a rap for him here — whereat Concini leapt into the air like an animal, and his face was like that of a beast of prey. He afraid of the King? Not a whit! The King had better take care or he would find himself in trouble.

The lady remained unruffled; she pitied this puling extravagance. The lackey went on raving after she had left the room. It was unheard of that a husband should make such an attack upon his wife's cavalier — and, moreover, such a husband! The King did not understand who he was and how he stood. On every side his death was reckoned on, and no art could help him now. For those who knew, the Queen's regency had already begun.

To all this she listened. But in her fury, and in Concini's fury, she did not remark what had been mentioned for the first time: her husband's murder. And Henri, when the affair was reported to him, decided that she had not taken the suggestion seriously. He did not learn of it from Madame de Sully, who kept her thin lips firmly closed, but from the Dauphin, who had listened from his quiet corner, in a flush of wrath which had left him paler than his wont. He swore that Monsieur Concini should die; and when he was King, he kept his word.

Said the Dauphin Louis, in his father's cabinet: " Sire, they mean to kill you. And my poor mother is in the conspiracy."

Henri: " My boy, I have known her nine months longer than you. She is violent and quarrelsome, and inclined to domineer, but she is not a she-wolf."

Louis: " The man was more savage than a whole pack of wolves and would have eaten me up, bones and all."

Henri: " But the Queen? "

Louis: " She obeys him, as you know, my Father."

Henri: " She does not sleep with him. And that, let me tell you, is the main thing. A woman is not ruled otherwise."

Louis: " Sire, tell me that I may destroy your murderer."

Henri: " He is not my murderer, and would be unworthy of your hand."

Louis, pallid, too tall for his age, choking down his tears: " Father — my dearest Father! These others must be given a terrible example. The corpse shall lie on the inner bridge of the Louvre, so that all who come in and out must step across it."

Which indeed was what was done, in the time of King Louis. But the father he so admired embraced and held him while he said:

" You will be a child for a long while yet. Do not forget: today we have talked together as men. Our deeds make us enemies, and we must do more deeds to strike those enemies down. And so it continues, a murder proves nothing. I am more fearful for your mother, who needs forbearance, for she is always pregnant."

The Dauphin was near to bursting into sobs. The King clapped a hand over his mouth; footsteps were approaching outside. When the door was opened, the King was galloping round the room on all fours, the Dauphin on his back, riding him with a handkerchief for bridle. It was the Spanish Ambassador who came in. Don Inigo de Cardenas had come to Paris on a special mission: to make exact inquiry into the armaments and intentions of the King of France. As occasion offered, he was to ask for explanations, and this seemed an excellent opportunity.

Don Inigo was a haughty Spaniard, but he could distrust himself at times. The barrier set by his long ancestry between himself and other men had at last produced an inverted feeling that was certainly not self-confidence. Don Inigo stood in the doorway observing these strange antics. He felt both disgusted and embarrassed, and the sight, though it did not shock him, made him feel sad. The King made a great bound, in an effort to shake off the Dauphin, who clung to him still harder, shouting with excitement and glee. His height and his pale grave face belied the child that he still was.

The King stopped; and without rising from the floor, he said: " Ambassador, pray have you children? Yes? Then I'll go on."

And he started on another round of the room. The Dauphin stammered: " This is the g-g-game we always p-p-play."

But while talking with his father, he had not stammered at all.

Don Inigo withdrew. His first impression of the scene was that this King was not a danger to the World Power.

The Plague

But the Ambassador did not for that reason forget his mission. Though the King's demeanour might not be dignified, he had a Grand Master and an army. His stock of gold was increasing, while that of Spain was running out. His Great Plan had not been in general much remarked, but Don Inigo's aloofness, which freed him from all prejudice, enabled him to take the measure of it. He, and, as it would appear, he alone, divined that a settlement of the world was in the way of being achieved without the aid of Habsburg. The tradition of a century had made this more difficult to realize than might appear: yes, the haughty grandee was much to be commended for that secret self-distrust and absence of conceit that had opened his understanding.

He of course put the Great Plan on one side, so far as he considered it at all. He never mentioned it; but he worked with all the more energy for the complete estrangement of Their Majesties, by means of two Spanish marriages. The Queen was promptly induced to consent to the betrothal of her Dauphin to the Infanta. The King rejected the proposal. He made no false undertakings, he openly said no. The attached condition was not needed to make Henri stand firm, Spain's proviso being that he should sacrifice Holland.

Don Inigo was more obstinate than anyone not at war with his own conscience. He importuned the King until one day Henri lost patience, blurted out an oath, and cried: " If the King of Spain provokes me any longer, I'll pay him an unexpected visit in Madrid."

" Sire," returned the Ambassador with great dignity, " you would not be the first King of France who has sojourned in that capital."

Yes — and in a cell no bigger than a hen-house. " Ambassador," said Henri, in a much milder tone, " you are a Spaniard, and I am a Gascon. If we begin in this fashion, where shall we stop? "

As a result of his retort and others of the kind, Don Inigo became the hero of the day; but he was more ashamed than flattered. The Queen discovered that he was a kinsman of hers. The court began to use the stilted Castilian turns of speech that he had introduced. The intention was to humiliate the King. Don Inigo, more easily offended than such gentlemen usually are, desired no privilege in the presence of the King. One day he noticed the King's sword carried past. He took it from the servant, turned it over and over, and eyed it carefully. Then he kissed the blade and said: " I have been so fortunate as to handle the gallant sword of the most gallant King now living."

Moreover, he remained behind in the capital when it was visited by another exalted guest: the plague.

Most of those at court fled to their estates. The plague was no new visitation; the Black Pest had been regarded with ever increasing terror since it first appeared three hundred years before. Within the memory of those yet living, there had been one epidemic, an infection of the blood or of the lungs, or both together, during the siege of Paris; but the worst had taken place fifty years before. The only hospital, called the Hôtel Dieu, usually sufficed the city's need; but in time of plague eight sick persons were packed into every bed. There was much surprise that in a place so dedicated to God most of the sick died. Eight-and-sixty thousand at the last outbreak but one, which the old could still remember. The last had been milder, possibly as a result of an order from the Archbishop that those stricken by the plague should be separated from all the other sick. Since then the plague bore a name that betokened a discovery: it was called the Infection.

The King refused to leave Paris, despite the insistence of the Queen, who for her part was pestered by the Galigai-Concini pair. As though Marie knew no better, she regarded her husband as solely responsible for the plague. On the former occasion he had brought it upon his capital, before the city was his, when he was trying to starve it out. The curse was latent in him, and now it was breaking forth once more. He who had become anathema remained so, said Marie, who was exceedingly afraid. Concini-Galigai did not spare her a single death; and several of the palace lackeys had already been carried out as corpses. She at last let herself be persuaded to have a ship made ready, the intention being to remain on the high sea while the plague lasted. She would take the Dauphin with her, as also her *cavalieri serventi,* of course, even those now out of service. And the King might give his whole mind to his beloved plague.

He was indeed solely set upon the plague. He thought to combat it by means of air and fire, two purifying elements. In the Louvre he had all the windows thrown open, and juniper fires everywhere. He had a supply of the wood brought from the forests to disinfect the populous quarters with its pungent smoke. His especial care was to stem the movement of the infection, which came, he thought, from over the Rhine. Germany was quickly falling into ruin, whether her present confusion was called war, or, for the time, by some other name. And the infection was but the forerunner of the misery she was about to bring upon the world. But near the frontier, in Lorraine, dwelt Catherine.

The Duchess of Bar, Madame, the King's sister, his beloved Catherine — he had compelled her to that marriage. Was it true that he was possessed by a curse? He must not listen to such idle gossip. How fared the devout in these days? During the processions through the streets, while all the saints were invoked and prayers for the dead were chanted, there were always some in the watching crowds who were struck down and infected. The pestilence was not a curse, nor even a punishment; it was fed by ignorance and terror. Be not afraid! You are not afraid, Catherine? See — your brother, who did you much injury in your life, sends a mounted messenger to fetch you, for you will be safest at his side.

He bethought him of one whom she might follow, and came upon his kinsman, the younger Condé. The Prince was by nature silent, or at least pretended to be so at that time. Later on he made some noise in the world. But hitherto he had been a rather melancholy and diffident personage, who had gratefully accepted a modest pension from the King, for he had no possessions of his own. He was the son of that cousin who had once tried to get the better of the young Navarre. Then he died, poisoned, as was generally believed, by the Princess, his wife. She had never confessed. Her imprisonment and trial were matters of the past. Now she lived at court, where everyone's reputation was in some way tainted. For the rest, her son was a silent and impenetrable young man. Henri said to him: " Go and fetch my sister. If you are the messenger, she will understand that I do need her presence."

Condé had gone, and Henri fell into a state of dire unrest. If only he had her in his arms! Alas, he had robbed her of happiness that should have been hers. The obeisance by his bed of state was a stroke of pride and could not be her purpose. " We stand alone, each for the other; we had the eyes of childhood, the dreams of youth; and love possessed our hearts. Catherine, I thwarted you in the end, and let you leave me with a man to whom you are indifferent; and by then you were weary. You were already on the way towards death, and I should have reached a hand to hold you back. I should have reached out to you. Oh, what have I done! "

In his remorse and fear he hurried daily to the Hôtel Dieu, to touch the sick. They believed that the King's touch healed them, and he persuaded himself that it was true. He touched the hard tumours, and the red inflammations called *charbons*. He washed his hands and made his way to where another quavering voice called out to him, though there were many whose voices were quenched when their consciousness was blotted out. If he could see but one arise and walk, then surely his sister would come; he would keep her safe and yet make good all that he had made her suffer. He begged an infected monk, who perhaps hated him, to pray that someone on a journey might safely reach her place of refuge.

Nights he would leave his bed, and in the light of the flickering fires he would wander through the palace. Once, high up in the building, he came upon a corridor where there was no window open, nor any hearth prepared for burning wood. The place would have been pitch dark except that from a far-off corner he saw a number of little flames flickering towards him, so near the ground that he could not believe his eyes: an apparition moving in a halo of moving light. A she-dwarf, plainly to be recognized, although she wore no clothes. Stark naked, smeared all over with red paint, between her outstretched fingers she carried eight tiny tapers. Henri would have looked at her more closely, but a man who was fleeing from the creature fell at his feet. And by the light of the tapers Henri recognized Concini.

He was far less like his usual self than the Queen's foster-sister, his wife. Sleek and sinister no longer; his hair in wild disorder; the taut shoulders and slim flanks had sagged into a flaccid sack of flesh. The face was a mere mask of pallid horror, scarce imaginable. What fear could do! The noble Concini regarded the noble Galigai as the pest personified. Red — the red of the pest-stricken bodies — and the tallow lights on those dread coffins: his terror deprived him almost of speech, and he yelled like a tortured cat.

"Sire! I have met the plague. Mercy, Sire, or I must die! Touch me, O sacred Majesty — Heaven has sent you, touch me." And the Queen's adorer lay gibbering and wailing on the floor. The Queen should have heard him amid her assembled court, but are there any warnings that the world remembers? The plague gave none. The red-smeared image passed so near that her tapers dripped upon the writhing wretch. He could bear no more and fainted. The pestilential foster-sister took no heed of the scene she had evoked. Her eyes were upturned, she was walking in a trance. Henri left the place.

The state of the capital grew worse, more by reason of the prevailing terror, which deepened as men met and talked. Indeed, the malady began to decrease as the King's doctors followed his measures. The colonnade of his Place Royale was transformed into large and airy lazarets. Suspected by the townsfolk as too magnificent, it served very well for the sick. Henri did not count the hours he spent there. In the streets he met either no one, or a few muffled figures hastening past with covered biers. When he arrived, he felt the free air upon his face, and smelt the smoke rising from the woodpiles all around the square. The smoke was blown by the wind into the open porticoes, but did not linger anywhere. Beyond and above it gleamed the blue of heaven, while the fragrant vapours wreathed round the prostrate forms, of which there were a thousand or even more. His own longing for his sister here found most relief.

The King by no means meant to conclude that day by touching his sick subjects — he had touched nearly two thousand. New faces were ever turned expectantly towards him, blackened by smoke, or sometimes blackened also by the plague. He did not weary. This was the day on which Catherine would come. The order had been given that he should be informed at once. And he bade all the sick be healed. This day his touch had virtue, though they were black all over with boils and pustules, and their breath already envenomed. He had not bandaged his mouth, for he knew himself strong and safe. Close at hand, behind a little cloud, a bell was tinkling to announce the presence of the Sacrament. The priest, his mouth unbandaged also, was repeating the prayers for the dying.

When the cloud passed, priest and King looked into each other's eyes. One of them was short and frail, gaunt of feature, but with shining eyes. And he said to the King: " You have as much courage as if you believed in God."

" I do," said Henri; then, not far away, he caught sight of a figure, stock-still and silent. Silent, and destructive of all hope. " Condé? " said Henri eagerly, but judgment was pronounced, as he well knew. " Condé! " The other merely bowed his head. And a smoke cloud drifted between them.

From beside the King came the moans of a sick man who wanted to die and could find no help. " He is a heretic," said the priest. " I have sent for a pastor, but he will come too late."

" We will go," said Henri. Had his Protestant sister there been lying on her bed of death, he would have knelt no otherwise. He dropped on both knees and chanted softly into the ear of the dying man: " Praise the Lord, O my soul."

He knew of one sole place in the palace of the Louvre where he could weep unhindered all night through. That was his bed of state; there he would lie, guarded, with curtains closed, secure in solitude. From his cabinet he stepped into the great hall; dusk was falling, and he did not notice the assembly of his court, though not one was absent. What remained of his court, about twenty or thirty persons, had sought the sanctity of Majesty, hoping, perhaps that it might preserve them against the plague. The King, as he hurried in, was wholly at variance with their idea of majesty. He looked dishevelled, his face was suspiciously blackened; here was no protector against the plague, but a harbinger of the plague itself. Nay, more — his time was over, his life of little moment, and, as it was said, the regency had already begun.

The door opposite swung open. God be praised! — the Queen, with the Dauphin at her side, preceded by lackeys carrying candelabra. The court — what was left of it — hurried out of the shadows to meet the rising glory. Their obeisances, their bended knees, and their murmured homage were offered to the Dauphin. At the other end of an empty room stood the King, alone.

The first to recover himself was the grave and melancholy Condé. Calm and composed, he made his way with dignity towards the King. Bellegarde and Bassompierre hurried after him, and Henri was soon the centre of a group; but for those few moments he had stood alone.

MARGOT OF OLD DAYS

The Queen of Navarre appeared when the plague had been overcome, and the festivities at court became more resplendent than ever. All the gentlemen and ladies left their castles, which were mostly damp and dirty, and found their way back to the only city where life could be properly enjoyed. Their twin delights were winning money and spending it. A winner at play appeared next day at the Louvre arrayed in all the glories of the noontide or the dawn or the starry moonlight. Many sold their dank castles that they might shine at court.

Marguerite de Valois came to the conclusion that her banishment had lasted long enough; it had lasted eighteen years. As a woman of thirty-four, she had been dismissed by her husband Henri — though the decision was not solely his. The last of the perished Royal House could not bear to see a successor, though he were her husband, on her dead brother's throne. Her hatred of him had risen to such a pitch that she had actually sent an emissary to murder him. But time had effaced all these matters; who now gave a thought to ancient murderers and ancient hatred? Forgotten love, too, could scarce show its face once more.

She appeared unannounced, but Henri received her with all due honour as the last of the Valois and his first wife. He essayed a friendly tone and inquired after the castle at Usson, where she had spent these eighteen years. And silently he reckoned that she must now be fifty-two. She looked it. " There is good eating in Auvergne, I fancy? "

" And good love-making," she answered with a boldness that in a flash recalled all that Margot had been in old days.

Beneath the sagging cheeks, the mask of paint, and the blond wig he could discern his companion in much enjoyment of the senses. The night of Saint Bartholomew had cast its shadow before, and pleasure had reached the point of pain. This woman had been the goddess of her age, lovely, luxurious, and learned. When a procession passed by, people forgot to salute the Host: Madame Marguerite was the object of their worship. " And this," thought Henri, " is what she has become in all these years." And what of himself? In his dismay, he assured her that she had altered little.

" Your amours have also kept you young, sir," said she, though she did not think so. He seemed to her cast down, almost oblivious of his good fortune and his fame. She herself had become good-humoured as the years passed, though still capable of terrible outbursts of passion. Nor was she more malicious than she ever had been. "You have the reputation," she went on, "of being always gay and always in love, and you deserve it. My eyes convince me that you are truly the *vert galant*."

There was still a melting look in them, and her words were well intentioned. He gave her his hand and bade her welcome, and reminded her of the pleasant days of old: King and Queen of Navarre, his petty battles, and their arcadian Court of Muses. To which she replied that she had come intending to form an Academy of the choicer spirits, but, alas, her means were sadly straitened.

He was more than generous, and gave her what she wanted at the moment, a pension, and a house in the Bois de Boulogne. But there he stopped short; other claims might follow, and he was afraid of Rosny, when a lady tried to delve into the treasury. For her part, she smiled a gratified smile; here was Henri as he was reputed — addicted to play, women, and money.

"I shall now await the Queen," she said. "I am a near kinswoman of hers through my mother, Madame Catherine. So it had to be a Medici once more." Whereupon she departed, in high good humour.

The Minister proved accommodating in the matter of money. His new complaisance towards the claims of the court would usually have been a matter for surprise. Henri knew the explanation. The King's diplomats had urged the King's cause everywhere; even the alliances with England and Holland were strengthened and secured. The Duke of Cleve had but to die, and Habsburg would certainly provide the pretext for a campaign. "Enough procrastination — we shall march." But the blow must not be expected, and to that end the court of France plunged into a riot of pleasure: gambling and love-making, and, instead of the usual parsimony, festivities and banquets went on from day to day.

The Queen of Navarre became a person of much consideration after her second and formal reception at the Louvre. This was very different from her first and unobtrusive visit, when she left her carriage in actual fear that she might be turned away. The King now came to meet his one-time wife with all due ceremony, as far as the centre of the new courtyard. Queen Marie de Medici awaited the returning exile at the foot of the staircase, attended by a brilliant retinue. All the bystanders were delighted to observe the two ladies and their solemn salutations; and all itched to dispose their persons in obsequious attitudes. Margot of old days and Henri, both alone upon the stage, met each other eye to eye; it was a solemn moment, but she had not thought it would have brought such bitterness. Their features were set in formal smiles of courtesy. And with unblinking eyes that soon were turned away, they said: " Yes, I am thinking of past days. No, I do not wish them back."

Thereafter the round of pleasure continued. There was gambling everywhere, especially in the Arsenal. Madame de Rosny had a great dining-chamber built. Monsieur de Rosny presented the King with a bag of gold pieces for his play, and provided a smaller one for the company. Henri, however, lost all he had, being intent on his anxieties. He was a disagreeable loser, but soon forgot his irritation in the cares that weighed upon his mind. Monsieur de Rosny positively indulged in a jest, which he had never before been known to do. He placed before the Queen's maids of honour two beakers, one containing red wine, and the other filled with wine of lighter colour, which they took for water. But it was in fact the stronger liquor. They thought to dilute the other with it, and soon became quite dizzy and extremely frolicsome. Their antics made a charming picture; all were dressed the same, wearing gowns of silvered tissue.

The Queen and the princesses were making holiday, so it was said; and each occasion called for a banquet. Marie de Medici did not appear until the ball. She evaded dining at the King's table, her reasons for which she was disposed to keep to herself, as being likely to disturb the general good humour. The ball and the ballets promptly followed. Under Henri's guidance, the gentlemen and ladies of the court learned all manner of homely and expressive country dances. He who could provoke a laugh had won his lady's favour. But this was nothing to the splendour of a spectacle, in the Louvre, against the background of the staircase and the great hall, the sumptuous decorations, and the costumes. After feverish preparations, and the intrigues of those eager to take part, every place was occupied. The King himself was drawn into this business and looked about to see whom he could identify. But those he had in mind had already vanished.

High personages figured in the spectacle; what they had to say was mostly of small moment; the music and the succeeding scenes were a mere pretext. The intention was to present to high and low, during the space of a single night, with all the glamour of gold and motley colour, what a lifetime could not compass: a galaxy of unimagined splendours. The spectators were as rapt as the performers, and the fantastic display reached its climax in the marvellous stage machines. These, rising from an abyss into an unearthly light, presented a group of feminine beauties, each arrayed as a star or a rose or a jewel, their lithe, soft limbs entwined in undulating nets. Then the machine revolved and presented quite another semblance: a masque of chastity. Here was disposed a concourse of angels in white and silvery draperies. A sudden and surprising transformation, upon which darkness in a while descended, and the vision was blotted out. Then came the comic interlude: camels, impersonated by acrobats, and others ingeniously riding on their backs. At the rear of the scene was a tower, with a Turk in each window brandishing a sabre and scattering lucky sweetmeats among the audience — while a number of fat women, who were in fact men padded in mimicry of women, belaboured each other and anticked about the stage. All of this, with the aid of the spectators, caused a fiendish uproar.

As an end of this interminable spectacle — which, however, wearied none of the onlookers save one — as a triumphant finale the whole company moved across a bridge through the clamorous assemblage, so that all could look their fill, as they might choose, at resplendent gentlemen, camels, smooth-limbed beauties, or clowns. The older spectators remembered that there had been just such a performance, though less gorgeous, at the Valois court. The last of that House, Madame Marguerite, had originated this one and was therefore much applauded. Henri was indifferent to it, mainly because of the memories that filled his mind.

He did his part with good humour; he even walked on to the bridge, arrayed as the god Mars. He merely hoped that no one would draw conclusions from all this, especially the Spanish Ambassador. Henri had to fill up time until the hour struck; it had been so agreed with Rosny. He was to divert the attention of the courts of Europe, and especially of his own, so that no eye should follow the moving hand upon the clock. But in all the throng and turmoil of festivity he had but one wish: to be alone, to contemplate his cause and gather up his strength, lest he might grow weary and be thus assailable by doubt.

It was a fact that hunting wearied him just then. Hunting had always refreshed him since his boyhood; now, when he dismounted, he went straight to bed. The question was how far his flagging energy was due to physical reasons. Even laughter then subjected him to too great a strain, much as he enjoyed making merry with his friends; and among his friends he ranked all those who had accompanied him through life. D'Epernon — everyone knew how matters stood with him, but he too was an ancient comrade. Now the gouty, deaf old man might easily have been made a mock of, if objects of ridicule were needed. The court, however, preferred the King's more reputable friends. Marshal Roquelaure kept a wife of some kind in his province, whom he never produced, none could tell why. Perhaps owing to some infirmity — his wife was deaf or crazy. The old soldier's domestic circumstances provided inexhaustible matter for jests; and it was natural that they at last became outrageous. But not because the King was present. On the evening that it happened, he was present and had to restrain Roquelaure from drawing his sword. He took him by the arm and they both left the company.

"I have laughed with these people a little too long," said Henri.

"I am an ass that I cannot take a joke," growled the other.

Henri: "But was it so, and against whom was it aimed?"

Roquelaure gave an astonished jerk of the head.

Henri: " Do you understand me? "

Roquelaure, with determination: " D'Epernon has too many friends here."

Henri: " Say, rather, accomplices."

Roquelaure, but without conviction: " Very well — accomplices."

Henri, looking all round the room: " Not in my cabinet. The inner door may be ajar. Roquelaure? "

" I am listening, Sire."

" Do you feel strong enough to take the field once more? "

" I do," said the Marshal, with rather too much emphasis. He thought there must be something behind the King's question. Was he to be dismissed? Henri drew him into an embrasure of the wall.

" We must beware of the Queen; she may be lying awake and she is pregnant. Since our expedition to Savoy — some years have passed. Have you observed that only the first two thirds of man's life can be exactly reckoned? Youth seems endless, age passes like a day."

Roquelaure, on the defensive: " Old Crillon and I often used to reckon up his doings all through your last war. And we wondered whether we should ever know such good days again."

Henri: " I commend you and my brave Crillon. But, for myself — better had I not seen the Queen of Navarre again."

Roquelaure, with conviction: " Women are a trial and a trouble; that is and always has been true. They should stay at home, and war is an excellent opportunity for leaving them there."

Henri, who had laid a hand on his shoulder and was now standing quite close to him, said, staring into vacancy: " Shall we find life easier as the years pass? Surely — surely we have outstayed our welcome. We have so long been in the foreground, and have set the mode — of gaiety, of free thought, of ruling a people for that people's good."

Roquelaure: " And of bravery, and steadfastness, of all that stands for France, and the mode of making love."

Henri: " Not forgetting cuckoldry. But enough. However it be named, they are weary of it, and of us too. They will soon demand the very contrary, though they will be then no nearer happiness. Think you my son Vendôme is well bedded with that Italian ruffian? "

But Marshal Roquelaure could give no comfort to the father, whose son by Gabrielle had become a pervert.

Henri, now full face to the wall: " What do I know? "

Thereby he in fact referred to more than the various forms of love. Had he a right to his Great Plan? A task so new and difficult, and so very real — at a time of his life when, in the face of all who wished him dead, the sense of reality had begun to fade.

Roquelaure saw that this was the King's weak hour; he had more intelligence than was commonly believed. After a moment of uneasiness he made up his mind, flung a rather tremulous arm about his master's shoulder, and said: " Navarre." And then, in his master's ear: " Prince Henri of Navarre."

The King turned, embraced him, and kissed him on both cheeks, and said: " Roquelaure, you were always the handsomest of us all, with that resplendent armour you always used to wear, especially in battle."

" Battle! " cried the Marshal. And as he saw his master put his finger to his lips, he whispered: " We shall not die in battle, but in a place like this."

Henri eyed him long and steadfastly. Simple minds were always right. Simplicity cleared the vision.

First they searched every corner and alcove, in case they had been overheard. Then Henri went into his cabinet.

Days Pass

It was just then that he made acquaintance with *Don Quixote*, the Brussels edition of 1607. Bassompierre read it aloud, but laughed so much that he could not go on. Henri put on his large pair of spectacles, took up the book, and in an undertone read out the ludicrous adventures of the Knight of the Doleful Countenance. He joined in his listener's laughter, not without a feeling of uneasiness. The King of Spain was said to have been delighted with the book. Why did everybody laugh at it? Here was someone who believed himself to be in conflict with his enemies when he was merely the victim of a hoax. He carried in his heart the image of a noble lady, who was in fact of very humble origin and whom he had never even seen. He mistook a flock of sheep for an army, a servant-maid for a goddess, and engaged in all manner of exploits, the absurdity of which was plain except to his beclouded mind. The only person who stood by him was his squire, the very pattern of a henchman. And a trusty henchman's understanding was of no great compass.

It was fortunate, thought Henri, with a burst of laughter, that his Grand Master was not a short, squat man, and his sovereign tall and gaunt. And now both he and Bassompierre were quite helpless from laughter — he had to stop. By way of composing themselves they had recourse to *Amadis of Gaul*, a romance of chivalry, in which real battles took place and the ladies were truly noble. Moreover, every day Henri devoted a strict half-hour to the *Théâtre d'agriculture*, which was the title of the work on husbandry that he most admired. There was no end to learning, especially in a matter that the King had so assiduously studied. Plough-land and grass-land, the State's twin suckling breasts, in Rosny's phrase. His King bore the words within him and busied himself with domestic matters, while his Plan made its way across the world.

To his mind, Europe was now ready to face and acknowledge a reality, so soon as the Habsburg ambition of a universal monarchy had been destroyed. There was indeed a much heavier task before him than tilting against windmills and flocks of sheep — that was much more like the practice of the universal monarchy, always a prey to chimeras. The clear concept of a league of free peoples must some time prevail. What he knew was here of little moment. "This we do know. And the proof is that, taking the longest views, we never lose ground, we pursue each simple task that comes to hand, just as we pursue the Great Plan, which is also simple in design."

Henri opened the Royal Library in Paris, which was to be for the people's use. And in the years that were left he was to found the handicraft museum. Much stood upon the existence of a single man. Hunting wearied him, and he hunted no more. But he was never too weary to inquire into the causes of distress. In the matter of agriculture he saw in person much more than he read. The peasants came in from the countryside and brought him their troubles. And he set himself to relieve them — as though no war were imminent. His feet upon the fields, his heart with his country, and in his mind a bold and simple scheme for the future: one man's life was indeed heavily burdened. And these were the years beyond all reckoning; they passed as a day passes.

The Marquis de la Roche, Royal Governor in Canada, Newfoundland, and Labrador, suffered shipwreck. His crew remained for five years upon a desert island; he himself at last found his way back to France in a small boat, a broken man. Others followed, old men of the Religion or new men of the trading companies. Monsieur de Monts received the full powers of a Viceroy and maintained a trade in furs under Royal privilege, which roused much jealousy. He equipped three strongly armed ships of war to combat smuggling. He sowed seed, built houses, and fortified the colony, consisting of seventy-two persons, of whom half died in the first winter. In the second, only six died of scurvy.

The King supported Monsieur de Monts, when he was generally derided or attacked, this being at the instance of the fur merchants, who could not stomach a system by which their trade would become a Royal privilege, and a business of the State. What would be the end of this? A King begins with certain wares, until he at last absorbs the entire foreign trade of the State. All solid citizens began to describe such notions as fantastic and absurd. Inwardly enraged, they so ridiculed the King's idea that he yielded, and they could fix prices once more. In this matter he stood alone, against the faithful Rosny, who did not understand the drift of such a policy; indeed, he would in the event have supported the merchants against his King and this strange notion of a State engaged in foreign trade.

One scheme succeeded where another failed. On two occasions Henri sent three ships full of workmen and their families to make a beginning with the "Christian-French Republics" across the seas. An old warrior of the Religion founded the city of Quebec. His name was Samuel de Champlain. It was not Henri's habit to allow his hardened adventurers to cross the ocean; his most daring enterprises were carried on without their aid. Natives who had learned the language visited him, and he had speech with them. When Champlain made his last journey, to report the discovery of the lakes of Huron, Michigan, and Ontario, the King would indeed have been overjoyed. But he was no longer there.

He had provided lodging in the Louvre for a number of craftsmen, and was often in their workshops. One of them was an engraver on wood, and one day Henri carried off a print which had just been taken and hung it in his cabinet where he could see it as he sat. He could not, as in old days, resolve his cares by pacing up and down, nor even now, while seated in his chair. The print depicted a skeleton digging in a field. The skeleton as husbandman. Though we be dead, we do not slacken: the work goes on.

JOY IN MISERY

Marie de Medici was ill-humoured in those days, prompt to take offence, and her condition worsened until she grew permanently shrewish. Henri confessed to Rosny that he could no longer talk to her, much less find any solace or comfort in her company. "When I come home, she looks at me with a cold, contemptuous eye. I try to kiss or fondle her or make her laugh; in vain, I have to seek distraction elsewhere."

She had commonly just broken off a colloquy with certain persons, as for instance D'Epernon, having indeed talked of her husband, though scarcely in terms that would have given him pleasure. But what was new, and amazed most people, was her sternness towards any traffic of the sexes. She wanted one of her maids of honour executed out of hand for such an offence. Henri shrugged his shoulders, but was forced to discuss the matter with the infuriated lady. She was in Spanish costume, he booted and spurred as though ready for a journey. This was a civilized court, he reminded the Queen. What she proposed was quite absurd; moreover, there was a matter that had caused general indignation, and was not unknown abroad: namely, that the palace was swarming with female spies, and in the most private apartments no one could rely on being unobserved.

" Least of all yourself," said she. " I am sick of hearing you described as an old lecher."

" You should forbid your friends the word," he retorted, struggling to maintain his patience.

" I will not have the Louvre called a brothel," she replied in icy tones.

" Who made it so? " he asked. " Madame, you brought in foreign customs here. Your changed mind should be a matter for congratulation; but, madame, you overdo your good intentions."

Then Marie burst out at him; she wanted the girl's head. But above all: " The Spanish Ambassador has guessed your purpose."

" He has taken some while to do so," observed Henri. " I have at last convinced him of my peaceful intentions. Don Inigo says publicly that a King who has done such great work in husbandry, and in the arts and industries — "

Marie: " — will lose his war. That is his conclusion, though he does not always utter it."

He had done so for her benefit, as Henri realized.

Marie, undeterred: " You will attack and be defeated: our unhappy Europe is at the mercy of such a paltry hero. But not for long."

She had to pause for breath. Her black lace garments made her anguished face look whiter still. The heavily flounced skirt concealed her condition. But it was not this alone that moved Henri to forbearance; he was grieved because she had turned her back upon the kingdom, his and hers, and so pitifully lost her way. She meant evil, that he saw, and she might utter any outrage, if she did not faint first.

Marie knew she must not yield an inch or she would never prevail. She brandished her heavy hands, stamped, and screamed: " You are worn out; has no one told you so? You cannot last much longer. Your infamies have been enough to exhaust one man. But I do not mean only lechery and play; you have your fingers in all the works of heaven and of earth, and even of hell. You are caught in the lawlessness you have yourself created, and you are impotent. Something must happen to you very soon."

"To you, I think," said Henri to himself. He stood ready to catch the great creature as she swayed and fell. But she did not: the Queen suddenly dropped her voice and went on, though every movement of her face and body betrayed an agonized intentness:

"Give me the regency!"

And as he did not answer:

"Think of your son. You will be dead, and he will lose the throne if you do not give me the regency in good time."

Henri smiled an indulgent smile and suggested a compromise. "In return for your regency, I demand this girl's life."

Thereat Marie did not faint, but had to crouch upon her haunches, the weight of her body being suddenly more than she could bear. Colic, no doubt; her complexion turned green, and she presented a pitiable sight. Henri was at her side in an instant; and he said in a voice that was both gentle and firm:

"Madame, you have been grossly importuned. Think no more of it; and remember that you have your best friend at your side."

She tottered to her feet. To profit by his melting mood, she spoke in the shrill, quavering voice that went so ill with her large person.

Marie, petulantly: "When will you give me the regency?"

Henri, softly: "When I am eighty."

Marie: "You will never live to be sixty."

She departed, the floor-boards creaking beneath her heavy tread. At the door she turned for a final warning. It was not that she was malignant. He knew that this poor soul's rage merely masked her desperation.

Marie: "No one can answer for your life."

That very same day she must have called off her female spies, for there was no more interference with traffic between the sexes in the palace of the Louvre, as was remarked by many, and especially by the girl who was to have been so promptly executed. The times of old Catherine seemed to have returned, to the King's shocked astonishment. But he said nothing, for he saw and scorned her purpose. He was to lay himself open to a flank attack, which was what in fact happened. The preachers seized with renewed zest on that most fruitful theme: the ageing libertine who drained the kingdom dry and ruined it, while he alone kept all Christendom in suspense and fear. Henri gave a warning, in his own fashion, to his confessor Cotton, who was probably in the background of this affair. He pretended to confess that his conscience was troubling him over the death, many years before, of a certain Monsieur de Lionne, a gentleman who had done no worse than warm his feet in the gashed bodies of young country girls. There was no lechery in that; an old gentleman who so warmed himself would be thoroughly approved.

" My son," said Cotton — and it was hard to tell whether he spoke in simplicity or guile — " take care of your reputation. He who has none to lose does not know what he might venture."

" My father," said Henri, " you are accountable for my reputation. Tell the preachers that of late the Crown has been vilified."

Whereat a sudden silence fell. But the effect was that the King grew dejected. Three years earlier he would have laughed. Well, let it be seen how much a man could face when dogged by an evil reputation. He had Europe on his side, which was his main advantage. He had been named King of Europe. In March 1609 died the Duke of Cleve. The peoples looked towards the King of France, the courts all held their breath. His Grand Master urged him to march. Henri insisted on acting in accordance with the law of nations. Habsburg took Cleve and Jülich, and then he set his German allies to besiege Berg and the city of Düsseldorf. There followed long negotiations, and no blow was struck. But his hesitation did at last confuse the issue. It was the conspiracies within his own doors that prevented his taking a decision.

The eve of the campaign arrived, but never the day. In due time the Great Plan was and would be the inspiring force within him; but had there been no Plan, no league of peoples for eternal peace, he must none the less march forth in defence of his throne; for the situation had now so far advanced. It would indeed be said that the King was now an exhausted libertine, good for nothing but fumbling in a woman's skirt, who had lost his common sense, and probably his wits as well. Such is the force of the spoken word; in the end Jesuit Cotton proved to be more knave than fool.

A Prince who ruled in spirit over the world as then existing, and the world that was to come, was transformed by common talk in the last year of his sojourn into a decayed debauchee; such is the force of reputation. It was created then and there, by his court and by his capital. In the hour before the last, this same reputation would cross the frontiers and cost him friends beyond them; but not the attachment of the peoples. They were no doubt guided by some deep essential wisdom in holding fast to their belief in him; and especially his own people. Such reputation, although called into being by those nearest to his person, should not have had the power to cast him down; he thereby lost the hours before the last. He became, what he had never been, ripe for his murderer.

In the days of his first encounter with a young — much too young — damsel, named Charlotte de Montmorency, he had just previously made a memorable expedition into the countryside. The King on foot, gouty d'Epernon in his litter, and some other gentlemen — they walked upon the hills that look down upon the great city. The King was talking in loud tones; even the deaf man in the litter could hear most of what he said. Henri had just left his cabinet, and during all his meditations there he had had before his eyes a certain woodcut, which now made him talk with all the greater assurance. When his capital lay outspread before him, he turned his back on it, bent down, and with the litheness of a boy thrust his head between his straddled legs. So standing, he exclaimed:

" I can see nothing but whorehouses."

" Sire," answered Roquelaure gaily, " I can see the Louvre."

It was kindly spoken, and intended to amuse the King. From the litter came a burst of giggling laughter that went on and on until the bearers had to clap their master on the back.

The King then fell a little behind his companions. A person whom he had not particularly observed was walking by the side of him, though at a due distance — one of those poets or scholars who frequent courts, that anyone so minded may claim them and luxuriate in their glory. The youth's father had been a hosier, or something of the sort; whereas the son was employed by the King to delight posterity by composing fluent verse for a ballet lately performed in the Louvre with much applause, or write a poem on one of the little feathered creatures that have their being in the aviary. One, for instance, who had begun life, like a mortal, full of confidence and joy: then seizes a brief authority, abuses it, pays the penalty of tyranny and is overthrown, retires into isolation, and cries out in terror at every outstretched hand.

But such was not the theme in the young man's mind today. The poet-scholar was secretly thankful for his trained wits, he would neither say nor do anything incautious, although great personages had taken him into their households for his skill in the art of words, as if he had been a sprig of nobility or a promising swordsman. He was careful not to approach the King on his walk, when companions were not wanted. What a plain citizen's son may mutter to himself from a due distance may be sensible but of no immediate moment. The King was quick of hearing, but it was not to be expected that he would lend an ear to this trivial monologue.

"Good fortune is a strain. Nothing can so test us as good fortune. My own, so trifling by contrast, I must keep within due limit, for it is only thus, self-circumscribed, that fortune remains what she appears to be. Suppose I become known through all Europe for my skill in the use of words; suppose even that my reputation reaches the shores of New France. What then? I must either increase my good fortune or resign it. Trifling as it is, and will remain, it will bring me enemies who will not hesitate to strike. But my fortune bids me grow yet more fortunate; to labour and to travel — and the end of it all will lie beyond the grave.

"The son of a small house must recognize the hour for departure from the stage. Let him find refuge in a cloister, an aviary, or a library — and be silent. He is not great enough to remain fortunate in evil fortune. He is no prince, upon whose existence a whole world stands, and falls when he falls. *Infelix felicitas* — upon him there is no such obligation laid. He who is born to greatness has no choice. He must tread the dark way; *infelix felicitas.*"

THE LAST BEFORE THE END

Not that Madame Marguerite de Valois would have improved the reputation of the Louvre, or her own. That was not within her power. By contrast with Marie de Medici, Queen Margot acted without dissimulation: she had no evil counsellors except her passions, and in them there was still much vigour. She was now living in a house lent her by the Archbishop. There she gave excellent dinners to her Academy of choice spirits — and in days to come her Foundation was to be honoured by the State. The rest of the house was occupied by her young favourites.

One morning she had gone to Mass; facing her in her coach sat a handsome youth of twenty. When they arrived home, a page of the Queen of Navarre leapt on to the step and shot the reigning favourite dead; he had been the predecessor. He tried to escape, but Madame Marguerite was so infuriated at her blood-stained dress, and the youth's death, that she had the murderer pursued and caught. He was led up to the corpse, kicked it, and said: "Is he truly dead? Then you can do your will on me, I do not care."

This to a lady whose patience he had so sorely tried. "Strangle him!" she screamed. She took off her garter — her legs were still good, though a little fleshy — and flung it to her lackeys. "Make haste, someone, and strangle him!" But no one obeyed. Queen Margot was beside herself. The youth of eighteen who had slain the youth of twenty with such satisfaction must be tried by the appropriate court. The King signed the death-warrant, and indeed he could do no otherwise. The ill-timed passions of his first wife, with their consequences, might well have been put to his account had he been lenient. The vengeful creature perverted the sentence of the court. Beneath her window, in the court of honour, only three yards away, the scaffold was erected. The youth was brave and firmly set, he had not begged for pardon. And so, for what satisfaction it might bring her, the faded idol of another day sat with sagging cheeks and open bed-gown and gloated as the young head fell.

Her former husband reflected that poor Margot was herself the victim of her own excesses. She could not tell beforehand how far she might go. Cotton could have advised her, not because he himself was wise, but out of the gathered wisdom of his predecessors. Be on your guard! — and with this precept in his heart he was present at a tilting match arranged by Madame Marguerite. A long time had passed since her adventure, and it troubled her no more. Henri was all the more alert to observe what would be her next vagary; he would regard it as in some sense an omen.

Margot, in fact, had nothing less in mind than to provide him with a new mistress. This was Mademoiselle de Montmorency, Marguerite-Charlotte, born in 1594. The child was in her fifteenth year when Queen Margot invited her guests to the tilting match. Several other ladies of the court, as though by a common understanding, had thought of the young beauty with the same end in view. The first reason was that the poet Voiture had compared her with the blush of dawn. Well, something could surely be made of a day that was but breaking — though all were well aware that such a creature, immature and with a face not really formed, was but a promise for the future. Viewed from near at hand, the little beauty was a discovery by Monsieur de Voiture.

The other ladies had selfish reasons for the scheme, in particular Madame de Sourdis, who seldom had any others. She proposed for the girl's hand on her son's behalf, offering to waive a dowry. Dame Sourdis had inherited from her niece Gabrielle a pension of fifty thousand livres. If she succeeded in what she had in mind, it might be turned into a hundred thousand. Montmorency, the father, was in disfavour; how could a Constable, whom the King called gossip, conspire against his master? He bewailed his folly; all would be well once more if he could recover the King's grace. The marriage was agreed upon, without a dowry, although Charlotte was a wealthy heiress.

Here an ancient Princess intervened — she too must have a finger in the pie. Madame Diane de France, a hoary old dame of bastard origin, took charge of the child when her mother fell sick, thus promptly upsetting all Dame Sourdis's calculations. It was just at this moment that Queen Margot invited her guests to the tilting match. She meant to hold it on her own ground.

She, too, was thinking partly of herself. Much money is needed for the building of a new house: painful memories had set her against the Archbishop's palace. Moreover, it irked her to be the only faded idol who found joy in tender blossoms. Here was one for the companion of her youth, who should lead him into temptation. Apart from the calculations that would be made by everyone, this Margot of old days was a sagacious humanist, who saw deep beneath the surface. " My one-time husband," so she told herself, " wants an impulse for his high undertakings " — she knew what they were, but she respected them — " and it will be a pity if he does not outstrip his fame and at last immortalize it." Enough — he needed something. He needed and he lacked what had in fact equipped him for all that he had done: a passion for a woman. It was comic that such things could be, women being what they were, and that he could continue in such passions now that he was a great King.

Not solely comic, Margot told herself. It was both childish and chivalrous to treat women seriously. So long as he still felt thus, nothing was lost, and he was hers; by which she meant she held him fast, by all her memories, the evil ones especially, as he was and had been, before her very eyes. So she resolved to build her house opposite his, so that she could see into his windows from across the river — with the aid of a pair of strong spectacles, of course.

The tilting match was a notable triumph for one who had been left out of account: Monsieur de Bassompierre. He overcame the Queen's cavalier, Concini, which threw Marie de Medici into a furious rage. The King was delighted. Bassompierre, in this long while, had gained in understanding and capacity; he was now seen to be a man of his hands as well. That hesitant, inquisitive personage had developed into an admirer of the King; he understood the burden of the King's greater glories. And Henri told himself he could not have a friend too many as the hero of the day rode round the stands.

He made his horse kneel before Their Majesties, swept off his hat, and awaited the command. What lady should he choose to be his partner in the reward of glory? The choice was difficult in the face of such an array of beauty. The Queen of Navarre decided; she bade Henri look at a very young girl who had enjoyed the privilege of a seat exactly opposite. He had had his eye on the new beauty for the past hour, without seeming to have noticed her. In the first place he was ill disposed to her father. The daughter had been presented to him; when and where he had promptly forgotten. A child like any other, without any presaging blush of dawn. In the meantime he felt several pairs of eyes upon him. Bassompierre merely waited; the others were expectant.

Henri was by this time only too familiar with this old, old manœuvre of offering him a woman. A sidelong glance at his immediate neighbours convinced him that the two Queens were certainly in agreement. Then he pretended to look at the young creature opposite; for the first time he really saw her — and was conscious of a shock, as though he were confronted by a miracle or an attempt upon his life. Indeed, he nearly fainted. He had always been excessive in his emotions.

Bassompierre, a man of quick intelligence, who knew his master, assumed that this was his command. He rode across the arena, and his horse knelt once more. Many a willing hand was outstretched to the Montmorency; all the ladies wanted to see Bassompierre lift the girl on to his saddle. The onlookers leapt from their seats to watch the new star rise. Bassompierre led his horse while the child, proud and radiant, looked down upon the gathered throng. She was enraptured, and the purpose of it all was quite forgotten. When they at last reached the other side, the King had gone.

He felt, no doubt, that he was too well understood. He wanted to be rid of women at last, he had had enough of all the trouble that they brought. Margot he knew too well, and could see her self-interest; her other motive he did not recognize. Those impulses of energy, born of a passion for a woman, had now quite faded from his mind and memory. However, the affair pursued its inexorable course. First, the Constable de Montmorency refused the previous proposal for his daughter Charlotte, and himself offered her hand to none other than Monsieur de Bassompierre. This gentleman had done little to deserve it, for it could well be said of the Blush of Dawn that there was nothing more beautiful beneath heaven.

What had he really to offer for so rich an heiress? Well, he was as brave as his own sword, and now self-trained into a man of no mean wit. A soldier of good fortune, and of no estate whatever, he had stepped into the light, and would soon have vanished if the King had tired of him. It was all one; Montmorency wanted to get back into favour. Said his crony d'Epernon: " How long do you think this King will live? " " Longer than you," retorted the Constable, vexed at having paid so much attention to the gouty old conspirator. Both then dined with Roquelaure and Zamet, lord of eighteen hundred thousand crowns, as he liked to describe himself. " What — back again? " thought Henri when he was told of the betrothal. It was indeed strange how old acquaintances always reappeared, the remnant of what once had been.

Henri took small account of what now passed in the house of Montmorency; he congratulated the chosen bridegroom and invited himself to the wedding. But in the meantime he had an attack of the gout, the common malady of ageing warriors. Both

Montmorency and the King were attacked at the same time; d'Epernon was never free from it. While lying on his bed of pain, Henri had himself read to by Bassompierre and young Gramont by turns. Both followed the fashion in admiring the novel of Monsieur d'Urfé, *L'Astrée*, wherein shepherds and shepherdesses lived in Arcadian innocence, the pleasures and the pains of life being left outside the picture — the sort of tale, in fact, that might appeal to a man in the throes of gout.

But the ladies of the court also visited the King upon his bed of sickness. Not one but was full of praises for the charms of the young Charlotte. Of these the rarest was a natural purity — oh, how far removed from courtly calculations! The mere sight of her inspired belief in the rosy landscapes of the shepherdesses, and their idyllic lambs. From the lips of Queen Margot such commendations seemed particularly out of place. And Henri answered: " The child wants to present herself as a little lamb, or, rather, a little goose. It is possible she may be so as yet. But when I have made her my mistress, she will want to be Queen. They all do."

But great pain can so far reduce a man that he may be imposed on by the merest fantasies. True, the background of the lambs and little geese is an earthly landscape also; none the less, we conceive of it as innocent of pain. Bed is wearisome. The romance of Monsieur d'Urfé, which is so likewise, seemed like an unimagined adventure that might be tried. Love in innocence was plainly a new experiment. What did Feuillemorte think of it?

Bellegarde, the Grand Master of the Horse, had been so long at court that he was now commonly known as *Monsieur le Grand*. In the matters now to hand, the King appealed to his trusty counsellor. When Henri invited him to speak as man to man, the old friend realized his responsibility, and he said: " *Distinguo*." He insisted on a distinction between the shepherdesses, of whom he thought but little, and a young lady of simple and virtuous exterior. " A child," said Henri, " Feuillemorte, a child."

" And why should Bassompierre be the only one to possess that child? " asked Feuillemorte. He had kept his handsome face and figure, but there was now a little drop of moisture always hanging from the end of his nose — a subject of constant derision at the court, like Marshal Roquelaure's wife.

In the silence that followed, Henri realized that Feuillemorte was no longer interested and no longer understood the case presented. The possession of a child — such an idea had never entered Henri's dreams. For his Grand Master of the Horse he had only the one command: " Bring her here! " His very words. But awhile ago they would have been: " Let me see her! " This was the sole thought in Bellegarde's mind; dead days passed once more across his inner vision.

The King lay awake all night. His two readers took it in turn to sleep. The romance called *L'Astrée* showed no signs of ending, and the King's impatience to figure as a shepherd drove him out of bed. In the morning he called the little Montmorency a little goose; just a plain goose, in fact, and he would not see her at all. This did not prevent him from confessing to Bassompierre, her betrothed, as soon as he appeared, that he loved Charlotte; indeed, he was madly in love with her.

Eight o'clock of a winter's morning: the illustrious monarch was leaning on his young and handsome favourite, who knelt upon a cushion by the bed. His tears dripped on the young man or trickled into his own grey beard. " If you marry her and she loves you, Bassompierre, I could not help hating you. You would hate me if she loved me. Let there be no rift between us — do not let us destroy our affection for each other. I am resolved to marry her to my nephew, the Prince of Condé. She shall be one of my family and comfort my old age."

Bassompierre, now stiff with fear, suddenly remembered what had happened at the tilting match. And yet he was quite sure that if someone dared ask his poor beloved master to describe the little beauty once again, it would be clear that he had no notion what she really looked like. All this was the caprice of a sick man. Hence he kept his feelings to himself; and he tried to calm the King with courtly phrases. " Sire, may this new love bring you joy equal to my sorrow at the loss of it, if indeed I could ever feel sorrow where Your Majesty was concerned."

There was a surprise in store for him. All that day the King lay and languished. When Henri had given up hope and had begun to play dice with his noblemen at a table set beside his bed — the three women appeared. Madame de Montmorency had duly recovered from her malady. The King sat outside the bed and talked across it to the mother and the daughter; and in truth he preferred the looks of the mother. But his head was full of the shepherdesses in the *Astrée* romance; here was one who looked like one of them and promised unknown raptures. Did she approve a marriage with Monsieur de Bassompierre? he asked the little one. Said she, with the face of innocence: " Since my father will have it so."

Poor Bassompierre stood aghast. Not long before, she had told him he would be the only love of all her life. When the King repeated the question, Charlotte merely lifted her shoulders. Bassompierre saw himself coldly disowned. His nose began to bleed; he left the room and remained invisible for two days. He neither ate nor drank, nor could he sleep. Henri slept once more. The old King could not see what his aggrieved favourite had discovered, at the price of torment, that here was no Blush of Dawn: the creature had no heart, and any traffic with her must bring degradation. The beauty of a child seemed to the King a guarantee of goodness. He would have given half his war treasure — in imagination, not in fact — for the goodness that he had never found.

Condé was agreeable and accepted the dispositions made on his behalf: his betrothal, a much increased allowance, and an equivocal position. The King was arranging a marriage for him, to get a mistress for himself. The King chose him in particular because he was suspected of perverted tastes: he would probably not touch his wife. Condé remained aloof for two months until the marriage was concluded. During this respite the King could indulge his raptures. It was plain enough that his attraction to the girl was innocent, in accordance with the precepts of Mon-

sieur d'Urfé, and that the verses that he commissioned for his
lady, or himself composed, left much to be desired. His court
poet, Malherbe, could usually do better. " How sweet it is to
think of joys now past! " is doubtless a correct sentiment, and a
neat summary of human experience. It suits a man getting on
in years, who may properly recall the past, but is beyond despair
or ecstasy.

Condé made plain his opinion of these unseemly transactions
as soon as he was married. First he pouched the ten thousand
livres which the King had given to the young wife, as well as
jewels from the Queen worth eight thousand more. He could
thus pay his debts, to his relief, and he had a quarter-year's allowance. The King had summoned the pair to Fontainebleau, and
there they showed themselves as what they were. The false child,
now a Princess of the Royal House, did her best to play off the
one against the other; she fanned her young husband's jealousy,
while she tormented her elderly admirer. One evening, by the
light of torches, she came out on her balcony with hair unbound.
The King was near to fainting, and this time without disguise.
" God! Is he mad? " said the young innocent.

Condé, to Henri: " Sire, you grow younger every day. You
change your clothes several times a day, you cut your beard in
different fashion, you not only wear a collar with perfumes sewn
into it, you wear my wife's colours in public. Sire, I dislike all
this, both on your account and on mine. You make us both
ridiculous."

Such was his tone, and he grew more and more insolent. He
was a short, lean, sharp-featured young man. He had given up
his brooding silence. He pretended to be easy-going and stupid,
but he knew where his interest lay. He had doubtless reckoned
up his prospects when he took his wife and fled. Behind remained a King whose fancied passion would be transformed into
fury. And all the sooner if his enemy Habsburg offered refuge
to the Prince of the Blood and his wife. This to him, a great,
victorious King — a defeat like this would never be forgiven; no
man would suffer it. He would run upon his own destruction,
now so carefully prepared. " Courage! " said the youthful in-

triguer. " The King will be killed, as every fool can see. Then I shall be nearest to the throne, and the Habsburg will set me on it. There will be no resistance in the kingdom. The Protestants regard their Henri's divorce as invalid, and the Dauphin as a bastard."

The President de Thou warned Henri. In vain; Henri insisted on the purity of his intentions. " Your past is evidence against you," observed de Thou. In vain. Henri had written to Rosny that he would soon lose patience with the Prince. Rosny had advised him to throw Condé into jail. He would soon have done so, as Condé reproached him with his " Egyptian tyranny," which was not agreeable to the ears of a popular King. Henri cut off the enterprising youth's allowances. The Bastille remained a threat.

" Courage! " said Condé. He first carried off his wife to his hunting lodge in Picardy — not far from the frontier of the Spanish Netherlands. In Brussels reigned the Archduke and the Infanta. Still within the domain of Egyptian tyranny, so beware! To avert suspicion they made some expeditions, one to Amiens, to visit the Governor, Monsieur de Traigny. The Prince, the Princess, and his mother too — she had in former days poisoned her husband; the Prince was supposed not to be his son, but the truth could never now be known. The child's mother would gladly have let the King have her as his mistress, and so would the Prince's mother. Several other ladies were no less assiduous in the matter. Queen Marie de Medici had said: " There are thirty she-pimps for this pretty piece of business. If I liked I could be the thirty-first." And she would certainly have lent her help, so soon as the matter had been decided. The General of the Jesuits had but to let Marie know that the sacrifice must be made. This was the last one before the end.

THE NEW HELEN

Saint Hubert's day brought lovely weather; the pair could hardly be surprised, while riding out, to meet a hunting party. They were the King's huntsmen, which seemed curious; and they

explained to the young Princess that a head forester in the neighbourhood — She listened no more; she had recognized the King.

The King was wearing livery. He had two hounds on leash.
There was a bandage over his left eye; and no one recognized him
except his little lady. She rode close by him and said: " I'll never
forgive you," and galloped away.

On this occasion Henri could hardly have forgotten how a
little old peasant, with blackened face, and a bundle of faggots
on his bent back, had in days gone by made his way through the
enemy lines to the Château of Cœuvres. Gabrielle d'Estrées had
told him how ugly he was. Then he touched her heart and won
her, and before him lay the years of greatness and possession. He
was trying to conjure up dead days and to reproduce himself as
he had been. Of all this a child knew nothing; she merely said
that she would never forgive him. But supposing she had actually understood!

Still, it was flattering to think that a King should disguise himself on her account; she must be an incomparable little person.
And the little person, or the little goose, resolved to hold her
tongue — though Bassompierre, who now knew her rather too
well, would have given her another name. Meantime the lady
of the house, whom they had ridden out to visit, prompted the
little goose to admire the landscape. In so doing she caught sight
of a window in a side-building: the King, with his hand upon his
heart, blowing kisses. " Good God, what is this! Madame, you
have the King here." Madame de Traigny wanted to take the
agitated child across to him; a good word is never thrown away.
But the little creature reflected that good words, though they
might mean but little, would be more appropriate later on. The
old gentleman must first get rid of his fat old Queen and all his
nine bastards. Then she would see about providing a real
Dauphin.

The Prince and the Princess of Condé mistrusted each other,
being unable to agree on anything. Both wanted to inherit the
sovereignty, but in different fashion. In the end they each departed empty-handed. The Prince's mother, in fear of a painful
scene, left the place, but not before she had tried to open her

son's eyes. Henri returned gloomily to Paris. Now or never;
Condé astutely carried his wife across the frontier by the aid of
some pretext of looking at an estate. From the first town in the
Spanish Netherlands he wrote to the Infanta and demanded protection of his honour, and safety against an Egyptian tyrant. The
lady, her own honour being securely guarded by the sacrifice of a
woman buried alive, received the persecuted victims in her palace
at Brussels. The admirable child was welcomed and entertained
with all the distinction due to her rank. But when she wanted
to go — that was a different matter. Her every attempt was
thwarted.

The King received the shattering news in the evening at the
card-table. Present were his cousin Soissons, the Dukes of Guise
and Epernon, Créqui and Bassompierre, the last next the King.
He said in an undertone, scarce wishing to be heard: " Sire, I
should not have acted like the Prince of Condé, and I would not
be in his shoes." But the King refused to discuss the matter with
any but Sully.

The Grand Master had gone to bed and would not get up until
the dispatch had been actually put before him; then he came.
The King, strangely enough, had gone to see the Queen, who lay
once more in childbed; and the atmosphere of the room suggested that of a death chamber. The King had been listening to
foolish or treacherous advice. The Minister Villeroy commended the method of diplomacy, just because it was the slowest.
President Jeannin knew only one, and that was force. Every sovereign who harboured Condé should be threatened with war.
And Henri actually wanted his wife's opinion. She lay turned
away from him, so that he could not see her face. He was never
to know that this was the night in which Marie finally inured
herself to the thought of his death. And here he was, hoping to
touch her heart.

As Sully entered, Henri took him by the hand. " Our man is
up and gone, and taken everything with him. What do you say
to that? "

Sully drummed a march on the window-pane. From long
familiarity Henri understood. " Our man might have been jailed

long ago," said the march. " But what now? " asked Henri.

Sully's advice was to do nothing. The less that was made of
the matter — as, in the present state of Europe, was their plain
interest — the sooner would the Prince return. If only from lack
of money.

Thus ended the Council of State, if such it could be called.
Sully had seen what, at the moment, was hidden from the King
in his existing mood — that nothing at all could be done; there
could be no war at present. The King had hung back while
Europe awaited him as the deliverer. How could he now march
to fetch a mistress out of Brussels? For matters now stood so
that he could not fail to give just that impression. Henri said to
the Papal Legate later on: " It is false to allege that I was influ-
enced by an infatuation. There are many lovelier women in
France." But it made no difference. The peoples never believed
him; the courts and their Jesuits merely pretended that such
was their view. But it was said and written and reported that it
was a modern Helen who had induced the King of France to unloose the furies of war.

Albrecht of Austria ruled the Spanish Netherlands with his
wife, the Infanta Isabella. He was an Archduke, and a very astute
official. His prompt move was to exploit to the utmost the King's
relatives against him, even by disputing the succession and stirring up revolt within the kingdom, alleging his doubts of the legal
position, as well as the point of honour. Was he, a Habsburg, to
give up another man's wife to an importuning lover because that
lover threatened him with war? Henri made known to him that
he would fetch the Princess at the head of fifty thousand men.
The Archduke awaited the event. It might indeed be that an
old man in love had lost his head, but it was improbable. The
Archduke suspected that Henri was after the Prince rather than
the Princess.

Since the arrival of a certain decree from the King of Spain,
Condé was heir to the throne. The Infanta's court celebrated
the event with eight hours of banqueting and dancing. The
Archduke could not explain precisely why he should refuse to
return a Prince of the Blood to the head of his family — and no

one can remain a member of the Royal House against the monarch's will, for he becomes a rebellious subject. As matters proceeded, the King pronounced a sentence of outlawry on Condé. That once melancholy youth began to bestir himself to some purpose. The Archduke recommended him to travel, and he did so — all through Germany, by the aid of Spanish money. At Trent he was arrested by the Venetians, and they would have delivered him to their allies. But he escaped to Milan, which was as safe as Madrid.

At this news Henri quietly withdrew. He had renounced the last love of his life, but the world was not to know it yet. The little lady in Brussels had as yet no notion of it; an attempt to kidnap her had lately been frustrated by her hosts. Hannibal d'Estrées, Gabrielle's brother, scarcely justified the King's confidence; Henri, who had already set out to meet his darling, called him a nincompoop. But he did not know that Hannibal was innocent of the mishap, and that the scheme had been betrayed before he reached Brussels. By whom, Henri was later on to learn.

The little goose, in her guise of the modern Helen, was luxuriating in her self-importance. Madame de Berny, at the instance of the King, reminded her that the King had been granted one divorce already. " As I understand you," Charlotte had said, " an old gentleman who regards me above everything is better than a young one with schemes of his own, like my husband. Madame, pray write to the King, for my letters here are read, and assure him that my sole devotion is to his greatness and his fame. And I will do my utmost to present him with a Dauphin whom none can question."

This the emissary took leave to doubt, for the dear child was receiving the homage of General Abrosius Spinola, the conqueror of Ostend. Rubens painted her at his commission; the Genoese merchant, whose wealth alone induced the Spaniards to admit him to a military career, had the ear of the Princess in all matters. His real ambition was not the possession of an evanescent beauty, but war against Henri. He was eager for the final glory of confronting the most famous captain of the day. The

Archduke, that astute official, postponed the war by specious concessions, until what he expected should have come to pass. Dead men wage no wars.

Spinola vehemently urged that the attacker's host could be divided and held until the Universal Monarchy could close in upon it from every side. But the Archduke knew Habsburg. Murder was the more certain method. Still, if, as was reported, Henri forgot his ardour in the loved one's absence and called her Dulcinea, there still remained Condé, the intriguer, and Spinola, as headstrong as Henri himself.

He had sent all manner of most heartfelt and appealing letters to Brussels, but the later ones were intended to deceive. He meant to be conceived as crazed with love, and so to escape observation. Meanwhile what he wrote to the little lady was scarcely to be distinguished from his usual amorous tirades. Little Goose certainly noticed no difference. She read out the great King's letters to the Infanta and received her meed of adulation; but she was not allowed to leave the city. Her answers reached Henri by the safest way; it was thought they would act like poison on his fevered mind. " I am called the new Helen," said Little Goose.

" And so you are," said the Infanta. " And why are you betraying your royal lover with Spinola? "

" He is used to such betrayals and would think it odd if I did not," said Little Goose. " May I ask Your Highness a question? Why did you prevent Monsieur d'Estrées from abducting me? I do not mean that he ought to have succeeded. But your soldiers could have rescued me from the King's men on the road. A fight for the new Helen — the story would have gone through all the courts of Europe."

" The Archduke is for proceeding quietly," said the Infanta.

" Don't you understand a woman either? " asked the little lady in a coaxing tone.

" Not a Frenchwoman," answered the Infanta, with a scorn that crushed that exhibition of ingenuousness. But the little creature did not understand the force of what was meant.

A MAN ALONE

At the beginning of the year 1610 the military position of the King was better than it had ever been before. He secured the treaty with Savoy against Spain; the Duke would have defended the south-eastern frontier. Maurice of Nassau and his veterans would have fallen upon the Empire before it could have made a move. The city of Hall in Swabia witnessed a meeting between the Protestant princes and the King's envoys. His Councillor Boississe constituted the League of Princes, including the Free Cities, against the Emperor, their inducement being the restoration of freedom to the Empire and the princes, of which they had been deprived by Habsburg's appropriation of the Imperial dignity. After that successful achievement the Dauphin was to have been proclaimed King of Rome.

Henri's idea was rather different, and he looked further ahead. To whom could he speak his mind? A Great Plan is conceived in solitude, by the lifelong labour of one man, who has come to regard it as reality. But when would the world regard it so? As soon as he tried to negotiate, he was confronted with alien claims that kept him baffled. His allies beset him with their disputes and intrigues, their fears of each other and the Emperor. The German levies, taken together, formed an army equal to his own, at least in numbers. But foreign troops followed the drum in the hope of plunder. A commander with no private interest was beyond their understanding. It was his task to teach them how to fight for an article of faith. Could he yet train champions of freedom and of conscience? It was ten years since his last war. The Great Plan came late to fullness.

He of course confided his doubts to Rosny, who dismissed them all. There were no more rebellious parties left in his kingdom or among the people. The conspiracy of the court against the King — well, it certainly existed, but it was well in hand. The conspirators could get no hold among the masses, despite the efforts of their preachers in the pulpits and at street corners. It would indeed be well to silence Monsieur Concini, and put

Monsieur d'Epernon in jail — and prevent certain persons from holding secret meetings, at least until war was declared.

Certain persons — Henri realized that one person only was intended: the Queen. As matters then stood, it was he, not she, whose comings and goings were under scrutiny. This colloquy was taking place in the Arsenal. This great King was not secure against traitors in his own palace.

This was a circumstance on which Rosny, who always watched the King closely, did not want the King to dwell. A man who based his faith both on calculation and on force commonly divided people into friends and enemies; and his enemies were seven in kind. But he alone could see into his master's heart.

" Sire," he said, " your power is not unbalanced, and will not be overset by its own weight. That is the defect of the Emperor and his realm, and of the Universal Monarchy in general. Do you remember the times when your fortresses were in ruins? Now they are the finest in Europe. The King of Spain is not what he was, nor — in confidence — is your British ally, since the Queen's death. Your Majesty is the richest sovereign of them all. Would you guess how many millions I have put by against the war? "

" Eleven," said Henri.

" More," said the Grand Master.

" Fifteen."

" More."

" Thirty."

" More — forty."

In his delight Henri repeatedly assured Rosny that he intended no less than an extension of his frontiers. The conquered territory should be divided among his allies. He would wage this war for an everlasting peace, for the freedom of nations, the happiness of mankind, and in defence of human reason.

He meant to be arbitrator of Europe, as Rosny realized. So far the reckoning was correct. Later on, perhaps, he might keep a few conquests for himself.

" Sire," said he, " I will answer for your Great Plan to the extent that you drive the House of Habsburg behind the Pyrenees."

This was the peak of the high latitudes whereon a man may move alone. The King left the Arsenal; no mention had been made of the now distant darling. None the less, in his own mind, that child in Brussels was involved in the purpose of his life. That living purpose was embodied as a woman whom he meant to get if he had to take fifty thousand men to help him do it. But he changed his mind abruptly when Condé reached Milan. The attempt to carry off young Charlotte failed; ruses and bribery — all were unavailing; her father's request for her was refused, though the Constable pressed the Archduke to send her back, in his anxiety to recover the King's favour. It was then that Henri first realized how matters stood. A letter from the Princess of Orange had been overlooked and laid aside; Henri, in his cabinet alone, picked it up and recognized, at last, that virtue was against him. An elderly prince, wrote Madame d'Orange, has no right to pursue so young a girl.

Virtue warned him to surrender this, his last belated love. He was forbidden by God to sacrifice the lives of thousands to his passion, and least of all the innocent girl who regarded him with such childlike awe. When his army withdrew she would be taken away from Brussels and sent to her husband, which was what she particularly dreaded, for he beat her. At this point Henri stopped reading. He now knew: the child was appealing to him from simple fear of persecution and maltreatment. Fate was dealing with him hardly; he was faced at the same moment by the limit of his royal power and of his right to love.

He would have suffered yet more sorely had it not occurred to him to contemplate her picture. He had no painting of her, she had never been long enough in his company. He meant to call her image up before his inner vision; and he tried, but tried in vain. Did she refuse herself because she would never be his? Seen but seldom, held for a moment — was she born of his own imagining? But when he ceased trying to envisage her, a face did actually appear — but not the unknown face, so far away, of her who had been named the new Helen. There before him he saw the woman who had been his dear lady, and was so yet. Gabrielle appeared and spoke: " Sire, my beloved lord! " And she went on:

" The Great Plan was made in the days that were mine. I know it, and I alone, for I at last became your flesh and blood. I am in no grave, I live within you. We do not die."

She said no more, and vanished: but he was well aware of what his bodily eye had seen during those moments of reunion: the digging skeleton, the dead man who went on with his task. He had been conscious of a thrill of exaltation so long as Gabrielle was with him — not as a memory, but a very presence, which brought solace and hope. He pondered, sat down, and began to recall Mornay's report of his wife's death. Madame de Mornay had known happiness only at the end of her austere existence. Was that the secret? The Joy that came upon her brought back her youth and beauty. Joy rises from the grave. Be brave, be resolute, and do not yield. Henri said the words aloud. Henceforth stand fast: his end will come upon him early or late, in the form predestined — and find him ready.

At the end of March the Louvre was uninhabitable. Sully had a room prepared in the Arsenal where the King slept under the protection of the Grand Master, his soldiers, and his guns. " Scarcely to the credit of the mightiest Prince in Europe," he said on the last evening in the month, as he sat on his bed in his silk bed-gown, and began to laugh. But the Duke of Sully maintained a strictly official demeanour, as though they were speaking in an assemblage and what they were now discussing was addressed to the whole world.

" Sire," said Sully, " there is more than one reason for your seeking refuge here. First, your reputation; second, the defection of your allies. The conspiracy at your court comes but third; yes, malignant as your enemies may be, they will never act. And what is a conspiracy without action? Consider the tyrant Dionysius of Syracuse; he was saved himself by minding his reputation instead of deliberately destroying it."

" I am not much interested in the tyrants of antiquity," said Henri; " we have to deal with those now living."

Sully raised his brows, and his forefinger. " The King of England — a poor creature at best — has merely been waiting until he could say that he has no mind to go to war on behalf of a modern Helen. His Secretaries of State are talking a great deal about the balance of power in Europe, which is always an ominous sign. Your Majesty has deigned to make matters easier for these waverers. You have, in your wisdom, let it be thought that you could not master your passion for the Princess of Condé, and have made the lady's return a condition of peace in Europe. Were you a different Prince — "

" Such as Dionysius the tyrant," suggested Henri.

Rosny: " I should have said: ' My Lord, a great King of Syracuse loves a little lady so long as he thinks fit. You have long since ceased to love this child. But you stand on your privilege and your royal authority. You will not yield. You are too proud to combat your deplorable reputation."

Henri: " When a man is as old as Dionysius — "

Rosny, with a sudden change of attitude, and in as pleading a tone as he could compass: " Sire, my dear master, do not confuse your last love with your life's end. That is far off yet. Rid at last of these fetters, a great heart throbs for great achievements."

Henri opened his lips, closed them, and quietly took his faithful servant's hand. Thereupon Rosny asked for fourteen days in which the matter might be considered. This interval was needed in order to proclaim that the part of the modern Helen had been played out and was ended. " Meantime, send out the recruiting-sergeant, but let him enrol no men as yet. We say we have no money. The King of Spain really has none. And yet the Archduke in Brussels is beginning to disband his troops. Sire, a modern Helen is a poor excuse for war, you can find a better one at any time in Cleve, Jülich, and Berg. It is ill advised to fight on two fronts."

War on two fronts would not usually have alarmed the Grand Master. The King rose from the bed and calmly announced his will.

" I'll give you fourteen days, Grand Master, and not a day more. I have had two suits of armour made, one for each front.

On those two fronts they will protect me; but will they do so here? Fourteen days is a long respite. Grand Master, you will see — they will kill me."

The King stretched himself full length and promptly went to sleep. Rosny kept watch at the bed's head. Had he always kept such watch!

When the King rose, it was the early morning of April the 1st. He returned to the Louvre with a strong escort. The King's own bodyguards never left him alone, they lined the doors and windows of his cabinet and stood over the very writing-table. At this news all the conspirators were seized with alarm. The King had come back from the Arsenal with a decision taken, and he would deliver them to the fate that they had earned. They were too late. The Marquise de Verneuil sought refuge with Monsieur d'Epernon; she put on a disguise and made her way by side streets to his house, with the report that all was lost. At a sign from the Duke, a man in a violet cassock left the room; but not even the Marquise's evil conscience told her who he was.

D'Epernon said Hey and Ha, as he usually did, but was not much disturbed by the news when he had understood it. The man might indeed be very much on his guard, but not knowing his enemies' design, he would give them an opening in the end. The cabinet would not be always full of soldiers. A Spanish Doctor of Theology had prophesied the death of a famous man this year; which did begin to interest the Marquise. And a German mathematician had himself predicted the exact day to the victim of his calculations, the 14th of May. The Marquise was half reassured. D'Epernon said that events not prophesied might never happen; but they became inevitable as soon as they were believed, especially by the person most concerned.

That same morning the Queen's foster-sister fell into a frenzy. The imagined bullet in her throat had begun to set her choking, and between her paroxysms the creature hunted for the gold she needed for her escape. Her handsome husband learned of hiding-places he had never dreamt of, alert as he had been. As every sack appeared he grew more affectionate; then fell into a sudden fury. People of family like us! A Concini, a Galigai —

to flee from a King who was a King no longer! Intolerable! And the Queen Regent at their feet.

" So long as she hates the King," replied the she-dwarf. " Afterwards? Well, you must sleep with her."

" It is your fault that I could not," he cried, lifting his fist to the agonized little creature.

" Fool! " she spoke in strangling gasps; " you should have done it long ago. Go — and let me not see your face until you have."

Whereat that much desired youth attitudinized round the room until she managed to slip through the door.

In the early afternoon Don Inigo de Cardenas was announced to the King. Henri had dined in his cabinet — with but little satisfaction, as was shown by barely touched dishes. The guards were posted round the walls. As the Ambassador entered, they brought their muskets to the ready. The Ambassador recoiled, not from fear, but from embarrassment. The coming interview was to be irksome enough already. He had postponed it until an order from Madrid allowed of no more procrastination. He could now see, without any need for preliminaries, that the King meant to treat him as man to man. This was no more than Don Inigo had expected; one who is inclined to self-distrust likes such plain dealings. Majesty, unless perverted, is straightforward. Don Inigo had always found much encouragement in an encounter with the King. And now these levelled muskets. Well, he knew how he must open his business.

The King swung his chair round, pointed to another five feet away, and said: " Do you understand a joke? "

To the Captain of his bodyguard he said: " This is not the man. Indeed, he would much regret it. Ground your muskets! "

The musket-butts rattled on the floor. A slow minute passed. And the Ambassador had to begin unbidden.

The Ambassador: " I have been sent by the King of Spain, my master, to inquire of Your Majesty for what purpose you have raised so powerful an army, and whether an attack on him is intended."

The King: " Had I dealt with him as he has dealt with me, he might indeed complain."

The Ambassador: " I humbly entreat Your Majesty to tell me wherein the King my master has offended." This in a challenging tone, the more so as Don Inigo could foresee the grievances of the King of France and was inclined to think them not ill-founded.

The King: " He has tried to rob me of my cities. He bribed Marshal Biron and the Count d'Auvergne, and now refuses to surrender the Prince of Condé."

The Ambassador: " Sire, he could not but receive a Prince who thus appealed to him; nor would you do otherwise if a foreign prince sought refuge at your court."

The King: " I would do my best to reconcile him with his sovereign and send him back to his own country. Moreover, though he had never in the past been willing to lend money to the Emperor, he has now provided four hundred thousand livres for the war against my friends and allies."

The Ambassador: " You have, in the face of the whole world, lent money to the Dutch Netherlands. Once more, I must ask whether you have raised this vast army against the King my master."

The King, rising from his chair: " I arm my person and my country to secure myself from attack; and I take my sword to attack whosoever provokes my anger."

The Ambassador rose and, though trembling, stood squarely to the King. " What shall I report to the King my master? "

The King, turning his back on the Ambassador: " What you please."

He sent to the Duke of Sully enjoining him to decide whether this meant war. Henri had given him fourteen days' respite. But if war it must be, he was willing, and would be alone accountable.

THE PARTY

If this was, in effect, a declaration of war, there was every effort made in Europe not to understand it so. Sully got his fourteen days, and more. Minister Villeroy and his like had their occasion to make a display of virtue. For God's sake, no bloodshed! By which he meant the blood of his own party. It was a minority within the city, though an active one; the King's enemies were in the majority, which was why Villeroy and his fellows were against the shedding of blood. In the contrary case he would have appeared much less lachrymose. With tears in his eyes, he uttered a warning to Monsieur Pecquius, the envoy of the disarmed Archduke. It was promptly given out in Brussels that the King was utterly besotted by his infatuation. The reports lately put about by Sully were intentionally misleading. The dispute over the modern Helen was proceeding as before. None the less, a closer scrutiny suggested an opposite view.

In the first place, the young captive in Brussels was no longer entertained with banquets and balls. Her letters to the King had to be forged; her own effusions, as also his, would have been scarcely convincing. Condé, for his part, felt himself aggrieved by Brussels. The Archduke and the Infanta indeed wished they had never met him. The Archduke, that astute official, would not have believed that his earnest appeal to honour and justice could end in such a way. His envoys dashed to and fro, to Madrid for money, and to Rome for mediation. Pope Paul V did in fact send a Legate Extraordinary; but the King of France, instead of waiting for his pronouncement, at once informed him of the route he meant to take: through Liége to Jülich. For the invasion of the Spanish Netherlands an enormous force had been collected. But even that was trifling compared with the real strength of the King and his allies.

The House of Austria had at its head two quite mediocre rulers, the Emperor Rudolf and the King of Spain, Philip V. They were not served by any minister of Sully's rank, and their armies had no faith in their one commander. There were matters at issue between their countries, and the people were inclined towards revolt. The Emperor himself was opposed by his own brother Matthias. Europe was, in fact, in arms against the World Power, with its impotent but intolerable pretensions. At the beginning of May 1610, there stood ready for action: on behalf of Italy, sixty thousand men, and six-and-forty cannon, French, Papal, Savoyard, and Venetian troops, all under the command of the Frenchman Lesdiguières. On the Spanish frontier two armies of twenty-five thousand men each, at either end of the Pyrenees. The Duke de la Force was appointed Marshal on the 13th of May by the King, the last day of the stipulated fourteen.

The German line of the House of Austria would see, advancing through Jülich and the Spanish Netherlands, twenty-five thousand Frenchmen with twelve thousand Swiss and landsknechts, under the orders of the King. England, which had in fact joined in, provided, together with Sweden and Denmark, twenty-eight thousand men; the Protestant princes in Germany sent thirty-five thousand; the United Provinces, as well as the Protestants of Hungary, Bohemia, and Austria, fourteen thousand each. In all, Europe raised two hundred and thirty-eight thousand men, with two hundred cannon, two fifths of the total being provided by France. The war treasury of the allies amounted to more than a hundred and fifty million livres.

These efforts, the like of which had scarcely been seen before, were made and borne in order to overthrow the tyranny of the World Power — and to avert the terrors that it threatened: the dissolution of Europe and its precious heritage; the spread of barbarism from the centre of the continent; the long-prevailing violation of conscience and of justice among nations; and the religious war that was in fact to last for thirty years. These preparations had begun immediately after Vervins, when the King conquered Spain. That was twelve years ago. His mind had to toil and to mature, until in due time the Great Plan could be conceived. It was only gradually that his diplomacy, his cause, and his own glory won the support of Europe as a whole. At last the power of the princes and republics, never before made manifest, their armies and their money, had been gathered into the hand of one man — after twelve years had passed.

It was scarcely a fair contention that the King of France had assembled his forces to fetch a mistress out of Brussels. But just that explanation was current. It sufficed that one party gave it credit — that party which, based solely upon the hatred of the people and mankind, will always and everywhere exist. One age passes over into the next, and is, in passing, changed; and the aspect of events may be ceaselessly transformed. Opinions bear other designations. But it is always true that on one side stand mankind and the people, and on the other their remorseless enemy. Have they a friend, Henri, once King of France? — he too is dimly felt to be immortal. He was killed, but only for the time. Enough that he was killed.

It should never have happened. Fate and history should have forbidden the deed. But in very truth he was not understood, except by the people in their inarticulate hearts. President Jeannin, the same who advocated the use of force when the King was sighing for a lady he had lost, watched the dawn of the Great Plan and said he was not convinced.

Two Suits of Armour

Henri demanded from Duke Albrecht a passage through the Spanish Netherlands: the 8th of May 1610. As the die was thereby cast, he was all the more anxious to be reconciled with the Queen. She would, while he was in the field, be Regent of the kingdom. And surely, in the end, she must stand for the interests of the kingdom. She was his ally by the force of circumstances, and if not her feelings, her advantage must win her to his side. In the meantime he relied on her mother heart. His own love for his children was utter and absolute, it was the paternal feeling of a simple nature. And simple he was in other matters too.

He now entered just as Marie was boxing the Dauphin's ears for having pushed her dog off a cushion on which he wanted to sit himself. Her fury far exceeded the provocation. " You will be the last," she said to Louis, who was gazing at her in bewilderment. At the sight of his father, he fled into his arms. " Your mother means," said Henri, " that you would never leave her though she were utterly forsaken."

The boy ran past his father and out of the door. The parents stood in silence, breathing heavily and at a loss how to begin. At that same hour the Duke of Epernon made his way to a part of his palace which he was not at all accustomed to frequent: a squalid attic, right under the roof. The silver-polisher, who here had his sleeping-quarters, was today dismissed, together with any lackeys who were lodged near by. The Duke put his head into the room, and a figure rose up from the floor, for there was nothing on which to sit. The former law-clerk, now a street-corner orator, merely shook his head. "Not here yet?" whispered d'Epernon. "Can he have given us the slip again, with his knife and his queasy conscience?"

Words which could not, of course, be allowed to reach the Louvre. Meantime the Queen stood expectant, her lips parted and her eyes astray. Henri, who had come to speak to her about the regency, recoiled, in sudden and inexplicable horror. He told her curtly that he had something of importance to discuss.

"You?" said Marie de Medici. Her wandering gaze slowly came back. Doubt first beaconed in her eyes: "Something of importance — you?" — such was their message; then their expression gradually changed to one of malice and infinite contempt.

"Madame, remember who you are," said the King with emphasis; he stopped short of a tone that would have sounded like a command. The Dauphin too had eyed her for a long while in bewilderment.

"I am remembering the Spanish marriages," returned Marie. "My highest ambition — that is what is in my mind."

Henri reminded her that she was already more than Spanish marriages could ever make of her. He spared her the reproach that, though Queen of France, she still conceived herself as a petty Italian Princess. He had, however, here encountered the real hindrance that had gone far to wreck his marriage — just as he knew this interview could come to no good issue.

Realizing, therefore, that the conversation must be futile unless, perhaps, it were solely left to chance, he said:

"What a magnificent gown, madame, and how radiant you look!"

At this she smiled an ecstatic smile. He had touched her, he did not know how deeply, for these were her thoughts: " And as soon as you are gone, my lover will come; my delicious, handsome lover. His is the child I carry. Oh, bliss and glory! You gaunt old cuckold, look at yourself in a mirror. If any ill befalls you, the fault is not mine, for I was elsewhere occupied. This is what I have been longing for; this is joy and ecstasy, and no more than I deserve."

Such were the thoughts of the ageing Queen, and a crass look came into her face. " You eye me very narrowly," said Henri; " no doubt you find me thinner. That is the result of my many cares."

" Oh, have you cares? " asked Marie, haughty and full-breasted.

Henri: " What would it cost you to relieve them? "

Marie, slyly: " I'll guess the riddle. You want me to write to Brussels."

Henri: " And to Madrid."

Marie, in astonishment: " Do you want Condé back as well? So the modern Helen is no use by herself. Pray, how is that adored young lady? Sire, I would not have believed it of you. You actually sat upon my bed to bewail the child's escape."

Henri: " I was your friend, and had no other friend."

Marie, loftily: " That I'll soon prove. Your scheme to abduct the little beauty from Brussels you confided to one person only."

Henri: " To you."

Marie: " To your friend. Yes, you were brazen enough for that. And whom did you send? Monsieur d'Estrées. Who played into your hands? Madame de Berny. Aha, your friend knew all about it."

Henri: " It was you who betrayed me? "

Marie, in great triumph: " My mounted messenger was there before Hannibal. Ha! Your baggage's brother was nicely tricked."

Henri, with contempt: " Madame, you have hitherto carefully hid your feelings. I would now hear all you have to say."

Marie, thrusting a forefinger into her temple: " The time will soon come for an old fool to be deposed and put in a safe place."

Henri, shouting: "You will not leave this room. You are under arrest."

Marie, with her forefinger still against her temple, in a tone that was almost gentle and caressing: "See how much power is still left to you. Unless I am mistaken, you will give the regency to your only friend — and in five days' time; on the sixth day the world will hear some news."

The last words were spoken in a truly gentle and caressing tone, and very softly. A listener might doubt if they had really reached his ears.

Henri controlled himself; and without a pause he said in a calm cold voice: "Madame, we part for ever. We know as much, but it is not to be made known to this court or to any foreign court. On the contrary, I suggest that we should come to some outward understanding, and each do his part to restore our damaged dignity. I not merely renounce the Princess of Condé, who is in any event no longer in my mind, I engage not to take another wife — on condition that you dismiss Monsieur Concini."

Marie suddenly began to gurgle and choke and groped helplessly for her handkerchief, which Henri handed her. But she could not control herself, and with a burst of convulsive laughter she fled sidelong from the room.

Outside stood the Dauphin, behind the balustrade of the great staircase. He spat into the depths below, and each time hurriedly took cover. Came a smacking sound, and the Dauphin said: "Hit him — right on the bald patch."

"Whom have you hit?" asked his father.

"No matter. They're all villains," said that sallow lad, quite without any satisfaction at his coup.

"Where are you taking me?" asked the King.

"Where we shall be alone," was the answer. "Sir, please let me see your two new suits of armour."

So they wandered on and on, hand in hand along tortuous corridors, up and down deserted stairways, and into regions long since left desolate. At that same hour a man was making his way through the palace of the Duke of Epernon. He was tall

and broad and extremely ugly. He thrust out a great red head
mistrustfully and peered round every corner before he turned it;
he counted the doors and at last stopped outside one, but lingered a long while before he entered.

The King produced a huge key, unlocked the secret chamber,
went in with the Dauphin, and immediately locked the door
behind him. The suits of armour were set up like figures in war
panoply, with legs of iron and visored helmets. " This," said the
King, " is that they may be taken for old armour, should anyone
find his way here and amuse himself by making them unusable."

Said Louis: " Sir, you should be wearing them day and night.
Especially in the place whence you have just come."

And Henri answered gravely: " I see, alas, that you have ceased
to be a child."

Louis's lips trembled so violently that he could scarcely speak.
" She loves her dog more than she loves me." He laid his hand
upon his heart. " I have not been listening at the door. I already
know too much. You will leave me, that I know. Sir, your son
is a weakling. What I tell you is the fear of a weak heart, but a
heart that loves you."

" I live for you alone," said Henri.

They wandered on and on, hand in hand, until they came
into the open air, and then they walked awhile in the garden
between the high hedges. Here they did not speak.

The Last One

When the murderer Ravaillac at length ventured to scratch
at the door in a manner prearranged, and was admitted into the
silver-polisher's attic, where he found two persons — at that same
hour the Spanish Ambassador, Don Inigo de Cardenas, was received by Queen Marie de Medici.

He wore an absent look, which made Marie dread the occasion more than she had ever done in her worst nightmares. She
was vexed, too, by his aloof demeanour. She had flattered herself that she would be expressly asked for her consent and her
commands. These were, in reality, no longer needed, but was

she not a chief personage in these events? Don Inigo's thoughts were, of course, elsewhere engaged; it was merely for form's sake that he paid her this uncomfortable visit. And such was his tone that he might have been speaking of events ten thousand miles away:

" The King has enemies. I betray no secret when I say that his life seems to be threatened." Here he paused, and added abstractedly: " It is degrading for well-disposed people to look on while a great ruler, who could never quite achieve his aims — "

The Ambassador remembered who he was.

" — is dragged down by the wolves," he concluded. Thenceforward he said no more than was his duty. He was back once more in that apartment with its great carved chairs, its piles of cushions and dark paintings; and beside him was a Chinese writing-table, a sumptuous gift from the General of the Jesuits.

" Your Majesty, I am assured, shares my anxiety; I may not say my abhorrence. It is the extent of the King's enterprises that has brought the fate we dread upon him. Such an unprovoked and overwhelming attack upon Christendom is not permissible from however pure a motive."

" The King's motives are not pure," said Marie de Medici — the first words she uttered.

Don Inigo threw back his head as the sole indication of his scorn, and so continued, speaking by virtue of his office. He repeated that for just these reasons he could not feel any abhorrence of the event now imminent. The sin of pride was visited by eternal death. " There is also the lesser penalty of bodily death, but that is trifling by comparison."

" Trifling, indeed," repeated Marie, but she blanched.

" The anxiety I share with Your Majesty," said Don Inigo with emphasis, " is another matter. It concerns no individual, however prominent; but the political consequences of the event foreseen. The policy of the courts of Europe would suffer certain disadvantages if there were no safeguard against military defeat but murder."

The Queen drew herself up and said in an imperious tone:

" You have uttered a word that I may not hear. I have not

heard it. Otherwise it would be my duty to stop this business and have you arrested by the King's bodyguard."

Don Inigo saw that the Queen's intention was to save her soul in any event. *Salvavi animam meam* — well, that accorded with what he had to do. By way of giving her time to make her chosen move he fell to examining the Chinese writing-table. The elaborate piece contained countless drawers, not to mention many secret hiding-places; and it glittered with pearl and mother-of-pearl inlay. Two idols to the right and left of it nodded their fat heads at every uttered word. In the centre stood a little tower, with bells on each of its seven roofs. He wished he could stand listening to their silvery peals and neither say nor hear another word.

But he stood up once more and said: " What can we do to prevent this? "

The writing-table was now between himself and the Queen. From ten or twelve paces she confronted him, a dark figure against a tall purple hanging. She had thrust her hands into its folds; only her face stood out white against this sinister background. This woman was hard and cowardly, though she need not, for his purposes, have been both. However, she would plainly be an excellent accomplice in this affair. He must pretend he was trying to prevent the King's murder. She would help him in this dissembling, and when the deed was done, his report would go out to all the courts in Europe.

" It is terrible; nor is it by any wish of mine," said the Queen. Her voice broke; it might have been from genuine fear. " And now we are nicely bogged," said she — a remark which much offended the Ambassador's ears. Such a notable occasion, and she so utterly beneath it!

" How can we get out? " he asked, as he might have addressed a groom when his carriage had stuck fast.

The Queen exclaimed wildly: " My regency! Surely you fools see that I must be crowned today or tomorrow. The whole World Power is useless if that is not understood. I should at once have the Duke of Sully executed. Then there would be no need of your murder."

" In the first place," the Ambassador replied, with a sick feeling in his throat, " it is not my murder. Or Your Majesty would certainly not see me here."

The place at which he pointed was the Chinese writing-table, and only the patient nodding of the idols helped him to swallow the nausea in his throat.

The Ambassador: " Your coronation will be magnificent, a State ceremony such as has never before been seen — it has been discussed in council for two hours. But the King is on the march with two thirds, if not three quarters, of the European armies. Would you depose that King and execute his Minister? Pray tell that tale to someone else."

The Queen shrieked as though she had been spattered with hot oil: " Then nothing will serve. And we are ruined."

" We are indeed beaten in advance," agreed the Ambassador, but there was a chill upon his chest, and his throat was still constricted. " But Your Majesty forgets — " He broke off; he was about to bear false witness, and this dissembling afflicted him much more deeply than the Queen, who had no self-respect.

The Ambassador: " You forget the good Fathers of the Society of Jesus."

The Queen burst into a shattering laugh. At this she felt the first indications of her condition, for which, on this occasion, she had to thank her adored and handsome lover, which made it all the more essential that the King should disappear — what need of all this talk? The lying murderer behind the writing-table must go. For what they might do or leave undone she cared nothing. She was awaiting her adored and handsome lover.

The Ambassador, unperturbed: " Cotton, the confessor, has an ingenuous heart. He can so prevail upon the King that he will let his hour go by."

The Queen: " You clod! Try to invent some other device. He has prevailed upon him to such purpose that the old fool no longer knows whether he is to believe in this affair or not. He must be made to believe in it."

Marie de Medici had now done her best, and so had the Ambassador. They could get no further. The Queen had suddenly to relieve herself, such was the violence of her colic. And the stench that suddenly filled the room was such that the Ambassador could no longer control his nausea. Leaning on his hands, he vomited over the Jesuit General's Chinese writing-table. The two idols nodded approval. And each time he retched and spat, all the little bells in the little tower rang a silvery peal.

For what purpose did these two great personages tear themselves to pieces? In another place, the silver-polisher's attic, there was a straw pallet which did not smell of roses either; but on it crouched, side by side, the Duke of Epernon, Governor, Commander of the Infantry; and the discharged law-clerk, who had caught the pox. The gouty nobleman said to his diseased companion: " You may well give your malady to others by biting them. The fellow we are waiting for knows neither shame nor decency. Bite him if he grows insolent."

The law-clerk bellowed laboriously into the deaf man's ear, but there were certain words that did not penetrate. " He'll do anything for money. He is, as I am, of the law, no more honest than myself, does the dirty work of both sides, and pilfers where he can, to grease the hands of such as I. He has been in jail twice, for a murder committed by another, and then for debt, which he had most certainly contracted."

The Duke observed that this rascally personage claimed to be an emissary from Heaven. A man who could see visions in the fire, such as a vine transformed into an archangel's trumpet, and blow into it until a shower of sacred wafers poured out of its mouth — fools of this kind no doubt had their uses, but they were likely to give trouble first. " A man like this is in league with the Devil, though he may not know it. Take a bite at him, say I."

" My lord," said the pox-ridden clerk, " it is clear that you are not well acquainted with the law. The dirty work there is more than even the Devil can stand; he'll have no traffic with lawyers. Now, our man has also been a student of theology. When I was looking for someone to suit your purpose, I found him in the house of Dame Escoman, one of Venus' priestesses now much in decline. She hires out rooms. There sat our man

poring over Jesuit tractates. I began by buying him everything
the Fathers had written on tyrannicide, which he much wanted
to possess, but had no money. May I remind you, my lord,
that you are still in my debt for my disbursements, costs and
charges?"

"Ha? Hey?" said d'Epernon. But, as one of them was deaf
and the other's corroded throat was growing hoarse, they reached
no understanding on this point.

"A true nobleman," snarled the clerk, "would take care not
to degrade himself by public traffic with so vile a rascal."

"What's that, you dog?" D'Epernon heard this without the
slightest effort. "Say another word and I'll have you strangled
and broken on the wheel."

"There is written evidence," said the other ominously.
"Dame Escoman gave me letters to be carried to high personages; she knew there was something afoot and wanted to save
the King. The whole business has almost driven the old harlot
crazy."

The Duke resolved to bear the name of Escoman in mind.
Then he said to his companion with all the dignity that a gentleman could muster while crouching on the silver-polisher's
straw pallet: "You yourself, and this chosen agent of yours, must
strictly do what you have undertaken. Obey orders or I'll dis-
own you," said he in his most martial voice. He gathered himself up, for, of the pair, it was he who was in most pain. And so
the murderer Ravaillac, when admitted by the clerk, found the
Duke of Epernon on his feet.

The clerk searched the corridor lest they might be overheard.
In the meantime the Duke surveyed the murderer, who was now
to serve their needs. He was tall and broad, with bones like a
beast and mighty hands. His face, a truly evil face, would have
been in his favour except that it made him conspicuous. His hair
and beard were red, a sort of blackish red not commonly seen.
An evil face is not, indeed, the sign manual of murder. It may
be that of a cheat, not of one athirst for blood; it may be so
deeply seamed that crime cannot mark it, either before or after

the deed is done. It does but tell the tale of the man's own vicious, squalid life. Here was a sordid jackal of the courts, a self-tormentor, a visionary at the mercy of his conscience, a weakling in a mask that was not his — no fit agent for what had come to be conceived as an act of justice.

The clerk returned, but stood by the half-open door, still on guard. He said some words of welcome to the murderer, while the Duke of Epernon wondered whether he would not do well to hand over both these ruffians to the city watch. The King had appointed three Protestant generals to command his armies. D'Epernon was to remain in Paris, having indeed a foreboding that the King would remove him from his post. With all proper consideration, on the sole pretext of his gout, since a commander of infantry must needs be able-bodied. The King would in fact have him put to death after the first victory; he could do no otherwise, despite his aversion to the executioner. He would spare his master the ordeal and deliver up the murderer in return for the command of an army. The whole of Paris was discussing the murderer and waiting to see whether he would appear in violet or green.

"Master Ravaillac," said the Duke, " you come from Angoulême. You conceive yourself, so I hear, as a chosen instrument. That is well."

Ravaillac, in a thick and menacing voice: " My lord, your memory has failed you. I have long been known to you, before ever I became a King's murderer and so recognized in the streets of Paris. You commended me to the Fathers of the Society of Jesus; I spoke my mind to them to ease my suffering conscience. Not one would understand me. And now, my lord, you are pretending to be deaf."

D'Epernon: " Ha? Hey? Do I hear aright? Famous are you? And you claim a conscience? On your knees, dog! "

Ravaillac, kneeling: " I am an outcast. How does it avail that the angel let me blow into his trumpet? "

D'Epernon: " Indeed — and why? "

Ravaillac: " That must be my own affair. No one speaks the

word, neither the archangel nor you, my lord, nor the Canon in Angoulême, who gave me a splinter of the Holy Cross set in a woollen heart."

D'Epernon: "Hear him! I fear you are a paltry fellow. So you would vaunt yourself as the King's murderer, known to all the city. Enough, you are not the man for our business and may go home."

Ravaillac, drawing a knife: "Then I'll stab myself before your eyes."

The clerk: "With a knife so blunted!"

Ravaillac, drawing himself up: "Cattle! What do you know of the conflict with the unseen? This is a stolen knife. A voice spoke to me in a tavern and said: 'You must use a stolen knife.' On the road, as I walked behind a wagon, I heard another voice say: 'Break it against that wagon.' And a third voice, in Paris at the Cloister of the Innocents —"

"Innocents," repeated the clerk.

Ravaillac: "At the bidding of the third voice, I shouted a warning to the King as he passed by. It would be ill done to kill him unwarned. But the King's bodyguard pushed me back."

The clerk: "Were you dressed in violet or green? Next time pray wear some other garments, that the King will not recognize you."

So saying, the clerk also drew a knife; but his knife had a point. He stood behind Ravaillac, and at a sign from d'Epernon he would have stabbed this man of so perilous a conscience right through the back into the heart, this being apparently the only means of preventing discovery of the murder before it was committed.

The Duke silently forbade it, and the clerk put away his knife — not without regret. For this corpse he could have demanded his price. But when the King was dead, who counted then? And the Duke had made the same reflection, to the clerk's disfavour. "Sure is sure," thought d'Epernon. "The King must go." He himself had felt a twinge of conscience, which was far too prone to pleading excellent excuses.

"Are you determined?" he asked the murderer. "Answer

clearly. You, Master Clerk, watch the door. This is no matter of theology, but of politics. What did you mean to say to the King at the Cloister of the Innocents?"

"I had to warn him," said Ravaillac once again. "He must not die unprepared."

D'Epernon: "It is goodwill thrown away. Everyone has warned him, but in vain. He wills his own end."

Ravaillac: "I meant also to ask him whether he intended war upon the Pope."

D'Epernon: "Ask his soldiers, they are longing for that war."

Ravaillac: "Last of all, whether the Huguenots intend to massacre all good Catholics."

D'Epernon: "Sharpen your knife again."

Ravaillac, in a sudden impulse: "This instant, my lord. A crucifix I lately saw commanded me to strike."

D'Epernon: "Hey! Not so fast! The regency must first be settled, and the Queen crowned. We must think of the kingdom. The day following the coronation shall be yours."

Ravaillac: "How could I strike too soon! The kingdom is all my thought and my desire. Hail to our good Queen Regent, death to the heretic who has brought disaster on us!"

The dialogue now dropped into the ranting tone of strolling players talking of great matters.

"You have the woollen heart, my brave Ravaillac, no harm can come to you. Your name shall be immortal and stand in the record of history."

The poor wretch was at last receiving the consideration from which he had always been debarred by his hideous countenance — his dream was fulfilled. Erect and rigid, Ravaillac saluted the Duke with lifted hand. D'Epernon tried to respond likewise, but gout prevented him.

The clerk aped the gesture with such energy that an ulcer on his face burst, and the pus ran into his eye. Cursing as he went, he followed the murderer from the room. He wanted to survive for a while, despite his pox. The sturdy fellow at his side would very soon be in fragments on the wheel.

The Duke of Epernon waited until they were out of the

house. He was bitterly chagrined at the trivial role that must be his; he could not present himself before the world with any great effect; the death of so extraordinary a King could not be staged very ceremoniously. Fame being what it was, a certain Ravaillac would certainly get into the history books. Who would ever remember the earlier would-be murderers of the King, eighteen or more of them? Some had been gallant soldiers, or fanatics not burdened by a queasy conscience. Who remembers those mystic lads, so nearly chaste, who thought to give up their place in hell to a greater sinner if they killed him? All forgotten, all vanished. The only survivor was this pitiful braggart, just because he was the last. The evil living of a century past was embodied in this petty villain's trickeries and his outworn superstition. Immortal in his degradation — he would be the last.

The Approach

Escoman, a lady of gallantry, had been toiling for a whole year to save King Henri's life. He had loved much; his last and unknown friend was a woman who had loved much.

Her hair, with a little aid, could still look fair, and her charms were well preserved. Boys admired her, and resorted to usurers on her account. But such callow lovers are not lucrative, and she equipped her house for the meetings of other women with their companions of an hour. Business began about dawn, when the dancing and gaming rooms closed and for various reasons many couples were homeless. Escoman usually came home alone; but if she were lucky enough to find a couple who would pay for her own bedroom, she would sit with all due dignity in her kitchen. She made no complaints. And she considered life in general rightly ordered.

The favour of chance could go still further. There came a knock, just as dawn was breaking, at the outer door. Escoman called from a window that the visitor must wait. Hurriedly she awoke her lodger, the occupant of the second bedroom, and bade him remove himself to the kitchen. The man, who had lodged with her the year before, made no protest. He was an obliging and pleasant fellow, and read for more hours than he slept. He brought his books with him. While the visitors used his bed, the lodger was applying his mind to serious matters. Nor did the company of a female, with her charms uncovered, divert him from his task. Escoman, as a woman of experience, could distinguish feigned from a real indifference; his she did not doubt. The man was tall and powerful, but such men tended to be chaster than shorter, weaker ones. His want of interest in her affairs stirred her curiosity.

In his absence, she looked over the objects of all this assiduous study. They were mainly writings of a certain Mariana, *Societatis Jesu*. She knew no Latin; and when they were together in the kitchen at night, she asked some cautious questions. He answered readily and seemed to be labouring under a long suppressed desire to open his mind. All his reading was on the subject of tyrannicide. Escoman, for her part, recognized no such right and did not believe that a pious Father could have sanctioned it. But she knew the tyrant's name; it was often in the mouths of preachers. Egyptian tyrant, they called him rather drolly, although they meant the King of France. And he showed his liberality by ignoring their tirades. Escoman was all for freedom, indeed, her calling claimed it, with more justification, she thought, than did these foul-mouthed preachers or street-corner orators. The woman came of a family of farmers. The King had replaced one of her brothers' cows; a cousin, who had once been her lover, he had helped with ready money.

She looked on the King as a good man. But her lodger was not on that account a bad one. His trouble was that he immersed himself in all the controversies of the time, as though they were his business and not far beyond his mediocre understanding. The priestess of love had at once seen through him and often tried to interest him in women, but in vain. She was sure if his full-blooded body were properly engaged, his mind would soon shed this ridiculous obsession. One day he said he must leave her house, and told her why. He intended to go home, to confess his supernatural mission to the Fathers. They must approve his purpose; he needed support. But his landlady was not the only person in whom he had confided. In all the streets he was pointed out by the passers-by as the man who would kill the King. Why he? said they, with a shrug of the shoulders. But they did not say so openly, lest they might become involved.

Escoman was proud to frequent a house where the King often appeared: that of the wealthy Zamet. He was glad to have these gallant ladies as an ornament and allurement for his gaming rooms, as long as the company was of the ordinary sort. At the arrival of more exalted personages, not to mention Majesty, people like Escoman vanished. It had never entered her head to present herself before the King. Unwearied and without regard for danger, she had gone up and down in search of any who might help her save the King's life. But she had never put herself in his way, nor were any of her countless letters addressed to him. Such was her reverence for the King.

She made known what she had discovered to the ex-shoemaker who had risen from her own station in life. Zamet hurried her into that discreet apartment where Gabrielle d'Estrées had once rested for a little while before the terrors of her end began. The shoemaker and the gallant lady mingled their sighs over the King. "His hour will soon be on him," whispered the man of wealth. But the poor woman in her bead necklaces was full of passionate hope.

"He will hear of the plot and take his measures. But how is it to be broken to the King? You must speak to him, Zamet."

"Escoman, you think me more powerful than I am. A word too much and I shall have them on my heels."

"Zamet, what do you fear? He is the King, you can claim his protection when you tell him that another murderer is near."

"Escoman, in the first place the King is not the man he was. The burden of his cares has soured him. Moreover, he always wants to be loved. He is now beset by hatred, and a life so burdened — I have known the King a long while — is not one to which he would cling."

"Zamet, I love him; you likewise. Everyone that knows his murderer has come must, from very love of him, tell him so."

" Escoman, how many have really told him the truth when you have made it known to them? Are there certain persons too that merely need enlightenment? "

" Zamet, how can you say so! Would you have it understood that the Queen knows of the plot and has a part in it? "

" Escoman, silence, for the love of Christ, or for our own safety's sake I shall have to lock you up in my deepest cellar."

" Zamet — among your sacks of gold. But are they there still? Several of your treasures seem to have vanished from your house. Are you already thinking of flight? "

" Escoman, see only what is permitted, and hear nothing that is forbidden. The Queen is raging for revenge, because Concini has been flogged by the King's magistrates, and has spent a day in jail for his insolence. The King is delighted. That sealed his fate."

" Zamet, one of the Queen's women has told her that I have knowledge of a very grave matter that concerns the King's safety and must see her. She has of course consented, and will receive me tomorrow."

" Escoman, the Queen went into the country today."

" Zamet, if only it were not you who said so! No and no, the Queen will have returned tomorrow. I had offered to show her letters that were ready for dispatch to Spain."

" Escoman, pray excuse me. I would be prepared for some sacrifice if you would repeat nothing of what has here been said."

" Zamet, I do not want your gold. And I fancy you get little good from it yourself."

" Escoman, I have been thinking all this while of someone who would listen to you. Her purposes probably run with yours, which does not mean that either she or you can prevail against destiny. But you shall meet her in my house — I will not say when, nor whom. You must discover her yourself. But now, in all seriousness, I ask you to excuse me."

Now, this light lady knew a youth in one of the King's offices who purloined letters at her request. Two youths, in fact; but the first, who told her about these fearsome letters, by way of enhancing her endearments, refused to get them for her afterwards. Plead as she might the terrible crime that he might thus prevent, that prudent young official merely answered: " Bread tastes good — everywhere, dear lady."

His friend, to whom she had paid no attention, one day slipped something into her hand as they passed in a crowded street. When she opened the packet afterwards, she sank back on her bed, and her heart turned over in a flush of exultation. She saw the King saved. Ah, but how? This unlooked-for chance, in which she could scarcely believe as she turned the letters over, made her yet more diffident as to what she should now do. Hasten to the Arsenal and ask for Monsieur de Sully? She had of course written to him long before, and had of course received no answer. Should she now show him the stolen letters? He was a man whom she dreaded; and she postponed the visit.

So she sewed the letters into her shift, betook herself to the Jesuits in the rue Saint-Antoine, and asked for Father Cotton. In doing so she did not reflect that if the King's murderer was known to all the city, his saviour would scarcely pass unobserved. She was treated with much abruptness, and Cotton was not visible. The Father Procurator received her and listened to what she had to say, but she was sensible enough not to mention the hidden letters. He treated her agitated story as though it were a matter of small moment. His demeanour as he bade her go in peace was positively icy. This was more than she could endure. " You let the King die," she cried, " that a dog like you may live? "

She struck the reverend Father in the face, whereupon he suddenly became kindly and amenable and asked her what she had in mind to do. " I'll stand at the street corners and rouse the mob against such murderers. Murderers! " she shrieked, but not a sound could penetrate those massive walls.

" Be calm, my daughter. I myself will go to the King at Fontainebleau."

" Do you mean that too? " she asked, but was only too ready to believe him. It seemed impossible that human beings could be more cruel than wild beasts. No, their faint hearts must be enlivened, were it only by a box on the ear.

She went, and did not notice that someone was at her heels all day. Another hurried from the house of the Society of Jesus to the Duke of Epernon. The day was the 8th of May. The King was not at Fontainebleau; at that hour he was wandering with the Dauphin between the tall hedges of his garden, while the Queen and the Ambassador dealt with various matters. At a street corner Escoman ran into her former lodger.

She was utterly aghast, nor did he wait for her to speak; as though he had left her but the day before, he went on where he had then stopped. The deed was to be done forthwith, the task was laid upon him, and he had the power. His tender conscience had at last been pacified — this since he had seen his old mother at home, receiving Communion. To him, the King's murderer, Holy Communion was refused. So he had laid the crime upon his mother, innocent as she was of any sin; it was now outside the world, and he did not need to fear the pains of hell. He would find there the famed figures who had done that very deed.

She replied that he certainly seemed to have learned enough chicanery in the courts to incriminate another for his own crime. "But take care! You will find that someone has been before-hand with you."

"Not you, surely? It is everywhere reported that you have lately lost your wits." Therewith he left her standing. Her face was suddenly wet with tears. At that moment an empty litter was carried past. She beckoned to it and named her house. Then she arrayed and beautified herself, as she well knew how to do; in the evening she meant to visit Zamet.

That day the Queen of Navarre also bethought her of that man of money and his gaming-tables. He had made known to her that if she was ever short of money for play, he would consider it an honour to lay a purse before her.

That was the least of her concerns, although she had, as usual, exhausted her allowance before the next was due and could now get no access to the King, her former husband. In the meantime she knew that his death had been decided.

Oh, she knew it as others knew it. It was unlikely that what had reached so many ears would be actually accomplished. When she herself in days gone by sent a murderer to the King, she had taken her measures in secret, but they had miscarried. He had most mercifully been preserved. If only this attempt might also fail! She caused her chaplains to say Masses for the salvation of a living person, whom she did not name. And all the time she said in her own mind: " Lord, spare him this time! This one time yet! " Margot prayed in secret that, her whole House having perished, she might not lose the companion of her youth and be left utterly desolate in the end. And she promptly dismissed an agreeable youth whom she had lately summoned from the country. Her whole mind and heart were set solely upon Henri.

He would not receive her. How indeed should he trust her after the attempt she had already made upon his life? How helpless she felt! Could Henri not recognize his enemies? Anyone could reckon them up for him, but no one did; there was a conspiracy of silence, and here was she, ready to speak. Suppose she wrote to him that the Queen, his wife — but he knew it already. If only a man would believe what he knew. Moreover, he would not get her letter. He was surrounded by the King's bodyguard. In other days it had been his will to live that kept him safe, for he had so longed to live. This was an Henri whom she did not know.

They would not dare kill him. All Paris shared the secret, the people would not suffer such a crime, they would rise up in revolt. The murderer was pointed out in the streets. And there was a woman now most actively intent upon saving the King's life. Marguerite resolved to act. None should deprive her of this, her last privilege. Why did the woman knock at every door except hers?

Madame Marguerite de Valois drove to the house of the said lady, Escoman, but was told that she was with Zamet. Thither she made her way, was received with every honour by the master of the house, escorted to the room set apart for more exalted guests, and a purse was duly put into her hand. Her partners were Monsieur d'Epernon and Monsieur de Montbazon, the fourth being a lady unknown. The Duke of Epernon told the Queen of Navarre in an undertone that she was a foreigner and very rich. He perhaps had this from Zamet and believed it. The purse from which the foreigner produced her money was observed by Margot to be like her own. D'Epernon, who was playing in partnership with the Queen, made blunder after blunder, and the pile of winnings in front of the strange lady grew and grew. Suddenly she made as though to get up and go, but the gouty d'Epernon barred the way with both his legs and demanded his revenge. It was abominable to relieve people of their ready money and then depart.

Escoman sat down once more. Escoman and Margot exchanged a long look and recognized each other. Escoman realized that this was the exalted personage who would help her; she would dismiss the two gentlemen, the word would be spoken, and the King saved. Margot observed that this was not a light lady, with her charms so well preserved, as the city knew her, but a woman who could be trusted. She looked haggard and emaciated, but there was not a hint of defeat in those burning eyes. Here was an incitement not to yield, either to scorn or weariness or danger. Margot opened her mouth — and at that moment the master of the house addressed her. He bent deeply forward, so that only Margot from where she sat could see his face; and she could not but compare the usual Zamet with this distraught creature.

" Madame," he stammered, " forgive me this intrusion. Your partner is looking for a certain person who has now arrived."

" I am well aware of that," said Madame Marguerite de Valois. " We are here," she added, eye to eye with Escoman.

" The person expected is without," he answered feebly.

" Ha? Hey? " spluttered the gouty d'Epernon.

Escoman leapt to her feet. Flinging Monsieur de Montbazon and his chair aside, she fled — and soon disappeared in the throng.

The veins in Montbazon's forehead swelled as he said: " D'Epernon, the strange lady and I have won all the money, and now she leaves it on the table."

The traitor's customary gurgling laugh was his sole reply; he swept the gold into a heap and pushed it in front of Madame

Marguerite. "Possibly she will need it no longer," he said at last. Margot gathered up the gold and flung it full into his face; then she hastened after the vanished lady; but she had vanished never to return.

Escoman tried to escape through Zamet's famous kitchen, but the Chief of the Police was there. Him she evaded, but ran into some of his men, who flung thick cloths about her head and soon had her bound and helpless.

From her prison she managed to send out warnings and appeals; one was received by the Queen's apothecary and reached the ears of Marie de Medici. Her precious papers were safely conveyed to Minister Sully. He did not withhold them from the King, after removing all the dangerous names, the first being that of the Queen: her coronation was clearly inevitable. The King rode through the streets encircled by his bodyguard. In a few days he would set out for the war. There was no reason to interfere with his comings and goings during that brief space.

The emissary chosen by fate to carry these documents from the prison was Mademoiselle de Gournay, adopted daughter of Monsieur Michel de Montaigne. Encounters of old days — their shadows are now gathering about your end, Henri. The wisest of your dead sends a last, vain message.

The Lord Approaches

The King's bodyguard was a new force, which had existed barely a year, only since the King knew his life to be endangered in his capital. Its standards were of white silk embroidered in gold, with a flash of lightning for a badge, and the inscription: "*Quæ jubet iratus Jupiter.*" Wherever Jupiter in his wrath had commanded, there the King's bodyguard was present. Wrath, and the menace of the lightning — Paris recognized its King no more. The streets had long seen him unescorted, on horseback or on foot. He would stop and talk to passers-by. A man dragged at his cloak — the King held him with a look; a knife dropped from a raised hand, and the King went on.

In a courtyard of the Louvre there was a may-tree planted,

which fell down three times. "A German prince," said the King, "would regard that as an omen, and his subjects would firmly believe him doomed. I waste no time on superstitions." Labrosse, the physician, bade him beware of the 14th of May, and he offered to describe the would-be murderer. Nor would this have been a feat of magic. The King shrugged his shoulders. He inspected his regiments, the old Huguenots, the warriors of Ivry, brave Crillon's French Guards, and his Switzers. Troops marched off to the frontiers every day. It was his purpose to be the last to cross them, at the risk of being too late. The King fled no man if he could but flee his fate. "I must meet fate with a cheerful countenance," he said.

He would allow no one about his person except soldiers. At the end of the day's work came the Grand Master, and their council of war at the Arsenal. All the plans and orders drafted by them both were there preserved, until they came into the hands of the various commanders. Nothing should be found in the King's cabinet, which he seldom entered. Once alone in his cabinet, his loneliness came upon him — and fear possessed him too. The heavy tramp of the guards outside the doors no longer brought him comfort, for how could any outward challenge avail against a failure of the inward man?

Not everything was false. Men told him to his very face that he was worn out. They talked and whispered and fell silent; they called him an old lecher, long past his prime, not fit to face the coming age. But he knew well he would have been more than fit to face it, and other ages yet to come. Life had taught him many kinds of lessons, such as would suffice humanity for some long while. Doubt he understood, and goodwill; exhaustion, retribution, exaltations, conquest, exuberance, and resignation. Above all, he had learned to despise nothing; and he was on his way to becoming a man of simple mind. Posterity as well as truth called for such a man, who had already trod some very thorny paths. But today? And here? The tramp of the bodyguard without was the only proof of his continued presence. He would not dally much longer now.

A man should not burn out his strength before the hour of

night. The Lord approaches and His servants are asleep. " Lord, what shall I do? Await Thee free from guilt? Thou dost punish me through that in which I erred. I should have loved less, played less, and striven less eagerly to shape mankind; then I should not now be weary beyond my years. What if I asked the meaning of it all? — were the senses to remain frozen, while the mind was alert enough to devise my Plan? Thou wouldst counsel me, Lord, wholly to resign myself, whether I approach Thee with curses or with prayers. And now I must leave Thee, Lord. Thou mayest bless me afterwards."

Was the hour so near? said Henri, eyeing the digging skeleton. It was nearly dawn, and a last taper flared up before the picture and went out. Was the hour so near?

On the 13th the coronation of Queen Marie de Medici, Regent of the kingdom, was duly celebrated. In Saint-Denis, after the ceremony was over, Henri presented to the crowds there gathered the Dauphin as their King. As in the days of King Henri, the stage was thronged by all ranks without distinction; a vast crowd had flocked into the town from Paris. It was the common folk who first responded when Henri thrust the Dauphin in front of him and cried out: " This is your King." But neither the common folk nor even the burghers understood. Those of higher rank, however, grasped his meaning: the Regency would pass, he and his successors would remain. This was confirmed by the Regent herself. Until then the cathedral had not been high or broad enough to contain her pride and glory. Suddenly she burst into tears.

Her joy had doubtless dissolved in tears because she knew that the new King, Louis, on whose behalf she would rule, would soon ascend the throne. Few being in the secret, there was much astonishment. A King who had often started on a campaign to achieve a purpose that was plain seemed now to be taking his departure for an unknown destination. It is hard enough for an individual to face with calmness an event that may be doubly significant; either alternative brings terror. And a mob, in such case, grows uncontrollable. King Henri was the man of the people, but they wanted to be sure of him. Not with impunity can a people be allowed to tremble for the life they treasure most. There in the cathedral many peered about them, seeking the murderer. They would have torn him to pieces, and the spectre would have been banished. It was a matter for thankfulness that the King had at least not left the kingdom without appointing his successor. The crowning of the Regent ended with a great sigh of relief, which she herself had least of all expected. Though this was her triumph, she had trembled so violently that she could scarcely stand. She could not have endured ten minutes more.

When Marie de Medici, her crown upon her head, returned to the Louvre, who was it that threw water at her from a balcony, and hailed her as " Madame Regent "? In a fury she replied: " The merry monarch may now go in to his lioness." The lady was a singer, with so superlative a voice that it would have put three nightingales to shame. Moreover, Marie learned that she was really not to have the Regency; she would be merely a member of the Council, and the other votes were to count equally with hers. And it could be foreseen that Monsieur de Sully's vote would count for more. Henri had admitted to him that he feared disaster from the coronation of the Queen. That he might well say.

The last person who warned him on this 13th of the month was his son Vendôme, Gabrielle's son. Henri, in friendly fashion, slipped his arm through that of the rather corpulent youth and led him through the great hall, from which the company promptly withdrew. The courtiers all wore a gloomy air, even those who were attached to the King; and they were too dejected even to listen for what was said. " What would you have? " said Henri to Gabrielle's son. " Consider: your beloved mother believed in every sort of prophecy; and I shared her fears in the matter of dreams. In the end she did not die of poison, she died a natural death, for which she, in her secret self, felt the hour had come. It is only in appearance that we run a race with murder, for it is a race that we always win."

"Sire, I am indeed thankful to hear that you feel so secure against attack; but this night until the 14th is the fatal time " — and Cæsar begged his father to beware.

Henri spent the night well; the Queen had several times to leave her bed. On the morning of the 14th he prayed for longer than usual. The tramp of his bodyguards disturbed him, and he was tempted to send them away. The Queen came to his room, as she had not done for a long while. She told him of a nightmare she had had — that he had been lying beside her as a corpse.

" Was I an unpleasant corpse? " he asked, a little too abruptly. She recoiled — he knew the truth. Her nightmare had come to her in waking hours. Dreams that will come true do not torment those who know too much and therefore cannot sleep.

" Fear not for my life, madame. Three days more, and I shall leave to join the army, taking all my guards."

The Queen swayed, and groped for some support; but she did not take her husband's arm. " Three days only? " she repeated. Her demeanour might be explained by her concern for his safety, supposing no other apprehension lay behind it. It is easy to be too late when only three days are left for so anxious an enterprise.

She was, in fact, at odds with her own self. Suddenly she begged Henri to stay in the palace all that day. Let him remember his son Vendôme's warning. Such was her condition, there was that in her that bade her save him — against her own will, indeed, but she tried, under cover of another's name. Henri objected that the fatal night was over.

Marie: " This whole day may be fatal — so says your son Vendôme, and he had it from Labrosse, the physician, whom you ought to have received."

Henri reflected that Labrosse, had he received the man, would have described the murderer. Whither would the trail have led in the end? He was sorry for the Queen, poor creature. He gave her his hand. But he could give no greeting to their life together, which he still more regretted. As she laid her hand in his, she swayed and almost fell. Once upon her knees, she would have confessed. This he did not want her to do, and he took her arms to hold her steady. " Madame," said he, " I would not be open to the taunt that you induced me to stay at home because I was afraid. But I will certainly lie down."

After dinner he was very cheerful for a while. But as no one could join him in his laughter, he grew suddenly weary, though not disposed for sleep. As he lay, he asked the time of everyone that entered. His guards and lackeys came and went. One answered: "Four o'clock," and added in the confidential tone which his humbler subjects always used to him: "You should take the air, my lord."

"You are right — send for my carriage," said the King. There appeared beside his couch his old First Chamberlain, Monsieur d'Armagnac; with outspread legs and arms he fairly blocked the King's departure. "My lord, if you are tired and do not care to mount a horse, you should receive some peasants who await you in the great courtyard."

"You are right," said Henri once more. "That will refresh me."

Down below he promptly recognized the peasants; they were those at whose table he had once eaten in a marshy meadow; he had been taken with a fever while among them, and treated them with disfavour because they let one useless belly eat for six while they went short. This time they had brought with them a sort of crate, such as might house poultry; through gaps between the boards could be seen a huddled human being, who replied to questions with inarticulate mumblings.

Among the men the King noticed one in dirty-coloured wool, a man gnarled in body as the result of years and years of cramping, straining toil and a grinding monotony of attitude and movement. He had once been as shapely as any nobleman, and indeed had made bold to fight a nobleman about his girl. He could never do that again. At the King's bidding he explained that it was his own brother, Jules Simon, in the hen-crate. He had always been diligent at digging in the fields until his mouth was eaten away by leprosy and he went blind.

"Has it come to that?" said Henri. "Must there be ever someone who eats you up — it used to be the man who ate for six." And he knew that if he asked them if they had a chicken in the pot on Sundays, they would certainly answer yes. Well, he must contribute to their leper. His First Chamberlain had to reckon how much money he had available. "Seventy-four crowns," said Armagnac; and Henri: "Give them to these men."

They all knelt in bewilderment at a sum which would have kept any one of them for a long while and was now to help one of them die. The oldest, with a shock of white hair covering his huddled shoulders, looked to be seventy years old, but the King knew better and took off twenty of those years — he, a man indeed of fifty, said: "Dear lord, as you rode past while hunting you caught sight of my house, which was near to falling down. You gave orders that it should be put to rights, laid down thirty crowns on the spot, and paid forty pence for your dinner."

"Ha!" cried the King; "so I ate my dinner with you, did I? What day in the week was it, and what was there to eat?"

"Sunday; a chicken."

Henri burst out laughing; it was his last real laugh. He waved his hand and turned to go, but stopped with his foot poised on the threshold. Oh, day of bitter sorrow, when we must part. The great courtyard was full of his bodyguards. Their Captain stepped forward and reported that the carriage had come.

What carriage? — for a moment his mind was blank, but he said nothing. "Sire," pleaded Monsieur d'Armagnac, quite in his old bluff fashion, "take me with you."

"Not even my guards," said Henri emphatically. "What would my peasants say? This is my people and I am their King. Where is the Queen?"

He turned back into the room. But Marie de Medici was not to be found.

As he went out, a one-armed officer confronted him. "Sire, I was hit by a bullet before Montmélian. I am discharged and in debt, and this very day I am to be arrested. Save an old soldier from such misery and shame."

The King: "I will pay your debts."

The officer: "You cannot do that. I do but ask for my freedom."

The King: "Friend, I will add your debts to mine, and pay

both. Armagnac, go to the Treasury office in the old courtyard and tell them to draw up an order; I will sign it when I come back."

The officer: " Sire, I shall be arrested before then; you must take me away from here."

The King: " They shall not catch you, Captain. Where will you be safest for the next hour? "

Armagnac, very softly: " In your carriage, Sire."

The King grew pale and eyed the man; he shifted from foot to foot, and then said: " Very well, Captain, come with me."

INTO HARBOUR

Through the corridors and by-ways of the Louvre echoed a far-off cry, as the King, followed by his veteran, hurried towards the outer doors: wild yells of fear and joy, the hysteric outburst of one utterly distraught. Armagnac hurried after his master; he fancied this must be the Queen, thinking she had better make her presence known. But Henri recognized the voice as that of the Marquise de Verneuil — she who had once been a very fleshly presence, and was now but a voice left desolate.

On his way the King was again stopped several times. Vitry, the Captain of the Guards, begged to accompany him. In expectation of the solemn entry of the Queen, the streets were packed with strangers and unknown persons. " You are trying to make favour with me," retorted the King sharply; " you would much prefer the company of the ladies." On the stairway from his cabinet to the outer door, he met the Duke of Mercœur, Marshal de Bois-Dauphin, and one of his sons, Anjou. He had a word for each of them, but scarce thought of what he said. What was in his mind was: Whither now, and why?

To Monsieur de Praslin, another Captain in his guard, who offered to protect him, he gave a very curt reply, and then, with a sidelong glance, made certain that his one-armed officer was still at hand. There he was indeed, now quite a different man, with an alert look in his eye and briskness in his gait. He had understood. What was there to understand? Henri asked himself.

The sight of those who were to accompany him should rather have banished any fear. They were standing beside the great State coach and talking about the weather. His old friends Lavardin and Roquelaure, in whom there could be no guile, and de la Force, promoted Marshal the day before, and eager to march down to the Pyrenees. Three more familiar figures, and last of all d'Epernon, who was better there than elsewhere.

On his right the King put d'Epernon, Lavardin, and Roquelaure, on his left Monsieur de Montbazon and de la Force: six persons, including the King, crowded on to the front seat of the huge creaking, swaying coach. There was room opposite for two or three. A third tried to mount the step — the one-armed officer. "Who may you be?" growled the Marquis de Mirabeau, thrusting the man back. "Sire, beware of people you do not know," said Roquelaure. The King was about to speak when his neighbour Montbazon handed him a letter, and someone gave the word to start, perhaps his other neighbour, d'Epernon. As the horses strained at the traces, the one-armed officer was knocked down. He picked himself up, ran after the coach, and managed to spring on to the driver's seat. The King had the curtains of the coach opened on all sides, his pretext being that he wanted to see the decorations for the Queen's ceremonial entry. The one-armed officer sat facing towards the King.

"What day of the month is it?" asked Henri suddenly. "The 15th," was the reply. "No, the 14th," said another. "Between the 13th and the 14th," said Henri to himself in an undertone. Several lackeys ran beside the lumbering coach, and some equerries rode on each side of the horses. One asked, on behalf of the coachman, where the King wished to be driven; and Henri answered that he was merely out to take the air. Whenever the coachman asked for orders, the King named some house or church. The Arsenal was in Henri's mind, but that he did not reveal. He might be intercepted.

The coach accordingly drove into the rue de la Ferronnerie, which is narrow and crowded and difficult for vehicles, being a continuation of the rue Saint-Honoré. At the junction of the two streets, Henri caught sight of a certain Monsieur de Mon-

tigny. He had once confided to this very commonplace gentleman that he would gladly die. He had confessed that he longed
for solitude, for the true peace of the spirit. But he had recovered
himself and added: " For princes there is no harbour on this sea
except the grave, and they must die at their task." Here, at the
entrance to the street, not far from his harbour, he cried: " Greeting, Montigny; I send you greeting! "

A press of people gathered round the royal coach, far beyond
the usual traffic. They jostled against the walls of the Cloister of
the Innocents, as though the passage were not already congested
enough by the shops and booths along the walls. All bared their
heads and stared at the King with a kind of witless bewilderment; and all were silent. Outside the House of the Salamander
there was a complete stoppage, caused by two wagons, one laden
with hay, and the other with casks of wine. The driver of the
coach had to deal with the situation without much help, for
the equerries and runners mostly evaded it by going through the
Cloister cemetery. Only a few of them remained to heave the
wagons out of the way. Here was a pause that could hardly offer
a better chance, if so be that someone had followed the coach
from the Louvre, watching for his opportunity. But the one-
armed officer in front sat facing towards the King, and not a hair
that moved, much less a man, could escape his eye.

At last. The wagons had been dragged to the right of the
street, the coach managed to pass them on the left — very carefully, to avoid a collision. The King looked up towards a house
and cried out something that none understood; the coachman
thought it was a warning to take care. All the occupants of the
coach looked up too. Over the archway there was a coat of arms:
a crowned heart pierced by an arrow.

The one-armed officer realized with a shock that, for a flash, he
had been taken unawares. His duty it was to be on guard, with
eye and hand. Too late: it had happened. He leapt to the
ground, dashed at the murderer, and hammered at his face with
the pommel of his dagger. " Take care! " cried the Duke of
Epernon. " Do not kill the King's murderer."

The officer was paralysed by fury — he had been a worthless, faithless watcher, tried and found wanting on the only day of his life that would be reckoned. What could he now say? — though the witness of his eyes and conscience could make clear what was, for all the rest, a turmoil of wild horror. The murderer had crept out from behind the coach while the King was looking up at the crowned heart pierced by an arrow. All had looked up, excepting only the Duke of Epernon; for he expected the murderer. The King, while his eyes were turned upward, had one arm round the traitor's neck, having just given him a letter to read; this enabled the Duke to jerk his head round, to see whether his man was in view. The King's other arm was resting on Monsieur de Montbazon's shoulder, and it was from that side that the murderer struck. Owing to the King's attitude, the first blow merely grazed the skin.

The King took his arm from Monsieur de Montbazon's shoulder. " I am wounded," he said; and his chest, now unprotected, took the second blow. This was the one that killed him: it reached the lung and severed the aorta. A third belated stroke merely pierced Monsieur de Montbazon's sleeve. Cried the latter in an anguished voice: " Sire, what has happened? " " It is nothing." And again — the last words he uttered: " It is nothing " — then the blood gushed from his mouth, and La Force cried: " Sire! Think of God! "

Those with the King, except La Force, left him and fell upon the murderer. The blood-stained knife was wrenched out of his hands, but he fought with his bare hands, truly potent weapons, against a throng that tore at him, but could not get him down. The lackeys and a certain Monsieur de la Pierre seized and bound him in the end; then Montigny appeared — " Greeting, Montigny; I send you greeting! " — and he proposed that the murderer should be lodged for the time being in the Palais Retz near by. Those who had accompanied the King, and many others, made their way thither with the murderer.

Marshal de la Force remained alone in the coach with the King. He spread his cloak over him and cried out to the street: " The King is only wounded." Monsieur de Gurson had also stayed; he had been first on the spot and had slit the murderer's nose with the pommel of his dagger. La Force charged him to clear the street and turn the horses, which, with help from willing hands, he managed to do. There was no attempt to crowd round the coach, from which blood was now dripping on to the ground. In stricken horror the bystanders shrank back against the walls and into the archways. Not a word was uttered.

La Force drew all the curtains of the coach. He and Gurson accompanied the King, who lay outstretched, with eyes closed and yellowing face. They took him back through the rue Saint-Honoré to his palace of the Louvre. They had not been near to him in life, but they paid their last duty to him like the honest men they were. Once more La Force cried out: " The King is only wounded " — but in the meantime from inside the coach, and down its steep steps on to the street, dripped a thickening runnel of blood. O people, it is the blood of your King Henri. They stood in silence. The swaying, creaking coach began to gather speed, leaving the dark trail behind it. On the way the onlookers said nothing about the decrees of Heaven, or the fulfilment of worldly designs. They merely took account of what had happened, and their minds were wholly possessed by pity and by terror. What would happen now? None knew — save for one thing only, which did happen.

The Duke of Epernon had had the murderer secured by others, being little inclined for violent encounters. He stood by and shouted orders, chiefly with the intent that the King's murderer might not be killed too soon. The woollen heart came into his mind, which should, by the usual prediction, have made our friend invisible. A woollen heart, bestowed by the Fathers, with or without a splinter inside it, that was no great matter; but invisibility would, he felt, have been a boon just then. Still, the deed was done. The King had fallen, and the deed was done. At this moment he found himself confronted by the one-armed officer, and promptly realized that he was in the power of the enemy.

The enemy looked merciless. He had lost his hat in the tumult, and his iron-grey hair was in disorder. His nostrils were distended, his mouth awry, and beneath the overhanging brows burned two hard eyes. With his only hand the discharged Captain knocked the General's hat off. Out of the corners of his eyes d'Epernon could see how matters stood; there was nothing to be hoped for from the people in the street. At that moment a great gob of spittle from the Captain's mouth struck him in the face, and there stuck.

The Captain was a man for his pipe, and his spittle was as thick as it was black, and it oozed all over the Duke of Epernon's face, his forehead and eyelids, cheeks and lips. And the Captain's single fist was thrust under the villain's chin. Such was the colloquy between that pair: no word uttered, but the meaning very clear. The Duke of Epernon obeyed; he hobbled in the direction of the Louvre, a very toilsome journey, following the dark trail on the ground. He would gladly have avoided it, but the fist commanded: "Step in it! You shall bear that blood upon your feet."

From walls and archways all manner of figures leapt forth, they also with clenched and lifted fists. D'Epernon first tried to cover his bespattered face. But it was made clear to him, still without words uttered, that he must display it for all to see. Towards the end of his journey he himself was solely intent upon displaying himself for who he was. The court should recognize him, and the Queen flee at the sight of him. The King was no longer living, but he would awake to look on his betrayer. Two men, one marked by madness and the extremity of shame, the other dark with wrath, iron-grey and hard, appeared before the guard-house of the Louvre.

The soldiers had turned out, and their musket-butts rattled on the stones. Like the people in the streets, they said no word, and the expression of their faces was that of the one-armed Captain. He advanced to the foot of the grand staircase; and he watched the Duke of Epernon walk up it, with head high and face bespattered, at the mercy of anyone who might wish to spit upon him. Whereupon the discharged and indebted officer betook himself to the Treasury office in the old courtyard.

He explained that the King had directed an order to be drawn which he was to have signed on his return. The clerks, who had hitherto stood in whispering groups, suddenly grew busy. They asked the officer to sit down, sent out a messenger with the document, and assured him that in a very short time his debt would have been discharged. He did not believe them; he expected to be arrested and taken away — to a deep and lifelong jail in which men are not put for debt. But the head of the office appeared in person. The money had been paid. And the gallant Captain, whom our King had favoured, was now free.

Seul Roi

Henri recovered consciousness, or, rather, a shadow of his former consciousness returned when he was lifted out of the coach. This happened on the way to the Queen's apartments, and wine was hurriedly sent for in the hope it might restore him. Monsieur de Cérisy, Lieutenant in his guard, lifted his head, and the King's eyelids fluttered several times. Then they remained closed. At each opening of his eyes a faint and far-away recollection floated into his mind. The first was: " The Arsenal, I wanted to see Rosny, and I was misunderstood."

The second recollection, faint and far away: " Gabrielle, beloved, your mouth breathes your very breath into me. Oh, stay." And the third recollection should have been the words: " We do not die." But that was not the thought that a living man had shaped and made articulate, to give him courage to confront time and posterity. Another had conceived it, not he who lay there dying. But at the third flutter of the eyelids, behind the great eyes that would soon close for ever, hovered, as the last conscious thought, those words: " We do not die."

They carried the body into the King's cabinet and laid it on the couch. The room was at once thronged. Few could see more than a blood-stained shirt, a forehead darkly discoloured, a chest charged with blood, closed eyes, and swollen lips. They were told that the King was alive, and as no one wanted to believe the contrary, this body was for a while the King. Beside the corpse stood the First Physician, who was then called Petit, and the Archbishop of Embrun, whose great cathedral stands in the

Alps. It was not the priest but the doctor who made bold to address the dead man and tell him to ask mercy from Jesus, son of David.

At last, when the stillness in the crowded room had become unendurable, someone covered the King's open mouth with his ribbon of the Holy Ghost. This was an admission that he had ceased to breathe. A movement ran through the huddled mass, which then began to melt away. When Marie de Medici hurried into the room, she had a clear view of the body. " The King is dead! The King is dead! " she shrieked. The Chancellor, an austere man of law, corrected Her Majesty. " Kings do not die in France," said he; he had brought the Dauphin, and pointed to him. " The King lives, madame." This abashed her and made her very angry. Her Concini had flung open her door and shouted through it: " *È ammazzato*. We are rid of him."

The Dauphin promptly left the room. He had indeed kissed the King's hand, bowed, and crossed himself, but all in rather perfunctory fashion. He did not weep; his mother wept. He hated every person in that room; they had all had a hand in the murder. What he now must see and must believe, his own anxiety that he thought so childish or feeble, had long since brought him enlightenment. And certain words came back into his mind: "Father, grant me one request. . . . Father, you will leave me, that I know. . . . Father, you, a great King, have a weakling for a son."

About midnight the body was arrayed in white silk. Next day it was opened by the Faculty, who took out the inner organs for removal to Saint-Denis. The heart was promised to the Jesuits; but in the meantime there were signs and circumstances that suggested it had better come into other hands, and the Fathers made no protest. The perfumed corpse was laid out in state, as was scarcely to be avoided, if only to banish the suspicion that the corpse was any one man's work. The room connected the King's cabinet with the grand gallery. The populace was admitted without hindrances, provided they made their way in from the street and were street people.

King Henri's will still prevailed. The people had been privileged to go in and out before him on all high occasions: when he made a feast, or when Majesty appeared and was made manifest before friend and foe and foreigner, or when Henri had come home a victor. Here, perhaps, were all these three occasions combined in one. His people of Paris now thronged into his house and into his room, where a bed, draped in fringed gold brocade, lay for all to see. It was set between two windows, which reached down to the floor; and below, the Seine flowed past.

The lying in state lasted until June the 10th, three weeks, time enough for the great concourse of people that poured in from the provinces. His capital and his kingdom used his house as theirs. They penetrated into the remotest rooms and there took up their abode. They kept watch over the empty vessel, as they had been forbidden to do and had failed to do so long as he was in their midst. It is but the truth that the palace of the Louvre was then occupied by King Henri's people: the court was swept away, the Queen vanished to resorts much more remote than those she frequented when the conspiracy was laid against his life. His soldiers, too, were merged into his people, they guarded and defended no one save him alone. And now he was gone.

One out of thousands could leap on to the table and cry havoc. He could say what all felt: " Our King Henri and we were of one mind. He ruled with us, and we in him. He wanted to better us and give us better lives. He was of our blood too, and therefore it was shed."

Now he is gone. When his people were keeping a vain watch over what was left of him — his men of law, his craftsmen, seamen, the warriors of freedom and of conscience — a tall peasant could leap on to a table, and no harm done. One who had shared a white loaf with Henri, and a jug of wine. " Now he is gone, we are left behind, and we are sorrowful." In the life of the people sorrow is the common lot; and then comes resignation — storms do but lower in the distance. The lying in state, the occupation of the palace, which is no longer his, will soon be safely at an end. The court will breathe again, after the grim populace have withdrawn with all their burden of affliction.

On the last day the Dauphin Louis — as King — the thirteenth of his name, caused great scandal, for which his mother resolved to correct him in very emphatic fashion when peace and order were restored. On his own authority and unattended, he went among the people — a shy lad, inclined by nature to fear and despise mankind, whether as individuals or in masses. At the threshold of the room where the semblance of his father lay at rest, he knelt, made the rest of the way kneeling, and kissed the floor at the foot of the bed. Now, the floor was dirty from the tramp of many feet, so that the whole action was quite at variance with the King's known character. There was one explanation: His father had often led Louis by the hand; he did it for the last time now.

There were many who were afraid that the King's death might make the Duke of Sully apprehensive for his safety: he had served his master only too well. In the first flush of fear he departed in secret from the Arsenal, hoping to be neither tracked nor recognized. When, in the street, he observed faces, very many faces, and all with the same expression, he set himself at the head of his mounted guard. He thus appeared at the Louvre and curtly demanded audience of the Queen, but was told on good authority that she was much overcome, and indeed quite distraught. This enlightened him, as only one of them could be free from anxiety or fear: he or she.

She never let him become an open enemy. For a while he kept his power, or the outward form of it, so that the great King seemed to survive in the person of his great Minister. This, on account of the people, and his own air of menacing gloom — until both the King's servant and the common folk were gradually bereft of their potency and could be sent home. Marie de Medici, as soon as she well could, abandoned herself to the pursuit of wealth, the festal enjoyment of her folly, and the glory of her empty sovereignty. Rubens, who painted it all, was much embarrassed at having to present such a figure as the centre point of his usual display of celestial voluptuousness.

King Henri's heart is where he promised it should be laid at last. In the meantime it had made many journeys, being displayed in all the provinces of France. It lay upon a Jesuit's knees, and so travelled through the land. Throngs of stricken people watched his heart appear as though of its own motion, and then depart once more; thus they did not need to descend upon the capital to fetch it. They will never forget that they have, for this one time, possessed their King. His heart did not beat solely for his people, but also for his privilege, for the greatness of France and the peace of all the world. But his people came first; and they were nearest to his heart, when they were poor.

The only King who still lives today among the poor.

Seul roi de qui le pauvre ait gardé la mémoire.

ALLOCUTION

D'HENRI QUATRIÈME
ROI DE FRANCE ET
DE NAVARRE

du haut d'un nuage qui le démasque pendant l'espace d'un éclair,
puis se referme sur lui

On m'a conjuré, on a voulu s'inspirer de ma vie, faute de pouvoir
me la rendre. Je ne suis pas très sûr, moi-même, de désirer son
retour, et encore moins, de bien comprendre pourquoi j'ai dû
accomplir ma destinée. Au fond, notre passage sur la terre est
marqué par des peines et des joies étrangères à notre raison, et
parfois au dessous de nous-mêmes. Nous ferions mieux, si nous
pouvions nous regarder. Quant aux autres, ils m'ont assurément
jugé sans me voir. Certain jour, jeune encore, quelqu'un, s'ap-
prochant par derrière, me ferma les yeux des ses mains; à quoi je
répondis que pour l'oser, il fallait être ou grand ou fort téméraire.

Regardez moi dans les yeux. Je suis un homme comme vous;
la mort n'y fait rien, ni les siècles qui nous séparent. Vous vous
croyez de grandes personnes, appartenant à une humanité de
trois cents ans plus âgée que de mon vivant. Mais pour les morts,
qu'ils soient morts depuis si longtemps ou seulement d'hier, la
différence est minime. Sans compter que les vivants de ce soir
sont les morts de demain. Va, mon petit frère d'un moment, tu
me ressembles étrangement. N'as-tu pas essuyé les revers de la
guerre, après en avoir connu la fortune? Et l'amour donc, ses
luttes ahannantes suivies d'un bonheur impatient et d'un déses-
poir qui perdure. Je n'aurais pas fini poignardé si ma chère maî-
tresse avait vécu.

On dit cela, mais sait-on? J'ai fait un saut périlleux qui valait
bien des coups de poignard. Mon sort de décida au même instant
que j'abjurai la Religion. Cependant, ce fut ma façon de servir
la France. Par là, souvent nos reniements équivalent à des actes,

et nos *faiblesses peuvent nous tenir lieu de fermeté. La France m'est bien obligée, car j'ai bien travaillé pour elle. J'ai eu mes heures de grandeur. Mais qu'est-ce qu'être grand? Avoir la modestie de servir ses semblables tout en les dépassant. J'ai été prince du sang et peuple. Ventre saint gris, il faut être l'un et l'autre, sous peine de rester un médiocre amasseur d'inutiles deniers.*

Je me risque bien loin, car enfin, mon *Grand Dessein* est de l'époque de ma déchéance. Mais la déchéance n'est peut-être qu'un achèvement suprême et douloureux. Un roi qu'on a appelé grand, et sans doute ne croyait-on pas si bien dire, finit par entrevoir la Paix éternelle et une Société des Dominations Chrétiennes. Par quoi il franchit les limites de sa puissance, et même de sa vie. La grandeur? Mais elle n'est pas d'ici, il faut avoir vécu et avoir trépassé.

Un homme qui doit cesser de vivre, et qui le sent, met en chemin quand même une postérité lointaine, abandonnant son œuvre posthume à la grâce de Dieu, qui est certaine, et au génie des siècles qui est hasardeux et qui est incomplet. Mon propre génie l'a bien été. Je n'ai rien à vous reprocher, mes chers contemporains de trois siècles en retard sur moi. J'ai connu l'un de ces siècles, et qui n'était plus le mien. Je lui étais supérieur, ce qui ne m'empêchait pas d'être même alors un rescapé des temps révolus. Le suis-je encore, revenu parmi vous? Vous me reconnaîtriez plutôt, et je me mettrais à votre tête: tout serait à recommencer. Peut-être, pour une fois, ne succomberais-je pas. Ai-je dit que je ne désirais pas revivre? Mais je ne suis pas mort. Je vis, moi, et ce n'est pas d'une manière surnaturelle. Vous me continuez.

Gardez tout votre courage, au milieu de l'affreuse mêlée où tant de formidables ennemis vous menacent. Il est toujours des oppresseurs du peuple, lesquels oncques n'aimai; à peine ont-ils changé de costume, mais point de figure. J'ai haï le roi d'Espagne, qui vous est connu sous d'autres noms. Il n'est pas près de renoncer à sa prétention de suborner l'Europe, et d'abord mon royaume de France. Or, cette France qui fut mienne, en garde le souvenir; elle est toujours le poste avancé des libertés humaines, qui sont liberté de conscience et liberté de manger à sa faim. Il n'y a que ce peuple qui, de par sa nature, sache aussi bien parler que combattre. C'est, en somme, le pays où il y a le plus de bonté. Le monde ne peut être sauvé que par l'amour. A une époque de faiblesse, on prend violence pour fermeté. Seuls les forts peuvent se permettre de vous aimer, puisque aussi bien, vous le leur rendez difficile.

J'ai beaucoup aimé. Je me suis battu et j'ai trouvé les mots qui saisissent. Le français est ma langue d'inclination: même aux étrangers je rappellerai que l'humanité n'est pas faite pour abdiquer ses rêves, qui ne sont que des réalités mal connues. Le bonheur existe. Satisfaction et abondance sont à portée de bras. Et on ne saurait poignarder les peuples. N'ayez pas peur des couteaux qu'on dépêche contre vous. Je les ai vainement redoutés. Faites mieux que moi. J'ai trop attendu. Les révolutions ne viennent jamais à point nommé: c'est pourquoi il faut les poursuivre jusqu'au bout, et à force. J'ai hésité, tant par humaine faiblesse que parce que je vous voyais déjà d'en haut, humains, mes amis.

Je ne regrette que mes commencements, quand je bataillais dans l'ignorance de tout ce qui devait, par la suite, m'advenir: grandeur et majesté, puis trahison amère, et la racine de mon cœur morte avant moi, qui ne rejettera plus. Si je m'en croyais, je ne vous parlerais que de cliquetis d'armes, et de cloches faisant un merveilleux bruit, sonnant l'alarme de toutes parts, les voix criant incessamment: Charge! charge! et Tue! tue! J'ai failli être tué trente fois à ce bordel. Dieu est ma garde.

Et voyez le vieil homme qui n'a eu aucune peine à vous apparaître, quelqu'un m'ayant appelé.

En guise de rideau, le nuage d'or se referme sur le roi.

This book is set in Electra, a linotype face designed by W. A. Dwiggins. This face cannot be classified readily as either "modern" or "old-style." It is not based on any historical model, nor does it echo any particular period or style. It avoids the extreme contrast between "thick" and "thin" elements that mark most "modern" faces, and attempts to give a feeling of fluidity, power, and speed. The book was composed, printed, and bound by The Plimpton Press, Norwood, Mass. The paper was made by S. D. Warren Co., Boston. The binding and typography are by W. A. Dwiggins.